Deuce Delaney

a novel by

Michael Justus Murray

Text copyright © 2012 by Michael Justus Murray
Cover images © 2012 by Michael Justus Murray

ISBN: 978-0615669380

Front cover art: Michael Murray and Austin Murray
Back cover art: Michael Murray, Austin Murray, Brent Robinson, and Neil Robinson

Website: http://www.facebook.com/deucedelaney

CHAPTER ONE

My name is Mansfield Stone Delaney the IV. I'm named after my dad, Dr. Mansfield Stone Delaney the III. He's a big, hot-shit surgeon. He's named after my grandfather and great-grandfather who also were big, hot-shit surgeons. Personally, I hate the name Mansfield Stone. It's a pansy name. So I go by an alias—Deuce Delaney. I named myself after the deuce in a deck of cards because we always make deuces wild when we play poker. I'm a wild card.

Today is my birthday. I'm thirteen years old. I'm a big, hot-shit teenager now. I figure I'm old enough to swear now—maybe not out loud yet, but in my mind. When I grow up, my dad wants me to be a surgeon. But ain't no way I'm going to be a doctor. When I grow up, I'm going to be a professional scuba diver like my hero, Mike Nelson, who's an ex-Navy frogman and professional scuba diver on my favorite TV show, *Sea Hunt*.

At breakfast Mom tells me she's going to have a little party for me tonight. She asks me what kind of cake I want. I request chocolate with penuche icing. It's my favorite cake. I ask her if Jack Arcudy, who's my best friend, can come. She says okay, but she doesn't look too happy about it. She doesn't like him. She thinks he's too wild and gets me in trouble.

I call Arcudy and invite him to my party. His Mom gives him permission. I invite him to come over this afternoon, but he says he has to work a funeral. His dad runs Arcudy Funeral Home. I always joke his dad buries my dad's mistakes. He has to put the little flags on all the cars that are going to the cemetery.

I wait for Mom to go to the grocery store. Then look for my birthday present. I'm dying to see what she got me. First I asked for an electric guitar, but she said no way, so I asked for a Blancpain Fifty Fathoms diver's watch. I saw a picture of the wrist watch on the cover of *Skin Diver* magazine. Lloyd Bridges, who plays Mike Nelsen on *Sea Hunt*, was wearing it. I search my parents' bedroom closet and under their bed—that's where my mom typically hides presents—but can't find it.

I run down to the mailbox when the mailman comes. Grandma Colleen always sends me twenty dollars on my birthday. Sure enough, there's a letter in the mailbox for me from her. I tear open the envelope and find a crisp twenty dollar bill, which I put it in my coin bank with a combination lock.

After lunch, I ride my bike to Denny Boebel's house and check out his scorpions. He captured three of them in the mountain wilderness at Philmont Scout Ranch in New Mexico this summer and brought them home on the train in a matchbox. He keeps them in a fishbowl—he says scorpions can't climb glass walls. They're hiding behind rocks on the dirt floor of the fishbowl. They're tan and about two inches long. I think it'd be cool to have a pet scorpion, so I buy one for five bucks. Approaching the scorpion from behind, Boebel picks it up with his fingers by the segment of its tail right below its stinger—so it can't sting him. He dangles the scorpion right in my face—it tries to pinch my nose with its claws. I jump backwards. He laughs and calls me a chicken. He says it will sting you only if it feels threatened. Holding the scorpion in the palm of his hand, he nudges it from behind into a jar with air holes in the lid. He tells me to feed it flies and crickets and to give it water every few days. He warns me that the chlorine in tap water will kill it, so I should let the water sit out for a day or two, so the chlorine evaporates.

I transport the scorpion to my house in the trap on the front fender of my bike. I smuggle it inside my shirt upstairs to my room, where I sit down at my desk and look at it in the jar. It's pointing its stinger right at me. I name it Sting.

I look up scorpion in the encyclopedia. I read that a scorpion is an eight-legged arachnid and that its sting is similar to a bee sting. I've been stung by a bee—it didn't hurt that bad.

I build Sting his new home. I get out my aquarium, which I got for Christmas two years ago, but never set up because Mom wouldn't let me have a pet piranha. I get a bucket, go outside, and get dirt, sand from Calley's sand box, and a few rocks. Go back inside and pour the dirt and sand in the aquarium. Then make a bridge out of the rocks for Sting to hide under. Then put a jar lid beside the bridge for his water dish.

I dare myself to pick up Sting like Boebel did. I let him out of the jar onto my desk. Carefully approaching him from behind, I pick him up by his tail and gently set him on the open palm of my other hand. Then lower him into the aquarium. At first he won't crawl off my hand onto the floor of the aquarium, but finally he does. He tries to climb up the glass walls but falls back down. He hides under the bridge.

I wonder if he's hungry. I go upstairs into the attic, where flies are usually buzzing around the windows this time of year. I catch some big, fat, juicy ones and pull their wings off so they can't fly away—I figure Sting would prefer to eat live flies. I drop them in the aquarium and watch to see if he stings them. I watch for about an hour, but he doesn't.

After I get bored of messing around with Sting, I set the aquarium on the top shelf of my bookshelves. I figure Mom won't notice Sting up there—I can't even see the rocks unless I stand on a chair.

At five o'clock Arcudy comes. While we wait on Dad to get home, I show him my new secret pet. I demonstrate how I pick up Sting and let him walk around on the palm of my hand.

"You wanna hold him? He won't sting you. Scorpions only sting if they feel threatened," I explain.

"Nope. I don't like spiders. They're creepy."

Six o'clock rolls around, and Dad still hasn't come home. I tell Mom I don't think he's going to make it. She says he better—he promised. I can't believe she fell for that. He promised last year and the year before but didn't make it. We wait and wait. Finally, he calls and says he's sorry, but he's tied up at the hospital—I knew it.

We eat without him. We have steak and cake and ice cream. Man, is it good. Then Mom gives me my present. It's this great, big box. I figure she wrapped the scuba watch inside it to fake me out. I open it—

"Hot damn!" I exclaim. "It's a Blancpain Fifty Fathoms. Just like Mike Nelson's."

Mom frowns at me. I'm not allowed to say swear words, but she doesn't yell at me since it's my birthday and I have company.

I check out my scuba watch. Man, is it cool! Mom says it's the official watch of the U.S. Navy Seals. It has luminescent hands and is waterproof to a depth of three hundred feet. A cool, red-and-yellow symbol that means no radiation and the words "NO RADIATIONS" are on the face of it. Mom says it's the civilian watch—the luminescent hands don't emit any radiation. She doesn't want me to get cancer from it. Then she says how much trouble she had finding it. No jeweler in town carried it. She ordered it from a skin diving catalog that she borrowed off the scuba instructor at the Y. I show it to Arcudy. He thinks it's really cool. I put it on, run out in the kitchen, and hold my wrist underwater in the sink. Sure enough, it doesn't leak. Then we run down in the basement and turn off the lights so it's pitch-black. Man, you can see the hands glowing clear over on the other side of the basement.

After my birthday party, I ask Arcudy to stay overnight. He calls and asks his Mom, but she says no. He has to go to the doctor and get his radiation treatment for his acne tomorrow morning.

∞()∞()∞()∞()∞()∞

After supper, Arcudy calls and asks me to stay overnight at his house tonight. At first Mom says no because I just spent the night there two weekends ago. "Please. It's the last weekend of summer,"

I beg. Finally, she gives in. I tell Arcudy I'll be right over and beat it out of here before Mom has a chance to change her mind.

I take my swimsuit and a towel in my gym bag. Since I broke the gear shift on my bike and it's at the bicycle shop being repaired, I have to walk to Arcudy's house. He lives on the other side of Luna Lake Park on Pinecrest Court. Mrs. Arcudy answers the door. She doesn't look too thrilled to see me. She doesn't like me. She thinks I'm too wild and get her son in trouble. Trying to be polite, I ask her how she's doing. She says fine, but I swear she's looking at me suspiciously. She says Jack is upstairs in his room.

Upstairs, I find Arcudy in the bathroom checking out his zits in the mirror. His face is sunburned from the radiation. When I say hi, he's startled and quickly looks away from the mirror.

We argue about what to do. I want to go to the pool since we only have a few days left to go swimming since the pool closes after Labor Day, but Arcudy wants to go downtown to Sky-Line Books and Mags and look for some book named *Candy*. My parents have expressly forbidden me to go to Sky-Line Books and Mags because the police are always raiding the place for selling dirty magazines. He talks me into it by telling me that the book is supposed to be really dirty.

We ride double on Arcudy's bike downtown to the bookstore, park on the sidewalk, and go inside. A sign in one section says Adults Only. We sidle over near the section. In one aisle, a sleazy-looking guy is checking out a dirty magazine. I spot *Candy* across the aisle on a bookrack marked Adult Literature. A picture of a pretty, blonde girl with alluring eyes is on the book cover.

"Boys, move away from there," a saleslady tells us.

We go outside the store to reconnoiter.

"She won't sell it to us. We're minors," Arcudy says.

"We'll hafta shoplift it," I reply.

"You do it."

"No, you do it."

We flip a coin to decide who shoplifts the book. I call tails and lose.

"Since I'm the one taking the risk, it's mine," I say.

I devise a plan. I tell Arcudy to create a diversion—buy a comic book and drop his money to distract the saleslady. Then I'll swipe the book.

Back in the store, Arcudy picks out a comic book and heads over to the cash register. At the same time, I mosey over to the Westerns bookrack, which is right next to the Adult Literature. When he pays the saleslady, he accidentally-on-purpose drops his money and coins go rolling across the floor. He and the saleslady bend over to pick them up. Right then I swipe *Candy*, hide the book inside my shirt, and slip out of the store. I run up the sidewalk a block and wait on Arcudy. When he exits the store, I wave at him. He hops on his bike and races up the sidewalk.

Excited, he asks, "You got it? You got it?"

With a sly grin, I nod my head.

"Let me see. Let me see."

"Take it easy." I pull the book out from inside my shirt and show it to him. He wants to read it right here. It's starting to get dark out. The streetlights have come on. "Let's go back to your house," I say.

Arcudy pedals us home as fast as he can. We go into his room, lock the door, and sit on the edge of his bed, reading *Candy*. We read the dirty words and scenes out loud, snickering. We completely lose track of the time.

All of a sudden, somebody tries to open the door. "Jack, unlock this door!" Mrs. Arcudy orders.

We hide the book under his pillow, and Arcudy opens the door.

"What are you doing in here?" she asks him.

"Nothing," Jack answers with an innocent expression on his face.

"It's time for you to go to bed."

We fake like we go to bed. We say good night to Mrs. Arcudy and turn off the ceiling light. Later, we turn on the desk light and drape a towel over the shade to dim it. Then we get *Candy* back out and start reading it again.

We don't go to bed until one thirty. Then we lie awake talking about girls. Tell the same old stories. Arcudy tells me about the time he played spin-the-bottle at a party at Sherry Spayde's house. I tell him about the time that I made out with Linda Logan—except I didn't really make out with her. The truth is I was spending the night with her brother, Jeff, and a girl named Carol Baker was spending the night with Linda. All of us were playing a board game called Life down in the basement. In the middle of the game, Linda turned off the lights and tried to kiss me, and Carol tried to kiss Jeff. The girls were in seventh grade and were interested in boys. Jeff and I were only in fifth grade and weren't interested in girls yet, so we fought them off and ran upstairs. But that's not what I tell Arcudy. I tell him we made out on the couch, and how romantic and sexy it was. I figure he'll never know the difference since the Logans moved to Torrance, California. After I finish telling that story, I wait for Arcudy to tell me about the time last year that he made out with Barb Shaffer at a make out party in her basement, but he doesn't say anything because he's sound asleep.

I close my eyes and go to sleep.

The next day we decide to go to the movie. We look in the newspaper and see an ad for *The Village of the Damned* that shows a picture of a kid with really weird eyes. Intrigued, we want to see this movie, but I figure Mom won't let me go because it has the word "Damned" in the title. So I call her and ask if I can go see *Son of Flubber*, which is a Walt Disney movie. She says okay, but I have to be home by five thirty.

Before Arcudy can go to the movie, he has to cut the grass at the funeral home. I volunteer to help so he'll get done faster. We ride the bus downtown to the square and walk to the funeral home. He hauls the mower out of the garage and mows the lawn. Using the clippers, I trim the grass around the flower beds, the Arcudy Funeral Home sign, and the flagpole. He sweeps the grass off the front walk and picks up the cigarette butts off the front porch.

By the time we finish, we're hot and thirsty. Arcudy takes me downstairs in the funeral home, where there is a kitchenette, and gets two bottles of root beer out of the refrigerator. We chug them. On the way back upstairs, I look down the dark basement hall.

"Hey, man. What's down there?" I ask.

"The embalming room."

"Really? Any dead bodies in there?"

"My dad embalmed some guy this morning."

I'm curious to see what a dead person looks like. "Let's go look."

"Nah, we can't. We're not allowed in there. You gotta have an embalmer's license."

"Can't we just sneak a peek? I've never seen a real-life dead guy."

He stares down the hall, hesitating…

"What'sa matter? You scared?" I taunt him.

"I ain't scared. C'mon, I'll show you."

Arcudy checks to make sure the coast is clear. Then we tiptoe down the hall to a doorway. He turns on a light switch. Fluorescent lights flicker on in a windowless room. We peek into it. A corpse is lying on a table under a sheet.

I whisper, "Oh, man—look. A corpse…"

Arcudy glances back up the hall. Then tiptoes across the room to the table. I follow him. Looking over his shoulder, I see the contours of a corpse's head, torso, legs, and feet under the sheet.

"I dare you to pull down the sheet," I whisper.

Arcudy checks to make sure no one is coming. Then slowly pulls the sheet down. I see the dead man's bald head, then his bony face, then his hairy chest. Arcudy stops the sheet at his navel.

"Damn—he doesn't look dead. He looks like he's just sleeping— except his skin looks kind of waxy. He doesn't look scary at all," I observe.

"My dad puts massage cream on the face and hands. And stuffs cotton in the nose and mouth to keep body fluids from leaking out."

"You know what he died of?"

"My dad said lung cancer. He smoked."

"My dad says that's why you shouldn't smoke. Cigarettes cause lung cancer."

Grinning deviously, Arcudy says, "Let's give him one last smoke." He checks again to make sure no one is coming. Then reaches in his pocket, pulls out a cigarette butt, and sticks it in the dead man's mouth.

We start laughing.

"Jack!" Mr. Arcudy calls from upstairs.

We startle and gape at each other…

Arcudy grabs the cigarette out of the dead guy's mouth and pulls the sheet back up over his head. Then we bolt out of the room, turn off the lights, and run upstairs.

We go into the room where the caskets are displayed. Mr. Arcudy is dusting them with a feather duster. He pays us each five bucks for mowing the lawn. Then the phone rings, and he disappears into his office.

Arcudy and I walk around the room, checking out the caskets. He shows me a fancy one that he says is the "Cadillac" of caskets. It's lined with satin cushions.

"It looks comfortable," I say.

"I dare you to get in it."

"I ain't afraid of caskets." I climb inside it and lay my head on the soft pillow. "Cool, man!"

Suddenly, Arcudy closes the lid of the casket. It's pitch-black. Fearful that I'm going to suffocate, I scream, "Let me outta here!"

The lid opens. Mr. Arcudy is glaring down at me.

"Get the hell outta there!" he orders. Man, is he mad!

I quickly climb out.

"God damn it! Look! You got grass in it!" he yells.

Some grass came off my tennis shoes.

"God damn it! People will think it's used!"

Mr. Arcudy yells at Jack and me for horsing around with his caskets. "Caskets are not toys," he lectures us. He makes Jack get out the portable vacuum cleaner and vacuum the grass out of the casket. Then kicks us out of the place.

"That was a dirty trick you pulled on me," I say to Jack.

"What?"

"Closing the lid of the casket on me."

He just laughs.

It's almost time for the movie to start. We run to the Madison Theater. Buy our tickets at the ticket window and run inside. Buy some popcorn and candy and go sit down in the front row. The movie is about these blonde-haired kids who have supernatural powers. They can read adults' minds. If they don't like what an adult is thinking, they get this glowing light in their eyes and take control of his mind—like they force this one adult to shoot himself. We like the movie so much that we stay and watch it again.

After the movie, we take the bus back to Arcudy's house. He invites me to stay for supper—they're having pizza. Pizza is my favorite food—I could eat it for dinner every day. When I call Mom and ask her if I can stay for supper at Arcudy's house, she says no. After I beg and plead for a while, she gives in but says I absolutely must be home by ten thirty tonight. They order a pizza from Georgio's with pepperoni, onions, and mushrooms on it. I pick off the mushrooms. If there's one thing I hate, it's mushrooms.

After supper, Mr. and Mrs. Arcudy go to a party. As soon as they leave, Jack and I look at his dad's *Playboy* magazines, which he hides in his closet. Mammary glands never cease to amaze me.

Later, we go around the house collecting cigarette butts out of the ashtrays. We take them into his parents' bathroom, turn on the ventilation fan, and smoke them. Check how cool we look in the mirror.

Next, we go down in the basement and raid his dad's bar. We each drink a shot of whiskey—it burns my throat.

All at once, I notice it's ten thirty. When I tell Arcudy I have to go home, he asks me to spend the night again. Then calls his Mom and asks her if it's okay. She says yes—I think she says it just to get him off the phone. I call Mom. Before I even get a chance to say one word, she says no. I start begging. She keeps saying no. She says I've already been here two days—I'll wear out my welcome. I tell her it's okay with Mrs. Arcudy. She says she's not going to argue with me—I have to go to church tomorrow.

"Aw, man," I gripe.

"You have ten minutes to get home. I mean it, Mansfield."

"Thanks a lot." I hang up on her.

I tell Arcudy my old lady said no. I get *Candy* out of his bedroom. I pack the book in my gym bag, say so long, and head for home. I figure there's no way I'm going to make it in ten minutes— not unless I take the shortcut through Luna Lake Park. The only problem is I'm not allowed in the park after dark. Mom expressly forbid me after a girl named Regina Wukela got child-molested and murdered there a few years ago. She says weirdos and perverts hang out there now. But I figure I don't have any choice. It's either that or be late and get in trouble.

I walk down Pinecrest Court and take the path through the park. The streetlight where the lane dead-ends helps light the way. I go past the statue of Johnny Appleseed. Come to the road that circles Luna Lake. Check to see if there are any cars parked on the road—sometimes couples go parking there—but don't see any.

I cross the road and walk through the playground to the lake. A ledge made of flat rocks circles the lake. I stand on it for a minute, gazing across the water. See the reflection of the moon in the water. Hear the bullfrogs croaking and the waves lapping against the boathouse. It's a nice atmosphere.

I walk along the ledge to the other side of the lake. Go past the pavilion. Cross the picnic area and come to the woods. I look for the path that goes through the woods, crosses the creek, and goes up the cliff past my tree fort to my house. But I can't find it in the dark.

Finally, I find the path. I walk down it through the woods. Man, is it dark out. I trip over a root and almost fall flat on my face. I start to get scared. I'm heading toward the place where Regina Wukela got murdered. She was murdered in a sewer pipe that drains into Possum Run, which is a small stream in Luna Lake Park. The police found her dead body hidden inside the sewer pipe. Now people say that the sewer pipe is haunted by her ghost. That sometimes you can hear a little girl crying in the night there. But I don't believe it. Personally, I don't believe in ghosts.

All of a sudden, I get a mad impulse to climb inside the sewer pipe. I've done it before in broad daylight but never at nighttime.

Don't be crazy, man. You have to get home.

I come to the creek. Climb down the bank to the sewer pipe. I can just barely see it in the moonlight shining through the trees.

Don't be a chicken.

I climb up a pile of rocks and look into the pipe. It's pitch-black.

C'mon, I dare you.

I climb inside the pipe. Crouching at the opening, I peer into the darkness. Listen to the water trickling between my legs. It smells kind of stinky—like sewage.

"Anybody home?" I yell. It echoes down the pipe.

"Nobody but us ghosts," I answer, laughing to myself.

I actually dare myself to walk up the pipe a ways. I take a step. Feel a spider web stick to my face. I brush it away with my hand. I'm afraid to go forward...

"Bawk, bawk, bawk, you big chicken. C'mon, just go ten steps."

Holding my gym bag in front of me to clear away any spider webs, I go one step...

Two steps...

Three steps—

Suddenly, I think I hear a noise up ahead in the blackness. Stopping dead in my tracks, I strain my ears...

I get this weird feeling like something is there—watching me. A shiver runs right down my spine.

I spin around, scramble back down the pipe, and leap out over the rocks. Landing in the mud, I slip and fall down—dropping my gym bag. Hopping back up, I grab my gym bag, leap across the creek, and take off up the path. Scamper up the cliff. Then run through the woods past my tree fort all the way to my side yard.

The kitchen light is on in our house. I run up the bank and the steps onto the back porch. Fling open the door and dash into the kitchen.

Mom is peeling potatoes.

"Hi, Mom! I'm home!"

"You're late."

"I came as fast as I could." I'm panting like crazy. I head toward my room.

"Wait a minute, young man."

I stop.

Pointing her finger in my face, she says, "Don't you ever talk to me like that on the phone again. And don't you ever hang up on me again. Do you hear me?"

I nod my head.

"That was very disrespectful."

"I'm sorry."

I go upstairs to my room and go inside my closet. A set of drawers is built into the wall. I pull the bottom drawer all the way out and set it on the floor behind me. There's a space inside the wall. It's my secret compartment where I hide all the things I'm not allowed to have. I stash *Candy* inside it.

I flop down on my bed. Think about what I just did and laugh. Man, I really scared myself tonight.

CHAPTER TWO

I'm watching a Tarzan movie on *The Big Show* on TV. I'm right at the good part where Jane and her friends from England are about to get tortured to death by a tribe of natives.

"Time to eat!" Mom calls.

I act like I don't hear her.

"Mansfield! Time to eat!" she calls louder.

"Just a minute."

"No just a minute! Turn that TV off!" she yells.

I leave the TV on and go into the kitchen. Mom and my sisters, Meg and Calley, are sitting at the kitchen table, eating TV dinners. A chicken TV dinner and a big glass of milk are on the table in front of my chair.

"Can I eat in the TV room?" I ask.

"No," Mom answers.

"But it's a TV dinner."

"So?"

"You're supposed to watch TV while you eat it. That's why they call it a TV dinner."

Rolling her eyes, she says, "Sit down, Mansfield. You need to eat supper with us. Supper is family time."

I sit down. Meg and Calley are pretending like they're feeding their troll dolls. With their ugly, cute faces and furry, fluorescent hair combed straight up, troll dolls are the latest fad. I scarf my food, so I can get back to my movie.

"May I be excused?" I ask.

"No. I have a P.T.A. meeting tonight. I need you and Meg to clean up the kitchen," Mom answers.

I groan. I figure the movie will be over by the time I'm finished.

"There are hardly any dishes. You can do it in a few minutes," she says.

Mom goes upstairs to get ready. Since the dishwasher is on the blink as usual, Meg and I have to do the dishes by hand. I try to get out of it by faking like I have to go to the bathroom. "Excuse me."

"Just where do you think you're going?" Meg asks.

"Nature calls."

"Oh, no, you don't. Get back here!" Meg screams and runs after me.

I dash into the bathroom off the kitchen, lock the door behind me, and sit down on the toilet with my pants up.

Meg pounds on the door. "Open the door!"

"I can't. I'm on the toilet."

"You big liar."

"Beat it, Meg. Or I'll pound you."

"I'm telling."

Meg goes away.

I just sit here, listening…

Through the door, I hear Meg say, "He's in there faking like he's pooping."

"Mansfield, come out of there!" Mom says.

I flush the toilet and open the door. "I'm done."

Mom looks at me like she doesn't believe me. Back in the kitchen, she hands me a dishrag. "Here. You wash. Meg, you dry and put away."

Mom goes back upstairs.

"You spastic creep," Meg calls me.

"You little rat-fink," I call her.

"I know you are, but what am I?" she replies.

"You ugly scag."

"I know you are, but what am I?"

"You anal pore."

Meg puts her hand to her mouth like she's shocked. "Mom! Mansfield called me an anal pore!"

Mom comes back downstairs, peeved. "Did you call your sister an anal pore?"

I nod my head.

"I told you not to call her bad words?"

"Anal pore is not a bad word. It's a scientific name. Mr. Gilbert says it in science class."

"It means a bad word when you call your sister that. Since you persist in calling her bad words, you can clean the kitchen by yourself. Meg, you're excused."

Meg hangs her dish towel on the towel rack and picks up her troll doll off the counter.

Mom heads upstairs again.

Standing in the doorway with a snotty grin on her face, Meg says, "Oooh....cut you down, tore you up, nailed you to the wall."

I turn on the garbage disposal to grind some garbage in the sink.

"Riveted," she says.

"Get outta here."

"Riveted, riveted, riveted—"

"I'm warning you..."

"Riveted, riveted, rivet—"

I snatch her troll doll out of her hand and shove it headfirst down the garbage disposal. Hear the sound of plastic grinding...

Trying to save her doll, Meg claws my wrist with her fingernails.

I let go of the troll doll and sock her in the arm.

She grabs hold of the doll's spinning feet and yanks it out of the garbage disposal. Its hair is chopped and its face is mutilated.

Bawling, she runs upstairs.

I turn off the garbage disposal and check the scratches on my wrist. Man, do they smart.

Mom storms into the kitchen. Meg is behind her, holding her mangled troll doll, sniffling. Furious, Mom asks, "Did you stick Meg's doll down the garbage disposal and hit her?"

I nod.

"Go to your room!" she yells, pointing upstairs.

"But what about the dishes?" I madly look around for the dishrag.

"Now!"

I beat it out of the kitchen and up the stairs.

"And you stay there until your father gets home!"

I go into my room, slam the door behind me, and flop down on my bed. "Jeez, what a grouch!"

I reach under my pillow and pull out the latest issue of *Mad* magazine. I read the Don Martin cartoon. He's my favorite cartoonist. Soon, I hear a car in the driveway and go look out the window. Mom is going to her P.T.A. meeting. Time for me to move upstairs to my Observatory. The door to it is in my bedroom. I go upstairs to the attic where the ladder to my Observatory is. Climb up it to the trap door. My "Radiation Warning Symbol–Enter at Your Own Risk" sign is coming loose again. I re-stick the tape. I climb through the trap door and latch it behind me so Meg can't bug me. I'm in a small room on top of our house—what Dad says is called a turret. The room is in the shape of an octagon and has windows on all eight sides. And, wow, talk about a bird's eye view. It sits three and a half stories off the ground. Then our house sits on top of Mount Airy, which is the highest hill in town. Really, it's practically a cliff. You're so high up in the air that you don't feel like you're in a house—you feel like you're floating in a helium balloon. So high up that I sometimes get this funny falling feeling in my legs when I look out.

I named it my Observatory because it's where I spy on the world. A wooden, octagon-shaped shelf runs around the room below the windows. I sit in the middle of the room in a reclining swivel chair with a headrest that I bought at Goodwill for only ten bucks. I had to haul it up here with a rope. The legs have rollers so I can roll around. I have all my spy equipment and stuff spread out on the shelf. My telescope. Dad's high powered binoculars. And his old, high-powered rifle scope that I took off his .30-06 and mounted on my toy bolt rifle. Which Mom doesn't like me to use because she's afraid someone will see me and think I'm a sniper. Especially since Lee Harvey Oswald assassinated President Kennedy from the window in the Texas School Book Depository Building last year.

I open the windows to get some fresh air. Man, is it nice out. The sun is going down—it makes Luna Lake look like it's on fire.

I turn on my transistor radio and sing along to "I Saw Her Standing There" by the Beatles, who are a new rock and roll band from England. I really like them. Mom says they're just a fad with their long hair and British accents and will be gone in a few months, but I don't think so.

I look through my binoculars at Possum Run Pool in Possum Run Park. Mick Uhde, who's the pool manager and swim team coach, is emptying the water out of it. I feel blue because summer is over and school starts tomorrow.

I see a car coming up Mount Airy. I think it's Dad and jump up but then see it's just Tecca's MG. She's coming home from cheerleading practice.

I sit back down, get out a deck of cards, and play solitaire.

Gradually, it gets dark out and the street lights come on down below in the town. I watch the moon rise. Man, is it beautiful. It's so big and orange that it looks like the sun. It slowly gets smaller and turns yellow. I look at it through my telescope. I can see craters on the lunar surface.

All of a sudden, I spot two sets of headlights pulling into the driveway. I scurry down the ladder, run down the stairs, and jump in bed with my clothes on. Soon, I hear voices coming through the register.

"Mansfield!" Dad calls.

I fake like I'm asleep.

"Mansfield, get down here! Right now!"

I tumble out of bed and hurry downstairs. In the kitchen, Mom tells Dad, "Look what your son did to Meg's doll. He put it down the garbage disposal." She shows him the mangled troll doll.

"And then he hit me," Meg tells him.

Narrowing his eyes, Dad asks me, "Why did you destroy her doll?"

"She was taunting me."

"And you hit her."

"She scratched me first." I try to show him the claw marks on my wrist, but he doesn't look.

"I don't care what she did. You're a boy. Boys don't hit girls. You're stronger. It's unfair for you to hit her." Man, is he mad.

I shut up.

"Meg is gonna grow up to hate you if you don't stop being mean to her. You want her to grow up to hate you?"

I shake my head.

"Don't you ever touch her again. Do you understand me?

I nod my head.

"What?"

"Yes." I stare at the floor…

"What did I tell you would happen if you didn't leave your sister alone?"

"You'd ground me," I mumble.

"Speak up."

"You'd ground me,"

"I warned you, Mansfield. You're grounded for a week. And you have to buy Meg a new doll. We'll take it out of your allowance."

I sigh.

"Now tell your sister you're sorry."

I look at Meg. She's loving it. "I'm sorry."

Dad looks at his wristwatch.

"Doc, don't forget about the Ark," Mom says.

"Oh, yeah. Mansfield, your mother and I have decided we want you to join the Ark."

"The Ark?" I question.

"It's the youth fellowship group at church," Mom says.

"I don't want to."

"That's too bad. It's time you got involved in a constructive organization. You need something to keep you out of trouble," Dad says,

Mom chimes in, "Listen, Mansfield, I talked to Mrs. Heasley about it at P.T.A. She said they hired a new Youth Director,

Reverend Roush, who's young and dynamic. He's able to relate to young people. She told me her son, Richard, goes and he really enjoys it.

"I know him from school. He's a real jerk. He's always trying to score brownie points with the teachers. And—"

"Alright, that's enough, Mansfield. I'm not gonna argue with you. You will join. And that's final," Dad says.

"Aw, man," I groan. This is the problem with being a kid. My parents can make me do something I don't want to do. I can't wait until I grow up and am free.

Dad turns to Mom. "Is that it?"

"I guess so," she says.

Dad looks at his wristwatch again. "Alright, it's ten-fifteen—time to get ready for bed. You've got school tomorrow."

Back in my room, I get undressed and put on my swim team tank suit, which I wear to bed instead of pajamas. I think pajamas look dorky.

I go into the bathroom and start brushing my teeth. Meg stands in the doorway, points her finger at me, and starts tee-hee-heeing with her hand over her mouth.

As I close the door in her face, I tell her, "I wish somebody'd drop an H-bomb on your face."

I lie awake in bed. I feel like crap. It's bad enough I have to go to school tomorrow, but now I have to join the Ark. I don't want to be stuck in a Bible study class with a dork like Richard Heasley.

Mom pokes her head in my room. "Goodnight, Deuce."

I don't say goodnight to her.

∞()∞()∞()∞()∞()∞

Early in the morning, I climb out of bed and go look out the window. Man, is it ever a crummy day. It's drizzling and so foggy that I can barely make out the woods. It feels cold and smells like rotten apples on the ground—the brown ones that feel like dog crap when you step on them. I stare at the birdbath, watching the raindrops sprinkle in it...

Man, am I depressed. Today I'm starting eighth grade at Johnny Appleseed Junior High School. The last thing I feel like doing is going to school.

I have an idea—I'll fake like I'm sick. I quickly empty my wastepaper basket and set it next to my bed. Then hop back in bed.

At twenty till seven, Mom sticks her head in my room and says in a cheery voice, "Time to get up, Deuce."

"Mom..." I moan.

She doesn't hear me or notice the wastepaper basket. She goes downstairs. I wait for her to come back and check on me.

After a while, Meg comes into my room. She's dressed and ready for school.

"Deuce, you better get up. You're gonna be tardy."

I groan, "Meg...go tell Mom I'm sick."

Meg looks in the wastepaper basket. "I don't see any puke. You're faking."

"Please, Meg." I hold my stomach like I'm on the verge of puking.

Meg goes downstairs.

A minute later, Mom yells, "Mansfield! You've got five minutes to get dressed and get down here!"

"Mom, I can't! I'm sick!" I yell back.

"Mansfield, don't make me come upstairs!"

I jump out of bed and get dressed as fast as I can. Put on my new school clothes—my madras shirt, reversible belt, and penny loafers. I put dimes in the half-moon cutout slots of the leather strips on the shoes, which I think looks cool. Instead of wearing my new khaki pants, I put on my tan jeans. They look cool.

"Mansfield!"

I run to the bathroom and pee as fast as I can. Then run downstairs and stagger into the kitchen with a sick look on my face.

Mom is standing by the stove with a spatula in her hand. A plate of French toast is on the table. Looking perturbed, she says, "Your breakfast is cold."

"Mom, I don't feel good." I rub my stomach.

"Forget it, Mansfield You're not missing the first day of school. Now sit down and eat your breakfast."

"Don't blame me if I puke on the floor."

I scarf down my French toast. My lunch money is laid on the counter.

"Mansfield, you have jeans on. The school dress code says no jeans."

"It says no blue jeans. These are tan jeans."

"You're not wearing jeans to school. They'll send you home. Go back upstairs and put on your new khakis right now."

I run upstairs and change into my new khaki pants. Look glumly at my baggy pant legs—they look uncool.

I try to slip out the side door without wearing my plastic raincoat and rubbers—they look uncool too.

"Mansfield, come back here and put on your raincoat and rubbers," Mom orders.

"Mom, it's not raining."

"Yes, it is. It's sprinkling. You're not gonna ruin your brand new clothes and shoes on your first day of school."

I go back inside and put on my raincoat and rubbers. "I look like a dork," I complain.

"At least you'll be a dry dork. Come straight home tonight. Don't forget—you're grounded. Goodbye, Mansfield. Have a nice day."

I don't say goodbye to her.

I walk to the intersection of Parkview Circle, Mapledale, and Shady Lane, where Arcudy is waiting for me by the mail collection box. "It's about time, Deuce. Where the heck've you been?"

"Antarctica."

"I almost left without you. We better not be tardy."

"Don't sweat it. We'll take the short cut."

We jog down Mapledale. Hang a left at Forrest Road, a right at Arlington Avenue. Take the short cut through the woods—the dirt path is shorter because it's the hypotenuse and the sidewalk is the right angle of a triangle. I hope that we don't run into any hoods. They hang out in the woods, smoking. They shake down kids for their lunch money to buy cigarettes. Luckily, we don't see any. We come out behind the school. I hear the bell ring—figure it's the 8:26 warning bell. We sprint across the football field and around the side of the building to the front of the school. No one is standing around the flagpole—they've all gone inside.

We run inside the school. Walk past the principal's office and then run down the hall in a way that looks like we're walking. All of a sudden, I smell puke. We rip around a corner—on the floor is a puddle of puke about as big as the Atlantic Ocean. Unable to stop in time, we madly tiptoe through it. The floor is so slick I almost slip and fall in it. It's right outside the Boys' restroom. Somebody didn't quite make it.

Mr. Turner is cleaning up the puke. He's the school janitor. He's an old geezer with really bad B.O., who cuts the longest farts in the world. I once heard him cut one when he was walking by, starting at my locker and ending at the other end of the hall at the janitor's room. Anyhow, he's mopping up the puke in slow motion. Wintergreen deodorizer is in the soapsuds—it's supposed to kill the most putrid smells in the world—but it sure isn't killing this one. This one is still putrid enough to gag a maggot.

We run downstairs in the basement to shop class and slam on the brakes. Walk into the drafting classroom just as the tardy bell rings.

"Boys, you're tardy," Mr. Hoffman says. He's our homeroom-shop teacher. He calls us to his desk, takes our names, and marks us tardy in his attendance book. He warns us that he'll send us to the office if we get another tardy mark. We go sit down at two empty drafting desks next to each other.

"Thanks a lot, man. You made us tardy," Arcudy whispers out of the side of his mouth.

"But we beat the bell," I whisper back.

"Tell it to the judge."

Mr. Hoffman assigns us our lockers in the basement hallway in alphabetical order. Arcudy and Jim Beck are assigned locker number 1. I'm assigned locker number 4 with Russell Ealey. I'm not crazy about getting stuck with Ealey as a locker partner for a year. He's a year older than me because he was held back a year in school. He's a really weird kid, who wears a glass eye. He has a reputation around the school for doing gross things for money. Like last year I saw him eat an earthworm for a dollar on the football field after lunch. Mr. Hoffman gives us a combination lock. Ealey claims the top shelf, so I take the lower shelf. Trying to be friendly, I tell him, "My name's Mansfield, but my friends call me Deuce."

"Beat it, shit-for-brains. I ain't your friend."

So much for trying to be friendly.

∞◊∞◊∞◊∞◊∞◊∞

When I wake up in the morning, I lie in bed, hoping that Mom oversleeps, so I won't have to go to church today. Unfortunately, she rousts me out of bed at eight thirty in time to go to both Sunday school and the worship service afterward. I dress up in my itchy wool suit, a white shirt, and a dorky, clip-on bow tie. I stash my transistor radio with the earphone in one breast pocket inside my suit coat and the latest issue of *Mad* magazine and some atomic fireballs in the other breast pocket to help me get through the sermon during the worship service.

Mom fixes Meg, Calley, and me cold cereal for breakfast. Then whisks us out the door, saying she doesn't want to be late to church again.

"Where's Tecca?" I ask.

"I let her sleep in."

"Why do I hafta go to church and she gets to sleep in?"

"She got home late last night from cheerleading at an away game. She needs her beauty sleep."

"Why doesn't Dad hafta go to church?"

"Because he's an agnostic."

"I'm an agnostic."

She rolls her eyes. "You don't even know what that means."

"Yes, I do. It's a person who doesn't know whether or not God exists. I don't wanna go to church like Dad."

"Your father and I agreed you need to go church until you're an adult. Christianity will give you the moral foundation to build your life upon. Once you're an adult, you can decide for yourself. Now get in the car."

I get into Mom's Buick Electra 225 convertible and sulk. I can't wait until I'm an adult and can be an agnostic.

I stare out the windshield at the sunny day. "Mom, it's nice out. Can we put the top down?"

"No. We don't have time."

"You never put the top down. Why did you get a convertible?"

Mom sighs like I'm trying her patience. "Mansfield, don't be difficult."

The church parking lot is full, so we have to park far away at the Red Cross building. Rushing to get out of the car, Mom runs her hose.

"God damn it," she swears.

"Mom, you broke one of the Ten Commandments. You took the Lord's name in vain," I say.

"God give me strength!" she exclaims.

I'm late for my Sunday school class. I slip in the door. Spot Nick Tridico sitting at a table in the back of the room. Girls like Tridico. They think he's good-looking because he has a Beatle haircut. He has made out with Karen Larson, who's the dreamiest girl in eighth grade at my school. I sit down next to him. He has a pencil and paper. While our Sunday school teacher teaches a Bible lesson, we play tic-tac-toe and hangman. I hang Tridico with the word phlegm. That word never fails to hang people because it only has one vowel.

After Sunday school, I ask Mom if we have to stay for the worship service. I hope not because I think sermons are really boring. She says Dr. Williams, who's the minister of our church, is giving a sermon on the subject of family, which I need to hear. I ask if we can sit in the balcony, which I think is more fun. Mom says no because she's afraid of heights. She makes me sit beside her in a pew in the front of the church. The first half of the service I look around at the stained glass windows, the religious paintings on the ceiling, and the chandeliers. I fake like I cough and slip an atomic fireball in my mouth as soon as the last spicy jawbreaker melts away. Dr. Williams announces that the Ark will meet in the parlor tonight to plan the retreat—Mom elbows me in the ribs to make sure I heard that.

I accidentally bump Meg on the leg with my foot, so she hits me on the leg, so I hit her back on the leg. We play "gotcha last." We keep hitting each other softer and softer—both of us are hoping that the other won't detect our last hit. Mom notices what we're doing and whispers "Stop" before I can hit Meg again. With a snotty grin on her face, Meg whispers in my ear "Gotcha last."

Calley and the other children go down front and listen to Dr. Williams tell the children's story. Afterward, they go to the children's room. I'm envious of Calley for getting out of listening to the sermon.

At the start of the sermon, I hide my *Mad* magazine in a hymn book, so it looks like I'm reading hymns. Soon, Mom taps me on the arm and shakes her head. I put away the *Mad* magazine.

I sneak the earphone out of my breast pocket and into my ear on the opposite side of Mom. Then turn on the transistor radio. The volume is turned up too loud—the sound just about pops my eardrum. I quickly turn it down. I tune in to WKYC, an AM station out of Cleveland, and listen to rock and roll through the sermon.

After supper this evening, Mom drives me to the Ark. I don't speak to her on the way. She drops me off at the side door of the church.

"Deuce, I think you're gonna have a good time."

"I doubt it."

I go to the parlor and peek through the open door into the room. A large group of junior high boys and girls is waiting for the meeting to start. I'm glad to see Tridico and the Lewis twins, who I know from swim team, sitting in the back row of chairs. I sit down with them. They're talking about how much they like the Beach Boys' hit song "I Get Around." I join in and say I really like it.

"Hey, Deuce. You swimming this year?" Doug Lewis asks.

"Yep."

A young man enters the room, carrying a slide projector. He's a short, chubby guy, who's going bald and combs his hair to hide it. He has rosy cheeks—he doesn't have a beard. Bad acne pockmarks are on his face and neck. His black glasses are broken and held together by white adhesive tape on the bridge. He's wearing a madras shirt, white jeans, and sandals, trying to look like the Beach Boys. A young lady is following him, lugging a portable tripod projector screen. It looks like something is wrong with her face—her left eyelid and the left side of her mouth are drooping.

"Who's that?" I ask.

"Reverend Rick and his wife. They're real winners," Tridico answers, meaning they're real losers.

While Reverend Roush sets up the slide projector, a boy calls the meeting to order. Tridico tells me he's Bob Sheldon, the president of the Ark, and calls him a wimp. Sheldon asks the recording secretary to read the minutes from last week's meeting. A pretty girl with big brown eyes and long brown hair reads the minutes. Tridico says her name is Sarah Williams—she's Dr. Williams' daughter.

Reverend Roush walks up to the podium. "Excuse me, Sarah, but I see a new face here tonight." He's looking right at me. "Young man, come up here."

Feeling self-conscious, I walk up front.

He looks at me earnestly. "Hi. I'm Reverend Roush, but you can call me Reverend Rick. Welcome to the Ark." He shakes my hand and won't let go of it. His palm is sweaty and feels like a dead fish.

Pointing toward his wife, he says, "That's my beautiful wife, Ruth."

The right side of Ruth's mouth forms a contorted smile, and she says something that I can't understand.

"What's your name?" Reverend Rick asks me.

"Deuce Delaney."

"Nice to meet you, Deuce."

Finally, he lets go of my hand. Then reaches down and actually rearranges his private parts right in front of everybody. He doesn't seem to be aware of it.

With a big smile on his face, Reverend Rick announces, "Listen, group. I want everybody to make Deuce feel welcome. We want him to feel like he belongs at the Ark."

I go sit down, feeling like I don't belong here.

Reverend Rick puts on a slide show of last year's retreat at Judson Hills. He says it's to get everybody in "the spirit of the Gospel" for this year's retreat at Judson Hills next weekend. He shows slides of a beautiful lodge where kids are eating in a dining room, studying the Bible in an assembly room, and singing along with a girl playing a guitar at a campfire. He shows pictures of a lake, but nobody's doing something fun like swimming, canoeing, or fishing. Reverend Rick keeps cracking corny religious jokes. I notice he has a speech impediment. I can't tell if it's a lisp or a stutter or what—he hides it very well.

During the slide show, I catch Sarah Williams looking at me. She smiles when I notice her. I quickly look away—I'm not interested in making friends with a minister's daughter.

After the slide show, Ruth serves refreshments. Then Reverend Rick says a prayer, and we adjourn.

Mom picks me up at the side door. She stops at a red light. Smiling at me, she asks, "So how'd it go? Did you have a good time?"

"Nope."

"Do you like Reverend Roush?"

"No. He's a loser."

"Why?"

'He's trying to be cool. But he's not. He's uncool..."

The light changes.

"So what'd you do?"

"We watched slides of last year's retreat at Judson Hills. It looked like it was no fun. There's a lake, but nobody went swimming. The kids were stuck inside, studying the Bible."

"I presume you don't wanna go this year."

"Nope. I wouldn't like it."

"Well, like it or not, you're going. It's time you started participating in something constructive."

"But I don't want to. Jack Arcudy doesn't hafta—"

"I don't wanna hear it. You will go. You will give it a chance. And that's final."

I feel like running away.

We don't speak to each other the rest of the way home.

CHAPTER THREE

On Thursday night, Mom makes me get ready to go to the retreat tomorrow. I pack my clothes, toothbrush, transistor radio, and a flashlight in a duffel bag. To spice up the retreat, I decide to take fireworks. I get three cherry bombs and my lighter out of my secret compartment. I also take *Candy* to show to Tridico. Last but not least, I make a smoke bomb. I sneak into the kitchen, measure a cup of sugar, and pour it into a paper bag. Then go to my room and get my hidden jar of saltpeter. I measure a heaping cupful, pour it into the bag with the sugar, and shake the bag. Presto—I got me a smoke bomb. This mixture burns and makes a lot of smoke but doesn't explode. I don't pack this stuff in my duffel bag. I'm afraid Mom might snoop in it while I'm at school. Instead, I hide it in the bottom of my rolled-up sleeping bag.

After school the next day, I change into Bermuda shorts, a T-shirt, and tennis shoes to wear to the retreat. Mom drops me off at the church parking lot. Ruth comes over to our car to speak to Mom. Mom presses the power window button and puts down her window. Ruth says something to her that I can't understand. Mom opens her purse, gets out her billfold, and gives her some money. After Ruth leaves, I ask, "Mom, what's wrong with Mrs. Roush's face?"

"The poor woman has myasthenia gravis. It makes the muscles in her face sag."

"She talks funny. I can't understand a word she says." I imitate her garbled talk.

"Don't make fun of her, Mansfield. We don't make fun of people with disabilities. It's insensitive."

Mom gives me some spending money in case we stop at a root beer stand. I get out of the car.

"Have a good time, Deuce."

"I won't."

"Not with that attitude. Why don't you try? You just might surprise yourself."

I grab my stuff out of the back seat.

"Mrs. Heasley said you can ride with Richard to the retreat."

"I ain't riding with him."

"Suit yourself. Bye, Deuce."

I slam the car door.

She drives away.

I look around for somebody to ride with to the retreat. Spot Tridico in the front passenger seat of a station wagon. His dad is driving a carload of kids there. The Lewis twins are in the back seat. I walk over to the car and ask Mr. Tridico if I can ride with them.

"Sure. We have room for one more," he answers.

Mr. Tridico has Nick open the tailgate on the station wagon for me, and I toss my stuff in the back. I hop in the back seat with the Lewis twins, who are glad to see me.

When it's time to leave, the drivers form a caravan in the parking lot to travel to Judson Hills. Then we hit the road with Reverend Rick leading the way. Tridico finds a rock and roll station on the radio. On the way out of town, Reverend Rick drives through two yellow traffic lights. Our car is the fourth one in line, so Mr. Tridico has to run red lights to stay in line. Then the caravan has to pull over and wait for the cars that didn't make it through the light to catch up. After Reverend Rick does it a third time, Mr. Tridico gets peeved at him.

We travel through Lucas and Perrysville far out in the country where I've never been before. Then turn onto a gravel road that runs along a river. Finally, we come to a sign that says Judson Hills. We turn into the lane and drive to a lodge overlooking a lake. I have to admit it looks cool.

As soon as Mr. Tridico parks, we kids pile out of the car and run down to the shore of the lake. Pick up flat rocks and skip them across the water. Mr. Tridico calls us back to the car and makes us unload our stuff. Then he and the other drivers head back to Waterbury—except for Mr. and Mrs. Stevens, who are going to be chaperones.

Reverend Rick leads the way to the cabins. He's wearing his white jeans, madras shirt, and sandals again. The group walks across a field of mowed grass. The girls' cabins are nestled against a pine forest at the edge of the field. Ruth, Mrs. Stevens, and the girls split off here. Reverend Rick guides the boys to the far side of the field. We follow a path through a hardwood forest and cross a footbridge with log railings spanning a creek. The boys' cabins are hidden in the trees.

Reverend Rick takes charge of the ninth grade boys and assigns cabin number 5 to them. I'm glad I won't be stuck in the same cabin as him. He puts Mr. Stevens in charge of the eighth and seventh grade boys and assigns cabin number 6 to us. Our cabin has two bedrooms filled with bunk beds. A bathroom is in between the bedrooms. Mr. Stevens puts the eighth graders in one bedroom and bunks with the seventh graders in the other bedroom. Tridico and I claim top bunks next to windows. Doug Lewis takes the bottom bunk under him. Greg Lewis takes the bottom bunk under me. Two guys who go to Sherman Junior High School, which is on the rich side of town, take another bunk. I don't know them. Richard Heasley takes a bottom bunk by himself by the door.

Tridico and the Lewis twins show each other the cans of shaving cream they brought for a shaving cream fight.

I fish *Candy,* my cherry bombs, smoke bomb, and lighter from my sleeping bag and spread them out on my mattress. "Look what I brought."

They huddle around me. Tridico's eyes light up when he sees *Candy*. "I've heard it's really dirty."

"It is," I reply.

"Where'd you get it?"

"I swiped it at Sky-Line Books and Mags."

"Can I read it?"

"Yeah. Tonight. After everybody goes to bed."

"Cherry bombs! Cool, man! Let's shoot one off!" Doug Lewis exclaims.

"Not now. We'll get in trouble," I tell him.

"What's in the bag?" Tridico asks me.

"A smoke bomb."

"It doesn't look like a smoke bomb."

"It's homemade."

"Homemade?"

"I made it by mixing saltpeter with sugar?"

"Where'd you learn how to do that?"

"I read about it in my *Van Nostrand's Scientific Encyclopedia*."

"Where'd you get the saltpeter?"

"I swiped it from a drugstore. I'm a pyro-kleptomaniac," I joke.

They laugh.

I see Heasley looking us. I put away my fireworks in my duffle bag.

Mr. Stevens enters our room. "Boys, time to eat."

We head down to the lodge. I'm feeling pretty cool. Tridico and the Lewis twins are walking with me. We sit down at a table at the back of the dining room. Reverend Rick sits at the head table with Bob Sheldon, Sarah Williams, and some other girls. It's really hot in here. Perspiration is running down Reverend Rick's forehead. Before dinner, he asks, "Would someone volunteer to say grace?"

I quickly raise my hand and say, "Grace."

The kids laugh.

Reverend Rick gives me a dirty look. He doesn't think I'm funny.

"Bob, would you please say grace?'

"Let us pray," Sheldon says, and everybody bows their heads—except me. I look around while he's praying. I notice Sarah Williams staring at me. I quickly look away.

We have a buffet dinner. Ruth and Mrs. Stevens serve sloppy joes, baked beans, potato salad, and brownies. It's not too bad. They let us go back for seconds.

After dinner, Reverend Rick announces that there will be a campfire with live music tonight. We're to meet in front of the lodge at eight thirty. We have free time until then.

Everybody cheers.

Tridico, the Lewis twins, and I explore the lodge. We open a sliding glass door and go outside onto a balcony that overlooks the lake. We spit over the railing into the water for a while.

We go back inside and go downstairs to a walkout basement. Ping pong tables are set up in a rec room. We play doubles—me and Tridico against the Lewis twins. Two ninth grade girls named Debby Foster and Kathy McDonald are playing next to us. Debby Foster is a pretty, blonde-haired, blue-eyed girl, who's a varsity cheerleader and very popular at Johnny Appleseed. Tridico tries to flirt with her, but she totally shuts him down.

At dusk we go back to our cabin and get ready for the campfire. I put on a sweatshirt and my tan jeans. Grab my flashlight. I wait on Tridico while he combs his long hair in front of the bathroom mirror. Then walk with him to the lodge.

"Man, that Debby Foster is really good-looking. I got the hots for her," he tells me.

"Forget it, man. She thinks she's better than you and you're too young for her."

He smirks. "She's just playing hard to get."

Reverend Rick leads the group to the campfire on a trail that runs along the wooded shore of the lake. The trail is dark. Tridico walks with Debby Foster and shines his flashlight on the ground ahead of them, so she can see. I do the same thing for Kathy McDonald.

Up ahead, I see a light in the forest. A campfire is blazing in the middle of a small clearing. Mr. Stevens throws a log on it.

Everybody gathers in a circle around it. Debby Foster spreads a blanket on the ground, and she and Kathy McDonald sit down. Tridico wheedles permission from Debby for him and me to sit on the blanket with them.

Reverend Rick begins by reading verses from the Bible. Then he says he wants to share with us young people some of his thoughts about God and Jesus. While he preaches, I tune him out and stare into the core of the fire. It's hypnotizing. It's like I can see a miniature world in the coals. Hell or somewhere. Finally, Reverend Rick quits preaching and asks if anybody wants to share his or her thoughts about God with the group. He's looking straight at Bob Sheldon. Sheldon talks for a while. Then Heasley has to give his two cents' worth. I think about asking, "What if there is no God?"—just to stir things up—but I don't.

Reverend Rick announces that Sue Robertson is going to play some songs for us. She gets out her guitar and plays "Puff the Magic Dragon," "Five Hundred Miles," "Where Have All The Flowers Gone?" and "Michael Row Your Boat Ashore." She's not bad. While she is singing, Tridico inches closer and closer to Debby Foster until she pushes him away.

"Does anyone have a request?" Sue asks.

"'Twist and Shout'" by the Beatles," I request.

This makes Reverend Rick mad. "That song should be banned. They sing, 'Shake it off, baby.' "

"Uh…I don't think so. They say 'up.' Not 'off,' " I say.

Reverend Rick glares at me for arguing with him.

I get the distinct impression he doesn't like me.

"I don't know that song," Sue says.

"Let's give Sue a big round of applause," Reverend Rick says.

Everyone claps.

Reverend Rick announces it's time for the floating cross. He says he wants the ceremony to be reverent—so no flashlights and no talking until we get back to the lodge. Then he asks Sue Robertson to play "Kumbaya." Everyone sings along while she plays it. Meanwhile, Reverend Rick and Mr. Stevens light candles that are stuck in holes in a wooden cross. Then they carry the cross to the shore and launch it. Burning candles in the shape of a cross float across the lake. It's supposed to be religious. Unfortunately, when the cross gets a little ways out in the lake, the wind blows the candles out.

Tridico walks with Debby Foster back to the lodge. On the way, he tries to slip his arm around her, but she slaps it away. I have to admit—the guy has nerve.

I walk Kathy McDonald back. It's really dark without a flashlight. "Watch out for Copperheads!" I whisper.

Scared, she asks, "Are they around here?"

"Just kidding."

"You go first."

"No talking," Reverend Rick scolds me.

Back at the lodge, I overhear Tridico tell Debby Foster, "Catch ya later."

The girls go to their cabins. The boys go to ours. On the way, Tridico pulls me aside.

"Hey, man. I asked Foster to meet me at the lodge tonight."

"Get outta here."

He just grins.

"What'd she say?" I ask.

" 'You wouldn't know what to do if I did.' "

"What'd you say?"

" 'Try me.' She's meeting me there at two o'clock."

"Really?"

"Yeah. She's bringing Kathy McDonald with her. You wanna come with me?"

I figure it would be fun to sneak out at night and meet girls. "Yeah. Sure."

Back at our cabin, Mr. Stevens makes us get ready for bed. Tridico and I slither into our sleeping bags with our clothes on, so we'll be ready to sneak out tonight.

Mr. Stevens enters our room and announces, "Lights out!" He turns off the light. Then leaves the door open and heads back to his room.

"Hey, Deuce. Lemme read *Candy*," Tridico whispers.

I toss him the book.

He reads it by the light of his flashlight. The Lewis twins want to read it too. I tell them after Tridico.

The Lewis twins and I lie awake talking. We tell fireworks stories. I tell about a kid who had an M-80 go off in his pocket. The idiot lit it in his driveway when a police car drove down his street. So he spit on the fuse and stuck it in his pants pocket. But the fuse wasn't out. "Man, the M-80 blew his gonads off!"

The Lewis twins groan.

"Knock it off over there!" Mr. Stevens yells.

One by one, people fall asleep. To stay awake, I listen to my radio through the earphone.

Finally, at one thirty, I figure it's time to sneak out. "Tridico," I whisper. He doesn't answer. He's sound asleep.

I crawl out of my sleeping bag, climb down the ladder, tiptoe to his bunk, and shake him. He acts like he wasn't asleep.

We take our flashlights. We're afraid to sneak out the front door—Mr. Stevens might catch us. I figure we should climb out a window. I climb onto my bunk, open the window, pop out the screen, and hand it down to Tridico. Look outside. I figure it'll be easy to hang and jump, but we could have trouble climbing back in. I unhook the metal ladder from my bunk and drop it out the window on the ground, so we can climb up it to get back in. Lying on my stomach, I back my legs out the window. Then hang and jump. A minute later, Tridico is right beside me.

We walk down the path through the woods, cross the footbridge, and come to the grass clearing. As we cross the clearing, we look for Foster and McDonald but don't see them. Tridico says they must already be at the lodge.

At the lodge, we peek in the front door. It's dark inside. Tridico says they must not be here yet. The door is unlocked. I want to go inside and raid the refrigerator, but Tridico wants to wait outside for the girls so we don't miss them. We wait by a mercury light. He asks me what time it is. I check my watch and tell him five till two.

"Oh, cool, look." I point at a huge cecropia moth flying around the mercury light. But Tridico isn't interested. All he can think about is making out with Debby Foster in the lodge.

We wait five minutes, ten minutes, fifteen minutes, but the girls don't show. Tridico starts getting worried. He keeps looking in the direction of their cabin and asking me every two seconds, "What time is it?" and "Where is she?"

At two thirty, I say, "Hey, man, I hate to say it, but I don't think they're gonna show."

"She stood me up," Tridico says.

"She's probably sound asleep."

"That stuck-up bitch."

I have a good idea. "Let's wake her up."

"How?"

"A cherry bomb."

His eyes get big. "Yeah!"

"Wait—I got a better idea."

"What?"

"The smoke bomb."

He snickers. "Let's do it!"

We run back to the cabin to get the smoke bomb and a cherry bomb. I prop the ladder against the side of the cabin and climb back inside. Everybody's still out like a light. I get the smoke bomb, a cherry bomb, and my lighter and climb back out the window.

We circle around the perimeter of the pine forest to Foster's cabin and reconnoiter. We look in the windows. It's dark inside. We sneak around the side of the cabin to the front door that opens into the pine trees.

Tridico checks the door. He whispers, "It's unlocked. Let's light the smoke bomb and toss it inside."

"No way. We don't wanna burn the place down. We could kill somebody."

"Oh."

We walk around to the other side of the building. I find a small door on the foundation. I open it and shine my flashlight into a crawl space underneath the cabin. The floor is compact dirt and the walls are concrete block. I don't see anything that can catch on fire.

I tell Tridico my plan. First, light the smoke bomb and toss it in. Then light the cherry bomb and toss it in. Then run like hell back to the cabin. But don't run across the clearing because somebody might see us. Go the back way through the woods.

"Here." I hand him the lighter. "You light. I'll throw."

He lights the lighter. I light the paper bag on fire and toss the smoke bomb into the crawl space. Wait until smoke is bellowing out. Then light the cherry bomb, quick toss it, and shut the door.

"Sweet dreams, ladies," I whisper.

We run into the woods.

Kaboom!

I glance over my shoulder. Smoke is pouring out of the cabin.

We run like maniacs. Tridico is ahead of me. He keeps pushing branches out of his way—they fly back and hit me in the face.

When we reach the cabin, we scramble up the ladder and dive in the window. Tridico leaps from my bunk to his. I jump into my sleeping bag without even taking my shoes off.

"Hey, where were you guys?" Doug Lewis asks.

"Nowhere. Go back to sleep," I say. I bury my face in my pillow—I can't stop laughing.

After a while, I hear voices outside at the other cabin and see flashlights shining around.

Doug Lewis gets up and looks out the window in the front door. "Hey, they're up next door."

"Who?" I ask.

"Reverend Rick and everybody," Doug says. He comes back to his bed and starts getting dressed.

"Where you going?" his brother asks.

"I'm gonna see what's going on."

"Wait for me," Greg says, and he jumps out of bed and starts getting dressed.

So does everybody else. Only Heasley stays in bed. They all run out the front door.

Tridico looks at me. "What are we waiting for?"

We jump out of bed and run out the front door. In the clearing, the girls are milling around, talking excitedly about what happened. They say that a big boom woke them up and there was smoke everywhere, and that Mrs. Roush thought the place was on fire and made them go outside.

I walk up to Bob Sheldon. "Hey, man, what's going on?"

"Something blew up in the girl's cabin," he answers.

"What?"

"I don't know. Reverend Rick is checking inside."

Tridico walks up to Debby Foster. She's standing with Kathy McDonald. "Glad to see you could make it," he tells her. She doesn't know what to say. She's too embarrassed about being seen in her nightie and hair curlers. Not that I blame her. She looks pretty dorky.

After a while, Reverend Rick comes outside. Shaking his head, he tells Ruth, "I don't know, honey. I can't find any sign of an explosion or fire. I checked the furnace...everywhere."

Ruth says something. I can't understand what, but I do know one thing—she's really upset.

"Calm down," he says to her. Then he tells the girls it's time to go back to bed, but they all say they're not going back in there. He tells them don't worry—he checked it out and it's safe. Finally, they go back inside.

Back at our cabin, the funny thing is Mr. Stevens slept through the whole thing.

In the morning, I put on my shorts, a different T-shirt, and my tennis shoes. Then Tridico and I walk to the lodge for breakfast, snickering about last night. Ruth and Mrs. Stevens serve scrambled eggs, bacon, toast, and orange juice in the dining hall. Debby Foster and Kathy McDonald are sitting at a table near the sliding glass door to the balcony. I follow Tridico to their table. He sits down beside Debby Foster. I sit down beside him.

"So where were you last night? You stood me up at the lodge," Triidico says to Debby.

"I couldn't sneak out. Mrs. Roush guarded the door."

"You should've climbed out the window. Like we did."

Debby is impressed that he snuck out to meet her. "Rumor has it somebody shot off fireworks at our cabin last night. Was that you guys?"

We act innocent, but she and Kathy suspect we did it.

After breakfast, Reverend Rick stands up and gives the morning announcements with a frown on his face. He announces that he found a burnt mark and ashes on the ground in the crawl space underneath the girls' cabin this morning. Then he warns us if he catches anybody with fireworks, he'll send them home. I realize I'd better get rid of the cherry bombs the first chance I get in case he searches the cabin.

Next, we have Bible study. Reverend Rick and Bob Sheldon hand out Bibles at our tables. Tridico and I share one. So do Foster and McDonald. Reverend Rick reads the lyrics to "This Is My Father's World." Then we study Bible verses about nature—how it's God's artwork. After a while, I look out the sliding glass door at the lake. It's sunny and warm out. I wish we could go swimming. If there's one thing I hate, it's sitting inside listening to a minister preaching about how beautiful it is outside. I figure if it's so beautiful outside, we should be outside enjoying it. I notice other people are becoming bored. They're yawning and talking and fidgeting in their chairs. Even Sarah Williams looks bored. Only Bob Sheldon, Heasley, and a few girls are paying attention. Reverend Rick gets more and more peeved. Finally, he stops in the middle of a verse and reminds us that this is a church retreat—not a slumber party.

Tridico whispers to Debby that he'd rather be reading *Candy*. When he tells her that we have the book, she and Kathy are interested in reading it.

Finally, Bible study ends. Reverend Rick says it's time to go on our "Walk with God." We're supposed to walk alone through the woods on the trails nearby and try to feel God's presence and talk to him. Then come back to the lodge in half an hour.

Outside, Debby and Kathy ask Tridico and me to show them *Candy*. The four of us sneak to our cabin. The girls wait outside on us. While Tridico gets *Candy*, I flush the two cherry bombs down the toilet. I hate to throw them away, but I can't take the chance of Reverend Rick finding them.

Tridico and I lead the girls to a big log out of sight in the woods, where they sit down and read *Candy*. Huddled over it, they snicker. In no time, we have to go back. I run back to our cabin and put *Candy* in my duffel bag. Then we rush back to the lodge.

It's time for lunch. We have hotdogs. At afternoon announcements, Reverend Rick announces that we have free time all afternoon. "Yay!" everybody yells. He tells us we can use the recreational equipment downstairs in the cabinets. Then he rearranges his private parts.

Tridico and Debby Foster slip out on the balcony. They hold hands at the railing and look at the lake. The next thing I know they're gone.

I go downstairs to the rec room with the Lewis twins. We start to play ping pong. Out of the corner of my eye, I see a kid running from another kid across the room. Looking over his shoulder, he runs into the sliding glass door. I hear him grunt and the sound of glass breaking. Stunned, he staggers backwards. Then he sees blood gushing from his arm. Holding his arm out, he starts jumping up and down and screaming.

I tell the twins to go get Reverend Rick. Then I rush over to the kid. I tell him to quit jumping up and down, but he won't listen to me, so I grab him and make him hold still. I see a long gash on the inside of his arm a few inches below his armpit. Blood is squirting out like a geyser. I slap my hand over the wound and apply pressure to stop the bleeding. Then make him lie down on the floor. I look around for something to make a tourniquet.

Reverend Rick and Mr. Stevens run into the room. They see blood all over the kid and panic. Reverend Rick screams at me to get out of the way and shoves me off to the side. Mr. Stevens asks Reverend Rick if he wants him to call an ambulance. Reverend Rick says no, the phone is disconnected. Then he picks up the kid and goes running upstairs with him. He carries him outside and puts him in his car. Then he and Mr. Stevens speed away.

I go to the bathroom in the lodge and wash the blood off my hands and arms. Then go back to the rec room. Ruth and Mrs. Stevens are cleaning up the blood and broken glass. Kids are gawking at it on the floor. Mrs. Stevens shoos them away.

The twins and I play ping pong for a long time. Eventually, we get bored and look in the cabinets for something else to do. We find equipment to play softball, volleyball, badminton, and horseshoes. I also find a long rope with knots tied in it every few feet—it looks like it's used for tug of war.

"Hey, man. I got an idea. Let's make a rope swing into the lake," I say.

"Cool, man," Doug says.

We go outside and look for a place to rig up the rope swing. I spot a tall tree right next to the lodge. I figure we can tie the rope to this limb that extends over the lake above the balcony and swing off the balcony.

"How are we gonna get the rope up there?" Greg asks.

"I'll show you," I answer.

I make a loop in one end of the rope and slip it over my shoulder. Then shinny up the tree to the limb. I estimate I'm about twenty feet high. Straddling the limb, I work my way out it about ten feet. Then I tie the rope around it. The rope hangs down to the water. I take off my tennis shoes and throw them onto the balcony, so they don't get wet. I don't care about my shorts and T-shirt. Then I shinny down the rope. Stick my toe in the water. Man, is it cold. I slowly lower myself in. The water is over my head. I swim back to shore with the rope and hand it to Doug Lewis.

"How's the water?" he asks.

"Nice."

I go up on the balcony. Doug throws the rope up to me. Then I climb onto the railing and leap off. I swing out across the lake—let out a Tarzan yell. At the top of the arc, I let go and drop into the water. I swim up to the surface. "Wow! Cool!"

"Lemme do it!" the twins holler.

The twins and I take turns swinging off the balcony. Soon, kids are watching us. We show off for the girls. I dive and do can-openers. Doug Lewis tries a back flip and does a belly-smacker. I notice Sarah Williams is watching me with a smile. The boys in our cabin who go to Sherman do it. Some seventh grade boys want to do it, but we tell them they're too young. I'm having so much fun that I completely lose track of the time.

All of a sudden, the sliding glass door opens and Reverend Rick comes storming out on the balcony. He sees me and Doug Lewis standing on the railing, holding the rope, about to go double.

"Get down off there!" he screams.

We let go of the rope and jump down onto the balcony.

"You're not allowed to swim here! Someone could drown!"

"We know how to swim. We're on swim team," I tell him.

"You could fall off this balcony and break your neck. Who put that rope up there?"

I slowly raise my hand and mumble, "Uh...me."

"Take it down right now!"

Man, is he mad. I figure I better not argue with him. I walk down to the shore and wade into the water.

"What are you doing?" he asks me.

"Taking down the rope."

I swim out to the rope and shinny up it to the tree limb. Then untie it and let it drop into the water.

"Alright, Mr. Smarty-pants, how do you get down?" Reverend Rick asks.

I figure I have two choices. I can either work my way across the limb to the trunk and shinny down it—which is the hard way. Or jump—which is the easy way. "Like this," I answer and jump. Banzai!" I holler. Plunge into the water and swim to the surface. Then swim to shore with the rope and climb out.

"Put that rope away!" he orders.

I take the rope into the rec room and put it in the cabinet. Then I get my tennis shoes and beat it back to the cabin with the twins. We change out of our wet clothes. I put on my tan jeans again.

Tridico comes into the cabin. He looks like he's on cloud nine.

"What'd you do this afternoon?" I ask.

Grinning from ear to ear, he answers, "I made out with Debby at the Chapel in the Pines."

I razz him by singing "Chapel of Love" by the Dixie Cups.

"What'd you do?" he asks.

I tell him about the rope swing.

"It sounds like fun," he says.

"It was till I got in trouble. Reverend Rick said we're not allowed to swim in the lake."

I have to take a crap. I go in the bathroom and sit down on the toilet. Tridico hollers through the door that they're heading back to the lodge. I tell him to go ahead—I'll catch up.

After I get done, I walk down the path through the woods. Up ahead, I see Sarah Williams standing on the footbridge, looking over the railing at the creek. As I go by, she turns around and says, "Oh—hi, Deuce."

I stop. "Hi."

"You're a dare devil—swinging off the balcony like that."

I smile modestly.

"You should've seen the look on Reverend Rick's face when you jumped out of the tree into the water. His teeth about fell out."

I laugh.

She looks at me with a sly grin on her face. "I heard about the dirty book you showed Debby and Kathy."

I play dumb. "What dirty book?"

"*Candy.*"

"Who's the big mouth?"

"Kathy."

"Don't tell anybody. I don't wanna get in more trouble."

"I won't."

"Can I read it?"

I'm surprised. I can't believe a minister's daughter wants to read *Candy.* I don't know what to say.

"Please, Deuce. I promise I won't tell anybody."

"Okay."

We sneak to my cabin. I check inside to make sure everybody is gone. Then I let her in. She shuts the door behind her and locks it.

We go to my bunk. I get *Candy* out of my sleeping bag and hand it to her. She sits down on the bottom bunk and looks at the picture of Candy on the cover.

"She's pretty," she says.

I nod.

She leafs through the book.

I watch out the window to make sure nobody is coming. Every now and then I hear her giggle.

She sets the book down on the bed. "Where do you go to school?"

"Appleseed."

"You like it?"

I shrug. "It's okay."

"I go to Sherman. I hate it. The kids are snobs. I wish I went to Appleseed. Where do you live?"

"The house on Mount Airy."

"The old mansion with the tower?"

"Yeah. That's my Observatory. I spy on the world up there."

"It's neat. Do you have any brothers or sisters?"

"Yeah. Three sisters. Tecca, Meg, and Calley."

"How old are they?"

"Tecca is seventeen. Meg is eleven. Calley is seven."

"You like them?

"Tecca is nice. Meg, can be a real pain in the butt. Calley is a riot."

"You're lucky. You have a big family. I'm an only child. I hate it. I wish I had a brother or sister."

We keep talking. I get tired of standing, so I sit down on the other end of the bed.

"What's your dad do?"

"He's a doctor."

"You like being a doctor's son?"

"It comes in handy when you're sick," I joke.

She laughs.

"Actually, he's not home much. He practically lives at the hospital."

"I hate being a minister's daughter. Nobody likes me. Everybody thinks I'm goodie-goodie. You got a girlfriend?"

"No. What about you? You got a boyfriend?"

"Bob Sheldon likes me. But I don't like him. He's a good boy. He's no fun. I like bad boys. They're more fun. Have you ever made out?"

I'm half-tempted to lie and tell her yes. But her honesty makes me tell the truth. "Nope."

She smiles. "Neither have I. Everybody thinks I'm a prude because I'm a minister's daughter. But I'm not. You wanna make out with me?"

For a second, I admire her pretty face and wavy hair.

She bats her doe eyes at me.

Something tells me don't do it. Not with Sarah Williams. She's our minister's daughter. That's just asking for trouble. Plus, I figure Tridico will razz me for making out with a minister's daughter. But I just can't resist the temptation. I figure this is my chance to find out what it's like to make out. I nod.

She scoots over next to me and faces me. She puts her arms around my shoulders, and I put mine around her waist. She gazes at me with a dreamy look in her eyes. Then she closes her eyes and puckers her lips. This is it—my heart is racing. I kiss her right on the lips. She opens her eyes and smiles at me. Nothing to it. We kiss again. I like it. Her lips feel soft and smooth. Then we start making out hot and heavy—just like in the movies.

Bam! Bam! Bam!

It startles us!

"Open this door!" somebody yells. They keep pounding on the door.

"Oh, God!" Sarah says. She looks scared to death.

I run to the front window and peek out. See Ruth and Mrs. Stevens on the front step. Mrs. Stevens looks in my direction. I duck.

They quit pounding on the door. I peek out the window again. Ruth is heading down the path. I figure she's going to get Reverend Rick. Mrs. Stevens is still standing guard on the front step.

I run back to Sarah.

"What're we gonna do?" she whispers.

"Quick. Out the window," I say.

We run to the back of the cabin. I climb up on a top bunk against the wall, open the window, climb out onto the window sill, and jump. Hit the ground and roll. Jump up and take off into the woods.

"Deuce! Wait!"

I look back. Sarah is crouched on the windowsill—scared to jump.

I run back. "Jump!"

"I can't."

"Yes, you can."

She turns around and starts climbing out the window backwards. I grab hold of her legs and start lowering her to the ground.

"Here they are! I found them!"

I turn my head and see Mrs. Stevens standing at the corner of the cabin, pointing at us. I quickly let go of Sarah, and she falls to the ground.

"They're back here!" Mrs. Stevens hollers.

Reverend Rick comes huffing and puffing around the corner with Ruth right behind him.

"I caught them sneaking out the window," Mrs. Stevens tells them.

Sarah staggers to her feet. Reverend Rick stares at her blouse which is torn open. You can see her bra. Shocked, he has to look away.

"What did you do to her?" he says to me.

"Nothing."

"Sarah, what did he do to you?"

"I didn't do anything to her," I say.

"You be quiet! I'm not talking to you!" he screams.

Sarah starts crying. Holding her blouse shut, she turns her back toward him.

"Did he try to t-t-touch you?" he stutters.

"No," I say.

"Where did he try to t-touch you?"

"Nowhere," I say.

Sarah just keeps crying.

Ruth is looking at me like I'm a sex fiend.

Reverend Rick stares intensely at Sarah. "Sarah, tell me, where did he...try..."—he's trying with all his might not to stutter—"to...t-touch you?"

Sarah sobs, "Please...leave me alone..."

Ruth puts her arm around Sarah, trying to comfort her. Then she and Mrs. Stevens take her away.

Reverend Rick says to me, "I don't know what you did to her, but I'm sending you home. You obviously cannot behave like a Christian."

I figure I'm in big trouble now—I knew I shouldn't have messed around with a minister's daughter.

He takes me around to the front of the cabin, reaches in his pocket, and pulls out a key ring, and unlocks the door. He's sweating like a pig. His madras shirt is soaked and bleeding red down his back into his white jeans—it looks like somebody shot him in the back.

We go inside to my bunk, where my stuff is. Out of the corner of my eye, I spot *Candy* on the lower bunk where Sarah and I made out. I pray, Please, God, don't let him see it.

He spots it. Picks it up and looks at the cover. Then blurts, "Did you show her this f-f-filthy smut?"

I act innocent. "I've never seen it before."

"I don't believe you. Did you try to t-t-touch her impurely?"

"What?"

His face is beet-red. "You know what I mean. Did you try to touch her br-br-breast?"

"No."

"Then how did her blouse get torn?"

"I don't know."

He looks at me like he doesn't believe me. Pointing up at the sky, he says, "God knows. He knows you did it."

He searches my duffel bag. I'm glad that I got rid of the cherry bombs.

After I gather up my stuff, Reverend Rick takes me to the lodge. Everybody's in the dining room, just sitting down for dinner, except Sarah Williams and Ruth. As he escorts me through the dining room, everybody hushes and watches me go by—they can tell I'm in big trouble but don't know why. He takes me into the kitchen, makes me sit down in on a stool in the corner next to the garbage cans, and tells me to stay here. Man, does it stink. He goes back in the dining room, where I hear him say grace.

Mrs. Stevens brings me my supper on a paper plate. She practically drops it in my lap and walks away. I eat by myself. I pick at my food—I'm not hungry. Then dump the plate in the garbage can. I figure my parents are going to kill me. Then I have an idea. If I tell Reverend Rick I'm sorry and want to be a Christian, maybe he'll change his mind about sending me home. I figure it's worth a try—I have nothing to lose.

I wait and wait on him. It's like everybody forgot about me. Finally, after evening announcements, he comes back into the kitchen. "Let's go, Delaney. I wanna be back by dark."

"Reverend Rick?"

"What?"

"Uh...I'm sorry. If you just give me one more chance, I promise I'll try to be a Christian."

He looks at me like he's not buying it. Glancing at his watch, he says, "We can talk about God and what it means to be a Christian in the car."

He takes me out to his car. He has an old, beat-up Ford Falcon. He tells me to put my stuff in the back seat. I try to sit back there, but he makes me sit up front with him. When he tries to start the car, he realizes he forgot the keys and goes back into the lodge.

I look out the window. See Tridico and the Lewis twins standing by the mercury light, talking to Debby Foster and Kathy McDonald. They keep glancing at me. Tridico comes over to the car. I roll down the window to see what he wants.

"Hey, man. Did you really try to feel up Sarah Williams?" he asks.

"No!"

"McDonald said you took her in the boys' cabin and ripped her blouse off."

"I swear all we did was make out."

Reverend Rick comes back out of the lodge. Tridico sees him and beats it out of here. Reverend Rick climbs into the car and starts the engine. When we pull out of the parking lot, Tridico and the twins wave—they're laughing at me. I prop my chin in the palm of my hand—so Reverend Rick won't see what I'm going to do—and give them the finger as we go by.

Reverend Rick gives a sermon all the way home. Seething, he calls *Candy* dirty, filthy smut. He says it demeans women and will corrupt my morals and poison my spirit. He gets so agitated talking about it I'm afraid he's going to wreck the car. Fortunately, he calms down and talks about sin and repentance.

"Mansfield, there's a battle going on between God and Satan for possession of your soul. I'm afraid Satan is winning. You need to repent before it's too late. God has a plan for you and it's to be a Christian."

He goes on and on and on. I figure if I tell him what he wants to hear, maybe he'll change his mind and take me back to the retreat.

"Jesus died on the cross for your sins. Have you been saved, Mansfield?"

"No."

"You need to be saved before you die or you won't get into Heaven. Do you want to get into Heaven?"

"Yes."

"Then you need to repent your sins. Do you repent your sins?"

"Yes."

"Do you accept the Lord Jesus as your Savior, Mansfield?"

"Yes."

"Then he will forgive your sins and save you."

"I'm forgiven?"

"Yes."

"Can I go back to the retreat?"

"No. The Bible says you must consecrate yourself to the Lord Jesus and be transformed first."

I sigh. I realize he's not going to change his mind. God may have forgiven me, but he's not going to forgive my sins no matter what I say. He keeps preaching, but everything else he says goes in one ear and out the other.

I wish I could listen to the radio, but his car doesn't have one. When he stops at a red light in Lucas, I have a mad impulse to jump out, but where would I go?

On the outskirts of town, we go past the Sunset Drive-In. I notice the movie *Psycho* is playing there. I'm dying to see it. It's supposed to be really scary. I wanted to see it last year at the theater, but Mom wouldn't let me. She said I'm too young. She's afraid it'll warp my mind. I figure I'll never get to see it now. My parents are going to lock me up and throw away the key.

When we get to Waterbury, Reverend Rick tells me to keep my mouth shut about what happened with Sarah Williams in the cabin. He doesn't want me to ruin her reputation. He doesn't know where Mount Airy Lane is so I have to show him. Then his poor clunker can barely make it up the steep hill—it keeps almost stalling. When he reaches our driveway, he looks at our house on top of the hill. He looks impressed.

"I don't believe I've met your father. What does he do?"

"He's a doctor."

"Does he come to church often?"

"Huh-uh. Sunday is his only day off. He likes to sleep in. He's an agnostic."

"I don't imagine he'll be happy that I sent you home, will he?"

"Nope."

"Well, I'm sure he'll understand why I had to do it."

I tell him he should turn around at the turnaround at the mail box and not try to drive all the way up to the garage. The driveway is so tight it's practically impossible to turn around up there unless you know what you're doing. And it's harder than hell to back out.

But he doesn't listen to me and drives all the way up. I notice Dad and Mom's cars are gone. I start praying for nobody to be home.

He parks the car and we get out. I get my stuff, and we walk up on the front porch. I open the door. It seems pretty quiet inside. I tell him I don't think anybody's here.

"Anybody home?" he yells. Nobody answers.

He waits around for a few minutes. Finally, he says he has to get back to Judson Hills and tells me to tell Dad he'll call him tomorrow afternoon after he gets home from the retreat. He gets back in his car and tries to leave. First, he tries to turn around but discovers he can't. Then he tries to back out. He keeps backing into the retaining wall. The whole time I'm going crazy—I want him to get out of here before somebody comes home. Finally, he leaves.

I sit on the steps of the front porch, getting more and more worried. My parents are going to yell at me. Then ground me.

All at once, I have a good idea—to sleep out in the tree fort tonight and come home tomorrow when I'm supposed to. This way my parents won't know that I got sent home. I can tell them Mr. Tridico drove me home. Maybe I could even call Reverend Rick myself tomorrow and fake like I'm Dad. I can disguise my voice by putting a handkerchief over the mouthpiece of the telephone. I've faked other people out before by doing that. I'd better get the hell out of here before somebody comes home. I grab my stuff and beat it out of there.

CHAPTER FOUR

I run downhill through our back yard into the woods. As soon as I'm out of sight, I slow down. At the tree fort, I haul my stuff up the ladder, which is made out of boards nailed to the trunk of the tree. I snag my shirt on a nail sticking out of one of the boards—I need to hammer it back in. I shove my stuff through the trap door and climb into the tree fort.

Damn it—somebody's busted in again.

The milk box is open—my old comic books and *Mad* magazines and a deck of cards are strewn all over the place. I suspect it was the bird-brain Byrd brothers, who live on Mount Airy Lane—they've raided my tree fort before.

I have a few hours to kill before bedtime. I have a good idea. I'll go to the drive-in and see *Psycho.* The only problem is how to get there. I'm scared to go home and get my bike, but it's too far to walk. Finally, I figure I have no choice.

I sneak back to the house and peek in the garage. Everybody's still gone. I dash into the garage, jump on my bike, and pedal as fast as I can down Mount Airy Lane. Fearful that I'll run into my parents coming up the hill, I hold my breath all the way. I make it.

Every time a semi passes me on the highway, I just about get blown off the road.

I get in the line of cars at the entrance to the drive-in. The guy in the ticket booth thinks it's funny that I rode my bike to the drive-in and lets me in for free. I park in the front row and prop the speaker on the handlebars. Then go buy some buttered popcorn and sit on my bike with the kickstand down.

The beginning of the movie is boring—there aren't any monsters, vampires, or ghosts. But then a pretty lady gets stabbed to death in the shower. Man, is it gory. It scares the crap out of me. I can hardly watch the rest of the movie.

When I ride home, I turn on the headlight on my bike—it shines a dim beam ahead. My house is dark inside—everybody's in bed. I sneak my bike into the garage. Then head for the tree fort. I hesitate at the path into the woods. Man, is it spooky in there. I wish I had my flashlight.

As I walk down the path, I keep looking behind me—I'm scared a psycho is following me. I walk faster and faster. Finally, I reach my tree fort. I climb up the ladder and close the trap door as fast as I can. Fish my flashlight out of the duffel bag and shine it on the ground—don't see anything.

My imagination is running wild because of that scary movie. I tell myself to relax. I look at my watch—it's almost midnight. I get undressed. All I wear to bed is a T-shirt and my underpants. I set my jeans and tennis shoes beside my sleeping bag.

I have to take a leak. I don't feel like climbing back down the ladder, so I just pee over the side. It makes a neat waterfall. I unroll my sleeping bag on the floor, crawl in, and get situated. Then turn off my flashlight. Man, is it dark. All I can see are a few stars shining through the trees. And quiet. All I can hear are the crickets chirping and the leaves rustling in the breeze.

I tuck my flashlight in a fold of the sleeping bag by the zipper— just in case I need it. Then close my eyes and try to fall asleep but keep picturing the psycho stabbing the lady to death in the shower. What if a psycho tries to get me? I'll be trapped up here with nowhere to run or hide. Nobody will hear me yelling for help this far away. I imagine a psycho lurking in the dark, waiting for me to fall asleep. He could be sneaking up on me right now...

All of a sudden, I hear a noise.

Grabbing my flashlight, I shine it at the trapdoor—don't see anything. I slip out of my sleeping bag, crawl over to the trap door, open it, and shine my flashlight on the ladder and ground—don't see anything down there. I shine it down the path toward the creek where Regina Wukela got murdered—nothing down there.

I laugh and tell myself it's just my imagination playing tricks on me—all because of that damn movie. But, just in case, I'll set up an alarm. I set the milk box on top of the trap door. Then balance an empty pop bottle on top of the milk box. I figure it'll fall off and wake me up if somebody tries to open the trap door. Then I crawl back inside my sleeping bag. I swear I'll never watch a movie like *Psycho* again unless I'm at home with the lights on.

A noise wakes me up.

Disoriented, I don't know where I am...then realize I'm in my sleeping bag in my tree fort.

Oh, my God! It was the pop bottle falling down that woke me up.

Petrified, I watch the trapdoor slowly open...

The milk box tips over.

A hideous face appears—

"Ahhh!" I scream.

The face disappears and the trap door slams shut.

I frantically squirm out of my sleeping bag, scramble over to the trap door, and crouch on it—using my weight to hold it shut.

"Help!" I yell louder and louder until I'm screaming at the top of my lungs.

It's no use—nobody can hear you.

I strain my ears—don't hear anything. Wait...then slowly move off the trap door, creep over to the side of the tree fort, and peer into the darkness down below...

Is it gone?

I faintly discern a white silhouette of a human being standing in a patch of moonlight on the path...

It's looking up at me...

I watch paralyzed with fear...

It vanishes down the path toward Possum Run.

Get outta here!

I bolt!

Flinging open the trap door, I scurry down the ladder. My bare foot slips off a rung—

I fall. As I plummet, my chest scrapes against the ladder. I land hard on my heels on the ground and fall backwards on my butt...

Run!

I spring to my feet. Then run for my life up the path through the dark woods, ducking under branches and stumbling over roots and rocks in my bare feet...

I burst out of the woods into my back yard. See our dim house on top of the hill. Sprinting across the yard, I glance over my shoulder to see if it's chasing me. Right then I trip over Calley's sand box and fall head over heels in the grass. Jump up and hobble across the yard—my shin is killing me.

I scramble up the bank on my hands and feet and dash around the side of the house to the front porch. Ring the doorbell, pound on the door, and yell, "Let me in!"

Ike starts barking in the house.

I keep glancing behind me. "Hurry up!"

Finally, I see a light come on in the house. Then see Dad coming down the stairs, fastening his robe. Mom is behind him in her nightgown. Dad turns on the porch light and looks out the window in the front door. Sees it's me and unlocks the door.

I shove the door open and run past him through the foyer into the living room. Just stand here, panting...

Dad and Mom just stand there, looking surprised to see me...

I gasp, "Something...tried...to get me."

"What?!" Dad exclaims.

I catch my breath for a second. "Something tried to get me."

"Oh, my God! He's bleeding, Doc," Mom cries, pointing at my chest.

My T-shirt is torn and there's a big splotch of blood on the front of it. Suddenly, I feel woozy.

Dad pulls off my shirt and examines me. Blood is oozing from a gash on my chest. "Hmm…this is a pretty deep laceration. But it's not life-threatening. He'll need a few stiches."

Mom looks relieved. Then bewildered. "Mansfield, what are you doing here? Why aren't you at the retreat?"

Dad hands me my shirt. "Mansfield, hold your shirt against the wound to stop the bleeding."

I do it.

"Doc, he should be at the retreat," Mom says. Flabbergasted, she throws her hands up in the air. "Why isn't he at the retreat? What is he doing here running around barefoot in his underwear?"

"Alright, calm down. Don't get hysterical. Let me handle this," Dad says to her. Then he says to me, "What the hell are you doing here?"

"Dad, please…listen to me…something tried to get me."

"Where?" Dad asks.

"Uh…the tree fort."

"The tree fort? You should be at the retreat. What the hell were you doing at the tree fort?"

"Uh…I…uh…" I stammer.

"Answer me."

"I…uh…got sent home."

"What?! Who sent you home?"

"Reverend Rick."

"Oh, no," Mom groans.

"God damn it, Mansfield!" Dad swears. Man, is he furious. "Now what did you do?"

"Nothing."

He gets in my face. "I don't believe you. You must've done something to get sent home."

"What's going on?" Calley asks. She's upstairs in the hallway, looking down over the bannister at us.

"Calley, go back to bed!" Mom yells.

"Is Deuce in trouble?"

"Calley, go back to bed!" Dad commands.

She runs down the hall to her room.

"Helen, let's suture his wound. Then we'll get to the bottom of this."

Dad steers me into the kitchen and makes me lie down on my back on the kitchen table. Then he gets his doctor's bag. Since Mom was a nurse before she married Dad, she assists him. He takes away my shirt and has Mom hold a compress against the wound while he washes his hands. Then he cleans my wound. Man, does that hurt. He dabs some ointment on the gash with a big, cotton-tipped swab. It burns like crazy. Mom hands him a clamp and a thin, curved needle with a black thread.

"Mansfield, this may sting a little. I don't have any local anesthetic," Dad warns me. He has Mom grip my shoulders so I don't move. Then he sews a stitch. It feels like somebody touched me with the head of a match right after it's blown out. Mom snips the thread with scissors and dabs the spot with cotton. I grit my teeth and watch the seconds tick by on the kitchen clock.

"There. That should do it," Dad says.

My eyes are watering a little, but I'm not crying. "How many stitches?"

"Six."

Dad applies antiseptic. Then makes a bandage out of gauze and strips of adhesive tape. "Alright, you can get down now."

I climb off the table.

"So how'd you get hurt?" Dad asks.

I try to remember what happened...

"I was asleep in the tree fort...and something tried to get me." I picture its face. "It had a hideous face. I was so scared I just tried to get away. I climbed down the ladder as fast as I could. My foot slipped, and I fell. As I fell, my chest scraped against the boards nailed to the tree. A nail must've got me."

"You'll need a tetanus shot."

Dad reaches in the pocket of his robe, pulls out a pack of cigarettes and his lighter, lights a cigarette, and takes a long drag. "So why'd Reverend Roush send you home?"

"Don't you care something tried to get me?"

"We'll come back to that later. Right now I wanna know why you got sent home."

"Uh...he thinks I tried something on a girl."

"What girl?" Mom asks.

"Sarah Williams."

"Sarah Williams?!"

"Helen, please—let me handle this. What does he think you tried to do to her?"

"Uh...touch her impurely."

"What do you mean?"

"Uh...he thinks I tried to touch her, you know, breast."

"Oh, God, no! Not Dr. Williams' daughter. Did you?" Mom asks.

"No!"

"You better not have."

"Why does he think that?" Dad asks.

"Well...uh...they caught me and her in a cabin and—"

"You were in a cabin with Sarah Williams?" Mom asks.

I nod my head.

"Just the two of you?"

I nod again.

"What did you do in there?" Dad asks.

"Nothing."

"Did you try something?"

"No."

"Then why does he think that?"

"Well...uh...her blouse was torn."

"Her blouse was torn?" Mom asks.

I nod my head.

"Did you try to feel her?" Dad asks.

"No."

"Then how did it get torn?"

"I don't know."

They look at each other with sheer panic on their faces.

"It...it must've happened when we tried to get away."

Mom rushes to the phone.

"What're you doing?" Dad asks her.

"I'm calling Reverend Roush."

"Helen, it's three o'clock in the morning. He's asleep."

"I don't care. I'll wake him up."

"You can't call him. The cabins don't have phones. And the phone at the lodge is disconnected," I say.

Mom puts down the phone. She looks like she wants to strangle me.

"He said he'd call you when he gets home tomorrow afternoon," I tell Dad.

"Helen, there's nothing we can do tonight. I'll talk to Roush tomorrow."

Turning to me, Dad says, "All I gotta say is you better not be lying. If you tried to feel her, I'll..." He doesn't say what he'll do to me, but the look on his face says he'll kill me. "How did you get home?"

"Reverend Roush drove me."

"When?"

"After supper."

"When we were gone?"

"Yeah."

"So you ran away and hid out at the tree fort, right?"

I nod my head.

"You didn't have the guts to face the music like a man. Did you?"

I shake my head.

He shakes his head in disgust. "You're confined to your room until I talk to Reverend Roush. Now go to bed."

"But—but something tried to get me."

"I suspect you had a nightmare."

"It wasn't a nightmare. I saw it. It had a hideous face."

"I told you to stop watching all those horror movies on *Ghoulardi*. They'd give you nightmares. Go!"

As I head up the stairs, I yell over my shoulder, "Jeez, you don't even care something tried to get me!"

Before I go to bed, I go into the bathroom. Pull back the bandage on my chest and look at my stitches. They look pretty gross. I figure they'll leave a pretty big scar. I rub the bump on my shin from when I banged into Calley's sandbox.

On the way to my room, I spot a crack of light under my parents' bedroom door. I creep to the door and put my ear to the keyhole.

"Doc, he truly believes he saw something," Mom says.

"It was a nightmare, Helen. Remember, he had vivid nightmares as a child. Go to sleep."

Their light goes out. I go to my room. I figure I'm in big trouble again, but I don't care. I'm just glad to be home safe and sound in my own bed. I roll over and try to go to sleep but can't. I keep picturing whatever it was that tried to get me—see its hideous face looking at me. All I know is it wasn't a nightmare.

∞◊∞◊∞◊∞◊∞◊∞

When I wake up in the morning, last night seems like a bad dream. But then I feel my stitches pulling, and I know it really happened. I check to see if they've healed at all, but they look even grosser.

I crawl out of bed and look out the window in the direction of my tree fort. Wonder what tried to get me last night. I want to go back there and investigate in broad daylight, but I can't since I'm confined to my room.

Mom opens my door. "Mansfield, we're not going to church. I can't face Dr. Williams this morning."

"Mom, can I go get my stuff at the tree fort?"

"Yes. But come right back."

I get dressed. I have to wear my old tennis shoes.

When I climb up the ladder to the tree fort, I examine the nail sticking out of the board. I think I see blood on it, but it could be rust.

In the tree fort, I find the fallen pop bottle and toppled milk box. I tell myself that's proof it wasn't a nightmare—something tried to enter the tree fort. I gather up my stuff, drop it down on the ground, and climb back down the ladder. Go to the spot where I think I saw whatever tried to get me and look around for footprints. Don't see any.

Looking for footprints, I go down the path toward Possum Run but don't see any. I pause at the top of the cliff. Even though I know I should turn back, I decide to investigate the place where Regina Wukela got murdered. I climb as fast as I can down the cliff to the creek. Hop from rock to rock to the pool of water below the opening of the sewer pipe. A rubber is floating in the brown foam on the surface—gross. I peer inside the sewer pipe. A trickle of water is running out of it and down a pile of rocks. I don't see any clues.

I hurry back to the tree fort, grab my stuff, and jog home. My stitches hurt. I pull up my shirt—see blood seeping through the bandage.

In the kitchen, Mom asks, "What took you so long?"

"My stitches slowed me down." I show her the blood seeping through the bandage.

She sends me back to my room.

At one o'clock, Mom calls me downstairs for Sunday dinner. During the meal, everybody ostracizes me. Nobody says a word about last night.

Dad drives me to his office to get my tetanus shot. On the way, I tell him about the alarm that I rigged last night in my tree fort and what I found there this morning. He just stares out the windshield.

"Dad, that proves something tried to get me."

"You probably knocked them over when you fled. Or maybe it was a raccoon."

We don't speak to each other the rest of the way home. Then he sends me back to my room.

I play solitaire at my desk. I'm just killing time until I get yelled at. As time goes by, I get more and more worried. Man, I wish they'd hurry up and get it over with.

At three o'clock I hear the phone ring downstairs through the floor register. I figure it's Reverend Rick calling Dad. I rush to the register and hold my ear against it. Sometimes I can hear people talking downstairs through the register, but I can't hear him.

I go back to my desk and play another hand of solitaire...

"Mansfield! Come down here!" Dad yells.

Feeling pins and needles in my stomach, I go downstairs. Dad and Mom are in the den. Dad is sitting at his desk smoking a cigarette, and Mom is sitting on the leather couch. Dad tells me to shut the sliding doors. Then tells me to sit down in the armchair in front of the desk—it's the hot-seat.

Dad stamps his cigarette out in the ashtray. "I just spoke to Reverend Roush. It appears you're telling the truth. The Williams girl said she ripped her blouse climbing out the window."

Man, am I relieved.

"But you're still in hot water. Did you take her into a cabin and lock the door?"

"She locked the door."

"What did you do in there?"

"Uh...we just talked."

"Is that all?"

I nod my head. I'm praying she lied.

"That's not what she said. She said you made out with her."

"Oh, yeah, I forgot. I guess we did that a little too."

Dad starts grilling me. "Did you show her a dirty book? Some book called *Candy?*"

I figure Sarah probably told the truth about that too. I nod again.

"Why?"

"Uh...she asked me to."

"Dr. Williams' daughter?" Mom says like she doesn't believe me.

"She did."

"Where'd you get this book?"

"I found it."

"Where?"

"In a trash can in Luna Lake Park."

64

Mom says, "That's where that book belongs. I'm really disappointed you took that trash to a church retreat and showed it to Dr. William's daughter. I thought I raised you better than that."

"Did you shoot off a cherry bomb and a smoke bomb under the girls' cabin late at night?" Dad asks.

"No." I figure Reverend Rick can't prove it was me who did it.

"Reverend Roush said a boy in your cabin saw you show another boy a cherry bomb."

It had to be Richard Heasley—that little rat fink squealed on me. I ought to pound him.

I sigh. I figure they got me now, so I say, "It was just a prank."

"Where'd you get the cherry bomb?"

"I bought it from Denny Boebel. His dad buys lots of them when they go to Florida."

"Cherry bombs are very dangerous. I've had to surgically repair fingers that have almost been blown off by them. Do you have any more?"

"No," I lie.

"Where'd you get the smoke bomb?"

"I made it."

"Out of what?"

"Saltpeter and sugar in a paper bag."

"You think you're real smart, don't you? Well, you're not. Don't you realize you could've started a fire? You could've killed somebody."

"I set it on the ground so it wouldn't catch anything on fire."

"That's how accidents happen. You have any more saltpeter?"

"No. I used it all up," I lie.

"Did you and your friends go swimming in the lake?"

"Yes."

"That's dangerous. Somebody could've drowned without a lifeguard."

"We all knew how to swim."

"Did you rig up a rope swing and swing off the balcony?"

"Yes."

"That's dangerous too. You don't know what's underwater in a lake. Somebody could've hit their head on a stump and been knocked unconscious."

"We didn't."

"You were lucky."

I don't say anything. It's no use arguing with an adult.

Dad looks at Mom and shakes his head. "I can't believe one kid can screw up so much in that short of time."

"You wouldn't think there're enough hours in the day," Mom replies.

Dad lectures me. Something is wrong with me. I can't do anything without getting in trouble and sent home. I deserved to be sent home—I behaved like a hellion. Mom says that she's ashamed of me and that she'll never be able to look Dr. Williams in the eye again.

The phone on Dad's desk rings, and he answers it. He tells Mom there's an emergency at the hospital, and he has to leave. He tells me we'll finish this later and sends me back to my room.

I sit at my desk, worrying about my punishment. I figure they'll ground me for at least two weeks. Then I work on my English composition. I'm hoping to score some brownie points by doing my homework. After I get done, I play solitaire again. Play hand after hand. Don't win one.

At six o'clock I hear somebody coming up the stairs. I hide the cards in the top drawer of my desk, pick up my pen, and act like I'm working on my composition. It's just Meg. She brings me my supper on a tray. When she sets it down on my desk, she says, "I don't know if I should come in here. I might get raped."

"Get outta here!" I pick up a deviled egg off my plate and act like I'm going to throw it at her.

She runs out of the room.

After supper, I get Sting out of the aquarium and play with him at my desk. I tell him my problems. "Sting, something tried to get me last night, and my parents don't believe me."

Dad doesn't get home until almost ten o'clock. He calls me downstairs again. I stop outside the door to the den and eavesdrop.

I hear Dad tell Mom that he stopped at the parsonage and talked to Dr. Williams on his way home from the hospital. Dr. Williams said wild rumors are already spreading around the church about Sarah and me. Outraged parents called him and the deacons after their kids came home from the retreat and told them what happened there. Mrs. Heasley demanded that they fire Reverend Roush. The deacons have decided to get rid of him for letting things get out of control.

Oh, shit!

"Mansfield! Get down here!" Dad yells. "God damn it—where is he?"

I walk in the den and sit down in the hot-seat. Dad is fuming. Mom looks shook up. I say, "Well, I finished my comp—"

"Christ Almighty, Mansfield! You've caused a scandal at the church. Everyone's talking about you and Dr. William's daughter," Dad says.

"You've ruined her reputation," Mom says.

"Because of you and your shenanigans, they fired Reverend Roush," Dad says.

"I...I didn't mean to ruin Sarah's reputation. Or get Reverend Rick fired."

"That's what's wrong with you. You always fail to see the consequences of your actions."

"I'm sorry."

"I'm afraid it's too late for that. You've caused serious harm. I have to severely punish you. I'm grounding you for two months."

"Two months?!"

"I'm imposing strict controls. I'm gonna keep a tight rein on you. You don't go anywhere without first getting permission from either your mother or me. That means no football games. No staying overnight at a friend's house. You go straight to school and you come straight home. No going to anybody's house or stopping at Ven-Mar or the park. If the only way to keep you out of trouble is to not let you out of the house, then that's what I'll do.

"And I'm docking your allowance—you'll only get lunch money.

"And no TV without our permission.

"And you're gonna have to apologize to Dr. Williams.

"And you're to stay away from Sarah Williams. Is that clear?"

I nod my head.

"It better be. Now go to your room."

Outside the den, I stop and eavesdrop again. I hear Mom say, "Doc, I feel terrible about Reverend Roush."

"So do I. But I don't think it was all Mansfield's fault. Dr. Williams said they were looking for an excuse to get rid of him. Apparently, he has a bad habit of unconsciously rearranging his private parts in public."

I go upstairs to my room and throw myself down on my bed. Man, am I mad. Two months. They actually grounded me for two months. That's almost until Thanksgiving.

I hate them. They have to be the meanest, strictest parents in the whole world.

I wish I had different parents. Ones like Arcudy's. I swear they let him get away with murder.

Someday I'm gonna run away. Just as soon as I turn sixteen, I'm gonna drop out of school and run away and become a professional skin diver just like Mike Nelson. I imagine myself cruising around the ocean on a great, big cabin cruiser—skin diving all day.

They'll never be able to ground me again.

They don't even care something tried to get me.

I think about last night again. Maybe it was just a nightmare or a raccoon...

No way.

I picture its hideous face in my mind. Then picture the white silhouette of a human being standing in a patch of moonlight.

It wasn't a nightmare or a raccoon.

I drift off to sleep...

I'm in my tree fort. It's dark and fog is swirling around. I see its hideous face. It disappears.

I'm in the woods at Possum Run. An invisible force pulls me to the opening of the sewer pipe. Powerless to stop, I climb into the pipe and walk into blackness. Turn around. The opening is a small circle of light far away. Then I sense something is right in front of me. I try to run, but it's like I have weights on my feet. I feel a cold, moist breath in my ear and long, bony fingers digging into my sides. Struggle with all my might but can't get away. Scream, but no sound comes out.

I wake up—heart thumping. Realize it was just a nightmare. Lying perfectly still, I look around the room to make sure nobody's lurking in the shadows. Then look at my wrist watch. It's three fifteen. I get up, go to the bathroom, take a leak, and get a drink of water.

I don't go back to bed right away. I'm scared I'll pick up where I left off in my bad dream. Instead, I go up in my Observatory and look out the window. I think about Regina Wukela—how people say her ghost haunts Possum Run where she was murdered.

Her ghost...maybe you saw her ghost...

But I don't believe in ghosts.

But then I think there weren't any footprints, and I remember how it looked like a white shadow. I decide to go to the library tomorrow to check out the newspaper articles on Regina Wukela and see if I can find any books on ghosts. Then I go back to bed.

CHAPTER FIVE

On the way to school, Arcudy asks me, "Hey, man, you wanna go to the Waterbury Senior High football game on Friday night? We can meet girls there."

"I can't. I'm grounded for two months."

"Two months! What'd you do? Rob a bank?"

I tell him about getting sent home from the retreat on the weekend. And then how something tried to get me at the tree fort.

"Are you kidding?" he asks.

"No."

"What was it?"

"I don't know. All I know is it had a hideous face."

He looks at me funny.

"Uh...you promise you won't laugh?"

He nods.

"Say it."

"I promise."

"I think I saw a ghost."

He laughs. "Get outta here."

"I swear it. It was white and sort of floated down the path towards Possum Run."

"Maybe it was a person."

"No human being has a face like that. I'm telling you—I saw a ghost...the ghost of Regina Wukela."

He just looks at me funny again.

On Saturday afternoon, I ask Mom for permission to go to the Waterbury Public Library. I tell her I need to find a book for my report in History class. She says okay, but I have to be home by five thirty, and I'm not allowed to go anywhere else.

I ride my bike downtown to the library and tell the lady at the reference desk that I want to read the newspaper articles on Regina Wukela. She brings me reels of microfilm and shows me how to work the microfilm machine.

I reel the machine to July 18, 1959. A big headline at the top of the front page of the Waterbury Times reads, "Waterbury Man Confesses To Killing Girl." A smaller headline underneath it reads, "Girl Sexually Molested, Tortured, and Drowned." There's a picture of the killer, Carl Hickey. Man, does he look creepy. There's also a picture of Regina Wukela. She looks cute. She's wearing glasses shaped like cat eyes and her two front teeth are missing. I read the article:

> Carl Hickey, 28, of 563 Wolfe Avenue, reportedly confessed to sexually molesting, torturing, and killing Regina N. Wukela, 9, of 63 Davey Avenue, yesterday afternoon in Luna Lake Park. The girl's body was found by Detective Lt. Robert Czarnecki last night in a storm sewer pipe that drains into Possum Run approximately one-quarter mile southeast of the park pavilion. First degree murder charges are expected to be filed against the 6 foot 2 inch, 200 pound man, who has tagged himself as a "lone wolf," by Fairland County Prosecutor Thomas C. Brown tomorrow.
>
> Hickey confessed to the crime which shocked the city after interrogation by Police Chief James T. Saxon, Detective Lt. Robert Czarnecki, and Detective Lt. Peter Wiley. Investigator J. B. O'Donnell and lie detector expert Albert Scott of the Ohio Bureau of Criminal Investigation also participated. Hickey was subjected to a lie detector test by Scott, but the results of the test have not been released.
>
> Hickey told police he first saw the Wukela youngster

while standing on the wooden bridge just south of the pavilion in Luna Lake Park. He placed the time around 1:00 p.m. He said the girl was wearing a red two-piece bathing suit and was walking towards the lake. Hickey told police he asked the girl if she wanted to go swimming in the shallow pool of water underneath the bridge. Hickey demonstrated to police how he held her by the hands and lowered her up and down in the water.

According to police, Hickey asked the girl if she wanted him to show her an even better "swimming hole." He then led her into the woods behind the pavilion to a large pool of water below the opening of the sewer pipe. Police said there he exposed himself to the Wukela girl. When she screamed and tried to run away, he dragged her into the sewer pipe where he sexually molested her. Hickey admitted to police that he gouged out the girl's eyeballs with his car keys so she would not be able to identify him. Fearing she could still identify him, he told police he held the girl face down in the water until she drowned. He placed the time around 2:30 p.m.

Police said Hickey showed no remorse during the confession.

According to police, Mrs. Norma L. Wukela, the mother of the victim, said her daughter left home after lunch to go to the Possum Run swimming pool. After she failed to return home for supper, the mother notified the Waterbury Police Department at 6:21 p.m. that her daughter was lost. Police then conducted a search of the park.

Detective Lt. Peter Wiley questioned Harold "Cappie" Smith, who operates the boat rental business in Luna Lake Park. Smith informed the police officer that he'd seen a man playing with a little girl, who matched the description of the Wukela girl, on the wooden bridge around 1:30 p.m. He told police he saw them walk behind the pavilion. An hour later, he saw the man drive away alone in a white 1954 Ford Sunliner. Smith said he wrote down the car's license plate number because the man was acting suspiciously.

Through the Bureau of Motor Vehicles, police determined that the car was owned by Hickey. Police said he immediately became a suspect because of his past criminal record of sex offenses. Hickey was arrested by Lt.

Wiley last night at the home of his mother, Sheila Hickey. Lt. Wiley said he offered no resistance. He was taken by police to the Waterbury Police Department for questioning.

Police searched Hickey's car and found the bottom piece of a red two-piece bathing suit in the glove compartment. Police then conducted a search of the woods southeast of the pavilion along Possum Run. Just before dark Detective Lt. Czarnecki found a rubber beach sandal floating in the creek near the sewer pipe. He then discovered the girl's mutilated body inside the sewer pipe.

Fairland County Coroner Dr. Willard Orewiler said the girl's body was sent early this morning to the Cuyahoga County Coroner's Office for examination.

Dr. Orewiler said his preliminary examination of the girl's body late Thursday night revealed evidence of sexual assault.

There's another article with the headline, "Crime Shocks City." It tells what people around town think about the murder. Everybody says Hickey is a "monster" or "sick." One guy says, "Fry him."

I skim the rest of the articles on Hickey. They say the jury found him guilty and gave him the death penalty. The judge sentenced him to be executed in the electric chair—"Old Sparky." I look for an article on his execution but can't find one. All I see is a picture of Hickey in his cell on death row in the Ohio State Penitentiary. He still looks as creepy as ever.

Next, I look for a book on ghosts. I find one called *The Ghost Busters* by Maxwell Finney. The author is a "professional ghost buster." His job is to drive ghosts out of haunted houses so the owners can sell them. In the chapter called "Characteristics of Ghosts," I read:

> A ghost is the disembodied spirit of a dead person. In cases where a person has died a violent death, his spirit may appear because it is unable to rest in peace. Usually the ghost is seen as a pale, shadowy apparition. However, it may be heard as a sound, felt as a wind, or smelled as an odor. Frequently, the ghost appears at or near the place where the violent death occurred. Sometimes it appears at the time of the day on the

date of the year that the violent death occurred. It may also choose to appear only to certain receptive people.

The more I think about this, the more I become convinced what I saw that night in my tree fort was the ghost of Regina Wukela. So how do I prove it? I need to stake out my tree fort at night and take a picture of it when it comes back. But that won't work. I can't take a picture of it at night. And I don't want to do this alone.

I need someone else to see it with me. Who? Arcudy. I'll ask him. He's my best friend. He'll help me.

Before I go, I check out a book on Tecumseh just in case Mom checks to see if I was really working on my report.

On Sunday, Dad removes my stitches and says my wound is healing nicely.

On the way to school the next day, Arcudy tells me he sat with Tammy Kramer at the Waterbury Senior High football game on Friday night. Tammy goes to Appleseed and is pretty good-looking. He says he walked her home after the game, and they held hands. Then made out in her garage. Man, he's on cloud nine.

"That's nice. Jack, I think I really did see the ghost of Regina Wukela."

He rolls his eyes like not this again.

I tell him about the newspaper articles that I read at the library. I read to him the paragraph about the characteristics of ghosts from *The Ghost Busters,* but he's only half-listening.

"It's like the book says. She died a violent death. Her spirit won't be able to rest in peace until Carl Hickey is electrocuted. He mutilated her face. That explains the hideous face I saw. My tree fort is near the place she was murdered. Who knows? Maybe I'm one of those receptive people."

He looks at me like I'm crazy.

"I can prove it. All we hafta do is stake out the tree fort."

"You can't. You're grounded."

"I'll sneak out."

"When?"

"Friday night."

"I'm going to a make out party with Tammy on Friday night."

"We can do it afterward. The ghost didn't come until late at night. C'mon, let's be ghost busters!" I plead.

"I don't know…"

"Arcudy, you're changing."

"No, I'm not."

"Yes, you are. You're more interested in girls than a mystery."

"Okay, I'll go."

At lunch on Friday, I remind Arcudy that we're sneaking out tonight. I arrange to meet him at the bridge at the bottom of Mount Airy at midnight. I figure my parents will have gone to bed by then. I make him promise to be there.

At eleven o'clock I say goodnight to Mom and Dad and go to bed. Get my flashlight out of the nightstand and read my book on ghosts under the covers. I don't trust myself to just lie here in the dark—I might fall asleep.

I read the chapter called "The Harrison House." It's about an old mansion in Worcester, Massachusetts, that's supposed to be haunted. There's a picture of it. It reminds me of our house—it has a tower. It's supposed to be haunted because a guy named Charles L. Harrison went nuts and murdered his wife and one-year-old daughter with an ax. Then hung himself from the stairway in the tower. People who've lived there have witnessed strange things like a phantom baby crying in the nursery at night, unexplained blood on the floors, and supposedly the ghost of Charles L. Harrison. It was suspended in mid-air from the ceiling of the tower stairs like a hanged man. It's pretty spooky.

At eleven thirty I tiptoe down the hall to my parents' bedroom. Don't see their light on under their door. I tiptoe back to my bedroom and get dressed. Put on dark clothes to camouflage me. Open my window. It feels pretty cool out, so I put on my hooded sweatshirt.

I get out Jerry Mahoney, my toy ventriloquist dummy, which I got for Christmas a few years ago. I lay him in bed and pull the covers up—just in case Mom peeks in my room during the night. In the dark, it looks like I'm still in bed.

75

I pop the screen out of the window and hide it under the bed. Then tuck the flashlight down the front of my pants, crawl out the window onto the ladder of the TV antenna, and climb down it to the ground.

I walk down Mount Airy Lane. When I get to the bridge, I look around for Arcudy. Don't see him. Check my watch. It's three minutes till twelve. At a quarter after twelve, he still hasn't shown. I think about walking to his house and throwing pebbles against his window, but then I see him coming up the street on his bike.

"Hey, Deuce!" he yells.

"It's about time. Where the heck've you been?"

"Sorry. I was talking to Tammy on the phone."

"I just hope we didn't miss the ghost."

We head back up Mount Airy Lane. Arcudy walks his bike next to me. On the way, I tell him about the Harrison House. By the time we reach my house, Arcudy is spooked.

Arcudy hides his bike in the bushes next to the mailbox. Then we sneak around the house and walk down the path through the woods. Arcudy tells me to turn on the flashlight. I tell him not until we're far away from my house. He keeps stepping on the back of my tennis shoe. Every time he does it I have to stop and pull it back up over my heel. I keep telling him to back up. He says if I'd just turn on the flashlight. Finally, I turn it on.

When we get to the tree fort, I shine the flashlight all around. Don't see anything. Then I look around for a hiding place. A great, big tree trunk is lying on the ground near the tree fort. We could hide behind it. If the ghost comes back to the tree fort, we'll have a ringside seat. I tell Arcudy my idea. He feels the ground and says it's too wet. He wants to sit in the tree fort. I try to explain to him that we'll be trapped up there if the ghost comes, but he's afraid he'll get his pants dirty sitting on the ground and his mom will yell at him.

Finally, I give in, and we climb up into the tree fort. I turn off the flashlight, and we sit down and wait for the ghost. Meanwhile, I tell Arcudy about how Carl Hickey child-molested Regina Wukela, gouged out her eyeballs, drowned her, and hid her mutilated body inside the sewer pipe. People say her ghost haunts the sewer pipe—you can hear a little girl crying in the night. My book on ghosts says that's just what ghosts do. Man, is he scared. He keeps saying, "Did you hear something? Shine the light over there!" Then I shine the light where he's pointing, and we see nothing.

After an hour goes by and the ghost doesn't appear, Arcudy's fear goes away. He tells me about the make out party he and Tammy went to in Candy Clark's basement tonight. Candy dimmed the lights and played Johnny Mathis records to create a romantic atmosphere. Tammy and he made out on the couch. The party ended when Candy's older brother screwed a hose onto an outside faucet, stuck the nozzle through a basement window well, and squirted everybody.

Arcudy cuts a squeaky fart. He laughs. "The ghost cut one."

"Very funny. Look, this is no laughing matter."

He yawns and stretches. "What time is it?"

I check my watch. "Two o'clock."

He pulls the hood up on his sweatshirt and curls up in a ball on the floor of the tree fort. "Wake me up if you see any ghosts."

He goes to sleep.

For the next three hours, I stare into the darkness, waiting for the ghost to appear. I have a hard time staying awake. Finally, at five o'clock, the sky begins to lighten.

"Jack, wake up." I shake him.

He wakes up.

"It's getting light out. We better get home before our parents wake up."

"So where's the ghost?"

"I don't know."

"You know what?"

"What?"

"I don't think there is a ghost. I think it was just your imagination."

"It wasn't my imagination. It was real."

"Right," he says like he doesn't believe me.

I sigh. No one believes me.

∞◊∞◊∞◊∞◊∞◊∞

Mom takes me to church on Sunday. She says the longer she waits to face Dr. Williams, the harder it'll be. Sarah is sitting with her mom across the center aisle. During the sermon, I notice her eyeing me, but I act like I don't see her. After the benediction, everybody files out the church. Dr. Williams stands by the front door and greets everybody as they go by. Mom apologizes to Dr. Williams for my behavior. Then says, "Mansfield has something he wants to say to you."

"I'm sorry, Dr. Williams," I say and stare at the floor.

"Youth is a period of great trials and tribulation," he tells Mom and me.

One good thing does come out of it though. I don't have to go to the Ark anymore.

∞◊∞◊∞◊∞◊∞◊∞

During lunch at school on Monday, Arcudy asks me, "You promise not to tell anybody?"

"Yeah."

"I'm gonna buy an ID bracelet. Then I'm gonna ask Tammy to go steady with me. If she says yes, I'm gonna give it to her to wear."

"Wow! It sounds like you're in love."

He just grins.

On Tuesday night, Dad and Mom go to open house at Appleseed. Before they go, I ask Mom for permission to watch TV tonight. She asks me if I have all my homework done. I tell her yeah even though I haven't done my Math problems yet. She says okay — I've been pretty good lately.

I watch three of my favorite shows. First *Combat!* I think it's cool that the exclamation mark after *Combat* is really a bayonet. And I think Sergeant Saunders is really cool the way he can be surrounded by practically the whole German army, and it just doesn't faze him. Then *McHale's Navy.* I think Ensign Parker is really funny. And then *The Fugitive.* Will Dr. Richard Kimble prove he didn't kill his wife—it was the one-armed man—before Lt. Philip Gerard catches him? When my parents come home, Mom sticks her head in the TV room and says, "Mansfield, come in the den. Your father and I need to talk to you."

"Just a minute. I'm watching *The Fugitive.*"

"Now!"

Uh-oh. Now what did I do?

I go into the den where Dad and Mom are sitting in their usual places with perturbed looks on their faces. I sit down in the hot seat.

Dad says, "Mansfield, we got a disturbing report on you at the open house. Your Math teacher, Miss Robinson, told us you haven't been doing your assignments. Is this true?"

Robinson is an ugly old maid, who's always cross and lives for one thing—math. She's really hard. At the end of every class, she collects our homework to make sure that we did the assignment. Then she assigns a whole slew of problems as homework for the next day's class. I turn in only the problems that I'm able to get done in study hall. I don't do homework—it interferes with watching TV. "Yeah, but I get 100s on all the quizzes."

"That's not the point. The point is the teacher assigns you homework, and you're supposed to do it. It teaches you good study habits," Dad lectures.

"But if I can get 100—"

"No ifs or buts about it. How do you expect to develop good study habits for college?"

"I'm not going to college."

"What do you mean you're not going to college?" Mom asks.

"You wanna grow up to be a garbage man?" Dad asks.

"I'm gonna be a professional skin diver."

"Well, even a skin diver needs to know math. You don't wanna run out of air at fifty fathoms."

"Not Mike Nelson."

"Mansfield, I'm not gonna argue with you. You need to do your Math assignments, and that's final. Do you have tomorrow's assignment finished?"

"Uh...I'm gonna do it in study hall," I lie. Math is third period and study hall is seventh period.

Dad shakes his head. "Go do it right now."

"I can't. I didn't bring my Math book home."

"From now on, bring your book home and do your homework before you watch TV."

"So can I finish my show?"

"No. I'm not gonna reward you for not bringing your book home."

Mad, I go to my room. It's not fair that I have to do homework if I can get 100s on the tests without doing it.

To make my parents happy, I start bringing my Math book home. But, instead, of doing my homework, I fake like I'm doing it. I sit at my desk with my book open and pencil and paper in case my parents come in the room. Then I read comic books or mess around for an hour or so. Then tell my parents that I did my homework and watch TV until it's time to go to bed.

∞◊∞◊∞◊∞◊∞◊∞

On my way to German class, I go into the Boys' restroom to take a leak. Skip Shalaya and Gordon Fox are paying Russell Ealey a dollar to lick a urinal cake. Using his index finger and thumb, Ealey picks up a urinal cake from a urinal. Holding it up to his mouth, he wiggles his eyebrows and grins like a maniac. Then touches the tip of his tongue to it for a split second.

"Mmmm. Nummy," he says.

"Gross," somebody groans.

"Hey, you didn't lick it. I ain't paying," Shalaya says.

Ealey holds it back up and actually licks it. That really grosses everybody out. "Mmmm—lollipop. Anybody wanna lick my lollipop?" he asks, and he sticks the urinal cake in Shalaya's face.

"Get it away from me!" Shalaya yells, and he knocks Ealey's hand away.

The urinal cake goes flying. Everybody leaps backwards to get out of its way. It lands on the back of Bob Parsons' neck and rolls down his back. Then rolls behind the waste can.

I take a leak and run to class before the bell rings. Ealey is sitting at his desk next to me. I notice that he has drawn a Nazi swastika in blue ink on the back of his left hand. Then notice them all over the cover of his notebook.

After school at our locker, I ask Ealey, "Do you feel sick?"

"Nope. Why?"

"I think urinal cakes are poisonous."

Grinning like a maniac, he shapes his hand like a gun, aims it at me, and burps.

"Russell, you're crazy."

Mr. Wilson is lecturing us about the Stamp Act in History class. Man, is it boring. I think about last Friday night in the tree fort with Arcudy. All of a sudden, it dawns on me why we didn't see the ghost of Regina Wukela. We were in the wrong place. We should've been at the sewer pipe. That's where she got murdered. Like the book says, ghosts haunt the spot they got killed. How dumb can you get?

On the way home from school, I tell Arcudy about the mistake we made. "Let's sneak out again this weekend. This time we'll stake out the sewer pipe."

"I can't. I hafta go with my dad to Elmira, New York."

"When?"

"We're leaving after school tomorrow and won't be back till Sunday."

"What for?"

"We're bringing back a body."

"Rats!"

"I don't get to see Tammy this weekend," he grumbles.

On Friday night, Dad, Mom, and Meg go to the high school football game to watch Tecca cheerlead. Since I'm grounded, I have to stay home and babysit Calley. Mom has mercy on me and says I can watch TV tonight. Calley is sitting with her legs crossed on the floor right in front of the television, watching *The Flintstones.*

"Calley, change the channel."

"No, I was here first."

"You wanna stay up past your bedtime tonight?" I ask.

She nods.

"Change it."

She changes the channel to what I want to watch—*Rawhide,* which is a western about cowboys on a cattle drive. I think Rowdy Yates is cool.

Before Mom leaves, she tells me Calley's bedtime is ten o'clock. At nine thirty, I tell Calley to get ready for bed. She begs me to let her stay up past her bedtime and watch *The Twilight Zone,* which comes on at ten thirty. She wants to watch it because I told her it's a scary show. I tell her okay. Then tell her to take her bath and put on her pajamas, so she can jump in bed when Mom and Dad come home.

Calley runs upstairs to take her bath. I feel like teasing her. I get a glass of cold water in the kitchen and sneak upstairs to the bathroom. She's playing in the bathtub with her Barbie doll. I tiptoe in and pour the glass of water down her back. She shrieks. She gets mad and throws a bar of soap at me.

Calley likes me to play monster and scare her when I babysit. So I get a needle and syringe out of my secret compartment. I swiped a box of them out of the storage cabinet at Dad's office. When she's putting on her pajamas, I walk into her room and announce, "Calley, time for your polio shot." She sees the needle and runs out of the room, screaming. I chase after her but let her get away. She runs down the hall into the bathroom and locks the door.

"Open the door, Calley. Dad said I'm supposed to give you your polio shot,"

"He did not!" she screams.

"You don't wanna get put in an iron lung, do ya?"

She won't open the door, so I get a coat hanger, straighten the wire hook, stick it through the hole in the doorknob, and unlock it. She tries to hold the door shut, but I force it open.

"Roll up your sleeve. This will just hurt a little," I say.

She backs into the corner and starts to cry.

"Calley, I'm faking. I'm playing monster."

Immediately, she stops crying and grins. "Do it again, Deuce."

"No. It won't be scary now that you know I'm faking."

Before *The Twilight Zone* comes on, I dim the lights in the TV room for a scary atmosphere. We watch an episode about a doll named Talky Tina that talks when you pull her string. Except instead of saying that she loves you, Talky Tina says that she's going to kill you. The show scares the crap out of Calley because she has a Chatty Cathy doll that talks when you pull her string. She asks me if Talky Tina is true. I tell her all of the *Twilight Zone* episodes are real-life stories. That really scares her.

Mom and Dad come home after *The Twilight Zone* ends. I tell Calley, "Quick! Get in bed!" She dashes up the back steps to her bedroom. I check the *TV Guide* to see what movie will be on *Shock Theater*, which is my favorite show because it's hosted by Ghoulardi, who is really cool. It says *Caltiki-The Immortal Monster*. It sounds like a good horror movie.

Mom comes into the room with an angry look on her face. "Mansfield, did you let Calley stay up and watch *The Twilight Zone?*"

"Uh...yeah..."

"Now she's afraid to go to sleep. I had to take her Chatty Cathy doll out of her room. She's afraid it'll come to life and kill her."

"Sorry." I could brain Calley for telling on me.

"Don't do it again."

"Okay."

"Go to your room."

"Can I watch Ghoulardi? He has a really good movie on tonight."

"No. You've had enough TV for one night. You're still grounded."

I go to my room and mess around at my desk. My Visible Woman model, which is my favorite model, is on my bookshelf. I check out her mammary glands and reproductive system. Then open my junk drawer, where I keep fun toys like my yo-yo and Silly

Putty and gag toys like fake puke, a joy buzzer, a whoopee cushion, and a plastic ice cube with a fly in it. I get out my vial of mercury, which I took out of Dad's old thermometers. I think it's cool that mercury is liquid at room temperature. I pour the silvery-white metal into a puddle on my desk and play with it. I rub a bead on a dime, which makes it shiny.

After a while, I get bored of messing around. I walk to the window. Stare into the dark woods where my tree fort is...

What tried to get me? Was it really just a nightmare or a raccoon like Dad said? Or the ghost of Regina Wukela?

It's warm and breezy outside—a perfect night for ghost-busting. Man, I wish Arcudy was here.

I could go by myself. Hide out of sight.

You gotta be crazy. Going to the sewer pipe alone at night would be scary.

I remember that the book said since ghosts are spirits and not physical, they can't actually hurt you. Like they can't shoot you with a gun or stab you with a knife. If it's an evil spirit, the most it can do is appear and scare you into doing something to hurt yourself. Like in one chapter about a haunted bridge, the ghost appeared and made a lady drive her car into a river. I figure as long as I stay cool, a ghost can't harm me.

I talk myself into going by telling myself if it's too scary, I'll just turn around and come back. I wait until the light is off in my parents' bedroom. Then sneak downstairs to the utility room and get Dad's big flashlight out of the wastepaper closet. It has a powerful beam that shines far away. On the way back to my room, I notice light flickering in the TV room and peek in. All of the lights are turned off in the room, and Tecca and her boyfriend, Scott, are making out on the couch. I spy on them and watch a blob-like monster attack and devour its victim on TV. The floor creaks under my feet, and Tecca asks Scott if he heard something. I beat it out there.

Back in my room, I put on my blue jeans and a dark shirt for camouflage. Lay the dummy under the covers in my bed. Then climb out the window and down the TV antenna. I decide not to take the path through the woods past my tree fort. I don't feel like climbing down the cliff in the dark. Even though it'll take longer, I decide to ride my bike down Mount Airy Lane to the bridge and take the path along the creek. I sneak my bike out of the garage and walk it down the driveway. When I reach the mailbox, I hop on it and coast down Mount Airy Lane.

Man, is it weird outside. Black clouds are rolling across a full moon. Gusts of wind are blowing through the trees. Branches are creaking back and forth and leaves are swirling around. Electricity is in the air. Off in the distance, I hear a dog barking.

At the bridge, I park my bike and look over the guardrail. Man, is it dark in the woods. I turn on my flashlight and shine it up the creek. Don't see anything.

This is your last chance to turn back.

You've come this far. Don't chicken out now.

I follow the path along the creek through the woods—shining the light ahead of me. Every step of the way I'm ready to turn and bolt. Finally, I reach the sewer pipe. I shine the light all around. Don't see anything. I scramble down the bank to the creek and climb onto a rock pile at the opening of the pipe. Then shine the flashlight up the pipe. All I see is light glimmering off the stream of water in the bottom of the pipe and reflecting in concentric circles off the concrete wall of the pipe. Far away is a small circle of blackness— like a bullseye.

I look around for a hiding place. Spot a big tree on the other side of the creek a short distance up the cliff. I can hide behind it and watch the sewer pipe. I cross the creek and climb a little ways up the path that leads to my tree fort. Then climb across the face of the cliff to the tree. Turn off the flashlight. It's pitch-black. Check the time. Ten till one. Standing behind the tree, I watch. My eyes are straining to see in the dark. I'm listening for any strange sounds. All I hear is water running out of the sewer pipe.

"Hoot!"

Man, it startles me.

I realize it was just an owl and laugh at myself. I tell myself to take it easy.

Soon, I get tired of standing and sit down on the ground. As time goes by and no ghost appears, I feel less and less scared and more and more ridiculous. What am I doing sitting in a woods watching some dumb sewer pipe at two o'clock in the morning? I have to be nuts. I should be home in bed sound asleep. But I keep telling myself just five more minutes.

At two thirty, I see flashes of lightning illuminating the sky to the west. It looks like a thunderstorm is coming, but it's still far away—I can't hear any thunder. I watch the lightning come toward me. Finally, I decide I'd better head for home. I don't feel like getting wet—let alone struck by lightning. I stand up and brush off the back of my pants. Then take one last look at the sewer pipe—

I freeze.

Something is coming toward me inside it.

I duck behind the tree. Peek out...

It stops at the opening. Peers out...

I see its hideous face in the moonlight.

It climbs out of the pipe and down the rocks. Stands beside the pool of water.

It turns toward me.

I duck behind the tree. Slowly peek out...

It crosses the creek and starts to climb up the path toward my tree fort.

Suddenly, there's a flash of lightning, followed by a faint rumble of thunder.

It stops—looks in the direction of the thunder. Then turns around, goes back across the creek, climbs into the sewer pipe, and disappears into the blackness.

I realize I'm shaking.

I hide behind the tree for a few minutes—to make sure it's gone. Then turn on the flashlight. I scramble down the cliff and across the creek to the sewer pipe. Shine the light inside. All I see is empty pipe—it's gone.

I shine the light on the stream of water in the bottom of the pipe—see splash marks.

Get the hell outta here before it comes back.

I run all the way back to my bike. Hop on it and pedal as fast as I can up Mount Airy Lane. By the time I reach our mail box, the thunderstorm has passed. It didn't rain. The storm missed us. Panting like crazy, I hop off my bike and walk it up the driveway. Our house is dark inside. Scott's car is gone. I sneak my bike into the garage. Then climb up the TV antennae into my room.

I get undressed and crawl in bed, but I'm so excited I can't fall asleep. I say out loud to myself, "I knew it. I knew I really saw something."

What the heck is it?

I picture it in my mind—milky white and shaped like a child.

It has to be the ghost of Regina Wukela.

But, man, it sure doesn't act like a ghost. It doesn't float. It left splash marks—it walks.

But what else could it be?

Where did it come from? And where was it going? It looked like it was headed toward my tree fort again. Why did it turn around and go back?

I gotta tell somebody. Who? Dad? Mom? No way. They'll never believe me. They'll just ground me even longer for sneaking out.

Arcudy. Nah, he won't believe me.

Nobody's gonna believe me. Not without proof.

Tomorrow—I gotta find proof.

CHAPTER SIX

When I wake up the next morning, all I can think about is what I saw last night. I'm dying to go back to the sewer pipe and check things out in broad daylight. I jump out of bed, throw on some clothes, run downstairs, and grab a bowl of cereal. As soon as Mom goes to the hairdresser, I run out the door. It's a beautiful morning. The sky is sky blue and the leaves are red, yellow, and orange. I hop on my bike and tear down Mount Airy Lane to the bridge. Then run up the path to the sewer pipe. I climb down the bank to the creek and look for footprints in the gravel. Don't see any.

I climb up the rocks and look inside the sewer pipe. The splash marks are long gone. I peer into the clear stream of water at the mud that has settled in the bottom of the pipe.

Oh, man! A footprint.

I climb inside the pipe, squat down, and examine it. I see what looks like the footprint of a small, human being in the clay-like sediment. My eyes trace the outline of its toes, arch, and heel. The footprint is pointing toward the opening of the pipe. All at once, it hits me—whatever it is, it's going barefoot.

I walk up the pipe a little ways and spot two more footprints, pointing away from the opening of the pipe. I walk farther and find more footprints. They disappear into the darkness. Man, I'd give my left nut to know where they go.

I'm so excited. The footprints prove that something was here last night. I need to take pictures of them before they wash away.

I hurry home to get Dad's Polaroid camera. As I think about it, I realize what will happen if I show pictures of the footprints to Dad. He'll say any barefoot kid playing in the sewer pipe could've left them. Then I'll have to tell him what I saw last night, and I'll get in trouble for sneaking out. So I scrap the idea of taking pictures of the footprints.

I go up in my Observatory. Gazing out the window at Luna lake Park, I ponder my next move. I tell myself this is a real-life mystery right in my own back yard. I have to solve it like Stuart Bailey on *77 Sunset Strip*. I need to find out where those footprints go, and there's only one way to find out—to follow them up the sewer pipe. The only problem is I'm scared to go alone.

At lunch I ask Mom if I can go to the library to do more research for my History report. She's pleased that I'm working so hard on it and gives me permission.

I sneak into Tecca's room, where I can talk on her phone in private. I call my other friends, trying to find somebody who'll go up the sewer pipe with me. I strike out. Joe Bosko says he and Jon Price are going to the James Bond movie, *Dr. No*. He invites me to go with them, but I tell him I can't—I'm grounded. Jim Chambers says he's going slot car racing this afternoon.

I think about waiting until Arcudy gets home, but I'm afraid the footprints will be washed away. Then it'll be too late for me to follow them.

I realize if I'm going to do it, I'll have to do it by myself. I figure it wouldn't be that scary if I was prepared. All I need are a flashlight, rubber boots, and a club in case I run into a sewer rat. It might actually be a pretty cool adventure—sort of like going on an expedition up the Amazon River.

I change into old clothes and put on my hooded sweatshirt. Then smuggle Dad's flashlight, my rubber boots, and mini wooden baseball bat into the garage and cram them in the trap on the front fender of my bike.

I get my notebook and say goodbye to Mom. She tells me to be home by four thirty.

I park my bike under the bridge on Possum Run, so Dad won't see it when he comes home from work this afternoon. Put on my boots. Then grab my flashlight and bat and walk to the sewer pipe. At the opening, I turn on the flashlight and shine it up the pipe. I can see all the way to the bend. It doesn't look scary. There are some cobwebs, which I figure I can knock down with my bat. It smells like sewer, but I figure I'll get used to that. I check my watch—ten till two.

I pull the hood over my head. With my bat in my right hand and my flashlight in my left hand, I start walking up the pipe. I have to walk hunched over to keep from hitting my head on the top of the pipe but don't have to straddle the water. I can walk in it since I have boots on. I shine the flashlight on the slimy sediment and follow the footprints, knocking down the cobwebs as I come to them.

When I get to the bend, I stop and look back. The opening is a small circle of light. As I walk around the bend, I keep glancing over my shoulder. When the opening disappears, I feel like the walls are closing in on me. I fight off the feeling by reminding myself that the opening is just around the bend. I force myself to concentrate on looking for footprints. Sometimes I'll see several in a row. Then they disappear for a ways. But they always reappear.

I keep following the footprints. Finally, I see light up ahead and scurry toward it. I step out of the pipe into light streaming down from a sewer grating overhead. The bars on the grating make me feel like I'm in jail. Looking through them, I see trees and blue sky. Man, is it nice to breathe fresh air again. I check the time—it's two minutes after two. I've only been gone twelve minutes, but it seemed like an hour. I sit down on a dry spot and rest…

That wasn't so bad. Really, it's all in your mind.

Here the pipe branches into two pipes—like a Y. I stand up and shine the light up each one. I spot a footprint in the pipe that goes to the right. Memorize right. Check my watch again—ten after two.

I turn right and head up the pipe. After a while, I see a faint light up ahead. Rushing to it, I look up and see two small circles of light.

Then spot metal ladder rungs embedded in the concrete wall that go up to them—realize it's a manhole cover. A drop of water drips from it and hits me in the forehead. I check my watch. Quarter after two. Only five minutes. I'm starting to get the hang of it.

Here the pipe goes straight ahead. I follow the footprints up it. After a while, I see a bright stream of light up ahead. Then come to a big sewer grating high above my head. Instead of having two gratings, it has three. Looking through them, I see it has clouded over. I stretch my neck and rub my lower back—I'm getting stiff from walking bent over.

Here four pipes intersect. I go up each pipe a few yards, looking for footprints, but can't find them.

Damn—I've lost them.

Searching more thoroughly, I find footprints about ten yards up the first pipe on the right. But I'm scared to follow them. I go back to the sewer grating and stare at all of the pipes.

What if I take the wrong pipe on my way back? Oh, man—I could get lost underground.

I should've brought a crayon. I could've marked the way. Man, was that dumb.

I'd better go back.

I shine the light down the pipe that goes back. See my footprints in the slime as plain as day.

You idiot—how stupid can you get? All you gotta do is follow your own footprints back.

I turn right and follow the footprints again. After a while, I see a faint light up ahead. Then come to another manhole cover. Here the pipe goes straight ahead, and another pipe shoots off to the right at a right angle. The footprints go straight ahead. I follow them around a bend and come to still another manhole cover. Here the pipe keeps going straight, and another pipe shoots off to the right at a right angle. I shine the flashlight up ahead—

Suddenly, I see beady, red eyes reflecting in the dark.

Oh, God! A rat.

I stop dead in my tracks. Swinging my mini bat, I yell, "Get outta here! Or I'll bash your brains in!"

The rat scurries up the pipe with its little tail wiggling. Disappears into the dark.

That does it—I'm getting outta here. No way am I going any farther. Not with a sewer rat up ahead. It's probably carrying the bubonic plague.

But then I notice something. Instead of going straight ahead, the footprints go up the pipe that turns right, so I'm able to follow them without following the rat.

I check the time—twenty till three. I've been underground for fifty minutes. Man, how far do they go?

Go back.

I can't go back now. Not after coming this far.

Five more minutes. Just five more minutes. If I don't find where they go by a quarter to three, I'm going back—the hell with it.

I turn right and follow the footprints. After a ways, I see light up ahead and rush toward it.

Please be an opening…

Shit! Another sewer grating. The grating is so low that I have to bend over to keep from hitting my head. I look through it, trying to see where I am. All I see are tree limbs.

Here the main pipe ends. Another pipe shoots off to the left at a right angle. This pipe looks too small for a human to go up it. I crouch in front of it. The opening is about two foot above the bottom of the pipe that I'm standing in. I shine my light up it. Man, does it look creepy. It's made of brick and mossy. No water is running out of it. A small mound of mud is at the lip.

What is that?

Looking closer, I see what looks like a handprint in the mud. I hold my hand next to it. Mine is much bigger.

I can't believe it. It must've gone up there.

Now what am I gonna do?

Turn back.

I examine the opening. There's no way I could walk bent over inside it. I wonder if I could crawl up it.

You gotta be crazy. Don't even think of it. You could get stuck in there and nobody would ever find you.

A shiver runs down my spine.

Forget it. Give up. It's time to go back. It's past a quarter to three.

I stand back up...but can't go.

You've come so far. Just see if you can crawl up it.

I squat and set my flashlight and mini bat inside the pipe. Then crawl inside on my hands and knees. Man, is it tight. When I inhale, my back presses against the top of the pipe. I pick up my flashlight and shine the light around—spot a spider web. I knock it down with my bat.

Just see how far you can go.

I crawl on my hands and knees up the pipe. Keep conking my head on the brick. My hood keeps falling down. I have to reach back and pull it up.

After I go about ten yards, my knees are killing me.

I run into a huge spider web—it sticks all over my face and hair. I drop my bat and try to brush it off—

Suddenly, I feel something crawling down my cheek.

A spider!

I smash it.

That does it—I'm getting outta here. I ain't getting bit by a black widow spider.

But I can't turn around. The pipe is too small. I try backing up, but my sweatshirt keeps getting caught on the pipe and bunching up under my armpits.

All of a sudden, I feel something wet on my hands. I shine the light in front of me and see water trickling down the pipe toward me.

What the heck?

Oh, no—rain.

I imagine being trapped underwater in the pipe.

I panic. "You gotta get outta here!"

I crawl backwards as fast as I can.

The next thing I know, water is rushing down the pipe, backing up against my body. Rearing in terror, I crack the back of my head against the pipe.

The flashlight goes out—it's pitch-black.

With my back slammed against the pipe, I scramble backwards.

Feel the water rising...

In no time, it's up to my chest.

The side of my face mashed against the pipe, I frantically try to keep my mouth above water...

Gasping for air, I suck water up my nose...

Start choking—gurgling—

I'm gonna die!

I tumble out of the pipe. See blurry light. Find myself lying on my stomach on the concrete in front of the pipe. Water is gushing out of the pipe and roaring all around me and tumbling down on me from the sewer grating above. I drag myself away from the torrent into the corner where the main pipe ends.

Kneeling in brown, foamy water, I sputter and cough water out of my nose and mouth. My nose burns...

My soaking-wet sweatshirt is scrunched under my armpits. I pull it down.

I stand up—hit my forehead on the grating. Trying to get out from under the water falling from the grating, I back up against the wall. Stand in swirling water up to my calves. My legs feel like rubber. I'm soaked to the bone.

Looking through the grating, I see a flash of lightning, hear a clap of thunder. Rain is pelting my face.

I look down the pipe—see water rushing into blackness. It looks like it would sweep me away.

I feel the water rising...

Soon, it's up to my thighs.

I panic at the thought of my face being trapped underwater by the sewer grating. Crouching, I grab hold of the grating and push— it doesn't budge. I press my back against it and push with all my might—still doesn't budge.

The water is up to my waist.

I press the side of my face against the bars and scream, "Help! Somebody! Please! Help me!"

The water reaches my chest.

I keep screaming for help at the top of my lungs, but nobody hears me.

"Wait…"

It feels like the water has stopped rising.

Looking up at the sky, I see the rain has slowed down.

"Dear God, please make it stop raining…"

My eyes are fixed on the water level…

"Yes!" The water is definitely going down. "Thank you…"

I hold on to a rod of rebar sticking out of the concrete wall and wait for the rain to stop. Keep checking the water level, then the rain…

The water goes down to my thighs.

I start getting cold…

Down to my knees.

I start to shiver…

Down to my ankles.

My teeth are chattering…

The water doesn't go any lower. It won't stop raining…

"Deuce, no one's gonna rescue you. You can't stay here."

I look at the water running down the pipe. It has slowed to the point where I think I can walk in it without getting swept away.

"You gotta go back.

"I can't. I have no flashlight. I can't see.

"If it starts raining hard again, the water will start rushing again…

"Now is the time. Go!"

I duck under the water falling from the grating and plunge into the pipe. Shortly, it's pitch-black. It's like I'm blind—I have to walk with one hand on the wall of the pipe.

The water gets deeper. I feel the current rushing around my calves. Struggle not to fall down. Keep wading forward…

Finally, I see a faint light up ahead. Rush out of the pipe and see the manhole cover above me.

"You made it.

"Keep going."

I remember I turned right here on the way up, so I turn left and head down the pipe. I start humming the theme song to *Combat!*

Hum it over and over. See another faint light up ahead, Come to the next manhole. Remember I went straight here.

"Don't stop. You should come to the four-way intersection next."

I imagine a hot shower…

Finally, I see a stream of light up ahead and wade as fast as I can to it. Overhead, water is streaming down from the three sewer gratings. I scurry out from under it and look out the gratings. Man, am I glad to see sky again.

I try to figure out which way to go. I'm not sure if it's the first or second pipe from the left. I go look in the first pipe for my footprints but don't see them. Look in the other pipes but they're gone.

Oh, my God…they washed away.

How will I find my way back?

I imagine getting lost in here and feel cold fear…

All of a sudden, I hear a motor rumbling and tires hissing on wet pavement—

"A car!"

I hear another one.

"Help!" I yell again and again…

"They can't hear you.

"You gotta keep going."

Looking at the pipes again, I'm pretty sure the first pipe on the left is the way back. I head down it…wade into the darkness…start humming the theme song to *Johnny Yuma.*

After going a ways, I stop singing and listen…

It sounds like the water is getting louder and feels like it's rising.

"Oh, God! It's raining harder."

Terrified that I'll be trapped underwater in the pipe again, I run blindly, splashing through the water down the pipe. In no time, I feel it flowing around my thighs…

Lurching into the wall of the pipe, I fall down…flounder in the black water…struggle to my feet…

Then the water is rushing through the pipe and swirling around my hips. It sweeps me off my feet. I fall headfirst into the water. My head goes underwater and I start to panic—

Don't panic!

I hold my breath. Surface. Take a gulp of air.

I feel myself being swept fast through the roaring blackness. Dog paddle frantically.

Swim!

I put my face in the water and start swimming—roll my face sideways and breathe. Swallow several mouthfuls of water.

Stroke and breathe…stroke and breathe…stroke and breathe…

All at once, I spill headfirst out of the pipe. Water is churning all around me—sweeping me toward the black opening of the next pipe.

I lunge sideways.

The torrent spins my legs around and slams my torso into the wall next to the opening.

I feel myself being sucked into the pipe. Clawing at the concrete, my fingers slip across the surface. I frantically grope and clutch onto a metal rung. Pull myself up a ladder out of the water.

Clinging to the ladder, I gasp for air. Stare at the water rushing by underneath me. Puke up some water.

I look up and see a manhole cover.

You're never gonna get outta here.

You're not gonna make it.

I start crying.

"Stop crying.

"Pull yourself together.

"You can make it."

I tell myself to just stay here until it stops raining. I don't care if it takes hours. Do not move until I'm absolutely sure it has stopped raining.

I wait and wait…

I start shaking all over…

Oh, God—the water is rising.

I climb higher up the ladder. Look up at the manhole cover.

Maybe I can open it.

I scramble up the ladder to the manhole cover. Planting my feet on the rungs, I press my back against it—then lift with all my might.

It lifts up an inch or two. I shove it sideways—see sky and feel raindrops hitting my face. Keep shoving it sideways until there's enough space to stick my head out.

Don't get your head knocked off by a car.

I peek out. Don't see any cars. I see that I'm near the blockhouse in the park. I open the manhole the rest of the way and climb out. Just stand here in the middle of the road in the pouring rain—beaming with joy.

I'm alive.

I slide the manhole cover back on and walk over to the side of the road. Sit down on the curb, take off my boots, empty the water out of them, and put them back on. I check myself for injuries. My fingertips and the palms of my hands are skinned and bleeding,

What time is it?

I check my watch—it's gone.

"Damn it! I lost it."

My Fifty Fathoms came off somewhere in the pipe. My watchband must've broken. I hate to lose my prize watch, but there's no way I'm going back down there to look for it. I also realize I lost Dad's flashlight and my mini bat. I must've dropped them when I was trapped in the small pipe.

I jog through the park and get my bike. Then race home. Park my bike and stash my boots in the garage. Grab my notebook and run into the house. My tennis shoes squish.

"I'm home!" I holler.

Mom's in the kitchen. She eyes me suspiciously. "You're late."

I try to look innocent. "Sorry. I couldn't help it. I got stuck at the library, waiting for the rain to stop. But it never did."

She sees my wet clothes. "What happened to your forehead?"

"What?"

"It looks like you scraped it."

"I wrecked my bike, trying to get home on time." I show her the nasty scrapes on my hands.

"Wash them and put antibiotic ointment on them."

I go upstairs to the bathroom. Take off my wet clothes and toss them down the laundry chute. I have a bruise on my hip from when

I slammed into the wall. I hop in the shower and let the hot water run on me. Man, does it feel good…

I recall being trapped in the small, brick sewer pipe when it first started to rain. I shudder. That was a close call. I got out in the nick of time. A few more seconds and I would've drowned.

I relive being swept through the black sewer pipe. Realize swim team probably saved my life. At practice, I learned how to swim dead-tired, with my eyes closed, swallowing water.

I picture grabbing hold of the ladder rung and pulling myself out of the raging torrent. That was lucky. I don't know what would've happened if I'd been sucked down that pipe.

I'm glad I thought of escaping through a manhole. I'd probably still be stranded on that ladder if I hadn't thought of it.

Chuckling, I tell myself, "Man, you used up a few of your nine lives today."

During the sermon at church the next day, I wonder where I was in town when I was trapped underground in the small, brick sewer pipe. Then I have an idea—I could retrace above ground the route I took underground and discover where I was. I can't wait to do it. Finally, Dr. Williams says the benediction.

At our Sunday dinner, I tell my parents I discovered that I lost my watch—my watchband must've broke when I wrecked my bike yesterday. I ask for permission to go look for it. They say that's too bad and give me permission.

I hop on my bike and tear down the hill to the bridge. I walk along the creek, looking for my Fifty Fathoms. I don't see it, but I do find my mini bat washed downstream from the sewer pipe. Then I find Dad's flashlight in the pool at the opening of the pipe. It doesn't work. I don't find my watch. I sigh. I figure it's lost for good.

To trace my route above ground, I look in the direction the pipe heads underground. It heads toward the pavilion. I go back to the bridge and get my bike. Ride up Mount Airy Lane to the back entrance of Luna Lake Park. Turn into the park and ride around Luna Lake. Come to a Y intersection at the pavilion. If you go left, you circle back around the other side of the lake. If you go right, you head toward the side entrance of the park. I look around for a sewer grating—spot one in the grass next to the road. Looking through the grating, I see that the sewer pipe branches in the direction of each road. This must be the first sewer grating I came to yesterday. I remember I followed the footprints up the right pipe.

I turn right, pedal past the blockhouse, and come to the manhole where I escaped yesterday. As I ride toward the side entrance, I realize this was where I was swept through the pipe. I come to the side entrance at the intersection of Parkview Circle, Mapledale, and Shady Lane. Spot three sewer gratings by the street sign on Shady Lane and remember there were three gratings yesterday. Climbing off my bike, I lie on the ground on my stomach and peer through a grating. I try to figure out which way I went yesterday, but it's hard to see all the way down to the dark bottom. I'm pretty sure I took the pipe up Shady Lane.

I ride up Shady Lane. Come to a manhole cover in the middle of the intersection of Shady Lane and Painter Road. I remember that I went straight here yesterday and then turned right at the next intersection. Continuing up Shady Lane, I come to Bird Cage Walk, which I think is a weird name for a street. Spot another manhole in the middle of the intersection.

I turn right and pedal up Bird Cage Walk. A sign reads Dead End. Tall trees line both sides of the street—it's like riding through a tunnel. The houses are old and sit up on steep banks. The street is made of bricks—moss is growing in the cracks. I ride slowly, looking for a sewer grating. The road dead ends at a wooden barricade in front of a pine forest. Beyond the pine trees is the Waterbury Cemetery.

I spot a sewer grating in the grass next to the road. Ride over to it and park my bike. Peering through the grating, I see the small, brick pipe where I almost drowned. Just looking at it makes me feel claustrophobic. I look in the direction the pipe heads—see a driveway that cuts into the grassy bank and disappears into a jungle of pine trees and bushes. A mailbox is by the driveway, so there must be a house here. Across the street is a vacant lot.

I walk over to the driveway. Peer through the pine trees but can't see the house. All I can see is the corner of a garage. I walk up the driveway. See an old, brick house. The front porch is almost hidden behind evergreen bushes. I look around for a sewer grating or manhole cover in the front yard—

"Hey you!"

I look and see a man standing on the front porch. He looks mean.

"Get the hell off my property!" he yells.

I do an about-face and beat it back down the driveway. When I get out of sight, I flip him the bird.

I hop on my bike and take off down the street. Turn right on Shady Lane and ride to the next street—Chestnut. Turn right and ride up Chestnut to Waterbury Cemetery. Park my bike next to the wrought-iron gate. A new double sewer grating is in the street by the entrance to the cemetery. Looking through the grating, I see that the pipe runs down Chestnut. Then spot an old grating in the grass by the mail box of the last house on Chestnut. Looking through it, I see a small, brick pipe that heads in the direction of the small, brick pipe on Bird Cage Walk—I figure they must be connected. Lying on the ground, I peer through the grating again. See that the small, brick pipe turns into the cemetery.

I go into the cemetery but can't find any sewer gratings or manhole covers.

I wonder where it goes—could it go to the grave of Regina Wukela?

There are thousands of graves here. I realize I can't find her grave, so I give up and head to the library.

After supper, I go to Tecca's room and call Arcudy.

"Hello," he says.

"Jack, guess what!"

"What?"

"I saw the ghost again."

"Get outta here."

"I swear to God. I staked out the sewer pipe on Friday night, and I saw it come outta the pipe. Then I went back Saturday and saw footprints in the mud in the pipe."

"Footprints?"

"Yeah. I followed them up the pipe and almost drowned."

I tell him the whole story.

"Are you kidding me?" he asks.

"No. It really happened."

"Damn...you're lucky you're still alive..."

"I know. Listen, man, you gotta go with me."

"Where?"

"To the sewer pipe. So you can see the ghost."

"When?"

"Friday night."

"I'm planning on seeing Tammy Friday night. I didn't get to see her this weekend."

"Jack, this is a big mystery. I need your help to solve it. Me and you will be like Stuart Baily and Jeff Spencer on *77 Sunset Strip.*"

"My ID bracelet is ready at the jewelry story. I'm gonna ask her to go steady with me."

"We'll sneak out after you ask her. You can tell me all about it."

"Okay...I guess so..."

He tells me about his trip. It sounds pretty grisly. He says the dead guy was killed in a head-on collision with a semi, and his body was mutilated. They had to bring him back in a body bag.

CHAPTER SEVEN

I madly try to finish my Math assignment in homeroom period the next day. I only get half way done before the bell rings. In Math class, Robinson calls on students to go to the blackboard and do problems. When she gets to the ones I haven't done, I sit nervously at my desk, trying to look inconspicuous. I make it to the last problem, which is the hardest.

Please don't call on me...

"Mansfield Delaney."

Man, I just about fall out of my seat.

I take my paper and book to the board and pick up a piece of chalk. Act like I'm studying my paper, but really I'm reading the problem. The whole class is watching me.

You're gonna make a fool out of yourself.

Ring!

Saved by the bell.

∞◊∞◊∞◊∞◊∞◊∞

On the way to school, Arcudy proudly shows me his new ID bracelet. His name is engraved on it.

"Cool, man. How much did it cost?" I ask.

"Twelve dollars."

"Twelve dollars! That's expensive."

"It's sterling silver."

"You're gonna give it to Tammy?"

"Yeah."

"You just got it. Don't you wanna wear it?"

"No. I got it for her to wear. It tells the world I'm her boyfriend. We're going steady."

I think he's girl crazy, but I don't tell him that. I'm afraid if I make him mad, he won't go with me to the sewer pipe on Friday night.

∞◊∞◊∞◊∞◊∞◊∞

On the way home from school, Arcudy tells me Tammy invited him to her house tonight. He's going to ask her to go steady there. I wish him good luck and tell him to meet me at the bridge at midnight.

"I'm not coming, Deuce."

"Why not?"

"I don't feel like it."

"You can't back out on me. I'm counting on you."

"I just wanna go home after I see Tammy."

"Jack, she's changing you. She's making you girl crazy."

He doesn't say anything.

"Please, Jack…just go with me one more time," I beg.

"Okay, okay."

"Thanks. You're a true friend."

After supper, it starts to rain. I go up in my Observatory. Read comic books and play Solitaire, killing time. I keep looking out the window to see if the rain has stopped. Finally, around ten thirty it stops.

At eleven thirty I fake like I go to bed. At a quarter to twelve, I get out my flashlight, tuck my ventriloquist dummy under the covers, and sneak out the window. Get my bike out of the garage and coast down Mount Airy Lane. Man, is it crummy out. It's cold and misty and it smells like dead worms in the road. I start worrying about whether Arcudy is going to fink out on me. I'm relieved to see him waiting for me under the streetlight at the bridge.

"Deuce, I did it. I gave Tammy my ID bracelet. We're going steady." He's grinning from ear to ear.

"Congratulations. Tell me about it."

I turn on the flashlight, and we walk up the path toward the sewer pipe. The path is really muddy. I hear the creek rushing in the darkness.

Arcudy tells me Tammy was babysitting her kid brother, so her parents weren't home. After she put her brother to bed, they made out on the couch in her family room. Then he asked her if she wanted to go steady and wear his ID bracelet, and she said yeah. Then he becomes secretive and makes me promise not to tell anybody what he's about to tell me. He confides she let him feel her up a little on top of her blouse. I ask him what it felt like. He says not like flesh—more like rubber. I say maybe she was wearing falsies. He says that's not funny—I'm talking about his girlfriend. I don't say anything else. Man, is he touchy all of a sudden.

"Damn it, Deuce! I'm getting mud all over my penny loafers."

"I can't believe you wore your good shoes."

"This is the last time I'm doing this!"

We reach the sewer pipe. Arcudy keeps griping about the mud.

"Shut up! You'll scare the ghost away," I tell him.

He shuts up. We creep up to the opening of the pipe. I shine the flashlight inside it. Water is pouring out.

"I don't see any ghosts," he says.

"Give it time." I shine the light on the rushing creek. "C'mon, let's cross the creek."

"What for?"

I explain how we can hide behind the tree on the cliff and have a perfect view up the pipe, like I did last weekend.

"We can't cross that," he says.

"Why not?"

"It's too deep."

"Don't be a pansy."

I hop from rock to rock across the creek—get a wet foot. "It's easy!" I shout.

"Shine the light so I can see," he says.

I shine the light on the creek in front of him. As he hops from rock to rock across the creek, his foot slips off a rock and he steps into the water.

"Damn it!" he swears.

When he gets across, he makes me shine the light on his loafers. They're soaking wet and caked with mud.

"Look, they're ruined," he says.

"No, they're not. With a little shoe polish, they'll look as good as new."

We climb up the path and across the face of the cliff to the place behind the tree. It's too wet to sit down on the ground, so we just stand here waiting. Arcudy tries to wipe the mud off his shoes with a leaf.

After a while, it starts sprinkling. I ignore it.

"Hey, man, it's raining," Arcudy says.

I look up at the sky. "I think it's gonna pass over."

It starts raining harder. We move closer to the tree trunk, trying to get out of the rain. I feel drops falling from the branches on my head.

"Let's get outta here," Arcudy says.

"Just a minute. I think it's slowing down."

It starts raining really hard. We just stand here getting wetter and wetter.

"This is nuts. I'm leaving," he says.

"Go ahead—leave. But if you do, you're not my friend anymore."

"You're crazy." He takes off.

"I mean it, Arcudy."

He doesn't even look back.

"Hey, wait for me!" I yell and go running after him.

I catch up with him at the creek and shine the light on it. The water has risen. All of the stepping stones are underwater.

"Great. Now how are we gonna get across?" Arcudy asks.

I work my way along the bank downstream, looking for another place to cross. He follows me. I find a spot. I shine the light on a rock above water in the middle of the creek. "Look, we can hop to that rock and, from there, hop to the other side," I point out.

"You go first."

Shining the light ahead of me, I take a short run, leap off my left foot, land on my right foot on the slimy surface of the rock—almost slip and fall—hop and land on the other side of the creek. "Made it!" I yell.

I shine the light on the rock for Arcudy.

He jumps. His foot lands on the rock and slips off it. He stumbles through the water the rest of the way across the creek and jumps out on the bank.

"Shit! I lost my shoe!"

I shine the light on his feet—see he's missing his right loafer.

"The mud sucked it off. I gotta find it. They're brand new. They're my school shoes."

He takes off his other shoe and socks. Then rolls up his pant legs. "Deuce, this is the last time I ever listen to you—I swear to God." Man, is he mad.

I'm trying with all my might not to laugh.

He tells me to shine the light on the creek. Then wades into the rushing water. Floundering around, he gropes underwater for his shoe but can't find it.

"It probably got swept away," I tell him.

Suddenly, he loses his balance—starts windmilling his arms. Then falls down in the water.

He clambers out of the creek onto the bank. Stands there with his arms out, water dripping off them. "God damn! Son of a bitch!" he yells. Man, is he furious.

I start laughing.

"Shut up, you dumbass!"

But I can't stop laughing. I keep picturing him windmilling his arms and falling down in the water.

He grabs his shoe and socks and storms away in a huff.

I run after him. "Hey, it stopped raining. Wait a second! Stop!"

He keeps walking toward the bridge.

"What's the matter?"

He won't speak to me.

When we reach the bridge, he hops on his bike and pedals up the street.

"Hey, c'mon. I'm sorry. Don't be mad," I say.

"Go to hell!" he yells.

"Aw, you big pansy! Can't take a little rain!" I yell back.

I get on my bike and ride home. I feel lousy. We didn't see the ghost, and now Arcudy is mad at me. I'll never get him to go ghost-hunting again. Plus, I'm drenched to the bone and freezing my butt off.

About half way up Mount Airy, my heart skips a beat—through the trees I see the garage and front porch lights on at my house. I pedal up the hill as fast as I can. When I reach our driveway, I see lights on inside the house. I pray it's one of Dad's patients having an emergency.

I sneak my bike into the garage and run to the TV antennae. A light is on in my bedroom.

Uh-oh...

I scurry up the TV antenna and climb into my room. The covers are pulled back on my bed and my ventriloquist dummy is lying on my desk.

Shit...they know I'm not in bed...

On the spot, I make up a story that I couldn't sleep and went up in the Observatory. My parents usually don't go up there since you have to climb a ladder. I undress as quietly as I can, but the floor keeps creaking. Tiptoe to the closet and toss my wet clothes back in the corner. Slip into my tank suit. Tiptoe toward the door to turn off the light—

Suddenly, Dad appears in the doorway. He looks mad. "Where the hell have you been?"

"Uh...nowhere."

"You went somewhere. Your bike was gone."

"Doc?!" Mom calls from the bottom of the stairs.

"I'm in his room! He's here!" Dad yells.

Mom comes upstairs into my room. She tells Dad that Mrs. Arcudy said Jack just got home. Jack told his mom that he snuck out with me.

"Where'd you go?" Dad asks.

I don't know what to say. I can't tell him what we were really doing. If I do, I'll have to tell him about sneaking out and going up the sewer pipe last weekend, which will just get me in more trouble. "Uh…we were just riding around on our bikes."

"Where'd you go?"

"Luna Lake."

"What were you doing there?"

"Uh…we were just meeting Tammy Kramer."

"Who's Tammy Kramer?"

"Arcudy's girlfriend."

"Who were you meeting?" Mom asks.

"Nobody. I just went along."

"What'd you do there?" Dad asks.

"Nothing. She didn't show."

"You weren't meeting Sarah Williams, were you?" Mom asks.

"No, mother. Tammy doesn't even know her. They don't even go to the same school."

They question me about sneaking out. They caught me because Mom came in my room to make sure it wasn't raining in my window and discovered I wasn't in bed. They're especially angry that I tried to deceive them by putting the dummy in my bed. They ask me how long I've been sneaking out. I tell them this was the first time, but they don't believe me. They say they suspect I've been sneaking out all along—this is just the first time I got caught. They says it's bad enough I snuck out but to sneak out when I'm grounded—that's really bad. They don't trust me. Since they wrongly thought I was behaving, they were considering ungrounding me. But not now—I blew it. Now they're grounding me indefinitely—I have to earn their trust again.

After they leave, I lie awake in bed, thinking about how much I hate my parents, and how I can't wait until I turn sixteen so I can run away. Also, I decide I'm never going to speak to them again.

I go on my talk strike the next day. The only time I say anything to my parents is when they ask me a question. Then I just say yes or no unless it's a question that can't be answered that way. Then I answer it in as few words as possible. They just ignore what I'm doing. I can tell they figure I'll give up sooner or later, but I'm determined not to.

Arcudy isn't waiting for me on my way to school on Monday morning. At school I see him at his locker.

"Hi, Jack," I say.

"Deuce, I'm not speaking to you."

"Why not?"

"I'm mad at you. You got me in trouble. Your mom called my mom, so I got caught sneaking out. My parents grounded me for a week. Now I won't be able to see Tammy this weekend." He shuts his locker and walks away.

I sigh. I just lost my best friend.

Man, is he lucky. He's only grounded for a week. His parents are so lenient.

∞()∞()∞()∞()∞

On Trick or Treat night, Meg and Calley put on costumes. Meg dresses up like a ballerina. I help Calley dress up like a ghost. I drape a sheet over her head and cut holes in it for her eyes and mouth. Meg is going Trick-or-Treating with some of her friends. Mom and Mrs. Murphy are taking Calley and Patty Murphy door-to-door in the Murphy's neighborhood. Mom stopped handing out candy on Trick or Treat years ago because kids wouldn't trudge all the way up Mount Airy to our house for a lousy candy bar.

At eight o'clock Mom and Calley come home. Calley is whining because she wanted to keep Trick-or-Treating until her bag was full. Mom says she has enough candy to last till Christmas.

Later, Meg runs into the house bawling. She says a big kid ran up to her, screamed in her face, and stole her bag of candy.

"It was horrible! He had only one eye."

"I'm sure it was just a mask," Mom says.

"No, it wasn't! I saw his hollow socket."

"Where did it happen?"

"Parkview Circle."

Mom consoles Meg by telling her Calley will share her candy.

"No, I won't. It's my candy," Calley says.

"Yes, you will. You don't need all that candy. It'll just give you cavities."

Mom makes Calley dump all her candy out on the kitchen table. Then tells her and Meg to divvy it up. After a while, Meg whines that Calley is hogging her candy. Then Calley whines that Meg is taking all the good candy and leaving her the crummy candy. Mom tells them if they don't quit fighting she's going to throw the candy in the wastebasket. That shuts them up.

We take our big nine-week test in Math at the end of the term. The first problems are pretty easy, but then they get harder and harder. I glance at Jane Burns, who sits next to me. She's a brain and is whizzing through the problems. She finishes first and turns in her test. I'm still working on mine when the bell rings. Robinson tells us to put down our pencils and turn in our tests. I didn't get the last problem done. When I turn in my test, Robinson tells me to come back to her room after school tonight—she wants to talk to me in private. I worry about it the rest of the day. It has to be bad—it's Friday the thirteenth.

After school, I go to her room and peek in the door. She's sitting at her desk, grading papers. She tells me to come in. She thumbs through the test papers, pulls mine out, and hands it to me. 96% is written in red pencil at the top of the paper. It's crossed out and 0% is written next to it.

"Mansfield, I gave you a zero because you cheated. If I catch someone cheating, I automatically give them a zero."

I'm stunned. "What?"

"I saw you copy off Jane Burn's test."

I shake my head. "I didn't copy off her."

"I'm changing your desk. So I can keep my eye on you." She assigns me a new desk right in front of her desk. "You can go now."

Man, am I upset. She falsely accused me of cheating. While I walk home, I stew over what to do. I think about telling my parents. But then I think—who are they gonna believe? Robinson or me? No way they're gonna believe me. They said they don't trust me. I can't tell them. Since I'm just a kid, there's nothing I can do about it.

At home everyone except Calley is getting ready to go to the football game tonight. Waterbury High School is playing Massilon High School, which is a big rivalry. Dad, Mom, and Meg are riding to Massilon on a bus that a group of parents chartered. Tecca is going with the cheerleaders on the pep bus. They're leaving at five o'clock and won't be back until after midnight. Since I'm grounded, I have to babysit Calley. Before they go, Mom tells me Calley is not allowed to watch *The Twilight Zone.*

After we eat our TV dinners, Calley says, "Deuce, play monster."

With a crazy look on my face, I tell her, "I'm a psycho."

She runs. I chase her around the house. When I catch her, I drag her down in the basement to the incinerator. Pretend like I'm lowering her into it. When she starts to cry, I stop, revert to my normal personality, ask "What am I doing?" and let her escape. She runs and hides. Then I revert to my psycho personality, go find her, and act like I'm going to incinerate her again. We do it again and again. She loves it.

When *The Twilight Zone* comes on, Calley begs me to let her watch it. I make her promise not to have nightmares and get me in trouble like last time. Then I tell her she can stay up and watch Ghoulardi until Mom and Dad get home. That really thrills her.

In homeroom period, Hoffman hands out our report cards. We have to take them around to our classes and have our teachers fill in our grades. Then take them home and have our parents sign them— to prove that we showed them to them—and bring them back to school by the end of the week.

I get a B in Industrial Arts and a C in Music. My Music teacher, Mrs. Crawford, tells me I sing flat. In Math class, Robinson calls us up to her desk in alphabetical order. I wait nervously. I'm praying for a C. When she calls my name, I traipse up to her desk and hand her my report card. Without looking in her grade book, she writes my grade on my report card and hands it back to me. I glance at it— F. Act like it doesn't faze me. Go back to my desk. Check again to make sure I read it right—F. I notice a 2 and a 5 in the box under it. Look at the comment code on the back of the report card. 2 means "Not working to best of ability." 5 means "Does not complete assignments."

Man, I can't believe it. I got an F on my report card. I've never got an F before. I feel like a dunce. But then I figure it's because Robinson gave me a zero on the nine-week test for cheating. This makes me mad because I didn't cheat. But I don't know what to do about it. She's a teacher, an adult. I'm just a student, a kid. Everyone will believe her. No one will believe me.

As I file out of the room after class, Robinson hands me a slip of paper and tells me to give it to my parents. I read it out in the hall:

PARENT-TEACHER CONFERENCE

Dear Dr. and Mrs. Delaney,

I'm requesting a parent-teacher conference to discuss Mansfield's F in Math last term. Please call me at the school (LA4-4595) between noon and 2:00 p.m. to schedule it. I'm very concerned about your son's failing grade and feel a conference is necessary to correct the problem. I request that he attend the conference with you.

Sincerely,
Martha Robinson

Shit…my parents are gonna kill me…

I get a C in History, Cs in English and Spelling, an A in Physical Education, and a C in German. I walk home from school in slow motion. I dread showing my report card to my parents. I think about forging Mom's signature on the report card and turning it back in without showing it to them, but I realize sooner or later they'll ask to see it. Then I'll get caught.

I slip into the house through the side door. Overhear Mom talking to Meg about her report card in the kitchen. Mom says, "You got straight As. That's great, Meg. At this rate, you'll be rich someday." Dad pays us a dollar for each A we get. Meg is thrilled because she's going to get $11.

I try to sneak up the steps to my room.

"Mansfield? Is that you?" Mom asks.

"Yeah…"

"Come here."

I go into the kitchen.

"Did you get your report card today?" Mom asks.

"Uh-huh…"

"How'd you do?"

"Uh…not so good…"

"Let me see it."

I hand my report card to Mom.

She pulls it out of the sleeve. Suddenly, she frowns. "You got an F in Math."

"You got an F?" Meg asks me.

"Meg, go!" Mom exclaims.

Meg leaves the kitchen with a big smirk on her face.

"I'm supposed to give this to you." I give Mom the Parent-Teacher Conference slip.

As she reads it, she starts to fume. Glaring at me, she asks, "How could you get an F in Math?"

"Mom, the teacher gave me a zero on the big test. She said I cheated. That I copied off Jane Burns. But I didn't."

She looks at me like she doesn't believe me. "Go to your room. We'll deal with this when your father gets home."

I go to my room and change out of my school clothes. I get Sting out of his aquarium and play with him. I set him on my desk. Then let him crawl around on the palm of my hand. He likes to do that…

"Sting, you're my only friend. I hate Robinson. She falsely accused me of cheating. You believe me, don't you?"

His two beady eyes on his cephalothorax just stare at me…

I fantasize about taking Sting to school and putting him on Robinson's chair—Sting stinging her bony butt.

"Heh, heh," I chuckle.

When I put Sting back in his aquarium, I notice he's out of dead flies. I need to feed him.

As soon as Dad gets home from work, my parents call me into the den. I take my seat. Dad is examining my report card at his desk. He flips it over and reads the comments on the back out loud. Then looks at me with disgust. "You got an F in Math because you failed to do your assignments like we told you to."

"Dad, that's not why I got an F. I got a score of ninety-six percent on the nine-week test. But Miss Robinson changed it to zero. She said I cheated. That I copied off Jane Burns. But I didn't."

"So Miss Robinson made this up?"

"I…I think she has it out for me or something…"

"I find that hard to believe."

"You don't believe me. You never believe me."

"That's because you lie to us."

I knew he wouldn't believe me. I shut up.

"Mansfield, your mother and I are really disappointed in you. You won't get into college if you get Fs in Math."

"I don't wanna go to college."

"If you fail Math for the year, they'll make you repeat it. You want that?"

That would be really embarrassing. "No."

"Fortunately, it's not on your permanent record since you're only in eighth grade. I know you're not dumb. You have a high IQ. You're just not applying yourself. You cannot get any more Fs. So we're instituting a new regimen. Starting next term, you have three hours of compulsory study time every weeknight. And we're gonna check to make sure you do your Math assignments. You have to get your grade up by next term."

"I got an A in Gym," I point out.

"That doesn't count."

"Since it's Friday, can I watch TV tonight?"

"No. There will be no TV until your homework is done."

After supper, I wait for my parents to go to the football game. Then I go up in my Observatory to spy on the world. Since it's dark out, there's nothing interesting to watch, so I read comic books.

I hear Calley calling me. I ignore her.

She sticks her head through the trapdoor. "Deuce, let's play psycho."

"Don't bug me, Calley. I'm in a bad mood tonight."

She sticks her tongue out at me.

"Beat it!"

"You big meanie!" She scurries down the ladder.

When I go back down to my room, I look for dead flies in the attic. There are only a few left. I'm going to have to find something else to feed Sting.

I go with my parents to the parent-teacher conference. Miss Robinson meets with us in her classroom after school. She tells my parents that during the nine-week test she caught me copying off of the paper of the A-student who sat next to me, so she gave me a zero on the test. She wondered how I was able to get 100s on all my quizzes without doing my homework. She suspects that I copied off of the A-student's quizzes. That's why she gave me an F this term. She doesn't tolerate cheating. It's not fair to the students who honestly earn their grades. In the long run, I'm only cheating myself. She moved my desk to the front of the class, so it won't happen again.

"He says he didn't cheat," Mom tells her.

"I distinctly saw him copying off of Jane Burn's paper," Robinson replies sternly.

"Miss Robinson, with all due respect, it's your word against his," Dad says.

"Dr. Delaney, every parent believes their child wouldn't cheat. Has your son ever acted dishonestly?"

"Well...yes..."

Robinson smirks.

"I didn't cheat. I'll take a lie detector test," I pipe up.

They disregard me. Dad glances nervously at his watch. "So how can we resolve this? What does he need to do?"

"He needs to do his assignments. Honestly, I think he's capable of doing the work. He's just not applying himself."

"We agree with that. We've instituted compulsory study time at home on weeknights. We're gonna check to make sure he does his Math assignments. We hope this will take care of the problem."

"I hope so too. I want Mansfield to be proficient at Math," Robinson says.

I ride home with my parents.

"It's not fair. I shouldn't't've got an F. I didn't cheat."

"Life's not fair sometimes," Dad says.

"You believe her. You don't believe me."

"I don't know who to believe. This is what happens when you lie and deceive us. We don't trust you. You have to earn our trust again."

Every weeknight my parents check to make sure I do my Math homework. I'm not allowed to watch TV until I show them that I finished it and get their permission.

∞()∞()∞()∞()∞()∞

On Thanksgiving, we go to Aunt Susan and Uncle Dave's house for a big family get-together. They live on a farm. I play with my cousin, Phil, who's a year older than me. We take turns riding their horse, Lady. I ride around the field at a fast gallop like Hopalong Cassidy—it's a blast. I wish I had a horse.

After horseback riding, Phil and I mess around in the barn. We climb up into the hayloft and build a fort out of bales of hay. Later,

Phil shows me the new bull. It has a humongous pair of testicles. We toss pebbles at them, but Phil says we'd better cool it when the bull starts kicking its stall door.

For Thanksgiving dinner, we have turkey and mashed potatoes and gravy and dressing and cranberry sauce. For dessert we have pumpkin and mincemeat pies. Man, is it good. After dinner, we watch family slides. Man, are they boring. Except for the slides of the time Uncle Dave got drunk and drove his tractor into the pond. Those slides are really funny.

CHAPTER EIGHT

On Tuesday night, Dad and Mom go to bridge club. I have to babysit Meg and Calley. Mom writes down a phone number in case of an emergency. I do my Math assignment, so I can watch *The Fugitive* on TV tonight. As soon as I finish, I realize I'm not allowed to watch TV without my parent's permission. I pick up the phone in the kitchen to call Mom, but Meg is on the phone in my parents' bedroom talking to Laurie Roberts. I try to listen in on them, but she tells me to get off. I tell her to hurry up—I need to call Mom before *The Fugitive* starts. I keep picking up the phone, but Meg won't get off. Finally, I go upstairs to my parents' bedroom. She's reclining on their bed, yakking away.

"Get off the phone," I say.

"I don't have to."

"Look, I'm the babysitter. I'm in charge here, and I'm telling you—get off the phone."

"You're not the boss of me."

"I mean it, Meg. You've been on long enough. Get off the phone—now!"

"Make me."

I walk toward her with my hand shaped in a fist.

"Don't you dare! I'll tell," she says.

I remember Dad told me not to touch her, so I drag my feet across the carpet to create static electricity on my body. Then shock her big toe on her bare foot.

"Don't touch me!" she screams.

"I didn't. It was electricity."

I drag my feet across the carpet again and point my finger at her toe.

She kicks my hand away.

I'm going to miss my show. "Meg, if you don't get off, I'll sic Sting on you."

"Who's Sting?"

"My pet scorpion."

"Sure," she says like she doesn't believe me. She goes right on talking.

I go get Sting. Holding him by the tail, I carry him to my parents' bedroom. Meg is lying on her back on the bed with the phone propped between her ear and her shoulder. I dangle Sting right in her face. "Sic her, Sting!"

Meg screams bloody murder. Then drops the phone, scrabbles off the bed, and runs out of the room.

"Good boy, Sting."

I put Sting back in his aquarium. Then go to the kitchen, call Mom, and tell her I did my Math assignment. She gives me permission to watch TV.

I start worrying that Meg will squeal on me when my parents come home. I need to make up with her. She's locked in her bedroom. I knock on her door. "Meg, I'm done with the phone. You can use it now."

"Get away from me!" she yells.

"Meg, I put Sting away. You can come out now," I yell through the door.

"I'm telling!"

"Meg, I was faking. I wouldn't let him sting you. Please don't squeal on me. Okay?"

"Leave me alone!"

I hurry downstairs to watch *The Fugitive*. Mom and Dad come home during the show. I hear them in the kitchen.

"Mansfield! Come here!" Dad yells.

I figure Meg must've squealed on me. I go into the kitchen. She's whimpering to Dad and Mom about me.

"She's terrified. What the hell did you do to her?" Dad asks.

"I didn't touch her," I say.

"He's got a scorpion. He tried to put it on my face."

"I did not."

"You have a scorpion?" Dad asks.

"Uh...yeah."

"Where?" Mom asks.

"In my room."

"Where in your room?"

"My aquarium."

They can't believe it. They take me to my room and make me get the aquarium down off the shelf. Sting points his stinger at them.

"See," Meg says. The little chicken is standing behind Dad.

"I want that thing outta my house," Mom says.

"He's harmless. Look..." I demonstrate how I approach him from behind and pick him up by his tail. Then set him in the palm of my other hand and let him crawl back into the aquarium. "See— they only sting if they feel threatened."

"Doc, I won't have a scorpion in my house," Mom says.

"Get rid of it, Mansfield," Dad says.

"How?"

"Flush it down the toilet."

"But he's my pet."

"You heard me."

"But—but he didn't do anything wrong."

"Now!" Dad yells.

I pick Sting up by the tail again and take him into the bathroom. Dad follows me to make sure I do it.

"Sorry, Sting." I drop him in the toilet. Then flush. He spins around in circles. "Bye, Sting. It's been nice knowing you." Then he gets sucked down the toilet.

Back in my room, Meg tells Dad and Mom, "I was talking on the phone, and he stuck the scorpion in my face and said 'Sic her!' "

"Did you do that to her?" Mom asks.

"I asked her nice to get off the phone, so I could call you to get permission to watch *The Fugitive.* But she wouldn't get off. You said I'm not allowed to touch her. So I didn't touch her."

Mom and Dad look at me like I'm a monster.

"Something is wrong with you to do that," Mom says.

"What if it had stung her?" Dad asks.

"I was just faking. I wouldn't let him sting her."

"She doesn't know that. She's not a mind reader. That's how accidents happen. You need your head examined scaring her like that."

Dad grills me about where I got a scorpion. Mom wants to know how long it's been living in her house. She thinks I'm strange because I had a scorpion as a pet. Finally, they tell me to go to bed. I don't believe it—all they did was yell at me. They didn't ground me any longer.

∞()∞()∞()∞()∞()∞

On Saturday morning, Dad wakes me up early in the morning and tells me to get dressed—we're going to Cleveland today. I ask him what for. He answers we're visiting a friend of his. He tells me to put on school clothes and goes downstairs.

I get up and get dressed. Dad always goes to the work on Saturday morning. I smell something fishy.

In the kitchen, Mom is in her robe fixing breakfast. Dad is sitting at the table, drinking a cup of coffee and reading the paper. He's dressed and ready to go. He tells me to sit down and have breakfast before we go. Mom brings me a bowl of hot cereal.

"Who are we visiting?" I ask.

Dad doesn't look up from his paper. "An old friend of mine from med school."

"He's a doctor?"

"Uh-huh."

"What kind of doctor?"

"A psychiatrist." He turns the page.

"A psychiatrist?"

"That's right. His name is Dr. Isch." He puts down his paper and finishes his cup of coffee. "Well, I think we better get going."

"Uh...do I have to go?"

"Yes."

"Why?"

"Because I said so."

"But I was gonna do homework today."

"You can do it tomorrow."

"You're taking me to a shrink."

Dad looks at Mom. She doesn't say anything.

"I ain't going," I say.

"Yes, you are," he says.

"Why?"

"Your mother and I think he might be able to help you."

"You think I'm nuts."

"No, we don't. We just think you're having trouble adjusting and need a little professional help. That's all."

"I won't do anything else wrong. I promise."

"I'm afraid it's too late for that."

"Aw, man. This isn't fair."

"I don't care whether you think it's fair or not. You're going and that's all there is to it. Now get your coat and go get in the car."

We ride in Dad's Cadillac. Dad keeps trying to strike up a conversation, but I refuse to speak to him. Finally, he says, "Mansfield, go ahead and pout—we're still going."

I don't say a word the rest of the way.

When we get to Cleveland, I start worrying about Dr. Isch. He'll probably make me lie down on a couch and probe my brain. I don't like somebody messing around with my mind.

Whatever you do, don't tell him any secrets. He's on Dad's side, and don't you forget it.

We go to Dr. Isch's office, which is in an old mansion on a main street in Shaker Heights. Dr. Isch is waiting for us in the reception area. He's bald-headed, has a beard, and wears round glasses. Dad introduces me to him. He shakes my hand. I stare at the floor. They talk about old times for a few minutes. Then Dad says he thinks he'll drive downtown and check out the med school to see how it's changed. He leaves me on my own.

"Would you like a cup of hot chocolate or a soda?" Dr. Isch asks.

Even though I'd like a cup of hot chocolate, I don't want to be friends with him. "No thanks."

"Let's go into the study where we can talk in private."

Dr. Isch takes me into a room lined with wooden bookcases and closes the door behind us. The drapes are drawn, so it's dim. He walks over to a great, big aquarium and turns on the light. Neon-colored fish swim to the surface.

"You guys hungry?" Dr. Isch asks. He gets out a can of fish food and sprinkles some in the water. They eat it.

"So what do you think of my fish, Mansfield?"

"They're the most beautiful fish I've ever seen."

"They're salt-water fish. See the seahorses?"

"Huh-uh."

"Over here. They're hiding behind the plant. They're shy."

I spot two small seahorses swimming behind a plant. "Cool."

Dr. Isch goes to his desk and picks up a manila folder, pen, and pad of paper. A couch and an armchair are arranged in a right angle around a coffee table. He sits down in the arm chair. Extending his arm toward the couch, he says. "Have a seat, Mansfield."

I go sit down in another arm chair way over by the fish tank.

"You go by Deuce, right?"

"Yeah."

"Deuce, would you mind moving over here, please?"

"Uh...what for?"

"I think it'll be easier for us to talk. What's the matter? Does it bother you to sit here?"

"No." I get up and walk over to the couch. "Do I have to lie down?"

He smiles. "Not if you don't feel like it."

I sit down. He's sitting caddy-corner to me, so I have to turn my head to see his face. I watch the fish.

"You know what I am, right?" he asks.

I nod. 'You're a shrink."

He smiles again. "I guess that is what some people call us, but actually I'm a psychiatrist. I'm a doctor just like your father. The only difference is he treats people's bodies and I treat their minds.

"Before we go on, I want you to know that it's my job to help you. But for me to help you, I need you to be honest with me. Okay?"

I nod.

"I want you to know everything we talk about is strictly confidential. It's just between you and me. Okay?"

"What about my dad? Won't you tell him?"

"Your father has asked me to do a psychiatric assessment. To be honest, I will give him my opinion as to your mental health, and my opinion will be based in part on things you tell me. But if you specifically ask me not to tell him something, I won't. Fair enough?"

"I guess so."

"Alright, tell me a little about yourself?"

"Like what?"

"How old are you?"

"Thirteen."

"So you're a teenager. Where do you go to school?"

"Johnny Appleseed Junior High."

"What grade are you in?"

"Eighth."

He takes notes while we talk. "What's your favorite class?"

"Study hall," I joke.

He laughs. "Seriously, what's your favorite subject?"

"Uh…science, I guess…"

"Why?"

"It's interesting."

"How so?"

"It can be used for good things or bad things. Penicillin or H-bombs."

"True. What's your least favorite?"

"Math."

"Why's that?"

"Uh...I don't like the teacher."

He writes something down on his pad of paper. "What do you do for fun?"

"Watch TV."

"What are your favorite shows?"

"Sea Hunt. Combat! Shock Theater—I like the host, Ghoulardi."

"Why?"

"He's really funny."

"What do you find funny?"

"I think it's funny when the hero and heroine always run toward the monster in a horror movie. And they project Ghoulardi into the movie, and he tells them they're running in the wrong direction and tries to get them to run away from the monster."

He cracks a smile. "What books do you like to read?"

"Comic books. *Mad* magazine."

"What's your favorite game?"

"Solitaire."

"Why's that?"

"You can play it by yourself."

"Do you have any hobbies?"

"I build models."

"That's interesting. What kind?"

"Mostly airplanes and boats. I asked for a Centuri Payloader model rocket for Christmas. It has a large payload capsule. I wanna launch a miniature camera or a biological specimen into the upper atmosphere."

"What biological specimen?"

"A white mouse."

"Won't it die?"

"No. The rocket has a parachute."

"What do you wanna be when you grow up—a rocket scientist?"

"No. A professional skin diver. I wanna search for sunken treasure."

"Do you belong to any clubs?"

"Uh...I used to belong to the Ark."

"The Ark?"

"It's a youth fellowship group at our church."

"Did you quit?"

"Uh...not exactly. I, uh...got kicked out."

He writes something down again. "Do you play any sports?"

"I used to be on swim team—but not this year."

"Why not?"

"Cuz I'm grounded."

"Do you have any other interests?"

"Uh...yeah, I like to spy on people up in my Observatory."

"What's your Observatory?"

"It's the turret on top of our house. Which is on top of Mount Airy. I can spy on people down in the town."

"So why do you like to spy on people?"

"It's interesting."

"How so?"

"You never know what you'll see."

"Let's switch gears for a minute." He opens the folder and pulls out a stack of cards. "This is a Rorschach test."

I sigh.

"What's the matter?"

"I don't like tests."

"This isn't a knowledge test. It's a personality test."

Dr. Isch moves over beside me on the couch and spreads out ten cards on the coffee table. "We'll start with the free association phase. What do you see?"

"Inkblots."

"What else?"

"Uh...they're symmetrical."

"Look at them and tell me what comes into your mind spontaneously."

I look at them again. "The Abominable Snowman."

"The Abominable Snowman?"

"Uh-huh." I randomly pick a card with black ink. "This one reminds me of the Abominable Snowman. You know—the ape monster in the Himalayas."

"Deuce, do you believe in the Abominable Snowman?"

"Yep. And the Loch Ness monster. And UFOs," I answer, grinning. I don't really believe in them. I'm just spoofing him.

Dr. Isch doesn't think I'm funny. With an annoyed look on his face, he says, "Deuce, I don't think you're taking this test seriously, which will invalidate my interpretation." Then he puts the cards away and moves back over to the armchair. "Let's talk about your family. How do you feel about your parents?"

"I think they're really strict."

"Why do you say that?"

"Cuz all they do is ground me. I've been grounded since September."

"How would you change them if you could?"

"I'd make them more lenient."

"How do you feel about your sisters?"

"I like my older sister, Tecca, and my kid sister, Calley. But I can't stand Meg."

"Why?"

"Cuz she does everything perfect and calls me the black sheep of the family."

"Deuce—do you know why you're here?"

I nod.

"Why?"

"Cuz my parents think I got a screw loose."

"I wouldn't put it that way. Actually, they just think you're having some problems adjusting. Do you think you're having any problem adjusting?"

"No way."

"Let's back up to your sister, Meg. Do you ever feel anger towards her?"

"Yeah."

"When?"

"All the time. We fight a lot."

"Can you think of any specific incidents?"

"Uh...not really."

"Your father mentioned to me an incident where you frightened her with a scorpion."

"I was just faking."

He asks me to tell him about it. I explain that Meg wouldn't get off the phone. I'm not allowed to touch her, so I used Sting to scare her off it. But I wouldn't have let him sting her.

"How did you feel about it afterwards?"

"Bad."

"What do you mean?"

"Dad made me flush Sting down the toilet, and it wasn't his fault. I felt like I got him killed."

"How did you feel towards your sister?"

"Mad."

"Why is that?"

"She didn't hafta squeal on me. I wouldn't've squealed on her if she did it to me."

"What would you have done?"

"I would've checked out her scorpion. But she'd never have one. She thinks bugs are creepy."

"Deuce, I hafta say I think a scorpion is a rather unusual pet. Why did you have one?"

"They're interesting."

"Aren't you afraid of getting stung?"

"Not really. They only sting if they feel threatened. You approach them from behind."

He looks at his notes. "Deuce, you told me you don't like your math teacher. Why is that?"

"Cuz she gave me an F in Math, and I didn't deserve it."

"What do you mean?"

I explain that she falsely accused me of cheating. "I'll take a lie detector test to prove it."

"That's not necessary. I believe you."

"You do?"

"Yes. I don't think you've lied to me so far. I wanna ask you about something else. Why'd you get kicked out of the Ark?"

"I got caught making out with our minister's daughter at the church retreat. Everybody thought I tried to feel her up because her blouse was torn. But I didn't. She tore it climbing out the window when we tried to get away. That's the truth."

"I believe you."

I smile. "You're the first person who believes me."

Dr. Isch questions me about when I got in trouble with the law this summer. Arcudy, Price, Bosko, and I slept out in Bosko's back yard. Bosko liked Nancy Owens, so he wanted to toilet-paper her yard. He had a whole case of toilet paper. His dad works at a paper company. In the middle of the night, we threw rolls of toilet paper all over the trees and bushes—they unrolled like gigantic streamers. By the time we finished, the place looked like a blizzard had hit it. The next day everybody in town drove by to look at it. We would've got away with it, but Bosko kept bragging about it to everybody. Finally, his bragging got back to the Owens, and they told the police. A cop went to Bosko's house and questioned him, and he ratted on everybody. We almost had to go to juvenile court, but Dad talked Nancy's parents out of pressing charges against us, so we wouldn't have juvenile records. We had to clean it up. It was a real mess because it had rained and turned the toilet paper soggy. We had to climb up in the trees. It took us a whole day.

Next, Dr. Isch questions me about the time in sixth grade Arcudy and I got in trouble for throwing water balloons at cars.

Next, Dr. Isch questions me about the time in fifth grade I got in trouble for taking a dirty picture to school for show and tell. The picture was in one of Dad's medical textbooks. It showed a man who had elephantiasis of the gonads. Man, was it gross. The poor guy had testicles the size of a grapefruit. I tried to say it was a scientific picture, but I still got in trouble.

"Deuce, let's talk about sneaking out at night. Your dad told me you snuck out with your buddy. What did you do?"

I don't know if it's the fish swimming around or the air bubbles bubbling to the surface, but I feel so calm and peaceful inside that I feel like telling him the truth—like I can trust him. "Well, I'd tell you the truth, but you'd probably think I'm crazy."

"No, I won't."

I shake my head. "You won't believe me."

"Try me."

"Okay."

First, I tell him about the night the thing with the hideous face tried to get me in the tree fort.

He listens to the whole story without interrupting me. "Do you think it could've been an animal? Opossums have ugly faces and climb trees."

"No. It had a hideously deformed human face…like the face of Reginal Wukela."

"Who's Regina Wukela?"

"This girl who got murdered in Luna Lake Park. They found her body in the sewer pipe. Her face was mutilated. People say her ghost haunts the creek—not far from my tree fort."

I explain this is a mystery that I wanted to solve. So one night I snuck out to stake out the sewer pipe. And, sure enough, I saw something that left small, barefoot footprints in the slime on the bottom of the pipe. "I thought it could be the ghost of Regina Wukela. So I talked my friend into sneaking out with me to stake out the sewer pipe. I wanted him to see it. But it rained, and we got caught."

"Well…that's interesting." He looks like he doesn't believe me.

"You don't believe me."

"I didn't say that."

"Then you believe me?"

"I'll be honest with you—I don't believe in ghosts. I believe there's either a physical or psychological explanation for every supernatural phenomenon. I believe there's one for what you experienced."

He looks at his watch. "I told your father to come back in an hour. We've run over. Let me ask you one last question. Do you ever talk to him about things that bug you?"

"Are you kidding?"

"Why not?"

"He's never home. He's too busy making money."

Dr. Isch writes down something on his pad. "Deuce, in the future, I want you to try something. If something bugs you, try to talk to your father about it. Will you do that?"

"I guess so."

"Good. I also want you to know if you have anything you want to talk to me about, feel free to call me. Alright?"

"Okay."

He gives me a business card with his name, address, and telephone number on it. I stick it in my wallet.

"Do you have any questions you want to ask me?" he asks.

"No."

"Anything you're worried or concerned about?"

I shake my head.

Dr. Isch stands up and sets his pen and legal pad on his desk. "The session's over. You feel any different?"

I feel my head. "I don't think it's any smaller."

He laughs. Then turns off the light in the aquarium and takes me back out to the reception area. Dad is sitting in a chair, reading a magazine. He smiles at me, but I won't even look at him.

In the car on the way home, Dad says, "Now that wasn't so bad, was it?"

I refuse to speak to him.

At home, Mom, Tecca, Meg, and Calley are decorating the Christmas tree. They went out and bought one while Dad and I were in Cleveland. Wouldn't you know it, they got a short one. Every year I try to talk Mom into buying a tall one, but she never does.

"Deuce, come help us decorate the tree," Mom says.

"Nah, I don't feel like it." I'm still mad.

I go to my room and flop down on my bed.

Man, I wish I had some salt-water fish.

I decide to start saving my money for them.

CHAPTER NINE

On the last day of school before Christmas vacation, we have our Christmas assembly in the auditorium. The school orchestra and choir put on a concert together for the whole school. They perform Christmas carols. The kids in the choir are wearing robes. The heat is turned on full blast in the auditorium. Between that and the stage lights, it's really hot on stage. Kids start dropping like flies. During "Joy to the World," Jerry Richards faints and falls backwards off the top row of the risers. He disappears into the curtain at the back of the stage—there's a big thud when he hits the floor. The music grinds to a halt. Then you can hear people running around behind the curtain and see the curtain moving in and out—they're trying to aid Terry. Mrs. Bell, the choir director, exits the stage to help. Later, she comes back, and they finish the song. Next, during "Away in a Manger," a big, fat girl, Lotebel Mathis, starts to faint. As she falls forward, she grabs on to the kid beside her, the two of them tumble and knock over some people in front of them, who knock over some people in front of them. Man, they're like bowling pins. The whole school laughs. Mrs. Bell, Mr. Hall, the orchestra conductor, and Mr. LaRue, the stage crew advisor, struggle to carry Lotebel off the stage. Mrs. Bell and Mr. Hall are so upset they cut the program short. Afterward, we learn it was no laughing matter because Terry Richards cracked his head open and had to have stitches.

On the first day of Christmas vacation, Mom ungrounds me so I can do my Christmas shopping. The only problem is I'm broke. Mom tells me to use my savings. I tell her I don't have any savings since they docked my allowance, so she gives me twenty-five bucks.

I take the bus downtown to the square and stop in Gorka's Pet Shop to see if they have any salt-water fish. All they have are fresh-water fish. I spot a fish tank with a sign that reads "Piranha." Now that Sting is gone, my aquarium is free. The price tag is $19.99. Another sign reads "DO NOT PUT HAND IN TANK." I see a small fish swimming around by itself. I can't believe it's a piranha. It doesn't look that ferocious. It looks more like a blue gill. I ask the saleslady if this is really a piranha. "That's what the sign says, sonny," she says. Then she goes to another tank, catches a goldfish in a fishnet, and dumps it in the piranha's tank. "Time to eat, Boris," she says. I watch Boris for about ten minutes, waiting for him to eat the goldfish, but he doesn't.

I buy a Giant Ant Farm for Calley's present. On the way out of the store, I take one last look at Boris. The goldfish is gone.

I only have seventeen bucks left to buy presents for everybody else, so I go to the Volunteers of America store. I get a bargain on four used bowling balls for sixteen bucks. I buy a solid black one for Dad, a blue one with white swirls for Mom, a black one with gold speckles for Tecca, and a black one with red speckles for Meg. When I ask the lady at the cash register if she'll gift wrap them for me, she calls me a smart aleck and puts them in a big cardboard box. Man, it weighs a ton.

I lug the box of bowling balls to the square. As I board the bus, the bottom falls out of the box. A ball lands on my foot and just about crushes it. Two balls roll down the steps of the bus and almost bowl over a little, old lady boarding the bus. The bus driver gets mad and tells me I can't take them on the bus. I tell him they're my family's Christmas presents. The little, old lady hears this and tells him to let me take them on the bus, so he does. I haul them two-at-a-time down the aisle and set them on the seat next to me.

After I get off the bus, I lug them two-at-a-time up Mount Airy to my house. My arms feel like jelly. I sneak them to my room and hide them in my closet. Then go see Mom in the kitchen.

"Mom, I know what I want for Christmas."

"What?"

"A piranha. They got one at Gorka's Pet Store. It's only $19.99."

"Deuce, we've been over this. No piranha. I just got rid of the scorpion."

"They make great pets. I really want one."

"What's it eat? Fingers?"

"Nah, you feed it goldfish."

"Gross." She imitates the way Meg says gross. "Deuce, I don't think I'd count on it if I were you."

"Aw, man. You never get me what I want for Christmas."

"Just be glad you're getting something. Some kids don't get anything for Christmas."

I turn around and walk out of the room mad.

∞◊∞◊∞◊∞◊∞◊∞

On Christmas Eve, it starts snowing. Mom says it looks like we're going to have a white Christmas after all. She decides we're not going to the Christmas Eve service at the church this year. She wants to stay home and spend a quiet evening with her family.

I go to my room and wrap my Christmas presents. The Giant Ant Farm is no sweat, but the bowling balls are a real pain in the butt. I wrap them in individual cardboard boxes. They take a whole roll of wrapping paper.

I go back downstairs to the living room. Dad has built a fire in the fireplace. Christmas music is playing on the stereo. All of the lights are turned off except the lights on the Christmas tree. Meg and I wait for Calley to go to bed, so we can put the presents under the Christmas tree. We have to wait because Mom says Calley still believes in Santa Claus. Calley is so wound up she doesn't want to go to bed. Mom tells her the sooner she goes to bed, the sooner Santa will come. They set out a glass of milk and a plate of cookies for Santa. Calley says if Santa comes down the chimney, he'll burn his butt. Mom tells her the fire will be out by then. Then makes her go to bed.

Mom waits for Calley to go to sleep. Then she tells me and Meg where the presents are hidden. I already know—they're in her sewing room. I already checked how many presents have my name on them when Mom wasn't home. I'm hoping that the long present is the Centuri Payloader model rocket that I asked for. I have to act like I don't know where they are. We carry them downstairs and put them under the tree. I go get the bowling balls. The presents cover half of the living room floor.

Dad and I assemble one of Calley's presents—the Susie Homemaker play kitchen. It comes in about ten boxes. We rip them open and spread the pieces all over the living room floor. We have to assemble a refrigerator, stove, dishwasher, sink, and cupboard. Dad curses because there aren't any directions.

Mom makes everybody hot chocolate with whipped cream. Meg and I take turns squirting whipped cream in each other's mouths. We polish off the whole can. I pitch it in one of the empty Susie Homemaker boxes. Then eat the cookies set out for Santa.

We don't finish assembling the Susie Homemaker set until almost midnight. Dad burns the cardboard boxes in the fireplace one at a time. They go up in a big roar and light up the whole living room—

Kaboom!

Embers fly all over the living room.

Dad stomps them out.

Mom rushes into the smoke-filled living room. "Should I call the fire department?!"

"No. I have the situation under control," Dad tells her.

There are a few burn marks on the carpet. Mom's not too happy about that.

Dad pokes around the logs in the fireplace and spots the can of whipped cream in the glowing coals. It's blackened and has a big hole where it blew apart at the seam. The pressurized can exploded when it was exposed to heat.

"How the hell did that get in there?" Dad asks.

"Deuce threw it in a box," Meg says.

Dad scowls at me.

"It was an accident. I didn't know you were gonna burn the box," I say.

Calley comes downstairs. The big boom woke her up. She sees all the presents under the tree. "I knew there was no Santa Claus."

Mom makes her to go back to bed. Then looks at me like I spoiled her quiet Christmas Eve with her family.

Man, I don't feel too crummy.

Bright and early on Christmas morning, Mom wakes me up. In a cheery voice, she exclaims, "Merry Christmas, Deuce! Time to open presents. Calley can't wait any longer." She seems to have forgotten about the explosion last night.

I get out of bed, throw on some clothes, and go downstairs to the living room. Calley and Meg are still in their pajamas, sitting on the floor by the presents. Mom is sitting on the sofa in her robe. Dad comes downstairs in his robe and gets out the camera. He takes family pictures. He doesn't mention the explosion last night either. Finally, Tecca comes down in her nightgown. She looks like she's still half asleep. She must've stayed up late with her boyfriend last night.

Dad takes pictures of everybody opening their presents. I open the long present first. It's the Century Payloader model rocket with the complete ignition and launching system. "Hot dog!" I exclaim. I thank my parents. I also get a microscope and a ski jacket. Tecca gets me a gas model airplane. Meg gets me the 45 record "Do Wah Diddy Diddy" by Manfred Mann.

Meg gets a record player, a lot of clothes, and an Etch A Sketch.

Tecca gets a diamond ring that Mom says is a family heirloom. It was her mother's engagement ring. She died of cancer when I was a little kid, so I don't remember her. Tecca also gets a set of luggage to take to college and a cashmere sweater.

Calley gets her Susie Homemaker set and a lot of toys. Most of them look pretty boring, but the Vacu-Form set looks pretty cool. You can make all sorts of things out of plastic with it.

Dad gets Mom a fur coat. She gets tears in her eyes and says he shouldn't have. Then he gives her a diamond ring. She starts crying and says he really shouldn't have.

Mom gets Dad a Rolex wrist watch made out of gold.

I give Calley her Giant Ant Farm. She thinks it's pretty neat—just as long as the ants don't escape and crawl into her bed.

I make everybody else open up their present from me at the same time since they go together.

"I wonder what this is. It's so heavy," Tecca says.

"You'll never guess," I say.

Nobody knows what to say when they first see their bowling ball.

"I figure everybody can go bowling together," I say.

"It's just what I wanted," Dad says.

"It's very thoughtful. Thank you, Deuce," Mom says.

"I'll take it with me to college. Thanks, Deuce," Tecca says.

"Mine's chipped," Meg gripes.

"Don't worry, Meg—it won't matter," I say. Meg's a terrible bowler. The last time she went bowling she bowled an 18.

Meg and I play "Do Wah Diddy Diddy" on her new record player again and again. She holds on to the record afterward.

After brunch, Dad makes me shovel the front porch, steps, and walk to the driveway. My cousins come in the afternoon. Phil tells me they got a new quarter horse for Christmas. I can't wait to ride it. Phil and I mess around with the bowling balls. We start to take them down in the basement, but Dad tells us, "No bowling in the house, Mansfield. Take them outside." We take them out in the garage, set up pop bottles like bowling pins, and bowl for a while. Then play marbles with them in the snow.

I have a cool idea—to throw the bowling balls out the window of my Observatory. Phil reminds me that we're not allowed to play with them in the house. I tell him we're throwing them out the window—that's not in the house. We sneak the bowling balls up to my Observatory and open a window. Earlier, Meg and Phil's younger sister, Julie, made a snowman in the front yard. I tell Phil it's a strike if you hit it. I chuck my bowling ball out the window. It rolls down the roof, jumps the gutter, crashes through the bushes in front of the house, and rolls to a stop in the snow. I miss the snowman by a mile. Then Phil throws his bowling ball like a shot put. It clears the roof and hits the ground with a thud, bounces down the front bank, and rolls down the front walk to the driveway. Picking up speed on the driveway, it bowls straight toward Uncle Dave's parked Volkswagon Bug. Our jaws drop...

The bowling ball slams into the side of the car. Then ricochets down Mount Airy Lane. Rolls out of sight.

We slip downstairs and out the door. Sprint down the driveway to Uncle Dave's car. It has a big dent in the running panel under the front door.

"Shit!" Phil exclaims with a scared look on his face.

"C'mon. Let's find the bowling ball," I say.

We follow the bowling ball's tracks in the snow down Mount Airy Lane. Near the bottom of the hill we see where it jumped the curb, bounced down the cliff, and went airborne into the creek. Then see where it slammed into a tree and bashed in the bark. I'm glad it didn't hit anybody.

I fish the bowling ball out of the creek and lug it back up Mount Airy Lane. When we get to our house, Phil asks me if I'm going to squeal on him. I tell him no way. He looks pretty relieved.

We eat Christmas dinner—standing rib roast. Man, is it good. For dessert we have chocolate mousse pie. It's my favorite dessert. After supper, we watch family slides on a screen with a slide projector. They go way back to when I was just a baby. My cousins don't leave until ten thirty. Dad makes me walk them down the driveway to the turnaround with a flashlight. He's scared somebody will slip and fall on the ice in the dark. I'm careful not to shine the light on the dent in the car. Nobody notices it in the dark.

Every day after Christmas I walk down to the mailbox and check the mail. I'm expecting Grandma Colleen's Christmas present. She goes to Florida every winter. At Christmastime she sends each of her grandchildren money. On Tuesday, I spot a letter in the mail to Dad from Dr. Isch. It has to be about me. I'm tempted to steam it open, but I'd better not risk it.

When Dad comes home from work, he takes the mail into the den and shuts the door behind him. He's in there for a long time. He doesn't mention the letter to me.

At night I wait for everybody to go to bed. Then sneak into the den. I find the opened letter in his top desk drawer. The typed letter reads:

Dear Mansfield:

This letter summarizes my diagnostic impressions drawn from my initial psychiatric interview with your son, Mansfield, at my office on December 12, 1964. I conducted the interview with the aim of making an initial diagnosis and formulating a treatment plan. Since you had already provided me with a history of the presenting problem, pertinent medical information, family and social history, and specific behavioral patterns, I used the interview to establish an initial rapport with Mansfield and to talk to him about the presenting problem.

Mansfield is exhibiting adolescent misbehavior that includes: minor vandalism; getting into trouble at school; repeatedly lying to his parents; sneaking out of the house at night; and exhibiting menacing behavior toward his younger sister. He recently was expelled from a church retreat for inappropriate conduct with a teenage girl. Despite having a high IQ, he received a failing grade in Math at school last term.

During the interview, Mansfield and I discussed his misbehavior in detail. At the beginning, he appeared guarded and apprehensive; his responses were somewhat evasive. However, as the session progressed, he became more open and cooperative. I believe that his responses were for the most part honest—except his Rorschach test responses. His stream of speech and mental activity showed no marked abnormalities. His affect and mood were appropriate. He appeared well-oriented. He seemed somewhat cool emotionally.

It is revealing that Mansfield expressed hostility towards you during the session. I asked him if he ever discusses his problems with you. He responded that this is impossible because you are never at home. He expressed that you are "too busy making money."

A rather strange thing surfaced during the session. In response to my asking him why he sneaked out at night, he confided that something tried to "get him" in his tree fort one night; that he believes it was the ghost of a little girl who was murdered in the neighborhood several years ago; and that he sneaked out to prove it.

Mansfield exhibits many of the behaviors and characteristics typical of the antisocial personality. He is emotionally immature. He lacks insight, judgment, and a sense of responsibility. He refuses to play by the rules of society. He tends to act impulsively without regard for the consequences. He habitually lies and commits other acts of dishonesty. He shows little anxiety or guilt about his behavior. He doesn't seem to learn from experience; when he's caught and punished for misbehavior, he repeats it. He doesn't seem to be influenced by authority or discipline.

However, I think it would be premature to diagnose Mansfield as antisocial at this stage. In my opinion, it is more plausible that he is misbehaving in order to get your attention; he has learned that the only way he can get your attention is by getting into trouble.

Mansfield's "ghost story" also may be symptomatic of a mental abnormality. However, I'm more inclined to believe that it is a normal adolescent fantasy. Adolescents' brains are still developing, which may lead to a teen's inability to separate fantasy from real life.

Mansfield's behavior also may be symptomatic of

sibling rivalry between him and his sister. However, I'm more concerned about your relationship with Mansfield at this point.

Based upon my initial psychiatric interview with your son, I recommend the following treatment plan. You need to get involved in a positive manner in his life as soon as possible. You should encourage him to participate in sports and extra-curricular activities at school and then take an active interest in them. You should look for recreational activities in which the two of you can participate. You need to do things which demonstrate your unqualified love for him. I recommend that you take a father and son trip to reconnect. I further recommend that you immediately discontinue his grounding. In my opinion, it only encourages his misbehavior. If this treatment fails to correct Mansfield's behavioral problems, I recommend continuing the initial psychiatric assessment, further diagnostic testing, and psychiatric treatment that may include psychoanalysis and/or psychotherapy.

If you have any questions or concerns, please feel free to call me.

Irv

P.S. Sorry it took so long to send you my initial assessment. I took some time off before the holidays. Happy New Year.

I put away the letter and go back to bed. I lie awake thinking about what Dr. Isch said. He tore me up pretty good—not that that surprises me. I knew he was on Dad's side to start with. I don't buy what he said about me misbehaving to get Dad's attention. Dad didn't even enter my mind when I did those things. I know why I did them—for the fun of it. And I knew I never should've told him about the ghost of Regina Wukela. No way it's an adolescent fantasy. You just can't trust a shrink. But I sure agree with him about one thing—ungrounding me.

After church on Sunday, Dad says he wants to talk to me. I madly rack my brain, trying to figure out what I did wrong. He takes me into the den and tells me to have a seat.

"Deuce, I wanna have a man-to-man talk. First of all, I wanna say I'm sorry. I've been doing some soul-searching lately, and I'm afraid I've been so wrapped up in my profession that I haven't spent enough time with you. I don't know…maybe if I'd spent more time with you, you wouldn't be experiencing some of the problems you're experiencing." Dad made a New Year's resolution to quit smoking. He plays with a silver dollar to keep his hands too busy for a cigarette.

"So I made a New Year's resolution—there's gonna be a new program around here. I'm gonna make time for you. I really want you and me to spend time together. Would you like that?"

"I guess so." I figure he's saying this because of Dr. Isch's letter.

"I thought we might go on a ski trip together. Would you like that?"

"Sure. But, uh...I thought I was grounded."

"Well, that's another thing I wanna talk to you about. I've decided you're no longer grounded. I fear it's counterproductive."

I act like I'm surprised.

"I want you to join swim team. I'd like to watch some of your meets. And I want you to join an organization at school. You need to get involved in some extracurricular activities."

"Like what?"

"Like a club or something."

"But I don't like clubs."

"How do you know unless you try?"

"I've tried."

"I'll make you a deal. If you join an organization, I'll take you skiing at Boyne Mountain."

"Where's that?"

"Michigan."

"Really?"

"Yep. They have a beautiful ski resort there. There's a lodge with an outdoor heated swimming pool. We'll spend the whole weekend there—just you and me."

"No Meg?"

"Just the men."

I have to admit I wouldn't mind going to a swank ski resort. "I don't have any spending money."

"I'm reinstating your weekly allowance. You can start saving for the trip. And Grandma Colleen will be sending you some Christmas money. Well, what do you think? We have a deal?"

"I guess so."

"Good." He smiles. "Well, I guess that takes care of everything I wanted to say. Do you have anything you want to say?"

I shake my head.

"Oh—one last thing. If anything bothers you, I want you to feel free to talk to me about it. That's what I'm here for. Okay?"

I nod my head.

"Good. You know, I'm really glad we had this man-to-man talk. I feel like it's the start of a whole, new relationship between you and me. I think next year is gonna be a good year for us. Now how about showing me your new microscope?"

We look at slides under my microscope of a hair and a thin piece of skin that Dad peels off his finger. Then he pricks his finger with a lancet, and we look at a blood smear. He points out the plasma, red blood cells, white blood cells, and platelets.

"Man, it looks alive," I tell him.

The next day I get my Christmas present from Grandma Colleen in the mail. She sends me a check for $100.00. Man, I'm rich. Everybody asks me what I'm going to spend it on. At first I think about buying salt-water fish, but then I decide to save my money for Boyne Mountain. Dad cashes the check for me at the bank and brings me five twenty dollar bills, which I put in my coin safe.

CHAPTER TEN

After school, Mom drives me to swim team practice at the Y. I run into Arcudy in the locker room.

"Hey, I thought you were grounded," he says.

I'm surprised that he spoke to me. He must not be mad at me anymore. I tell him my parents ungrounded me. He takes off his I.D. bracelet and puts it in his locker. We walk down to the pool together.

"So are you still going steady with Tammy?" I ask.

"Nope. We broke up."

"Really?"

"Yeah. She dumped me for Tom Bradley." He shrugs like he doesn't care, but I can tell he's heartbroken. "Deuce, there's always more fish in the sea."

"Right."

At the pool I do a racing dive off a starting block and swim a length of butterfly. Man, does it feel good to be back in the water. Coach Campbell puts us through a two thousand yard workout. I'm pretty whipped by the end. I can tell I'm out of shape. My eyes are bloodshot since I'm not used to the chlorine. When Mom picks me up, she gives me grief for not drying my hair—says I'll catch cold.

I have a swim meet on Saturday. Dad and Mom both attend. They sit in the stands and cheer for me and the team. I take a first in the 50-yard Butterfly and a second in the 50-yard Freestyle. Arcudy beats me. My time is slower than usual since I'm out of shape. Our medley relay takes first place. I swim the butterfly leg and Arcudy swims the freestyle leg. Our freestyle relay also takes first place. I swim first-man and Arcudy swims anchor. Dad and Mom think I do great.

The next day Dad helps me assemble my Centuri Payloader model rocket. He says we'll launch it when the weather gets nice.

It's snowing really hard when Mom picks me up at the Y after swim team practice. She has a hard time driving up Mount Airy Lane. The car's tires keep spinning in the snow. We barely make it up the hill.

After supper, I turn on the lamppost in the front yard and keep looking out the window at the snowstorm. I start hoping for a snow day tomorrow. It would get me out of a quiz in Math class. By the time I go to bed, the snow is getting deep. All night long I hear the wind howling.

When I wake up in the morning, I jump out of bed and look out the window. It's still dark out. The snow looks really deep in the light of the lamppost. I run downstairs in my tank suit to the kitchen. Mom's listening to school cancellations on the radio. Meg and Calley come into the kitchen in their pajamas. Finally, they announce Waterbury City Schools are closed.

"Yay!" we holler.

I scarf down a piece of toast with peanut butter and quickly get dressed. Then go up to my Observatory and look out the windows. The snowstorm is gone. It's perfectly still and quiet outside. Slowly, the golden sun rises in the turquoise sky. It's a winter wonderland. The ground and trees in Luna Lake Park and Possum Run Park are covered in deep, sparkling-white snow. There are no tire tracks or even footprints.

"Mansfield! Come down here!" Dad yells.

I go back downstairs to the kitchen.

Dad's eating breakfast. "I need you to shovel the driveway."

I hate to shovel the driveway. I groan. "But it's a snow day."

"Not for me. I hafta make it to the hospital."

"But it's dangerous. I could have a heart attack. Arcudy's grandpa died of a heart attack shoveling snow."

Dad rolls his eyes.

I buckle my rubber galoshes over my shoes and put on my ski jacket, stocking cap, and gloves. Then get the snow shovel and start shoveling the driveway. Man, is it hard. The snow is up to my knees. After I shovel in front of the garage door, Dad gets in his Cadillac, which has chains on the tires. He backs out of the garage and tries to maneuver his car around, so he can go forward down the driveway. He makes me shovel the snow in front of and behind his tires. Finally, his car is facing forward, and he plows down the driveway and Mount Airy Lane.

Calley comes outside in her snowsuit with Ike. We explore the yard. We slog through snowdrifts that are up to Calley's waist and over Ike's head. Back in the driveway, I shovel snow in a big mound and dig a tunnel into it—like an igloo. Calley burrows inside it with Ike. She gets cold, so we go in the house. Mom fixes us hot chocolate with marshmallows to warm us up.

In the afternoon, I go sledding with Arcudy, Price, and Bosko in Possum Run Park. We meet at the park entrance on Parkview Circle, which is near the sledding hills. I pull my Flexible Flyer sled and our Adirondack wooden toboggan there. Younger boys and girls are sledding down the baby hill. Older, more daring boys are sledding down Suicide Hill. Kids call it Suicide Hill because it's really steep and you crash into the creek not far from the bottom of the hill if you don't turn your sled in time. Naturally, my friends and I want to go down Suicide Hill.

First, we ride our sleds down the hill. Since it's a sheet of ice from kids sledding down it, we go superfast and really close to the edge of the creek bank—the ride is thrilling. Then we pull our sleds back up the hill, which is practically impossible. The hill is so steep and slippery that we keep sliding back down.

Next, the four of us scrunch onto the toboggan, push it over the crest, and streak down the hill. At the bottom, everybody leans sideways to turn away from the creek, but we're not going to make it, so we roll off the toboggan before we crash. The toboggan flies into the creek. We fish it out of the creek and pull it back up the hill. We're having a blast.

Later, two girls, who look like they're in grade school, want to ride down Suicide Hill. They have a plastic saucer sled, which you can't steer. We try to warn them about the creek, but they say they're not afraid. Sitting cross-legged on the saucer and holding the handles, the red-haired girl streaks down Suicide Hill. Screaming with glee, she speeds straight toward the creek and doesn't roll off the saucer. Sailing off the bank through the air, she crashes into the creek out of sight. Immediately, I hear her wailing. Everybody runs down the hill to the creek. The girl is lying on the rocks with her legs in the water. Blood is streaming down her face. She has a deep gash on her forehead. Everybody is gawking at the sight of blood.

Jack and I help the girl stand up and crawl up the creek bank. Dazed, she says she feels dizzy and has to sit down on the ground. She might have a concussion and be in shock. Since she can't walk, I tell Arcudy to get the toboggan. I tell Price to run to the nearest house and call an ambulance. I tell him we'll tow the girl on the toboggan to the park entrance on Parkview Circle. They take off.

Blood is dripping off the girl's nose into the white snow. I give her first aid. To stop the bleeding, I untie her scarf and tie it around her forehead. She keeps crying.

"What's your name?" I ask.

"Sharon," she whimpers.

I put my hand on her shoulder. "Sharon, next time roll off the sled before you get to the creek."

She nods and sniffles.

As soon as Arcudy brings the toboggan, we lay Sharon down on it. Since Suicide Hill is too steep and icy to pull her up it, Arcudy, Bosko, another boy, and I tow her through the woods where the hill is not as steep and icy. Her friend walks beside her.

We take Sharon to the park entrance on Parkview Circle. Price is waiting there for us. He tells us he went to the house across the street, told the lady who lives there about the sledding accident, and she said she'd call an ambulance. Soon, the lady comes outside and says Sharon can wait for the ambulance inside her house where it's warm, so we tow Sharon across the street to her front door, and Sharon staggers inside. We hang around and watch the ambulance arrive with its siren blaring and take her away.

All the way home, my friends and I talk about how exciting the girl's crash was.

"It was gory. You see all the blood in the snow?" Arcudy asks.

I show him the blood on my gloves. "My dad says head wounds bleed a lot."

"I can't believe she didn't bail out," Price says.

"Girls are dumb. Man, she flew into the creek—like a flying saucer!" Bosko exclaims.

"That's why they call it Suicide Hill," I say.

On the way home from the Ashland swim meet, Dad asks me when I'm going to join an organization at Appleseed. I tell him after swim team season is over. He reminds me of our deal—no extra-curricular activity at school, no ski trip to Boyne Mountain.

At the end of the term, I take the nine-week test in Math. I know that I answered all of the problems right, so I should get 100% on the test. Since I got As on all of the quizzes and did my homework this term, I should get an A on my report card. And I won't have to worry about failing Math anymore.

The next day Robinson makes me come up to her desk at the end of class. I get a bad feeling. She shows me my score on the nine-week test. I got an 80%—a C. She explains that she gave me zeros on the last two story problems—which were worth ten points apiece—even though I got the right answers because I didn't follow directions. The directions said I had to show how I arrived at my answer—I just wrote down the answers. That cost me 20 points. I explain that I solved the problems in my head. She tells me to follow directions next time.

I fume all the way to my next class. It's not fair. I had the right answers. Who cares how I arrived at them? I can't wait until I'm sixteen and can drop out of school.

We carry our report cards around the next week. Robinson gives me a C in Math. When I show my parents my report card, they're pleased that I got a passing grade and encourage me to pull my grade up to a B next term. I don't tell them what happened on the nine-week test. I figure they'll just yell at me for not following directions.

I start the third term. Since I'm halfway through the school year, I change some subjects. I take Art in place of Music for the rest of the year. Mr. Henry is the art teacher. He wears a beret and speaks with a lisp. Even though he's American, he makes the class pronounce Mr. Henry the way the French say "Henri." He calls us "mes petits oiseaux." He says the French words mean "my little birds" in English.

I take General Science in place of Shop. Mr. Frazier is my teacher. He says he's going to divide the remainder of the school year into three six-week units—Physics, Chemistry, and Biology. We're going to do a lab experiment every two weeks. It actually sounds interesting. Then he announces the annual Appleseed Science Fair will be held on March 2. Anyone who does a project will get extra credit. I'll pass.

At dinner Dad asks, "Deuce, have you joined a club?"

"Uh...not yet. I'm still looking for the right one."

"If you keep procrastinating, it'll be too late to go to Boyne Mountain. Winter will be over."

I have an idea. "What if I do a science fair project?"

He thinks about it for a minute. "It's not a club. But it's a step in the right direction. Okay, I'll make you a deal. If you get a Superior on your project, I'll take you to Boyne Mountain."

We shake hands on it.

On Groundhog Day, the fire alarm goes off during a spelling test in English class. Our teacher, Mrs. Nash, instructs us to put down our pencils and exit the room in an orderly manner. We evacuate the school in single file and congregate around the flagpole. I try to spot the fire but don't see it. Don't even see any smoke. Soon, I hear a siren, and a fire truck pulls up out front. Firemen jump out and run into the building.

Without coats, we're freezing our butts off. There's melting snow on the ground. People start asking Mrs. Nash when we can go back inside. She says as soon as there's no danger of fire. "Great. In the meantime, we'll freeze to death," I wisecrack to Greg Fisher, who sits behind me in class.

Eventually, the firemen get back in the fire truck and leave. Then the bell rings, and Mrs. Nash says we can go back inside. Everybody wonders if it was a fire drill, but I figure it was a false alarm. There's no way the school authorities would stage a fire drill in the middle of winter and actually make the fire department come.

In study hall, I read an article in the Appleseed Press about our new assistant principal, Mr. Joseph Kruse. I've seen him patrolling the school to catch kids running in the halls and hoods smoking in the restrooms. He has a crew cut, is built like a gorilla, and talks with a southern drawl. The article says he used to be a drill sergeant in the Marines and a football coach at William Barksdale Junior High School in Jackson, Mississippi. He says he "believes in using corrective discipline and corporal punishment to make students behave." That means he paddles them. I figure I'd better steer clear of him.

In homeroom period a few days later, Mr. Hoffman gets called down to the office. While he's gone, the person leading the Pledge of Allegiance comes on over the P.A. system and says, "Stand please." Everybody in the class stands, faces the flag, puts their hand over their heart, and recites the pledge—except for Buford Hickman. Buford has the reputation around the school for being a tough hood. He slouches in his chair with his legs crossed, feet propped on his desk, and hands folded behind his head. Suddenly, Mr. Kruse storms into the classroom and shouts, "Su-un, wipe that smirk off your face!" Then he picks Buford up by the scruff of his neck and hauls him down to the office. Kruse was standing out in the hall, watching Buford through the open door the whole time. When Kruse brings Buford back to class, it's obvious that he paddled him from the way Buford's hobbling. Buford looks white as a sheet, totters into the room, and faints. Kruse makes him sit at his desk with his head between his legs to aid blood flow to the brain.

In the locker room before Gym class, guys are changing into their gym clothes. I overhear some hoods razzing Buford for fainting after he got paddled by Kruse.

"I couldn't help it! He beat me! Look at my ass!" Buford exclaims. He drops trou and shows them the nasty welts on his butt. "He left marks. I'm gonna sue Joe No-toe." Joe No-toe is the nickname the hoods have given Kruse because he got half his foot blown off in World War II.

"How many whacks did you get?" Lonnie Butsavage asks.

"Five."

"Shit, only five. You pussy," Butsavage says.

"His paddle has holes in it. So it hurts more."

In homeroom period the next day, Kruse announces over the P.A. system proper behavior for the Pledge of Allegiance. In his southern drawl, he says, "All pupils are required to stand, face the flag, place your hand over your heart, and respectfully recite the Pledge of Allegiance. I will not tolerate any pupil disrespecting our country's flag. I've seen men die for our flag."

On a Saturday morning, I go to the Waterbury Public Library and leaf through science magazines, looking for an idea for my science fair project. In *Popular Mechanics,* I come across an article called "Build the Shotgun Sound Snooper." There's a picture of it. It looks like a Browning .50 caliber machine gun mounted on a tripod.

The article tells how to build a shotgun microphone out of metal tubes. How it works is the different lengths of tubes pick up and amplify the different frequencies of sound. The article says you can aim it at somebody who's 250 yards away and hear what he's saying. I could put it up in my Observatory. Not only would I be able to spy on people, I could eavesdrop on them. Cool, man. That's what I'm building for my project. I copy the article on the coin-operated copying machine.

As soon as Dad gets home from work, I tell him I want to build a shotgun microphone for my science fair project. Then show him the bill of materials in the article, which lists the items needed to build the microphone and the amplifier. He says it doesn't look too expensive and tells me to charge everything. I ask him if he'll help me build it. He says he'll help me if I run into any problems, but he's not going to build it for me—it's my project.

Over the next couple of days, I look in the Yellow Pages and call places for the parts to the shotgun microphone. I order ten six-foot lengths of 3/8 inch aluminum tubing, four pieces of aluminum stripping, and one aluminum box from the Waterbury Tube and Steel Company. At first they don't want to do such a small order, but when I tell them it's for a science fair project they say okay. Then I call Hohler's Electronic Distributing Company and order a Crystal microphone cartridge and a Lafayette PK-544 amplifier. Then I track down a camera tripod at Max's Camera Shop and a set of headphones at King TV and Appliances.

There's a teachers' meeting on Wednesday, so I don't have school. Mom drives me around town, and I pick up the parts for my shotgun microphone. The people at Waterbury Tube and Steel Company are real nice. They throw in an extra six-foot piece of aluminum tubing for a spare. So is the guy at Hohler's. He double-checks my amplifier parts list to make sure I have everything. When I tell him I'm making a shotgun microphone, he smiles and says I'll probably work for the CIA someday. The only hitch happens when I go to King's. The guy says they don't have any headphones in stock. He'll have to order me a set, but it'll only take a week. When we go home, I take everything down in the basement to Dad's workshop. I'll build it on the weekend.

On Saturday afternoon, I start building the shotgun microphone. First, I build what the article calls the tube cluster. I cut the aluminum tubing into thirty-six pieces with a hacksaw. The pieces range from one inch to thirty-six inches in length and are graduated in one-inch steps. Then I glue them together with epoxy. A diagram shows how to arrange the tubes in the shape of a hexagon. While I'm waiting for the epoxy to dry, Dad comes down in the basement. He says it looks like I'm making progress. After he goes back upstairs, I make the support brackets out of the aluminum strips.

After supper, I mount the microphone cartridge. I connect a piece of mike cable to the cartridge and glue it inside a funnel. Then attach the tube cluster to the microphone cartridge by taping the flush end of the tube cluster inside the funnel. That creates the tubular microphone. Then I mount the tubular microphone on the camera tripod with the support brackets.

Dad comes downstairs again. I call it quits for the night. We admire what I've built so far. Dad says it looks just like the one in the picture. I tell him I have the hard part to do tomorrow—the amplifier. I ask him if he'll help me. He says if I get in a jam, but he thinks I can do it myself.

I get up early the next morning and work on the amplifier. It gets me out of going to church. I have to mount and wire all the electronic components in the aluminum box. I follow the schematic and look at the photo of the inside of the amplifier. Using Dad's soldering gun, I solder the wires. I learned how to solder in metal shop at school this year. It takes me all day, but I do it.

After supper, I mount the amplifier to the support bracket of the shotgun microphone. I grin—I'm done. I'm dying to try it out. Man, do I wish I had those headphones. Dad and Mom come down in the basement and check it out. They're really impressed. Dad says we'll have to test it next week.

I call King's every day after school to see if the headphones are in. Come Friday they're still not in. I start worrying about whether I'll have them in time for the science fair next Tuesday. Finally, they come in on Saturday. Man, am I relieved. Dad and I go pick them up. At home I plug them into the shotgun microphone and put them on. Turn on the amplifier and listen. Don't hear anything. Damn—I must've made a mistake. Then it hits me—I forgot the battery. How dumb can you get? So Dad and I go buy a nine-volt transistor battery and try again. This time it works—I can hear Dad talking into the tubes.

We test the shotgun microphone outside. We get Calley and drive to Luna Lake. We drop her off on one side of the frozen lake and tell her to sing something when we give her the signal. Then we drive around to the other side of the lake, park the car in the picnic area, and set up the shotgun microphone on a picnic table—I don't want to set it in the snow. Dad says we're a good two hundred yards away. I put on the headphones and aim the shotgun microphone at Calley. Dad waves his arms. A few seconds later I hear her sing:

Great, big gobs of greasy, grimy gopher guts,
Mutilated monkey's meat,
Little birdie's bloody feet,
And me without a spoon.

Man, am I excited. It actually works. I take off the headphones and let Dad listen.

"You hear her?" I ask.

He smiles and nods his head.

We test it in the woods. Dad drives back to Calley. They disappear into a clump of pine trees. Aiming the shotgun microphone at the trees, I pan it back and forth. At first I only hear birds chirping, but then I actually hear them talking.

By this time, everybody's freezing. In the car on the way home, Dad says, "Good job, Deuce."

I have to admit I feel proud of myself.

I do my science fair report the next day. The title is "Shotgun Microphone." I explain how it works, tell about sound waves, and compare it to a parabolic reflector microphone, which is another kind of long distance microphone. Tecca types it for me. It's three pages long not including the title page, table of contents, and bibliography. I also draw diagrams and graphs on frequency resonance, which I attach to poster board.

On the day of the science fair, Dad drives me and my shotgun microphone to school early. We carry my project to the gym and set it up on a card table. Randy Walters sets up his project on The Human Eye beside me. He checks out mine. I can tell he's impressed. He says he thought it was a machine gun.

In Science, Mr. Frazier takes the whole class to the science fair to look at the projects. Everybody really likes my shotgun microphone—especially Mr. Frazier. He asks me if it really works. I turn it on and aim it at Mr. Wilson and Miss Blake, the French teacher, on the other side of the gym. We hear them talking about meeting at a motel room on Friday night. Mr. Frazier tells me to aim it somewhere else.

I mosey around the gym, checking out the other projects. There are projects on The Atom, The Cell, and Crystals, just to name a few. Some of them are pretty cool. Bob Davidson, who did his project on The Heart, actually has a cow's heart in a jar. Mary Richardson did hers on The Skin and its Functions. She made a model of a cross-section of skin out of foam rubber. Her report is twenty pages long.

When I come back during lunch period, I see that the judges have judged the projects. I rush to my table and look at the judges' rating—Superior. I almost got a perfect score. They knocked off one point for my report being too short.

Man, am I happy! Boyne Mountain here I come.

I look at the scores other students got. Most people got either a Good or an Excellent rating. There aren't many Superiors. Mary Richardson got one. Steve Maxwell, who's a real brainy ninth grader, got one for his project on Ultrasonic Waves. Robin Burr, who's another real brainy ninth grader, got one for his project on Mitosis. There's only one perfect score—Jane Burns got it. She did her project on Logarithms. It looks boring. There are only two Poor scores. Ann Carr got a Poor for her project—A Hornets Nest. They had to remove her dormant hornets' nest from her display because hornets started flying out of it. Russel Ealey also got a Poor score. The title of his project is:

Falling Off Water Tower

Did Cat Live?

On a poster board, Ealey glued snapshots of a cat falling from the Waterbury water tower. The pictures show Ealey dropping the cat over the railing on the catwalk, and the cat falling upside down, turning sideways, and landing on its feet in the grass lawn at the base of the tower—then running away. Ealey had to climb up the ladder with the cat. That's his whole project. He has no report. One of the judge's comments says, "This is not science. This is cruelty to animals."

In the evening, the science fair is open to the public. I show Dad and Mom my Superior. Man, are they proud! They say they knew I could do it. I ask Dad when we're going to Boyne Mountain. He says he'll check his calendar at work and set something up tomorrow.

In Science class the next day, Mr. Frazier calls me up to his desk. I wonder what I did wrong. He tells me I advanced to the district science fair at Waterbury College on April 8 since I got a Superior on my project. Then he asks me if I want to be his lab assistant. I can earn extra credit by helping him set up lab experiments. I say okay.

At supper I tell my parents about advancing to the district science fair and becoming Mr. Frazier's lab assistant. Man, are they pleased! Dad tells me we're going to Boyne Mountain next weekend. We'll leave Friday morning and come back Sunday afternoon. Man, I can't wait! I get to get out of school.

∞◊∞◊∞◊∞◊∞◊∞

We do a lab experiment on Work in Science class. I help Mr. Frazier set up levers, fulcrums, and pulleys. When we finish the experiment, he hands me the key to the storage room and has me put things away. While I'm in the storage room, I find a *Nasco Biological Science Catalog* on the counter. I leaf through it. The catalog shows scientific items that science teachers can order for their classrooms. Mr. Frazier comes in and sees me looking at it. I quickly set it down and get back to work. He smiles and tells me I can take the catalog home—he has another one. I thank him.

After supper, I go up in my Observatory and look through the *Nasco Catalog*. Right away I see something I want—the Nasco-ject Preserved Rat. The ad says they take white rats and painlessly euthanize them—how do they know it's painless? Then inject them with a preservative, so all the internal organs are preserved exactly as alive—even the animal's weight remains approximately the same as when living.

I figure a preserved rat would make a nice pet. I wouldn't have to feed it or clean its cage, and it wouldn't poop in my hand. It only costs $7.50 plus 85 cents for shipping and insurance. I fill out the order blank—where it asks my Position I fill in Lab Assistant. I raid my safe for the money, go downstairs to the den, and get a stamp and envelop out of Dad's desk. I'll drop it in the mailbox on my way to school tomorrow.

On Saturday morning, Dad leaves orders for me to clean up the workshop today. I go down in the basement. Tools and materials that I used to build the shotgun microphone are strewn all over the place. I hate to throw away the scrap aluminum tubing.

Out of the blue, I have an idea to make a James Bond weapon gadget. It'd be cool to make a blow gun disguised as a pencil. I find a pencil in a drawer of Dad's workbench. Then find a piece of aluminum tube the same diameter as the pencil. Cut off a piece of tube five inches long with a hacksaw. Then get a paintbrush and a bottle of yellow model airplane paint. Paint the tube yellow. While the paint dries, I saw off the two ends of the pencil, file them down, and stick them in each end of the tube. Presto—I have a blow gun disguised as a pencil. The piece with the eraser even reads "No. 2" on it. Only if you look close can you see where the fake pencil ends fit in the tube.

Next, I make a dart. I cut a 3/8 inch cube of surgical sponge and insert a surgical needle through it.

I try shooting it. I pop out the fake pencil ends, stick the dart in the tube, aim at a wooden door about ten feet away, and blow. Man, the needle sticks right in the door.

I make nine more darts—so I'll have plenty of ammunition. Hide them in an empty metal throat lozenges case. Then practice shooting at my dart board down in the basement. After a while, I'm a pretty good aim.

On Monday, I take my blow gun to school. I carry it in my shirt pocket with my dart case. They look like a harmless pencil and throat lozenges. The blow gun is loaded with a dart. Arcudy and I go to our lockers and take off our coats. When he turns his back on me, I pull out the blow gun, pop out the fake ends, and blow—shoot him right in the butt.

"Ow!" he yells and jumps. He looks at his butt.

I quickly stick the fake ends back in the blow gun and put it back in my pocket.

He finds the needle sticking in the seat of his pants. Pulls it out and looks at it. Then looks suspiciously at me. "You butthole! What is this?"

"I don't know." I try to act innocent but can't help laughing.

He chases me down the hall with the needle. Coach McNeely comes around the corner. We cool it. As soon as McNeely is gone, he asks me again what it is. I show him my blow gun. Shaking his head, he says, "You're sick, man."

In study hall, Arcudy and I get passes to go to the library. We sit at a table with Price and Bosko. Fake like we're reading.

"Show them your blow gun," Arcudy whispers.

I get out my blow gun. Pop out the fake ends. Look around for a target. Spot a photograph of the new librarian, Mrs. Brandt—she's a real battle-ax—tacked on the bulletin board. I aim and shoot at it. The first two darts miss, but the third one sticks right between her eyes. Everybody cracks up.

"Hey, man, let me try it," Bosko says. He tries to grab the blow gun and knocks it out of my hand onto the table.

"Boys! Cut out the monkey business!"

Mrs. Brandt is coming towards us.

I quickly cover the blow gun and the fake ends with my book.

"What do you got there?" she asks me.

The blow gun is sticking out from under my book. "Uh...just a pencil."

She picks up my book and sees the blow gun. Then sees the fake ends. "That's no pencil."

She looks at the bulletin board and spots the dart sticking in her face. Then storms over to her photograph and removes it.

She confiscates all the pieces of my blow gun. "Young man, come with me."

Shit...

She marches me to the office in a huff and tells the office receptionist, Mrs. Richards, she wants to see Mr. Kruse.

Oh, God...what if he paddles me?

Mrs. Richards makes me sit on the bench outside Kruse's door and escorts Mrs. Brandt into Kruse's office.

I wait—scared shitless...

Oh, no...what if they suspend me? There goes Boyne Mountain.

A few minutes later, Kruse comes out of his office with Mrs. Brandt. "Don't you worry, ma'am. I'll handle it," he tells her.

"Thank you, Mr. Kruse."

"My pleasure, ma'am."

She gives me a dirty look as she walks away.

"Su-un, get in here!" he yells.

I hustle into his office.

He shuts the door behind me and sits down in the chair behind his desk. Then orders me to sit down in the chair in front of his desk.

I spot my blow gun on his desk.

"What's your name, su-un?"

"Mansfield Delaney, sir."

He makes me spell my name and writes it down on a sheet of paper. "What grade are you in?"

"Eighth."

He picks up my blow gun. "Where'd you get this?"

"Uh...I made it."

He holds up the dart. "You got any more of these?"

I nod my head.

"Give 'em to me."

I take the dart case out of my pocket and hand it to him.

He opens it and sees the darts. "You know what I do with this crap?"

I shake my head.

He takes my blow gun and the darts and tosses them in the wastebasket. "I won't tolerate pupils bringing dangerous weapons into my school. You could put out somebody's eye."

"But...but I didn't shoot anybody," I say meekly.

All at once, he jumps out of his chair, leans across his desk, and sticks his finger in my face. His face is scarlet. "Don't talk back to me!"

I shut my mouth.

He sits back down. "Su-un, yooou think yooou know it all, but yooou don't! I doooo!" he yells in his southern drawl.

I just stare at the floor.

He holds up the sheet of paper. "Do you know what this is?"

"No, sir."

"This is my list of school troublemakers. And you're on it now. I'm gonna watch you like a hawk." He folds his hands on his desk. "Are you sorry, su-un?"

I'm hoping he won't paddle me if I say I'm sorry. "Yes, sir. I shouldn't've brought it to school."

"For your punishment, I was gonna give you five whacks. But, since you're sorry, I'm only gonna give you three."

He opens his desk drawer and pulls out this great, big paddle with small holes drilled in it. With a smirk on his face, he says, "I call this the Board of Education." Then he makes me take my wallet out of my back pocket, stand on two footprints taped to the floor, and brace myself against his desk. I feel my knees shaking...

"Bend over, su-un."

I bend over and shut my eyes—my heart is pounding...

Whack!

My eyes pop open—I jump and cry, "Ow!"

"Bend over."

I plant my feet on the floor, brace myself against the desk, and bend over again. Grit my teeth and stare straight ahead at the sign on the wall that says, "No Horseplay."

Whack!

I don't make a sound or move my feet.

Whack!

I let go of the desk and hop around, rubbing my butt—it feels like it's on fire.

My eyes are watering.

Don't cry. Whatever you do, don't cry.

"Su-un, you wanna sit down for a minute?"

My butt is too sore to sit down. I shake my head.

After a few minutes, Kruse asks me if I'm ready to go back to class.

I nod.

He gives me back my wallet.

I put it in my front pocket.

"Su-un, I'm warning yooou once and for all," he drawls, pointing his finger at me again. "I better not see your face in here again— yooou understand me?"

I nod.

He writes me a pass and sends me back to the library. As I walk into the room, I think to myself, "Whatever you do, don't faint." Mrs. Brandt and everybody's looking at me—they all figure I got the wood. I smile like it didn't faze me. I give my pass to Mrs. Brandt and walk to the table where my friends are. Sit down very carefully—my butt is still burning. It's still vibrating when the bell rings.

On the way home from school, I ask Arcudy if he could tell that I'd got paddled when I entered the library. He laughs and says he could tell I got the wood from the funny way I was walking.

At home I go straight to the bathroom, drop trou, and look at my butt in the mirror. Big, red welts are on my cheeks. A really wicked-looking one is on the back of my right leg. Man, does it hurt. I don't show them to anybody. I'm afraid Dad will find out that I got the wood at school and cancel our ski trip.

When I get home from school on Thursday, Dad's car is in the garage. I wonder what he's doing home so early. In the kitchen, Dad, Mom, and Meg are standing around with worried looks on their faces. I ask what's wrong. Dad answers Grandma Colleen had a stroke and is in the intensive care unit at a hospital in Sarasota, Florida—she might not make it. Then says he has to catch a plane to Florida tomorrow morning, so we're going to have to postpone our ski trip to Boyne Mountain. He promises that we'll do it another weekend. Man, am I disappointed—of all the rotten luck.

A few days later, Dad comes back from Florida. He announces to the family that it looks like Grandma Colleen is going to pull through. She's paralyzed on one side and can't talk too hot, but she's a tough old bird. Everybody's relieved. I ask him about our ski trip. He says he'll call and make the arrangements tomorrow.

The next day Dad tells me it's all set up—we're going to Boyne Mountain March 26-28. I'm afraid the snow will be melted by then. He says that's the earliest date they had a vacancy, and it stays cold in Michigan for the whole month of March.

In English, Mrs. Nash makes the class change desks because kids are talking too much. Kelly Rudolf is assigned the desk behind me. She's a cheerleader and one of the most popular girls in eighth grade. She's good-looking. She has blonde hair and blue eyes.

On Saturday morning, my Nasco-ject Preserved Rat comes in the mail. I open the package in my room. Man, he looks like he's alive. I name him Flatus.

In the afternoon, I go with Arcudy downtown to the record store. He wants to buy a 45 record called "Louie-Louie" by the Kingsmen—he says he heard it's really dirty. They've banned it on all the radio stations. When he finds it, he's afraid the saleslady won't sell it to him since he's a minor, but she does. She must not know it's dirty. At his house, we go into his room, lock the door, and slap it on his record player. We listen to it about ten times but can't understand the words. We try playing it at 33 speed and we still can't understand the words. All I know is they sound really dirty.

On Monday at school, we have an assembly in the auditorium. I'm happy because it gets me out of Math class. Milton T. Petty, who's the principal of Johnny Appleseed, stands on stage at the podium and addresses the student body. Students call him Mouse because he's short, fat, and bald-headed, and has beady eyes and buckteeth. Petty introduces Congressman White, who speaks about the challenges facing today's youth and fighting communism in some place called Vietnam. Man, is he boring. He talks on and on about the domino theory that if one country falls to communism, its neighboring countries will fall to communism—until the United States of America falls to communism. He talks right into our lunch period. A few guys start coughing, hoping he'll get the message that they're hungry and don't want to miss lunch, but he can't take a hint. Soon, half the guys in the auditorium—including me—are coughing just because they think it's funny. Petty, who's sitting on stage, is boiling. Finally, Congressman White gets so flustered that he stops in the middle of his sentence, thanks us for our attentiveness, and sits down. People applaud weakly. Then Petty goes to the podium, thanks the congressman for his fine speech, and apologizes for those students who think lunch is more important than saving democracy in the world.

During English class, Petty comes on over the P.A. and lectures the whole school about how rude and discourteous we were to Congressman White. He says he doesn't care if Congressman White did talk into the lunch period—nobody was going to starve to death. Then he announces there will be no more assemblies this year. At this moment Kelly Rudolf coughs. Mrs. Nash thinks that I did it and yells at me for mocking Petty. Then she gives me detention after school. I don't bother to tell her that I'm innocent. I doubt she'd believe me anyhow.

After class, Kelly Rudolf tells me she's sorry for getting me in trouble. She couldn't help it—she really has a cough. I tell her it's no big deal. It's not the first time I've got detention and probably won't be the last.

I take Flatus to school the next day. While I'm standing by the flagpole waiting for the bell to ring in the morning, I take him out of my pocket and set him on the ground with a piece of string tied around his neck—like he's on a leash. Kids crowd around watching. I pull him along on the string—like he's going for a walk with me. Everybody laughs. Then make him do tricks. "Sit up, Flatus," I say and pull up on the string—he sits up. "Roll over, Flatus," I say. With a flick of my wrist, he rolls over. "Play dead, Flatus," I say and roll him over on his back. Man, can he play dead. Everybody thinks it's a riot.

In English, I set Flatus on Kelly Rudolf's chair before she comes into the classroom. She almost sits down on him—she screams. But I can tell she loves it. Then Mrs. Nash comes in the room—I quickly put him away.

After school on Wednesday, we have our last dual swim meet with Ashland. Mom comes all by herself. Dad's at work tying up loose ends before we go to Boyne Mountain this weekend. Our team slaughters them. After the meet, Mom takes Arcudy, the Lewis twins, and me to the root beer stand to celebrate the end of the season. I order three coneys, onion rings, and a root beer float, but the funny thing is I only eat about half of it. I'm just not hungry.

When I wake up the next morning, I have a sore throat and ache all over. I tell Mom I feel sick. She feels my head, says I don't have a fever, and makes me go to school. In History class, I feel like I'm burning up. I'm so weak that I have to lay my head on my desk. At the beginning of lunch period, I go to the nurse's office. The school nurse makes me lie down on the examining table and sticks a thermometer in my mouth. A few minutes later, she pulls it out and reads it. "You're sick, alright," she says. She goes around the partition to her desk and calls Mom at home. "We have a very sick boy on our hands. He has a fever of 103," she says to her.

Shortly, Mom picks me up at school. In the car, I look at her with a pitiful expression on my face. "I told you I was sick," I say. She doesn't say anything, but I can tell she feels pretty guilty.

At home Mom makes me take some aspirin, get undressed, and get in bed. I fall asleep in about two seconds…

I'm sitting at my desk at school and look out the classroom window. I see a big flash of light and a mushroom cloud off in the distance—it's an H-bomb. I dive under my desk—

I wake up and see Dad hovering over me. He takes my temperature—103.6 degrees. Using a tongue depressor, he looks down my throat. He looks in my ears with an otoscope. Then feels my throat—says my glands are swollen. Dad tells Mom it could be strep throat. Mom asks me if I want any supper. I tell her I'm not hungry. I start worrying about being too sick to go to Boyne Mountain. Take some more aspirin and go back to sleep.

I wake up in the middle of the night. My bed is spinning in circles, and I feel like I going to puke. I jump out of bed and run to the bathroom—madly feel for the light switch. Make it to the toilet in the nick of time. Mom hears me puking and checks on me. She makes me drink ginger ale to soothe my stomach, but it doesn't work. I puke all night. Mom puts a wastebasket next to my bed, so I don't have to run all the way to the bathroom.

In the morning, Dad asks me how I feel. I tell him horrible. He takes my temperature—102.4 degrees. Then says he's going to have to cancel our reservations for Boyne Mountain. I feel like crying. I knew something would go wrong.

I puke all weekend. I can't hold anything down—not toast, soda crackers, ginger ale, or even water. I have the dry heaves. All that comes up is greenish-yellow bile—it tastes really putrid. My guts feel like they're turning inside out. Dad gives me some pills to make me stop puking, but I puke them up. Then he inserts suppositories up my butt. Man, they feel awful. And I still don't stop puking.

On Sunday night, Dad says if I don't quit puking tomorrow, he's going to put me in the hospital where I can be fed intravenously—he's concerned about me becoming dehydrated. I don't know if I'm going to make it to tomorrow.

When I wake up in the morning, I feel a little better. I make it all morning without puking. Then Mom fixes me a poached egg with soda crackers, and I hold it down.

But I don't get well. My fever won't go away. It hovers between 100 and 101 degrees. Every morning I get up and move into my parents' king-size bed and watch TV all day. Mom brings me my meals on a tray. I got life made. It sure beats going to school.

While I'm home sick, we get our report cards for the third term. Mom goes to school and picks mine up. Mr. Frazier gives me an A in Science. He writes a note saying he automatically gives an A to anyone who gets a Superior on his science fair project. He tells me to get well—he misses his lab assistant. Mom and Dad are thrilled about it. I get Cs in all of my other subjects—except Math. Robinson gives me an Incomplete because I missed the big nine-week test. My parents aren't too happy about that. I tell them at least I didn't get an F. They give me a big lecture about how I'm going to have to make up the work when I get well, so I don't fail Math for the year.

Mr. Frazier takes my shotgun microphone to the district science fair on April 8. The next day he calls Mom and says I got a Superior score again. If I'd gotten one more point, I'd be eligible for the state science fair in Columbus.

Four days later my temperature still hasn't gone away. Dad takes me to the hospital to get a blood test. The next day he tells me the test didn't come back conclusive, but it looks like I have mononucleosis. I have too many mononuclear cells in my blood. He says it's called the "kissing disease" because it can be transmitted by kissing. Meg hears that and says, "Deucey's got V.D." I tell her to shut up or I'll pound her, but the trouble is I'm too weak. Dad says all I have to do is rest and eat right and it'll go away on its own.

I fall way behind in my school work. Not that I care. But my parents do. Mom goes to school and gets my Math assignments from Robinson, but I don't do them. I don't feel up to it.

∞()∞()∞()∞()∞

On Easter Sunday, Mom asks me to hide Meg and Calley's Easter baskets for her. When I ask her why I'm not getting one, she answers I'm too old to get an Easter basket. I hide Meg's basket in the kitchen oven and Calley's basket up in my Observatory. It takes

Calley about fifteen minutes to find her basket, but Meg can't find hers. She gets more and more frustrated.

"Tell her where you hid it," Mom says to me.

"The stove," I tell Meg.

"Where?" Mom asks, alarmed.

"The oven," I tell her.

Mom runs into the kitchen, flings open the over door, and takes Meg's Easter basket out of the oven. It's a big melted chocolate mess. Mom groans and says she turned on the oven a while ago to preheat it. She asks me why I hid it in the oven. I tell her I thought it was a good hiding place. She says I should've told her I hid it there. Meg starts crying and says I ruined her Easter basket since her candy is melted. I tell her it's not ruined—I'll eat it. She says I did it on purpose. I say I'm sorry—it was an accident. Mom asks me why I have to ruin every holiday.

I go back to school the next day Dad makes me go even though I still have a fever of 99.5 degrees. He says it's only a low grade fever. If it spikes, I'll have to stay home again, but he doesn't want me to miss any more school. He's afraid I'll never catch up.

Kelly Rudolf asks me what I had. I answer Pukeitis. Then tell her I puked twenty-five times over a period of three and a half days. Actually, it was only around sixteen or seventeen times, but I exaggerate a little. Kelly says she's never heard of Pukeitis. I tell her it's a very rare disease caused by Pukococus bacteria.

CHAPTER ELEVEN

Ealey and I are at our locker putting on our coats after school. Out of the corner of my eye, I see him showing Bill Sweat something that makes a clicking sound. Ealey keeps looking around nervously to see if anybody's coming. I peek over his shoulder. Man, I can't believe it! He has a switchblade.

"Cool, man. A switchblade. Where'd you get it?" I ask.

"It ain't no switchblade, shit-for-brains. It's a stiletto. The blade comes out the front—not the side," Ealey informs me.

"Oh."

With a fiendish grin on his face, he says, "All you gotta do is stick it in the guy's gut and—"

He presses the button, and the blade comes shooting out.

Miss Ramsey, who's a girls' gym teacher, comes down the hall. Ealey sticks the stiletto in his pocket.

On my way home from school, I think about how I sure would like to have that stiletto. Then wonder if Ealey might sell it to me. The only problem is I'm sort of scared to ask him—he's too weird.

At home Mom tells me I need a haircut and gives me two bucks to pay the barber. Then says Dad said I'm supposed to get a crewcut. The snow is melted on the roads and sidewalks, so I ride my bike to Bernie's Barbershop. There are just a few guys in front of me. I hang up my coat and leaf through the stack of comic books, looking for an interesting one. A *National Enquirer* in the adult stack of reading material catches my eye. The headline reads "Mother Uses Baby's Face As Ash Tray." I pick up a few comic books and the *National Enquirer*—Bernie doesn't say anything. Then sit down and read the article in the *National Enquirer*. It's about a mother who burns her baby's face with a cigarette. Man, is she sick. She lives in New York City. I wonder if any sickos like her live in Waterbury. I doubt it—Waterbury is like Mayfield on *Leave it to Beaver*.

When it's my turn, I sit down in the barber chair. Bernie asks me what style of haircut I want. I tell him I want to look like the Beatles. He calls it a mop-top cut. He snips a little hair off the sides and back of my head and spins the chair around. I look in the mirror—my hair looks cool. I tell him I like it and pay him.

As soon as I get home, I duck into the bathroom by the side door and comb my hair in such a way that it's not hanging down over my forehead. Plaster it down with water, so it looks shorter. Then go into the kitchen, where Mom is fixing supper.

"Hi, Mom. What's for supper?"

"Did you get a haircut?"

"Yeah."

"It doesn't look like it. Your hair doesn't look any shorter. You paid two dollars for this?"

I nod.

"What a waste of money. Your father said a crewcut. This is not a crewcut. It's a Beatle haircut. He won't be happy when he sees this."

The phone rings, and Mom answers it. I beat it to my room. I'm hoping my parents will forget about my haircut. But, as soon as Dad gets home, he calls me downstairs into the kitchen.

"Look—he got a Beatle haircut," Mom says to Dad.

Dad looks at my hair and frowns. "This is not a crewcut, Mansfield. Go back to the barber tomorrow and get it cut right."

"Dad, the crewcut is out of style."

"The Beatle haircut may be the style in England. But it's not the style in the USA."

"It will be."

"Mansfield, you cannot have a Beatle haircut."

"Why not?"

"Because your hair hangs down over your forehead and ears. It'll interfere with your studying."

"Meg has long hair and it doesn't interfere with her studying. She gets straight As."

Dad blinks. "Because it violates the school dress code for boys. You're supposed to be able to put two fingers between your hair and your eyebrows." He puts two fingers against my forehead. "I can't even get one finger between your hair and your eyebrows."

"But—"

"Mansfield, I'm not gonna argue with you any longer. Tell Bernie I said he's to give you a crew cut. And this time you pay for it out of your allowance."

"Aw, man. This isn't fair. It's my hair. I should be able to wear it the way I want. I don't tell you and Mom how to wear your hair."

"As long as you live in our house, you'll wear your hair how we tell you."

"I can't wait till I grow up." I storm out of the room.

At our locker before homeroom period the next morning, I ask Ealey if he'll sell me his stiletto, but he says it's not for sale. Man, is he weird to talk to. I try to look him in the eye, but his glass eyeball points in a different direction than his good eyeball, so I can't look him in both eyes at the same time. I end up looking him in his good eye.

After German, Ealey follows me out of class. In the hall, he sidles up to me and says out of the corner of his mouth, "I'll sell it to you for twenty-five bucks."

"Twenty-five bucks?!"

"Take it or leave it."

"Forget it."

At home I think about that stiletto. I know Ealey's trying to gyp me, but I really want it. Since I'm no longer saving my money for Boyne Mountain, I decide to pay him the dough. I open my safe and get out twenty-five dollars to buy it tomorrow.

The next morning I tell Ealey I changed my mind—it's a deal. He makes me give him the dough first. Then he slips me the stiletto. I'm afraid to carry it in my pocket, so I hide it in my locker.

At my locker after school, I wait until the coast is clear. Then slip the stiletto in my pocket. I'm dying to show it to Arcudy, but he didn't come to school today. He had to go to his uncle's funeral. He'll be so envious. I walk home by myself. I keep reaching in my pocket to feel my stiletto but don't take it out—there are too many kids walking on the sidewalk and cars driving by. I can't wait to get home where I can play with it in the privacy of my Observatory. But as soon as I walk in the door, Mom pounces on me and reminds me I have to go to the barber again. I run to my room and hide it in my secret compartment.

At the barbershop, Bernie looks surprised to see me so soon. I explain that my dad said I have to get a crewcut. In the chair, he turns on the clippers and buzzes the sides and back of my head. I start getting worried. I can tell he's cutting a lot off—my head feels really cool. Then he shaves the back of my neck. When he's finished, he spins me around—I look at myself in the mirror. Man, I barely recognize myself—I look practically bald. I figure he scalped me because he was afraid Dad would send me to a different barber if he didn't get it right this time.

Everybody's just sitting down at the dinner table when I get home—except Dad. He's still at work. Meg takes one look at me and says, "Hey, look—Yul Brenner."

"Alright, Meg—that's enough," Mom says. "Your hair looks very nice, Mansfield."

"No, it doesn't. I look like a dork."

I sit down at the dinner table. Mom passes me the meat loaf. "So, did you have a nice day at school today, Mansfield?"

"Nope."

"What happened?"

"Nothing."

"Jeez, you're really in a good mood tonight," Meg says to me.

"Meg," Mom says and shakes her head. "If he wants to pout, let him."

I don't speak to anybody the rest of supper. As soon as I finish doing the dishes, I get my stiletto and go up in my Observatory. Then spend the rest of the night pushing the button and watching the blade shoot out. Later, I sneak into the bathroom and check myself out in the mirror pulling my stiletto. I look pretty tough.

In Science class, Mr. Frazier does a lab experiment on acids and bases. We set out bottles of acids and bases on the lab table at the front of the class. Mr. Frazier sticks pieces of litmus paper in the bottles—they turn red or blue depending on whether they're an acid or a base. Next, he mixes hydrochloric acid and zinc. The chemical reaction generates hydrogen gas, which he collects in a bottle. Then he lights a wooden splint and sticks it into the bottle. Poof—the gas explodes. Everybody thinks it's pretty cool. But my favorite is butyric acid—it smells just like puke. It would make a great stink bomb.

∞()∞()∞()∞()∞()∞

Sitting behind me at her desk, Kelly Rudolf taps me on the shoulder and whispers, "Wanna piece of gum?"
I nod.
While Mrs. Nash is diagramming a sentence on the blackboard, Kelly slips me a rolled-up stick of gum. Faking a yawn, I slip it into my mouth. It tastes odd. I hear her snickering. I ask her what's so funny. She tells me she pulled a prank on me—the gum is a laxative. I spend the rest of the period wondering if I'll need to go to the restroom, but I don't.
I try to think of a prank to pull on Kelly. Up in my Observatory after supper, I have a good idea. I'll swipe butyric acid from the science storeroom, make a stink bomb, and put it in her locker.
The next day I take a big empty mayonnaise jar to school in my gym bag. After school, I tell Arcudy, "Come with me."
"Where to?"

"Mr. Frazier's room."

"What for?"

"To swipe some butyric acid."

"What for?"

"To make a stink bomb."

He makes a face like he's afraid we'll get in trouble.

"Don't sweat it, Jack. I'll do all the dirty work. You just stand lookout in the hall."

We hang around outside Mr. Frazier's room until everybody's gone. Then I peek in the room. Don't see anybody. I tell Arcudy to fake a sneeze if he sees anybody coming. Then I slip into the room, snatch the key out of Mr. Frazier's desk, and unlock the door to the storage room. Then duck into the storage room, find the bottle of butyric acid, and fill the jar halfway with acid. Then stash the jar in my gym bag, lock the door, put the key back in Mr. Frazier's desk, and beat it out of there.

"See—nothing to it," I tell Arcudy.

As soon as I get home, I make my stink bomb. I sneak into the kitchen and get stinky food from the refrigerator—Dad's goose liver and Limburger cheese, onions, left-over canned tuna, and a hard-boiled egg. Then smuggle everything up to my Observatory. I peel the egg and dump everything into the jar with the butyric acid. Presto—I got me a stink bomb. I smell it to see if it works. Man, does it work! I swear it's putrid enough to gag a maggot. I quickly screw on the lid. I have to open the windows to keep from gagging.

The next day I take the stink bomb to school in my gym bag. I show it to Arcudy on the way. I unscrew the lid and hold the jar under his nose.

He sniffs—gags. "What are you gonna do with it?"

Grinning deviously, I tell him, "I'm gonna put it in Kelly Rudolf's locker. It'll be hilarious."

His eyes light up. "Cool, man. This I gotta see."

"But I need your help."

"How?"

"My plan is I'll divert her away from her locker. Then all you hafta do is unscrew the lid and put the stink bomb on the top shelf of her locker—in the back where she can't see it."

"I don't know about this..."

"C'mon, man—it's just a harmless prank." I explain to him that I'm getting even for the prank she pulled on me with the laxative gum.

"What if something goes wrong?"

I scoff, "What could go wrong? My plan is foolproof. If she doesn't think it's funny, all we gotta do is put the lid back on to stop it."

He nods.

At school I spot Kelly Rudolf in a crowd of girls milling around the flagpole. When the bell rings, Arcudy and I follow her into the school to her locker bay. I hand Arcudy my gym bag. As soon as Kelly opens her locker and takes her coat off, I stop by and ask her to show me our Language assignment. While she shows me our assignment in her Language book, I maneuver her around so her back is toward her locker. Behind her, Arcudy sneaks up, gets the stink bomb out of my gym bag, unscrews the lid, and slips it into her locker. He finishes in the nick of time because Barb Scott, who's Kelly's locker partner, comes along. We hang around for a minute to see if they discover the stink bomb. Scott hangs her coat and tosses some books in the locker. Then they lock up and head to class.

Arcudy and I run down in the basement, cram our stuff in our lockers, grab our books, and run back upstairs to Science class—just beat the tardy bell.

During homeroom period and Science, I can't look at Arcudy. Every time I do, we snicker at the secret stink bomb. I can't wait for English—I figure I'll hear all about it from Kelly.

When the bell rings, Mr. Frazier opens the classroom door, and we file out of the room. I smell the stink bomb the second I step into the hall.

"Whoa!" Arcudy exclaims with a panicked look on his face.

As we run down the hall toward Kelly's locker, the putrid smell gets stronger and stronger. Students are gagging and saying somebody must've puked in the restroom down the hall. We stop at Kelly's locker bay, which reeks of vomit.

"Give me the lid!" I say to Arcudy.

"I don't have it."

"Where is it?"

"I left it in your gym bag."

"Wait here. Nab Kelly or Barb Scott if they come by and get them to open the locker while I go get the lid."

I race downstairs to my locker. Spin the combination on my lock—mess up. Spin it again. Open my locker and grab the lid. Race back upstairs to Kelly's locker.

Arcudy's skulking around the hall near her locker bay. With a worried look on his face, he whispers, "They didn't come."

"Shit!" I have no idea what class either of them is in to find them.

"I gotta get to Music," Arcudy says. He takes off.

I stand here praying for Kelly or Barb Scott to come along, but they don't.

The tardy bell rings. I race to Art and run into the classroom. Luckily, Mr. Henry is back in the supply room, so I don't get nailed for being tardy. I get out my clay turtle, which I'm supposed to glaze today. But I'm too worried to work on it. I rack my brain trying to figure out what Kelly's class schedule is, so I can intercept her between classes and get her to open her locker.

Twitching his nose, Mr. Henry asks the class, "What's that icky smell?"

"Puke," Bill Burton says.

I look out the window across the teachers' parking lot at the other wing of the school where Kelly's locker is. Teachers in the classrooms on the second floor are opening their windows.

Shit—it's the stink bomb, man.

I get a sick feeling in my gut...

The fire alarm goes off. Students pour out the back door of the school into the teachers' parking lot. A teacher has a handkerchief over her mouth.

Oh, God...they're evacuating the school.

Mr. Henry tells the class to put down our clay, leave our belongings behind, and go out the front door by the auditorium. We file down the hall and stairs to the first floor. I smell the stink bomb clear down here. We exit the school and stand by the flagpole.

I hear a siren off in the distance getting closer and closer. All of a sudden, a firetruck comes roaring up in front of the school.

Oh, Jesus! What have I done?

Firemen jump out and run in the front doors of the school.

We wait. Everybody is whining about how cold it is. Then it starts sprinkling. After a while, Mr. Henry says, "This is ridiculous. We're going to catch pneumonia. Wait here, mes petits oiseaux..."

Mr. Henry comes back a few minutes later. Everybody's wet and freezing their butts off. He tells us there's no fire—just icky fumes on the second floor. Then says we're supposed to go to the auditorium—it's safe there.

They herd the entire school into the auditorium. I look around for Arcudy but don't see him—he must be up in the balcony. Then Petty comes on stage and addresses the student body. He announces that there's nothing to be afraid of. The school is not on fire. There are just some offensive fumes on the second floor. They are not poisonous. That's just a rumor. Right now they're trying to find out what's causing them. Then he leaves the auditorium.

The whole school is in a tizzy over the stink bomb. I listen to the girls in the row in front of me talk about how horrible it was. One girl says it smelled just like vomit—only ten times stronger. Another girl says it almost made her barf. Then I hear a guy behind me talk about how his class got out of taking a test. Then somebody says he heard they're going to send us home—everybody says they hope so. I get more and more scared.

Oh, God, what did I do? I never dreamed this could happen...

At eleven Petty comes back on stage. He says they've determined the cause of the problem and are taking care of it right now. I figure they must've found the stink bomb. He says classes will resume as soon as the school airs out. When the bell rings, we're supposed to get our stuff and go to our fourth period classes. Everybody groans since we're not getting to go home.

Fifteen minutes later, the bell rings. Everybody files out of the auditorium. I go to Art, put away my clay turtle, and get my books. Then go to History class. It's on the same wing of the school as the stink bomb but on the first floor. I smell it a little out in the hall. I go into the classroom. Arcudy is sitting at his desk. He looks pretty scared. He sees me and quickly looks away. I don't say anything to him because Mr. Wilson is in the room.

As soon as Mr. Wilson dismisses us to go to lunch, Arcudy bolts out of the room. I catch up with him out in the hall. He acts like he doesn't know me.

"Man alive, Jack—I didn't see that happening," I say in a low voice.

"I had nothing to do with it," he whispers.

"The heck if you didn't."

"It was all your idea. You made it and everything."

"Hey, you're in on it too. You put it in her locker."

He quits speaking to me.

"Listen, man, we gotta stick together if we don't wanna get caught. We need to get our stories straight. You know—if they question us," I tell him.

He won't look at me, but I can tell he's listening.

I follow him through the cafeteria line. All I get for lunch is a carton of milk and a pack of creme-filled sandwich cookies—I'm not hungry. We sit down by ourselves at our assigned table.

"The way I figure it is—how are they gonna know we did it?" I ask.

"Rudolf will tell."

"But she didn't see us do it. All she saw was me asking her for our assignment. Nobody saw us do it."

"So?"

"So they can't prove it. The only way they can prove it is if one of us rats on the other. Now I promise not to rat on you, if you promise not to rat on me. Okay?"

He nods his head.

"Say it."

"I promise."

"I promise too. Now if Kruse or anybody else asks you what we were doing at Kelly's locker this morning, just tell them I was getting an assignment. Got it?"

He nods his head.

"And if they ask you about the stink bomb, just act like you don't know what they're talking about. You know—play dumb. Got it?"

"Yeah...okay."

I get the jar lid out of my pocket and wipe my fingerprints off it with a napkin under the table. Then go toss it in the trash barrel. I start breathing a little easier—I just might get away with it. I even feel a little hungry and eat my lunch.

After lunch, we go to our lockers and switch books. I tell Arcudy I'll see him in Gym—then make a sign like I zipped my mouth shut. On my way to English, I tell myself that I have to play dumb about the stink bomb with Kelly. But I don't see her in class. She must be down at the office getting questioned about it. Just the thought of that scares me.

While Arcudy and I are putting on our gym uniforms in the locker room before Gym class, I remind him of our promise. He nods. We jump on the trampolines in the gymnasium. Arcudy and I are standing at one end of a tramp, spotting Ed Norris, when Arcudy nudges me in the side and glances across the gym. I look— see Kruse. He's standing in the doorway, staring right at me. I quickly look away. Watch him out of the corner of my eye. He walks across the gym and says something to Coach McNeely.

"Delaney! Arcudy! Get your butts over here!" Coach McNeely yells.

My heart starts beating like crazy.

We walk over there.

"You boys come with me," Kruse says.

Kruse marches Arcudy and I in our gym uniforms down to the office. He orders me to sit down in the chair outside his office. Then hauls Arcudy inside his office and shuts the door. I try to listen but can't hear…

They sure have been in there a long time. I wonder what Arcudy is telling him…

What if he's ratting on me?

Finally, the door opens, and Arcudy comes out. Man, does he look shook up. He doesn't look at me. Kruse tells him to sit down out there. Then calls me in. Tells me to shut the door and sit down in the chair across from him. I feel myself shaking.

Glaring at me, he asks, "Su-un, did yooou put a stink bomb in Kelly Rudolf's locker?"

I try to look innocent. "What?"

"Yooou heard me."

"Uh...I don't know what you're talking about, sir."

"That's not what your buddy told me. He told me yooou stole butyric acid from Mr. Frazier's room. Yooou made a stink bomb and put it in Kelly Rudolf's locker."

That dirty rat!

"It was an accident, sir. It was just supposed to be a harmless prank," I confess.

He looks at me with a smirk on his face. "Well, su-un, I'm afraid you're up the creek without a paddle."

I sigh. "I'm sorry..."

Kruse tells me Arcudy said all he did was watch and asks if that's true. I figure this is my chance to get even. I tell him that's a lie. Arcudy put the stink bomb in Kelly's locker and stood lookout when I took the acid. Then he sends me out of his office and makes Arcudy come back in. After a few minutes, they both come out. Arcudy looks like he's really mad at me. He sits down in the chair farthest away from me. Kruse tells us to wait here. Then he goes into Petty's office.

"You butthole," Arcudy whispers.

"Hey—you ratted on me first."

"I oughtta pound your face into the ground."

"Try it." I know he won't try anything here in school.

We wait and wait. Don't speak to each other. Finally, Kruse comes out of Petty's office and sends Arcudy in there. He takes me back into his office and shuts the door.

Eyeing me suspiciously, he says, "Su-un, someone set off a false fire alarm here at school two months ago. He pulled the alarm down in the basement—right across from your locker." Then he points his finger at me and yells, "Yooou did it, didn't yoooou?"

I shake my head. "No, sir!"

"Su-un, don't yoooou lie to me!" he yells, shaking his finger right in my face.

"I'm not lying. I didn't do it."

"Then whooo did?"

"I don't know."

"Arcuuudy?"

"I told you. I don't know."

The intercom buzzes on Kruse's telephone. He answers it. "Yes, sir. I'll be right there." He hangs up and tells me to come with him.

Kruse takes me into Mr. Petty's office, where Petty, Mom, Arcudy and his parents are all sitting around a big table. Mom looks very upset. Mrs. Arcudy looks at me like—now what did you get my son into? I sit down next to Mom at the table. Kruse sits down beside Petty. Petty starts to tell everyone about the stink bomb but is interrupted by a knock on the door. It's Mrs. Richards with Dad. He looks calm on the outside, but he's seething inside. He takes a seat beside me at the table.

Fiddling with his pen nervously, Petty says, "Dr. Delaney, I'm sorry to bother you at the hospital, but we have a very serious disciplinary problem here." Then he starts telling about the stink bomb again. I find out that it was Mr. Frazier who discovered butyric acid leaking out of the bottom of Kelly Rudolf's locker, the fumes got sucked into the ventilation system, a fireman had to cut the lock off the locker, the jar got knocked over inside the locker, butyric acid spilled all over the girls' books and ran down on their coats and ruined everything in the locker, and their moms are really mad and want it all paid for. Dad says he'll pay for it.

In his high, squeaky voice, Petty reads the school's disciplinary policy from the *Pupils' Handbook* For minor offenses like running in the halls or smoking in the restroom, they can give the pupil detention. For major offenses like fighting, theft, or vandalism at school, they can either suspend or expel the pupil. Petty says the stink bomb is a major offense—somebody could've got sick from the noxious fumes, and the vandalism damaged personal property. Also, I stole the butyric acid from the science stockroom. Dad says he'll accept whatever the school deems appropriate. Arcudy's parents say the same thing—except they keep dropping hints they don't feel he was as bad as me. I was the ringleader—their son was just a follower. Petty says the police said he could press charges against us for criminal mischief, but he's reluctant to do that—he doesn't really want us to have a juvenile record. Then he talks about suspending us. He says this is the first time Arcudy has been in trouble at school—so they can be more lenient with him—but I've been in trouble before. Kruse informs my parents about my blow gun. Dad says he hopes they don't suspend me for a period of time that could permanently damage my academic record. Finally, Petty suspends Arcudy for five days and me for ten days.

While our parents wait in the office, Kruse sends Arcudy and I one at a time down to the locker room to change into our street clothes. When I go past the back entrance to the school, I have a mad impulse to bolt out the door and run away, but I don't know where to go and have no money.

After I change clothes, I stop at my locker and grab my coat and gym bag. Back at the office, Mr. Frazier wants to talk to me and my parents. We go into the conference room. He tells me that he's disappointed in me for stealing the butyric acid and making a stink bomb. He thought he could trust me but was wrong. He's sorry, but I can't be his lab assistant anymore. My parents say they understand. I feel bad for having let him down.

Before we leave, Dad asks me where my books are. I tell him I didn't bring any. "Just because you're suspended, don't think you're gonna get out of doing your homework," he scolds me. Then he sends me back to get my books.

In the parking lot, Mom starts to cry.

"Look—you made your mother cry," Dad says. Then he tells me to get in the car with him. As soon as I get in, he yells, "Of all the lame-brained stunts you've pulled, this one takes the cake. Do you know where I was when the school called? I was in surgery. If you think I like getting called out of surgery for an idiotic stunt like this, you got another thought coming." Man, is he furious.

He doesn't say another word the rest of the way home. I wish he'd yell at me or hit me—anything but the silent treatment. When we get home, he tells me to go to my room and stay there until he calls me. I sit at my desk. Get Flatus down off the shelf and talk to him. I tell him he's the only friend I got and ask him if he wants to run away with me.

Later, Dad calls me back downstairs. He and Mom are waiting for me in the den. I sit down in the hot seat. First, they yell at me for stealing the butyric acid. Dad says I violated Mr. Frazier's trust. Mom says they didn't raise me to be a thief. Then they yell at me for putting the stink bomb in Kelly Rudolf's locker. What a stupid thing it was to do. Acids are dangerous chemicals.

"Just look what it did to those girls' belongings—it completely destroyed them. Don't you have any respect for other people's property?" Dad asks.

"It was supposed to be a joke," I say.

"A joke? You think evacuating the school and the fire department coming is funny?"

"We didn't mean that to happen."

"Well, it did, didn't it? Your joke backfired on you like it always does. You're just damn lucky nobody got hurt."

I just stare at the floor.

They yell at me about how somebody could've got hurt. Mom says the acid could've spilled on one of those girls and disfigured her for life. Dad says somebody could've burned to death in a real fire somewhere else while the fire department was at the school. Then I would have that on my conscience for the rest of my life.

They yell at me for getting suspended. They say that it'll be a black mark on my academic record for the rest of my life and could hurt my chances of getting into college. Then Dad says I'm damned lucky Mr. Petty didn't expel me for the rest of the year—that would've really screwed up my academic record.

They tell me they're worried I'm becoming a juvenile delinquent and will be getting in trouble with the law next.

Finally, they get around to my punishment. Dad says he's going to deduct two dollars a week from my allowance until I've paid for the damages to the girls' property. I'm to use my suspension to get caught up in all my subjects—especially Math. This is not going to be a vacation. They're going to check my progress daily. But they're not going to ground me. Confining me to the house won't solve the problem.

Dad says, "And we absolutely forbid you to associate with Jack Arcudy. You two can't do anything without getting into trouble. And you must join a constructive organization. And since you can't seem to find one, we've picked one for you—the Boy Scouts."

"The Boy Scouts?" I ask.

"That's right. There's a troop that meets at the Lutheran Church."

"But-but I hate uniforms...and marching..."

"We feel it's crucial that you join an organization with rules and discipline. You need a constructive outlet for your energy—especially since you lost the lab assistant position."

"But—"

"No buts about it—that's final."

I spend my entire suspension in my room faking like I'm studying. Really what I do is sit at my desk all day, reading comic books, *Mad* magazines, and the *Encyclopedia,* playing Solitaire, and messing around. I have my Math book open and a pencil and paper with problems on it ready on my desk. Whenever I hear somebody coming, I quickly hide what I'm doing in my top desk drawer and act like I'm studying.

On my first day back at school, I'm standing by the flagpole before school starts, when Denny Boebel walks up to me. "Hey, look—it's the Mad Bomber," he says with a big grin on his face. Then he turns secretive. "Was that you yesterday?"

"What?"

"C'mon—I won't tell anybody."

"I don't know what you're talking about."

He tells me about a bomb scare yesterday. He says somebody called the school and said there was a time bomb in a locker. They had to evacuate the school again. When they didn't find a bomb and the school didn't blow up when it was supposed to, they let everybody come back inside. He figures it was just me faking them out to get even for suspending me.

"Well, it wasn't. And don't go telling people it was." That's all I need—somebody blaming me for that.

"Okay, okay. You don't hafta get mad about it."

During homeroom period, Petty comes on over the PA and tells me to report to the office. I wonder what he wants. I hope he just wants to warn me to stay out of trouble but get scared it has something to do with that bomb scare. I swear everybody in the room is looking at me like I did it.

Kruse is waiting for me at the office. He marches me straight into his office, picks up the telephone, and dials a number. Then hands me the telephone and the Pupils' Handbook open to the first page.

"Su-un, read this out loud," he orders.

"What for?"

"Read it!" he yells.

I start reading out loud over the phone a letter from Petty to the students.

"That's enough." Kruse takes the phone away from me and hangs it up. Then leaves the room, closing the door behind him.

I listen. Through the door, I hear Kruse talking to Mrs. Richards about what I just read but can't hear what she says.

Soon, Kruse comes back into his office. He snatches the handbook from me, hands me the phone again and a piece of paper with typing on it, and orders, "Read this out loud!"

I read, "Do you know how many lockers there are in Johnny Appleseed Junior High School I do. 568. I hid a time bomb…"

I stop. Read the rest to myself, "…in one of them. It's set to go off at ten."

Oh, God! He's trying to frame me for the bomb scare.

"Keep reading!" Kruse yells.

I shake my head.

He snatches the paper out of my hand, leaves the room, and shuts the door behind him.

Again, I hear Kruse talking to Mrs. Richards but can't make out what they're saying.

After a while, Kruse comes back into the room with another young man, who flashes a badge at me and says he's Sergeant Boyle from the Waterbury Police Department.

Oh, God! It's the police.

"Sit down. I wanna ask you a few questions," he says.

I sit down.

"I'm investigating an incident that happened at the school yesterday. Someone called in an anonymous bomb threat. Said he hid a time bomb in a locker. Said it was set to go off at ten o'clock. Was that you?"

"No."

"Mr. Kruse informed me that you hid a stink bomb in a girl's locker two weeks ago. This makes you a suspect."

"I didn't do it."

"Why'd you set off the stink bomb?"

"It was just a prank that backfired on me," I explain tensely.

"How did you feel about being suspended?"

"Bad."

"Were you mad about it?"

"No."

"What did you do while you were suspended?"

"Studied."

"Did you go anywhere?"

"No. I was confined to my room."

"You got a phone in your room?"

"No, sir."

Sergeant Boyle starts drumming his fingers on Kruse's desk. "Look, Delaney, we know it was you. The person who called had a boy's voice. The lady who received the call has positively identified you as the person who made the bomb threat. She recognized your voice this morning."

"I didn't do it."

"C'mon—admit it. It'll go a lot easier on you."

"I told you—I didn't do it!" I start to cry.

Sergeant Boyle looks at Kruse and shrugs his shoulders. Kruse makes me go sit down outside his office. I'm afraid Sergeant Boyle is going to take me to the police station.

Kruse comes out of his office alone and sends me back to class. I figure Sergeant Boyle must've been bluffing that Mrs. Richards positively identified me as the person who made the bomb threat since he didn't arrest me.

I walk around on pins and needles all day. I expect to get called back to the office any minute. It seems like school will never end. I think about talking to Arcudy to find out if they questioned him but don't since I'm mad at him. In English, I try to say I'm sorry to Kelly Rudolf, but she gives me the cold shoulder. As soon as the final bell rings, I beat it out of the school.

On the way home, I decide not to tell my parents about what happened. They'll have a hemorrhage if they find out the police are after me for the bomb scare. I try to slip into the house, but Mom nails me the second I walk in the door. Man, is she upset. She says Mr. Petty just called and told her the police questioned me today about a bomb threat at school yesterday.

"You didn't do it, did you?" she asks.

"No."

"I hope not—because that's a very sick thing to do. Only somebody with a very disturbed mind would do something like that."

"I know."

She looks relieved, but I still see some doubt in her eyes.

Minutes later, Dad rushes into the house. "Alright, tell me exactly what happened," he says to Mom.

Mom tells him about Mr. Petty's phone call. Then Dad really puts me through the third degree. He wants to know exactly what the police asked me and what I told them. He gets angry when I tell him Kruse made me read those lines over the telephone. Mom tells him Petty said they don't know who did it. The police questioned me only because of the stink bomb.

"You didn't have anything to do with this, did you?" Dad asks.

"No."

"You see what you get yourself into by pulling these stupid pranks?"

"Yes."

"Well, all I gotta say is—I hope you've learned your lesson this time."

"I did. I'm not gonna do anything bad again."

CHAPTER TWELVE

At school the next day I read about Fred Baker in the Appleseed Press. Fred was the star halfback on the Appleseed Pioneers football team. His spinal cord was severed when he was tackled in a football game last year. He's paralyzed and confined to a wheelchair. Student Council is sponsoring a candy sale to raise money for the Fred Baker Benefit Fund. They're giving prizes to the students who sell the most candy. I have a good idea. Instead of selling the candy door-to-door like everyone else is doing, I'll see if Dad and Vivian, who's his receptionist, could sell it to his patients for me. I'm hoping that raising money for Fred Baker will improve my reputation at school.

At supper I tell Dad about the candy sale at school. He says no soliciting is allowed at his doctor's office. I explain it's to raise money to pay for Fred Baker's orthopedic devices that aren't covered by his insurance. Dad says that's a good cause, so he'll make an exception. Then he asks me if I'm going to the Boy Scout meeting tonight. I tell him I can't—I have a test in Math tomorrow to study for.

On Saturday morning, Mom drives me to the candy sale at the school cafeteria. I sign out ten cases—240 boxes of chocolates. I lug the cases out to Mom's station wagon in the parking lot and load them in the back.

"That's a lot of candy to sell," Mom remarks.

"It's for Fred Baker. And I wanna win a prize."

After work on the following Friday, Dad hands me an envelope stuffed with candy sale money. Over the past five days, he and the other three doctors in his medical complex sold all but six boxes of the candy to their staff and patients. Everyone said it was for a worthy cause. I thank him and sell the last six boxes to Mom for a total of $240. I'm thrilled. I just might win a prize.

I'm up in the Observatory. Man, is it nice out. It's so warm I open the windows. Listen to the wind humming through the TV antenna. It smells like spring. Down below everything's turning green. The leaves are coming out. The dogwood tree in the front yard is blossoming white flowers.

I browse through my *Nasco* catalog. Check out the Cap-Chur Gun for the umpteenth time. It's a tranquilizer pistol for animals. It looks really cool in the picture. It resembles a German Luger pistol. How it works is a CO_2 cylinder fires a needle and syringe with a tail piece up to a distance of fifteen yards. A powder charge behind the rubber plunger in the syringe explodes on impact with the animal and instantaneously injects an immobilizing drug through the needle into the muscle tissue. What catches my eye is the Special Notice that reads: "The CO_2 powered weapon is NOT regulated and we can ship it to anyone without restriction." I figure that means me.

Man, I wish I had a Cap-Chur gun. I fantasize that I'm an African big-game hunter on safari—like John Wayne trying to capture a white rhino in the movie *Hatari!* He chases after it in a jeep and shoots it with a tranquilizer gun that knocks it out. The problem is the pistol costs $115. I don't have that much money. I could ask for it for my birthday, but there's no way my parents would buy me a tranquilizer gun. They wouldn't even buy me a BB gun.

During homeroom period on Monday, I go to the cafeteria and turn in my candy sale money to Mr. Ryan, who's the Student

Council Advisor. He's impressed by how much money I raised for Fred Baker. He pats me on the back and says, "You're in the running for a prize."

At supper Dad tells me I have to go to the Boy Scout meeting tonight. I tell him I can't—I have another Math test to study for.

"That's what you said last week."

"I can't help it if Miss Robinson keeps giving us tests."

"When is it?"

"Friday."

"That's four days from now. You have plenty of time to study for it."

"Don't blame me if I flunk it."

After supper, I ride my bike to the Lutheran church. I try opening the front door, but it's locked. I start hoping there's no meeting tonight. I try the side door. Rats—it's unlocked. I wish Arcudy was with me. Inside, I follow the lights down the hall to the Assembly Room. A sign by the door says Troop 113. I'm late for the meeting. Peeking in the doorway, I see about fifty Boy Scouts in green uniforms and green caps with red neckerchiefs standing at attention in neat rows. The guys in the front rows look like they're in high school, and the guys in the back rows look like they're in junior high. I'm glad to see Denny Boebel standing in the back row.

A big guy, who looks like he's in high school, is standing at the head of the troop, facing the scouts. He leads the troop in what he calls the Scout Oath and Scout Law. The scouts raise their right hands, with their three middle fingers pointing straight up, and recite the words in unison.

The big guy spots me. He smiles and waves at me. "Come on in. You interested in joining the Boy Scouts?"

"Yeah," I say.

We walk up to each other.

"Great. What's your name?" he asks.

"Mansfield Delaney."

"I'm George Rhodes. I'm the troop leader." He shakes my hand and just about crushes it. He has a butch haircut and looks clean-cut. A silver eagle is pinned on the front of his uniform, and he's wearing a sash with rows of badges on it. He's what my parents would like me to be.

Rhodes introduces me to a grownup named Mr. Buckmaster, who's sitting at a table, counting money. He's the scoutmaster. He looks like Howdy Doody. He's wearing a green uniform too and a hat like Smokey the Bear wears. He has me fill out an application and gives me a paper that tells about dues and where I can buy my Boy Scout Manual, uniform, and camping gear.

"Congratulations, Mansfield. You're automatically the rank of Scout when you join." When he shakes my hand, he extends his left hand with his little finger separated from the others. He interlocks his little finger with the little finger on my left hand and won't let go. Grinning, he says, "That's the BSA Left Handed Three-Fingered Hand Clasp. It means you belong to a worldwide brotherhood…"

"Thanks." I slip my hand out of his.

"Fall in, Scout," he orders.

I go stand at attention at the end of the back row.

Buckmaster reminds the troop about the field trip this Saturday to the Westinghouse factory. He says it'll count toward the Citizenship merit badge. He asks how many people are going. A lot of guys raise their hands. Not me—I ain't volunteering for anything. Then he announces there won't be a meeting on Memorial Day holiday—good. Then says that's because the troop is marching in the Memorial Day parade—not good. He tells everybody they have to be in full uniform to march in the parade. That leaves me out since I don't have a uniform.

Rhodes announces we're going to break up for patrol meetings. Everybody should report back in an hour for drills. "Fall out," he commands. The scouts head to their patrol meetings. Rhodes asks me which patrol I'm joining. I tell him I don't know. He tells me to join his brother's patrol, which meets in room number 4. As soon as he leaves, Boebel tells me not to join that patrol—they're nerds. He takes me to room number 2, where a dozen guys are sitting at a table, horsing around. We sit down with them.

A guy wearing a white canvas sailor hat with the brim turned down enters the room, shuts the door, and sits down at the head of the table. "Hey, everybody—listen up."

Everybody just keeps right on talking.

"Shut-up, you nerds!" he hollers.

Everybody turns and looks his way.

He grins. "That's more like it." Sneering at me, he asks, "Who are you?"

"He's a friend of mine," Boebel answers.

"Who asked you, man?" he asks Boebel.

Boebel doesn't say anything.

"Sheik slaves don't talk without permission," the guy in the sailor hat says.

Boebel shuts up.

"Slave, down on the floor—five pushups."

Boebel gets down on the floor and does five pushups.

"Alright, what's your name?" the guy in the sailor hat asks me.

"Deuce Delaney."

"You're a friend of Boebel's, huh?"

"Uh-huh."

"You wanna join this patrol, huh?"

"I guess so."

"Well, we might let you—if you're lucky," he says, snickering.

Everybody laughs.

Some guy barges into the room. "Hey, Huey, Sheik wants to talk to you."

The guy in the sailor hat exits the room. I ask Boebel who he is. He says his name is Huey DeWeese. He's the patrol leader.

A few minutes later, DeWeese returns and calls the meeting to order. He says the first item of business is the "Sheik-mobile." I ask Boebel what's the Sheik-mobile. Boebel says the Sheiks are buying an army surplus jeep for $250.

"Sheik said we still need 110 bucks. So he passed a Sheik tax. All Sheik slaves hafta shell out ten bucks," DeWeese announces.

" Gol! Ten bucks?!" Boebel exclaims.

"You heard me. Bring it next week. You don't pay—you don't get to ride in it."

The next item of business is the broken chainsaw. DeWeese announces that Sheik passed a Sheik tax to fix the chainsaw. The Sheik slaves have to pay another dollar. Then he discusses something called a "Tote-Box." Boebel tells me it's a big wooden box with aluminum poles. The patrol totes their food in Tote-Boxes to their campsite—it's more convenient than carrying food individually in knapsacks. DeWeese announces that Sheik passed a new Sheik law. From now on, Sheik slaves have to tote the Tote-Boxes. The Sheik slaves groan. DeWeese tells them to grin and bear it. Then he adjourns the meeting. Everybody starts messing around again. I ask Boebel who's Sheik. He says he'll tell me later.

Rhodes sticks his head in the room and announces, "Time for drills." Boebel rolls his eyes and tells me, "Time for General Buckmaster." He says Buckmaster was a cook in the Army but acts like he was in charge of D-day. We go back to the Assembly Room, where Buckmaster leads the drills. He makes everybody line up one arm's length away from the guy in front of him and the guy next to him. We're supposed to look at the back of the guy's head in front of us. We practice Attention, Right-face, Left-face, About-face, and At ease. Man, I swear it's just like being in the Army.

Finally, Buckmaster says, "Troop dismissed." I walk my bike home with Boebel and Steve Schroeder, who's another guy I know from school. They tell me about the Sheiks. They say it's a secret organization—Sheik calls them the "anti-scouts." "Who's Sheik?" I ask. They tell me Sheik is a high school guy named Phil Poth. He's the Maharajah—the highest Sheik. He's the founding father of the Sheiks. Everybody calls him "Sheik." He's really cool. I ask them about DeWeese. They say he's a Rajah—the second highest Sheik. There are only three Rajahs—DeWeese, John Gillespie, and Craig Spurlock—all high school guys. They tell me all of the junior high guys in the patrol are Sheik slaves. They have to be Sheik slaves for three years. After they pass their Sheik initiations, they'll be Sheiks and have their own Sheik slaves. I ask them about the Sheik initiation. They say Sheik thinks up some Sheik test. Like on one campout, he made Jeff Miller sneak into Buckmaster's tent, open his knapsack, and rub poison ivy all over the crotch of his undershorts. They ask me if I'm going to join the Sheiks. I tell them I don't know—I'm not crazy about being somebody's slave for three years.

"C'mon—don't be a nerd," they say.

"What's a nerd?"

"Sheik says it's somebody who farts in the bathtub and bites the bubbles," Schroeder answers.

"I'll think about it."

When I get home, I go into the TV room, where Dad is watching *Ben Casey*. "So how'd it go? Did you have a good time?" he asks me.

"Nope."

"What'd you do?"

"Drills."

"They're good for you. Teach you self-discipline."

"I hate them."

"That's because you have a bad attitude. Give it a chance, Mansfield."

I leave in a huff. Go upstairs to my Observatory. Get out my *Nasco* catalog and admire the Cap-Chur gun again. This time I add up what everything would cost with pencil and paper. The pneumatic pistol. CO_2 powerlets. Syringes. I'd need a couple of 1cc syringes for little animals like rabbits and a couple of 3cc syringes for big animals like deer. The Cap-Chur charges. The Cap-Chur Sol drug. And shipping. It all adds up to $162.55.

I go to my room, open my safe, and count my money. I have $85 left from my birthday and Christmas money. I'm $78 short. I wonder where I could get the money. I come up with an idea how to sucker Dad out of some money. I go back downstairs and tell him I need a dissecting kit for Science class. We're going to dissect live frogs. I show him the kits in the *Nasco* catalog. When I tell him that I think I want to be a surgeon like him when I grow up, he picks out the most expensive one in the catalog—the Medical Anatomy Kit. It costs $26, including shipping. He says I can use it through high school, college, and medical school. I tell him I need it in two weeks. He tells me to get the money out of his wallet, which is on his bedroom dresser. I say I'll mail the money tomorrow. He tells me to fold the order blank around the bills so you can't see them. I figure I'll tell him the kit must've got lost in the mail when it never comes.

When I get the money out of his wallet, I discover that he's loaded. I count $243. I swipe an extra ten dollar bill. He won't notice it. Mom is always taking money out of his wallet to buy stuff. I don't feel guilty about stealing it or suckering him. The way I figure it is he got out of paying for a ski trip to Boyne Mountain.

Now all I need to do is figure out how to get the last $42.

During morning announcements over the PA, Mr. Petty announces the candy sale winners to the school. I take first place. I get called down to the office, where they take my picture to be put in the Appleseed Press with the first and second place winners. I smile for the camera. I went from bad guy to hero at the school in ten days. I win a 13-inch Playmate Admiral portable TV, which I lug home after school. When I tell Dad and Mom they took my picture for the Appleseed Press, they're so pleased they let me keep the TV.

I haul the TV up into my Observatory. Then run an extension cord from an electrical outlet in the attic up to the TV. The rabbit ears get lousy reception, but it's cool having a TV in my Observatory.

On Saturday, I go to Possum Run Pool. Mick drafted the boys on swim team to help get the pool ready to open on Memorial Day weekend. Arcudy is here. We don't speak to each other. Mick has us scrub the bottom of the pool with brushes before they fill it with water. Hoses are running into the pool, and water is blasting out of jets in the side of the pool. We start in the shallow end and scrub our way to the deep end.

The slope between the shallow end and deep end is slippery as ice from the soap suds. Everyone slides down it into the standing water in the deep end, which is two feet deep and freezing cold. We try to scramble back up the slope but keep sliding back down into the water. The only way out is to wade through the water and climb the ladder in the deep end. Then everyone starts pushing each other down the slope. Everybody's clothes are soaking wet, but nobody cares because we're having so much fun. Arcudy pushes me down, and I drag him with me. We're laughing. Then everybody starts sprinting across the shallow end and sliding down the slope into the water. Man, it's a riot. Finally, Mick makes us get out before somebody gets hurt.

On Memorial Day, the pool opens. The water is still murky and freezing cold, but I go swimming anyhow. I play tag with Arcudy and some other guys. During rest period, we actually speak to each other about racing together on swim team. We don't say anything about the stink bomb or getting suspended.

On the way out of school, Denny Boebel asks me if I heard about the strip fight. I tell him no. He says Charlene Bonham and Connie Bush are meeting behind the greenhouse after school. They're two ninth-grade hood girls. They're fighting because Bush called Bonham a "rip."

Boebel and I make a beeline to the greenhouse, which is across the street from the school. Already a big crowd of kids is milling around. All of the hoods in the school have formed a big circle around Bonham and Bush. Boebel and I can't see the girls, so we climb up on the roof of a nearby shed. Man, we have a ringside seat for the strip fight. I spot Arcudy looking around for a place to watch the fight.

"Hey, Jack! Up here!" I holler.

He sees me and climbs up.

The hood girls start screaming and swearing at each other. Then Bonham tears into Bush with her fingernails. Bush grabs Bonham by her hair and yanks it. Then Bonham claws at Bush's blouse.

"Rip it off!" Lonnie Butsavage yells.

Bonham tears Bush's blouse open, exposing the girl's bra.

Out of nowhere, Kruse charges through the crowd. Everybody scurries out of his way.

"Break it up!" he hollers.

The girls keep right on fighting.

Kruse tries to pull them apart.

All at once, Bonham spins around and slaps Kruse in the face—she knocks his glasses off. Kruse doesn't know what to do. He can't put a girl in a half-nelson like a guy. Man, I love it. Then Coach McNeely rushes up. He grabs Bush, and Kruse grabs Bonham. They escort them away.

Petty arrives at the scene and tells everybody to go home. He yells at us to get down off the roof. We jump down. I walk home with Boebel and Arcudy. We talk about the strip fight. We say it was the coolest fight we've ever seen. We just wish Kruse and McNeely hadn't broken it up so soon.

Boebel congratulates me on winning the portable TV and asks me what I did with it. I tell him I set it up in my Observatory. He says he'd love to have a TV in his room at home. Trying to make money for the Cap-Chur gun, I offer to sell it to him. He says he can scrape together $25. "It's a deal," I say. At Fairlawn Avenue Boebel turns off toward his house. Before he goes, he says he'll get his money and pick up the TV later.

Arcudy and I continue to walk home together. I tell him about the Cap-Chur gun.

"I'm gonna go deer hunting with it," I say.

His eyes light up. "I'd like to go deer hunting."

"We could go deer hunting together as soon as I have enough money to buy it."

"I could kick in ten bucks."

"Great. Now all I need is seven bucks."

"I'll bring the dough to school tomorrow."

"So...we're friends again?"

He nods.

I smile. I'm glad that Arcudy and I are friends again.

Later, Boebel comes to my house and buys the portable TV. I sneak it out of the house. He ties it to the rear carrier on his Schwinn Jaguar bike and rides away happy. I put the dough in my safe.

During lunch at school the next day, Arcudy gives me his dough. Then we discuss how we could go deer hunting when both our parents have forbidden us from associating with each other. I suggest that he join the Boy Scouts like I did—just don't tell his parents that I belong. I lie and tell him how much fun it is. I tell him about the Sheiks and that I'm thinking about joining them. He says he'll think about it.

All I need to buy the Cap-Chur gun is seven bucks. After school, I sneak into Meg's room. Unbeknown to her, I know the combination to her safe. It was written on a slip of paper that came with the safe, which she tossed in her waste basket. Backyard burning of the trash is my chore. I found the combination when I was burning the papers in the burn barrel. I dial the combination. Her safe is stuffed with one dollar bills. I swipe seven of them. I figure she won't notice them missing.

I sneak into the den and get an envelope and stamps. Then go up in my Observatory and fill out the blank order. I gaze fondly at the picture of the Cap-Chur pistol. Soon, it'll be mine.

I hop on my bike, speed to the mail collection box at the intersection of Parkview Circle, Mapledale, and Shady Lane, and drop the letter in the mailbox. Man, I can't wait to get my Cap-Chur gun.

When I get home from school the next day, I ask Mom if I got anything in the mail today. She says no and asks me if I'm expecting something. I tell her I sent away to *Nasco* for a dissecting kit. We're dissecting live frogs in Science class. Now she won't be suspicious when the package from Nasco with the Cap-Chur gun gets here.

It's cold and rainy all weekend, so the pool isn't open.

After school Mom tells me she picked up my Boy Scout uniform and camping gear at the store today. She spent all afternoon sewing the troop numbers and emblems on the shirt—so I could wear my uniform to the Boy Scout meeting tonight. She laid everything out on my bed—my uniform and cap, neckerchief and neckerchief slide, knapsack, flashlight, canteen, Boy Scout pocketknife, mess kit, collapsible cup, silverware, compass, collapsible toothbrush, First-Aid Kit, Boy Scout Manual, and a waterproof container to hold matches. There's even a Snake-Bite Kit. Man, I can't believe it. When Mom buys Boy Scout equipment, she doesn't mess around.

I put on my uniform after supper. Mom folds the neckerchief, wraps it around my neck, and slips the ends through the slide. Then puts the cap on my head. Stepping backwards, she looks at me and smiles proudly. "Deuce, you look sharp."

I look at myself in the hall mirror. "No, I don't. I look like a dork."

"Let me take your picture." She runs and gets her camera. Then makes me pose on the front steps. She keeps snapping picture after picture.

"Mom, I gotta go."

She gives me two dollars to pay my dues.

At the Boy Scout meeting, Buckmaster takes attendance and collects dues. I notice that the Sheiks say "Present" instead of "Here" when he calls their names.

Frowning, Buckmaster lectures the troop for their bad conduct on the field trip to Westinghouse. He says he's not going to name individual names—it was the scouts who call themselves the "Sheiks" who misbehaved. The plant manager, Mr. Jones, was so mad he'll never invite Troop 113 again. In the future, there will be no more field trips—it's a shame a few bad apples have to spoil the whole barrel.

Next, Buckmaster says the troop embarrassed him again at the Memorial Day parade—the whole troop marched out of step. The troop needs to drill more.

Rhodes announces the camporee. For those of us who are new, he explains the camporee is a three-day campout at Camp Emory Davis every summer. All of the Boy Scout troops in the Johnny Appleseed Council are invited. It's to be held June 18, 19, and 20.

At the patrol meeting, DeWeese shakes down the Sheik slaves for money for the Sheik-mobile one at a time. Some don't have it. He warns them if they don't bring the money next week, they'll have to be Sheik slaves for an extra year.

"You got any money?" DeWeese asks me.

"He's rich. His dad's a doctor," Schroeder says.

"What kind?" DeWeese asks.

"A surgeon."

"We could use a rich kid. You wanna join the Sheiks?"

I shrug my shoulders.

"C'mon—don't be a nerd."

"I'm thinking about it."

"It's up to you. You can be a nerd. Or you can be a Sheik."

Next, DeWeese announces all of the Sheik slaves have to shell out $7.50 a piece to pay for food and beverages at the camporee. He says Gut has to have the money by next Monday night, so he can buy the groceries.

"Gol!" the Sheik slaves all gripe.

"You ever tried eating air?" DeWeese asks them. "Hey, where is Gut tonight?"

"He couldn't make it," a kid says.

"Why not?"

"He's grounded."

"What for?"

"For suckering Mr. Jones."

Everybody breaks up laughing. I ask Boebel what's so funny. He tells me Gut suckered the plant manager on the field trip to Westinghouse. While Mr. Jones was leading the tour of the factory, Gut sneaked up behind him on the left side, reached around his back, and tapped him on the right shoulder. Boebel says Gut really suckered the poor sap—he turned all the way around looking for some guy who wasn't there. Sheik made him do it for his Sheik initiation.

Rhodes breaks up the patrol meeting early, so we have more time to drill. Buckmaster orders the troop outside. We march around the church parking lot for an hour. I hate it.

∞◊∞◊∞◊∞◊∞◊∞

Tuesday is my last full day of school. Man, am I happy—only one more day. We go to our classes but don't have any work to do. All we do is turn in our books. Robinson fines me two bucks for damaging my Math book. She tells me to bring the money to school tomorrow. Then asks me how the book got so damaged when I hardly opened it. I don't tell her that I dropped it in the creek cutting through the woods on the way home from school.

After school, I clean out my locker. No more homework. No more books. No more Robinson. No more Kruse. When I walk out the front door, I holler, "I'm free!"

The next day we have a half day of school. We're allowed to wear Bermuda shorts and tennis shoes. We carry our report cards around for the last time. My stomach is in knots when I go to Math. I'm praying that I'll pass. When Robinson calls my name, I walk up to her desk and hand her my report card and two bucks for the book fine. She marks down my grades for the fourth term and the whole year and hands it back to me with an envelope. She tells me to take the note home to my parents. Uh-oh. I walk back to my desk and sit down. Brace myself and look at my report card.

Man, I just about crap my pants. She changed the Incomplete last term to a D, gave me an F this term, and gave me an F for the whole year. She flunked me. Under the Fs, she marked the same old 2 and 5 and added a 10—the Comment Code says "Work Not Made Up."

I seethe the rest of the period. Call her every name in the book to myself. Give her the finger—hide it behind my other hand.

After the bell rings, she intercepts me on my way out of the room and tells me she's going to call my parents this afternoon to make sure they get the note.

By the time I get home, I'm a nervous wreck. My parents are going to crucify me. Mom is fixing lunch in the kitchen.

"It's not fair," I say.

"What?" Mom asks.

"She flunked me."

"What?"

"Robinson flunked me." I show her my grade card.

Mom looks at it—reads the comments. I watch her get madder and madder. She frowns at me. "Just wait till your father sees this."

"There's this too." I hand her the note.

She opens it and reads it. Glaring at me, she says, "Go to your room."

"What's it say?"

"Now!"

I go to my room and flop down on my bed. I fantasize about running away out west. Finally, I hear a car pull in the driveway. I go look out the window. It's Dad. He came home from work early because I failed Math—I'm dead.

A few minutes later, Dad yells, "Mansfield! Get down here!"

I go downstairs into the kitchen.

Shaking his head in disgust, he asks, "Mansfield, how could you fail Math?"

"I don't know. I passed all the tests."

"Did you do all your makeup assignments?"

"Most of them," I lie.

My parents keep asking me how I could fail. I keep answering I don't know. Finally, I say, "I guess I'm just dumb."

Dad says, "I don't believe you're that dumb. You're just not applying yourself. What the heck did you do in your room every night? What the heck did you do the weeks you were suspended?"

I just stare at the floor…

"Well, we'll find out why Friday. Miss Robinson is holding a parent-teacher conference Friday morning. You have to attend," he says.

"But…but it's summer vacation."

"Not for you. Be dressed in school clothes and ready to go by seven thirty in the morning."

I dread going to the parent-teacher conference.

"This is another black mark on your academic record. At this rate, you'll never be a surgeon," Dad says.

I just sigh. I don't bother to tell him I don't really want to be a surgeon. All I want to be is a professional scuba diver. While my parents keep yelling at me, I fantasize about scuba diving and finding treasure in a sunken shipwreck.

On Friday morning, Dad and Mom take me to the parent-teacher conference. They listen with very concerned looks on their faces while Robinson tells them why she flunked me. Dad asks Robinson if he can see my test scores. She shows him her grade book. He says my grades seem low for my test scores. She explains I failed to make up all of the work and tests that I missed when I was sick and suspended. Then she suggests that they enroll me in summer school. She's teaching a remedial Math class for students who did poorly. It'll focus on basic concepts and better study habits. Without it, I can't take ninth-grade General Mathematics or Algebra. It starts on Monday.

"We'll enroll him," Dad tells her.

"Wait a minute...I don't wanna be stuck all summer in the slow-learners' class. I'm not a slow learner," I say.

"Young man, we don't call them slow learners anymore. That's not nice. We call them retarded. That's the legal and polite term," Robinson scolds me.

"Miss Robinson, he'll be there on Monday," Dad tells her.

After the parent-teacher conference, my parents take me to the office, where they enroll me in summer school against my will. As soon as we get in the car, I say, "I ain't going."

"Yes, you are. It's the only way they'll let you take Algebra next year," Dad says.

"It'll ruin my whole summer."

"You should've thought of that before you failed Math."

"Just wait till I'm sixteen—I'm gonna drop out!"

"No, you won't. You're a minor. You need our permission."

I don't speak to them the rest of the way home.

My parents and I fight about summer school all weekend. I tell them I can't go to it because of the Boy Scout camporee, but they say summer school is on weekdays and the camporee is on the weekend. Then I say I can't go because of swim team, but they say summer school is in the morning and swim team practice is in the afternoon. Then they say they don't want to hear another word about it, so I pout.

On Monday, Dad and Mom move Tecca to Cedar Point Amusement Park. She graduated from high school over the weekend and is working there this summer before she goes to college in the fall. They take Meg and Calley along. After they move Tecca, they're going to go swimming in Lake Erie and ride the rides at the amusement park. I miss out on the fun because I have to go to summer school this morning and the Boy Scout meeting tonight. I get up early, put on my school clothes, and walk to school all by myself. It's weird being in Johnny Appleseed during summer. Hardly anybody is here. I feel lonely.

I see Russell Ealey in the restroom. "Hi, ex-locker partner."

"Hi."

"You're going to summer school too, huh?"

"Yeah."

"What are you taking?"

"Math."

"Me, too. You got Robinson?"

"Yeah."

"She flunked you too?"

"Yeah."

"We're the retards," I joke.

She's a bitch. I hate her guts."

"Me, too. She has it out for me."

In class, Robinson hands out our textbooks and assigns our desks. Ealey is assigned a desk right next to me. Robinson makes us solve problems on the blackboard. I stare out the window, depressed. It's a beautiful day—there's not a cloud in the sky—and here I am stuck inside with Robinson and every retarded kid in the school. It's so hot out she has the windows open. Somebody's mowing the lawn. I smell cut grass. I imagine riding the Blue Streak rollercoaster at Cedar Point.

All of a sudden, Robinson calls on me. I don't even know what problem we're on. She yells at me for not paying attention and tells me what problem we're on. Then makes me go to the blackboard and solve it for the class.

On my way home from summer school, I see a Parcel Post truck stop at the turnaround by our mailbox. Hoping that my Cap-Chur gun is here, I dash to the truck. The deliveryman hands me two packages from Nasco. Excited, I run into the kitchen and open the big box first. Sure enough, it's the Cap-Chur gun. Man, is it cool. It looks like a real gun. I start dancing the Twist. Inside the other box are the syringes, Cap-Chur Sol drug, Cap-Chur charges, and CO_2 powerlets. I get out the directions. First, I assemble a 1cc syringe. Fill it with the Cap-Chur Sol drug and insert a Cap-Chur charge behind the rubber plunger. Then figure out how the safety on the gun works and where the CO_2 powerlet goes. Each powerlet has fifteen shots. Then load the syringe—I'm all set.

I go outside in the woods. I pretend like I'm an African big-game hunter tracking the elusive white rhino. Finally, I spot a squirrel sitting on a branch in a tree. Switch the safety to off. Aim...pull the trigger—

Blam! Man, it sounds just like a real gun.

I miss. The squirrel scampers inside a hole in the tree. I look around for the syringe. Finally, I spot the tailpiece by a log on the ground.

I go back in the house and hide my Cap-Chur gun and ammo in my secret compartment.

At swim team practice I tell Arcudy, "Hey, man! I got the Cap-Chur gun. Man, is it cool! It looks just like a German Luger. I went hunting and just missed a squirrel."

His eyes get big. "I can't wait to see it."

"You wanna shoot it tonight?"

"Yeah. How?"

"I have an idea. I'm going to a Boy Scout meeting this evening. You come along. We'll slip out and shoot the Cap-Chur gun."

He grins deviously. "Okay."

I tell him the time and place of the Boy Scout meeting. We arrange to meet at the corner of Marion Avenue and Parkview Boulevard at ten till seven.

For supper, I eat a TV dinner. Afterward, I put on my Boy Scout uniform. I get out my Cap-Chur gun and load a 1cc syringe. Then put on my hooded sweatshirt and hide the gun in my pouch.

I ride my bike to the meeting place and wait on Arcudy. When he doesn't show on time, I fear that he finked out on me, but then I see him pedaling his bike up the street. He sees me in my uniform, snaps to attention, and salutes me.

'Spare me," I say.

"Where is it?"

I point at my pouch.

"Let me see it."

"Not now. We gotta go to the meeting first."

"Let's skip it."

"I can't. My parents will nail me."

We arrive late for the Boy Scout meeting and slip into the back row of scouts. Buckmaster is reading out loud to the troop a letter from the President of the Johnny Appleseed Boy Scout Council about the scouts who call themselves the "Sheiks." In the letter, the President says he has received numerous complaints from other local scoutmasters about the Sheiks' delinquent activities at Boy Scout camp. The Sheiks are giving the Boy Scouts of America a bad name and are a disgrace to traditional scouting. Then the President threatens to kick Troop 113 out of the Council if the Sheiks don't disband immediately. If the troop loses its local charter, it will not be allowed to use the name Boy Scouts of America and will be denied access to Camp Emory Davis in the future. After he finishes reading the letter, Buckmaster orders the Sheiks to cease and desist for the good of all the Boy Scouts in Troop 113.

Next, Buckmaster announces information about the camporee this weekend at Camp Emory Davis. He says cars will pick everybody up at the church at 4:00 p.m. on Friday and bring us back at 2:00 p.m. on Sunday. Tents will be provided, but everyone has to bring their own sleeping bag, food, and cooking utensils.

While Rhodes gives a first-aid demonstration to the troop, Buckmaster nabs Arcudy and signs him up to join the Boy Scouts. I don't think Arcudy was ready to join, but Buckmaster pressures him into doing it.

The troop meeting breaks up for patrol meetings. Arcudy and I follow Boebel to his patrol meeting. DeWeese calls the meeting to order. Pointing at Arcudy, DeWeese asks, "Who's this nerd?"

"I'm Jack Arcudy," Jack answers.

"You any relation to Arcudy Funeral Home?" DeWeese asks.

"Yeah. That's my dad."

"Does your old man ever bring his work home?"

Everybody laughs. Poor Arcudy—he's always getting razzed about his dad embalming dead bodies.

DeWeese spends most of the meeting collecting dough from the Sheik slaves for the Army surplus jeep, chainsaw, and food for the camporee. Then he assigns them to their work details at the camporee—half get assigned to KP, half to firewood.

Rhodes sticks his head in the room and says it's time to drill. On the way to the Assembly Room, I whisper to Arcudy, "Let's get outta here." We let everybody go past us. Then slip out the side door.

We ride our bikes to Luna Lake Park and park at the statue of Johnny Appleseed.

"C'mon, man. Let me see it," Arcudy says. He's dying to get his hands on the Cap-Chur gun.

I look around—see a man walking his dog. "Let's get out of sight."

I lead Arcudy into the woods. Then pull the gun out of my pouch and show it to him.

"Cool, man! Let me hold it."

I hand it to him. We creep around the forest, hunting for an animal to shoot. Don't see anything. It starts to get dark in the forest, so we leave.

I hide the gun in my pouch, and we ride over to Luna Lake.

Arcudy spots three swans on the lake and gets a gleam in his eye. Looks around and doesn't see anybody. "Gimme the gun."

I pull the gun out of my pouch and give it to him.

He aims at one of the swans and fires. The syringe makes a little splash when it hits the water. He misses the swan by a mile. "Just missed. Let me try again."

"I only brought one syringe. C'mon, let's get outta here." I'm scared somebody might've heard the bang and called the police.

We hop on our bikes and take off.

On the way home, I talk Arcudy into going to the camporee with me this weekend by telling him we can go deer hunting at Camp Emory Davis. I say I've heard there are herds of deer there.

"Cool, man," he says.

CHAPTER THIRTEEN

On Friday afternoon, I get ready to go to the camporee. I lock my bedroom door and open my secret compartment. Get out my Cap-Chur gun and two CO_2 powerlets—one for shooting and one spare. Fill two 3cc syringes and one 1cc syringe with Cap-Chur Sol drug. We'll use the 3cc syringes to knock out the deer, and we'll have the 1cc syringe in case we run into any rabbits, groundhogs, or little animals like that. I empty out the First-Aid Kit and hide the CO_2 powerlets and syringes in it. It makes a perfect ammo box. I hide my Cap-Chur gun and ammo box in the bottom of my sleeping bag. Then pack my sleeping bag and camping gear in my knapsack.

I put on my Boy Scout uniform. Then go down in the kitchen and pack my food in my knapsack. Mom watches me. I wrap hot dogs in aluminum foil. Mom says I should eat them tonight because they might spoil. I pack cans of pork and beans and spaghetti and meatballs, three cans of pop, and a bag of red licorice for treats. Then Mom packs several cans of soup and vegetables and fruit cocktail.

I pick up the knapsack. "Mom, this weighs a ton."

"You can't live on hot dogs and pop and candy for three days."

While she looks for her car keys, I go out in the garage and dump some of the cans of food in the garbage can.

Mom drives me to the Lutheran church and drops me off in the parking lot.

"Deuce, be sure to wash your face and brush your teeth before you go to bed."

"Mom, I gotta go."

She looks around at the mothers dropping off their sons. Suddenly, she gets a big frown on her face. "What's Jack Arcudy doing here?"

Arcudy is getting out of his mom's car. "His parents made him join the Boy Scouts."

"Why this troop?"

"Mom, it's a free country."

"You stay away from him, you hear me?"

"I will."

"I don't want you getting in any trouble."

"Don't worry. I won't."

As soon as Mom leaves, I lug all my gear over to where Arcudy is standing with a suitcase and sleeping bag. He didn't have time to buy a Boy Scout uniform or knapsack.

"You bring the gun?" he asks me in a low voice.

I nod.

We go into the church and sign out a two-man pup tent. Then hitch a ride to Camp Emory Davis in Mrs. Schroeder's station wagon with her son, Steve, and Denny Boebel.

We drive far out in the country. Finally, we turn onto a private gravel lane and go past a wooden sign that reads "Camp Emory Davis." Long lines of cars are dropping off scouts and leaving. Mrs. Schroeder drives slowly through a forest and across a mowed field to a lodge. She spots Buckmaster standing with scouts from Troop 113 in the parking lot and parks near them. We pile out and unload our gear. I hoist my knapsack onto my back.

Buckmaster and Rhodes assemble the troop. Then lead us to the camporee. We hike across the field toward a forest. I carry the tent. I check out the Sheiks on the way. Their knapsacks are mounted on aluminum frames with their sleeping bags tied on top—they look like they hardly weigh anything. Sheik slaves are carrying the two

Tote-Boxes. Each box has a pole on each side. Four Sheik slaves are on each pole—two in front and two in back.

We follow a trail through the forest up and down ravines. Hiking with a walking stick, Buckmaster is huffing and puffing and sweating like a pig. He commands the troop to halt and rests. My arms are killing me from carrying the tent, and my shoulders are sore where the straps on my knapsack are cutting in. I check out the Sheiks again. They've barely broken a sweat. I tell Arcudy it's his turn to carry the tent. He struggles to carry the tent and his suitcase and sleeping bag.

Finally, we come to a great, big grass clearing where all of the troops are setting up camp. Buckmaster and Rhodes pick a campsite for Troop 113 at the bottom of a hill. DeWeese leads the Sheiks to the top of the hill. Arcudy and I follow them. From the hilltop, there is a panoramic view of hundreds of scouts pitching tents and making campfires in the clearing. DeWeese tells the Sheik slaves to set up the Sheik citadel here. Arcudy and I start to pitch our tent next to them.

DeWeese and two other high school guys walk over to Arcudy and me. Hands on hips, DeWeese says, "Hey, you nerds. Get off Sheik property."

Arcudy and I lug our stuff back down the hill to where the rest of the troop is camping.

All of a sudden, a jeep with a bad muffler roars across the field. Waving on top of the hill, the Sheiks yell, "Hey, Sheik! Up here!" The jeep barrels past us up the hill—the engine backfires loudly. A guy riding shotgun is wearing an African safari helmet. The driver is wearing a World War Two leather aviator helmet with goggles and an Army field jacket. Grinning from ear to ear, he has a silver front tooth. He must be Poth.

Arcudy and I pitch our tent beside the forest at the edge of our troop's campsite. Put our stuff inside and unroll our sleeping bags. I let Arcudy have a peek at the Cap-Chur gun. Then hide it back inside my sleeping bag.

We borrow a hatchet off the scout next door and collect firewood in the forest. We hear a motor running and check it out. A big, burly high-school guy is cutting a log with a chain saw. Boebel, Schroeder, and some other Sheik slaves are carrying firewood back to the Sheik citadel.

Arcudy and I haul our firewood back to camp. The scout next door shows us how to build a teepee campfire. It takes us about an hour to light it. When I get out my hot dogs for supper, I realize I forgot hot dog buns and mustard. I'll have to eat them plain. I also forgot a can opener to open my can of pork and beans. I try opening it with the contraption on my Boy Scout pocketknife but can't get it to work, so I end up borrowing a can opener off the scout next door. I open my mess kit, pour my beans into a pan, and set the pan on the fire.

Boebel and Schroeder visit Arcudy and me at our campsite and invite us to tour the Sheik citadel. We drop what we're doing and tour their campsite. Arcudy and I are impressed. The Sheiks have pitched three twelve-man army tents. Two of them are bunkhouses—one for the Sheiks and one for the Sheik slaves—and the other one is the mess hall. At the mess hall, a big, fat guy they call Gut is fixing supper. He's their Sheik chef. He's barbecuing chickens on spits mounted over a fire in a pit. Rotating them, he bastes them with barbecue sauce. Man, do they smell good. Potatoes wrapped in bacon in aluminum foil are roasting around the outer coals. For desert, he's baking cherry pies in a contraption called a reflector oven.

They show us what's going to be the Sheik fire tonight. It's a humongous pile of firewood—brush, branches, and logs—stacked at least twelve feet high. Some of the logs are as big around as telephone poles.

"Like Sheik says, it ain't a Sheik fire unless it melts tin cans," Boebel says.

"Where is he?" I ask.

Boebel points to a hammock-tent strung between two trees at the edge of the woods. I see a guy lounging inside it through the mosquito netting. A Sheik slave takes him a can of pop.

"Nothing like having your own slave to bring you pop," Arcudy says.

Grinning, Boebel says, "It ain't pop. It's beer."

Gut blares a pressurized air horn.

"Sheik feast!" Schroeder yells.

I remember my pork and beans and take off running down the hill. When I reach the campfire, I see they're burnt. They're like tar stuck to the bottom of my pan—I can't even scrape them out with my pocketknife. I have to pitch the pan.

I whittle a stick to a point with my pocketknife. Then roast a hot dog. When it's golden-brown and juicy, the stick breaks where it's burned, and the hot dog falls in the fire. By the time I fish it out, it's charred and coated with ashes. I roast another one, using a fork. I roast this one without dropping it in the fire but roast my hand in the process. While I eat my hot dog and sip on my pop, I imagine eating barbecued chicken, potatoes wrapped in bacon, and cherry pie.

"You know, Jack, it can't be that bad being a Sheik slave."

Arcudy is eating a MacDonald's cheeseburger and fries leftover from last night. He nods.

"They're feasting like kings."

Munching on a cold French fry, he nods again.

"I think we should join the Sheiks."

"Yeah."

After supper, we go up to the Sheik citadel. Boebel is in the mess hall, cleaning the spits with steel wool.

"Hey, man. We decided we wanna join the Sheiks."

"It's about time," Boebel says. He tells us we have to get Poth's permission, but it's against Sheik law for Sheik slaves to bug him in his tent-hammock.

We look for DeWeese. Find him in the woods running the chainsaw.

"Hey, Huey, they wanna join the Sheiks."

DeWeese has trouble hearing Boebel over the noise of the chainsaw. He shouts, "Don't bug me! I'm busy!"

When we return to the Sheik citadel, Poth is talking secret-like to a high school guy in the Sheik-mobile. Boebel says the guy is

Gillespie—he's the Sheik spy. Since Poth isn't in his tent-hammock, Boebel says we can ask him now.

We go over to the Sheik-mobile. Poth and Gillespie shut up when they see us coming.

"Hey, Sheik, these guys wanna join the Sheiks," Boebel tells Poth.

"Beat it!" Poth yells.

Boebel does an about-face and shoves Arcudy and me back to the mess hall. "Now is a bad time. They're probably planning a Sheik raid," he tells us.

"What's a Sheik raid?" I ask.

"Gillespie cases the other troops' campsites for loot. Then the Sheiks raid them in the middle of the night."

"When can we join the Sheiks?" Arcudy asks.

"Not today. Come back tomorrow," Boebel answers.

Arcudy and I go sit down at our campfire. Man, are we disappointed. We start to worry about whether Poth will let us join the Sheiks. We decide to try again first thing in the morning.

At dusk, Rhodes invites Arcudy and me to the camporee bonfire. Since we don't have anything better to do, we decide to go. The troop falls in at Buckmaster and Rhodes' tent. I notice that none of the Sheiks are going. Buckmaster and Rhodes march the troop to a ring of rocks at the center of the clearing. In the center of the ring, firewood has been piled in the shape of a tall teepee. It's puny compared to the Sheik fire. As soon as all of the troops arrive, the scouts assemble in a huge circle around it and sit down on the ground. Then one of the scoutmasters tries to light the bonfire. The funny thing is he can't get it started. Somebody forgot to leave an opening in the teepee to light the kindling. Finally, another scoutmaster hands him a can of charcoal lighter, and he gets the bonfire started.

A scoutmaster stands and leads the scouts in singing "The Happy Wanderer." I don't join in. I don't feel like singing dorky scouting songs. Next, they sing "Caissons" and a song about the Titanic.

Buckmaster stands and tells a corny joke.

Another scoutmaster tells a ghost story. He tells it in a spooky voice. When he gets to the climax where he's lying in bed and hears the ghost coming up the stairs one step at a time, I yawn—

Kaboom!

It sounds like a cherry bomb went off at the Sheik citadel. I turn around and look up there but don't see anything. The scoutmaster pretends like nothing happened and continues telling his story. The ghost gets a few more steps up the stairs. Then scouts on the other side of the fire start pointing at something. I turn again and watch a fire at the Sheik citadel grow bigger and bigger. The scoutmaster tries to finish his story but nobody's listening. Everybody's watching the Sheik fire and "Ooohing" and "Ahhhing." Soon, it's humongous. Finally, the scoutmaster just quits. He's mad at the Sheiks for ruining his story. They end the camporee bonfire with "Taps." The scoutmaster, who led the singing, gets out his bugle and plays it. It sounds nice, except right in the middle—kaboom!— the Sheiks blow off another cherry bomb.

Arcudy and I walk back to our tent by ourselves. Our campfire has died down, so we drag our sleeping bags outside, lie down on top of them, and watch the Sheik fire. Man, it's spectacular. The flames must be thirty feet high. Every now and then, there's another kaboom inside the fire, and hundreds of sparks go soaring up into the night sky.

I gaze at the stars. Man, is it nice out. Not too hot, not too cold. I find the Big Dipper and think I see Saturn. Then see a falling star.

"Hey, Jack, you see that?"

He doesn't answer me. He's sound asleep.

After a while, I start to doze off, but every time I do another kaboom wakes me up.

At midnight I see two flashlights coming toward our campsite. They stop at Buckmaster's tent. I hear two grown-ups complain to Buckmaster about all the noise the Sheiks are making—they say nobody can sleep. Buckmaster says he'll take care of it. He and Rhodes go up to the Sheik citadel and everything gets quiet. They return to their tent. I figure the party's over. I wake up Arcudy and tell him it's time to go to bed.

Inside the tent, I turn on my flashlight, take off my tennis shoes and socks, and get some red licorice out of my knapsack for a midnight snack. Then crawl into my sleeping bag and nudge the Cap-Chur gun and the ammo box with my toe over in the bottom corner. Turn off my flashlight and munch on a piece of licorice.

Kaboom!

The Sheiks howl with laughter.

I lie awake, listening to the Sheiks. Finally, they quiet down. I have to take a leak. I get my flashlight, crawl outside the tent, and walk barefoot over to the woods. After I finish peeing, I spot dark figures creeping down the hill in the moonlight. I shine my flashlight at them. It's the Sheiks. They're wearing masks. They've pulled their neckerchiefs up over their faces like stage coach robbers in the western movies. "Douse the light, asshole," somebody whispers. I quickly turn off my flashlight. Then watch them walk across the field toward the other troops' campsites and disappear into the darkness.

Several minutes go by and nothing happens. I start to go back inside my tent—

Kaboom! Kaboom! Kaboom!

Off in the distance, I see flashlights beaming and hear guys screaming and an air horn blaring for a minute. Then the flashlights go off and the commotion stops. Soon, I see dark figures running back up the hill. They're laughing and panting like crazy. Then I see flashlights shining helter-skelter and hear guys yelling and cursing off in the distance for a while.

I go back inside my tent.

Arcudy has woken up. "Deuce, what's going on?"

"I think I just witnessed a Sheik raid," I answer. Then crawl back into my sleeping bag and go to sleep.

I don't sleep well. Something hard keeps poking me in the back.

In the morning, I wake up with a headache. The tent is hot and stuffy. I have a crummy taste in my mouth, and there's a line of dried spit across the side of my cheek. My back hurts. I reach underneath my sleeping bag and pull out a big rock. I can't believe I slept on it all night.

I crawl out of my sleeping bag, put on my shoes and socks, and go take a leak in the woods. The sun is shining, and it's hot outside already. Back in the tent, I rummage around in my knapsack for breakfast. All I have is spaghetti and meatballs, tomato soup, or green beans. I wish I hadn't thrown the can of fruit cocktail I in the garbage. I save the tomato soup for lunch and the spaghetti and meatballs for supper. Our campfire went out in the night. Cold green beans aren't very appetizing. Arcudy has gotten up and is having his breakfast. He's eating a snack-pack box of cereal. The only problem is he forgot milk. He has to eat it dry.

As soon as Arcudy and I finish breakfast, we go find Boebel at the Sheik citadel. He's sitting on a log in the mess hall with the other Sheik slaves, eating breakfast. Gut fixed blueberry pancakes with syrup and bacon and sausage. Man, does it look and smell good. I tell Boebel we came back to join the Sheiks. He says Poth is still in bed and can't be disturbed. A Sheik slave pours a cup of Tang and fixes a plate of buttered pancakes, sausage, and bacon. Then serves Poth breakfast in bed.

The Sheik slaves tell Arcudy and me about the Sheik fire last night. How they couldn't stand within twenty feet of it without getting first-degree burns on their faces. I ask them what the kabooms were. They say Sheik kept tossing cherry bombs and aerosol cans in the fire. I ask them about the Sheik raid that I witnessed last night. Boebel swears us to secrecy. Following Poth's plan, the Sheiks created a diversion. They sneaked up on Troop 110, shot off three cherry bombs, and then ran through the campsite pulling tent stakes, screaming like Banshees, and blaring the air horn. All pandemonium broke loose. Then Poth and Gillespie slipped into the campsite and walked away with the loot. They swiped a watermelon, two cartons of soda, some Jiffy-Pop popcorn, and a dozen eggs. The Sheiks ate the watermelon last night, Gut needed extra eggs to make blueberry pancakes this morning, and they'll eat the Jiffy-Pop popcorn tonight.

After breakfast, the Sheik slaves do K.P. Boebel gets put in charge of garbage. Gut gives him a rotten egg to put in the Sheik ammo. I ask Boebel what the Sheik ammo is. He shows me a

218

garbage can full of watermelon rinds and rotten tomatoes to throw at Troop 110 if they counterattack today.

Finally, Poth comes out of his hammock-tent. Today he's wearing aviator sunglasses. The first thing he does is let out a blood-curdling scream that's a string of swear words combined into one long word.

Poth walks into the woods.

"Now's the time to ask him," Boebel says.

We look for Poth in the woods but can't find him. Finally, I spot him high up in a tree, looking through binoculars in the direction of Troop 110.

We trot over there.

"Hey, Sheik, what are you doing up there?" Boebel asks.

"I'm taking a Sheik shit! Whaddaya think I'm doing?"

Sure enough, he's sitting on a forked branch with his pants down—a bare cheek parked on each fork of the branch.

We scurry out from under him. We don't want to get hit on the head with a turd.

"Sorry, Sheik," Boebel says.

We beat it back to the Sheik citadel and wait on Poth.

Boebel says nervously, "Gol, how was I supposed to know he was crapping in a tree?"

"Man, I hope he's not mad." I'm scared it'll hurt our chances of getting in the Sheiks.

After a while, Poth comes back to the Sheik citadel. He walks up to Boebel. "Twenty push-ups, Sheik slave."

"What for?" Boebel asks.

"It's against Sheik law to bug me when I'm taking a Sheik shit."

"Gol, I didn't know that."

"Tough shit. You know it now. Down on the ground."

Boebel drops to the ground and does twenty push-ups.

Smirking at Arcudy and me, Poth asks, "What the hell are these nerds doing on Sheik property?"

"We wanna join the Sheiks," I blurt.

"We ain't taking any new members. Now get the hell off Sheik property."

Arcudy and I traipse back down to our tent. Man, are we mad.

"He can go to hell. I don't wanna be a Sheik anyhow," I say.

"What a jerk," Arcudy says.

"I don't wanna be no slave."

"Yeah. Now what?"

"Let's go hunting."

"Good idea."

I start to get the Cap-Chur gun, but Rhodes shows up at our tent and says Buckmaster wants to see Arcudy and me. We walk over to their tent. Buckmaster is sitting on a collapsible camp stool. He gets out his Boy Scout Manual and shows us what we have to learn to earn the rank of Tenderfoot—the Scout Oath and the Scout Law. Then they start teaching us the knots we have to learn how to tie. He and Rhodes make us practice tying knots the rest of the morning. Man, is it boring. While they're teaching Arcudy how to tie a sheepshank, I secretly tie the collapsible camp stool to the belt loop on the back of Buckmaster's pants, so when he stands up, the stool hangs from his butt. I think it's funny, but Buckmaster doesn't think so. He tells me learning to tie knots is a serious business—it could save my life someday. Then sends us back to our tent. I get the distinct impression he doesn't like me.

By now, it's lunch time and I'm starving. Arcudy and I restart our campfire, and I eat my can of tomato soup, but I'm still hungry. So I trade the guy next door my Snake-Bite Kit for a peanut butter and jelly sandwich and some chocolate-chip cookies. I talk him into it by telling him that I've heard there are poisonous copperhead snakes at Camp Emory Davis. Arcudy eats a big bag of potato chips that are all crushed from being in in his suit case.

"C'mon, let's go deer hunting," I say.

"Yeah, I wanna bag a twelve-point buck," Arcudy says.

I go into the tent, get my Cap-Chur gun and the ammo box out of my sleeping bag, and hide them inside my shirt. Then Arcudy and I slink off into the woods. As soon as we get out of sight, I pull out the Cap-Chur gun, flip on the safety, and load the CO_2 powerlet and a 3cc syringe in it.

Stalking through the forest like big game hunters, we hunt deer. Soon, Arcudy says it's his turn to carry the Cap-Chur gun. I let him carry it. We come to a ravine. Climb down the bank, jump the creek, and climb up the other side. I make Arcudy go in front of me, so he doesn't accidentally shoot me in the back. We keep going and going. Don't see any game. Not even a chipmunk.

Finally, we come to a private camp lane. It's two earth tire tracks with weeds in the middle. We stop and rest for a minute—wonder where all the deer are. Turn here and walk down the lane—

Suddenly, I hear a motor—spin around and see the Sheik-mobile barreling down the lane toward us. The jeep beeps at Arcudy and me. We jump out of the way. Poth, Gillespie, DeWeese and another guy are riding cross-country in it. They beep again when they go by. Then disappear down the lane.

We enter a pine forest. It's cool and clean and smells like Mom's air freshener. The ground is covered with pine needles—it's like walking on a carpet. It's so soft I feel like lying down and taking a nap. If I was a deer, this is where I'd hang out. I tell Arcudy it's my turn to carry the Cap-Chur gun again. But we don't see any in here either.

Arcudy stops to take a leak. When he turns his back toward me, I have an idea. I quickly unload the syringe and hide it in my hand.

"Hey, Arcudy."

While he's peeing, he looks back over his shoulder and sees me aiming the gun at him.

I pull the trigger—bang!

Man, he just about has a heart attack.

I laugh my butt off. Hold up the syringe. "Faked you out, man. It wasn't loaded."

"Very funny. Don't you know you're not supposed to point even an unloaded gun at somebody?"

We head across a field. It's pretty rough going. I keep getting snagged in briars and brambles, and my feet keep getting tangled in weeds. Deer flies keep landing on our heads—they're driving us crazy. By the time we reach the other side, we're hot and sweaty and have deer fly bites and scratches all over our arms and hands. And we still haven't seen anything to shoot at.

Arcudy stops, looks around, and spits. "Hey, man, you're full of crap. There ain't no deer around here."

"Yes, there are."

"Oh, yeah? Well, where are they?"

"I don't know. Maybe they're sleeping."

"I'm tired of this. Let's do something else."

"What?"

"Let's do target practice."

"Okay. We can each take one shot. I don't wanna waste ammo."

I look around for a target to shoot at. Spot a No Hunting sign on a tree in a strip of woods beyond the field. I figure we can shoot at it. We walk over to the edge of the field. An old, barbed-wire fence separates it from the woods. I get down on my hands and knees, and tell Arcudy to hold up the wire. Then crawl under it. Then I do the same for him.

We walk over to the No Hunting sign. I load a 1cc syringe in the gun. Arcudy wants to go first. He stands pretty far away from it. He's scared the syringe might ricochet off the tree trunk, stick in him, and knock him out. He aims and fires. He completely misses the tree.

I laugh. "You couldn't even hit the tree, let alone the sign."

I look around for the syringe. Find it sticking in the ground about twenty yards behind the tree. The charge in the syringe didn't even explode. I load the syringe back in the Cap-Chur gun. Stand about ten feet from the tree, aim at the sign, and fire. The syringe hits the tree and shatters. I go look at the sign. Spot the needle sticking in it. "Hey, look, I hit—"

Arcudy freezes. He sees something.

"What?" I ask.

He signals me to shut-up. "Deer," he whispers.

I quickly load a 3cc syringe in the gun. Look around. Don't see it. "Where?"

"Give me the gun."

"No. Let me."

"Give me the gun. I saw it."

I hand him the gun. He creeps through the woods. I follow him. We come to the edge of the woods.

A herd of cows is grazing in a field. They stare at us and chomp on their grass. Arcudy saw the cow nearest to us.

"It's a cow—you butthead!" I almost split a gut laughing.

He doesn't feel too stupid. "It looked like a deer through the trees."

I have to admit the cow looks a little like a deer. It's brown and has a deer face and big doe eyes, but I don't tell Arcudy that. "C'mon, Davey Crockett. Let's get outta here." I start to go.

"Hey, Deuce."

I turn around.

He's aiming the gun at the cow. With a crazy grin on his face, he snickers and says, "Bet'cha I can hit it."

The cow is about ten yards away from him. I figure there's no way he could hit it. "You couldn't hit the broad side of a barn."

"Oh, yeah?"

"Yeah."

He squints his eye.

He's faking. He wouldn't really shoot a cow. He's not that crazy.

"I dare you."

Bang!

The cow springs and the herd stampedes a short distance. Then they halt.

I look around for the syringe—don't see it. Then I spot the tail piece sticking in the rump of the cow.

"Jesus Christ! You shot it!"

We stand as still as statues—our eyes fixed on the cow...

The cow's butt twitches slightly where the syringe is sticking out—like when a deer fly lands on its hide. Seconds go by and nothing happens...

Maybe it won't harm it.

Oh, God, I hope so...

The cow starts mooing like something's wrong with it. I get a sick feeling in my gut. Then it totters around. Then goes down on its front knees with its rump up in the air.

Oh, God! No!

I fear it's dying.

Dear God—please don't let it die…

"Hey!" I hear a man shout.

I look in the direction of the shout—see a farmer standing by a barn off in the distance. He runs toward us across the field.

We bolt. Run as fast as we can through the woods to the barbed wire fence. Arcudy dives under the fence.

"Go!" I push him from behind.

The back of his shirt gets snagged on a barb. He struggles to get free.

I frantically try to unsnag him. "Damn it! Hold still!" Finally, I get him unsnagged.

He wiggles underneath the fence, jumps to his feet, and takes off running.

I need him to hold the fence up for me. "Hey! Come back! Help me!"

He bounds across the field.

I glance over my shoulder—don't see the farmer. Then drop onto my belly and slither underneath the fence. Jump up and take off running again.

I sprint through the briars and brambles across the field. Keep glancing over my shoulder for the farmer. Don't see him.

Arcudy disappears into the pine forest. I follow him. Spot him peeking out from behind a pine tree and run over to him. Panting, I keep on the lookout for the farmer…

"Oh, shit! We shot it," Arcudy says. He tries to laugh about it but is too scared.

"Not me. You shot it—you dumbass."

"Here's your gun." He tries to hand the Cap-Chur gun to me.

"I don't want it." I walk away from him.

Arcudy follows me. "What do we do?"

"Don't look at me. I had nothing to do with it."

"Yes, you did. You dared me."

"So? I never thought you'd actually shoot. I thought you were faking."

"It's your gun."

I don't say anything. He has me there. I try to think what to do, but I'm so shook up I can't think straight.

Calm down. Think…

"I think we got away," I say.

"You sure?"

"Yeah. He's not chasing us."

As I think about it, I realize that the farmer probably can't identify us. We were too far away and standing back in the trees. Even if he figures out that we're Boy Scouts and comes looking for us at Camp Emory Davis, there's no way he can pick us out of all those scouts.

"Look—the way I figure it is he can't identify us."

"He can't?"

"No. He was too far away. We need to get back to the campsite before anyone notices we're missing. Hide out in our tent. C'mon, let's get outta here."

We run through the pine forest and down the service lane to the place where we turn into the woods near our campsite. Arcudy has to slow down—he has a side ache. We jog.

When we reach the ravine, Arcudy says, "I'm getting rid of this." He starts to throw my Cap-Chur gun down in the ravine.

"No, don't. Give it to me. I'm not pitching it unless I have to. Not after I paid a hundred and fifteen bucks for it."

He hands it to me, and I hide it inside my shirt.

We cross the ravine and head back to our campsite. When we reach the edge of the woods, we scout out the situation. Everything looks normal. I look around for the farmer. Don't see him.

"Okay. Look innocent. And if anybody asks you anything, play dumb."

We walk out of the woods into our campsite. Nobody pays any attention to us. We go inside our tent. I take the Cap-Chur gun and ammo box out of my shirt and hide them in the bottom of my sleeping bag. Then I make him change his clothes. I'm scared that the farmer might recognize his clothes. I don't change mine. I figure my uniform will blend in with all the other uniforms.

We hide in the tent. Every few minutes one of us peeks out the tent flaps to see if the farmer is looking for us. We don't see him.

At suppertime we figure he would've been here by now if he was looking for us. I start getting hungry. I tell Arcudy I think it's safe to go outside now—let's eat. We restart the fire. I keep an eye out for the farmer while I cook my spaghetti and meatballs. Arcudy opens a can of sardines and eats them. He asks me if I want to trade some spaghetti for some sardines. I take a whiff of them and tell him no thanks.

I sit down beside the campfire and eat my spaghetti and meatballs. The guy next door is frying city chicken. Man, does it smell good. I think about what I could trade for a piece.

All of a sudden, Arcudy comes up to me with a worried look on his face. In a low voice, he says, "Look."

I look where he's looking. An old pickup truck slowly pulls into the clearing and stops next to the first campsite it comes to. A man opens the door on the driver's side and gets out. He looks like the farmer. Then a young man wearing a uniform, badge, and gun gets out on the passenger side—he's a cop. I put down my spaghetti and meatballs.

Arcudy and I duck inside our tent. I close the flaps—then peek out between them. Arcudy is hunched over right behind me. I watch the cop and the farmer walk to a tent and talk to a scout. The kid runs and gets the scoutmaster who led the songs at the camporee bonfire last night. The cop, the farmer, and the scoutmaster talk for a minute.

"What are they doing?" Arcudy asks.

"I don't know."

The cop and farmer walk to the next campsite and do the same thing there.

They walk toward our campsite. The farmer is wearing bib overalls tucked into clodhopper boots. The cop is carrying a paper bag. They spot Buckmaster and Rhodes eating supper in front of

their tent, walk up to them, and start talking. I strain my eardrums
to hear.

"What are they saying?" Arcudy asks.

"Shut up—I can't hear."

All at once, Buckmaster and Rhodes get concerned looks on their
faces and set down their plates. They, the cop, and the farmer walk
toward our tent.

"Sit down!" I whisper.

We sit down on our sleeping bags.

My heart starts pounding.

"Where's Arcudy?" I hear Buckmaster ask.

"In his tent, I think," the guy next door answers.

"Arcudy? You in there?" Buckmaster asks. He's standing right
outside our tent.

Arcudy doesn't say anything—he's scared shitless.

Somebody opens the tent flaps. "Arcudy, get out here. You, too,
Delaney," Buckmaster says.

We crawl out of the tent.

The cop, the farmer, Buckmaster, and Rhodes are all standing
there. Scouts trot over and crowd around.

"Which of you is Jack Arcudy?" the cop asks. The name plate on
his shirt says Deputy Taylor."

"Uh...me," Arcudy answers.

Deputy Taylor frisks Arcudy. He doesn't find anything. Looking
sternly at him, Deputy Taylor asks, "Did you shoot Mr. Sterkel's
cow?"

"What?"

"You heard me. Did you shoot this man's cow?" He's pointing at
the farmer.

"Uh...I don't know what you're talking about, sir."

"Liar," Mr. Sterkel says.

Deputy Taylor reaches inside the paper bag, pulls out a wallet,
and shows it to Arcudy. "This your wallet?"

"Uh...no, sir," Arcudy answers.

"Then why does it say Jack Arcudy on this YMCA card?"

Arcudy doesn't know what to say.

Mr. Sterkel says to Buckmaster, "I found it on the ground by my fence—right where I seen these boys run."

Deputy Taylor pulls out a rag and unrolls it. Inside is the needle and syringe. He shows it to Arcudy. "What is this?"

"Uh...I dunno," Arcudy mumbles.

"Liar. That's what they shot into one of my Jerseys. Knocked her out cold," Mr. Sterkel says.

Buckmaster looks at it. He doesn't know what to make of it.

"They got some kind of gun. I heard it fire," Mr. Sterkel says.

The word gun really shakes up Buckmaster. "You boys have a gun?" he asks.

"No, sir," I say.

"No, sir," Arcudy says.

"They're lying," Mr. Sterkel says.

Deputy Taylor puts Arcudy's wallet and the needle and syringe back in the paper bag. Then hands the bag to Mr. Sterkel.

He frisks me and finds nothing. "I'm gonna search their tent," he tells Buckmaster.

Deputy Taylor reaches inside the tent and pulls out my knapsack and Arcudy's suitcase. Then dumps them out on the ground.

Buckmaster says to Deputy Taylor, "I don't see anything."

"They hid it," Mr. Sterkel says.

Deputy Taylor crawls in our tent and pats down Arcudy's sleeping bag. I realize that I made a big mistake. I should've let Arcudy get rid of the Cap-Chur gun when we had the chance. Then he pats down my sleeping bag. He feels something inside it and unzips the zipper—there's my Cap-Chur gun and ammo box.

"There it is. See—I told you," Mr. Sterkel says.

Everybody crowds around to get a closer look. Deputy Taylor picks up the Cap-Chur gun very carefully. Checks to see if it's loaded. "What the hell is this?"

I figure it's no use lying anymore—they got us. I answer, "A Cap-Chur gun."

"A what?"

"A Cap-Chur gun. Uh...it's an animal tranquilizer gun."

"Who does it belong to?"

"Me."

"Where the hell did you get it?"

"A science catalog."

He opens the ammo box and takes out a syringe. Shows it to Buckmaster.

"What is this?" he asks me.

"It's a needle and syringe with an explosive charge that injects an immobilizing drug into an animal."

"What's your name?"

"Mansfield Delaney."

"How old are you?"

"Thirteen."

"How old are you?" he asks Arcudy.

"Fourteen."

He turns to Buckmaster. "Sir, I'm arresting these boys for juvenile delinquency. It's against the law to possess this weapon."

"No, it's not. It uses a CO2 cylinder," I say.

He looks at me like I'm a smart aleck. "Well, it's against the law to shoot livestock. You punks are under arrest. I'm taking you to the sheriff's office."

As Deputy Taylor escorts Arcudy and me through the crowd of scouts, we walk past Poth. He winks at me.

Deputy Taylor orders Arcudy and me to get in the bed of Mr. Sterkel's pickup truck. "I'll charge your asses with Escape—which is a felony—if you try to run." Then he and Mr. Sterkel get in the cab of the truck. We ride back to the lodge. On the way, I blame everything on Arcudy and call him a dumbass for losing his wallet. He says he couldn't help it—it must've fallen out of his back pants pocket. I call him a dumb ass again—he's always losing his wallet. Then he blames everything on me and calls me a dumb ass for not getting rid of the Cap-Chur gun when we had the chance. I call him a dumb ass again and tell him if he hadn't lost his wallet, it wouldn't have mattered that we didn't get rid of the Cap-Chur gun. Then we quit speaking to each other.

At the lodge, Deputy Taylor makes Arcudy and me get into the back seat of his patrol car. He reports over the radio that he's arrested two juveniles for delinquency. Then he drives to Waterbury. Nobody says a word. I stare blankly out the window. Slowly, it sinks into my head that I've been arrested by the police. I'm in trouble with the law. I've never been in trouble with the law before. I wonder if they're going to put me in jail with murderers and rapists.

At the sheriff's office, Deputy Taylor pulls into a garage and takes Arcudy and me into the juvenile bureau, where they book us. Then he makes me sit down in a chair and takes Arcudy into his office and shuts the door. I look at gory pictures on the bulletin board of teenagers who've been killed in drunk-driving car accidents after school proms.

After a while, Arcudy comes out. He won't look me in the eye. Deputy Taylor calls me into his office, where he's sitting at his desk. He tells me to sit down in the chair across from him.

"What happened to the cow? Did it die?" I ask.

"No. The vet gave it a cortisone shot, which saved it."

Man, am I relieved.

Deputy Taylor turns on a tape recorder and questions me. I keep calling him "sir." I confess that I ordered the Cap-Chur gun out of the *Nasco Science Catalog* and that I dared Arcudy to shoot the cow. I tell him I didn't think he would actually do it—I thought he was faking. He says that's not what Arcudy told him. Arcudy says he dared me, and I shot it. Man, does that make me mad. I should've known he'd blame it all on me. I tell him Arcudy's lying through his teeth.

Deputy Taylor calls Arcudy back into his office and tells him what I said.

"No, sir. He shot it," Arcudy says.

"You dirty liar," I say.

"Well, one of you punks is lying," Deputy Taylor says.

He sends Arcudy and me back out in the waiting room.

"Jean, keep an eye on these punks," he tells the lady sitting behind the counter.

"Tell the truth, Jack."

"Make me," Arcudy says and starts to walk away.

I grab him by the arm—

Suddenly, Arcudy spins around and tries to slug me in the mouth—his fist glances off my ear.

I take a swing at him but miss.

"Boys, stop fighting!" Jean screams.

Deputy Taylor runs out of his office. "Break it up!" he yells and separates us. He makes me sit down on one side of the room and Arcudy on the other. "No more fighting or I'll kick both your asses." He goes back into his office and closes the door.

Arcudy and I glare at each other like we hate each other's guts.

A few minutes later, Deputy Taylor comes out of his office. "Well, boys, I'm afraid I'm gonna hafta lock you up."

Man, I just about crap my pants! "Uh...you're putting us in jail?"

"That's right—until whoever's lying tells the truth."

Deputy Taylor takes us down the hall to an elevator. Opens the elevator door with a key. Orders us to get in. Then uses the key to take us up to the second floor, where we get off.

He takes us down a narrow hallway to a guardroom with thick glass windows. In the room, a guard is sitting at a counter, monitoring TVs with black-and-white images of jail cells. A clock on the wall reads a quarter till nine.

Deputy Taylor says, "Hey, Charlie. I got a present for you—a couple of punks. Lock 'em up."

Charlie comes out of the guardroom with a big ring of keys. He and Deputy Taylor take us down a hall to a sign that reads Range 1. I see a long row of cells.

"You better not put them in the same cell. They're fighting," Deputy Taylor warns Charlie.

Charlie opens the first cell. It's empty. Extending his hand for me to enter, he grins and says, "Be my guest."

I go in, and he shuts the door behind me. I hear it lock.

Charlie and Deputy Taylor take Arcudy down the range and lock him in another cell.

I look around my cell. All I see is a bunk bed and a toilet right out in the open. Man, does it stink in here. It smells like a cross between BO, puke, and pee.

In the cell next to me, an old geezer is sleeping right on the toilet. Man, he looks like death warmed over. His hair is stringy and uncombed, he's unshaven, and his mouth is hanging open—he has no teeth. Drool is running down his chin. I can't believe anybody can sleep in that position.

Charlie and Deputy Taylor walk back past my cell.

"Uh...sir, how long do I hafta stay here?" I ask.

"I told you— nobody's getting outta here until whoever's lying tells the truth," Deputy Taylor answers.

I sit down on the bunk. Wait...

All of a sudden, the geezer next door falls off the toilet. He hits the concrete floor—thud—and cuts a huge fart. Then just lies there with his pants down around his ankles. Soon, his eyelids start fluttering, and he starts cursing in a loud voice—I swear he's looking right at me.

That does it—I gotta get out of here.

I holler to Charlie that I want to talk to Deputy Taylor. I figure I'll tell him I shot the cow just to get out of here. But by the time Deputy Taylor gets here, the geezer has fallen back to sleep right on the floor with his pants still down around his ankles. So I just ask Deputy Taylor if he called my Dad.

"Not until one of you punks confesses," he answers.

I wait and wait. Wonder what time it is. Man, I wish I had my watch. I figure at least two hours must've gone by.

Arcudy calls Charlie. A few minutes later, Deputy Taylor goes back to his cell. I hear them talking but can't hear what they're saying. Then Deputy Taylor has Charlie open Arcudy's cell. They walk past me. Arcudy's crying. He must've spilled his guts.

I keep waiting. Finally, Charlie and Deputy Taylor come and get me.

"Did you call my dad?" I ask Deputy Taylor.

"Yeah. He said he oughta leave you here."

When we go by the guardroom, I look at the clock. Man, I can't believe it—it's only twenty till ten.

Deputy Taylor takes me back downstairs to the juvenile bureau. I don't see Arcudy or his parents. I wait for Dad. When he doesn't come, I start wondering if he's so mad he's really going to leave me here—like Deputy Taylor said.

Finally, Dad comes into the juvenile bureau. If looks could kill, I'd be dead. Deputy Taylor releases me to him. We go out in the parking lot. Man, am I glad to get out of there.

We get in the car. For a minute, Dad sits there, gripping the steering wheel—seething. Then he points his finger at me and says, "Alright, you listen to me, buster, and you listen good. This is the last time I ever bail you out of jail. Do you hear me?"

"Yes."

"I should've left you there this time. Maybe that'd teach you a lesson."

I don't say a word.

He starts the car and pulls out of the parking lot. "What the hell ever possessed you to pull a stunt like that?"

"I don't know."

"You know what I think? I think you have a screw loose up here," he says, pointing at his head. "Anybody who'd shoot a defenseless animal like that has to have a screw loose."

"But I didn't shoot—"

"Shut up! I do not want to hear any of your lame excuses!" he yells. Man, he is absolutely livid. I've never seen him this mad before. "You oughta have your head examined."

"I did."

"What?"

"I did have my head examined."

"Don't get smart—"

Suddenly, he slams on the brakes. I fly into the dashboard. The car skids to a stop about a foot behind the car in front of us. He's so mad we almost got in a car wreck.

Dad lights a cigarette. He's smoking again. He doesn't say anything the rest of the way home. He takes me into the den, where Mom is waiting for us. Her eyes are red from crying. She asks me, "How could you do such a cruel thing? It shows an utter disregard for life. What is wrong with you?"

I shrug.

"Where'd you get this animal tranquilizer gun?" Dad asks.

"I ordered it out of the *Nasco* catalog."

"I'm confiscating that catalog right now. Go get it."

I get the *Nasco* catalog.

Dad puts on his reading glasses and reads the ad for the Cap-Chur gun. Then looks at me with disgust. "Don't you realize you could've killed that cow?"

I just stare at the floor—feel two inches tall.

"Nicotine alkaloids can be toxic," he says. He reads out loud from the ad: "'...an adverse reaction is possible and a heavy overdose could be fatal.'" Then he says, "You're damn lucky you didn't kill it."

I nod my head.

"Do you have any idea how much a cow like that costs?"

Shake my head.

"It's a Jersey dairy cow. A cow like that could be worth hundreds of dollars."

Dad looks at the ad again. "This gun cost a hundred and fifteen dollars. Where'd you get the money to buy it?"

"I used my Christmas and birthday money."

"Did you use the money I gave you to buy the dissecting kit?"

I nod.

Shaking his head in disgust, he says, "You conned me."

Mom chimes in, "I can't believe you shot the animal, and then just ran away. Left the poor thing lying on the ground. You didn't try to help."

"But I didn't shoot it. Arcudy did."

Dad jumps back in, "Don't give me that bullshit. You were there. That makes you just as guilty as the person who shot it."

"What were you doing with Jack Arcudy after we specifically forbid you to associate with him?" Mom asks.

"Mom, he's the only person I know in the scouts," I lie. "And I thought he was my friend. But now I know he's not—he tried to blame it all on me."

Dad rubs his eyes and lets out a long sigh—like he's tired. "Let's table this, Helen. Mansfield, go to your room."

I go to my room and sit down at my desk. I feel terrible. This has to be the worst night of my life. Not only did I get put in jail—my own parents hate me.

I get Flatus down off the shelf and pet him. "Flatus, I'm gonna change. Tomorrow I'm gonna tell them I'm sorry, I've learned my lesson, and from now on I'm not gonna get in any trouble. I'm gonna be good from now on."

On Sunday morning, I wake up early and go downstairs looking for Mom. Find her in the kitchen, fixing a pot of coffee.

"Hi, Mom. Are we going to church today?"

"No," she answers coldly.

"Darn, I really wanted to go."

She looks at me like she doesn't believe me.

After I get dressed and eat breakfast, I go outside and mow the lawn without being told.

During Sunday dinner, I ask Dad if he has any other chores he'd like done today. He says I can wash and wax his car, but I shouldn't expect him to cut me any slack for it. I tell him I know. As soon as I get done eating, I go out in the garage and get started.

At three o'clock Mom calls me into the house. We go into the den, where Dad is smoking a cigarette, waiting for me.

"I'm almost done with your car," I tell him.

He ignores that. "Mansfield, I spoke to Bob Buckmaster. You're kicked out of the Boy Scouts. He said you're not scouting material.

"And I called Mr. Sterkel and apologized and offered to pay any damages. Even though the cow survived, he has a costly vet bill and the cow's milk was spoiled. Any damages I hafta pay are coming out of your allowance—I don't care if it takes five years.

"And I spoke to our lawyer, Mr. Gray. He said charges are gonna be filed against you, and you'll hafta go to juvenile court. They could commit you to the Department of Youth Services and send you to Boys Industrial School."

This scares the heck out of me. I've heard B.I.S. is where they send really tough hoods who steal cars and knife people. I wouldn't last a day.

"You're mother and I have talked things over at great length and reached a decision. We feel we've tried everything, but nothing works. First, we punished you by taking away privileges and grounding you. When that didn't work, we got you psychiatric help. For the last six months, we tried a new, more positive approach. We tried to get you involved in constructive activities, but that didn't work either. You've used it as a license to do whatever you please. You continued to associate with bad company. You got suspended from school. Failed Math. Got kicked out of the Boy Scouts. And now you're in trouble with the law—the thing we feared most.

"So...your mother and I have decided we have no choice but to send you to a private school next fall."

"A private school?"

"That's right."

"What private school?"

"Sheets Military Academy."

"Military school?"

Dad nods.

"You're sending me to military school?"

"Yes. It's for your own good. You're too wild for us. We can't control you. We're afraid you're gonna do something that'll really hurt somebody. We feel it's our duty as parents to take action before it's too late."

"Not military school. Ground me for a year."

"We're not grounding you anymore. That didn't work."

"Anything—but military school."

"We feel the discipline and regimentation might straighten you out."

"It straightened out the Allen boy," Mom chimes in.

"Dad, I'm sorry. I really learned my lesson this time. I never wanna go to jail again. Believe me—from now on, I'll be good."

"We've heard this too many times. It's a broken record," Dad says.

"I promise."

"You've broken too many promises."

"You broke your promise too."

"What promise?"

"You promised you'd take me to Boyne Mountain."

"I can't help it your grandmother had a stroke—"

"You broke it."

"—and you got mono."

"Just give me one more chance."

Dad looks at Mom like he's weakening.

"Please..." I beg.

"We'll think about it," he says.

I go back out in the garage and finish waxing Dad's car. Man, am I sweating. Military school—that's the last place on earth I want to go. They make you wear uniforms and treat you like you're in the Army. Turn you into a robot. I'll run away before I'll go there.

Before supper, Mom calls me back into the den.

Dad lights a cigarette. "Mansfield, your mother and I talked it over, and we've decided to give you one more chance."

Oh, man, am I relieved. "Thank you."

"But this is it. If you get in anymore trouble, we're sending you to military school. No ifs, ands, or buts about it."

"You won't regret it."

"We hope not."

"I'm gonna go to my room and work on my Math assignment for tomorrow right now."

When I get home from summer school, Mom hands me a letter with a stern look on her face. "Here—this came in the mail for you today."

"What is it?"

"It's your summons to appear in juvenile court in two weeks."

The words "Juvenile Delinquency" and "Vandalism" on the summons jump out at me. I try to act like the summons doesn't faze me, but it scares me. "They're not gonna send me to B.I.S., are they?"

"I don't know. You'll hafta ask Mr. Gray."

CHAPTER FOURTEEN

On Wednesday night, I start worrying about going to juvenile court tomorrow. We have to be in court at two o'clock. Dad tells me to come straight home from summer school tomorrow. We're meeting with Mr. Gray at the courthouse at one o'clock to get ready for my case. I ask him if they're going to send me to Boys Industrial School. He says he doesn't know—that's what we have to talk to Mr. Gray about.

I don't sleep too hot. I have a nightmare about B.I.S. I dream a hood chases after me with a stiletto—stabs me right in the gut.

At summer school the next day, I get more and more nervous about going to court as the morning goes by. I wish I could hurry up and get it over with. By the time school lets out, I'm ready to have a nervous breakdown.

When I get home, Mom makes me put on my suit. Then she fixes me lunch, but I'm too nervous to eat. She keeps looking at the clock and wondering where Dad is. She's scared we're going to be late. At twelve thirty, he's still not home. She starts to call his office, but right then he walks in the door.

We drive downtown to the Fairland County Courthouse. On the way, Dad tells me how to behave in court. I'm to show respect for the judge—call him sir—act like I'm sorry, and not make any "smart-aleck remarks." Most of all, I should tell the truth.

At the courthouse we go upstairs to the juvenile court and sign in. Then go into the courtroom. It's empty. I take one look at the high judge's bench and get scared. We sit down in the spectator section and wait.

A few minutes later, a man comes in. He has gray hair and is wearing a gray suit and carrying a briefcase. Dad introduces Mom and me to him. He's Mr. Gray—my lawyer. He leads us out of the courtroom and down the hall to the law library. Then into the Gongwer Room. He shuts the door and says we can talk in private here. We sit down at the conference table in big leather chairs. He and Dad light up cigarettes and flick their ashes in big brass ash trays. He makes me tell him about the Cap-Chur gun, shooting the cow, and what I told Deputy Taylor. I ask him if they're going to send me to B.I.S., but he doesn't answer me. Then he tells Dad he has to meet with the judge and the prosecutor in the judge's chambers. I ask him who the judge is. He says Judge Princehorn. I ask him if he's strict, but he doesn't answer me.

We go back into the courtroom. Mr. Gray disappears through a door behind the judge's bench. I see Arcudy with his parents. We sit on one side of the room, and the Arcudys sit on the other. Nobody says a word to each other. We wait and wait. More kids come in with their parents—they all look scared. Finally, Mr. Gray comes out of the judge's chambers with another man who's wearing a phony-looking toupee. The man with the bad rug talks to the Arcudys. I figure he must be Arcudy's lawyer.

Mr. Gray tells my parents that he wants to talk to them in private, and they leave me alone in the courtroom. I wonder what they're talking about behind my back.

After a while, Mr. Gray comes and gets me. He takes me back to the Gongwer Room, where my parents are. He lights up a cigarette and tells me that he has worked out a plea bargain. Then he explains that the cops charged me with Vandalism, which is a felony. A felony means big trouble with the law. But because I've never been in trouble with the law before, the prosecutor is willing to reduce the charge to Criminal Damaging, which is only a misdemeanor. A misdemeanor means little trouble with the law.

And the prosecutor is willing to recommend to the judge six months' probation with the condition I pay restitution to Mr. Sterkel. The prosecutor is willing to do this only if I cooperate and admit to the charge today. But if I don't cooperate and deny the charge, the judge will set the case for trial at a later date. Then we'll have a trial, the prosecutor will put on his evidence, and the judge will decide if I'm innocent or guilty. Then Mr. Gray says I don't stand a chance of being found innocent since the evidence is overwhelming—I confessed to Deputy Taylor, Arcudy will testify against me, and all the physical evidence. "So I advise you to take the deal and admit," he says to me.

"What do you mean—admit?" I ask.

"I advise you to admit to the charge."

"But I didn't do it. Arcudy did."

"I'm afraid that's no defense."

"All I did was buy the gun. That's not against the law."

"That makes you an accomplice."

"But I didn't shoot the cow—Arcudy pulled the trigger. I'm innocent of shooting the cow."

"Look, this isn't Perry Mason," Mr. Gray says.

"Don't argue with him, Mansfield," Dad says.

"But what will the judge do to me?" I ask.

"That's up to Judge Princehorn," Mr. Gray says.

"But what if he sends me to B.I.S.?"

"Just do what he says," Dad says.

I shut up.

We go back to the courtroom. On the way, Dad whispers in my ear, "You let Mr. Gray do the talking in court."

The courtroom has filled up with people. Mr. Gray goes back into the judge's chambers. We sit in the spectator section. Man, am I upset. There's no way I want to admit to shooting the cow. I figure they'll send me to B.I.S. for sure. But I don't have any choice. They're all forcing me to do it. My parents don't care if I go to B.I.S.

Soon, Mr. Gray and Arcudy's lawyer come back into the courtroom with a young man who's carrying a big stack of manila folders. Mr. Gray whispers to Dad that the judge is going to call my case first, so he won't have to sit through all the other cases—he can get back to the hospital right away. That makes me mad. They're making me admit to something I didn't do just so Dad can get back to the hospital right away. Then Mr. Gray has me sit down with him at a table right in front of the judge's bench. Arcudy and his lawyer sit down next to us. The young man with the stack of manila folders sits down at the table next to us. Some lady sits down at a machine right below the bench.

A man enters the courtroom through the door behind the judge's bench and shouts, "All rise. The Fairland County Juvenile Court is now in session with the Honorable Judge James Princehorn presiding." Everybody stops talking and stands up. Then Judge Princehorn comes through the door dressed in a black robe. He sits down behind the bench, and everybody sits down. Man, does he look mean and strict. I get really scared. The courtroom is so quiet you could hear a pin drop. Judge Princehorn glances at the young man sitting at the other table with the stack of manila folders, and then asks the lady sitting at the machine to please make a note for the record that Mr. Martin is here from the prosecutor's office.

Judge Princehorn puts on his black glasses, opens a manila folder, and calls out my name. Mr. Gray stands up—he motions me to stand up. The judge looks at Mr. Gray and says, "Mr. Gray, you represent Mansfield Delaney, is that correct?"

"Yes, your honor."

"Are his parents here?" Judge Princehorn asks.

"Yes, your honor." Mr. Gray looks back at Dad and Mom. They stand up, and Dad says, "We're his parents, your honor."

Judge Princehorn starts talking in legal talk. He says I'm charged with Juvenile Delinquency for violation of General Code Section 12480, Vandalism. Then he turns to Mr. Martin and says, "I understand the prosecutor wishes to amend the charge. Is that correct, Mr. Martin?"

Mr. Martin stands up and says, "Your honor, we've engaged in plea negotiations. As a result thereof, we have agreed, in exchange for the juvenile's admission, to amend the charge to General Code Section 12481, Criminal Damaging. We further recommend probation for a period of six months with the condition that the juvenile pay restitution in the amount of $119.00."

"Mr. Gray, is that correct?"

"Yes, your Honor. The prosecutor has correctly stated the agreement we've reached," Mr. Gray says.

Judge Princehorn talks to me. He tells me I have the right to a trial, to examine and cross-examine witnesses, and all this other legal jargon. Finally, he looks me straight in the eye and says, "Mansfield, how do you plead to the amended charge?"

"Uh...I'm not sure..."

"Do you admit or deny you shot Mr. Sterkel's cow with this tranquillizer gun?"

"Well...uh...actually...ah...I didn't pull the trigger...your honor."

Judge Princehorn looks at me with raised eyebrows. "Are you telling me you didn't do it?"

"Uh...I'm just saying I wasn't the triggerman. Uh...some other...uh...juvenile delinquent in this court was the actual triggerman...your honor."

Judge Princehorn looks at Mr. Gray like he's really annoyed. Mr. Gray has a pained expression on his face. I start thinking maybe I made a mistake.

Judge Princehorn frowns at me. "Young man, you're raising a legal technicality. And I don't appreciate legal technicalities. Do you want to admit to the amended charge or not?"

All eyes are on me.

I nod my head.

Judge Princehorn tells me, "Mansfield, the court reporter can't transcribe a nod. You must say either 'I admit' or 'I deny' for the record."

"Uh...I admit."

"Why did you shoot this farmer's cow?"

"I don't know, sir," I say, shrugging my shoulders. Then mumble, "I'm sorry."

"I don't want your apology if it's not sincere."

"I apologize. It was a retarded thing to do," I say as sincere as I can.

There's a long, dead silence while the judge stares over his glasses at me. "I hope so. For your own good." Then he says, "I accept your admission and adjudicate you a delinquent juvenile for the commission of Criminal Damaging."

Judge Princehorn calls out Arcudy's name and goes through the same spiel with Arcudy and his lawyer. Arcudy says he admits and is sorry, and the judge finds him a delinquent juvenile too.

The judge gives me and Arcudy a long lecture. He says what a senseless thing we did. It shows a total disregard for life. We endangered valuable livestock. Mr. Sterkel depends on his dairy cows to make a living. And that it was stupid of me to order the tranquilizer gun. It's intended to be used by zookeepers and professionals who handle wild animals. Not juveniles. It's not a toy—it's a dangerous weapon. There's no excuse for our behavior since we both come from decent homes and have parents who obviously love and care for us. It's not a situation of parents abusing or neglecting their children like he so often sees. Maybe that's the problem—we've been spoiled.

Finally, he gets around to our sentence. He says he considers this a very serious offense because it involves a weapon. "It's bad enough you shot valuable livestock—what if you'd shot a person? You could've wounded or even killed somebody."

That really shakes me up.

He's gonna do it—he's gonna send me to B.I.S.

"I could commit both of you to the Youth Commission for this..." he pauses.

Oh, God—that's B.I.S.

"...but, in view of the fact neither one of you has been in trouble with the law before, I'm going to give you a second chance."

Thank you, Judge Princehorn!

He puts us on probation for six months. We'll have a ten o'clock curfew. We'll have to report to a probation officer every month. We're not allowed to associate with each other. We'll have to make full restitution to Mr. Sterkel for damages and pay court costs. And we're not allowed to even look at any kind of a gun.

Looking sternly at us, Judge Princehorn warns,"I'm giving you boys a break this time, but I better never see you in my courtroom again. Do you understand me?"

"Yes, sir," we say.

"Next time I won't give you a break."

"Yes, sir."

"I see a lot of troubled teenagers come through here. They all think they can beat the law, but they can't. You cannot beat the law."

"No, sir."

He lets that sink in for a minute. Then tells us to report to Mr. Williams when he gets back from vacation next week. He'll be our probation officer.

The lawyers thank the judge and it's over.

Man, am I relieved. I don't have to go to B.I.S.

We go out in the hall. Dad and Mr. Gray light up cigarettes and talk for a while. Then Dad talks to Mr. and Mrs. Arcudy for a minute. I wish he'd hurry up. I want to get out of here before the judge has a chance to change his mind. Finally, we leave.

When we get in the car, Dad lights up another cigarette, shakes his head, and says to Mom, "Do you believe the nerve your son had? Gray had it all sewed up, and he almost blew it." Then he says to me, "You just had to tell the judge you weren't 'the triggerman,' didn't you?"

"Well, you told me to tell the truth. I didn't pull the trigger. Arcudy did."

"Yeah, well, you won't be seeing Jack Arcudy anymore. I took care of that with Paul Arcudy. We'll be monitoring you."

Dad tells Mom that Mr. Arcudy heard the Boy Scouts of America forced Mr. Buckmaster to resign as scoutmaster of Troop 113 because of Arcudy and me shooting the cow. Mom feels bad about that. Dad says it wasn't entirely my fault. Mr. Arcudy said it was also because Buckmaster failed to control some scouts called the Sheiks, and some parents questioned why he slept in the same tent with George Rhodes.

Mom starts sniffling. "He has a criminal record. And his name will be in the newspaper."

"Gray said juveniles' names aren't reported in the newspaper. And he said if Mansfield stays out of trouble, his juvenile record can be sealed."

Still, Mom keeps on crying. "Doc, where'd we go wrong?"

Dad flicks his ashes outside the window. "I don't know, Helen."

"Mom, don't worry. It won't happen again. I promise."

"It better not. Because you aren't getting any more chances—you heard Judge Princehorn," Dad says.

I just stare out the car window. It's official now—I'm a juvenile delinquent.

CHAPTER FIFTEEN

Bored to death in Math class, I glance at the clock on the wall. It's broken. Russell Ealey is sitting at the desk beside me, chewing on his pencil. He has already chewed most of the paint off it. I look at his wrist watch.

Wait a minute—that looks like my watch.

I look closer. Sure enough, it looks like my Blancpain Fifty Fathoms. It even has the No Radiations symbol and words. All that's different is the band.

As soon as the bell rings, I say to Ealey, "Hey, man, that's a cool watch."

He shows it to me.

It is a Blancpain Fifty Fathoms.

"Where'd you get it?" I ask.

"None of your beeswax," he answers and takes off.

All the way home, I think about Ealey's watch. The more I think about it, the more I suspect that it's really mine. I remember Mom saying how hard it was for her to find a Blancpain Fifty Fathoms. She had to order it from a skin diving catalog because none of the jewelry stores in town carried it. He must've found it.

I think about how to handle the situation. I figure I'll have to make friends with him first. When the time is right, I'll tell him that I lost my Blancpain Fifty Fathoms in Luna Lake Park and ask him if he found it there. I could even offer him a reward for finding it. I'm not crazy about befriending a weirdo like Russel Easley, but I don't have any choice—not if I want to get my watch back.

After summer school the next day, I walk out of the school with Ealey.

"Hey, Russell. What're you doing today?"

"What's it to you?"

"Nothing. I just thought if you're not doing anything today, you might want to come over to my house and mess around."

"Bug off!"

"Okay." I go my own way—so much for trying to make friends with him.

When I take the shortcut through the woods, I notice that Ealey is following me. He spies on me from behind tree after tree. When I speed up, he speeds up, keeping me in sight.

At a bend in the path, I run ahead and duck behind a tree. When Ealey walks by, I step in front of him. "Quit following me."

"I can walk here if I want. This ain't your property."

"Look, man, you're welcome to come over to my house. But quit following me." I start walking up the path again.

He walks along with me without saying anything…

"Hey, Russell. I notice you have a Blancpain Fifty Fathoms watch. Are you interested in scuba diving?"

"Nope. I can't swim."

I figure this is circumstantial evidence that it's my watch.

Suddenly, he points at a tree trunk. "Hey, man—look at that bug."

A cicada is attached to the bark. It's crawling out of its exoskeleton.

He catches it by the wings between his thumb and index finger. Then tries to scare me by sticking it right in my face.

I act like it doesn't faze me. "It's just a cicada. They don't bite."

Grinning like a maniac, he tilts his head back, opens his mouth, and dangles the cicada right over it like he's going to eat it.

"I dare you."

"How much you pay me?"

"A dollar."

"Down the hatch." He pops the cicada in his mouth, chews it up, and swallows it. Then licks his lips. "Mmm, nummy."

Shaking my head, I say, "I don't believe you ate a live cicada."

He opens his mouth—it's gone.

"That is gross."

He picks the exoskeleton off the tree and pops it in his mouth. "Dessert."

"You're nuts, man."

"You owe me a buck. Pay up, man."

I get out my wallet and pay him.

We exit the woods and walk up the sidewalk on Arlington Avenue.

"Russell, where'd you get your Blancpain Fifty Fathoms watch?"

"Heil Hitler!" he yells and shoots out his arm in the Nazi salute. Then goosesteps up the street. "I wanna be a Nazi when I grow up. Do you like the Nazis?"

"Not really. The Nazis were the bad guys. Don't you watch *Combat?*"

Grinning fiendishly, he asks, "You know how the Gestapo would make a guy talk?"

"Huh-uh."

"Cut off his balls with hedge clippers."

I grab my gonads and groan.

"You know who the best torturers were?"

"Huh-uh."

"The Spanish Inquisition. Have you read "The Pit and the Pendulum?"

"Nope."

"I read it in English class. It's a short story by Edgar Allan Poe."

He tells me the story on the way home. The Spanish Inquisition shackles a prisoner to the floor in a pit. Then they slowly lower a huge blade swinging back and forth on a pendulum—swish, swish—toward his chest.

"It was really good till the ending. I didn't like the ending," Russell says.

"Why not?"

"The guy gets rescued at the last second when the blade is cutting his skin."

"You don't like happy endings, huh?"

"No. I wanted the pendulum to cut open his heart."

We come to the entrance of Luna Lake Park. Instead of going to wherever he lives, Ealey tags along with me. He talks nonstop about the Spanish Inquisition and their ingenious tortures. I hear about the Wrack—which stretches the victim until his limbs pop out of his sockets. The Head Crusher—which first breaks the victim's teeth, then cracks his jaw, then pops his eyeballs out of his sockets, and finally crushes his skull until his brains ooze out his ears. The Pear of Anguish—which is a pear-shaped device that they stick in the victim's mouth or up his butt and then slowly expand until he ruptures.

"Russell, you're a walking encyclopedia on torture."

He just grins fiendishly.

We turn onto Mount Airy Lane.

"Hey, man. Where do you live?" he asks.

I point to our house on top of Mount Airy.

"You live in a mansion."

I shrug.

"Your old man must be rich. What's he do?"

"He's a doctor."

"Is he home?"

I shake my head. "He's at work."

"When does he get home?"

"Suppertime."

When we reach our driveway, he asks me if anyone is home. I don't see Mom's car in the garage. I tell him I don't think so. I invite him into the house. Man, is he nervous. He keeps looking over shoulder.

I find a note to me from Mom on the kitchen counter by the phone. It says she went to the pool with Meg and Calley and will be home around 3:00. Two baloney sandwiches are in the refrigerator for my lunch. It orders me to burn the papers—that's written in all capital letters and underlined.

Eying the phone, Ealey asks, "What's your telephone number?"

"It's not in the telephone book. We have an unlisted number because my dad's a doctor. It's LA5-1613. I write it on the back of the note and give it to him.

We eat lunch. I give Ealey one of my baloney sandwiches. He scarfs it down. He acts like he's starving, so I give him the left-overs in the refrigerator. He eats the rest of the baloney, cold chicken, and two hard-boiled eggs.

We go upstairs to my room. I show him my models. While I change clothes, I notice him checking out the Visible Woman's private parts.

"Hey, Russell. You wanna see my Observatory?"

"What's your Observatory?"

"It's where I spy on Waterbury."

This intrigues him. I take him up to my Observatory.

Gazing out the windows, Ealey exclaims, "Wow! I can almost see all the way to my house."

I show him my spy equipment—my high powered binoculars, telescope, and toy bolt rifle with Dad's old, high-powered rifle scope mounted on it. Then demonstrate how I can aim the rifle and watch through the scope what people are doing at Luna Lake Park and Possum Run Pool. Ealey thinks that's really cool.

We go back downstairs to the kitchen. I get a book of matches out of the match drawer and the wastepaper basket out of the utility closet. Man, is it full. Wastepaper is falling out all over the place. I stuff it all down inside the basket.

I carry the waste basket to the burn barrel in the back yard. Ealey tags along. I dump the papers in the barrel and light them. Mesmerized by the flames, he tells me about a bird that flew into a window at his house and ricocheted off the glass and was lying in the grass stunned. He poured gas all over it and waited for it to come around. Then he threw a match on it. The bird flew away in a ball of flames—then crashed and burned. He exclaims, "Man, it looked really cool! Like a fireball."

Man, are you weird.

I have an idea. I show Ealey a huge hornet's nest that's hanging from a branch in a tree in our back yard. "You wanna blow it up with a cherry bomb?"

His eyes light up.

"Here's my plan. We'll tape a cherry bomb to a pole and stick it inside the hornets' nest from a safe distance. You know—so we don't get stung."

Excited, Ealey asks, "Can I do it?"

"Sure."

We go back in the house, where I get two cherry bombs out of my secret compartment—just in case the first one doesn't do the job. They are my last two cherry bombs.

We go out in the garage, where I get a long bamboo pole and a roll of masking tape.

Back at the hornets' nest, I set the cherry bombs and the tape on a rock in the yard. Test to make sure the bamboo pole reaches the hornets' nest. Tape a cherry bomb to the end of the pole. Then Ealey holds the pole, and I go to the end where the cherry bomb is.

"Ready?" I ask.

He nods.

"You only have a second or two before the fuse burns down," I warn him.

He nods again.

I light the cherry bomb and take off running.

With a determined look on his face, Ealey swings the pole around and sticks it inside the hornet's nest. Hornets fly out.

Kaboom!

Man, alive—the cherry bomb blows the hornets' nest to smithereens. In a cloud of smoke, it flutters like confetti to the ground.

Ealey just stands there with a crazy grin on his face. A few hornets are buzzing around his head. Man, are they mad.

"Get away from there!" I holler.

He walks up to me with the pole. The cherry bomb blew about a foot off the end of the pole. He rubs his forehead. He has a welt where a hornet stung him, but it doesn't faze him.

After things die down, we check out the damage. A few hornets are flying around looking for their nest, but it's gone. All that's left is a small piece of nest still attached to the tree. We find another piece on the ground. Dazed hornets are crawling out of it. We run back into the garage and get the gas can. Douse it with gas and light it. That takes care of them.

We had so much fun blowing up the hornets' nest that we look around for something else to blow up. Ealey wants to find a bird's nest. I look for an ant hill. But we can't find anything.

Ealey gets an idea to blow up one of my models. I tell him it would be cooler to light a model on fire than blow it up with a cherry bomb. Plastic looks cool when it burns, a cherry bomb will instantly blow a plastic model to smithereens. We go back to my room to get a model. I pick out an old aircraft carrier—tell him we can set it on fire in the bird bath. But Ealey wants to light my Visible Woman on fire. I tell him no way—she's one of my favorite models. He keeps begging me, and I keep telling him no. Finally, he says he'll get me a new one. I tell him only if he gets me a new Visible Woman and a Visible Horse. It's a new model that just came out. He says it's a deal.

We take the Visible Woman out in the garage. I hang her by a piece of wire from a nail in a rafter. Then set an old metal bucket on the floor underneath her to catch the molten plastic when it drips. Then shut the garage doors and turn off the light so it's dark. I strike a match and start to light her foot. Ealey stops me. He says he wants to light her. I give him the book of matches. With a crazy look in his eyes, he strikes a match and lights her feet. She starts slowly bubbling and melting—colorful globules of burning plastic fall into the bucket. They make a little "thsst" sound as they fall and leave smoke trails in the air. The fire slowly spreads up her legs to her abdomen. It looks really weird when her internal organs and face melts. I look at Ealey. He's hypnotized. At the end, a big blob of burning plastic falls into the bucket.

The garage is so full of smoke that it's hard to breathe. I fling open the garage doors and let the place air out. Then toss the bucket in the garbage can. I get done in the nick of time. I see Mom's car turn into the driveway. Ealey runs out the back door of the garage. Mom pulls into the garage with my sisters. When she gets out of the car, she sniffs the air and asks me if I've been burning something. I tell her just the papers. She goes into the house.

I look around for Ealey, but he's gone. He didn't even say goodbye. And I didn't find out about my watch.

I start to go into the house but then remember the cherry bomb that I left in the back yard. I go back to the rock. The tape is still there, but my cherry bomb is gone.

That creep—he must've stole it.

After summer school the next day, Ealey gloms on to me on our way out the door. As soon as we get off school property, he pulls a pack of Camel cigarettes and a book of matches out of his shirt pocket. Then lights a cigarette. With a tough look on his face, he takes a drag. "You smoke?"

"No. Cigarettes cause cancer."

"Pussy."

"How do you get them? You're a minor."

"It's easy. I just tell them I'm buying them for my dad. Or shoplift them."

On Mapledale, he says, "Hey, Deuce. Let's blow up something."

I'm surprised that Ealey called me Deuce—that's the first time he has ever called me my name. "Like what?"

"Let's find another bees' nest. I loved blowing up that bees' nest. That was so cool."

"I'm out of cherry bombs. Did you steal my last one?"

He ignores my question. "Let's make a Molotov cocktail."

"What's a Molotov cocktail?"

"It's a fire bomb. You fill a glass bottle with gas. Soak a rag with gas and stick it in the bottle. Then light the rag and throw the bottle at something. When the bottle breaks, the gas explodes into flames. I threw one at the fire station at Safety Town one night. It was really cool."

Safety Town is a kid-sized town set up on the playground at Brinkerhoff grade school. It has miniature, wooden buildings and houses, a traffic light, and stop signs. Streets, sidewalks, and lawns are painted on the surface of the asphalt playground. Preschool kids learn traffic safety rules by riding tricycles around the streets of Safety Town. I remember hearing that the fire station had burned down. The police said it was arson. "You were the arsonist, huh?"

He nods with a creepy smile on his face. "Don't tell on me."

I nod.

"I'll get you if you rat on me," he threatens.

"I won't. What if it blows up in your hand?"

"That's why you gotta throw it fast. You only have a few seconds before it explodes."

"I'll pass. I don't wanna end up looking like Vincent Price in the *House of Wax.*"

"What's the *House of Wax?*"

"It's my favorite horror movie. Vincent Price plays a sculptor whose face is hideously disfigured in a fire."

"You chicken. I love to play with fire…"

"Russell, where'd you get your Blancpain Fifty Fathoms watch?"

He eyes me suspiciously. "Why do you keep asking me that?"

"Uh…because I used to have one. I got it for my birthday. I lost it in Luna Lake Park."

"Where?'

"The sewer pipe."

"Finders, keepers. Losers, weepers."

I sigh. I'm getting nowhere on getting my watch back.

Suddenly, he stops and backs up the sidewalk to a telephone pole. He looks around to make sure nobody is watching. Then lifts up the cover on the fire alarm on the pole.

"What are you doing?" I ask.

With a weird grin on his face, he asks, "How much will you pay me to pull it?"

"Don't!" I don't want to get accused of setting off a false fire alarm.

He holds the lever in his hand like he's going to pull it.

"I want nothing to do with this," I say and take off running.

He lets go of it and runs after me. "What's the matter? You chicken?"

"Look, man, I'm already in trouble with the law."

"What'd you do?"

I tell him about shooting the cow with the Cap-Chur gun.

He howls with laughter.

I start thinking Ealey is a living time bomb. He's going to get me in trouble with the law again. Since I'm on probation, I cannot get in trouble with the law again. I need to ditch him.

"C'mon, let's make a Molotov cocktail. You got any gas?" Ealey asks.

"No. I just mowed the lawn. Our gas can is empty," I lie.

"We can go to the gas station."

"Russell, I can't mess around with you today. I don't have time to go to the gas station. I have swim team practice this afternoon," I tell him even though it's not till four o'clock.

We come to the intersection of Mapledale, Parkview Circle, and Shady Lane at the side entrance to Luna Lake Park. I'm hoping that he turns here to go to his house, but he follows me into the park— it's like he can't take a hint. I'm afraid he's going to follow me home again.

I stop. "Russell, where do you live?"

"Bird Cage Walk."

Bird Cage Walk—that's where the footprints in the sewer pipe led me.

"Where on Bird Cage Walk?"

"The last house on the street."

Damn...that's where I almost drowned.

This is my chance to play private eye and investigate.

"You got gas at your house?" I ask.

"Yeah..."

"Let's go to your house."

"Uh...we can't," Ealey answers nervously.

"Why not?"

He starts biting his fingernail. "Skarl."

"Who's Skarl?"

He glances fearfully over his shoulder. "My stepdad. No one's allowed on his property."

All at once, I remember that mean-looking man telling me to get off his property. "Isn't he at work?"

"He don't work. He stays home and guards the house. He don't let anyone set foot on his land. Not without permission."

"Why not?"

"Cuz he's a fucker!" Ealey snarls. For a split second, I see intense hatred in his eyes. Then it's like a mask comes down over his face.

A mailman walks by us.

"I gotta go," Ealey says. He takes off up Shady Lane.

I picture the look of fear and then hatred on Ealey's face when he talked about his stepdad, Skarl. I wonder what he has done to Ealey.

It's weird Skarl doesn't allow people on his property. There's something fishy going on there...

As soon as Ealey is out of sight, I walk up Shady Lane. I go past Bird Cage Walk. I don't want to run into Ealey again, and I'm scared to set foot on Skarl's property. I turn onto Chestnut and walk to the last house on the right side of the street. I sneak around the house to the back yard. A wooden fence surrounds the back yard of Ealey's house. I jump and try to look over the fence, but it's too high.

I give up investigating today and head for home.

The next morning Ealey is not at summer school. I wonder if he's sick.

It's Guest Day at Possum Run Pool for the junior high kids. We have the pool to ourselves all afternoon and are allowed to bring a person who's not a member. My parents let me go. On my way out the door, I overhear Meg talking to Mom in the kitchen about a boy she saw duck into the bushes at the end of our driveway.

"It wasn't Jack Arcudy, was it?" Mom asks.

"No. I've never seen him before. He was weird-looking," Meg answers.

I stuff my rolled-up towel and tank suit in the trap on the front fender of my bike and ride down our driveway. At the mailbox, Ealey suddenly steps out of the bushes in front of me. I slam on the brakes.

"Here you are," he says, and he gives me a new Visible Woman model and the Visible Horse model.

"Thanks."

"I shoplifted them for you. You're my first friend."

I'm not crazy about him thinking that I'm his friend, but I want the models. I park my bike and run them up to the house. Ealey stays at the mailbox. He's scared to come up the driveway since Mom is home.

When I return, Ealey's still here.

I hop back on my bike.

He trots along beside me. "Where you going?"

"The pool. I'm going swimming." I don't tell him it's Guest Day. I'm afraid he'll ask to be my guest. I don't want people thinking we're friends.

"Let's do something," he says.

"I told you—I'm going to the pool."

He keeps running along beside me, huffing and puffing...

I wonder how I can ditch him. "Russell, you gotta be a member to get in."

"You like Ghoulardi?"

I slow down. "Yeah."

With a ghoulish grin, Ealey says, "I love Ghoulardi. I think it's funny when he blows up model cars and Froggy." Froggy is a toy frog that Ghoulardi blows up with firecrackers.

"Cool it with the boom booms," I say, imitating what Ghoulardi always says.

"Turn blue, you purple knif," Ealey replies in a perfect imitation of Ghoulardi. Ghoulardi calls people a "knif," which is fink spelled backwards. Then Ealey starts singing "Papa Oom Mow Mow" by the Rivingtons, which Ghoulardi plays when he shows a film clip of what I read in the newspaper is called "the hypnotic eye gurning man."

I hop off my bike and walk it. "You watch Ghoulardi, huh?"

Smirking, he says, "Skarl don't allow anybody to watch his TV. The fucker calls me 'shit-for-brains.' But I outsmart him. I watch his TV on Friday night after he gets drunk and passes out. I just gotta make sure I leave it on the right channel and the right volume when I turn it off. So he don't catch me."

"What would he do if he caught you?"

"Whip me with his belt."

"Where's you real dad? Why don't you live with him?"

"He died. He fell in a vat of molten steel at the steel mill."

"Oh…that's too bad."

"Skarl jokes he's in the bumper of some car. If my dad was alive, he'd kill the fucker. He's sponging off Wanda."

"Who's Wanda?"

"My old lady."

"You got any brothers or sisters?"

"Nope. I'm an only child."

We arrive at the pool. I park my bike in the bike rack and walk to the pool gate. Ealey tags along behind me. I figure they won't let him in, but Mick thinks he's my guest and lets him go into the bathhouse.

While I put on my tank suit, Ealey rummages through the Lost and Found, looking for a swimsuit. He finds a pair of Waterbury Senior High gym shorts and puts them on. Man, does he look funny. They're about five sizes too big, but he doesn't care.

I go out on the pool deck. Ealey follows me. My friends, Jon Price and Jim Chambers, look at me like "You brought this creep?" I act like he's not with me, but he keeps tagging along behind me. I do a racing dive into the pool. Ealey stands at the side of the pool at the shallow end. He's afraid of the water. I figure this is my chance to ditch him. I swim to the deep end and go off the high board with Price and Chambers.

I keep an eye on Ealey. Watch him inch his way down the steps in the shallow end, When he's waist-deep, somebody accidentally splashes him. He turns around and runs back up the steps. The gym shorts are stuck to him—they go up inside his butt crack—and you can see right through them. Gross.

My friends and I start doing can-openers, trying to splash these girls who are sunbathing on the pool deck. They go to Appleseed. Their names are Lynn Burkholder, Michelle Phillips, and Kathy

Hamilton. Hamilton is a scag, but Burkholder and Phillips are pretty good-looking. I really nail a can-opener. It splashes the lifeguard, Vic, who's sitting in her lifeguard chair. She blows her whistle and makes us quit doing them. We move to the shallow end. Those girls get in the pool and start splashing us, so we start dunking them. It's a riot. Ealey is hanging on the side of the pool. He's dying to get in on the action, but he's scared to let go of the gutter.

Kathy Hamilton accidentally backs into him. Ealey grabs her from behind and dunks her. He holds her underwater and won't let her up. Her arms start madly thrashing around. Vic spots them and blows her whistle. But he still doesn't let her up. It's like he's in a trance. Then Vic jumps down out of the lifeguard chair and runs over to him. She gets there in the nick of time. Hamilton is about to pass out. Vic helps her out of the water and has her sit down on a bench to catch her breath.

Vic yells at Ealey and kicks him out of the pool. He goes into the bathhouse and changes. A few minutes later, I see him out in the parking lot by the bike rack. He gives Vic the finger. Then Mick goes out there to nail him, but Ealey runs off. When Mick comes back, he asks me, "Who is that little creep?"

"Russell Ealey."

"Was he your guest?"

"No. He followed me in."

"You see him, you tell him he's banned from this pool."

At nine o'clock on Saturday morning, I have a swim meet at Possum Run pool. Everybody's waiting for Mick to unlock the gate. We wonder where all the pool furniture is—it's vanished. Mick arrives and unlocks the gate. Everybody follows him to the pool. We discover that all of the pool furniture is lying on the bottom of the deep end. Somebody dumped it in the pool. Then somebody goes in the bathhouse and yells that all of the baskets are gone. They threw them in too. Mick says somebody vandalized the pool last night. He asks me if I did it. I tell him no—I don't know why everybody always suspects me.

They postpone the swim meet while Mick makes the swim team

dive down to the bottom of the pool and retrieve the furniture. Mick spots some rocks lying on the bottom of the deep end. He asks Scott Hitchcock to go down and get them. Hitchcock dives down and picks one up, but it disintegrates in his hand. He shoots back up to the surface. "It's a turd!" he hollers. Everybody says "Gross!" and starts laughing at him. Nobody will touch the other ones.

We don't have summer school on Monday—there's a teachers' meeting. Yay!

After lunch, I get a phone call. At first I think it's a prank call. The person doesn't say who he is and is talking in a whisper.

"Who is this?"

"It's me, Deuce."]

"Russell?"

"Yeah. Skarl's on the toilet. I can only talk for a minute. I made a Molotov cocktail. Come over to my house. We'll throw it at something."

I almost tell him no—I'm afraid he'll get me in trouble with the law. But then I think this is my chance to play private eye and check out Skarl's house. "Okay."

"Meet me at the corner of Bird Cage Walk and Shady Lane."

"Okay."

"You gotta come right now. Skarl and Wanda are going to the store. They'll be gone till three."

"Okay."

He hangs up without saying goodbye.

I tell Mom I'm going to the pool. Then ride my bike to Ealey's house. When I reach the stop sign at Bird Cage Walk, he steps out from behind a bush. "Come on. Hurry up," he says, and he takes off running up the street toward his house. I pedal along beside him. When we reach his driveway I start to turn in, but he grabs my handlebars and stops me. "No. I told you—you ain't allowed on his property."

I follow Ealey past his house to where the street dead ends. He makes me get off my bike and walk it around the barricade. Then leads me into a pine forest. He tells me, "Skarl can't see us in here." I park my bike out of sight from the street.

Ealey leads me through the pine trees to a large rock by the cemetery fence. Sitting on the rock is a beer bottle with a rag sticking out of it. The bottle is filled with a liquid, which I figure is gas.

He picks up the beer bottle and announces, "Here it is. Here's my Molotov cocktail." He proudly shows it to me.

"Cool, man."

He sets his Molotov cocktail back down on the rock. Beside it is a six pack of beer. Grinning from ear to ear, he says, "I bought beer."

"You drink beer?"

"Yeah. I like to get drunk. It feels good."

"How do you get it?"

"I steal it from Skarl. He keeps it locked in the garage. He locks the house when he's gone. The dumbass don't know I got a key," he snickers.

"Doesn't he notice it's missing?"

"Nah. He's got cases of it."

Ealey reaches in his pocket, pulls out a pocket knife, and opens a blade that's a bottle opener. Then opens a bottle of beer.

"Watch this, Deuce," he brags. He chugs the whole bottle.

He aims his hand at me like a gun and lets out a huge burp. Then laughs. "You want one?"

I figure I'd better not since I'm on probation. "No, thanks."

"Don't be a pussy."

I decide to humor him. "Okay."

Ealey opens a bottle for me and another for himself. We sit down on a log and drink them. While he guzzles his beer, I sip on mine. It's warm. I don't really like the taste—it's bitter.

"You like it?" he asks.

"It tastes good," I lie.

"I gotta piss."

Ealey sets his bottle on the rock. Then walks over to a pine tree and pees on the trunk. While he pees, he sings "Wooly Bully" by Sam the Sham and the Pharaohs.

He reaches in his pocket and gets out his watch—which is really my watch—and checks the time.

"Hey, Russell. It's a wrist watch. You're supposed to wear it on your wrist."

"I can't. Not at home. The fucker will steal it. C'mon, let's toss the Molotov cocktail before he comes home."

He chugs the rest of his beer. Then throws the bottle against the rock—it shatters.

I set my half-empty bottle on the rock.

"Folla, me, Deuce!" he says loudly.

I follow him.

Clutching his Molotov cocktail, Ealey teeters through the pine forest. "We gotta find the right place to light it. Somethin' hard to throw it at." He's slurring his words—I think he's getting drunk.

We walk along the chain-link fence that surrounds the cemetery. Go past the tombstones. Soon, we come to a life-size statue of a lady with wings like an angel. She's standing at the head of a coffin-shaped tomb that's close to the fence.

Ealey stops. "Look—it's the angel of death." He gets a lighter out of his pocket.

I back up to a safe distance.

He lights the lighter. Then lights the rag and throws the Molotov cocktail like a hand grenade over the fence. It hits the tombstone and shatters.

Whoosh!

Flames shoot up in the air. They lick the lady—like she's on fire.

Ealey watches mesmerized…

I keep looking around—I'm scared someone is going to see us.

Slowly, the flames die down. Then go out.

Ealey grins like a maniac at me. "Man, you see that? She looked like a witch being burned at the stake. Whaddaya think of that, Deuce?"

"I think you're a real pyromaniac, Russell."

He snickers.

We walk back to the rock.

Ealey checks the time. Then lights a cigarette, opens another bottle of beer, and sits down on the log. He chugs his beer. Lights his lighter and stares at the flame…

"Hey, Deuce. Did you read about Colonel Crawford getting burned at the stake in History class?"

"Yeah."

"I love the painting of the Indians torturing him and mutilating his naked body. I painted a picture of it in Art. The teacher hated it. Said it was icky. He's a homo."

I remember that Skarl will be coming home at three. I need to investigate.

Puffing on his cigarette, he says, "Hey, I got an idea. Let's find the spot."

"Where is it?"

"Near Bucyrus."

"That's too far away. How would we get there?"

"Hitchhike."

"I'm not allowed to hitchhike."

"Why not?"

"I'm not allowed to get in a car with a stranger. My parents are afraid of child molesters."

Ealey nervously checks the time.

"Russell, why are you so scared of him?"

"Who?"

"You know who—Skarl."

"I ain't afraida him."

"Then why do you keep checking the time?"

He stares at the burning ash on his cigarette.

Suddenly, his face twists in anger. "You wanna know why? I'll show ya why." He extends his arms. "See them?" He points at little, round scars on the inside of his arms.

I nod.

"Them are cigarette burns."

I'm horrified.

He pulls up his shirt. Points at more scars on his chest and stomach. Then he points at a red, crusty scab in his navel. His finger is trembling with rage. "See that?"

I look wide-eyed.

"The fucker put his cigarette in my belly button."

I'm speechless…

"He's a sick fucker." He pulls his shirt back down. Then takes a gulp of beer.

"Why don't you tell your mom?"

"I did. That crazy bitch did nothin'."

He tells me that once when a nurse gave him a shot, she noticed the scars on his arm and asked Wanda about them. Wanda told her that chicken pox caused them.

"Why don't you tell the police?"

"The fucker said he'll kill me if I tell the cops. If I wind up dead, he did it."

He takes a last drag on his cigarette and drops the butt in his empty beer bottle. Then stares off into nowhere with a weird smile on his face. "But he ain't gonna kill me."

"He's not?"

He shakes his head. "Nope—not if I kill him first."

"You…you're gonna kill him?"

He nods his head. "I'm gonna kill both of 'em."

"When?"

"The next time that fucker burns me."

"How?"

"I'm gonna wait till he's passed out. And the bitch is asleep. Then blow 'em all to kingdom come. And steal the fucker's car and get away…"

"Where are you gonna go?"

"Mexico. When I get there, I'm gonna go to the Temple of the Sun. That's where the Aztec priests did human sacrifice. They cut open people's chests and offered their hearts—while they was still beating—to the gods."

I don't know whether or not to believe him—if it's just drunk talk or he really means it. "How…how're you gonna blow them all to kingdom come?"

"A bomb."

"A bomb?"

"Yeah. I made a time bomb."

No way. How would he know how to make a time bomb? "You

really made a time bomb?"

Smirking, he nods.

I shake my head. "Get outta here!"

His face turns red. "I did!"

"Let me see it."

He starts chewing on his fingernail furiously...

"C'mon—prove it."

He checks the time. "Okay. I'll prove it."

He stands, steadies himself, and walks to a nearby pine tree. Then reaches into a small knothole in the trunk of the tree and pulls out a key.

That's where he hides his key.

I follow Ealey through the pine forest back to the street barricade, where we hide behind some bushes. Peering out from behind the bushes, he tells me, "Wait here. Lemme make sure he didn't come home early."

Ealey disappears up Skarl's driveway. Soon, he reappears and shouts "The coast is clear!"

I walk up the driveway.

"Hurry up—we ain't got all day!" He takes off up the driveway.

I trot after him. On the way, I glance around the front yard, looking for a sewer grating—don't see any.

He motions me to hurry up.

I speed up.

Ealey leads me into an alcove between the house and the garage where there are two doors—one goes into the house, the other into the garage. He unlocks the door to the garage and opens it. We duck into the garage. Leaving the door open, he runs across the garage to another door. I follow him. He unbolts the door, opens it, and steps into the back yard.

"C'mon!" He runs across the back yard to a shed.

I run after him, looking around the yard. A tall hedge runs around the yard in front of the wooden fence. I slow down, trying to look closer.

"Hurry up!" He's holding open the shed door.

Ealey pushes me inside the shed. It's filled with old machinery and piles of junk. I trip over a push reel lawn mower. He weaves his way to the back of the shed and stops at a block of concrete with a rusted sheet of metal on top of it. He slides the metal sheet sideways, exposing a hole in the block of concrete.

"What is this?" I ask.

"It's the old well. It's where I hide stuff."

Ealey lowers himself into the hole.

I look down into the gloomy hole. He's standing at the bottom. The top of his head is about a foot below the rim. He bends down— I can't see what he's doing.

Suddenly, he pops up, holding a metal gas can. He sets the gas can on the concrete block. Then climbs out of the hole.

Grinning diabolically, Ealey says, "This is it—my time bomb. It's filled with gas."

"How is it a time bomb?"

He lifts the gas can high in the air. A cherry bomb is taped to the bottom of it, which I figure is the cherry bomb that he stole from me. Pointing at the cherry bomb, he says, "That's the detonator. I'm gonna set the can on the burner on the electric stove in the kitchen. Then I'll turn on the burner and run out in the garage and steal the fucker's car. Get my ass outta there before the burner lights the fuse on the cherry bomb."

Jesus Christ…

He's not fooling…

He jumps down into the hole with the gas can. Bends downs and stands back up. Grinning like a maniac, he yells, "Titties!" He's holding up the centerfold in a *Playboy* magazine.

"Hey, let me see that."

He bends over again.

"What're you doing down there?" I ask.

All at once, Ealey sticks a pole with the skull of an animal on the end of it right in my face. The skull still has decomposed flesh on it.

I jump backwards.

Ealey is laughing down in the hole.

"What is that?"

"A pootey-tat," he answers like Tweety-bird in the cartoons.

"What happened to it?"

"He was a bad pootey-tat so I doused him in gas and lit him on fire. It was so cool. He leaped in the air in a ball of flames. Hissing and screeching and clawing at the air."

This guy is sick...

Ealey pokes the cat's skull at me. "Wanna pet him?"

"Get it away from me!" I shove the pole away.

"Ohhh...poor pootey-tat. Deuce doesn't like you."

I'm getting out of here.

I peer into the hole. "Russell, I'm leaving."

He puts the pole down and checks the time. "Shit! We gotta get outta here!"

Terrified, he climbs out of the hole and slides the metal cover over it as fast as her can.

"Move!" he yells.

Rushing, I bang my shin against a wheel barrel.

Ealey shoves me out the shed door and slams it shut behind him. Dashes across the back yard with me right behind him to the back door of the garage. Peeks through the open door. I look over his shoulder—don't see a car.

"C'mon!" he says.

We run into the garage. Ealey shuts the door behind us and quickly bolts it. We run across the garage and out the door to the alcove. He shuts that door and frantically tries to lock it—but can't the key in the keyhole. Finally, he gets it locked.

"Go, go!" he shouts.

We sprint down the driveway. Don't stop until we get back in the pine forest. Panting like crazy, Ealey peeks out at his house. "Phew, we made it," he says, giggling like a maniac.

He gets out my watch and checks the time again. "It's almost three. That was a close call."

"Hey, Russell, where'd you find my watch?"

He eyes me suspiciously. "It ain't your watch. It's mine. I didn't find it. I bought it."

"Where?"

"Goldsmith's Jewelry Store."

"You're lying. My mom bought me a Blancpain Fifty Fathoms watch for my birthday. She said she called all the jewelry stores in town, and none of them carried it. She had to order it from a scuba diving catalog."

Ealey glares at me. "Bug off, shit-for-brains!"

"Doggone it, Russell! That's my watch. I lost it in the sewer pipe in Luna Lake Park. I'll pay you a reward for finding it."

"I don't want a reward. You lost it. I found it. It's mine now."

"I love that watch, I want it back. That's why I tried to make friends with you."

"I thought you were my friend, but you're not. You just want your watch back." He turns his back toward me and starts messing around with his face.

"Russell, give it back—now."

All of a sudden, Ealey spins back around—

I see his hollow eye socket—he popped out his fake eyeball.

"Wha...what are you doing?"

"I'm gonna get you."

"Stop it, Russell!"

"I'm gonna kill you." He walks toward me like a monster.

I bolt through the pine trees, grab my bike, and run with it back out to the street. Hop on it and pedal as fast as I can down the street. Look over my shoulder and see him standing at the barricade.

"You psycho!" I holler.

Suddenly, I hear tires screeching and a horn blaring at me.

I spin around—see a big, black car heading straight at me!

I swerve and slam on the brakes—just miss it.

The car stops. In the driver's seat, a mean-looking man shakes his finger at me as I pedal past. In the passenger seat, a mousy woman peeks around him at me.

Man, am I shook up. Hear in my mind the tires screeching, the horn blaring. Picture the big, black car driving straight at me—it almost ran over me.

I picture the mean-looking man shaking his finger at me.

That's him.

Skarl.

I stop and look up Bird Cage Walk. Sure enough, the car turns into the driveway at Skarl's house. I look toward the barricade. Ealey is gone.

As I ride home, my mind is racing…

Ealey is a psycho.

He's going to kill his parents. Blow them up with a time bomb.

Lighting that cat on fire.

Popping out his eyeball like that.

I keep picturing the gross image of his hollow eye socket. Man, it looked like a hole that went clear to his brain.

Acting like a monster coming to kill me.

That's the last time I do anything with that psycho.

And Skarl.

Burning Ealey with cigarettes.

What a sicko!

I picture the ugly scab on Ealey's navel. Shudder. I can't believe something like that actually happened in Waterbury. It's like something you'd read about in the *National Enquirer*.

Tell Dad. He'll know what to do.

Wait a second…

If I tell Dad, he'll grill me and find out that I went to Ealey's house when I was supposed to be at the pool. He'll probably find out about the beer and Molotov cocktail.

I'll be in even worse trouble.

He'll send me to military school for sure.

I need to keep my nose out of it. Mind my own business.

That time bomb — I don't know if Ealey will really do it.

But what if he does?

People may die — bad people.

Man, I don't know what to do.

All I want to do is get my watch back.

I think about telling Arcudy, but I can't. There's nobody I can tell.

Wait…Dr. Isch…

I remember he said I should call him if I needed help, and he wouldn't tell Dad. I'll call him as soon as I can.

After supper, I go into the den and shut the door. I get Dr. Isch's business card out of my wallet.

Suddenly, the phone on Dad's desk rings. I answer it, "Hello."

I hear breathing.

"Hello," I say again.

Somebody whispers, "I think he knows you was here."

"Russell?"

"He questioned me about the footprints."

"What footprints?"

"The footprints in the back yard. In the mud."

"What are you talking about?"

"Your footprints. He said they didn't match."

"Match what?"

"The footprint of my shoe." Man, is he scared. His voice is shaking. "I made it all up."

"What?"

"He didn't burn me with cigarettes."

"What about those scars?"

"Chicken pox."

"Are you still gonna blow him up?"

"No. They'd put me in the electric chair."

There's a long silence.

"Russell? You still there?"

"I hear him coming. I gotta go."

"Russell, if you're scared he's gonna harm you, don't call me. Call the police."

Click—he hung up on me.

Now I don't know what to do. Ealey said Skarl didn't really burn him with cigarettes—he made it up. I suspect that Skarl really did it. The scab on Ealey's navel was fresh. I figure he's backpedaling because he's afraid of Skarl. But he said he's not going to kill him and Wanda. I decide not to call Dr. Isch. I figure I can't prove Ealey's going to kill them if Ealey says it's not true.

In bed at night, I lie awake thinking about what I'm going to say to Ealey in Math class tomorrow. I realize that it's impossible to be friends with him—he's a psycho. I figure I'll tell him I'm not going to be his friend anymore unless he gives me back my watch. Then if he gives it back, I'll tell him I'm busy every time he asks me to do something with him until I finally get rid of him.

CHAPTER SIXTEEN

On Tuesday, I'm late for school. I run down the hall to Math class. As I go past the Boys' restroom, I smell smoke. I back up and open the restroom door.

Smoke comes pouring out.

I duck inside. A dense cloud of smoke is hanging in the air on the side of the restroom where there is a wall of sinks and mirrors.

Man alive! Flames are leaping out of the trash barrel across the room in the corner.

I run to the sink that's closest to the fire, turn on the faucet, and frantically splash water on the flames. But it doesn't extinguish the fire at all.

Pull the fire alarm.

I run back out the door and tear down the hall.

Mr. Wilson comes around the corner.

I almost run into him.

"No running!" he exclaims.

"The restroom's on fire!" I exclaim.

He sees smoke coming out of the restroom door and runs down the hall into the restroom. I follow him. The fire is spreading up the walls in the corner. He runs back out in the hall and grabs a fire extinguisher out of the glass case on the wall. Runs back in and squirts it on the fire. It shoots out this white stuff that smothers the flames. After a minute or so, it looks like the fire is extinguished.

Mrs. Olson sticks her head in the door. "What's going on in here?"

"There was a fire," Mr. Wilson answers.

"Should I pull the fire alarm?"

"No. I have it under control. Would you please report it to the office?"

I hang around. I know I'm supposed to be in Math, but I figure I have a good excuse for not being there. After all, I discovered the fire. If it wasn't for me, the school might've burned down. Mr. Wilson checks out the damage. The trash barrel is burned, and the paint on the walls in the corner is charred. He spots water on the floor. I tell him I tried to put out the fire, but it didn't work. A paper towel hanging form the dispenser by the trash barrel is burned.

Mr. Wilson and I walk around to the other side of the restroom where the urinals and toilet stalls are. We discover that the ends of the rolls of toilet paper in some of the stalls were set on fire. Burnt matches and ashes are on the floor underneath them.

Arson—somebody tried to set the restroom on fire.

We also discover that the arsonist tried to set the other trash barrel on fire, but, luckily, it went out by itself.

Kruse rushes into the restroom. Mr. Wilson shows him where the fire was. Since Kruse doesn't like me, I'm afraid I might get in trouble for not being in class. I slip out the door.

When I walk into Math class, Robinson looks at me crossly. "Mansfield, why are you so late?"

"There was a fire in the Boys' restroom. I helped put it out."

I describe the fire to her and the class. "It looks like it was arson," I say and describe the signs. I notice Ealey isn't at his desk. He must not be here today.

Suddenly, Kruse charges into the classroom and collars me. Man, does he look mad. He says to Robinson, "Ma'am, I need to question this boy. I'm taking him to the office."

Kruse hauls me to the office. In the hall, I ask, "What? What'd I do?"

He doesn't answer.

I fear it has something to do with the fire. He must suspect that I started it. So much for being a hero.

He takes me into his office, shuts the door, and shoves me into a chair. Then sticks his finger in my chest and yells, "Yooou started that fire! Didn't yooou?"

I madly shake my head. "No, sir!"

"Yes, yooou did. Mr. Wilson saw yooou running away from it."

"I was running to pull the fire alarm."

"Don't yooou lie to me!" he yells.

"I'm not!"

His face turns scarlet, and he clenches his fist. For a second, I think he's going to hit me. Then someone knocks at the door. Kruse answers it. It's Petty. Kruse steps out in the hall to talk to him. He closes the door so I can't hear them. I sit here getting more and more scared. I'm in really big trouble now. I should've known Kruse would blame it on me. I never should've gone into that restroom. I should've let the school burn down.

Kruse comes back in. He's calmed down now.

"Mr. Kruse. Here's what happened. I swear it." I tell him exactly what happened.

"Don't give me that bull crap, su-un. I know it was yooou who started that fire. And yooou who set off that fire alarm. And yooou who made that bomb threat. Yooou are a very disturbed boy."

Somebody knocks on the door again. Kruse answers it. Mrs. Richards says, "The police are here."

Oh, God.

Kruse steps out of the office and shuts the door behind him. I look at the clock radio on his desk every two minutes. I'm scared the cops are going to arrest me and throw me in jail again.

Twenty minutes go by.

What is taking them so long? What are they doing?

My hands are sweaty and I feel sick to my stomach.

The door flies open—it startles me.

Kruse storms into the room, followed by two men. I recognize Sergeant Boyle—he's the cop who questioned me about the bomb scare—but not the other guy. They surround me.

"You remember me?" Sergeant Boyle asks.

I nod.

"I'm here to question you about the fire in the restroom."

"I didn't do it."

"What were you doing in the restroom?"

I'm so shook up I can hardly talk. "I…I was on my way to Math class, and I saw smoke coming out the restroom door. So I went in and saw the restroom was on fire. And I tried to put it out by splashing water on it. But that didn't work. So I ran out in the hall to pull the fire alarm. That's when I ran into Mr. Wilson…"

"Delaney, you're in big trouble with the law. This is Investigator Hardesty from the fire department. He's an expert at investigating fires. Tell him what you determined, Lieutenant."

Investigator Hardesty's eyes bore into me. "I determined that the fire was caused by arson. The arsonist set two trash barrels on fire. One of them caught on fire. The other one didn't. I found burned matches on the floor by the trash barrels. And a matchbook in the trash barrel where the fire went out. The arsonist tried unsuccessfully to burn the evidence."

"It wasn't me."

"Look, Delaney, it's no use denying it," Sergeant Boyle says. "We know you did it, and we can prove it. A witness saw you running from the restroom. All we have to do is take fingerprints. So why don't you just admit it and make things easier on everybody?"

"Because I didn't do it."

"Delaney, I'm losing my patience."

"That's the truth. I swear to God."

"Don't force me to get rough with you."

"Please…I wanna go home."

"You little prick, you're not going anywhere until you admit it."

"Leave me alone!"

Somebody knocks on the door. Kruse answers it. It's Petty again. He nervously peers over Kruse's shoulder at me. He and Kruse talk for a minute. Then he leaves, and Kruse shuts the door.

"Listen, Delaney, either you admit it, or I'm gonna hafta take you down to the station and lock you up," Sergeant Boyle says.

I start crying.

"If you just admit it, we'll take you home. C'mon, confess. Make it easy on yourself."

Somebody knocks on the door again. Mrs. Richards tells Sergeant Boyle that Captain Jones is on the phone. He tells her just a minute.

"You wanna think it over for a minute?" he asks me.

I nod.

"Alright, you think about it."

They all leave the room.

I sit here crying…

I don't know what to do…

I gotta get outta here before I confess to something I didn't do.

I look around the room.

The window.

I rush over to it. Outside is the back parking lot. Beyond it is the woods.

I glance at the door to make sure no one is coming.

Go!

The window is hinged on the top and opens from the bottom. I open it all the way. Then climb onto the register and slither like a snake out the window onto the window ledge. Tumble headfirst into a shrub.

I spring to my feet and sprint across the parking lot into the woods. Out of sight from the school, I stop and catch my breath. Madly try to figure out what to do…

The cops will be after me any minute.

I need to find a hiding place. Somewhere I can lay low till I figure out what to do…

I can't go to my tree fort. They'll nail me there for sure.

The library. I'll hide in the stacks. They won't think of looking for me there.

I run through the woods toward downtown. At the edge of the woods, I stop and peek out at Euclid Avenue. Don't see any cop cars. I step out of the trees onto the sidewalk and walk nonchalantly down the street a few blocks to the hospital. Then circle around front to the bus stop on Sycamore Street. I check if I have enough money to ride the bus downtown. I have fifty-five cents in my pocket. Bus fare is a quarter. A crowd of people is waiting for the bus. I stand inconspicuously in the middle of them. Wait on pins and needles for a bus to come.

Suddenly, I spot a cop car driving toward me on Sycamore. I duck behind a fat lady. The cop car drives past me. I breathe a sigh of relief.

Finally, the bus comes. I hop on and drop a quarter in the box. Ride downtown and get off at the square. Make a beeline to the library. Hide at a desk way back in the stacks of books. I grab a book off a shelf and act like I'm reading. The library doesn't have air-conditioning, so it's really hot and stuffy in here. I'm sweating.

I ponder what to do. I know I'm in big trouble with the law. Arson is almost as bad as murder. They lock arsonists away in prison for life. On top of that, I escaped.

I have one choice—run away. Go west to California. Become a scuba diver.

How can I get there?

I'm afraid the police will nab me if I hitchhike.

I think about taking a bus, but I don't know how much a bus ticket would cost. I go downstairs to the lobby, where there is a pay phone. I look up Greyhound's telephone number in the telephone book, drop a dime in the slot, and call them. A lady tells me a one-way bus ticket to Los Angeles, California, costs $98.

I go back to my desk. Try to figure out where I can get the money for a bus ticket. Think about borrowing it from Arcudy, but we're enemies. He wouldn't have that much dough anyhow. I rack my brain but can't think of a way.

I hide out at the library for hours. In the middle of the afternoon, I start getting hungry. I haven't eaten anything since breakfast. Man, I wish I could go home. I wonder what my parents are doing.

Mom is probably a basket case by now, and Dad is probably ready to disown me. I think maybe I should turn myself in, but I don't want to go to jail. I remember Dad telling me next time he won't bail me out.

But I can't stay here forever. They'll kick me out at closing time. I have nowhere to go.

What do I do?

I need someone to help me.

Dr. Isch…

He said I could call hem if I ever needed help.

Call him.

I go back down to the lobby. I get Dr. Isch's business card out of my wallet. Then call the operator and tell her I want to make a long-distance phone call to Cleveland, Ohio. She asks me which way — station-to-station or person-to-person. I ask her which way is cheaper. She says station-to-station. So I call station-to-station. The operator tells me to please deposit fifty cents for the first three minutes. For a second, I don't know what to do—I only have thirty cents. But then I remember the two dimes in my penny loafers. I slide them out and drop my dough in the slot. The operator puts the call through.

"Dr. Isch's office," a lady answers.

"I need to talk to Dr. Isch."

"I'm sorry. He's not taking any more calls today. You need to make an appointment."

"I can't. I need to talk to him right now It's an emergency."

"Are you his patient?"

"Yeah. He told me to call him if I needed his help."

"What's your name?"

"Deuce—Mansfield Delaney."

"Just a minute."

I wait…

"Hello, Mansfield. What's the problem?" Dr. Isch asks.

I blurt, "Dr. Isch, I'm in big trouble with the law. The cops arrested me for arson. But I escaped. I'm on the run. I need money to go to California."

The operator interrupts, "Your three minutes are up. Please deposit another fifty cents."

"I can't. I'm broke," I tell her.

"Then you'll hafta hang up."

"Ma'am, it's an emergency," Dr. Isch says.

"Sorry, but I'm going to have to disconnect you. Do you want to reverse the charge?"

"Yes," Dr. Isch answers, raising his voice.

"Go ahead," the operator says.

"Dr. Isch, I need to borrow a hundred dollars for a bus ticket to Los Angeles. I promise I'll pay you back someday."

"Slow down, Mansfield. Tell me what happened."

I tell him the whole story. I have to talk in a quiet voice because a lady is standing right behind me, waiting to use the phone. I fear that she's eavesdropping and will alert the police about me. She keeps giving me dirty looks for talking too long.

"I gotta hang up, Dr. Isch."

"Why?"

"There's a lady behind me waiting to use the phone. I think she's eavesdropping. I'm afraid she's gonna alert the police about me."

"Where are calling from?" he asks.

"A pay phone."

"Where?"

"Uh...I don't wanna tell you."

"Okay. What's the telephone number posted on the phone? You can let the lady make her call. I'll call you back after she hangs up."

I figure there's no harm in telling him that, so I read him the telephone number that's posted on the pay phone.

"Don't go anywhere. Wait for me to call you back," Dr. Isch says.

"Okay." I hang up.

"It's about time," the lady says to me.

I act like I'm looking at the bulletin board while I wait for Dr. Isch to call me back. After a while, the lady hangs up and leaves. Two minutes later the phone rings. It's Dr. Isch.

"Mansfield, you can tell me the truth. The police cannot find out what you tell me. The law makes it confidential. It's called doctor-patient privilege. Do you understand?"

"Yeah."

"Tell me the truth. Did you start this fire at school?"

"No. I'm innocent. But the police suspect me because of all this other trouble I got it."

"What other trouble?"

I tell him about the butyric acid bomb at school and shooting the cow with the Cap-Chur Gun. He's never heard of a Cap-Chur gun, so I have to explain that to him. Then I start to tell him about my watch and Ealey.

Suddenly, out of the corner of my eye, I see Sergeant Boyle stride in the front door.

I drop the phone and run. But I'm trapped.

He and another cop corner me by the bulletin board.

He puts me in a half-nelson. "Got'cha, you little prick!" Then handcuffs me with my hands behind my back. "You're not escaping this time."

He hauls me outside and shoves me into the back seat of a police car. He sits beside me, gloating that he caught me. The other cop drives us to the Waterbury Police Department. I wonder how they found me, but I'm too scared to ask.

At the police station, Sergeant Boyle asks the other cop, whose name is Officer Morgan, to book me while he goes to see the judge. Officer Morgan searches me. Then removes my handcuffs. Takes my mug shot. After he finishes booking me, he doesn't put me in a jail cell. Instead, he makes me wait in the booking area. I look at the Ten Most Wanted posters on the wall. At the rate I'm going, my mug shot will be up there someday. I wait here for an hour.

Sergeant Boyle comes back holding a piece of paper in his hand. Smirking, he tells me, "I'm gonna nail you now, you little prick." Then he takes me to a room where they take my fingerprints.

"Sergeant Boyle, you'll find my fingerprints on the restroom door. I pushed it open. And the sink faucet. I tried to throw water on the fire."

"I don't give a damn about the door or the faucet. We're checking the matchbook."

"I didn't touch any matchbook."

After they fingerprint me, a lady says to Sergeant Boyle, "Dr. Delaney is here with his lawyer. They demand to see the boy right now."

"Send 'em in,' Sergeant Boyle says.

A few minutes later, Dad and Mr. Gray enter the room. Man, am I glad to see them.

"I found your boy," Sergeant Boyle says to Dad.

"What are you holding him for?" Mr. Gray asks Sergeant Boyle.

"Arson."

"Have you charged him?"

"No. But we will."

"Then I insist that you release him."

"Fine. He's all yours," Sergeant Boyle says.

Mr. Gray notices the ink all over my fingers. "What the hell are you doing fingerprinting him? He's a juvenile."

Waving that piece of paper in the air, Sergeant Boyle says, "You got a complaint? Take it up with Judge Princehorn. Your client even has the judge pissed at him."

Mr. Gray reads the paper and frowns. Then says to Dad, "I'll meet you at my office."

Dad takes me out of the police station. Man, am I relieved they didn't put me in jail.

As soon as we get in the car, I say, "Dad, I didn't do it. I swear it."

He just lights a cigarette. He won't even look at me. He acts like I'm not here.

Dad drives to the Farmers Bank Building on the square. We take the elevator to the tenth floor and go into Mr. Gray's law office. Mr. Gray sits down at his big, wooden desk, and Dad and I sit down in big, leather chairs across from him. He gets out a pen and a yellow legal pad of paper. Looking steely-eyed at me, he says, "Mansfield, tell me everything that happened, starting at the beginning. Don't leave anything out."

I tell him everything. He listens carefully and writes down what I say. Then starts firing questions at me.

"What did you tell the police?"

"Just what I told you. That I saw smoke coming out of the restroom. And that I went in and tried to put out the fire. And that I didn't start it."

"Are you sure you didn't admit it?"

"I'm sure."

"Why did you flee from the school?"

"I was scared."

"You shouldn't' have run."

"They were pressuring me to confess. I panicked."

"Flight is evidence of guilt."

"Mr. Gray, I didn't do it. I swear it."

"Listen to me, Mansfield. You're in real trouble. You're accused of arson. This is a serious felony. You're on probation. It's very important for you to tell me the truth—for me to be able to defend you."

"I am telling you the truth. I'm innocent."

Mr. Gray sends me out in the waiting room while he talks to Dad in private. I strain my ears but can't hear what they say.

Finally, they come out. All of us ride down the elevator together. Mr. Gray tells Dad he'll call Tom Martin at the Prosecutor's Office tomorrow.

Dad and I ride home in silence. When we pull into the driveway, I say to him, "You think I did it—don't you?"

"I think you shouldn't've run."

"Dad, you don't understand. They were really pressuring me. I was afraid I was gonna confess to something I didn't do."

"You heard Mr. Gray. Flight is evidence of guilt."

I just sigh.

Mom is waiting for us in the kitchen. She's a nervous wreck. She's smoking a cigarette. I've never seen her smoke in my life. She tells Dad, "Milt Petty called. They expelled him."

"Jesus Christ, they at least could've waited until they charged him," Dad replies.

"They're gonna charge him?"

"That's what the police said."

"With what?"

"Arson."

"Oh, God!" She bursts out crying. "How could you do such a thing?" She's looking at me like I'm some kind of sicko.

"I didn't!"

"Alright, calm down. Don't get hysterical," Dad tells her.

Dad asks Mom to fix us some supper. He and I sit down at the kitchen table and wait in silence. Mom dries her eyes with a dish towel. Then gets out the electric skillet and starts fixing cube steaks.

"Doc, did he do it?"

"He says he didn't."

Dad tells Mom everything that I told Mr. Gray. They keep talking about me, but they won't speak to me. It's like I'm invisible.

"So he was hiding at the library all day? How'd they find him?" Mom asks.

Dad tells her that I gave Dr. Isch the telephone number of the pay phone at the library where I called him from. Dr. Isch then called the police and gave them the number. The police then called the telephone company and found out it was the pay phone at the library.

That dirty fink! I knew I should never trust a shrink.

"So why do the police think he did it?" Mom asks.

"They said they have an eye witness who places him at the scene. And he ran. That makes him look guilty."

"But he says he didn't do it. He says he tried to put out the fire."

"I know. But nobody believes him."

"What'd Gray say?"

"He said he's gonna call the prosecutor tomorrow. Find out what evidence they have."

Mom hands me my cube steak. She sees the black ink on my fingers. "Go wash your hands. What is that?"

"They took my fingerprints," I say.

She gets a shocked look on her face and starts sniffling again. "He's just a boy."

"Gray says Judge Princehorn authorized it. He's even got the judge mad at him," Dad tells her.

"Mom, don't worry. I can explain my fingerprints." I wash my hands and sit down at the kitchen table, but I barely touch my cube steak even though I haven't eaten all day. I have no appetite. Judge Princehorn already doesn't like me. Now I got him mad at me. He'll send me to B.I.S. for sure.

The phone rings. Mom answers it. She tells Dad it's Dr. Isch.

Dad sends me to my room. I plop down at my desk.

"Flatus, nobody believes me. Not Dr. Isch. Not my lawyer. Not even my own parents. And if they don't believe me, there's no way Judge Princehorn is going to believe me. I'm going to B.I.S., Flatus!"

After a while, Dad comes into my room. "You're confined to your room until you hear otherwise, you hear?"

"Yes."

"Go to bed," he says and leaves.

I get undressed and climb in bed but can't fall asleep. It's too hot and muggy in my room. I stick to the sheets. I lie on top of them, tossing and turning...

Finally, I go up into my Observatory. I open all the windows. There's a nice breeze outside. I cool off. I sit in my swivel chair, watching the fireflies flash down below. There are thousands of them. Man, are they beautiful.

I hear a train off in the distance. I should've run away when I had my chance—hopped a train. I could've been on my way to California. I picture myself on my cabin cruiser out in the blue Pacific Ocean, skin diving in a coral reef where nobody can find me.

I lean back in my chair and watch the moon rise. Listen to the crickets chirping. I wish I could just hide up here. Everybody leave me alone. Just watch the world go by. I drift off to sleep...

Nazis with machine guns are chasing me across a rooftop. I stop at the edge of the building. Below is a bottomless chasm. I leap toward the rooftop of another building that's a short distance away. The rooftop moves away from me, and I fall into the chasm—

I wake up. Looking around, I see that I'm sitting in my Observatory. It was just a nightmare.

Clouds are rolling across the sky in front of the moon. I wonder what time it is—it feels late. There's a reddish glow in the sky in the direction of the steel mill. They must be pouring steel.

On Possum Run Road, I spot a car turn off its headlights and turn into the parking lot at Possum Run Pool with only its parking lights on. It parks back in the corner in the shadows with the tail end facing me. Then the parking lights go off. It's probably a couple parking. I wish Arcudy and I were there—we could bushwhack them. I try to spy on them with my binoculars, but it's too dark to see anything.

A light comes on inside the car. I look through my binoculars, but it goes out before I can focus in on it. Then the trunk light comes on, and I think I see the silhouette of somebody getting something out of the trunk. Then the light goes out.

I spy on the pool. Mercury lights by each of the bathhouses illuminate it. After a few minutes, I think I see someone moving around in the shadows. They must be some high school kids skinny-dipping. I look through the binoculars, but it's too dark to see anybody. Then think I see somebody throwing stuff in the pool. Somebody's vandalizing the pool again—probably whoever did it last weekend. I smile—if only they knew I'm watching them.

Later, I see the light come back on in the car for a second. Then see the taillights and license plate light come on. I try to read the license plate number but can't get my binoculars to focus. I pick up my bolt rifle and try the rifle scope. Aim at the car and adjust the scope. See the backup lights come on, and the car backing up. Zero in on the license plate. Spot the license plate number—HWJ 481. Just for the heck of it, I play private eye and jot down the license plate number on the front of a *Mad* magazine.

I watch the car pull out of the parking lot and turn onto Possum Run Road. It drives a ways—then the headlights come on. I watch it cross Mount Airy Lane and enter Luna Lake Park. Then circle around Luna Lake and go out of sight. I think how lucky those guys are for not getting caught. If it was me, the cops would've nailed me and thrown me in jail.

I go down to my room and back to bed.

When I wake up in the morning, yesterday seems like a bad dream. But then I realize it all really happened. I stare at the ceiling, feeling impending doom.

The shit is gonna hit the fan today...

I remind myself that I'm innocent. My story is true. I'm not worried about the police finding my fingerprints. I can explain them. And they won't find my fingerprint on that matchbook.

Mom comes into my room, carrying a tray with my breakfast. She fixed me French toast.

"Bread and water," I wisecrack.

She sets the tray on my desk. Before she goes, she reminds me, "Your father said you're not to leave your room today."

I get up and wolf down my breakfast. It feels like it's going to be really hot today, so I put on a T-shirt and Bermuda shorts. Then go up to my Observatory. Right away I spot two police cars in the parking lot at the pool. Mick must have reported the pool being vandalized to the police. Looking through my binoculars, I see Sergeant Boyle and some other cops talking to Mick and Vic. I glance at the license plate number on the *Mad* magazine. Then tell Sergeant Boyle, "Hey, fuzz, you're talking to the wrong people. If you wanna know who did it, you should be talking to me."

I watch the swim team haul stuff out of the pool again.

Eventually, Sergeant Boyle drives away in one of the cop cars. Later, the other cop car drives away.

To kill time, I read *Mad* magazines and comic books. They help take my mind off my problems.

In the afternoon, I see Meg ride her bike down Mount Airy Lane. She's wearing her bathing suit and has her towel in her bike rack. She's going to the pool. Man, I'd give anything to be in her shoes.

At supper time I see Dad's car pull into the driveway. I tiptoe downstairs. Standing on the landing, I eavesdrop on Dad and Mom talking in the kitchen.

"Helen, I...I feel like I don't know my own son. He could be an arsonist."

"Are they gonna charge him?"

"You guys won't believe what happened at the pool today," Meg says. She just got home from the pool.

"Meg, please leave," Dad says.

"A kid—"

"Right now!" Dad orders.

Meg beats it out of the kitchen.

Dad tells Mom, "It doesn't look good. Gray said they have a lot of evidence. They have a teacher who actually saw Mansfield run out of the restroom at the start of the fire. And Mr. Kruse says he hung around the restroom after the fire—the way arsonists do."

Wait a second. First I'm guilty because I ran. And now I'm guilty because I didn't run.

"But that's not what Gray is really worried about. He's really worried about a matchbook that the police found in a trash barrel in the restroom. They're checking it for his fingerprints right now. He's gonna call as soon as he hears about the lab report."

I'm not afraid of that. They won't find my fingerprint on it. I didn't touch any matchbook.

"Helen, I'm really afraid Mansfield did it. The matches are Kissel's campaign matches."

"What?"

I hear Dad walk across the kitchen and open a drawer. "These. I handed them out for him at my office. I brought some home after he won."

"But he handed them out all around town."

"I know. Gray said he's working on a deal. He's trying to get probation. But the problem is Mansfield. He has everyone pissed off at him. Petty says he could've burned down the school. He has this cop—Boyle—pissed off because he's taking a lot of grief over letting a thirteen-year-old escape. And he has Martin and Judge Princehorn pissed off because they gave him a break and he blew it. They don't wanna get burned again."

"It sounds like he's tried and convicted."

"Gray's hoping they won't find his print on the matchbook. If they do, he says Mansfield's sunk. But if they don't, he says that creates a reasonable doubt. He may be able to leverage that into a deal we can live with once tempers cool down."

The whole time I'm listening to this I'm getting more and more upset. They're talking about making a deal when I'm innocent. Finally, I can't stand it anymore, and I run around the corner. "Wait a minute!"

Man, are they surprised to see me.

"I'm innocent."

The phone rings. Mom answers it. "I'll get him," she says. "It's Gray," she tells Dad and hands the phone to him.

"Hi, Tom. What did you hear? Uh-huh...uh-huh...that's what I was afraid of," Dad says in a grave voice. He looks sick.

Dad motions Mom to get him pen and paper—she runs and gets it. Then he listens intently to Mr. Gray. Keeps saying "Uh-huh," and writing stuff down. They're talking about a plea bargain.

I spot the book of matches on the counter. Go over and pick it up. Read "Re-Elect Kissel Coroner" on the matchbook cover.

I go back to listening to Dad on the phone. Hear him talking about a mental hospital in Cleveland where Dr. Isch works. Finally, Dad sighs and says, "It sounds like we'd better take the deal. Yeah...thanks, Tom." Then he hangs up.

"I'm not taking a deal," I say.

"Shut up," he says to me. Then says to Mom, "They found his print on the matchbook."

"Oh, God, no..." Mom says in a hushed voice.

That shocks me...

How did they find my fingerprint on the matchbook? I didn't touch it.

She starts crying.

"But listen, Helen. Gray said he was still able to negotiate a pretty good deal with the prosecutor."

"What?" Mom sobs.

Dad reads his notes to her. "He pleads to Arson. He'll be committed to the Department of Youth Services for an indefinite period—somewhere between one year and his twenty-first birthday. But the commitment will be suspended, and he'll be placed on probation with these conditions—psychiatric evaluation and treatment to be monitored by the court. And here's the crucial factor for Mansfield—Gray got the Martin to agree to let him go to Irv's private hospital in Cleveland."

"Oh, God, no...I don't want him committed to a mental hospital, Doc..." Mom sobs, shaking her head. She looks devastated.

"Helen, he thinks we should take the deal. He says if the judge actually commits him to the Youth Commission, they can send him anywhere in the state.

"He'll end up with a felony record, but Gray says he can get that sealed.

"And they'll drop the flight charge.

"He still has to get Judge Princehorn to go along with it. But he thinks he can persuade the judge. He says he's played poker with him for years."

Dad turns to me and says, "But the prosecutor said you gotta come clean. You gotta go to the police department tomorrow morning and give them a statement admitting everything. Or it's no deal. If you don't come clean, he'll see us in court, and there'll be no deal later."

He says to Mom, "We're supposed to meet Gray and Boyle there at nine."

"But I didn't do it," I say.

"They found your fingerprint on the matchbook," Dad says.

"That can't be. I didn't touch it."

"I don't believe you. I can't believe a word you say."

"I'm not going."

"Yes, you are. It's the best deal you're gonna get. You're not blowing it."

"No, I'm not. I'll run away first."

"You listen to me, buster. You are one screwed up kid. You need psychiatric help and you're gonna get it whether you like it or not."

"I hate you!" I yell at him. I start to go upstairs.

Mom grabs me by the arm. "Come back here! We're trying to help you!"

I jerk my arm loose. "Fuck you!" I yell at her.

Pow! Dad smacks me right in the mouth. I see stars.

The next thing I know I'm sitting on the floor, stunned…

Dad is glaring at me. "Don't you talk to your mother that way!"

"You…you hit me…"

He points his finger in my face. "You don't set foot out of this house. You're under house arrest. You hear me?"

I nod.

I taste blood and touch my lip—see blood on my fingers.

Dad sees the blood and becomes a doctor again. "Let me see, Mansfield." He bends over and examines my lip.

"Leave me alone!" I cry. I get up and run upstairs.

I go into the bathroom and look at my mouth in the mirror. There's a gash on the inside of my lower lip from my teeth. I spit blood in the sink. Rinse my mouth out with water. My lip swells.

I go to my room and slam the door behind me. Throw myself down on my bed and bury my face in my pillow. I start to cry…

"They don't believe me. My dad and mom don't believe me…

"They're making me confess to something I didn't do…"

I imagine myself at the police station—everybody pressuring me to confess. The cops. Gray. Dad and Mom. I don't stand a chance—I'll confess to anything.

"Deuce, here's your supper," Mom says.

"I'm not hungry."

She sets the tray on my desk.

"Mom, please! Listen to me. I didn't do it. Don't make me go to the police station tomorrow."

"Your father and I have decided you need psychiatric help. We're just trying to do what's best for you."

She leaves.

I start crying again…

"They're sending me to the nuthouse…"

I imagine being surrounded by men in white coats and nuts in straightjackets.

What if they put me in a straightjacket?

I feel the walls closing in on me…can't breathe—

I scurry up to my Observatory where I can breathe. I try to read a *Mad* magazine but can't concentrate, so I turn on the radio and play hand after hand of solitaire—can't win a game.

I see Dad's car pull out of the driveway.

The sun goes down.

Finally, I chuck the cards.

Somehow I gotta prove I'm innocent…

Think…

How did my fingerprint get on that matchbook?

It's impossible. I didn't touch it.

Boyle. He hates my guts. He's out to get me. He must've framed me. Doctored the fingerprints.

Tell Dad.

I go look for Mom. Find her sitting at the kitchen table. She looks shattered.

"Where's Dad? I really need to talk to him."

"He got called to the hospital."

"Mom, I swear to God I'm innocent. The police framed me."

"Why would the police frame you?"

"Sergeant Boyle hates my guts. He's out to get me. He took my fingerprints. He must've doctored them."

She looks at me like she doesn't believe me.

"I need you to call Mr. Gray. Tell him Boyle framed—"

"I'm not calling Mr. Gray and telling him the police framed you."

"Please, Mom. Don't send me to a mental hospital."

She puts her hands over her ears and cries, "Deuce, why do you put me through this? Where is your father when I need him? I cannot handle you by myself anymore."

The phone rings. Mom pulls herself together and answers it.

"Is it Dad?" I ask.

She motions me to go away and turns her back on me.

It's Dr. Isch. I'll tell him about Sergeant Boyle framing me. "Mom, let me talk to Dr. Isch."

"Go back to your room!" she yells.

She starts talking to him about the mental hospital.

She doesn't believe me.

Nobody's gonna believe me.

I go back up to my Observatory and play solitaire again. It's dark out now. I watch a full moon rise.

Later, I see Mom drive out the driveway.

Maybe the police didn't frame me. If they didn't frame me, how did my fingerprint get on that matchbook?

I picture the matchbook on the kitchen counter with the words "Re-Elect Kissel Coroner" on the cover—

All at once, I picture Ealey striking a match and lighting my Visible Woman on fire with a crazy look in his eyes. The matchbook cover read "Re-elect Kissel Coroner." Then I remember that I handed him the matchbook so he could light it. That was the day I burned the papers. I got a book of matches out of the match drawer in the kitchen.

Ealey...

The time bomb, the Molotov cocktail, the cat he lit on fire all flash through my brain.

He's the nut. He's the pyromaniac.

He started the fire with that book of matches.

And if they found my fingerprint on it, maybe they can find his on it.

That'd prove he did it!

I go look for Meg. Find her reclining on her bed, playing with her Magic 8-Ball.

"Meg, do you know where Mom went?"

"She ran to the drugstore to get her medicine. Did you set the school on fire?"

"No. I'm innocent."

"Right," she says like she doesn't believe me. "You won't believe what happened at the pool today."

"I don't know, and I don't care. I need to talk to Mom."

"A kid drowned."

"Really?"

"Yeah. Some kid named Russell Ealey."

"What?!"

"They found him floating face down in the pool this morning. Mick tried to give him artificial respiration. But it was too late.

"Cindy Roberts saw his body. She said he had dead eyes. And water dribbling out of his mouth. She said she'll have nightmares about it the rest of her life.

"Mick said the cops think he's the guy who's been vandalizing the pool. He threw all the lawn chairs and benches in the pool. They think he was drunk and fell in cuz they found beer bottles in the water and lawn.

"Vic said he didn't know how to swim. She kicked him out for holding a girl underwater."

I'm stunned…

"Dad said you're supposed to stay in your room," she reminds me.

I walk slowly back to my room.

Ealey's dead.

I sit down at my desk.

Now what do I do?

All of a sudden, I picture the car I saw last night at Possum Run Pool.

Wait a second…something's not right here…

I try to remember exactly what I saw last night. Picture the car pulling into the parking lot with just its parking lights on…somebody throwing stuff in the pool…the car driving away…

Who was that? What were they doing?

There's something fishy going on here.

Oh, God…

What…what if Ealey didn't really drown?

What if Skarl murdered him? Then dumped him in the pool to make it look like an accident?

I picture the cigarette burns on Ealey's arms and stomach. If Skarl could do that to Ealey, he could murder him.

I remember how scared Ealey was of Skarl the last time he called me—his voice was shaking with fear. Then remember him saying if he wound up dead, Skarl did it.

I picture the trunk light coming on. Suddenly, a chill runs down my spine.

Oh, God—what if that was his body?

I need to tell Dad this.

Wait a minute…

Dad won't believe me. He'll say that could be someone else's car. Ealey could've gone to the pool and accidentally drowned after that car left. I'll look like a fool if I accuse Skarl of murdering Ealey and it's someone else's car.

If only I knew that was Skarl's car…

All at once, I picture looking at the license plate on the back of that car through the scope on my bolt rifle last night. The license plate number—I wrote it down.

I run up to the attic. Scurry up the ladder to my Observatory. There it is—HWJ 481—on the cover of my *Mad* magazine. Oh, man, am I glad I wrote it down!

I could find out if that was Skarl's car I saw. All I have to do is go to his house and check the license plate number on his car. Knowing that he could be a murderer, I'd have to be super careful. I figure his car will be parked in the garage. It's dark out, so he won't see me. I don't want to go inside the garage—that would be too dangerous. I figure I could shine a flashlight through the window in the garage door at the tail end of his car.

But I'm under house arrest…

I could slip out of the house, ride over there on my bike, check the license plate number, and be back in twenty minutes. Beat Mom and Dad home.

If it turns out that I didn't see Skarl's car last night, I'll just tell Dad about Ealey and the matchbook. And pray that the police find Ealey's fingerprints on it. That'll prove I'm innocent, and they won't send me to the nuthouse.

If I did see Skarl's car last night, I may have solved a murder.

Man alive! I'd be a hero.

Decide...

Do it.

I rip the license plate number off the *Mad* magazine—I don't want to get all the way over there and forget the number. Leave the lights on in my Observatory just in case Mom beats me back—that way she'll think I'm up here. I know she won't try to come up the ladder. She won't even climb up on a chair. She's afraid of heights.

I hurry down to my room. Change out of my Bermuda shorts into blue jeans, so I'll be harder to see in the dark. Grab my flashlight out of my nightstand. Test it—it's really dim. I grab my penlight out of my desk. Test it—it's brighter. Stick it in my pocket.

I crawl out my bedroom window, so Meg doesn't see me sneaking out. Climb down the TV antenna.

This is it.

CHAPTER SEVENTEEN

I sneak my bike out of the garage. Afraid that I'll run into Mom coming home, I pedal as fast as I can down the driveway and Mount Airy Lane. Breathe a sigh of relief when I make it.

I turn into Luna Lake Park and tear around the lake—the same way that car drove away last night.

Heat lightning flashes in the sky. Sweat is running down my forehead. Man, is it muggy.

There's a full moon. It's so light out that I can see my shadow pedaling up the street.

I hear a weird sound. Slow down and listen. It sounds like a baby crying. I figure it's a cat. Cats make that sound when they're in heat. It gives me the creeps.

At the intersection of Parkview Circle, Mapledale, and Shady Lane, I see headlights coming toward me on Mapledale off in the distance. I steer off the road and duck behind a bush. I'm afraid it might be a cop car. Watch the car go by. It's not.

I ride up Shady Lane and turn onto Bird Cage Walk. Man, is it creepy at night. There aren't any street lights, so it's real dark where the road dead ends into the cemetery. I get scared.

I ride slowly past Skarl's house—it's hidden in the darkness behind trees and bushes. At the dead end, I put my kickstand down and park my bike next to the barricade for a fast getaway. I sneak over to his driveway and creep up it. When I get past the bushes, I see the black silhouette of the house. I look for lights on inside—don't see any. I figure he's in bed asleep and breathe easier.

I creep toward the house ready to run if I see anything move or a light come on. I listen for a dog barking—don't hear one.

I reach the garage. I peek in the garage door windows—see the moonlight reflecting off the rear window of Skarl's car but can't see the license plate.

I get out my penlight, click it on, and shine it through the window. I still can't see the license plate—his car is parked too close to the garage door.

Damn!

Now what do I do?

I shine the light on the garage door—spot the garage door handle. Click off my penlight and stick it back in my pocket.

If Skarl hasn't locked the garage door, I could raise it a foot or so and shine the light on the license plate without going into the garage...

Gripping the door handle, I very slowly try to turn it and raise the garage door. The door won't budge.

Shit! It's locked. I should've known he'd lock it.

Oh, man...I didn't think it'd be this difficult. I thought all I'd have to do is peek in the windows in the garage door. What do I do now?

I remember the door to the garage in the alcove but figure it's locked too. Then I remember the key Russell hid in the knothole in the pine tree. If the key is still there, I could unlock the door and go in the garage.

Don't even think of it. That's breaking into what could be a murderer's garage.

I turn around and sneak back down the driveway to my bike. I'm really disappointed. I snuck out of the house and rode all the way over here for nothing.

I wonder if Ealey put the key back in the knothole.

Just see if it's still there.

I enter the pine forest. Turn on the penlight. Weave my way through the pine trees to the cemetery. The tombstones look creepy in the moonlight. At the fence, I shine my penlight on the ground, looking for the big rock that Ealey set his Molotov cocktail and beer on. I can't find it.

I shine the light on the statue of the lady with wings like an angel—that helps me get my bearings. The big rock wasn't far from her.

Light reflects off the broken glass on the pine needles where Ealey smashed his beer bottle against the big rock. I spot the rock. From there, I find the knothole in the pine tree and shine the light inside it. Nestled in the hole is the key.

I could unlock the door, slip into the garage, check the license plate number, and be gone in less than a minute. If Skarl is in bed asleep, he couldn't catch me in that short of time.

I grab the key.

I go back to the driveway. As I slowly creep up it, I watch the house for any sign of Skarl.

Curiosity killed the cat. I should go home. Tell Dad.

I picture him saying to me, "I don't believe you. I can't believe a word you say."

He won't believe me—not without proof.

I'm so close. I can't go back without checking Skarl's license plate number.

I check the house—still pitch dark inside...

Eyes riveted on the house, I creep toward the alcove...

I reach the alcove and creep to the garage door...stick the key in the keyhole...turn it...

It unlocks.

Turn the doorknob...slowly open the door a crack—

All of a sudden, I think I hear a noise.

Grabbing the key, I bolt down the driveway and hide behind bushes. Peek out of the bushes and watch the house...don't see anything. It stays dark inside. I put the key back in my pocket.

Get the hell outta here! It's too dangerous. I could get trapped in the garage. The guy is a murderer. If he catches me, I'm dead...

But look, man—he's sound asleep. You could be in and out in no time. Man, if you chicken out now, you won't find out. There's only one way to find out. You gotta check his license plate.

I creep back up the driveway. In the quiet darkness, my eyes and ears are straining to see and hear...

Creep into the alcove...over to the door...

It's open about an inch.

Check the house again—still pitch-black.

Push the door open and step into the garage. It's so dark I can barely see.

Get out my penlight.

Don't turn it on. Not yet.

Leave the door open in case you have to run.

Feeling in front of me, I creep toward the car until I feel the headlight. Inch my way around the bumper. Bump into boxes. Click on my penlight and see cases of beer stacked against the wall in front of the car. Tiptoe sideways over to the middle of the hood. Crouch down and shine my penlight on the license plate...

HWJ 481.

My heart skips a beat.

That's it.

Check to make sure.

I reach in my pocket, pull out the slip of paper, and shine my penlight on it.

HWJ 481.

It's him. He did it. He murdered Russell.

Suddenly, I feel the hairs on the back of my neck stand up. I look up and see the silhouette of a man in the doorway, looking at me—

Startled—I gasp and drop the license plate number...

A light comes on and I see Skarl aiming a double-barreled sawed-off shotgun at me. All he's wearing are underpants and a leather holster with handcuffs dangling from it.

"Don't move or I'll blow yer head off!"

I freeze.

"Put yer hands up!"

Heart pounding, I raise my hands...

"Drop the flashlight!"

I drop it.

He moves toward me.

I start shaking like a leaf...

"Git down on the floor!"

I get down on my hands and knees. See untied army boots on his feet.

"On yer belly!" He stomps on my back.

I fall flat on my stomach.

The next thing I know he's kneeling on my back—crushing me against the floor.

Unable to breathe, I gasp for air...

He climbs off me. He frisks my back side and turns my back pockets inside out. Then rolls me over onto my back, frisks my front side, and turns my front pockets inside out. The key falls out of my pocket, and he picks it up.

Standing over me, straddling my waist, he points the shotgun right between my eyes.

I look up two huge gun barrels—imagine the blast ripping through my face and blowing my brains out. Clamping my eyes shut, I cower in terror...

"What the fuck are you doin' in here?" he yells.

My mind is paralyzed with fear. "Please...don't shoot me..."

"Bo-oy, I'll shoot you if I want. I know the law. The law says I can shoot you if you bust into my house." He prods me in the side with his boot. "Open your eyes!"

I open my eyes. I can't bear to look at the gun barrels and turn my head sideways.

"What the fuck are you doin' in my garage?" he yells louder.

Static noise is roaring in my brain...

He presses the gun barrels against my temple. "Talk! Or I'll blow yer fuckin' head off!"

I spot a carton of Falstaff beer out of the corner of my eye. "St-stealing beer," I stammer.

He knits his brow. "You was stealin' beer?"

"Me and my friend were just stealing beer," I tell him, so he thinks someone knows I'm here.

He lowers the gun. Squints out the garage windows. "Where is he?"

"I don't know. He was supposed to stand lookout. He must've run."

He squints at me. "I've seen you before. Where the hell have I seen you?"

"I don't know."

"How'd you know there was beer here?"

"Russell showed me. He invited me here to mess around."

"When?"

"Uh...a few days ago."

"I knew I've seen you before. You're the little fucker I almost run over."

"We took a six-pack in the woods and drank it."

"How'd you get a key to my garage?"

I act like I don't know Russell is dead. "Russell has one. I saw where he hides it. That's the truth—I swear to God. Just ask him if you don't believe me."

He reeks of beer, cigarettes, and BO. He stares at me suspiciously. His eyes are bloodshot. His hairy beer belly is hanging over his underpants. "What's yer name, bo-oy?"

"Ma-Mansfield Delaney, sir." My mouth is so dry I have to keep licking my lips.

"Mansfield," he snickers. "Where do you live, Mansfield?"

"Mount Airy Lane."

"Where on Mount Airy Lane?"

"The house on the hill."

"You're a fuckin' rich kid. What's yer old man do?"

"He's a doctor."

"He's probably a quack. What's yer buddy's name?"

"Jack Arcudy. He's staying overnight at my house. We snuck out."

"Where's he live?"

"Pinecrest Court, sir."

Glaring at me, he mutters, "Fuckin' punks!"

"Please, mister...can't you just let me go? I-I'm really sorry."

He shakes his head. "Ain't no way. You're in big trouble, bo-oy. This is breakin' and enterin' in the night season. This is a felony. I'm callin' the cops."

Feel a flood of relief.

"Please, mister...don't call the police. My parents will k-kill me."

"Shit, what're you worried about? Yer ol' man will just buy off the fuckin' judge."

He holsters his shotgun. Rolls me over onto my stomach, picks me up, and stands me on my feet. Then grabs hold of the handcuffs with one hand, presses the gun barrel against the back of my neck, and prods me forward. "Move!"

I stumble in a daze around the car toward the door. He stops at the door, sticks his head out the doorway, and looks around. Then prods me across the alcove to the side door of his house. He puts his gun in his holster, opens the screen door, and shoves me inside. Then shuts the door behind him—locks and bolts it.

He turns on a light. We're in a short hallway.

"Ersel, is that you?" a lady's voice asks.

"Go back to bed, Wanda," Skarl says.

"Did Russell come home?" she asks.

"Hell, no! I toldja he drowned. The cops toldja he drowned. He ain't comin' home, Wanda. Git that outta yer crazy mind."

A lady in a nightgown peeks around the corner of a doorway at me. "Who's he?"

"Some little fucker I caught bustin' inna my house. Now go back to bed."

She rushes toward me. "Have you seen my boy, Russell?"

"Git back in yer room, Wanda."

She grabs onto my arm—she has a crazy look in her eyes. "Do you know where he is?"

"God damn it, Wanda! How many times do I hafta tell ya? He's dead! D-e-a-d—dead! Now get the fuck outta here!" he yells.

She scurries back down the hall and disappears through the doorway.

Skarl clamps his hand around the back of my neck, steers me down the hall to a door, and opens it. I peer down steps into a pool of blackness.

He's taking me down in the basement.

He turns on the basement light. "You stay down there till the cops get here."

I freeze.

"Go on! Git yer ass down there, bo-oy!" He shoves me down the steps and shuts the door. I hear him bolt it.

I stand at the top of the steps—dazed...

Oh, my God...

Jesus...

I'm locked in Skarl's basement. I could die. He could kill me...

I am so afraid...

I tiptoe up to the top step and listen—don't hear him. Even though I know the door is locked, I turn around on the top step. Stand on my tiptoes and grope for the doorknob. Grasping it, I frantically twist and turn it. Then throw my back against the door harder and harder—

Suddenly, I lose my balance and tumble headfirst down the steps. I lie on my side at the bottom of the steps, moaning in pain— it feels like I broke my tailbone...

You gotta get outta here!

I try to stand up...

I can't get up because of these damn handcuffs.

Trying to slip my wrist out of the handcuff, I pull and twist my hand harder and harder—feel a sharp pain and stop pulling.

I roll over onto my stomach...struggle to my knees...stand up. Then rush around the basement looking for a door...window ...some way out...

All I see are stone walls.

I run underneath the basement steps. It's dark so I can barely see...

I spot a door. Back up against it, find the doorknob with my hand, and try turning it—locked. I throw my shoulder against it as hard as I can again and again. But it won't budge.

I go back to the bottom of the steps.

There's no way out...

Oh, God...

I'm trapped in a murderer's basement.

If he finds out what I know, I'm dead. He'll kill me.

I snivel, "I don't wanna die. Oh, dear God, please don't let me die..."

"Stop...get...get a grip on yourself."

I close my eyes. Take a deep breath. Force myself to concentrate...

Think...you gotta think if you wanna get out of this alive.

I still got a chance...if he believes my story and calls the police...

What did he see? How long was he standing there? Did he see me looking at his license plate?

I picture myself crouched in front of the car—shining my penlight on his license plate.

He couldn't see what I was doing. The car would've blocked his view.

All at once, I recall dropping the slip of paper with his license plate number on it.

Oh, God...if he finds it, I'm dead.

I start hyperventilating...

"Oh, dear God, please don't let him find it. Please..."

Why did I bring it? How could I be so stupid?

All of a sudden, I feel faint...

"Don't faint...do not faint..."

I bend over...breathe in through my nose...out through my mouth...

"Pull yourself together."

Think...you gotta think of an explanation why you had his license plate number...

I wrack my brain...but there's only one logical explanation—I saw him dump the body.

I'm an eye witness.

I can testify against him. Prove he murdered Russell.

I can put him in the electric chair.

He's gotta kill me.

I break out in a cold sweat...then feel like I'm going to vomit...

"Do not puke...do not puke..."

The nausea passes.

"You gotta get outta here before he comes back."

Jimmy the door.

I scurry around the basement, searching for a tool to jimmy the door. I see an old washing machine. Metal sink. Hot-water tank. A cot with an army blanket. A sign on the wall above it reads "Shit-for-Brains." This must be where Skarl sent Ealey when he was bad. I feel pity for poor Russell.

I keep looking for something to jimmy the door but can't find anything.

Find something to pick the lock.

I run over to a shelf beside the sink. Look for a safety pin or a piece of wire. See a box of detergent. Measuring cup. A bar of soap. Nothing sharp.

"Shit!"

I shuffle back to the bottom of the steps...

There's no way out.

I can't believe it. This cannot be happening to me. This is all just a nightmare. I'm gonna wake up in my bed safe and sound...

This is real...

I wanna go home.

Feel so alone.

Picture Mom and Dad.

Wait—sooner or later they'll discover I'm gone. They'll start looking for me.

Oh, God, no—they'll think I ran away. They won't know to look for me here...

You stupid idiot—you should've waited on Dad. Or, at least, written a note that said where you were going...

"Oh, God, what have I done?"

I picture my parents discovering that I'm gone—Mom looking upset and worried. Dad looking sad and tired.

I'll never get to see my family again. Calley. Meg. Tecca. Ike...

Never get to live my life...

I feel tears rolling down my cheeks...

"I don't wanna die. I wanna live.

"Oh, dear God, please give me one more chance...just one more chance. I promise I'll never do anything wrong. Please..."

I feel pins and needles in my hands—the handcuffs are cutting off my circulation. I wiggle my fingers—the numbness slowly goes away.

The police—they're my only chance.

Did he call them? What's he doing?

Suddenly, I get a weird feeling like someone's watching me and look up at the ceiling.

Maybe he's watching me.

I quickly look down. Then go sit down on the cot and act like I'm waiting patiently for the police to come. While I wait, I peek up at the ceiling, looking for a peephole, but don't see any.

Where are the police? Why don't they get here? How long does it take for him to call the police and for them to get here? How long has he been gone? I wish I had my watch...

Every minute that goes by and the police don't come, I know my odds of surviving are going down and the fear in my gut intensifies...

What is he doing? What is taking him so long?

It doesn't take this long to call the police.

He's suspicious. He's checking out my story. He's gonna find out I know he killed Ealey.

I am so scared—my hands won't stop shaking...

Damn it—where are they? Why don't they come? What is taking them so long? They should be here by now.

Something's wrong.

He didn't call them. He tricked me.

He found that piece of paper. I know he found it.

He's gonna murder me! Just like Russell!

I imagine him shooting me. Making me kneel handcuffed. Then pointing the shotgun at the back of my head.

Me cowering defenseless...

Boom—the blast blowing my brains out.

A weapon. I gotta find a weapon.

I spring to my feet and run around the room, looking for a weapon. I spot a cardboard box on the floor behind the furnace and rush to it. I run into a huge cobweb hanging from one of the octopus-like arms of the furnace. The web sticks all over my eyes, nose, and mouth—I can't brush it off with my hands. I try to blow it off but can't.

I scoot the box with my foot out of the shadows into the light. It's filled with *True Crime* magazines. I see a magazine cover with a photograph of a creepy murderer torturing a lady who's bound and gagged—

I reel backward in horror—

"Ow! God damn it!"

I cracked my head on another octopus-like arm of the furnace. As the pain subsides, I realize I couldn't use a weapon even if I found one—not with these handcuffs. "Give up. It's no use..."

My legs are so weak that I have to sit down. I stagger back to the cot and sit down. Stare hopelessly at the cement floor...

I picture that lady being tortured.

"Oh, God! What if he tortures me? What if he tortures me to make me talk?"

I imagine him burning me with a cigarette—violently shudder.

I start crying again...

"Oh, dear God, please don't let me suffer..."

Creak! Creak! Creak!

I leap to my feet. Spin around and look up. Hear footsteps walking across the ceiling toward the basement door.

He's coming.

I start shaking all over.

I move unsteadily to the bottom of the steps. Hear him unlock the door and turn the doorknob. The door swings open...

Skarl stands at the top of the steps in the dark where I can't see his face.

Uh-oh—I don't see the police with him.

He pulls the door shut behind him and comes down the steps. He has put on pants and an A-shirt with grease stains.

I don't see his gun, which gives me a glimmer of hope. "Er...the police, uh...are they coming, sir?"

He doesn't answer me.

At the bottom of the steps, his face comes into the light...

I see cold fury in his eyes.

He knows...

Terrified, I back up.

He shoves me backwards against the cot. Standing with his hands on his hips, he towers over me. He sticks his finger in my face. "You're lyin'."

"No, I'm not." My voice cracks with fear.

"You wasn't stealing beer."

"Yes, I was."

All at once, he grabs me by the scruff of my necks and hauls me to the door behind the furnace. He unfastens a key ring from his belt and unlocks the door. Opens it and turns on a light in a dingy room.

He drags me across the room to another door, opens it, and turns on a light switch. A fluorescent light slowly blinks on...

It's his workshop.

My legs buckle with fear—I fall on the floor...

He kicks me into the room. Then slams the door shut behind us.

"I called yer buddy's house. He's home in bed. You lied to me!" he rages. His face is purple and contorted, his eyeballs are bulging out of their sockets, and a vein is popping out of his neck.

He reaches in his pocket, pulls out the slip of paper with his license plate number on it, and sticks it right in front of my eyes. "What the fuck is this?!" he screams in my face.

"I-I don't know..."

He kicks me so hard it knocks the wind out of me. "This is my license plate number. You saw something. What did you see?"

I gasp, "I...I don't know what you're talking about..."

"You fuckin' liar! What the fuck did you see?!" he screams louder.

I start bawling.

Suddenly, he picks me up off the floor and lays me face down on a table.

Glancing around, I see that I'm lying on a table saw. Then hear a whirring sound—

He clamps one hand on the back of my neck, grabs hold of my hair with his other hand, and lifts my head up—so I'm facing the spinning saw blade. Then screams, "What the fuck did you see?!"

"Nothing…I swear to God…"

He pushes my face toward the blade! "Talk!"

Utterly terrified, I beg, "Oh, God…no…please…don't…"

He pushes me closer! "Talk! Or I'll saw your fuckin' face in two!"

"Don't!" I frantically struggle—

"Talk!"

The whirring blade is just inches in front of my eyes!

"Ahhh!" I scream hysterically!

The blade is almost touching my face!

I cry, "Your car!"

He pulls my face back.

Sobbing, I spill my guts. "I saw your car at the pool last night…"

"Where was you?"

"My Observatory…"

"What?"

"My Observatory."

"What the fuck are you talkin' about?"

"The turret on top of our house."

"You're lyin'! How could you see my license plate number from up there?"

"A rifle scope. I can see things far away through it…"

"You…you was spyin' on me. You shouldn't've done that…" His voice is quivering with rage.

I choke back the tears.

"Who'd you tell?"

"Nobody."

"You're lyin'."

"I swear it!"

He starts pushing my face toward the whirring blade again! "You fuckin' liar! Who'd you tell?!"

Clamping my eyes shut, I plead, "No! Please! I didn't tell anybody!"

He pushes my face so close to the whirring blade that I feel the wind of it!

I blubber, "I didn't! I didn't know if that was your license plate number. That's why I came here. To find out..."

He pulls my face back. "Is that yer bike I found by the barricade?"

I nod.

"Does anybody know you're here?"

I shake my head. Snot is bubbling out of my nose. Sniffling, I say, "I didn't tell anybody what I saw. I won't tell anybody. I swear to God. Please...please don't kill me."

He lifts me off the table saw and sets me on my feet.

I collapse on the floor, whimpering...

He unfastens the handcuff on one of my wrists and fastens it around the leg of the table saw. Then turns off the machine.

He goes to a workbench and roots around. Holding a big knife and a roll of duct tape, he comes toward me.

He's gonna kill me!

"Please! Don't hurt me!"

He unpeels a long strip of duct tape and cuts it off the roll with the knife. Crouches in front of me and holds my chin still. Presses the tape against my mouth and wraps it around my head until my mouth is taped shut.

"Don't mess with this gag. Or I'll saw your face off. You understand me, bo-oy?"

I nod.

He stands, walks out of the room, and shuts the door.

I listen—hear him stuff something under the door. Then don't hear him anymore.

He's gone.

He didn't kill me...

Maybe he's not gonna kill me. Maybe he's gonna keep me prisoner down here...

No, he isn't. He's gonna kill me sooner or later. He has to.

I gotta get out of here.

I roll over and kneel beside the table saw. Look at the handcuff fastened around the metal leg. Slide it up and down the leg.

Maybe I can lift up the leg and slip the handcuff off the end of it.

Squatting, I grip the base of the saw. Teeth clenched, grunting and groaning, I lift with all my might...

It doesn't budge.

Shit!

All of a sudden, I hear a noise up by the ceiling. Look up and see dryer duct poke through a hole in the wall.

What's he doing?

I hear a car start.

He's leaving. Where's he going?

Then hear the engine revving...

Soon, I smell car exhaust.

Oh, my God! He's gassing me!

I frantically scream—hear my muffled cries.

I claw frantically at the handcuff. Then twist and pull my hand as hard as I can. Something pops inside my wrist—a fiery pain shoots up my arm. I stop pulling.

I slide the handcuff up the leg of the table saw as far as it'll go. My eyes are just above the edge of the table. Looking desperately around the room, I spot the roll of duct tape lying on the table. Then spot the knife behind it.

I lunge for it but can't reach it. Stretching, my fingertips are just inches away.

I swing my leg up onto the table, hook my foot around the knife, and slide it within my reach. Then grab the knife.

I madly try to cut the chain between the handcuffs.

It's steel. You can't cut it.

Your hand. Cut your hand.

You gotta do it. Before you black out.

I look at the palm of my left hand—see where the handcuff is caught on the base of my thumb. Then press the blade of the knife against the skin right above the handcuff.

Do it.

I start cutting—feel a sharp pain.

Don't stop...

Moaning, I cut deeper and deeper.

Oh, God, it hurts.

I feel faint.

Dropping to my knees, I hold my head between them and take slow, deep breaths.

Do not faint...do not faint...

A pool of blood forms on the floor.

I set the knife down and try to slip the handcuff over my hand, but it won't go. Inserting my finger inside the incision, I feel the handcuff caught on the bone at the base of my thumb.

I place my hand on the floor, pick up the knife, and work it inside the incision until the blade is pressed against the bone.

Feel dizzy and hear a ringing in my ears...

Shake my head.

You gotta do it...before you pass out.

One...

Shut my eyes.

Two...

Clench my teeth.

Three!

I cut as hard as I can.

"Ahhh!"—I see gold spots dancing in front of my eyes and feel white-hot pain in my hand.

I writhe in agony on the floor, hands and feet twitching...

I feel my hand slip out of the handcuff—I'm free. Hold my hand up and stare at it. The thumb is dangling by the muscle and tendon. A gaping hole is where the thumb used to be. Pinkish-white bone is glistening inside red tissue, and a small geyser of blood is spurting from the artery.

You're gonna bleed to death.

I slap my hand over the wound. Then just sit here in shock— clutching the thumb in my hand, holding my hand against my chest, rocking back and forth. Feel warm blood running down my arm.

The gas!

Holding my wounded hand against my chest, I stagger to my feet. Cross the room and climb up on the workbench. Reach up and grab the dryer duct. Yank the tube through the hole in the wall into the room and throw it on the floor.

Get outta here!

I jump down off the workbench. Stumble over to the door and open it—see the rags stuffed under it.

Run across the room to the door and turn the doorknob—locked.

I glance around the room for some way out...

All I see are stone walls.

He's gonna come get you.

The knife.

I run back into the workshop. Grab the knife off the floor and run back out. Shut the door and stuff the rags back under it.

The door—barricade the door.

I spot a refrigerator against the wall—I could barricade the door with it. Slipping the knife under my belt, I try pushing the refrigerator with one hand across the room—it won't budge. Hurl my body against it—still won't move. Pressing my chest against it, I shove as hard as I can and swivel the refrigerator side to side. Slowly, I slide it across the floor until it is barricading the door.

Panting, I lean against the refrigerator and hold my throbbing hand against my chest. The front of my shirt is soaked with blood. Blood is smeared all over the refrigerator. I examine my hand. Blood is still running down my arm, but it's not spurting out anymore. I stagger back to the workshop door, grab a rag off the floor, and wrap it in a bandage around my hand. Then unpeel the long strip of duct tape around my head and wrap it around the bandage to hold it in place.

All at once, the room starts spinning in circles and a wave of nausea hits me. Then I vomit—it explodes out my mouth and nose.

Finally, I stop heaving. My nose is burning. Vomit is hanging from my lip. I spit.

I hear a noise at the other end of the room.

I freeze. What's that?!

I hear it again—a weird voice-like sound coming from behind stacks of newspaper.

I pull the knife out. Creep over there with the knife raised. Peek over the stacks of newspaper. It's so dark I can't see...

I go behind the stacks of newspaper. Straining my eyes, I see a small door back in the corner. I dash to it. Clenching the knife in my teeth, I grope in the dark for the doorknob. Feel a metal bolt. Unbolt it and jerk the door open. It's pitch black inside. The smell of shit comes pouring out.

Holding my breath, I duck my head inside. Feel in front of me. Touch a chain hanging down. Grab it and pull down. A light comes on.

"Oh...my...God..."

Huddled stark naked in the corner is this...this creature with a hideous face...

It squints at me.

The face in the tree fort flashes through my brain—

Dumfounded, I realize that's it...

It moves toward me.

I stagger backward out of the room.

I hear someone unlocking the door—Skarl!

I run to the refrigerator. Throw my body up against it with the knife clenched in my hand.

I hear him twist the doorknob again and again—trying to open the door. Then silence...

"Open the door."

I don't make a sound.

"Open the door, Mansfield. I ain't gonna hurt you."

Seconds go by...

"Mansfield—don't make me break down this door..."

More seconds go by...

"Open the fuckin' door!" he screams and starts furiously ramming the door.

I hold the refrigerator against the door with all my might. Hear the door straining...

Oh, God—he's gonna bust it down!

He stops.

I hear him lock the door. Strain my ears...

Don't hear him. He's gone.

I feel dizzy again. Brace myself against the refrigerator, holding my knife. Then feel like I'm going to vomit again.

I groan, "Oh, God, help me...somebody please help me..."

Out of the corner of my eye, I see that creature peeking at me over the stacks of newspapers.

I cry, "Please...help me. He's gonna kill me…"

Wham!

I hear the sound of Skarl hitting the door with an ax. I hurl myself against the refrigerator.

Wham!

Wham!

Wham!

A pickax smashes through up by the hinge.

"Oh, no!"

Wham!

Wham!

The top of the door breaks off the hinge.

"No!"

Skarl peeks through the crack with a gas mask on. Then rams that side of the door open, pushing the refrigerator toward me.

My rubber soles slide backwards on the cement.

"No! No! Please! No!" I scream.

Desperately glancing around, I see that creature lying on the floor in the corner—

All at once, it disappears through the wall.

I dash over there—see this hole at the base of the wall.

Drop my knife and dive into it—my shoulders get stuck...

Furiously twisting and squirming, I squeeze my shoulders through the hole, then my hips—

A hand grabs my foot and pulls me backwards!

I frantically kick! My foot slips out of my shoe and I break free.

I crawl on my belly as fast as I can through some kind of tunnel toward a faint light. Dive out of the tunnel and see light up above. Spot a skull on a pole.

I'm in the well.

I scramble to my feet. Then jump up and grab on to the rim of the well. My bad hand loses its grip—I fall back down.

I leap and grab on to the rim again. Fingers clawing at the concrete, toes slipping and sliding down the wall, I pull my chest up over the rim...swing my legs over...

The moon is shining through the open shed door.

I stand up and run out the door. Duck under a clothesline. Sprint across the back yard toward the fence. A hedge runs around the yard in front of the fence. I try to burrow through the hedge but get caught in thorns—

"Help! Somebody please help me!" I scream at the top of my lungs.

A floodlight comes on by the house.

I wriggle out of the thorns. Look desperately around the yard. Spot that creature in the moonlight back in the corner.

It disappears into the ground.

I run over there. In the grass is an open manhole. Crouching, I grope in the hole for the ladder...

Skarl bounds out of the garage. He spots me and raises his gun—

I jump into the manhole—fall through the air, land on my heels, and fall down on the cement.

I spot the sewer pipe and dive into it. Blindly scramble down the pipe on my hands and knees. See a dim light up ahead. Then come to the opening of the pipe. Peek up at the sewer grating—in case he's waiting up there to blow my head off.

Boom!—buckshot rips into my backside and I fly headfirst out of the pipe!

I lie on the concrete under the grating, thrashing around in pain—my butt and the back of my legs feel like they're on fire.

Boom!—buckshot ricochets off the walls and the gunshot reverberates through the pipe.

Get outta here!

I scramble sideways into the larger sewer pipe. Fall down. Ears ringing, I gingerly touch my backside—feel shreds of my jeans embedded in my flesh and a warm wetness…

Blood!

Oh, God! I'm shot.

I hear splashes coming toward me…a foot steps on me…then a hand feels my head…

I moan, "Help me…please…"

The splashes fade away back down the pipe…

I tell myself, "Get up…"

I get back up and try to walk…something's wrong with my leg…

My good hand feeling the wall, I limp down the pipe, dragging my leg behind me…

I visualize a black pool of water in front of me…

"Four laps…just four laps…"

Keep limping along…

I'm so thirsty I drop to my knees…cup some water in my hand and drink it…

"One more lap…just one more lap…"

I get back up and keep going…hobbling badly now…can't bend my leg…

Finally, I feel the opening of the pipe. Looking up, I spot two small, faint circles of light—the manhole cover.

This must be the intersection of Bird Cage Walk and Shady Lane.

All I gotta do is climb up the ladder and open the manhole cover.

But what if he's out there waiting for you?

Get farther away.

I feel pins and needles radiating down my leg…don't know if I can make it…

Go one more. Go to Painter.

I turn left and hobble down the pipe through the blackness…

"One more stroke...just one more stroke..."

My leg goes numb. I take a step with my good leg. Then drag my numb leg behind me...

Keep going and going...

Where am I?

I'm in a pitch-black pit of quicksand...it's sucking me down...slog through the quicksand...legs feel like they weigh a ton—

All at once, I stumble out of the pipe. Find myself lying on the cement, looking up at the manhole cover...

You made it. You made it to Painter.

Groping around on my hands and knees, I find the ladder...pull myself with my good hand up the ladder rung by rung...

When I reach the top of the ladder, I'm panting like crazy. Sweat is running down my face. My legs feel like rubber. I can't let go of the rung to lift up the manhole cover...

I climb up another rung and press my back against the manhole cover. Then push up and lift it open, and push it sideways—

Suddenly, my gimpy leg spasms—

I cling to the ladder...

"Don't fall...don't fall..."

Finally, the spasm stops. I climb up another rung and peek out...

Don't see anybody...no cars...

I look up and down the street. It's very dark since there are no streetlights. I spot a house with a light on inside a few doors down Shady Lane.

If you can just make it there...get help...

I climb out of the manhole and hobble down the street— dragging my leg. Reach the house and head up the driveway.

You're gonna make it.

All of a sudden, headlights appear on Bird Cage Walk. A car turns onto Shady Lane and drives slowly down the street...

Oh, God! It's Skarl! He's hunting me!

I hobble desperately across the front yard. Hide behind a bush at the corner of the house. Peek out.

He slows down to a crawl at Painter. Then stops next to the manhole. Shines a flashlight out his car window at the open manhole…

Oh, God! I should've closed it.

He pulls the car over to the curb and parks. Climbs out and walks over to the manhole. Then shines the flashlight around on the pavement—like he's looking for something…

The flashlight beam fixes on a spot on the pavement. Then slowly trails me down the street—

Oh, God! He's tracking my blood!

I madly hobble around the house and across the back yard…across the back yard of the house on Mapledale into its side yard…

Glancing back over my shoulder, I spot a flashlight shining around the yards—

I duck behind a bush against the house. Peek out.

The flashlight is coming closer…

I frantically look around for a hiding place. Spot a window well behind the bush. Jump into it and crouch at the bottom. Peek out.

The flashlight is coming straight toward me. I see Skarl's murderous face in the glow of his flashlight. I duck and crouch as low as I can in the window well.

What if he saw me?

I hear his footsteps running toward me. Hold my breath…

He stops near me…

Hear him wheezing…

My heart is pounding so hard I fear he'll hear it…

His flashlight shines through the bush right above me…

No!

The light passes over me…

Hear his footsteps going away…

Terror-stricken, I don't move a muscle. My leg starts shaking…then cramps…still I don't move…

Finally, my leg buckles, and I slump against the wall of the window well…

You're safe here. Hide here until morning…

After a while, my leg starts hurting again. Then my hand...

The pain gets worse and worse until it becomes unbearable.

I get back up and peek out. Don't see him...

I climb out of the window well. Crawl through the grass to the front of the house. Peer up and down Mapledale. Don't see him. Ponder crawling up on the front porch and ringing the door bell, but I'm terrified he'll see me and kill me before the police come.

I spot a red box on the telephone pole in front of the house—the fire alarm.

I crawl across the front yard...down the bank...across the sidewalk to the telephone pole...grab on to the telephone pole and stand up...

I feel hot prickly needles in my head and see black spots in front of my eyes...

"Don't black out."

Clinging to the box for support, I grope at the face of it...lift the cover...feel the lever and yank it—

The bell starts ringing loudly.

Terrified that Skarl will hear it, I try to stop the ringing but can't.

I spot a car parked a little ways down the street. Hobble over to it and dive underneath it. Lie in the gutter, peeking out...

Watch for his headlights...

Don't come back...please don't come back...

A light comes on in the house in front of the fire alarm. Then one comes on in the house across the street.

Somebody please come outside...

I hear a siren off in the distance...listen to it get closer and closer...

"Hurry up. Please, hurry up and get here..."

I see flashing lights on Parkview Circle—

Suddenly, a firetruck turns onto Mapledale and barrels up the street.

Lights are coming on in houses up and down the street.

The firetruck screeches to a halt at the fire alarm. Firemen pile out, looking for a fire...

I crawl out from under the car and cry, "Help! Help me! Over here! I pulled the fire alarm!"

They walk toward me. "Where's the fire?"

"There—there is no fire. Call the police. A man is trying to kill me..."

They shine their flashlights at me—see my blood-soaked shirt. One fireman tells another to radio for an ambulance and the police. They make me lie on my back in the grass. Then cover me with a fire coat. They prop my feet up—my one tennis shoe is missing.

I notice people standing around in their bathrobes and nightgowns—gawking at me.

One of the firemen kneels beside me. "Kid, what's your name?"

"Mansfield Delaney."

"Where do you live?"

"55 Mount Airy Lane. Please...don't let him kill me..."

"Who's trying to kill you?"

"Skarl. He lives in the last house on Bird Cage Walk. He's trying to kill me because I know he murdered Russell..."

"Who's Russell?"

"Russell Ealey. His stepson. He murdered him and dumped his body in Possum Run Pool to make it look like an accident. He tried to murder me because I saw it. He locked me in his basement and tried to gas me. I had to cut off my thumb to escape. See..." I hold up my wounded hand for the fireman to see. The bandage is soaked in blood.

"Jesus..." the fireman mutters.

I break down crying. Grabbing his arm, I beg, "Please don't let him kill me...he...he was hunting me..."

He puts his hand on my shoulder. "It's okay, kid. You're safe now. We won't let him hurt you."

I watch for Skarl. I'm terrified that he's going to come out of the bushes and kill me.

Soon, an ambulance arrives with its siren blaring and lights flashing. Attendants jump out, strap me on a gurney, and load me in the ambulance. As we drive away, I stare out the back window in shock...

CHAPTER EIGHTEEN

I'm floating on a raft at the seashore—drifting out to sea. Mom and Dad are standing on the beach—waving towels over their heads, hollering for me to come in. I paddle as hard as I can, but my arms feel like lead. I keep drifting farther and farther away. Mom and Dad become dots on the horizon...

"Mansfield...Mansfield..."

A woman is calling my name. Her voice sounds like a 45 record played at 33 speed.

I try to open my eyes, but my eyelids feel like they weigh a ton. They flutter open...

"I think he's coming around," she says.

A nurse is hovering over me. I'm in a bed with rails around it. I feel something binding my hand. Look and see a bandage. Instantly, I recall the pain and horror of cutting off my thumb.

I picture Skarl's murderous face. Fearful that he'll come to the hospital to kill me, I scream, "Don't let him get me!" I struggle to get up and run.

Dad appears out of nowhere. Holding me by my shoulders, he comforts me, "It's alright...it's alright..."

"Please, Dad, don't let him get me..."

"Who?"

"Skarl. He's trying to kill me."

"Calm down. Nobody's gonna get you. You're safe here."

I grab on to his hand with my good hand. "Please don't leave me."

"I won't."

Clutching his hand in mine, I fall back onto the bed and close my eyes. The bed feels like it's swirling. I break out in a cold sweat.

"Mansfield, do you know where you are?" Dad asks.

"Hospital."

"What day is it?"

I can't remember...

"Mansfield, what day is it?"

"I...I don't—"

I vomit. I'm so weak that I can't lift my head. They roll me onto my side. The puke runs out on the pillow.

The nurse lays a towel on the pillow, and I vomit into it. All that comes up is some spit.

"Here. Sip on this," the nurse says. She holds a paper cup filled with ice chips to my lips.

I sip it. Hold it down for a few seconds. Then vomit it up.

Dad says, "It's the anesthetic. It'll wear off shortly."

They keep making me sip on the water, and I keep vomiting it up. I feel something jagging my wrist and try to pull it out. Dad tells me to leave the IV alone.

Finally, I stop puking. Doc tells a nurse he wants to move me to a private room. They wheel my bed out of the recovery room. I hold on to Dad's hand through the railing. They wheel me down a maze of halls, up an elevator, past the Pediatrics sign, and down a hall into a room with one bed. They lift me and lay me down in the bed. When my backside touches the mattress, I cry out in pain. I have to lie on my side. Slowly, the pain dies down.

Dad lets go of my hand.

"Don't leave me!"

"I'm just shutting the door."

He comes back and takes hold of my hand.

Mom rushes into the room and to my bedside. Stroking my hair, she asks, "Doc, how is he?"

"He's been shot. He's lost a lot of blood, but he's gonna pull through."

"What—what happened?"

"I don't know. I haven't had a chance to talk to him. He just came out of surgery."

There's a knock on the door. Dad goes to see who it is. He comes back a minute later. "Deuce, it's the police. They wanna talk to you. Okay?"

I want the police to catch Skarl. I nod weakly.

Dad lets two cops in suits into the room. They introduce themselves as Detective Hansen and Detective Edwards and say they want to question me. Detective Hansen gets out a tape recorder, lays a microphone against my pillow near my mouth, and turns it on.

"Mansfield, tell us what happened—starting at the beginning."

I struggle to think...my mind is groggy...

Slowly, I tell them what happened—starting at the night I saw the car at Possum Run Pool. When I get to the part where Skarl put me on his table saw and pushed my face toward the blade to make me talk, Dad and Mom listen with horrified looks on their faces.

When I tell them that Skarl tried to gas me and that I had to cut off my thumb to get out of the handcuffs, I break down crying...

"Oh, dear God..." Mom cries.

Dad puts his arms around my shoulders, and Detective Hansen turns off the tape recorder. After I stop crying, I have to pee. The detectives go out in the hall while Dad helps me pee into a bed pan. Then they come back in and start the tape recorder again.

Detective Hansen asks, "What happened next?"

"Once I got loose from the handcuffs, I escaped from his workshop. But I was still locked in his basement. So I barricaded the door with a refrigerator. Then Skarl tried to break down the door with an ax—"

Suddenly, I remember the creature. "Then it showed me the way out."

"What?"

"I don't know...this...this...creature..."

The detective looks at me strangely. "What do you mean creature?"

"There was this creature locked in a closet in the basement."

"Was it human? Or an animal?"

I picture it in my mind. "Sort of human."

"Male or female?"

"Male. He was naked. I saw his penis."

"How old?"

"He's small. So he must be just a boy."

"Can you give me a description?"

"He has a hideous face."

"What do you mean hideous?"

"Uh…his face is really deformed…"

"How so?"

"Like…like bad birth defects."

"Right…"

"I let him out of the closet. Then he showed me the tunnel out of the basement. We escaped through it before Skarl could murder me…"

I explain about the well and the manhole in Skarl's back yard. And that we escaped through the sewer pipe.

"Where is this boy?"

"I don't know. He disappeared in the pipe."

In my mind, I hear the gunshots and the buckshot ricocheting in the sewer pipe. "That's where Skarl shot me."

I have trouble remembering what happened next—there's a black void.

"I remember climbing out a manhole on Shady Lane. I made a big mistake and didn't put the cover back on—which almost cost me my life. Skarl drove by in his car and saw it. He got out and tracked me by following my blood. He was hunting me. I hid in a window well. He came within a few feet of me. Luckily, he didn't find me…" My teeth start chattering.

Mom gets a blanket out of a closet and covers me.

The detectives question me for a long time. I tell them about the fire at school and that the police charged me with arson because my fingerprint was found on the matchbook. But I didn't do it. Russell Ealey did. I tell them that I gave him the matchbook at my house one day and that he was a pyromaniac. The police should check it for his fingerprint.

Detective Hansen shuts off the tape recorder. Scratching his head, he says, "Son, I've been a homicide detective for twenty years and that's the damnedest story I've ever heard."

"Do you believe me?"

"Yeah. Nobody could make up that story." With a grim face, he tells me and my parents, "We'll investigate it right away."

My parents tell the detectives that they fear for my safety while Skarl is free.

"We'll post a guard outside your son's door," Detective Edwards says.

"Will he have a gun?" I ask.

"Yeah."

As soon as the detectives leave, Dad asks, "Deuce, why didn't you just tell me—instead of going there alone?"

"I...I didn't think you'd believe me. Not without proof."

Dad sighs and looks away.

"Nobody would've believed me."

He looks at me with his doctor face. "You need to get some sleep. You heal when you're asleep."

But I can't go to sleep. I'm too scared Skarl will try to kill me. Dad tells me not to be afraid—he's here. And there's an armed policeman out in the hall. He sits down in a chair next to my bed. I make him promise not to leave my bedside if I fall asleep. Then keep checking to make sure he's still here...

I see my thumb in a pile of garbage. Maggots are burrowing into the flesh—

I wake up in a cold sweat. Look for Dad. See the chair is empty— he's gone. I panic and start hollering for him.

A policeman runs into the room. "Your dad had to leave. He was called to the emergency room."

Man, am I upset! I knew I couldn't trust him.

I lie awake watching the door for over an hour...

Finally, Dad comes back.

"You left," I say.

"I'm sorry, Deuce. I had to go to the ER—Skarl's been shot."

"What?"

"The police shot him."

"Is he dead?"

"No. But he's in critical condition. They're operating on him right now."

"He's here?"

"Don't worry. He can't harm you. Not in his condition."

"I hope he dies."

Later, there's a knock on the door. Dad goes to see who it is. He comes back a minute later with Detective Edwards. He tells Dad and me that the police got in a standoff with Skarl at his house after he took his wife hostage. It ended when the police shot him.

"Mansfield, I need to ask you some more questions," he says.

"Okay."

Detective Edwards asks me if Skarl's garage was locked when I went there. I tell him yes. Then he asks me how I got into the locked garage. I tell him about the day I went to Ealey's house and explain about the key in the knothole in the tree. He says that's how Skarl knew I was there. All the doors and windows on the first floor of the house and garage were wired to an alarm system inside the house. The alarm went off when I opened the door to the garage.

He questions me about Ealey. I tell him that Russell was scared to death of Skarl and said that Skarl had burned him with cigarettes. And that Russell said if he ever wound up dead, Skarl did it. Then tell him about Ealey's time bomb.

He says the police found a small room in the basement with human feces and urine on the floor but no boy. I explain that's where Skarl caged the boy. I unbolted the door and opened it, looking for a way out. That's when I let him out of his cage.

He says the police found two stones had been removed from the base of the basement wall in one corner, which made a hole to a tunnel that ran to an abandoned well. I tell him the boy must've removed the stones when I was holding the refrigerator against the door. We escaped through that hole. He says they're looking for the boy but haven't found him.

I tell him about seeing the deformed boy at my tree fort one night and following his footprints up the sewer pipe and almost drowning last fall. But nobody would believe me. I also tell him that I lost my Blancpain Fifty Fathoms watch in the pipe and that Ealey must've got it somehow.

After Detective Edwards finishes questioning me, he tells Dad they're going to try to question Skarl tomorrow morning—assuming he lives through the night. And they may need me to be a witness against him at his trial. Then he leaves.

Dad just sits in a hospital chair, staring at the floor. He looks kind of old. He takes off his glasses, rubs his eyes, and puts them back on.

"Deuce, I don't know what to say. I owe you an apology. I'm sorry for not believing you. I want you to know I love you and...and I don't know what I would've done had I lost you. I—I don't think I could bear it. And now all I want is for you to get well."

He sees me eyeing the bandage on my hand. "I'm sorry, but I'm afraid they couldn't save your thumb. Fortunately, it's your left hand. It shouldn't keep you from living a perfectly normal life."

"I'm deformed."

"Just be thankful you're still alive."

"I want it."

"What?"

"My thumb."

"What?!"

"I want it."

"Deuce—"

"Please."

"What for?"

"I don't know. I just want it."

"It'll decompose."

"No, it won't. Not if they put it in formaldehyde."

"This is crazy, Mansfield."

"I don't care. I want it. Where is it?"

"They've probably already disposed of it."

"Go get it."

"Mansfield, I'm not gonna—"

"Then I will." I struggle to get up.

"Okay. I'll go check on it."

"You promise?"

"Yes."

"Say it."

"I promise."

I lie back down. Dad leaves the room. I think about my thumb. God, is it depressing. I look at my bandaged hand. My wrist and forearm are swollen and black and blue. I wonder what it looks like underneath the bandage. It must look really gross. I start crying.

After a while, a nurse comes in. I quickly wipe my eyes. She unhooks my IV. Then a lady brings me a tray with ginger ale, a bowl of chicken noodle soup, and soda crackers. She asks me if I'm hungry. I shake my head. She sets the tray down on a hospital bed table in case I get hungry later.

I just stare out the window—wondering what my thumb looks like.

Dad comes back.

"Did you get it?" I ask.

"Yeah."

"Where is it?"

"It's being taken care of."

"You promise?"

"I promise." He looks at my food and frowns. "Deuce, it doesn't look like you've even touched your food."

"I'm not hungry."

"You gotta eat if you wanna get better."

I don't say anything.

Mom and Tecca come. They ask me how I feel. I tell them bad. They all sit around talking. The sound of their voices makes me drowsy. I doze off...

"Deuce...Deuce..."

"Huh?"

"We're gonna go," Mom says.

"I'll be back first thing in the morning," Dad says.

Instantly, I'm awake. "No. Don't leave me."

"There's nothing to be afraid of. You're safe. He—"

"Don't make me stay here alone. Not with him here."

"He can't hurt you."

"Did he die?"

"I don't know."

"Go check."

"Even if he's still alive, I guarantee you he's not in any condition to hurt you."

"Please," I beg.

"Doc, why don't you check? It'll make me feel better too," Mom says.

"Me, too," Tecca says.

"Alright, alright," Dad says.

He leaves. Mom sits beside my bed with her hand on my arm. Tecca tells me she's going to bake me some chocolate chip cookies.

Dear God…please don't let him live…make him die…

Dad comes back.

"Is he dead?" I ask.

"No. But he can't hurt you. Fritz Frontz said the bullet severed his spinal cord. They don't expect him to make it through the night."

"You're sure he can't get me?"

"Positive."

"But he's not dead."

"Mansfield, the man is paralyzed. How can he get you if he's paralyzed?"

"Are you sure?"

"Yes. He's on life support. You need to go back to sleep. The best thing you can do is sleep. Give your body a chance to heal. I'll check on you in the morning."

Mom kisses me, and everybody says goodnight. They leave.

I try to go back to sleep but can't. My hand and butt are killing me. I lie here whimpering. Finally, I can't take the pain any longer and call the nurse. She gives me a pain shot. It knocks me out...

I hear someone breathing in the hall...

Skarl!

I try to get up and run but can't—it's like my body has weights on it.

He creeps into my room and pins me down on the bed...

I'm on the table saw and he's shoving my face toward the saw blade—

I wake up—thrashing in bed, heart pounding. I lie awake with my eyes fixated on the door until dawn.

Finally, a nurse comes in. She takes my temperature, checks my bandages, and gives me some pain medication. I ask her if she knows if Skarl died. She says she doesn't know.

Dad comes in and asks me how I slept last night. I say terrible and tell him about my nightmare. I ask him if Skarl died. He says he doesn't know.

A lady brings scrambled eggs, toast, and bacon for breakfast. I don't touch it.

"Deuce, you have to eat," Dad says.

"I'm not hungry."

A doctor comes in. Dad introduces me to Dr. Larsen. He's the doctor who operated on me after the ambulance brought me to the emergency room. He asks me how I'm feeling today. I tell him worse. He checks my hospital chart and asks me if I'm feeling any pain or numbness in my hand or my buttock. I tell him pain—but not in my hand, in my wrist. He says that doesn't surprise him—my wrist was severely dislocated. He had to manipulate it back into place. I figure that must've happened when I tried to pull my wrist out of the handcuff. Then he undoes the bandage on my hand and checks the sutures. I don't look. Then he makes me roll over on my stomach, pulls down the bandage on the back of my leg, and examines my wound.

"Hmm...I don't see any signs of infection. When I cut off your pants, your hind end looked like raw hamburger. I had to extract twelve gauge OO buckshot and shreds of blue jeans from your butt.

You're gonna have a hard time sitting for a while. I'll prescribe some pain medication."

I'm embarrassed that I got shot in the butt. "Dr. Larsen, please don't tell people I got shot in the butt."

"Why not?"

"It's not cool. Like an arm or a leg. My friends will laugh at me."

Dr. Larsen scoffs. "Mansfield, you're lucky you got shot in the butt. That's the best place to be shot. There are no vital organs."

Later, Mom brings me a bag full of stuff—a brand new bathrobe, slippers, and a toothbrush. She takes one look at me and says she can't stand looking at the dried blood on me any longer. She leaves the room and comes back a minute later with a nurse. They take off my hospital gown. I'm stark naked with bandages on my butt. Man, is it embarrassing. The nurse is about twenty years old. They give me a sponge bath. I keep flinching—it hurts every time I bump my butt on the bed.

The hospital pages Dad and he leaves.

Mom and the nurse dry me off. Put a clean hospital gown on me. Mom makes me brush my teeth.

All of a sudden, Dad flies into the room. "They found the boy!"

"Really?"

"Yes. He's in a room right down the hall. I'm going down there now. I'll be right back."

A few minutes later, Dad walks into the room shaking his head. "Incredible..."

"You see him?" I ask.

"No. It's a circus freak show down there. Doctors and nurses and cops and reporters all over the place. But I talked to Dr. Clark, who's one of the doctors treating him. You were right, Mansfield. The boy is severely deformed. He has multiple birth defects, and his growth is extremely stunted. The reporters want to talk to you too, but I told them they'll have to wait until you're better."

There's a knock at the door. It's Detective Hansen. He tells Dad and Mom that he just got done questioning Skarl. He says Skarl confessed to everything. Gassing Russell. Locking the kid in the basement. Trying to kill me. Skarl said he had to kill me because I could put him in the electric chair—so instead, he put me in the gas chamber. He used carbon monoxide because it's difficult to detect. He planned on making my death look like an accident by smashing my skull against a tree at the bottom of Mount Airy Road, and then laying my bike at the base of the tree so it looked like I crashed into the tree.

"Are the police guarding him?" I ask.

"Son, he ain't goin' nowhere. He's paralyzed from the chest down. They're gonna hafta wheel him into the electric chair."

"Really?" Dad asks.

"The prosecutor said he'll be seeking the death penalty for the murder of the Ealey boy."

I'm glad to hear that. He can't harm me if they execute him.

Detective Hansen leaves.

A Chinese doctor comes into the room. Dad introduces me to Dr. Chang. He's going to run an EEG on me to make sure the carbon monoxide poisoning didn't permanently damage my brain. They put me in a wheel chair. It hurts so bad to sit that they have to put a pillow under my butt. They wheel me to the EEG room, where Dr. Chang makes me lie on a bed, attaches small metal discs with wires to my scalp, and reads my brain waves. When he finishes, he says it looks like everything is normal.

They wheel me back to my room and put me back in bed. A lady brings me a toasted cheese sandwich for lunch. I eat about two bites and set it down.

"Deuce, you gotta start eating," Mom says.

"I'm not hungry."

"I thought you love toasted cheese sandwiches."

"Food makes me nauseated."

Mom and Dad say they're going to stay all afternoon with me. They sit beside my bed. I fall asleep.

When I wake up, Mom is gone. Dad is sitting in a chair reading the newspaper.

"What time is it?" I ask.

"Five o'clock."

"I wanna go home. I hate this place," I grumble.

"Cheer up, Deuce. You're a hero." He holds up the newspaper.

I can't believe it—my picture is on the front page. They took it out of the Appleseed yearbook. The headline above it reads "Youth Rescues Boy Locked in Basement." Underneath it is a smaller headline that reads "Night of Terror." I ask him if I can read it. He hands me the paper and says he's going down to the snack bar to get something to eat.

I scan the front page. Look at a sequence of pictures—Skarl hiding behind Wanda and pointing his sawed-off shotgun at her in front of his house, then a man crouched at the corner of the garage shooting Skarl in the back, and then Skarl lying in a pool of blood in the driveway with Wanda sitting beside him handcuffed to him. The caption under the pictures reads "Photographs capture dramatic shooting: Ersel Skarl uses wife as human shield; then is shot by policeman." Above the picture is a headline that reads "Police Shoot Waterbury Man."

In the middle of the page is a picture of Russell Ealey. They took it out of the yearbook too. The headline above it reads "Skarl kills stepson; locks other stepson in basement for ten years." Underneath it is a smaller headline that reads "Prosecutor will seek death penalty."

First, I read the article about Skarl:

> **Ersel W. Skarl, 42, of 43 Bird Cage Walk, was shot by police during a hostage crisis at his home yesterday. After holding his wife at gun point for nearly nine hours, Skarl attempted to escape by using her as a human shield but was shot in the back by a Waterbury policeman. Skarl was rushed by ambulance to Waterbury General Hospital, where he is listed in critical condition in the surgical intensive care unit. Wanda Skarl, his 39-year-old common-law wife, escaped unharmed.**
>
> **At approximately 5:00 a.m. on Thursday morning, Waterbury police went to the Skarl residence to question him about the attempted murder of a Waterbury boy and reported gunshots in the neighborhood earlier in the night. Police parked their cruisers out of sight from the secluded house and approached it on foot with guns drawn.**

"We walked right into an ambush. When we reached the mailbox at the end of the driveway, he (Skarl) opened fire on us from a second-story window," Detective David Edwards told reporters.

Within minutes of the shooting, backup units of Waterbury police, Fairland County Sheriff's Department, and State Highway Patrol troopers surrounded the house and sealed off the area. Residents were evacuated from the immediate vicinity because of fear of gunfire.

With rifles mounted in windows, Skarl barricaded himself behind mattresses in the house. He then telephoned the Waterbury Police Department and informed police that he was holding his wife hostage and would shoot her if they attempted to storm the house. He remained holed up in the house while police tried to talk him into releasing his wife and surrendering.

The standoff came to a bloody climax Thursday afternoon when police lost telephone contact with Skarl. Fearing for Mrs. Skarl's safety, police fired tear gas through windows into the house in an attempt to force him out.

Minutes later Skarl emerged from the front door with his wife handcuffed to him. Using her as a human shield from police and brandishing a sawed-off shotgun, he moved across the front sidewalk to the garage. When he attempted to enter the garage, he was shot from behind by police officer Gerald Jenkins, who was hiding around the corner of the garage.

Authorities cordoned off the crime scene and maintained surveillance of the area during the night. Investigators were back at the scene this morning. Police said a search of the house uncovered a small arsenal of weapons and ammunition.

"The house was like a fortress," Detective John Hansen told reporters. Police said the doors and windows on the first floor of the house and the garage were wired into an electrical alarm system. The doors leading into the house and the basement were also specially reinforced and equipped with heavy-duty deadbolt locks.

Investigators questioned the unemployed electrician at Waterbury General Hospital this morning. Paralyzed from the chest down as a result of his bullet wound, Skarl told police he was waiting with a rifle at his bedroom window when police approached his house in the dark. He told them that he expected to be arrested after his twelve-year-old stepson, who had been kept locked in a closet in the basement for over ten years, escaped from the house late Wednesday night. Police said the "closet boy" was freed from his tiny cell by thirteen-year-old Mansfield Delaney who discovered the secret. Skarl said that after the two boys made their escape from the house, he vowed police would never take him alive.

Next, I read the article on Russell:

At a press conference hastily called late this morning, Fairland County Prosecuting Attorney Thomas Brown informed reporters that he will file first degree murder charges against Ersel Skarl sometime next week. He told reporters he will also seek the death penalty against Skarl.

As a result of their investigation, police allege that Skarl murdered his fifteen-year-old-stepson, Russell, late Tuesday and then attempted to make it appear like the boy accidentally drowned. Skarl confessed to the bizarre murder from his hospital bed at Waterbury General Hospital this morning. Paralyzed from the chest down from a gunshot wound sustained yesterday, Skarl told police that he "put the boy to sleep" by gassing him with exhaust fumes from his car.

"First, I got him drunk. Then I took him down in the basement and gassed him. I done it that way so it wouldn't leave marks," he admitted to police. He informed police that he used carbon monoxide poisoning because he had read it is difficult for the coroner to detect.

Skarl said that he ran a hose from the exhaust pipe on his car in the garage to the room in the basement where the boy was gassed. Police said that they recovered the hose in the basement.

He further told police that he put the boy's body in the trunk of his car and drove to Possum Run swimming pool, where he dumped the body in the pool. He then threw pool furniture and beer cans in the pool to make it appear like the boy accidentally fell in the pool and drowned while vandalizing it.

Fairland County Coroner Willard Oreweiler indicated that an autopsy will be performed on the Ealey boy together with blood tests over the next several days to determine that the cause of death was carbon monoxide poisoning.

Skarl told police that he killed his stepson in self-defense after the boy threatened to kill both he and his wife. Skarl said that the boy made the threat after he disciplined him for starting a fire in a restroom at school. Authorities at Johnny Appleseed Junior High School confirmed that a restroom had been set on fire Tuesday morning.

Skarl also confessed to police that he kept a twelve-year-old stepson locked in a tiny closet in the basement of his house for over ten years. Skarl told police that he "confined the freak for his own protection." Police said that the closet boy escaped from the house late Wednesday night. He was found by Patrolman John Barclay of the Waterbury Police Department scavenging garbage in the back yard of a house on Bird Cage Walk early this morning.

"When I first saw him, I couldn't believe my eyes. He didn't look like a human being because of his deformities. He was naked and filthy. I had a heckuva time catching him. He can really scoot," Barclay said.

Police said that the closet boy was taken to Waterbury General Hospital, where he was examined by doctors, cleaned, and fed.

Police said the tiny basement closet was littered with urine-soaked newspapers and reeked of human excrement.

"'When I found out that a human being had been imprisoned in there for over ten years, it hit me like a sledgehammer. I wanted to cry," Lieutenant John Hansen said.

Wanda Skarl told authorities that she gave birth to the boy, who she named Earl, on April 29, 1953, in Lorain, Ohio. She said that the boy's father was named William Ealey, and that he died in an industrial accident shortly before the boy was born. She said that the boy's birth defects are congenital.

The woman further told police that she met Ersel Skarl several months after the boy was born and that they moved to Waterbury and bought the home at 43 Bird Cage Walk with proceeds from William Ealey's life insurance policy. She said that Skarl rejected the boy and hid him from the outside world because of his deformities. She told police that Skarl would not allow her or Russell to speak the boy's name, and that Skarl called him "the freak." She said as soon as the boy was able to walk, Skarl locked him in the basement. She said that her husband refused to spend any money on medical treatment for the boy, and he allowed him to eat only table scraps and dog food.

When asked why she never notified police, she said that she "feared for her life."

Wanda Skarl is being held in the Fairland County Jail. Police said they will meet Monday with Prosecutor Thomas Brown to determine what charges will be filed against the mother.

I save the article on me for last:

The Skarl house at 43 Bird Cage Walk looked like any other house in the quiet, middle class neighborhood, but it held a bizarre secret in a dark, squalid closet in the basement—a severely deformed boy. Thirteen-year-old Mansfield Delaney, of 55 Mount Airy Lane, discovered the secret and freed the "closet boy" late Wednesday night.

"The boy is a real hero. I don't know many cops who could've survived what he did," Detective David Edwards told reporters.

The article tells the whole story. It reads that I "walked right into a death trap" after I triggered the alarm inside Skarl's house. And that Skarl "cold-bloodedly handcuffed me to a table saw and tried to gas me."

"Like a coyote gnawing off its paw to escape a steel-jawed trap, Delaney escaped the handcuffs by cutting off his thumb with a knife."

It tells how I "rescued the closet boy from his infernal cage." And how he revealed "the secret tunnel out of the basement only seconds before Skarl would have hacked the Delaney boy to death with an ax."

It reads that Skarl shot me "in the backside" in the sewer pipe. Which is not true. He really shot me in the back of the leg.

It tells how the closet boy and I escaped through a pitch-black maze of underground sewer pipes. It reads: "In shock and bleeding profusely, the Delaney boy limped and crawled for two blocks underground before climbing out a manhole."

It reads that "the Delaney boy hid in the window well of a house on Mapledale Avenue while the cold-blooded killer relentlessly tried to hunt him down like an animal."

It ends with: "Mansfield Delaney's night of terror finally came to an end when he was rescued by Waterbury firemen after he tripped a fire alarm on Mapledale Avenue."

I stare blankly out the window. God, am I depressed. The world knows that I'm missing a thumb now.

Dad brings me a cheeseburger, fries, and a chocolate milkshake from the snack bar. He thinks I might like this better than the hospital food. I tell him I'm not hungry. He says they won't let me go home until I start eating. I force myself to eat some.

After supper, Mom comes. She says the phone has been ringing off the hook all day with people asking about me. She says Grandma Colleen called. So did Aunt Susan and Uncle Dave. And all their friends.

Tecca, Meg, and Calley come. Tecca baked me a batch of chocolate chip cookies, but I don't feel like eating any. Everybody tries to be real nice to me—even Meg. Nobody says anything about my hand—not even Calley. Meg and Calley want to turn on the TV and watch "Seventy-Seven Sunset Strip," but I don't feel like it. The place in the theme song where they click their fingers will remind me that I'll never be able to click my fingers on my left hand again.

After my sisters leave, Dad and Mom say they have some good news—I don't have to go to the psychiatric hospital in Cleveland. Prosecutor Brown himself called Dad and apologized and said he's dropping all charges against me. And he'll be charging Skarl with attempted murder. Then they say Mr. Petty called and said they're dropping the expulsion and reinstating me in school.

Before my parents leave, Dad asks me if I'm still feeling pain in my hand or leg. I tell him only when I bump them. He says he's going to discontinue my pain medication, but he's going to prescribe a mild sedative to help me sleep. I ask him what a sedative is. He says it's just a sleeping pill.

After they leave, I can't stand it any longer—I have to see what my hand looks like. I carefully unwrap the bandage and look at my wound. Oh, God is it gross. Where my thumb used to be, there's just a line of black stitches holding together flaps of skin. The wound is an ugly red color and fluid is oozing out. I stare at it horrified. All I can think is I'm deformed now. No girl will want to be touched by my hand. I start crying and can't stop. The tears run down my face onto my pillow.

At ten the nurse checks my bandage, takes my temperature, and gives me my sleeping pill. I have horrible nightmares all night. First, I dream an airliner up in the sky is going to crash. I keep running but can't get away from it. Then I dream the hospital gets me mixed up with another kid who's supposed to have brain surgery to remove a brain tumor. I tell everybody they have the wrong guy, but nobody will believe me. They hold me down on the operating table, clamp the gas mask over my face, and turn on the ether. I black out but can still feel the doctor hacking away on my brain with his scalpel. Then I dream a wasp flies inside my ear—I can feel it buzzing around inside my head. I'm petrified that it's going to sting my brain. I wake up with a splitting headache and don't go back to sleep.

Dr. Larsen sees me again when he makes his rounds the next morning. He looks at my chart and asks me why I'm not eating. I tell him I'm not hungry.

Later, Dad tells me Dr. Isch will be seeing me this afternoon. I ask him what for. He says he's worried about the traumatic effect Skarl has had on me. He thinks it might help if I talk to Dr. Isch about it. I tell him I don't want to talk to Dr. Isch about it—I don't want to talk to anybody about it anymore.

Detective Edwards stops in to see me. He says he recovered something that belongs to me and sets my Fifty Fathoms watch on the bed table. He says they found it in the well with Ealey's other stuff. They don't need it as evidence. And they recovered my bike— they found it hidden in the woods by the barricade. Dad can pick it up at the police station. Dad thanks him. I realize I'm supposed to be grateful, but I don't really care. I can't wear the watch—not with my bandage. And I won't be able to ride my bike anymore—how can I hold on to the handlebars?

Detective Edwards tells Dad and me that he talked to Wanda Skarl yesterday afternoon to tie up some loose ends. She told him that the tunnel I escaped through used to house the waterline from the well house to the basement. When Skarl hooked up the house to city water in 1954, he disconnected the waterline and patched the hole in the basement wall with stone. Then Detective Edwards says he thinks he knows how the closet boy was getting out of the basement last fall. Wanda told him that around Halloween last year Skarl punished Russell because he discovered that Russell wasn't bothering to bolt the door on the closet boy's cage after he took him his supper. For some unknown period of time, the closet boy was able to escape his cage into the locked inner room of the basement. Once free, he was able to work loose the stones in the patched hole and escape into the well house. From there, he used the sewer pipes to scavenge for food.

After Detective Edwards leaves, Dad says it was nice of him to bring me my watch—I should've thanked him. He asks me if I want to put it on. I look at the bandage on my left wrist and tell him I can't. He says I can wear my watch on my right wrist and offers to help me put it on. I shake my head.

When Dr. Isch arrives, Dad says he has to go check on some patients and leaves.

"You're quite the celebrity now. I read about you in the Cleveland Plain Dealer," Dr. Isch says.

I shrug.

"How are you doing?"

"Okay."

"So you found your ghost, huh?"

"I guess so."

"Do you wanna talk about it?"

"No." I don't trust him—not after what happened at the library.

"Are you having any problems as a result of what happened?"

"No."

"Your father told me you're having nightmares, you're not eating, and you appear to be depressed. These are all behaviors typically exhibited by people who have been victims of trauma or violence. It's really important for you to work your way through the experience by talking about it—so the nightmares will go away."

I tell him about my nightmares and how I'm afraid to sleep at night. He just listens.

"And I feel bad about losing my thumb."

"That's normal. You'll have to go through a period of grief just like a person grieves the loss of a loved one. But, ultimately, it shouldn't stop you from living a normal, productive life."

"That's easy for you to say—it's not your thumb."

"True."

"I feel like I'm deformed. I'm scared girls will be grossed out by it."

"I'm aware of a woman who's happily married to a man who lost an arm and a leg."

Dad comes back. Dr. Isch says he wants to see me again in two weeks and gives me a prescription for something that'll help me sleep.

After supper, Dad, Mom, and Meg visit me. They turn on the TV and stay until nine thirty. At ten the nurse brings me a new pink pill. I figure it's what Dr. Isch prescribed. I pop the pill and hope I don't have any nightmares tonight. Then turn off the light.

When I comb my hair, I look at myself in the mirror.

I recoil in horror…

My eyes are bulging. My face has a gaping hole from my upper lip into my nose. I have no ears.

My hands are claw-like appendages.

Oh, my God! I'm the closet boy…

I struggle to wake up from my dream but can't...

Help!

My eyelids crack open. I can't move or speak. I dread that I'm the closet boy...

I sit up in bed. Trembling, I realize I was stuck in a nightmare that I'm the closet boy. The nightmare seems so real that I climb out of bed, hobble into the bathroom, and look at myself in the mirror to make sure I have a normal face.

"That was the worst nightmare yet," I tell myself in the mirror.

I go back to bed. I look at my watch on the bed table. It's three thirty in the morning. I'm dead-tired, but I'm afraid to go back to sleep. I'm afraid I'll return to that nightmare.

I try to put my watch on my right wrist using only my index and middle finger on my left hand. After several minutes, I succeed.

I crawl out of bed and sit in a chair on my right butt cheek with the light on waiting for morning to come. It seems like it's so far away. I start crying, but no tears come out—I fear that I'm cracking up.

I turn on the TV, but all the stations have signed off. I read all the newspaper articles again. Then the rest of the paper. I'm still sitting in the chair—reading my hospital chart—when the nurse comes in at seven.

She notices that I'm reading my chart. Annoyed, she snatches it from me and says, "I'll take that." She brings me another pink pill.

"Nurse, what's in the pink pill?" I ask. I'm wondering if it made me have that nightmare last night.

"Medicine," she answers. "How do you feel?"

"With my hands," I reply.

She gives me a dirty look. "Have you had a bowel movement?"

"No. I think the medicine makes me constipated."

"You need to take your medicine."

I fake like I take the pill but really go flush it down the toilet after the nurse leaves—I'm not taking any more pills. Then climb back in bed and try to sleep a little now that it's light out.

At eight thirty Dad comes. He says everybody else will be coming after church. He takes one look at me and says, "You look terrible. You have dark circles around your eyes. How'd you sleep last night?"

"Horrible."

"Did the medicine help?"

"No. It made it worse. What is it?"

"It's a mood elevator. Give it time."

"Dad, what's gonna happen to the closet boy?"

"I don't know. The paper said Fairland County Children's Services got emergency custody of him on Friday."

"Can I see him?"

"They're not letting the public see him—only his doctors."

"I have a right to see him. I set him free."

He thinks about it for a moment. "Okay. I'll go check on it."

A few minutes later, Dad comes back and tells me I can see the closet boy—he cleared it with Dr. Clark.

"Right now?"

"Yep. Chris said this is a good time because things are pretty quiet down there."

Dad helps me put on my robe and slippers. Then pushes me down the hall in a wheelchair to Room 411.

"Come on in, fellas," Dr. Clark says.

Dad slowly wheels me into the room. The lights are off and the window blinds are shut tight. Dr. Clark is sitting in a chair in the dark. He's wearing a doctors' headlight on his forehead—using it to read a medical chart.

Dad introduces me to him.

"Mansfield, I read about you in the paper. You're quite the hero. How ya doin'?" Dr. Clark asks.

"Okay."

"You're probably wondering why I'm sitting here in the dark. He doesn't like the light. It hurts his eyes."

I look at the closet boy's bed—it's empty.

"He's hiding behind the chair. He's extremely shy. Extremely afraid of people—especially adult males," Dr. Clark explains. "Actually, he's like a wild animal. The medical literature refers to them as 'feral boys.' "

345

Dr. Clark and Dad talk medicine. Dr. Clark tells Dad "the boy appears to have a fairly severe case of Treacher-Collins Syndrome." Then he explains to us, "It's a birth defect characterized by underdeveloped facial bones and tissues. Lower eyelid colobomas. Conchal type microtia.

"The good news is he doesn't seem to have any breathing or feeding problems, which is the primary concern with Treacher-Collins.

"The bad news is the boy is severely malnourished. He's only three feet eight inches tall and weighs only fifty-one pounds. He's twelve and has the physical development of a six to eight-year-old. He has bow legs and chest deformities. I suspect he may have Ricketts as a result of malnutrition and lack of sunlight and exercise.

"I'm afraid he's been abused too. The x-rays show multiple old fractures."

I see the closet boy peeking out at me from behind the chair over in the corner—gnawing on his hand.

"Hi," I say.

He steps out from behind the chair and creeps toward me—holding a teddy bear.

"You remember me?" I ask.

"He can't talk. And he doesn't hear very well," Dr. Clark says.

The closet boy creeps up to my wheelchair and squints at me. I can't tell if he recognizes me. I try not to stare at him but can't help it. This is the first time that I've seen him close-up. God, is he weird-looking! Since his forehead, cheekbones, and jaw are underdeveloped, his eyeballs protrude and his whole face droops badly. And his ears are tiny and missing parts. His hair is like cobwebs, his skin like watery milk.

All of a sudden, he drops his teddy bear, bends over, and looks closely at my Fifty Fathoms. Then starts feeling my watch. I notice that his hand has no thumb. Repulsed by his deformity, my impulse is to pull my hand away, but then I remember my missing thumb and don't. Using my teeth, I take off my watch and let him play with it. I swear he recognizes it.

"He likes your watch," Dr. Clark says.

"What's gonna happen to him?" I ask.

"Fairland County Children's Services is gonna take him to Rainbow Baby and Children's Hospital in Cleveland tomorrow for further testing and evaluation."

"What about after that?"

"Well, physically, I think his growth is permanently stunted, although he has put on two pounds in two days. The kid loves ice cream.

"I don't think he's mentally retarded. His EEG was normal. Intelligence is usually normal with Treacher-Collins. I just think he's extremely developmentally delayed as a result of being locked in that basement all those years. But with hearing aids and speech therapy, who knows? Maybe he'll learn to talk someday."

"His facial deformities..." He sighs and says, "He has severe ocular hypertelorism and severe hypoplasia of his cheek bones, jaw, and chin. He's looking at a lot of bone reconstruction surgery.

"Will he ever be psychologically normal?" He shakes his head and says, "After what that—pardon my language—son of a bitch put him through and these kind of birth defects, I doubt—"

Water is splashing on the floor.

"Whoops!" Dr. Clark says.

The closet boy is peeing on the floor.

Dr. Clark hollers for a nurse.

Soon, a nurse runs into the room. There's a big puddle of pee on the floor. She gets a towel and mops it up.

Dad says we better go. He starts to wheel me out of the room.

"Hey—you forgot your watch," Dr. Clark says.

"That's okay. He can keep it."

"You sure?"

"Yeah."

On the way down the hall, Dad asks, "Deuce, are you sure you wanna give him your watch? I'll go back and get it for you."

"I'm sure. He saved my life. It's the least I can do."

When I get back in my room, I think about my watch—how the closet boy seemed to recognize it. I figure he must've found it in the sewer pipe, and then Russell must've taken it from him.

347

Everybody in my family, except Tecca, visits me after church. I ask Mom to bring me a deck of cards. Dad makes me get out of bed and walk around. After a while, my butt hurts, so I let Calley push me in the wheelchair around the pediatric ward.

"Deuce, let's go see the monster."

"What monster?"

"The closet boy."

"Calley, he's not a monster. He saved my life."

"Meg says he looks like a monster."

"He's just deformed. Monsters are imaginary creatures in horror movies. They're not real."

I direct her to the closet boy's room. I'm hoping we can say hi to him, but his door is closed.

After supper, Mom brings me the deck of cards. At bedtime Mom and Dad go home. A nurse brings me my pills. I fake like I take them and go flush them down the toilet. I've made up my mind—I'm not going to sleep tonight. I can't take any more of those nightmares. I'm going to stay up and play solitaire all night. I sit in bed and play solitaire on the bed table. But I'm so tired I can't stay awake...

It's night. I'm riding my bike down a dark, creepy road...see a dead end sign...

Even though I can't see him, I know Skarl is waiting for me in the darkness at the barricade...

I put on the brakes, but my bike is pulled by an invisible force toward him...

I'm petrified...

At the last second, my bike takes off...

I float over Skarl's outstretched hands...up...up in the sky...

I turn and pedal toward Luna Lake Park. Up above, the stars are sparkling. Down below, the street lights are shining. Floating in midair—man alive! It's exhilarating...

I float over the houses and trees. I'm high enough to clear the power lines and nobody can see me.

I pedal to Luna Lake. Float a few feet above the water across the lake. Hover over the island...

I head toward Arcudy's house. On the way, I see a light on in a room on the second story of a house. Pedal to the window and peek in. A pretty girl is lying in the bathtub. She starts to stand up—

A nurse wakes me up. It's morning. The bed light is still on and the cards are spread out on the bed table. I try to go back to my dream but can't.

They bring me my breakfast. Man, am I hungry. I eat all of it and want more.

Dad arrives. I show him that I ate all of my breakfast and ask if I can go home. He tells me Dr. Larson said I have to have a bowel movement before he'll release me from the hospital. I hobble into the bathroom and try to go but can't. I can't sit down on the toilet seat because it presses against my wound. And I'm constipated. I hobble back to my bed and tell Dad I'm constipated. He says he'll prescribe me a laxative.

"What about my thumb?" I ask.

"What about it?"

"Did you get it?"

"Uh...no. You still want it?"

"Yes."

"What're you gonna do with it?"

"Put it on my shelf. Kenny Ward had his appendix out. He keeps it in a jar on a shelf in his room."

"Your mother thinks it's a bad idea. She thinks it's morbid."

"It's my thumb. I want it."

"Alright."

Later in the morning, a reporter named Roscoe Smith from the Waterbury Times asks to interview me. He tells Dad and me the newspaper wants to do a human interest story on me. He says all you ever hear about today's youth is their rebellion and juvenile delinquency. They want to do a story on what's good about young people. Dad asks me if I feel up to it. I say okay. Mr. Smith asks me questions about what he calls my "night of terror." As I tell the story again, my heart races and I breathe fast.

Shaking his head in disbelief, Mr. Smith says, "Truth is stranger than fiction."

I nod.

"You should write a book about it. It'd be a best seller."

"Maybe I will someday."

"So…how does it feel to be a hero?"

I shrug. "I don't know. I…I didn't feel like a hero…not while it was happening…"

"What did you feel?"

"Terrified."

"Mansfield, I hafta ask you a painful question. That was quick-thinking to cut off your thumb while Skarl was gassing you. How were you able to do it?"

I flashback as if it were happening again. I gulp. "It was either cut off my thumb or die. I wanted to live."

"That took courage."

I feel pain in my hand. "Uh…I don't wanna talk about it…"

"Okay. What do you think should happen to Ersel Skarl? Should he get the death penalty?"

"I don't wanna talk about him either."

"What do you wanna talk about?"

"The closet boy."

"What about him?"

"He saved my life. I'm glad I set him free. That makes it worth it."

"Worth what?"

"Losing my thumb."

Mr. Smith asks me some questions about my family, school, and interests. "Mansfield, what do you wanna be when you grow up?"

I think about his question. "I thought I wanted to be a Navy frogman. And a professional scuba diver. But I don't know now. I might wanna be a doctor."

"What kind of doctor?"

"A plastic surgeon. Fix kids' birth defects."

After the interview is over, Mr. Smith shakes my good hand. "Good luck in your future endeavors, Mansfield."

After lunch, Jack Arcudy peeks in my room. With a big grin on his face, he says, "Hey, man!"

"Come on in, Jack. Man, am I surprised to see you. I thought you're not allowed to associate with me."

"I told my mom I had to come see you. She said it probably wouldn't hurt this one time. She figures me and you can't get in trouble at the hospital. I had to sneak past the lady at the desk. She said I couldn't visit you by myself. I had to be accompanied by an adult. So...how ya doing?"

"Okay."

"Deuce, everybody's talking about you. Man, you're famous! The paper said Skarl shot you."

I nod.

"So...how's your butt, man?"

I roll my eyes.

"Of all the places to get shot, you get shot in the butt."

"For your information, I didn't get shot in the butt. I got shot in the back of the leg."

Laughing, he razzes me, "You got two buttholes."

"Spare me, Jack."

"Man, you're lucky he didn't kill you."

I nod. "Hey, Jack, let me ask you something. Did Skarl call your house the night he caught me? I told him you and me were stealing beer out of his garage. He said he called your house to check my story. You know if he did?"

Arcudy's jaw drops like he just remembered something. "That night Dad woke me up and said there was a man on the phone named Mr. Smith accusing me of stealing beer out of his garage. Dad told him that was impossible because I was home in bed sound asleep. Was that Skarl?"

"Yeah. It had to be him."

"Damn...I don't believe it. A murderer actually called my house. So are you afraid of him trying to kill you here at the hospital?"

"No. My dad says he's paralyzed. He's on life support."

"Damn, Deuce, you were right all along about the ghost. Except he wasn't really a ghost."

"He's a closet boy."

"The paper said he's badly deformed. What's he look like?"

"It's hard to describe. The bones in his face are underdeveloped. He looks sort of like a cross between a cicada and a warthog."

"Weird. So how's your hand? Does it hurt?"

"This is strange, Jack. Sometimes I feel pain in my missing thumb."

"Huh...that is strange."

"I haven't showed it to anyone. It's gross. You wanna see it?"

"Yeah, I guess so."

I peel back the bandage and show him the wound.

He looks at it curiously. "It's not as gross as I thought it would be. Do they make artificial thumbs?"

"I don't know."

"Deuce, it's a helluva story. We should make it into a movie."

"A horror movie. Maybe Ghoulardi would show it."

"Stay sick," Jack says like Ghoulardi.

A nurse comes in. She says if I want to go home, I have to get up and move around. Moving in slow motion, I crawl out of bed and put on my bathrobe and slippers.

Arcudy and I go out in the hall. I limp down to the elevator—my leg is killing me. I spot a wheelchair in a sitting area and sit down in it.

"Hey, wanna go visit Skarl?" Arcudy asks.

"That's not funny."

"We can pull the plug on him."

I snicker.

"Hey, I got an idea. Let's go find the operating room," he suggests.

"Okay."

He wheels me into the elevator. I remember the way to the recovery room. We stand outside the doorway in the hall, listening to a lady moaning and puking. The problem is I don't know how I got from the operating room to the recovery room since I was unconscious.

We go down the hall a ways. Come to two great big automatic doors. A sign on one of them reads "DO NOT STAND IN RED AREA." There's red tile on the floor in front of the door.

"I think the operating room is in there," I say.

"I wonder what the sign is for…"

"It's to keep nosey people like you from looking in."

Arcudy looks around—doesn't see anybody. Then walks up to the doors and peeks through the crack between them.

"See anything?" I ask.

"I don't—"

Wham! The doors fly open and knock Arcudy backwards on his butt.

A nurse and orderly wheel a patient out of surgery. The orderly asks, "What are you boys doing here?"

"Nothing," Arcudy answers. He gets up off the floor and wheels me away.

We go back to my room. I picture Arcudy getting knocked on his butt by those automatic doors and can't help but laugh.

Rubbing his forehead, he says, "Quit laughing. It's not funny."

Arcudy goes into the bathroom. I stand in the doorway and watch him look at his head in the mirror. He already has a lump on his forehead. He touches it gingerly.

"I hafta go to the bathroom," he announces.

"Pee or poop?"

"Pee."

"Can you poop?"

"What for?"

"So I can get out of this place."

"I'll try."

"Don't flush it."

I get back in bed.

After a while, Arcudy comes out of the bathroom. Grinning, he tells me, "Mission accomplished."

"Thanks. You're a true friend."

"Don't mention it. That's what friends are for."

Dad and Mom come. They don't look too happy about Arcudy being here but don't say anything. He takes one look at them and says he better get going. He beats it out of here.

Dr. Larsen comes.

"Dr. Larsen, I had a bowel movement. I left it in the toilet if you wanna see it."

"That's okay. I'll take your word for it."

He says he's going to release me. He checks my wounds, changes my bandages, and gives me instructions about how to take a bath and stuff.

"Any questions?" he asks.

"Dr. Larson, do they make artificial thumbs?" I ask.

"I know they make artificial hands. I don't know about thumbs. I'll look into it for you."

"Thanks."

Mom brought me clothes and new tennis shoes. She helps me put on Bermuda shorts and a T-shirt. She slit the sleeve so it'll go over my bandaged hand. It feels pretty good to be dressed again. I don't feel so much like an invalid.

An orderly comes into my room with a brown paper bag. "This is for Mansfield Delaney."

"That's me."

Looking strangely at me, she hands me the bag.

I tell my parents I have to take a leak. I take the bag into the bathroom and open it. My thumb is in a jar filled with clear liquid. But it doesn't look like I remember it. It's a weird gray color and all wrinkled and looks like it shrunk. I sigh...

Dad calls me. In the room, a nurse is waiting for me with a wheelchair.

"I can walk," I tell her.

"I hafta take you in the wheelchair to the lobby. Hospital rules."

I sit down in the wheelchair with the bag in my lap.

The nurse wheels me down to the lobby and parks me in the waiting area. Dad goes to get the car. She and Mom wait at the front door for Dad to pull up.

A kid is sitting in a chair next to me. He looks like he's about ten or eleven years old. His mom is over at a desk filling out papers.

"Hey kid. Wha'cha here for?" I ask.

"I'm having my tonsils taken out."

"You scared?"

"Nah. They said there's nothing to be scared of. I get to eat ice cream afterward."

"Oh, yeah? Well, that's what I was here for. And that's what they told me." I open up the paper bag and pull out the jar with my thumb in it. "Look what they did to me."

He stares at the jar. "What's that?"

"My thumb." I hold up my bandaged hand.

His jaw drops.

Out of the corner of my eye, I see Dad pull up out front. The nurse comes to get me. I drop the jar back in the bag. "Whatever you do, don't let them cut off the wrong organ."

ACKNOWLEDGMENT

I want to thank my good friend, Mark Smith, who held the umbrella for me when I took the picture of the sewer pipe in the pouring rain in South Park and never let me forget that a thriller must have some body count.

I also want to thank my good friend, Bob Castor, a career prosecuting attorney, who helped me get the courtroom and plea bargaining scenes right.

ABOUT THE AUTHOR

Michael Justus Murray was a lawyer who metamorphosed into a writer.

OTHER NOVELS BY
MICHAEL JUSTUS MURRAY:

WILD HORSES OF CURRITUCK
FOUR-BOOK SERIES

Made in United States
Troutdale, OR
07/16/2024

21258138R00219

Biblical Discipleship:

Essential Components for Attaining Spiritual Maturity

Biblical Discipleship

Essential Components for

Attaining Spiritual Maturity

Todd M. Fink

Biblical Discipleship
Essential Components for Attaining Spiritual Maturity

by
Todd M. Fink

Published by Selah Book Press

Cover Illustration Copyright © 2016 by Selah Book Press
Cover design by Selah Book Press

ISBN:
ISBN-13: 978-1-944601-02-7

Library of Congress Control Number: 2015921340

First Edition

ABBREVIATIONS

ESV	English Standard Version
NIV	New International Version
NKJV	New King James Version
NASB	New American Standard Bible
NET	New English Translation

Acknowledgement

My prayer in writing this book was that it would be something the Lord and I did together. I can honestly say that I felt God's grace and direction throughout the process. He gave me ideas and brought things to mind in such a way that let me know He was involved.

I also desired that this book would be biblically based because I wanted to allow the Lord to speak as much as possible. For this reason, this book contains a great deal of Scripture.

Thus, I want to acknowledge God for His help and give Him all the glory for this book. I believe it was He who gave me the idea to write it and the strength and grace to complete it. May He receive all the praise and glory for any role this book might have in His Kingdom.

Endorsements

As president of a Bible college and seminary, I am regularly asked if there is a discipleship book that I can strongly recommend. Thanks to Todd M. Fink, I finally have an answer. *Biblical Discipleship* addresses one of the greatest needs in the modern church. It takes into account the current cultural situation and the effects of bad theology, while suggesting practical strategies for personal growth. This book is, no doubt, going to push the ball forward.

 —— Dr. Braxton Hunter, Ph.D. President of Trinity
   Theological Seminary

To be a Christian is to be a disciple. To grow as a Christian demands pursuing the life of discipleship. Todd M. Fink has devoted his life to cross-cultural ministry and helping people know and grow in Christ. His many years of experience in the ministry and devotion to the Scriptures have made him a man with great wisdom on this vital topic. I'm thankful he has written this helpful resource to help God's people grow.

 —— Dr. Erik Thoennes, Ph.D. Professor of Theology/Chair
   Undergraduate Theology at Biola University/Talbot
   School of Theology; Pastor at Grace Evangelical Free
   Church, La Mirada, California

Todd M. Fink's *Biblical Discipleship: Essential Components for Attaining Spiritual Maturity* will prove to be a valuable resource to many who are interested in growing a deeper devotion to Christ. Fink opines an analysis of the major problems/issues in the contemporary Evangelical church that he believes are hindrances to a healthy discipleship focus. He offers a corrective vision for those who desire to go against this Evangelical sub-culture, as he describes it, and be faithful to God's call on their lives.

 —— Dr. David Talley, Ph.D. Professor/Chair Old Testament
   Department, Biola University

Table of Contents

Foreword

By Dr. Braxton Hunter, Ph.D.

Much of the modern church is spiritually malnourished. Contributing to this daunting dilemma are the realities of neglected, theologically corrupt, poorly devised, half-hearted and shallow forms of what some call discipleship. This is not an overstatement.

If it's not the result of an obvious human effort to distort the Christian teaching, much of the blame rests with the Western Evangelical proclivity to offer a consumer-driven church experience. Rather than choosing a local congregation based on doctrinal perspectives and spiritual growth possibilities, it's now common for individuals to join an assembly because of the amenities it offers. This sort of thinking has been suggested to the community by the local church herself. "Come visit us. We have a great _____!" One can fill in the blank with any number of services or benefits: praise band, exercise classes, gymnasium, coffee bar, and so on. It's not that there's anything wrong with these things. It's just that many local congregations have entered into an invisible contract with the community that says, "We are valuable, primarily because of these benefits," instead of one that says, "We will train you in the truth."

In other cases, the reason for this poor spiritual diet is spiritual fatigue. It seems hard enough for church leaders to care for the needs of a congregation of believers. Doing proper discipleship and training congregants to disciple each other is a time-consuming project that requires great effort and discernment. This hindrance is particularly the case for ministry leaders and churches in ministry contexts that require the majority

1

of their efforts to be spent on evangelism. However, a proper emphasis on discipleship can bolster those other efforts. More discipleship breeds more servants and more evangelism.

Nevertheless, it is often the case that the lack of rich and robust discipleship is because of an ignorance of how to accomplish it. Simply put, many ministry leaders and individuals need specific instruction on this vital matter. What they ultimately need is an explanation of how to reach spiritual maturity in their lives.

Fortunately, Todd M. Fink has provided us with just that. Though the shelves of Christian bookstores are replete with discipleship training materials, *Biblical Discipleship* is a welcome addition. It is unique in its clarity and insight. As a practical minister and an academic, I consider this book to be required reading.

Dr. Braxton Hunter, Ph.D.
President of Trinity Theological Seminary

2

Introduction

Today, we have many ways of defining success in life. Some define it as being a sports hero, others as being wealthy, others as being popular and well liked, and still others as being happy. How does God define success? He defines it as being spiritually mature!

How do we become spiritually mature? There's only one way, and it's called discipleship. However, statistics show that discipleship is in a state of crisis today. Many Christians are not growing in Christ and are stuck in the process of reaching spiritual maturity. A Barna study reveals that almost nine out of ten senior pastors of Protestant churches assert that spiritual immaturity is one of the most serious issues facing the church.[1]

Sadly, what discipleship meant in the time of Christ and what it means today is vastly different. Moreover, the importance Christ and the Apostles gave to discipleship is also stunningly different than the importance many Christians and churches today give it.

Unlike the disciples who had much of Scripture memorized, a whopping 81% of Christians today don't read their Bibles regularly. Unlike Christ's disciples who were "Fishers of Men," 61% of believers today have not shared their faith in the past six months. And sadly, unlike Christ and the Apostles who made discipleship the central focus of their ministries, 81% of pastors today have no regular discipleship programs in their churches. Discipleship is being neglected today, and the consequences are crippling many Christians and churches. This book hopes to change that!

---

[1] C. S. Lewis Institute, *Sparking a Discipleship Movement in America and Beyond,* cslewisinstitute.org, http://www.cslewisinstitute.org/webfm_send/210, Accessed 08/19/2015.

Chapter 1 focuses on the state of discipleship today and exposes the sad truth that it's in crisis mode. Chapter 2 reveals 13 key factors contributing to the lack of discipleship today. Chapter 3 defines biblical discipleship based on central phrases Christ used in His ministry. Chapter 4 brings to light 14 essential components of the discipleship-making process that must be understood and practiced in order to attain spiritual maturity. Chapter 5 provides practical, "how-to" help for growing in Christ. It includes self-assessment tests for measuring your level of spiritual maturity in each essential component of discipleship and gives hands-on, useful ideas for taking steps toward spiritual maturity.

This book contains a great deal of Scripture, of which some you probably have read before. However, I want to encourage you to slow down, be reflective, and allow God to speak to you afresh. God's Word is living, so no matter how many times we've read a verse, if we'll ponder and allow it to sink in, God will bring new insights and change to our lives.

Discipleship is a command for all believers and is our highest calling. This book provides biblical help for fulfilling this calling and seeks to discover what God says about genuine growth in Christ. It's both an informative book and a "how-to" book. It deals with the barriers that are hindering discipleship, and offers practical help for overcoming these barriers and attaining spiritual maturity.

So, are you ready to grow? Would you like to be pleasing to God? Would you like to fulfill the reason for which you've been created? Would you like the full blessings of God in your life? Would you like to become spiritually mature? Would you like to hear Christ's words, "Well done, good and faithful servant," when you arrive in heaven? If so, this book is for you.

Chapter 1

The State of Discipleship Today

In This Chapter

1. God's View of Discipleship Versus Today's View of Discipleship

2. The Lack of Discipleship Today

3. The Consequences of Neglecting Discipleship

1. God's View of Discipleship Versus Today's View of Discipleship

Dallas Willard, in his book *The Great Omission*, makes an incredible observation regarding the importance of discipleship when stating that the word "disciple" occurs 269 times in the New Testament, but "Christian" is only found three times.[2] Willard defines discipleship as the foundational aspect of what it means to be saved and be a true follower of Christ.

Anthony Robinson, in his article "Follow Me," picks up on Willard's statement and believes that because the word "disciple" occurs 269 times in the New Testament, it defines the mark of a genuine believer.[3] Robinson also contends that the church today is focusing primarily on conversion and neglecting the way of life here and now, which is discipleship.[4]

What Is Discipleship?

Discipleship is the process of becoming like Christ in our nature, character, values, purposes, thoughts, knowledge, attitudes, and will. In other words, it's the process of becoming spiritually mature. It lasts a lifetime and isn't relegated to a temporary study or dedicated class taken for a time and ended. Bill Hull claims, "It's not a program or an event; it's a way of life. Discipleship is not for beginners alone; it's for all believers for every day of their lives."[5]

---

[2] Dallas Willard, *The Great Omission* (HarperCollins, Kindle Edition, 2009-10-13), p. 3.
[3] Anthony B. Robinson, *The Renewed Focus on Discipleship: 'Follow Me'* (Christian Century, 124 no 18 S 4 2007, pp. 23-25. Publication Type: Article. ATLA Religion Database with ATLASerials. Hunter Resource Library), p. 23, Accessed 12/10/2014.
[4] Ibid., p. 23.
[5] Bill Hull, *The Complete Book of Discipleship: On Being and Making Followers of Christ* (The Navigators Reference Library 1, 2014, NavPress, Kindle Edition), Kindle Locations 436-437.

Discipleship Is the Only Way to Spiritual Maturity

Discipleship is the vehicle God uses to make us spiritually mature. There is no other way! It's the pathway we must follow in order to be transformed into the image of Christ and reach spiritual maturity. Through discipleship, God grants us life, love, joy, peace, healthy minds, healthy relationships, healthy families, and healthy churches. It's our life's calling and the highest purpose to which we can give ourselves.

Howard Hendricks went so far as to claim, "When a person makes a profession of faith and ... is never taken through a formal discipleship process, then there's little hope of seeing genuine spiritual transformation."[6]

To the degree we are committed to discipleship will be the degree to which we attain spiritual maturity. To the degree we neglect our commitment to discipleship will be the degree to which we suffer destruction, devastation, and eternal loss.

The Role of Discipleship in the Ministry of Christ

I've had the splendid privilege of standing on the mountain where it's believed Christ gave the Great Commission. It's called Mt. Arbel and has a spectacular view of the Sea of Galilee. It's estimated that Jesus spent 70% of His ministry time around the

Sea of Galilee, so Mt. Arbel would have been the perfect backdrop for Christ to have spoken some of His last and most important words to His disciples: "Go therefore and make

---

[6] C. S. Lewis Institute, *Sparking a Discipleship Movement in America and Beyond,* cslewisinstitute.org, http://www.cslewisinstitute.org/webfm_send/210, Accessed 08/19/2015.

disciples of all nations, baptizing them in the name of the Father and of the Son and of the Holy Spirit, teaching them to observe all that I have commanded you. And behold, I am with you always, to the end of the age" (Matt. 28:19–20).

A large part of Christ's earthly ministry entailed making disciples. During this time, He invested heavily into 12 men. Then, upon leaving, He commanded these men to go into all the world and make disciples.

The Great Commission Mandate given by Christ contains the summation of His purpose for the original disciples and all believers for all time. It would make sense then that the essential components of the discipleship-making process should be fully understood and obeyed. Unfortunately, there appears to be an immense lack of understanding in this vital area, and the gap between the command and implementation is alarmingly wide.

The Role of Discipleship in the Ministry of the Apostles

In addition to Christ's Great Commission Mandate to make disciples, the Apostle Paul sums up his, and the other Apostles' life work with the following statement: "Him we proclaim, warning everyone and teaching everyone with all wisdom that we may **present everyone mature in Christ**. For this I toil, struggling with all his energy that he powerfully works within me" (Col. 1:28–29). This verse highlights the central purpose and work of the Apostles, which was to present every person spiritually mature in Christ.

Because presenting every person mature in Christ would logically incorporate discipleship, and because the Apostles took seriously Christ's command to make disciples, it's safe to say that the summation of the Apostles' work was discipleship as well.

Therefore, in the Great Commission, we see the summation of Christ's work and purpose, and in Colossians 1:28–29 we see the summation of the Apostles' work and purpose, each focusing on discipleship as its central theme. For this reason, the role of discipleship is paramount in the life of every believer and church, if we're going to be serious about becoming spiritually mature.

How Discipleship Is Viewed Today

Unlike the high priority Christ and the Apostles gave to discipleship, and despite Christ's command to be and make disciples, discipleship today is a low priority in the life of most churches and Christians. John Stott affirms this trend by acknowledging, "The state of the church today is marked by a paradox of growth without depth. Our zeal to go wider has not been matched by a commitment to go deeper."[7]

In the majority of churches today, discipleship is not a central focus nor are there clear strategies for making disciples taking place. A recent survey done by Richard J. Krejcir reveals that 81% of pastors have no regular discipleship program or effective effort of mentoring their people to deepen their Christian formation.[8]

Many of these churches seem to have the idea that discipleship isn't that important, or they hope it will somehow be fulfilled through preaching, Sunday School, home Bible studies, and small groups. However, most churchgoers aren't involved in all these activities, and even if they were, most of these activities aren't primarily focused on discipleship. The passion for fulfilling the commandment to make disciples through an intentional, strategic process seems to be lacking in the average Evangelical church today.

When the average churchgoer is asked what the discipleship process should entail, head scratching and bewilderment sets in.

---

[7] Ibid., Accessed 08/19/2015.
[8] Richard J. Krejcir, *Statistics on Pastors: What is Going on with the Pastors in America?* 2007, www.churchleadership.org/apps/articles/default.asp?articleid=42347&columnid=4545, Accessed 08/06/2015.

David Platt shares his concern about Christians today and their understanding of discipleship: "If you ask individual Christians today what it practically means to make disciples, you will likely get jumbled thoughts, ambiguous answers, and probably even some blank stares."[9]

Many believe discipleship is optional or only applies to an elite group of radical Christians. Moreover, for the average churchgoer who does believe discipleship applies to them, most think of it as general growth that takes place through casual church attendance and occasional Scripture reading. It's not thought of as a comprehensive, intentional set of disciplines that must be seriously engaged in for discipleship to occur.

There's even significant debate regarding the essential components of the discipleship-making process among leading theologians. While there has been ample discussion and much written on the topic, there's still significant confusion surrounding what discipleship should involve.

Spiritual Maturity: the Overlooked Elephant in the Room

God's purpose for us in this life is that we would be transformed into the image of Christ: "For those whom he foreknew he also predestined to be **conformed to the image of his Son,** in order that he might be the firstborn among many brothers" (Rom. 8:29). Discipleship is how God transforms us!

Sadly, for most Christians and churches, this is not their focus. As a result, the elephant in the room (what we should be focused on) is neglected and overlooked. While becoming spiritually mature should be a believer's highest goal and priority in life, for the vast majority of Christians, becoming spiritually mature isn't even on their radar screen.

---

[9] David Platt, *Follow Me* (Carol Stream, Tyndale House Publishers, 2013), p. 69.

2. The Lack of Discipleship Today

You would think that the importance of the Great Commission Mandate to make disciples (Matt. 28:19–20), and the focus on discipleship by the Apostles as the means to present every person spiritually mature in Christ (Col. 1:28–29), would bring to the forefront the importance of discipleship. However, many adversarial winds are pushing against it, and the church is in a perilous state of health as a result.

Bill Hull states, "I find it particularly puzzling that we struggle to put disciple-making at the center of ministry even though Jesus left us with the clear imperative to 'make disciples.'"[10] Again, Hull sounds out, "Let's start with the obvious. Discipleship ranks as God's top priority because Jesus practiced it and commanded us to do it, and his followers continued it."[11] However, discipleship is being neglected and discarded by many today as optional or only for the "radical believer." As a result, most Christians today are spiritually immature.

Neglected Warnings

In addition to the importance Christ and the Apostles placed on discipleship, a number of well-known pastors, authors, and theologians have sounded the alarm over the years as well. Unfortunately, their voices seem to be lost in our busy, fast-paced lifestyles.

Dietrich Bonhoeffer, in his classic work *The Cost of Discipleship*, strives to help us understand that genuine salvation

---

[10] Bill Hull, *The Complete Book of Discipleship: On Being and Making Followers of Christ* (The Navigators Reference Library 1, 2014, NavPress, Kindle Edition), Kindle Locations 441-443.
[11] Ibid., Kindle Locations 458-459.

should include discipleship. He states, "Cheap grace is the preaching of forgiveness without requiring repentance, baptism without church discipline, communion without confession, absolution without personal confession. Cheap grace is grace without discipleship, grace without the cross, grace without Jesus Christ, living and incarnate."[12]

Bonhoeffer claims that today we often exchange discipleship with emotional uplifts instead of steadfast adherence to Christ's command regarding discipleship and its role in every believer's life.[13] Bonhoeffer cries out, "If our Christianity has ceased to be serious about discipleship, if we have watered down the gospel into emotional uplift which makes no costly demands and which fails to distinguish between natural and Christian existence, then we cannot help regarding the cross as an ordinary everyday calamity, as one of the trials and tribulations of life."[14]

Dallas Willard makes the lack of discipleship a major theme in two of his books, *The Great Omission* and *The Spirit of the Disciplines*. In *The Spirit of the Disciplines,* Willard claims, "One specific errant concept has done inestimable harm to the church and God's purposes with us — and that is the concept that has restricted the Christian idea of salvation to mere forgiveness of sins."[15] Willard also makes a bold statement regarding the importance of discipleship when he declares, "I believe there is nothing wrong with the church that a clear minded resolute application of discipleship to Jesus Christ would not cure."[16]

Bill Hull has also recently weighed in on the lack of discipleship today and states, "Unfortunately, non-discipleship

[12] Dietrich Bonhoeffer, *The Cost of Discipleship* (SCM Classics, Hymns Ancient and Modern Ltd., Kindle Edition, 2011-08-16), Kindle Locations 604-606.
[13] Ibid., Kindle Locations 1265-1267.
[14] Ibid., Kindle Locations 1265-1267.
[15] Dallas Willard, *The Spirit of the Disciplines* (2009-02-06, HarperCollins, Kindle Edition), p. 33.
[16] Dallas Willard, *Transformed by the Renewing of the Mind* (Lecture given at Henry Center for Theological Understanding, 2012), https://youtu.be/jkzeUcnzYbM, Accessed 10/15/2015.

'Christianity' dominates much of the thinking of the contemporary church. In addition to sucking the strength from the church, Christianity without discipleship causes the church to assimilate itself into the culture. And sadly, whenever the difference between the church's and culture's definition of morality ceases to exist, the church loses its power and authority."[17]

Hull goes on to warn, "Many mainline churches depart from orthodoxy because they reject the absolute authority of Scripture. However, many Evangelical churches pose an even more subtle danger by departing from the gospel that calls on all believers to be disciples and follow Christ in obedience."[18]

George Barna is also concerned about the lack of discipleship today. He says, "My study of discipleship in America has been eye-opening. Almost every church in our country has some type of discipleship program or set of activities, but stunningly few churches have a church of disciples. Maybe that is because for many Christians today, including Christian leaders, discipleship is not terribly important. If we can get people to attend worship services, pay for the church's buildings and salaries, and muster positive, loving attitudes toward one another and toward the world, we often feel that's good enough."[19] Barna stresses, "The strength and influence of the church are wholly dependent upon its commitment to true discipleship. Producing transformed lives and seeing those lives reproduced in others is a core challenge to believers and the local church."[20]

Greg Ogden is also troubled by the lack of discipleship today;

---

[17] Bill Hull, *The Complete Book of Discipleship: On Being and Making Followers of Christ* (The Navigators Reference Library 1, 2014, NavPress, Kindle Edition), Kindle Locations 341-344.

[18] Ibid., Kindle Locations 341-344.

[19] George Barna, *Growing True Disciples: New Strategies for Producing Genuine Followers of Christ* (Barna Reports, p. 20, 2013, The Crown Publishing Group, Kindle Edition), p. 18.

[20] Ibid., p. 21.

he says, "If I were to choose one word to summarize the state of discipleship today, that word would be superficial. There appears to be a general lack of comprehension among many who claim Jesus as Savior as to the implications of following him as Lord."[21]

Cal Thomas, a Christian syndicated columnist and social commentator, calls on Christians to look at the quality of our discipleship instead of directing our indignation at the moral decay. He writes, "The problem in our culture isn't the abortionists. It is not the pornographers or drug dealers or criminals. It is the undisciplined, undiscipled, disobedient, and biblically ignorant Church of Jesus Christ."[22]

---

[21]Greg Ogden, *Transforming Discipleship: Making Disciples a Few at a Time* (2010, InterVarsity Press, Kindle Edition), p. 21.
[22]Ibid., p. 22.

3. The Consequences of Neglecting Discipleship

The level of spiritual maturity among many Christians today is extremely concerning. This is primarily due to the misunderstanding of what discipleship entails and the neglect of an intentional, strategic plan for making disciples. While there are many positive things happening in the church today, there's a grave concern in the area of discipleship. According to recent statistics, the state of the average Christian and Evangelical church of the Western world today is in crises mode and suffering the consequences of neglecting discipleship. Consider the following stats:

- Only 19% of Christians read their Bibles daily or regularly (this means 81% don't read their Bibles daily or regularly).[23]
- About 40% of Evangelical Christians rarely or never read their Bibles.[24]
- Most Christians are biblically illiterate. Fewer than half of all adults can name the four Gospels, and many Christians cannot identify more than two or three of the disciples.[25]
- Atheists, agnostics, and Mormons scored better on biblical literacy than Evangelical Christians (Pew Research).[26]
- Of self-identified Christians, 27% believe Jesus sinned while on earth (Barna).[27]
- 61% of Christians have not shared their faith in the last six

---

[23] Russ Rankin, *Study: Bible Engagement in Churchgoer's Hearts, Not Always Practiced*, Nashville, 2012, http://www.lifeway.com/Article/research-survey-bible-engagement-churchgoers, Accessed 07/23/2015.
[24] Ibid., Accessed 07/23/2015.
[25] Albert Mohler, *The Scandal of Biblical Illiteracy: It's Our Problem*, Christianity.com, http://www.christianity.com/1270946, Accessed 08/18/2015.
[26] C. S. Lewis Institute, *Sparking a Discipleship Movement in America and Beyond*, cslewisinstitute.org, http://www.cslewisinstitute.org/webfm_send/210, Accessed 08/19/2015.
[27] Ibid., Accessed 08/19/2015.

months.[28]

- 48% of Christians have never invited a friend to church.[29]
- Only 25% of church members attend a Bible study or small group at least twice a month.[30]
- The average Christian prays somewhere between 1–7 minutes a day.[31]
- 81% of pastors have no regular discipleship program or effective effort of mentoring their people to deepen their Christian formation.[32]
- 20% of Christians say they rarely or never pray for the spiritual status of others.[33]
- 42% of Christians say they find it difficult to find time on a regular, disciplined basis to pray and read the Bible.[34]
- 18% of Christians say they don't have a fixed pattern of prayer, but only pray when the chance or need arises.[35]
- 60% of Christians pray on the go.[36]

---

[28] Jon D. Wilke, *Churchgoers Believe in Sharing Faith, Most Never Do,* 2012, Lifeway.com, http://www.lifeway.com/Article/research-survey-sharing-christ-2012, Accessed 08/19/2015.

[29] Jon D. Wilke, *Churchgoers Believe in Sharing Faith, Most Never Do,* LifeWay.com, http://www.lifeway.com/article/research-survey-sharing-christ-2012, Accessed 08/04/2015.

[30] Richard J. Krejcir, *Statistics on Pastors: What is Going on with the Pastors in America?* 2007, www.churchleadership.org/apps/articles/default.asp?articleid=42347&columnid=4545, Accessed 08/06/2015.

[31] Deborah Beeksma, *The Average Christian Prays a Minute a Day; Prayer by the Faithful Helps Their Relationships,* GodDiscussion.com, 2013, Accessed 07/27/2015. Victory Life Church, VictoryLifeChurch.org, *Intercessory Prayer—Praying Always,* http://www.victorylifechurch.org/pdf/Intercessory_Praying_Always.pdf, Accessed 08/19/2015.

[32] Richard J. Krejcir, *Statistics on Pastors: What is Going on with the Pastors in America?* 2007, www.churchleadership.org/apps/articles/default.asp?articleid=42347&columnid=4545, Accessed 08/06/2015.

[33] Jon D. Wilke, *Churchgoers Believe in Sharing Faith, Most Never Do,* 2012, Lifeway.com, LifeWay Research, http://www.lifeway.com/Article/research-survey-sharing-christ-2012, Accessed 08/19/2015.

[34] Cath Martin, Evangelicals Admit Struggling to Find Time for Daily Bible Reading and Prayer, 2014, Christianity Today, www.christiantoday.com/article/daily.bible.reading.and.prayer.is.a.struggle.for.aany.evangelicals/36765.htm, Accessed 08/18/2015.

[35] Ibid., Accessed 08/19/2015.

[36] Ibid., Accessed 08/19/2015.

- Only 26% of Christians feel they have been equipped by their church to share their faith with others.[37]
- Numerous studies show that self-identified Christians are living lives indistinguishable from non-Christians (Jim Houston).[38]
- Only half of Christians believe in absolute moral truth (Barna).[39]
- 5% of Evangelical Protestants are living with their partner outside of marriage.[40]
- 14% of Evangelical Protestants are divorced or separated.[41]
- 39% of Protestant pastors believe it's okay to get a divorce if a couple no longer loves one another.[42]
- Church discipline, an intensive form of discipleship for believers involved in serious sin, is virtually non-existent.[43]
- Churches today are often growing without depth (John Stott).[44]

Now to be fair, some of these stats fluctuate between various studies, but if they are even remotely accurate, the problem is still alarming. The stats reveal that the spiritual state, as a whole, of Evangelical churches and Christians in the Western world today is

---

[37] Ibid., Accessed 08/19/2015.
[38] C. S. Lewis Institute, *Sparking a Discipleship Movement in America and Beyond,* cslewisinstitute.org, http://www.cslewisinstitute.org/webfm_send/210, Accessed 08/19/2015.
[39] Ibid., Accessed 08/19/2015.
[40] Pew Research Center, *Evangelical Protestant,* Pewforum.org, http://www.pewforum.org/religious-landscape-study/religious-tradition/evangelical-protestant, Accessed 08/19/2015.
[41] Ibid., Accessed 08/19/2015.
[42] LifeWay Research, *Views on Divorce Divide Americans,* 2015, LifeWayResearch.com, http://www.lifewayresearch.com/2015/08/12/views-on-divorce-divide-americans, Accessed 08/19/2015.
[43] R. Albert Mohler Jr, The Disappearance of Church Discipline–How Can We Recover? Part One, 2005, AlbertMohler.com, www.albertmohler.com/2005/05/13/the-disappearance-of-church-discipline-how-can-we-recover-part-one, Accessed 08/20/2015.
[44] C. S. Lewis Institute, *Sparking a Discipleship Movement in America and Beyond,* cslewisinstitute.org, http://www.cslewisinstitute.org/webfm_send/210, Accessed 08/19/2015.

very troublesome and distant from what God intended. Michael Ramsden is disturbed about this and claims, "The American church is dying, not from the lack of evangelism, not from lack of resources, but from lack of effective discipleship."[45]

According to the stats, we're reaping damaging consequences for neglecting discipleship. As a result, most Christians are stuck in their growth in Christ and are failing to reach spiritual maturity. Dennis Hollinger cries out, "I'm convinced that what the world needs is not just more converts, but men and women who are authentic disciples of Christ, who love Christ with their whole being, and who will take their faith into the trenches of every sphere of life."[46]

Some things we can neglect and not adversely affect our spiritual health, but some things are foundational and critical to get right: understanding discipleship and the essential components of the discipleship-making process must be gotten right. Therefore, it's paramount we understand what's negatively affecting our commitment to discipleship. By neglecting discipleship, we reject God's nature and image, choosing instead to retain the image of sin and remain spiritually immature.

We can be certain that if the summation of Christ's and the Apostles' ministries was the command to make disciples, then Satan and his demonic cohort will do all they can to confuse and deter us in the process. We must not let them succeed!

Conclusion to Chapter 1

In this chapter, we analyzed the state of discipleship and spiritual maturity today, concluding that they're in critical condition and being grossly neglected. In the next chapter, we'll investigate 13 key factors contributing to this neglect.

---

[45] Ibid., Accessed 08/19/2015.
[46] Ibid., Accessed 08/19/2015.

Chapter 2

Key Factors Contributing to the Neglect of Discipleship Today

In This Chapter

1. The Distractions and Cares of Life

2. Materialism and the Pursuit of Wealth

3. The Refusal to Pay the Cost of Discipleship

4. The Lack of the Fear of the Lord

5. Being Ashamed of Total Devotion to Christ

6. The Effects of Prosperity Gospel Theology

7. Misunderstanding Heavenly Rewards

8. Misunderstanding the Purpose of Discipleship

9. The Lack of Church Discipline

10. The Belief in Salvation Without Discipleship

11. The Belief in Salvation Without Obedience

12. The Belief in Salvation Without Works

13. The Belief in Grace Without Effort

In chapter 1, we analyzed the state of discipleship and spiritual maturity today, concluding that they're in critical condition and being grossly neglected. In this chapter, we'll investigate 13 key factors contributing to this neglect. This will be a hard-hitting chapter, so prepare yourself to be challenged!

---

1. The Distractions and Cares of Life

Many Christians today are not devoted disciples of Christ because there are way too many distractions in their lives. They claim they just don't have the time for the level of dedication that discipleship requires. People are busy these days with important things in their lives: work, school, getting ahead, acquiring an attractive home, having nice cars, sports, enjoying the pleasures of life, and so forth. While these things are not necessarily bad in and of themselves, they can be if they are getting in the way of being a devoted disciple of Christ.

Many of these good and important things can also be thorns in our lives that choke out the Word of God and His plans for us. Christ told a story about four kinds of soils (four kinds of responses from people who hear His Word). Upon each soil (heart), fell God's Word, and each heart had a different response:

> And he told them many things in parables, saying: "A sower went out to sow. And as he sowed, some seeds fell along the path, and the birds came and devoured them. Other seeds fell on rocky ground, where they did not have much soil, and immediately they sprang up, since they had no depth of soil, but when the sun rose they were scorched. And since they had no root, they withered away. **Other seeds fell among thorns, and the thorns grew up and choked them**. Other seeds fell on good soil and produced grain,

some a hundredfold, some sixty, some thirty. He who has ears, let him hear" (Matt. 13:3–9).

A few verses later, Christ clarifies that the thorny soil represents the cares of this life that choke out the Word of God: "As for what was sown among thorns, this is the one who hears the word, **but the cares of the world and the deceitfulness of riches choke the word, and it proves unfruitful**" (Matt. 13:22).

Notice that the seed (the Word of God) which fell among the rocky ground and thorny ground did show life for a while, but then died out. Only the last soil produced fruit. Notice too, that for those who did produce fruit, some produced less than 100%. It's very likely that even among the good soil (lives of committed believers), the reason they only produced 30% or 60% was due to the thorns (distractions) in their lives that inhibited their fruitfulness.

This parable reveals the importance of God's Word as the key to fruitfulness in a Christian's life. However, many Christians are too busy to read it because of busyness. We should take a serious inventory of the distractions in our lives that are choking out God's Word and causing us to produce little or no fruit and eliminate them.

Today, We Have Unprecedented Distractions Pulling Us Away from Christ

In our age, we have a record amount of options facing us. Gone are the days when life was simpler, less tangled, and had fewer details and problems. We're now faced with countless impulses and stimuli from things like sports, social media, texting, phone calls, emails, Internet, TV, magazines, billboards, friends, work, entertainment, and on and on. People have a hard time focusing on God because they are "on" and connected all the time.

Television alone has revolutionized the Western world in staggering ways. Here are recent statistics on how much the average person in the U.S. watches TV:[47]

- Average time spent watching television per day ~ 5 hours and 11 minutes
- Years the average person will have spent watching TV in their lifetime ~ 9 years
- Percentage of U.S. homes with three or more TV sets ~ 65%
- Number of minutes per week the average child watches TV ~ 1,480 (24.66 hours)
- Percentage of Americans that regularly watch TV while eating dinner ~ 67%
- Hours per year the average American youth watches TV ~ 1,200
- Number of violent acts seen on TV by age 18 ~ 150,000
- Number of 30 second TV commercials seen in a year by an average child ~ 16,000

In addition to TV, we have countless other distractions in our lives. Many of these things are not wrong in and of themselves; it's just that we allow them into our lives in an excessive amount so that they choke out discipleship and fruitfulness. Consider the following items:

- Work
- Wealth
- Large homes
- Nice cars
- Possessions
- Hobbies
- Entertainment

- Facebook
- Social Media
- Internet
- Pleasure
- School & excessive homework
- Retirement
- Sports

---

[47] Statistic Brain Research Institute, *Television Watching Statistics,* 2015, www.statisticbrain.com/television-watching-statistics, Accessed 08/07/2015.

These, among others not listed, can take us away from our priority in life of being disciples of Christ. They are activities that can choke out God's Word and thus become thorns. They are choices we make that result in "saving our lives" instead of losing them for Christ.

It's obvious, according to the statistics, that we have time for the activities we love, but often don't make time for discipleship. The problem is that we're making soft choices. We're saying yes to the thorns and cares of this world instead of saying yes to Christ and discipleship.

Now it should be mentioned that "losing our lives" is where we find true life. The thorns are what actually rob our attention from laying up treasures in heaven. They are things that distract us from eternal rewards and cause us to focus on temporal pleasures instead.

By utilizing just a portion of time many Christians spend on activities like TV, sports, hobbies, entertainment, and social media, they could easily take Bible courses or get an online Bible degree. This would position them to be much more fruitful for Christ, which would result in storing up riches in heaven instead of on earth. Instead of frittering away their lives, they could invest them in eternal matters.

If we're wise, we'll say no to the thorns (distractions) of this life and say yes to losing our lives for Christ. If we do so, we'll not only find our lives in this life, but in the one to come as well. You see, happiness is a byproduct of serving and pleasing God. If we make happiness our primary goal, we'll never be happy because we'll be "saving our lives." However, if we lose them for Christ, then He will add joy to our lives despite the suffering, persecution, and trials we may endure for His sake.

Happiness and Entertainment: the Gods of the 21st Century

Many Christians today need to make some radical changes to

their lifestyles and priorities in order to be obedient disciples of Christ. The lofty place they give to pleasure and entertainment is crippling them. Many are not engaged in serious discipleship because they are distracted by the pleasures of life. The gods of our day are happiness and entertainment, and many Christians are lost in the pursuit of them. If it's not fun, thrilling, and exciting, they want no part of it.

It's almost become standard procedure today that everything we do must first be run through the filter of pleasure and convenience or we want no part of it. Many would even try to run discipleship through this same filter. They ask themselves, "How can we make it fun, exciting, attractive, thrilling, entertaining, and convenient?"

It's just not realistic to think we can make the cost of discipleship that involves denying yourself, taking up your cross, losing your life, dying to self, hating your life, and being persecuted for Christ convenient and entertaining. I fear we've become "lovers of pleasure rather than lovers of God," and we're trying to import our fun and entertainment syndrome into the discipleship-making process.

Happiness and Obedience

Some Christians even think it's okay to disobey certain commands of Scripture as long as it makes a person happy. They view happiness as supreme. They believe God wants us to be happy, so even if our lifestyles don't quite harmonize with Scripture, it's okay to disobey because God will forgive. They've bought into the lie that God's primary goal for us is happiness. This should be of no surprise as the message many pastors preach today is a continual focus on the blessings of God while neglecting the cost of following Him.

Today, the scales are so tilted towards happiness that many believe it's their Christian right. They fail to understand that God hasn't called us to be happy and entertained, but devoted and fruitful. God wants to replace our pursuit of happiness and pleasure with genuine joy and purpose. He wants us to lose our lives for Him so we can find them.

Entertainment and Spiritual Battles

Many Christians are ignorant of the spiritual battles being waged in high places because following the news and keeping up with current events is not fun or entertaining. They are blind to what's happening in the spiritual realm of the political arena and how it's affecting the moral fabric of our culture. They are unaware of the currents of philosophy spoken of in the last days and the dangers of the Great Apostasy. Many don't keep up on the news, don't vote, don't care, and have basically "checked out" regarding most things that aren't fun or thrilling.

Entertainment and the Last Days

Life for many Christians is primarily about entertainment, thrill, and having a good time, and if it's not, they have no interest. Essential godly character like self-discipline, responsibility, hard work, patience, endurance, suffering, faithfulness, and service are lacking in the lives of many. We're living in the last days as described in 2 Timothy 3:1–5:

> But understand this, that in the last days there will come times of difficulty. For people will be **lovers of self, lovers of money**, proud, arrogant, abusive, disobedient to their parents, ungrateful, unholy, heartless, unappeasable, slanderous, without self-control, brutal, not loving good, treacherous, reckless, swollen with conceit, **lovers of pleasure rather than lovers of God**, having the appearance of godliness, but denying its power. Avoid such people.

> This pretty well sums up our culture today, and

unfortunately, it's affecting the lives of Christians as well. Many believers are "lovers of pleasure rather than lovers of God."

We must understand that discipleship is not necessarily fun. Denying yourself is not a great thrill. Taking up your cross is not that exciting. Losing your life for the cause of Christ is not the latest fad. Suffering family division because of Christ is painful. Being ridiculed by society for holding to biblical truth is hard. Training yourself in godliness is not popular. Exercising self-discipline for the purpose of discipleship takes patience and fortitude. Not following the winds of modern day morality is challenging. Reading the Bible instead of watching TV takes self-discipline. Praying requires commitment and patience, and losing friends because of Christ is lonely.

However, these challenges are the core principles of discipleship that bring deep, genuine joy and eternal rewards in heaven. Those who are wise will choose the eternal riches over the fleeting pleasures of our day. They will be like Moses who, "When he was grown up, refused to be called the son of Pharaoh's daughter, choosing rather to be mistreated with the people of God than to **enjoy the fleeting pleasures of sin**" (Heb. 11:24–25).

Entertainment and the Church

In many churches today, there's a strong focus on entertainment. They ask how the music, preaching, adult, youth, and children's ministries can be entertaining so people will attend.

I am all for making church as attractive and professional as possible, but I don't think we should alter our message or promote the concept that "if it's not fun and exciting, we don't do it." Church is not a theater, a club, a sports activity, or a show where the goal is to entertain. Its purpose is to glorify God through preaching His Word, making disciples, and worshipping Him in Spirit and truth.

I don't believe we should get caught up in the entertainment trap. Attempting to eliminate the reality that discipleship is costly and inconvenient is deceitful. We need to be careful we don't join in the modern day belief that following Christ is supposed to be entertaining. If we build on this flawed foundation, we'll produce weak followers who will be the first to bail when they encounter any hardship.

Some churches are trying to satisfy the culture's appetite for entertainment and are incorporating a high dose of amusement into their church services to draw a crowd. They make sermons humorous, entertaining, upbeat, lighthearted, and short. What kind of disciples are these churches producing, and are they subtlety teaching their followers to "save their lives" instead of losing them?

Modern Day Conveniences and Discipleship

We live in an unparalleled time in the history of mankind. Advancements in technology have given us every modern convenience under the sun. While there are positives to these advancements, there are negatives as well. On the downside, in our effort to make life easier, we've become a soft and tender society. Toughness, suffering, hard work, endurance, self-discipline, and perseverance are lacking commodities.

My folks are from the Great Plain States of Nebraska and South Dakota. They grew up without electricity, indoor bathrooms, and running water in their homes. They had to walk or ride a horse to school, had no air conditioning during the hot, blistering summers, and didn't have heating throughout their uninsulated homes during the sub-zero winters. My mother tells of how she took a heated rock to bed at night to stay warm and milked 26 cows before and after school. My father was extremely poor, worked hard, and was raised on side pork (the trash meat from pigs). He milked several cows twice daily and rode a horse 10 miles to school. My parents were tough, rugged, disciplined, hardworking folks who knew how to suffer and endure hardship, and it was the same for many others in their day as well.

Discipleship Is Not Convenient

I fear that a great negative of our modern day conveniences is that we've become spoiled, soft, and tender. We know little about suffering hardship and going without. Today, if we have an inconvenience in our lives, we buy something to fix it or take a pill to make us feel better. We're not tough soldiers for Christ, but generally delicate and weak.

About the only thing left today that requires much hardship in life is sports. Other than that, almost everything else is convenient and easy. Unfortunately, the side effects of our conveniences are producing a soft and fragile society.

I believe our modern conveniences are also affecting our Christian lives. We don't like to be inconvenienced. We like instant gratification, ease, fun, and entertainment. Without realizing how much we've become products of our culture, deep within our subconscious mind is the belief that if something is hard we need to find a way to alleviate it.

Unlike what many would like, this attitude doesn't apply to discipleship and the Christian life. There's a cost to discipleship, and it's not convenient! It takes self-discipline, commitment, toughness, endurance, patience, and long-suffering. There's no modern convenience that can make discipleship easy. We can't throw disciples in the microwave for a few minutes and pop out mature believers. Spiritual maturity had a cost during the time of Christ, and it has a cost today. It has never been, and it will never be, convenient!

Busyness: an Enemy of Discipleship

People's lives are extremely occupied with countless activities and stimuli each day. In fact, many are addicted to it, and it has become their god. Cath Martin reveals that, because of our modern day busyness, many Christians are even trying to sustain their relationships with God while on the move: "In the face of busy lives, many evangelicals are doing faith 'on the go' and utilizing digital media to help them maintain their spiritual lives. A third of these busy Christians now use Bible apps, with daily devotional apps and the Book of Common Prayer app among the popular choices."[48]

Many Christians say they don't have time for discipleship because they're too busy, yet they have plenty of time for all their other activities. Why is this so? The stats show that it's because many Christians are saying no to Christ and discipleship and are saying yes to their own desires and plans. Putting God first is sacrificed or eliminated, while other activities are kept intact and prioritized.

Adding to all of the pleasure-oriented stimuli available to us today is the pursuit of wealth, power, and prestige that we believe bring pleasure and happiness. In many households, both father and mother are working long hours in order to have large homes, nice cars, good retirement, vacations, and a host of other pleasures money can bring. The time in which we live is marked by busyness and the motto of our day is activity.

Even though spending time with God and His Word is critical for growth in Christ, busyness distracts many away. A recent Barna Group survey reveals this startling fact: "Like all other forms of analog media, the Bible is pushed to the side in part because people are just too busy. Among those who say their Bible reading decreased in the last year, the number one reason was busyness: 40% report being too busy with life's

---

[48] Cath Martin, *Evangelicals Admit Struggling to Find Time for Daily Bible Reading and Prayer*, 2014, Christianity Today, www.christiantoday.com/article/daily.bible.reading.and.prayer.is.a.struggle.for.many.evangelicals/36765.htm, Accessed 08/18/2015.

responsibilities (job, family, etc.), an increase of seven points from just one year ago."[49]

Boredom Is at an All-Time High

Despite all our busyness and activity, boredom is at an all-time high. Why is this so? Why do children, students, and adults feel unsatisfied today? If busyness and pleasure bring happiness, why is boredom plaguing many today? It's because God made us to serve Him and not ourselves. Until we understand this, we can gain the whole world and all its pleasures, but still be empty.

Distractions in the Formative Years

As a former youth pastor, I remember the difficulty I had with some of my students. It was a struggle getting them to youth group, to church, and to discipleship activities because they just didn't have the time. They were too busy with school, sports, and jobs. Youth group and discipleship were in competition with their other pursuits, and unfortunately, most of the time the spiritual activities lost out. Growth in Christ and discipleship just weren't as high a priority. The good things in their lives were in the way. And sadly, most of their parents supported them and made schooling, sports, and jobs a priority for them over youth group and discipleship.

I often felt like I was fighting a losing battle and was grieved by their lack of growth. I've been able to trace the lives of many of these youth over the past 30 or so years, and today, many of them who made God and discipleship a low priority have paid a heavy price. Some no longer even walk with the Lord. The eternal consequences of the busyness in their lives have been, and will always be, an enormous cost to them.

---

[49] Barna Group, *The State of the Bible: 6 Trends for 2014*, 2014, https://www.barna.org/barna-update/culture/664-the-state-of-the-bible-6-trends-for-2014#.VdNGKTZRGUk, Accessed 08/18/2015.

In order to grab their attention, I often threatened to give these students a spiritual grade — a grade like they received in school for classes they attended. After all, they earned grades in school for how well they performed. What if I gave them a spiritual grade to help them see how well they were doing spiritually? Unfortunately, many would have flunked out.

Today, the average student spends around 7–8 hours in school a day, an hour or two on homework, an hour or two on extracurricular activities like sports, and then some have jobs on top of it all. And of course, we can't leave out TV, video games, and social media. When do they have time for God? Their lives are so stuffed full of other activities that being a disciple of Christ is shoved to the wayside.

The average person will spend a year or so in kindergarten, 12 years in primary and secondary education, and four years in college. During these years, the amount of time spent learning about earthly knowledge is astronomical. However, the time spent learning about biblical knowledge is minuscule and scarcely measurable in comparison. We've elevated secular knowledge to such a high degree that we feel justified in sacrificing eternal knowledge on its altar.

I believe God is in favor of us being responsible in school, but I can't help but think He's more concerned that we acquire eternal knowledge so we can build our lives on a solid foundation, and not on sand.

Building Upside Down

In biblical times, secular knowledge was built upon the foundation of Scripture. Critical factors like character, honesty, respect, self-discipline, diligence, hard work, and responsibility formed the foundation upon which secular knowledge rested.

Today, we have it backward. We make secular knowledge the foundation of life and demote eternal, biblical knowledge as subservient. In other words, we build biblical knowledge on the foundation of secular knowledge instead of building secular knowledge on the foundation of biblical knowledge. We give secular knowledge priority and, if we have time, squeeze in a little Bible knowledge.

For example, how many parents "stress out" if their children don't spend time studying their Bible like they do if they don't spend time doing their homework? Most parents are responsible regarding their children's secular knowledge, but irresponsible regarding their children's biblical knowledge! We're doing just the opposite of the biblical model and then wonder why our sons and daughters aren't serious about their relationships with Christ. We wonder why, according to Rainer Research, "approximately 70% of American youth drop out of church between the age of 18 and 22."[50] Moreover, the Barna Group estimates that "80% of those reared in the church will be 'disengaged' by the time they are 29."[51]

Our priorities are backward, and we're paying a high price. By elevating secular knowledge over biblical knowledge and discipleship, many parents are participating in damaging their children's spiritual future, which will have consequences, not only in this life, but in eternity as well.

Today, we're building on a shallow foundation. Many are building their houses on the sand. The state of the family is in disarray, our lives are harried and scarred, we're busy going every direction under the sun, and much of the free time we do have is spent on pleasure and entertainment. I'm afraid the average Christian today is falling far short of what Christ calls us to be.

Many are more concerned about their careers than Christ;

---

[50] Drew Dyck, *The Leavers: Young Doubters Exit the Church,* 2010, ChristianityToday.com, www.christianitytoday.com/ct/2010/november/27.40.html, Accessed 09/28/2015.
[51] Ibid., Accessed 09/28/2015.

more concerned about their earthly home than their eternal home; more concerned about sports activities than godly activities; more concerned about secular knowledge than Biblical knowledge; more concerned about their physical condition than their spiritual condition; and more concerned about their present life than their eternal life.

Getting Rid of Unnecessary Weights

Many Christians today need to lighten up! They have too many activities — even good ones — in their lives that are distracting them away from discipleship. Scripture calls these activities "weights." It says, "Therefore, since we are surrounded by so great a cloud of witnesses, let us also lay aside every **weight**, and sin which clings so closely, and let us run with endurance the race that is set before us" (Heb. 12:1).

In this verse, two things can deter us from our commitment to discipleship: sin and weights. Weights refer to the activities in life that are not bad but take away our time. God wants us to slim down in these areas so we can have more time for discipleship and attaining spiritual maturity.

When we give priority to the "weights" in our lives, we have less time to give God our best. As a result, we wind up giving God our leftovers: leftover time, leftover energy, and leftover service. When Christ called the original disciples, He didn't call them to give Him their leftovers. Today, Christ doesn't call us to give Him our leftovers either. He calls us to put Him first and give Him our best.

Distractions and Discipleship

In 1 Corinthians 7, God reveals how He feels about all the distractions in life that take us away from Him and discipleship:

But I want you to be free from concern. One who is

unmarried is concerned about the things of the Lord, how he may please the Lord; but one who is married is concerned about the things of the world, how he may please his wife, and his interests are divided . . . This I say for your own benefit; not to put a restraint upon you, but to promote what is appropriate and to **secure undistracted devotion to the Lord** (1 Cor. 7:32–35, NASB).

In this passage, the Apostle Paul is promoting the benefits of singleness. While he clearly states in the context that marriage is honorable and desirable, he also highlights how God feels about the distractions of life that can draw us away from Him.

Christ gave a warning as well about the distractions of life that would affect many in the last days: "But watch yourselves lest your hearts be weighed down with dissipation and drunkenness and **cares of this life**, and that day come upon you suddenly like a trap" (Luke 21:34).

God desires that we might be free from the distractions and concerns of the world so we can focus more fully on Him and discipleship. I wonder how He feels about us today?

Conclusion

Never in the history of any civilization have there been so many stimuli and activities available. How is this affecting Christians and discipleship? It's reeking catastrophic consequences according to the state of the average Christian today.

My mother made a wise statement about time management many years ago, saying, "We always have time for what's important to us." I believe she's right! It's not that we don't have time; it's that our priorities are out of line. We're so caught up in the distractions of our current age that we don't take time for Christ and discipleship.

2. Materialism and the Pursuit of Wealth

In Christ's call to discipleship, He exposes a trap that hinders many Christians from being fully devoted disciples of Christ and reaching spiritual maturity. They are being sucked into the deception that materialism, pleasure, and prestige are the true riches of life, not discipleship and living for Christ.

The fact that 81% of Christians don't regularly read their Bibles, 61% of believers have not shared their faith in the last six months, and the average Christian prays between 1-7 minutes a day reveals that many Christians are lost in materialism and neglecting discipleship.

Many believers are invested so heavily in this life that they're blind to eternity. They are working so hard to have a pleasant and enjoyable life now that spiritual maturity and the things of God are neglected. They have the eye impediment of shortsightedness. In our unprecedented age of materialism and consumerism, we're more susceptible than ever to this danger.

In Christ's call to follow Him, He bluntly states that materialism is an enemy of discipleship. We must choose one or the other, for no one can serve two masters (Matt. 6:24).

Following Christ means He has complete priority over our pursuit of materialism and pleasure. It means He is number one in our life, and not just in theory, but in reality. However, if we choose materialism over Christ, we might enjoy this life now, but will lose many of our rewards in heaven and fall into countless temptations and snares in the meantime.

Most Christians would strongly argue that their possessions aren't more important than God. However, the time they spend devoted to them reveals just the opposite.

Physical possessions are nothing more than what allows us to exist, and our purpose for existing is to know God and attain spiritual maturity, not getting lost in materialism. If our possessions become more important than God, then they are out of balance and can become our modern day idols.

Loving the World More Than God

We live in wonderful times with abundant luxuries and blessings. However, many are lost in the blessings and love this world too much. We need to heed God's warning: "Do not love the world or the things in the world. If anyone loves the world, the love of the Father is not in him. For all that is in the world — the desires of the flesh and the desires of the eyes and pride of life — is not from the Father but is from the world. And the world is passing away along with its desires, but whoever does the will of God abides forever" (1 John 2:15-17).

While our earthly activities aren't wrong in and of themselves, they can be if we're so occupied with them that we don't have time for following Christ and discipleship. If we're so absorbed in worldly activities that we have little time for eternal matters, then we love this world more than we should.

God loves to bless us and richly provides us with everything to enjoy (1 Tim. 6:17). However, if we focus more on the blessings of God rather than on God Himself, then it indicates we love the blessings more than God. We can become guilty of worshipping the idols of wealth, fame, and pleasure instead of God. As a result, we fail to be rich toward God and invest in our eternal home. We might be rich in earthly possessions but poor in heavenly riches.

Many Christians today are poor spiritually. They are like the lukewarm Christians in the church of Laodicea: "For you say, I am rich, I have prospered, and I need nothing, not realizing that you are wretched, pitiable, poor, blind, and naked" (Rev. 3:17). Many Christians are blind to their spiritual poverty, having no idea of their condition before God and of their possible loss of eternal rewards in heaven. Their eyes are locked on this world and are honed in on storing up their treasures here. As a result, they are poor and naked but don't know it.

The Cost of Materialism

Christ told a parable that perfectly illustrates the foolishness of being so absorbed in materialism and the pleasures of this life that eternal riches are neglected:

> And he said to them, "Take care, and be on your guard against all covetousness, for one's life does not consist in the abundance of his possessions." And he told them a parable, saying, "The land of a rich man produced plentifully, and he thought to himself, 'What shall I do, for I have nowhere to store my crops?' And he said, 'I will do this: I will tear down my barns and build larger ones, and there I will store all my grain and my goods. And I will say to my soul, 'Soul, you have ample goods laid up for many years; relax, eat, drink, be merry.' But God said to him, 'Fool! This night your soul is required of you, and the things you have prepared, whose will they be?' So is the one who lays up treasure for himself and is not rich toward God" (Luke 12:15–21).

This rich man had it all. He worked hard to have a good life. In fact, he worked so hard that he reached the point of retirement where he thought it was time to reap the rewards of his labor. He said to himself, "Soul, you have ample goods laid up for many years; relax, eat, drink, and be merry."

His desire is really the inner desire of us all. We long for the time when we can kick back, relax, eat, drink, and be merry.

In our Western culture, retirement is elevated as the time to eat, drink, and be merry. We're told to work hard so we can "kick back" and enjoy life during retirement. We need to be careful not to buy into our culture's message and neglect serving God in our latter years, or we might end up being fools like the rich man.

Those in retirement have the most wisdom, time, and experience to offer, yet many are eating, drinking, and being merry instead of serving God.

Modern Day Fools

Christ calls those who focus primarily on this life and aren't rich toward God, "Fools"! They work hard at acquiring a good life; they get a large house, nice cars, a good job, a good education, and gain recognition and status before others. However, they are poor in the eyes of God and will pay the consequences for all eternity. They give more importance to this life than heaven. Their aim is to accumulate money, influence, recognition, and happiness. They believe, as the rich man, that these are the true riches of life, but Jesus says to those who pursue them and neglect serving God, "You fool"!

The unbelievable oversight of this rich man was that he was so invested in this life that he completely overlooked eternity. He was like a story told by Steven Cole:

> In 1981, a man was flown into the remote Alaskan wilderness to photograph the natural beauty of the tundra. He had photo equipment, 500 rolls of film, several firearms, and 1,400 pounds of provisions. As the months passed, the entries in his diary, which at first detailed the wonder and fascination with the wildlife around him, turned into a pathetic record of a nightmare. In August, he wrote, "I think I should have used more foresight about arranging my departure. I'll soon find out." He waited and waited, but no one came to his rescue. In November, he died in a nameless valley, by a nameless lake, 225 miles northeast of Fairbanks. An investigation revealed that he had carefully provided for his adventure, but he had

made no provision to be flown out of the area.[52]

What a tragedy! This man prepared for everything but his departure. His story applies to many Christians today. We're so focused on this life that we forget to plan for our departure. We're not focused on eternity, but on our jobs, education, homes, cars, hobbies, sports, pleasures, activities, TV, Internet, Facebook, and on and on. We have time for all these activities, but don't have much time for reading our Bibles, serving the Lord, leading Bible studies, being Sunday School teachers, sharing Christ, developing our gifts and abilities, and deepening our knowledge of God.

Getting Our Priorities Right

Many believers are doing the same as the rich man and are neglecting the call of discipleship because they'd rather eat, drink, and be merry. They prefer enjoying the pleasures of life rather than pursuing spiritual maturity. For this reason, Christ told us not to worry or be so engrossed in materialism and the pleasures of this life that we neglect His eternal kingdom:

> Therefore, I tell you, **do not be anxious about your life**, what you will eat or what you will drink, nor about your body, what you will put on. Is not life more than food, and the body more than clothing? Look at the birds of the air: they neither sow nor reap nor gather into barns, and yet your heavenly Father feeds them. Are you not of more value than they? And which of you by being anxious can add a single hour to his span of life? And why are you anxious about clothing? Consider the lilies of the field, how they grow: they neither toil nor spin, yet I tell you, even Solomon in all his glory was

---

[52] Steven J. Cole, *Why You Should Hate Your Life.* Bible.org. 2014, bible.org/seriespage/lesson-67-why-you-should-hate-your-life-john-1224-26, Accessed 08/11/2015.

not arrayed like one of these. But if God so clothes the grass of the field, which today is alive and tomorrow is thrown into the oven, will he not much more clothe you, O you of little faith? Therefore, **do not be anxious**, saying, "What shall we eat?" or "What shall we drink?" or "What shall we wear?" For the Gentiles seek after all these things, and your heavenly Father knows that you need them all. But **seek first the kingdom of God** and his righteousness, and all these things will be added to you (Matt. 6:25–34).

Notice that Christ doesn't say that earning a living and working hard are wrong. In fact, the Book of Proverbs is loaded with verses that speak of being responsible and hard working. Also, the Apostle Paul says, "For even when we were with you, we would give you this command: If anyone is not willing to work, let him not eat" (2 Thess. 3:10). Moreover, Paul includes, "But if anyone does not provide for his relatives, and especially for members of his household, he has denied the faith and is worse than an unbeliever" (1 Tim. 5:8).

God expects us to be responsible, diligent, and hardworking in providing for our families, and if we don't, we are worse than unbelievers. However, Christ's call to "Seek first the Kingdom of God" is not in conflict with working hard and providing for our families. What God is against is the excessive pursuit of materialism that causes us to neglect being fully devoted disciples of Christ. We can be responsible and seek first the Kingdom of God at the same time.

We are commanded to give the Kingdom of God our highest priority. For Christians who make materialism their priority instead of being disciples of Christ, they'll miss out on the life God intended now and have few rewards in heaven.

Are We Too Involved in Materialism and Pleasure?

How do we know if we're too involved in materialism? Here's a simple answer: if we don't have time to read and study our Bibles, don't have time to pray, don't have time to evangelize and make disciples, don't have time to develop our gifts, don't have time to deepen our knowledge of God, don't have time to serve God and others, don't have time to faithfully attend church, then we're too busy with the affairs of this life and are not seeking first the Kingdom of God.

Preoccupation with this life is robbing many of the priority of discipleship and the treasures it brings.

Consumerism and Our Modern Day Culture

The day in which we live is unlike any other time in history. We're called consumers and for good reason. Virtually every advertisement we hear, every commercial we see, every billboard we drive by, every magazine we pick up, and every newspaper we read is screaming at us to buy their stuff. We're told that without their products we're unhappy, but with them, the happiness we've always longed for can be ours. We're told by friends, acquaintances, and the world that happiness is found in possessions.

Our society is drowning in a sea of materialism, but most can't see the danger. From early childhood we're indoctrinated in the belief that earthly possessions bring happiness, so we get on board the train early and ride it till death — never realizing that there's a life much richer, much deeper, with more purpose and meaning, and with the promise of eternal rewards. It's called the life of discipleship and is God's best.

Only What's Done for Christ Will Last

Being a disciple is where true life and meaning reside. It's our life's calling and the highest purpose to which we can give ourselves. It's the vehicle through which life and spiritual maturity are attained. However, it has a cost, and the cost is seeking first God's Kingdom.

Seeking God's Kingdom first means that we put God as the highest priority in our lives. It means we are fruitful and productive in His Kingdom, not absorbed and lost in acquiring worldly possessions. Because materialism is an enemy of discipleship, God warns of its danger:

> But godliness with contentment is great gain, for we brought nothing into the world, and we cannot take anything out of the world. But if we have food and clothing, with these we will be content. But those who desire to be rich fall into temptation, into a snare, into many senseless and harmful desires that plunge people into ruin and destruction. For the love of money is a root of all kinds of evils. **It is through this craving that some have wandered away from the faith and pierced themselves with many pangs** (1 Tim. 6:6–10).

The only thing we're going to take out of this life is our works and service for Christ. As a stanza from the popular poem by C. T. Studd says:

> Only one life, yes only one,
> Soon will its fleeting hours be done;
> Then, in "that day" my Lord to meet,
> And stand before His Judgement seat;
> Only one life, twill soon be past,
> Only what's done for Christ will last.[53]

If we're rich in good works for Christ, faithful as His disciples, committed to the priority of seeking His Kingdom first,

---

[53] C. T. Studd, *Only One Life Twill Soon Be Past,* http://hockleys.org/2009/05/quote-only-one-life-twill-soon-be-past-poem, Accessed 08/27/2015.

and devoted to serving Him no matter the cost, then we will be rewarded richly in heaven. But if we're lazy servants who are neglecting these commitments, then we'll suffer loss and have few or no rewards. We will have spent our lives lost in materialism and blind to eternity's riches, choosing a few fleeting years of pleasure at the expense of endless, eternal rewards in heaven.

Conclusion

The lure of the world and materialism is calling at every corner, countless voices all singing the same song. All are drawing our attention to the pleasures of this life and dulling God's voice that calls us to follow Him and store our riches in heaven. The wise person will listen to God's voice and choose the eternal riches over the temporal. Unfortunately, many won't.

Sadly, many Christians are being deceived by materialism and believe it will fulfill the deep longings of their souls. Instead, God tells us that joy and purpose are found in our commitment to discipleship and following Him.

We're consumers! Consumers of materialism, consumers of pleasure, and consumers of entertainment. Unfortunately, many Christians aren't consumers of God's Word or seriously involved in discipleship. Materialism and the pursuit of wealth are weeds choking out discipleship in our lives today, and most don't realize the severity of the problem. In fact, we're so busy we don't even know there is a problem!

3. The Refusal to Pay the Cost of Discipleship

In today's world, everyone wants a bargain. The cost of living drives us to be discount consumers. We're trained early in life to cut costs, be frugal, look for the best deal, and stretch our money.

We also look for the easiest and most efficient way to accomplish tasks. In fact, virtually all inventions have been born out of the desire to reduce work and make life easier. This mentality works fine in the physical realm but creates havoc in the spiritual realm.

It's great to enjoy the blessings of modern technology in our physical lives, but this same desire for ease can be a curse in our spiritual lives. Christ clearly highlighted the cost of discipleship, and there's no modern invention to make it easier. There's only one way to spiritual maturity, and it's by paying the cost of discipleship.

Christians Today and the Cost of Discipleship

In 1937, Dietrich Bonhoeffer produced a classic book called *The Cost of Discipleship*. In it, he addressed those within Christianity that he felt embraced "easy Christianity" or "cheap grace" in the Western world. Even in Bonhoeffer's day, he felt many Christians were neglecting discipleship and seeking a bargain spiritually. They wanted spiritual maturity without discipleship, heavenly rewards without serving, salvation without obedience, and the blessings of God without submission to Him.[54]

Today, not much has changed. The reason many Christians don't embrace discipleship is because they frankly don't want to pay the price. For them, the cost of spiritual maturity is too high.

---

[54] Dietrich Bonhoeffer, 2011-08-16, *The Cost of Discipleship,* SCM Classics Hymns Ancient and Modern Ltd. Kindle Edition.

They'd rather watch TV, play video games, spend time on their electronic devices, and do something fun rather than invest in discipleship. Scripture would define them as lazy servants who are lovers of pleasure rather than lovers of God (2 Tim. 3:4).

Many Christians Today Are Spiritually Lazy

Christ told a parable about spiritual laziness to show its devastating effects on our lives. In the Parable of the Talents, Christ gave talents to three different servants, and then called each into account for how they used them. Two of the servants used their talents wisely and were rewarded. However, one servant didn't use his talent but wasted it. To this servant, Christ said, **"You wicked and lazy servant!"** (Matt. 25:26, NKJV). Christ expects us to use our talents in serving Him, and He'll call us into account at the end of our lives for how we did. Christ called the servant who didn't use his talents "wicked and lazy," making it very clear how He feels about laziness.

The talents Christ gives us represent our time, abilities, resources, money, spiritual gifts, knowledge of God, skills, and so on. Unfortunately, many Christians waste much of their time on pleasure instead of developing and using their talents. They are highly adept at mastering video games, are extremely knowledgeable about TV and movies, are sports buffs and up to date with the latest fads and viral videos. However, they are not adept with God's Word, are unskillful in using their spiritual gifts, and uninvolved in ministry.

It's easy in our day to succumb to spiritual laziness and not be engaged in discipleship as Christ commanded. Laziness is destructive to discipleship and brings with it a high price in this life, and an even higher price in eternity.

Many Christians Are Undisciplined

Christians today, by and large, are undisciplined. Most know what they should do, but don't have the self-discipline to do it. The word "disciple" is related to the root word "discipline." Therefore, a believer must possess self-discipline in order to be a disciple.

Dallas Willard claims, "Full participation in the life of God's Kingdom and in the vivid companionship of Christ comes to us only through appropriate exercise in the disciplines for life in the spirit."[55] And Bill Hull sums up the thinking of many when he says, "Most of us want to reap the harvest of discipline while living a life of relative sloth."[56]

Spiritual maturity is unattainable without self-discipline. Therefore, if we expect to get anywhere in the Christian life and be the kind of disciples Christ calls us to be, we must begin by building discipline into our lives. We need to heed God's counsel in 1 Timothy 4:7–8: "Rather **train yourself for godliness**; for while bodily training is of some value, godliness is of value in every way, as it holds promise for the present life and also for the life to come."

The Cost of Non-Discipleship

For those unwilling to pay the cost of discipleship, they might feel they are getting a bargain by taking the easy road, but in the end, they'll pay a higher price for non-discipleship than discipleship. Dallas Willard claims, "The cost of non-discipleship is far greater — even when this life alone is considered — than the price paid to walk with Jesus, constantly learning from Him."[57]

Willard continues, "Non-discipleship may very well cost a Christian such things as abiding peace, a life penetrated throughout by love, faith that sees everything in the light of God's

---

[55] Dallas Willard, 2009, *The Spirit of the Disciplines* (HarperCollins, Kindle Edition), p. 26.
[56] Bill Hull, *The Complete Book of Discipleship: On Being and Making Followers of Christ* (The Navigators Reference Library 1, 2014, NavPress. Kindle Edition), Kindle Locations 451-452.
[57] Dallas Willard, *The Great Omission* (HarperCollins, Kindle Edition, 2009), p. 9.

overriding governance for good, hopefulness that stands firm in the most discouraging of circumstances, and power to do what is right and withstand the forces of evil. In short, non-discipleship costs you exactly that abundance of life Jesus said He came to bring (John 10:10)."[58]

Willard concludes, "The cost of discipleship, though it may take all we have, is small when compared to those who don't accept Christ's invitation to be a part of His company in The Way of life."[59] The cost of non-discipleship is greater than the cost of discipleship, and if we're discerning believers, we'll take it to heart. We'll choose the road that leads to life and spiritual maturity rather than the easy road many Christians are traveling today.

Conclusion

The reason many Christians don't embrace discipleship is because they frankly don't want to pay the price. For them, the cost of spiritual maturity is too high.

Christ clearly highlighted the cost of discipleship, and there's no modern invention to make it easier. There's only one way to spiritual maturity, and it's by paying the cost of discipleship.

---

[58] Ibid., p. 9.
[59] Dallas Willard, *The Spirit of the Disciplines* (Harper Collins, Kindle Edition, 2009), Kindle Location 170.

4. The Lack of the Fear of the Lord

What does the fear of the Lord have to do with a lack of discipleship? Doesn't it seem a little out of place here?

It can be strongly argued from Scripture that the fear of the Lord is the foundation upon which discipleship rests and is its number one requirement. In fact, a compelling case can be built that the fear of the Lord is not only the foundation for discipleship, but for salvation and every other aspect of the Christian life. God says, "The fear of the Lord is the beginning of wisdom; all those who practice it have a good understanding" (Ps. 111:10).

To the degree a person fears the Lord is the degree to which they will even care about discipleship in the first place. And to the degree a person fears the Lord is the degree to which they will be very careful to obey God and all His commands, despite what family, friends, and society say.

The fear of the Lord is the value we give God and the perspective from which we look at Him. It sets our worldview and establishes our priorities in life. It's a major theme and doctrine of Scripture that is extremely positive and healthy. It's a fountain of life, brings riches, honor, and wealth, and endures forever.

Because the fear of the Lord is so foundational to discipleship and has been greatly overlooked, I believe it deserves some time and attention.

Defining the Fear of the Lord

Considerable controversy over the past 40 or so years has arisen regarding what the fear of the Lord means. There are four main interpretations:

1. Some define the fear of the Lord as soft or nonexistent. They believe God loves us and is not to be feared. God is our friend, and we're on a buddy system with Him. As Roger Barrier points out, "Too many Christians want, in fact, not so much a Father in Heaven as a 'Grandfather in Heaven' — a senile benevolence who, as they say, 'liked to see young people enjoying themselves' and whose plan for the universe was simply that it might be truly said at the end of each day, 'a good time was had by all.'"[60]

2. Others would define the fear of the Lord as simply respect for God. JoHannah Reardon responds to this view by saying, "I often hear people explain the fear of the Lord as a mere respect or reverence. But the Bible uses the word *fear* at least 300 times in reference to God, so we make a mistake when we downplay it."[61] Reardon continues, "While respect is definitely included in the concept of fearing God, there is more to it than that. A biblical fear of God, for the believer, includes understanding how much God hates sin and fearing His judgment on sin — even in the life of a believer."[62]

3. Others would define the fear of the Lord as reverence and awe of God. They believe Hebrews 12:28–29 provides a good description of its meaning: "Therefore, since we are receiving a kingdom that cannot be shaken, let us be thankful, and so worship God acceptably with **reverence and awe**, for our God is a consuming fire." This reverence and awe is believed by some to be exactly what the fear of the Lord means and is the motivating factor for us to surrender to God. One author

---

[60] Roger Barrier, *What Does it Mean to "Fear the Lord?"* 2013, Crosswalk.com, http://www.crosswalk.com/church/pastors-or-leadership/ask-roger/what-does-it-mean-to-fear-the-lord.html, Accessed 08/15/2015.
[61] JoHannah Reardon, *What Does It Mean to Fear God?* ChristianityToday.com, Accessed 08/15/2015.
[62] Ibid., Accessed 08/15/2015.

elaborates on this view by stating, "Each of us will give an account of our lives to God, and He is fully aware of everything we think, desire, speak, and do. The fear of the Lord is an awareness of these truths. It can be defined as a continual awareness that you are in the presence of a holy, just, and almighty God, and that every motive, thought, word, and action is open before Him and will be judged by Him."[63]

4. And still others would see the fear of the Lord as a much stronger term synonymous with extreme fear or terror of God. They believe that there are other words in Hebrew and Greek for mere respect, reverence, or honor that God could have used if the fear of the Lord meant to simply respect or revere Him. As one scholar states, "With this distinction in both Hebrew and Greek, some still assert that fear merely means reverence. As if God through His Spirit could not select the right word hundreds of times! Some would prefer to believe this than to understand that God really ought to be feared. Why is it we will not accept the fear of God? Why do we try to 'explain away' the fear of God in Scripture?"[64]

Which of these four interpretations is correct? I believe the biblical evidence supports interpretations three and four.

The Meaning of the Fear of the Lord in Hebrew and Greek

The word "fear" in the phrase "fear of the Lord" comes from the Hebrew word *yirah* (transliterated), and means "to be terrified" (Jonah 1:10), "to be in awe" (1 Kings 3:28), and "to have

---

[63] Institute in Basic Life Principles, *What is the Fear of the Lord?* Iblp.org, http://iblp.org/questions/what-fear-lord, Accessed 08/15/2015.
[64] Acts 17:11 Bible Studies, *The Fear of God*, http://www.acts17-11.com/fear.html, Accessed 08/17/2015.

respect" (Lev. 19:3).[65]

"The fear of the Lord is the reverence one would pay to a king because he is the majesty. But if one has offended the king and punishment is coming, the fear of the king's wrath in Hebrew is *yare*. *Yare* is used in the phrase "fear the Lord" 31 times in the Old Testament."[66]

In summary, *yare* and its variant forms mean: to fear, revere, be afraid, to stand in awe of, be awed, honor, respect, to be fearful, be dreadful, to cause astonishment and awe, be held in awe, to inspire reverence or godly fear or awe, to make afraid, and terrify.[67]

The use of the Greek word *phobo* carries the same meaning as the Hebrew word *yare* (Matt. 28:4; 1 Pet. 2:17).

Biblical Texts on the Fear of the Lord

The following are key verses that explain the meaning of the fear of the Lord:

- **Hebrews 12:28:** "Therefore let us be grateful for receiving a kingdom that cannot be shaken, and thus let us offer to God acceptable worship, with **reverence** and **awe**."

- **Jeremiah 5:22:** "Do you not **fear** me? Declares the Lord. Do you not **tremble** before me?"

- **Psalm 2:11:** "Serve the Lord with **fear**, and rejoice with **trembling**."

- **Matthew 10:28:** "And do not **fear** those who kill the body but cannot kill the soul. But rather **fear** him who can destroy both soul and body in hell."

---

[65] Neverthirsty.org, *Bible Questions & Answers,*
http://www.neverthirsty.org/pp/corner/read2/r00664.html, Accessed 08/15/2015.
[66] Ibid., Accessed 08/15/2015.
[67] Lumina.bible.org, https://lumina.bible.org/bible/Deuteronomy+10, Accessed 08/16/2015.

These verses support the interpretation that the fear of the Lord is much more than simple respect or reverence. It carries the sense of awe, deep reverence, extreme wonder, dread, and trembling.

What Does the Fear of the Lord Mean?

The "fear of the Lord" is a common term Scripture uses to define the value and worth we should give God in our lives. For the person who fears the Lord, they will be extremely careful to love and obey God as they should. For the person who does not fear the Lord, they will care little or nothing about God. They are a hard-hearted person who can know what God wants them to do but could care less about doing it.

Is There a Conflict Between Fearing the Lord and Loving the Lord?

Some believe the fear of the Lord no longer applies to us today, but just the love of the Lord. They cite 1 John 4:16–18 as the text that nullifies the command to fear the Lord:

> So we have come to know and to believe the love that God has for us. God is love, and whoever abides in love abides in God, and God abides in him. By this is love perfected with us, so that we may **have confidence for the day of judgment**, because as he is so also are we in this world. There is no fear in love, but perfect love casts out fear. For fear has to do with punishment, and whoever fears has not been perfected in love.

According to this passage, some claim that it's wrong to fear the Lord, and if we do, we don't understand God's love correctly. However, what about the other 300 references to the fear of the Lord we find in Scripture, of which many are direct commandments? How do they fit with 1 John 4:16–18?

Additionally, Christ says that if we obey and keep His Word, then our love for Him is perfect:

> And by this we know that we have come to know him, if we **keep** his commandments. Whoever says, "I know him" but does not **keep** his commandments is a liar, and the truth is not in him, but whoever **keeps** his word, in him truly the love of God is perfected (1 John 2:3–5).

God's Love Does Not Remove Accountability

First of all, it should be noted that God's love does not remove our accountability to Him for our actions in this life. God is clear that both the non-believer and the believer will give an account to Him for how they lived their lives.

1 John 4:16-18 talks about how we can have confidence before God on the Day of Judgment, not that there will be no judgment. It speaks of how we can be perfected in love so we don't have to fear punishment, not that there will be no punishment.

With this being said, what does the Day of Judgment mean in this passage and how can we have confidence on that day?

For the believer, the glorious good news is that their sins have been forgiven in Christ and **no condemnation** awaits them. Therefore, they have nothing to fear regarding hell and God's wrath upon them. They need not fear punishment because they have placed their faith in Christ and have passed from death to life. They have responded to God's love and can now have full confidence that they are saved and will not incur God's wrath. For this reason, God's love should cast out any fear of His judgment and punishment upon them.

However, believers will still give an account for how they served God with their lives. The Apostle Paul gives reference to this when addressing believers. Note how he even includes himself in this time of accountability:

For we must all appear before the judgment seat of Christ, so that each one may receive what is due for what he has done in the body, whether good or evil (2 Cor. 5:10).

At this place, the believer is not judged as to whether or not they will be saved and going to heaven, but judged based on how they used their talents and served Christ in this present life.

How We Can Have Confidence at the Judgment Seat of Christ

The love of the Lord motivates us to live in obedience to God, and as we do, we are filled with peace and confidence before the Lord. While we aren't perfect, we can rest assured that if we're seriously following Christ and have no major sins in our lives, then we have nothing that would cause us to fear anything when we give account to the Lord. Once again, this doesn't mean we will be perfect or perfectly love and obey God, but it refers to the overall joy and peace a believer has when they know they are sincerely following the Lord with all their heart and are being pleasing to Him.

To the degree that we love God and keep His commandments will be the degree to which we'll have no fear when we give account at the Judgment Seat of Christ. We'll have peace and confidence regarding this day because we are loving God and being obedient to Him.

For the believer who is living a casual Christian life or living in unrepentant sin, they will not have the peace that things are right between them and the Lord, and in their case, they should rightly be concerned about how it will go for them when they give account to Christ. Their concern should not be about judgment and hell, but about losing heavenly rewards and being displeasing to the Lord.

In summary, we as believers should have a deep reverence and awe of God, giving Him the value and worth He deserves.

We should be extremely careful to love and obey Him as we should, being very attentive to please Him in every aspect of our lives. We should understand that nowhere in Scripture are we commanded **not** to fear the Lord. But just the opposite is true. Countless times we are directly commanded to fear the Lord and give Him the worth and value He demands.

The Fear of the Lord Applied to the Non-Believer

For the non-believer, there ought to be an expectant horror, terror, trembling, and dread before God for the judgment and wrath that awaits them. The reality of spending eternity in hell should shake them to their core.

For those who trample underfoot the sacrifice of Christ, and turn their back on Him and His salvation, they should shudder and tremble before God Almighty:

> For if we go on sinning deliberately after receiving the knowledge of the truth, there no longer remains a sacrifice for sins, but a fearful expectation of judgment, and a fury of fire that will consume the adversaries. Anyone who has set aside the Law of Moses dies without mercy on the evidence of two or three witnesses. How much worse punishment, do you think, will be deserved by the one who has trampled underfoot the Son of God, and has profaned the blood of the covenant by which he was sanctified, and has outraged the Spirit of grace? For we know him who said, "Vengeance is mine; I will repay." And again, "The Lord will judge his people." **It is a fearful thing to fall into the hands of the living God** (Hebrews 10:26–31).

Therefore, for the non-believer who could care less about God and does not give Him the worth and value He deserves, there ought to be an expectant horror, terror, trembling, and dread before God for the judgment and wrath that awaits them.

Fearing the Lord and Loving the Lord

The phrases "fear the Lord" and "love the Lord" go hand in hand. To love the Lord is to fear Him, and to fear the Lord is to love Him: "For as high as the heavens are above the earth, so great is his **steadfast love** toward those who **fear him**" (Ps. 103:11). "But the steadfast **love of the Lord** is from everlasting to everlasting on those who **fear him**, and his righteousness to children's children" (Ps. 103:17). These verses show that the fear of the Lord and the love of the Lord are harmonious, not conflictive truths.

Christ defines, in large part, what it means to love God. He says, "Whoever has my commandments and keeps them, he it is who loves me. And he who loves me will be loved by my Father, and I will love him and manifest myself to him" (John 14:21).

Keeping God's commandments is the mark of a person who truly loves and fears the Lord. Words are cheap; obedience is costly. A person who truly loves the Lord will not only say so, but will show it through obedience.

How the Fear of the Lord Is Viewed by Many Today

Many Christians and churches have a strong focus on the love of God, and a weak or practically non-existent focus on the fear of God. Just ask yourself if you've recently heard an entire message devoted to the topic of hell or the fear of the Lord? Then ask yourself if you've recently heard a message about the love of God?

If you're like most, the messages you've heard about the love of God versus the messages about the judgments of God and hell are extremely disproportional. Our focus today is on the love and grace of God. The fear of the Lord is unpopular and viewed negatively, while love and grace are viewed as far more appealing and positive.

Yet, when analyzing Christ's message in the Gospels, we see that He talked far more about the judgments of God and hell than about heaven. He did just the opposite of what most do today.

Now to clarify, God is love, and His love is an overarching truth of Scripture, but God is also a just God and will punish those who reject His love. To only focus on His love and omit His justice is not a balanced treatment of Scripture. We see this in the following text: "The Lord is slow to anger and **abounding in steadfast love**, forgiving iniquity and transgression, but **he will by no means clear the guilty**, visiting the iniquity of the fathers on the children, to the third and the fourth generation" (Num. 14:18).

The Biblical View of the Fear of the Lord

As mentioned, the "fear of the Lord" is a common term Scripture uses to define the value and worth we should give God in our lives. For the person who fears the Lord, they will be extremely careful to love and obey God as they should. For the person who does not fear the Lord, they will care little or nothing about God.

We can measure how much we fear the Lord by measuring how concerned we are about carefully obeying and loving Him. If we have areas in our lives where we are not fully obeying God, then this reveals a lack of the fear of the Lord on our part. For example, when 81% of Christians today are not regularly reading their Bibles, this reveals that they do not fear the Lord much.

There are few themes in Scripture that speak of such rich blessings in the believer's life as the fear of the Lord. Rather than being viewed as something negative, God views it as exceedingly positive. Consider the following verses that speak of the benefits and blessings the fear of the Lord brings to our lives:

- **The fear of the Lord brings church growth, discipleship, peace, and comfort:** "So the church throughout all Judea and Galilee and Samaria had peace and was being built up. And walking in the fear of the Lord and in the comfort of the Holy Spirit, it multiplied" (Acts 9:31). Contrary to most popular church growth philosophies, the fear of the Lord was a central cause of growth in the early church.

- **The fear of the Lord is the whole purpose of mankind:** The summation of our purpose in life is summed up at the end of the Book of Ecclesiastes: "The end of the matter; all has been heard. Fear God and keep his commandments, for this is the whole duty of man" (Eccl. 12:13).

- **The fear of the Lord brings riches, honor, and life:** "The reward for humility and fear of the Lord is riches and honor and life" (Prov. 22:4).

- **The fear of the Lord motivates us to know Scripture:** "Then they will call upon me, but I will not answer; they will seek me diligently but will not find me. Because they hated knowledge and did not choose the fear of the Lord" (Prov. 1:28).

- **The fear of the Lord causes us to live carefully:** "Now then, let the fear of the Lord be upon you. Be careful what you do, for there is no injustice with the Lord our God, or partiality or taking bribes" (2 Chron. 19:7).

- **The fear of the Lord causes us to be faithful:** "And he charged them: 'Thus you shall do in the fear of the Lord, in faithfulness, and with your whole heart'" (2 Chron. 19:9).

- **The fear of the Lord is wisdom:** "And he said to man, 'Behold, the fear of the Lord, that is wisdom, and to turn away from evil is understanding'" (Job 28:28).

- **The fear of the Lord is clean and endures forever:** "The fear of the Lord is clean, enduring forever; the rules of the Lord are true, and righteous altogether" (Ps. 19:9). Interestingly, the fear of the Lord is an eternal reality that will always be a part of God's Kingdom.

- **The fear of the Lord brings understanding**: "The fear of the Lord is the beginning of wisdom; all those who practice it have a good understanding. His praise endures forever" (Ps. 111:10).

- **The fear of the Lord is to hate evil:** "The fear of the Lord is hatred of evil. Pride and arrogance and the way of evil and perverted speech I hate" (Prov. 8:13).

- **The fear of the Lord is a fountain of life:** "The fear of the Lord is a fountain of life, that one may turn away from the snares of death" (Prov. 14:27).

- **The fear of the Lord brings life and satisfaction:** "The fear of the Lord leads to life, and whoever has it rests satisfied; he will not be visited by harm" (Prov. 19:23).

- **The fear of the Lord is required by God:** "And now, Israel, what does the Lord your God require of you, but to fear the Lord your God, to walk in all his ways, to love him, to serve the Lord your God with all your heart and with all your soul" (Deut. 10:12).

- **The fear of the Lord brings blessings:** "Blessed is the man who fears the Lord, who greatly delights in his commandments" (Ps. 112:1).

- **The fear of the Lord brings friendship with God:** "The friendship of the Lord is for those who fear him, and he makes known to them his covenant" (Ps. 25:14).

- **The fear of the Lord causes us to turn from evil:** "By steadfast love and faithfulness iniquity is atoned for, and by the fear of the Lord, one turns away from evil" (Prov. 16:6).

- **The fear of the Lord brings the love of God in our lives:** "But the steadfast love of the Lord is from everlasting to everlasting on those who fear him, and his righteousness to children's children" (Ps. 103:17).

- **The fear of the Lord motivates us to evangelize:** "Therefore, knowing the fear of the Lord, we persuade others" (2 Cor. 5:11).

- **Those who fear the Lord lack nothing:** "Oh, fear the Lord, you his saints, for those who fear him have no lack!" (Ps. 34:9).

- **God hears the prayers of those who fear Him:** "He fulfills the desire of those who fear him; he also hears their cry and saves them" (Ps. 145:19).

- **The Lord takes pleasure in those who fear Him:** "But the Lord takes pleasure in those who fear him, in those who hope in his steadfast love" (Ps. 147:11).

As these verses indicate, the fear of the Lord is a positive doctrine that brings some of the deepest blessings known to mankind. It's a theme pastors should be promoting and elevating in their churches, a doctrine that should run throughout all preaching and teaching. Discipleship rests on the foundation of the fear of the Lord and instead of avoiding it, Christians and churches today should be embracing it. But for some reason, they are reluctant and afraid to do so. I hope they are doing it out of ignorance, not because they fear man more than God.

The Fear of Judgment and the Human Heart

Interestingly, we get a glimpse into how God made the human heart by noting the way He uses the fear of judgment in dealing with mankind.

When the children of Israel entered the Promised Land, they

gathered at Shechem to renew their covenant with the Lord (Deut. 27, 28). Half of the tribes of Israel stood on Mt. Gerizim to pronounce blessings for obedience to God's commands (Deut. 28:1–14) and the other half stood on Mt. Ebal to pronounce curses for disobedience to God's commands (Deut. 28:15–68).

The tribe of Levi had a separate role in that they pronounced pure curses for disobedience, with no mention of blessings (Deut. 27:9–26).

In total, God spoke 65 verses (83%) that dealt with curses for disobedience and 14 verses (17%) that dealt with blessings for obedience. This significant difference should cause reflection. Why would God be so imbalanced in the attention given to the curses over the blessings? He also used this same tendency throughout the rest of the Old Testament.

We see a similar pattern in the life of Christ as well. He spoke overwhelmingly more about hell than heaven, and the judgments of God were a continual theme in His preaching. In fact, Christ is the leading voice on the subject of hell and spoke of it more than any other New Testament figure.

What do the themes of curses and blessings found in Deuteronomy, and the strong focus on judgment and hell in Christ's preaching, teach us about the human heart? It seems to indicate that the human heart is created in such a way by God that it responds better to the fear of judgment than the reward of blessings. It doesn't mean that blessings don't have an impact, as God did refer to them quite a bit.

Speaking About the Judgments of God

God made us and knows we respond better to judgment than blessings. We can take or leave blessings, but we can't take or leave judgment for disobedience. In other words, blessings are optional, but judgment is not.

If Christians and pastors don't speak of the judgments of

God, people may only choose to obey God if they think His blessings are worth the effort. If they don't think they are worth it, they'll "pass" on them as they'll have no fear of judgment for doing so. In other words, if judgment is removed from the table and blessings are the only option from which to choose, then people will just decide whether the blessings are worth it or not. If they decide the blessings aren't worth it, then in their minds they'll have nothing to lose but the blessings. For example, a child might choose to take or leave a reward for good behavior, but they can't choose whether or not they might be disciplined for bad behavior. It's the same with us.

However, when judgment is brought into the equation and put on the table, then people are faced with the realization that their misbehavior will incur God's judgment. By communicating clearly the reality of the judgments of God, people will realize they have two options. For the non-believer, they'll have to decide whether or not they want to pay the eternal price of suffering in hell for rejecting Christ. And for the believer, they'll have to decide whether or not disobedience to God is worth incurring His discipline in their lives, the loss of fellowship with Him, and the loss of eternal rewards.

Because it seems clear that the human heart responds better to judgment than blessings, it's imperative that we include the judgments of God in communicating Scripture to others.

Prophecy and the Fear of the Lord

One of the principle purposes of prophecy is to help us see the coming judgment that awaits those who don't fear the Lord. Unfortunately, books of the Bible that are prophetic in nature are largely overlooked today.

The Book of Revelation is unique in this aspect as it dramatically reveals the sobering reality of God's wrath upon those who reject Him and sell themselves to sin instead. For this reason, it's the only book in the Bible that begins with a promise for reading and hearing it: "Blessed is the one who reads aloud the words of this prophecy, and blessed are those who hear, and who keep what is written in it, for the time is near" (Rev. 1:3).

Most pastors and Christians feel the Book of Revelation is too difficult to understand, so they neglect it. Rather than mining its rich treasures, they disregard it because to them it's not worth the effort. However, in so doing, they disregard one of the most powerful books of the Bible.

The Fear of the Lord and the Gospel

The avoidance of the fear of the Lord affects the message of salvation. Today, in an attempt to eliminate negativity from the church atmosphere, many evangelistic salvation calls soften or pass over the sinfulness of mankind, the consequences of sin, judgment, and hell. They primarily focus on the love of God and His blessings.

A gospel that omits the sinfulness of mankind and the judgments of God is an incomplete gospel. It fails to clarify the reality of coming judgment and the consequences of sin. It's like hiding the truth from a cancer patient that they are sick and will die without treatment.

Hiding the truth about judgment presents a gospel that views the judgment of God as non-existent or as not that important. It's a gospel very different from that which Christ and the Apostles preached.

Consequences for Neglecting the Judgments of God

If the theme of judgment and hell is neglected or not taught, then there can be severe consequences. In addition, if there's an unbalanced focus on the love and grace of God, and little on the judgment and justice of God, then we can cause great deceit and destruction in the lives of many.

63

If we lead non-Christians to believe that there are basically no consequences for rejecting God, then we will have participated in the greatest deception of all time, and our omission of the truth can result in their eternal damnation.

I believe that if we leave out the hard truths of Scripture, we'll answer to God for doing so. This is why James 3:1 gives us this warning: "Not many of you should become teachers, my brothers, for you know that **we who teach will be judged with greater strictness.**"

If we leave out the sinfulness of mankind and the judgment of hell, then we can promote a false gospel that encourages non-believers to continue in their sin, and as a result, sends them to hell. The neglect of the judgment of God can lead others to believe that it doesn't really matter how they live their lives because God's love and grace will remove all the consequences for their disobedience to Him. To promote this mentality is not love, but deception.

Conclusion

The fear of the Lord is a foundational doctrine that applies to both the believer and non-believer. For the non-believer, there should be an expectant horror, terror, trembling, and dread before God for the eternal judgment that awaits them in hell.

For the believer, it's a theme that provides some of the deepest and richest blessings found in life. It endures forever and will never fade. Believers should not fear the judgment of hell, but the consequences a lack of the fear of the Lord produces. Consequences such as:

- The lack of discipleship
- Failing to reach spiritual maturity
- Sinful or poor choices
- The discipline of the Lord for serious unrepentant sin

- The loss of fellowship with God
- The loss of blessings
- The loss of eternal rewards

The fear of the Lord is the value and worth we should give God. It is developed as we grow in understanding and applying the Bible to our lives. It's God's gift to us and brings life, blessings, and rewards. It casts out the fear of judgment and gives us peace and confidence before the Lord.

The fear of the Lord can be summarized as having a right view of God, putting Him first, loving Him more than anything and anyone, and living in reverent awe and wonder at who He is and all He's done.

As mentioned, pastors and Christians today should not avoid its theme, but instead, should run to it and embrace it. After all, the fear of the Lord is what brings church growth, discipleship, and comfort to the church: "So the church throughout all Judea and Galilee and Samaria had peace and was being built up. And walking in the **fear of the Lord** and in the comfort of the Holy Spirit, it multiplied" (Acts 9:31).

Contrary to most popular church growth philosophies, the fear of the Lord is healthy and is one of the foundational truths that should be taught in churches today. It's one of the most important factors in discipleship and without it, very little, if any, will happen.

5. Being Ashamed of Total Devotion to Christ

"For whoever is **ashamed of me and of my words** in this adulterous and sinful generation, of him will the Son of Man also be ashamed when he comes in the glory of his Father with the holy angels" (Mark 8:38).

There's a growing hostility towards Christians today, and our culture now sees biblical principles as politically incorrect. Rather than stand against the turning tide, many Christians are instead choosing a path of peace and conformity to our culture's declining values.

It's not popular to be totally devoted to Christ as that's viewed as too radical and extreme. Moreover, for the person who holds to the truths of Scripture, they are often considered abrasive, hateful, intolerant, and judgmental.

How is being ashamed of Christ and His words affecting discipleship? Many Christians are ashamed to be fully devoted disciples for fear they'll become outcasts and marginalized among their friends and families. They prefer a kind of Christianity where they can enjoy all the blessings of God and those of their culture at the same time. They want the best of both worlds. In order to get the best jobs, gain recognition, be popular, and fit in, many Christians choose to avoid being devoted disciples as this would disrupt their world. They fear losing friends, family members, and general status in life so being a fully devoted Christian is avoided, and discipleship is glossed over and neglected.

Signs of the Times

Scripture clearly teaches that in the last days there will be a great falling away from the truth. People won't tolerate sound doctrine; there will be a great rebellion against God, and the times will be like the days of Sodom and Gomorrah. Even the church will be affected as many church members will prefer messages that are positive and upbeat rather than the truth of Scripture. "For the time is coming when people will not endure sound teaching, but having itching ears they will accumulate for themselves teachers to suit their own passions, and will turn away from listening to the truth and wander off into myths" (2 Tim. 4:3-4). Unfortunately, this verse describes the state of many Christians and churches today.

How should we deal with the mounting pressure to conform to our culture's increasing immorality, political correctness, and false philosophies of the last days?

For roughly 1,850 years of church history, there was solidarity on most moral issues. Yes, there was disagreement regarding some major doctrinal matters, resulting in the Reformation, but largely, on the moral issues, there was unified agreement.

However, moral tenants of the faith that began to erode in the Enlightenment Period—increased in pace during the 1850s, when science and evolution came to the forefront—have gained further acceleration since the 1960s. Scriptural morals are now being challenged on every front, and there's a new progressive move to radically alter civilization as we know it and usher in an entirely new morality. This morality is really nothing new; it's just the unleashing of the same old dark and twisted immorality of the sinful nature moved by the currents of Satan and the demonic realm.

How are Christians today responding to this challenge? Sadly, not very well according to the statistics. Rather than holding to the traditional moral values of Scripture the church has embraced for thousands of years, many are throwing much of it out the window and embracing the new "progressive" moral standards our culture is adopting.

With a scarce 19% of Evangelical Christians reading their

Bibles regularly, it's easy to see why evangelicalism is in trouble and we're caving into our culture's values. Many Christians are just simply ignorant and naive regarding what Scripture says about many of the moral issues of our day.

Key Issues Facing Christians Today

Some of the biggest issues facing Christians today are homosexuality, transgender issues, gender roles, abortion, divorce, sex outside of marriage, and childrearing philosophies. Many Christians hold views on these matters that are contrary to Scripture. Do they do this because they are ignorant of God's Word and simply don't know what it says, or do they love their culture and friends more than Christ? Are they ashamed to be totally devoted to Christ and His Word?

Many pastors today are also avoiding these key issues because they don't want to offend church attenders who have adopted our culture's values. Many churches now permit divorce with no biblical reasons, marry divorced people who are not biblically free to remarry, approve of homosexuality, overlook premarital sex, and wink at other questionable behavior. They believe the church today should just accept and support any lifestyle that both the Christian and non-Christian choose to embrace despite the clear teaching of Scripture that these acts are sinful.

Being Ashamed to Speak the Truth

Some Christians today propose a version of love they believe is best expressed by accepting, embracing, supporting, and celebrating certain sinful lifestyles that, according to God's Word, are immoral and wrong. I believe Scripture teaches that love is best expressed by telling the truth, not by allowing a person to continue in a destructive lifestyle for which they will destroy their lives, the lives of those around them, and incur the judgment of

God.

The moral issues of our day are nothing new, and the Apostle Paul had to confront them as well. Instead of approving, celebrating, remaining silent, or overlooking these issues, he dealt with them head on by stating the truth: "Or do you not know that the unrighteous will **not inherit the kingdom of God?** Do not be deceived: neither the sexually immoral, nor idolaters, nor adulterers, nor men who practice homosexuality, nor thieves, nor the greedy, nor drunkards, nor revilers, nor swindlers will inherit the kingdom of God" (1 Cor. 6:9).

Approving of the sinful choices of those involved in these sins would be similar to supporting an alcoholic's damaging lifestyle. We love best by speaking the truth, not by enabling people to continue their destructive activities. Unfortunately, many Christians are ashamed of the truth, remain silent, and shy away from being fully devoted disciples of Christ for fear of losing their status or popularity.

Being Ashamed to Choose Christ over Our Culture

Many Christians and churches today lag behind adopting the values of their culture by just 10 or so years. They change their message, morals, and values in order to fit in and not lose respect. Are they doing this because they are ashamed of being totally devoted to Christ and His words?

The pressure to conform to the values of our families, friends, and culture is a mounting force many Christians and churches are fiercely battling. It's a battle between staying true to God's Word despite the pressure or making concessions in order to alleviate it.

To relieve this tension, many pastors and churches are choosing a path of peace and positivity over conflict and strife. They don't want negativity in their churches, so they try to create a positive atmosphere that's loving and upbeat. They might have good motives, but are they ashamed to be fully devoted followers of Christ and His Word? Are they compromising and passing over certain hard truths and sins because they don't want any negativity in their churches? Are they afraid of offending church attenders and visitors who have adopted the values of their culture and would think they are crazy for truly preaching the hard truths of the Bible?

The call to discipleship is a call to total devotion to Christ. However, many churches are setting a poor example of discipleship because they are ashamed to fully obey the truths of Scripture that are not politically correct. While these churches may say discipleship is important, their example says something different. It says that they are ashamed of being fully devoted followers of Christ.

Being Ashamed to Address Gender Role Issues

Since the 1960s, the societies of the Western world have undergone major transformations regarding gender roles. In all fairness, I believe some of these modifications have been positive. However, some of these changes are highly concerning from a strictly biblical perspective. These changes deal with a new view of the gender roles in the church and family that our culture now embraces.

For almost two millenniums, the church understood the gender roles very clearly. They unanimously believed that Scripture taught clear distinctions regarding the roles of men and women within the church and home. But things have changed drastically in recent years.

Egalitarianism (the belief that men and women share the exact same roles in both the church and home) believes there is no distinction anymore regarding gender roles. This was not the case during four millenniums of Old Testament history and two millenniums since the New Testament. Therefore, for around six millenniums, believers understood clear distinctions in the gender roles, and there are virtually no examples to the contrary.

It's logical to ask why this change has all of a sudden occurred in correlation with the changes in our culture. Why were believers blind to the teachings of egalitarianism for almost six millenniums if they are found in Scripture? If there were sufficient biblical evidence supporting egalitarianism, then it should have surfaced eons ago. But why hasn't it? We should also see numerous examples of egalitarianism in church history as well. But we don't. Why is this so?

I believe it's because there's little support for it in Scripture. I've done significant research on this topic, and the evidence is overwhelmingly clear from Scripture that egalitarianism has very weak arguments supporting it. That's why, during the whole history of the church, we find virtually no support or examples upholding its position.

It appears, from an unbiased perspective, that Christians embracing our society's new values may be going to Scripture looking for wiggle room to support their beliefs instead of honestly going to the text and letting the text say what it says.

What has changed over the last six millenniums that would now cause us to question everything? The only thing that has changed is the values of our culture within the past 50 or so years that now challenge the gender roles and many other social issues.

Being Ashamed to Be Salt in Our Culture

Christ calls us to be salt in the world: "You are the salt of the earth, but if salt has lost its taste, how shall its saltiness be restored? It is **no longer good for anything** except to be thrown out and trampled under people's feet" (Matt. 5:13). What was the purpose of salt in Christ's day? It had three main functions: (1) to preserve food, (2) to add flavor, and (3) to provide minerals for bodily health.

Today, we are salt by preserving the truth of God's Word

instead of sacrificing it on the altar of political correctness. We are salt by adding flavor to life through demonstrating what it means to follow Christ's commands in all areas of our lives. And we are salt by providing health to the world as we speak the truth about the destructiveness and eternal consequences of sin. However, many Christians are ashamed to say anything and go against the tide of our culture's values.

Being Ashamed to Be Light in Our Culture

We're also called to be lights in the world: "You are the light of the world. A city set on a hill cannot be hidden. Nor do people light a lamp and put it under a basket, but on a stand, and it gives light to all in the house. In the same way, let your light shine before others so that they may see your good works and give glory to your Father who is in heaven" (Matt. 5:14–16). We are called to live in such a way that others can see the difference in our lives from that of the world.

What difference should they see? They should see believers who are living pure lives according to the commandments of God, who don't just say one thing and do another, but are genuine followers of Christ. They are not hypocrites, but practice what they preach. However, numerous studies show that "Self-identified Christians are living lives indistinguishable from non-Christians."[68]

The purpose of light is to illuminate and break the darkness. We're called to be lights by knowing God's Word and shining it into our culture. We're not to join the works of darkness, but reveal the evil deeds of our culture by shining God's Word upon it. "For at one time you were darkness, but now you are light in the Lord. Walk as children of light (for the fruit of light is found in all that is good and right and true), and try to discern what is

---

[68] C. S. Lewis Institute, *Sparking a Discipleship Movement in America and Beyond,* cslewisinstitute.org, http://www.cslewisinstitute.org/webfm_send/210, Accessed 08/19/2015.

pleasing to the Lord. Take no part in the unfruitful works of darkness, but instead, **expose them**" (Eph. 5:8–11).

Rather than celebrate, support, or approve the works of darkness, we should expose them. We should speak the truth in love, but nonetheless, we must speak the truth. However, many Christians are not living the truth and are not shining the light of God's Word upon the values of their culture. They are afraid and remain silent. And sadly, some join in the works of darkness, celebrating them rather than exposing and standing against them like the great prophet Isaiah did when he said, "Woe to those who call evil good and good evil, who put darkness for light and light for darkness who put bitter for sweet and sweet for bitter" (Isa. 5:20).

Being Ashamed to Speak for God

Scripture is full of examples of those who chose to please their families, friends, and culture rather than obey God. For example, Pilate chose to offer Christ up to be crucified in order to please a crowd, and Peter chose to deny Christ instead of acknowledging Him before His accusers.

On the other hand, God provides us with many examples of those who didn't bow to political pressure despite the enormous tension to do so. Among them is the Prophet Micaiah. Even though he was under extreme pressure to gloss over the Word of God to protect his life, he chose to obey God instead. His incredible story is recounted in 1 Kings 22.

During Micaiah's day, King Ahab (a wicked king over the 10 northern tribes of Israel) invited King Jehoshaphat (the king of Judah, who was a godly king) to go with him to war to take the city of Ramoth-gilead, a city once belonging to Israel but now lost to another nation.

King Jehoshaphat asked King Ahab to inquire of the Lord to see whether or not God would bless their plans. So King Ahab gathered all the prophets of Israel together, and these prophets unanimously affirmed God's blessing to bring victory if they went to battle.

King Jehoshaphat, for some reason, still had doubts and asked if there was any other prophet who could inquire of the Lord about their mission. King Ahab said, "There's this prophet Micaiah, but he never prophesies anything good from the Lord concerning me." Nonetheless, King Jehoshaphat insisted that this man be brought forth.

An officer, sent to summon Micaiah, warned the prophet not to stir up trouble by saying anything that differed from what the other prophets had already spoken. Micaiah responded, "As the Lord lives, what the Lord says to me, that I will speak" (1 Kings 22:14).

So Micaiah stood in the presence of King Ahab, King Jehoshaphat, all the prophets of Israel, all the officials of the two king's royal courts, and probably many army officials and commanders as well. All the power of two kingdoms were represented in this gathering. What would Micaiah do? What would he say? Would he be loyal to God and speak His words or yield to the pressure of those present and save his life? What would you do?

Micaiah chose to speak the truth of God's Word into his culture and as a result, was scorned and beaten by the other prophets, and then thrown into a dungeon by King Ahab. Nonetheless, Micaiah's words came true, and King Ahab lost his life because he refused to listen to Micaiah and the Word of the Lord.

Many other prophets in the Old Testament also spoke the Word of God to their culture and were beaten, persecuted, and killed. And the greatest example of all is Christ. He spoke the truth of God's Word into His culture and lost His life as a result. In addition, the Apostle Paul, the Apostles, and many others in

Scripture suffered great persecution for standing up for God and the truth. We applaud and admire them!

However, when it gets closer to home and affects us, many run from persecution and choose the values of our culture instead of standing with Christ. It's hard to stand against the tide of our culture, and it's especially hard to stand against family and friends. It's also hard for pastors and church leaders to stand against some within their congregations as they don't want a church split, lose members, see giving and tithes reduced, and have conflict.

Nonetheless, we have a choice to make. We can be like Micaiah, who chose to speak the Word of the Lord regardless of the cost, or we can choose the safe, easy route and appease our culture. What choice will you make?

Being Fearful of Losing Family and Friends

We naturally love our family, friends, and church family, and don't want to lose them. They provide us with the relationships we so desperately need. However, we must make a choice. Will we love family, friends, and our culture's values more than God? Will we remain silent on biblical issues out of fear of losing relationships? Will we conform to our society instead of being conformed to Christ? Will we fear being labeled intolerant, judgmental, dogmatic, and even hateful for speaking the truth? Will we be ashamed of what God says about moral issues and biblical truth, or will we speak the truth in love to our culture?

Recall what Christ said, "For whoever is **ashamed of me and of my words** in this adulterous and sinful generation, of him will the Son of Man also be ashamed when he comes in the glory of his Father with the holy angels" (Mark 8:38).

Unless we want to suffer shame and embarrassment before Christ, we need to be faithful in saying what God says about our culture. We're His mouth and voice. Unfortunately, many

Christians are ashamed to be fully devoted disciples as it causes problems in their relationships.

One of the ways we show our love and devotion to Christ is by being faithful to what He teaches in His Word. By holding fast to His teachings, regardless of the pressure to do otherwise, we demonstrate our love and devotion to Christ. Christ said, "Whoever has my commandments and keeps them, he it is who loves me" (John 14:21). If we don't keep Christ's commands, we have little right to claim we love Him. We can raise our hands in church, close our eyes in worship, and say whatever we want, but it's in our actions and commitment to keep Christ's commandments that we truly display our love for Him.

Being Ashamed to Be Small "p" Prophets to Our Culture

We are supposed to be like Christ and genuinely love people by telling them the truth. We also, in a sense, are called to be similar to the prophets of old. These prophets were called to speak God's Word into their culture. However, their hearers didn't want to hear their words and most of the prophets suffered great persecution or were killed for speaking the truth.

Today, I believe we're called to be like the prophets and speak the Word of God into our culture. However, the words we speak are the words of God already revealed in Scripture. Let me be clear: we don't speak our own words, but the words of Scripture! They are the only authoritative and inspired words known to mankind. Sadly, our culture, like the culture of the prophets, doesn't want to hear that they are sinners and their lifestyles are wrong.

Instead of hearing God's Word with open arms and repenting, our culture tends to get angry and attack the messenger. Nonetheless, our calling is to be small "p" prophets. We don't make up new Scripture, we just faithfully repeat what has already been revealed. We are also not to water it down, change its nuances, alter it, or adapt it so that it blends in with our culture's values. Instead, we are to speak the truth in love. We don't concern ourselves with how those in our culture might respond. How they do so is between them and God. We are called to be like the Prophet Ezekiel:

> So you, son of man, I have made a watchman for the house of Israel. Whenever you hear a word from my mouth, you shall give them warning from me. If I say to the wicked, O wicked one, you shall surely die, and you do not speak to warn the wicked to turn from his way, that wicked person shall die in his iniquity, but his blood I will require at your hand. But if you warn the wicked to turn from his way, and he does not turn from his way, that person shall die in his iniquity, but you will have delivered your soul (Ezek. 3:17–19).

God told Ezekiel that He would hold him accountable if he didn't faithfully warn the wicked people of his day to turn from their sins. I believe God will hold us accountable as well if we don't do the same. If we smooth over the sins of our culture, or remain silent because we're afraid, then I believe God will hold us accountable.

Why do many Christians remain silent and don't speak the words of God into their culture? Possibly, it's because they fear being labeled intolerant, judgmental, dogmatic, or hateful. Certainly that's what every culture in the Bible said to those who spoke God's Word to them as well. Whether it was the Prophets, Christ, the Apostles or us, it always has been and will always be the same.

A sinful society just doesn't want to be told that what they are doing is wrong and sinful. Therefore, when we speak God's words to them, they will naturally respond by accusing us of being intolerant, judgmental, dogmatic, or hateful. They'll attack the messenger who bears the message instead of heeding their warnings and repenting.

Sadly, many Christians are choosing to go along with our culture's sinful lifestyles because they are unwilling to be different and stand with God. Rather than being fully devoted followers of Christ, they settle for a mild version of Christianity that complies with their culture's values.

Being Ashamed to Use Good Judgment

One of the most misunderstood verses in the Bible is "Judge not that you be not judged" (Matt. 7:1). It's spoken so frequently that many believe we can't say anything contrary about anyone's sinful behavior or we're guilty of judging them. They claim it doesn't matter what God's Word might say; we have no right to weigh in on any matter.

What does this verse about judging really mean? We must see it in its context to fully understand it, as a verse taken out of context becomes a pretext. In other words, a verse lifted out of the other verses around it becomes what we want it to say rather than what it truly says. Here's the context:

> Judge not, that you be not judged. For with the judgment you pronounce you will be judged, and with the measure you use it will be measured to you. Why do you see the speck that is in your brother's eye, but do not notice the log that is in your own eye? Or how can you say to your brother, "Let me take the speck out of your eye," when there is the log in your own eye? You hypocrite, first take the log out of your own eye, **and then you will see clearly to take the speck out of your brother's eye** (Matt. 7:1–5).

First of all, it's true that our role is not to pass sentence upon another, that's God's job. However, in this passage, Jesus is not saying that we should never make any judgment about right and wrong. He means that we should not do it in a hypocritical manner.

God clearly calls us to use good judgment about right and wrong. Note how the passage ends: "You hypocrite, first take the log out of your own eye, and then you will **see clearly** to take the speck out of your brother's eye" (Matt. 7:5).

Therefore, this passage is **not** saying we are not to use good judgment, but instead, that we are **not** to use our good judgment hypocritically. We shouldn't say, "Don't do that," while we do the very same thing. It's failing to practice what we preach.

The point of this verse is to teach us how to judge correctly, not that we can't speak the truth of Scripture regarding sinful matters. For this reason, we are given the responsibility to judge between right and wrong, but must first get the beam out of our own eye in order to **see** clearly.

There are other verses in Scripture that also teach we have a responsibility to judge correctly using the Word of God in dealing with others. Consider the following verses:

- **Galatians 6:1:** "Brothers, if **anyone is caught in any transgression,** you who are spiritual **should restore him** in a spirit of gentleness. Keep watch on yourself, lest you too be tempted."

- **1 Corinthians 5:11–13:** "But now I am writing to you not to associate with anyone who bears the name of brother if he is guilty of sexual immorality or greed, or is an idolater, reviler, drunkard, or swindler—not even to eat with such a one. For what have I to do with judging outsiders? Is it not those inside the church **whom you are to judge?** God judges those outside. Purge the evil person from among you."

These verses affirm that we have a responsibility to evaluate right and wrong in order to minister God's Word to others.

We must remember that to simply repeat what God says is not being judgmental. We are not passing judgment on others when we proclaim what God's Word says to them; it is God's Word that is passing the judgment. Therefore, we must not be ashamed to exercise good judgment in order to help others. We are to be like doctors who prescribe medicine (God's truth) based upon our patient's needs.

Being Ashamed to Confront Our Inconsistencies

When we tell others that they are wrong while we're committing the same sin, we are inconsistent and guilty of being hypocritical. This can be done on an individual or a church-wide level. The world often claims we say one thing and do another, or that we single out some sins and pass over others.

For example, they see Christians speaking out against society's sins while at the same time, overlooking divorce, sexual immorality, etc., among their own church members. They see anger against some sins, but apathy toward others. They see these inconsistencies in our conduct, and as a result, say we're judgmental. Unfortunately, they have a point. We have no right to say one sin is wrong if we turn right around and allow other sins in our midst without confronting them.

Some years ago, David Kinnaman wrote a book called *Un Christian*. It highlighted the belief that many non-Christians view Christians as hypocritical. [69]

While the church never has and never will be perfect — and we would have no right to say anything if perfection was the standard bearer — when the gap is significantly wide between what we say and what we do, then we simply lose our moral authority and become guilty of hypocrisy in the world's eyes. We preach, "Thus says the Lord," yet we don't practice what we preach.

The importance of speaking a clear, biblical message and

---

[69] David Kinnaman and Gabe Lyons, *Un Christian*, (Grand Rapids, MI, 2007).

practicing what we preach is paramount if we want to have any influence and moral voice in our culture.

Misunderstanding the Nature of Truth

We must understand that truth by its nature is intolerant, judgmental, dogmatic, and absolute. Sadly, however, only half of Christians believe in absolute moral truth (Barna).[70] This reveals that for around half of Christians our culture's values have more influence over them than Scripture.

If I were to say, "Gravity exists, and if you jump out a window you will fall," that statement would be intolerant, judgmental, dogmatic, and absolute. However, even though some might think my statement is too dogmatic and absolute, what they think doesn't change the reality that gravity exists, and if you jump out a window, you will fall. My statement simply defines the essence of gravity.

And so it is with the essence of truth. Truth cannot be truth if it's not absolute. However, in our day of relativism (the belief that there are no absolutes), truth doesn't fit well. Nonetheless, it doesn't matter at all if the majority of people think gravity doesn't exist—it still exists. And it doesn't matter what they say or how angry they may get, gravity is an absolute, intolerant, dogmatic reality. Truth is the same!

If we repeat the words of Christ, "I am the way, and the truth, and the life. No one comes to the Father except through me" (John 14:6), we are repeating an intolerant, judgmental, dogmatic, and absolute statement. However, we are not passing judgment and setting up our own standard of right and wrong, but just simply repeating God's divinely revealed truth.

---

[70] C. S. Lewis Institute, *Sparking a Discipleship Movement in America and Beyond,* cslewisinstitute.org, http://www.cslewisinstitute.org/webfm_send/210, Accessed 08/19/2015.

Building a Crowd Instead of a Church

Some churches soften or eliminate the hard truths of Scripture in their desire to be more appealing to non-believers and grow their churches. This can be a form of deception as it hides and distorts the truth. In so doing, they can subtly communicate that they are ashamed of being totally devoted to Christ and His words. They could be more concerned about building a crowd than building a church.

As a result, non-believers may respond to God in an entirely different way than they should because they've been misled. Richard J. Krejcir comments, "I need to make this clear; in my many years of research (since the late 1970s), the churches that do and/or want to water down the message to attract more people make a huge mistake. They neuter the power and purpose of the Church to which Christ called us."[71]

Krejcir continues, "It's imperative we understand that growth statistics are just one aspect of an indicator of a healthy church. True success is being obedient to what God has called us to do and realizing that although we're responsible to serve, we're not responsible for the results. Our surrender to the will of God over our will and desires equals success; we are called to have the focus that God has and the passion and prayer to follow through. These are the marks of a successful church leader."[72]

Our faithfulness to God is determined by the degree to which we choose to obey His Word over pleasing others. We must realize that our priority in life is to love God more than our family, friends, and culture. We're called to be disciples who speak the truth of Scripture, not take the liberty to alter it because

---

[71] Dr. Richard J. Krejcir, *Statistics and Reasons for Church Decline*, 2007, Church Leadership.org, http://www.churchleadership.org/apps/articles/default.asp?articleid=42346&columnid=4545, Accessed 08/07/2015.
[72] Ibid., Accessed 08/07/2015.

we're ashamed to be fully devoted followers of Christ.

Being Ashamed of the Gospel

Today, some Christians and churches are ashamed of the gospel of Jesus Christ. For this reason, they omit parts of it that are unappealing to non-Christians. Aspects that are largely omitted or neglected include truths like the sinfulness and depravity of mankind, the consequences of sin, confession of sin, repentance, the judgments of God, the fear of the Lord, discipleship, denying self, taking up your cross, and hell. They pass over these uncomfortable truths and rush to the blessings of salvation instead. They focus on the benefits of receiving Christ, but leave out the consequences of rejecting Him.

Are they ashamed of Christ and attempting to remove the "offense of the gospel"? Interestingly, unlike many churches today, Christ focused more on the judgments of God and the cost of following Him than blessings.

The Apostle Paul was persecuted all over the known world because the gospel he preached was offensive: "But if I, brothers, still preach circumcision, why am I still being persecuted? In that case, the **offense of the cross** has been removed" (Gal. 5:11). When Christ and the Apostles preached the gospel, it was very offensive to many at that time.

The gospel was offensive to the Jews who believed that following the Law brought salvation. It was offensive to the Romans who believed in many false gods, and therefore, rejected the claim that salvation was found only in Christ. The gospel was folly to the secular mind who considered it ridiculous (1 Cor. 1:18). It was foolish to the Greeks who thought salvation came through wisdom and knowledge, and it's offensive to our culture today for many of the same reasons. There's no way to remove the offense of the Cross except by changing it to appease others. Unfortunately, some Christians and churches are doing just that.

However, in so doing, they are proclaiming a different gospel.

According to Scripture, a gospel that omits or alters the sinfulness of mankind, who Christ is, the judgment of God, and hell is an incomplete gospel. It's a false gospel that fails to communicate that from which a person is saved. It's a false gospel similar to cults like the Jehovah Witnesses, Mormons, Seventh-Day Adventists, and others who don't believe in the judgments of God and hell.

Conclusion

Being ashamed of total devotion to Christ affects discipleship and causes us to choose a path of peace and conformity instead of obedience and transformation. It allows the fear of losing family, friends, status, and popularity govern our lives instead of Christ. It opts for a version of Christianity that stands with our culture instead of standing with Christ. It causes us to be ashamed of full devotion to Christ because that would make us stand out and be different—something many Christians are unwilling to choose.

6. The Effects of Prosperity Gospel Theology

I believe another factor affecting the lack of discipleship today is the teachings of the Prosperity Gospel movement. Much of what they promote is now creeping into the Evangelical church.

There has been considerable debate in recent decades over what many have labeled the "Prosperity Gospel" or the "Health and Wealth Gospel" (also known by other phrases such as, "Name It and Claim It," "Confess It and Possess It," and "Word of Faith"). Their theological views vary from a more radical version to a softer, lighter version.

Beliefs of the Radical Version of the Prosperity Gospel

This version of the Prosperity Gospel believes God wants us to be rich, healthy, and happy, so we should partner with Him in faith to pursue these things. It teaches that Christians should expect miracles to provide physical healing and material riches. In addition, it claims Christians have a right to prosperity, money, wealth, big houses, expensive cars, large bank accounts, and profitable investments. It believes that our financial and health problems can be solved by sending "seed-faith" contributions to faith healers. Moreover, it teaches that if we do experience suffering or hardship, it's because we're guilty of sin and have a lack of faith.[73] The Prosperity Gospel movement began in the 1970s and has grown extensively over the years.

Beliefs of the Softer Version of the Prosperity Gospel

In recent years, there has been a more modern version of the Prosperity Gospel that is making its way into mainstream

---

[73] David E. Pratte, *Does God Promise Miracles to Give Us Healing and Prosperity?* 2011, Light to My Path Publications, www.gospelway.com/god/health-wealth.php, Accessed 08/22/2015.

Christianity. What began in the 1970s is gaining steam today. This softer version is more dangerous than ever because it contains subtler lies in its message. It promotes half-truths as whole truths, and a half-truth presented as a whole truth becomes an untruth.

When talking about the attraction and longevity of the Prosperity Gospel, Kate Bowler notes a major change that has extended its longevity: "The ascent of a smoother, more sophisticated 'soft prosperity' message — touted by more relaxed, corporate figures like Joel Osteen, Joyce Meyer, and Paula White — replaced the more theologically — explicit 'hard prosperity' teachings of an earlier generation. This helped the movement's appeal within a more therapeutic, secular context."[74]

A recent scholar has noted, "In the Prosperity Gospel, the believer is told to use God, whereas the truth of biblical Christianity is just the opposite — God uses the believer. Prosperity Theology sees the Holy Spirit as a power to be put to use for whatever the believer wills."[75] The main premise of the Prosperity Gospel is that God exists to serve mankind rather than mankind existing to serve God. It believes God's main purpose is to make us happy, healthy, and wealthy.

John Piper calls the Prosperity Gospel deceitful and deadly: "Luring people to Christ to get rich is both deceitful and deadly. It's *deceitful* because when Jesus himself called us, he said things like: 'Any one of you who does not renounce all that he has cannot be my disciple' (Luke 14:33). And it's *deadly* because the desire to be rich plunges 'people into ruin and destruction' (1 Tim. 6:9)."[76]

---

[74] Larry Eskridge, *The Prosperity Gospel Is Surprisingly Mainstream*, 2013, ChristianityToday.com, http://www.christianitytoday.com/ct/2013/august-web-only/prosperity-gospel-is-surprisingly-mainstream.html, Accessed 08/22/2015.
[75] Gotquestions.org, *What Does the Bible Say About the Prosperity Gospel?* http://www.gotquestions.org/prosperity-gospel.html, Accessed 08/22/2015.
[76] John Piper, *Prosperity Preaching: Deceitful and Deadly*, 2007, Desiring God, DesiringGod.org, http://www.desiringgod.org/articles/prosperity-preaching-deceitful-and-deadly, Accessed 08/23/2015.

The Preaching Style of the Prosperity Gospel

The Prosperity Gospel's preaching focuses on "felt need" messages about success, encouragement, positivity, wealth, health, happiness, blessings, purpose, love, and relationships. Preaching is nearly exclusively positive and upbeat, entertaining, and with virtually nothing negative mentioned.

The sinfulness and depravity of mankind, confession of sin, repentance, the judgments of God, the fear of the Lord, discipleship, denying self, taking up your cross, losing your life, suffering, church discipline, transformation through trials and suffering, and hell are virtually omitted and considered negative themes.

It's important to note that, biblically speaking, God does desire to bless us, and there's nothing wrong with positive, encouraging messages, but when parts of the gospel are eliminated or passed over because they are viewed as too negative, then this is where the great error exists. The main problem lies in what's eliminated, not so much in what's included.

Theological Problems of the Prosperity Gospel

While there are elements of truth within the Prosperity Gospel movement, much of their beliefs are only half-truths. The following are key issues that are problematic and untrue:

- **It omits many truths from the gospel:** Its biggest problem is not what it includes but what it excludes. While some of what it includes is unbalanced and twisted, it still does contain some truth. However, its omission of foundational truths is what's extremely concerning and leads it to be classified by many (myself included) as a false gospel. It virtually omits the sinfulness and depravity of mankind, the consequences of sin, and hell.

- **Salvation means something entirely different:** The Prosperity Gospel's version of salvation is salvation from poverty, sickness, failure, and unhappiness, not salvation from sin and hell.

- **It teaches we can have God's blessings without following His principles and commands:** It promotes a "lazy man's" approach to acquiring blessings as it advocates a "fast track" approach that eliminates the need for discipleship. Instead of attaining God's blessings through a lifelong, faithful application of God's principles, Prosperity Theology believes blessings can be attained immediately and miraculously without much effort on our part.

- **It teaches wealth and health are guarantees:** It treats God like an ATM Who is obligated to give us what we want when we want it. It diminishes His personhood and turns Him into a machine, making Him our servant rather than us being His servants.

- **It teaches happiness can be acquired without departing from sin:** The sinfulness of mankind is passed over and in its place is preached success, happiness, prosperity, positivity, health, etc. People are taught they can attain all the blessings of God while, at the same time, violating God's call for purity, confession of sin, holy living, and fellowship with God in the inner heart.

- **It reveals a shallow and ignorant understanding of the Word of God:** For the student of Scripture, it becomes quickly apparent that the beliefs of the Prosperity Gospel movement come up short. Verses are taken out of context and omitted, biblical themes are overlooked, and many verses are twisted and changed. It's clear they have gone to Scripture with the intent of making it say what they want instead of letting the

Scriptures say what they really say.

- **It fails to understand that God's main purpose for our life is that we would be transformed into His image, not have an easy life (Rom. 8:28–29):** In order to transform us into His image, God uses trials (James 1:2–3), suffering (2 Cor. 4:16–18), and pain. Prosperity Theology bypasses this truth and focuses on that which satisfies many of the desires of the sinful nature instead. Purpose and success are defined as being wealthy, healthy, and happy.

- **It wrongly defines God's blessings:** Instead of allowing God to define what His blessings are, Prosperity Theology defines them for Him. Proponents cherry pick the blessings they like and omit the ones they don't. Among their handpicked favorites are happiness, wealth, ease of life, health, and success. To the astute believer, it can be seen that some of these so-called "blessings" are just a dressed up version of what the Bible calls "fleshly" and "worldly" desires.

The True Blessings of God

God defines His blessings much differently than what Prosperity Theology advocates. Consider the following verses:

- **Matthew 5:3:** "Blessed are the **poor in spirit**, for theirs is the kingdom of heaven."

- **Matthew 5:4:** "Blessed are those **who mourn**, for they shall be comforted."

- **Matthew 5:5:** "Blessed are the **meek** [teachable], for they shall inherit the earth."

- **Matthew 5:6:** "Blessed are those who **hunger and thirst for righteousness**, for they shall be satisfied."

- **Matthew 5:7:** "Blessed are the **merciful**, for they shall receive

89

mercy."

- **Matthew 5:8:** "Blessed are the **pure in heart**, for they shall see God."

- **Matthew 5:9:** "Blessed are the **peacemakers**, for they shall be called sons of God."

- **Matthew 5:10:** "Blessed are those who are **persecuted** for righteousness' sake, for theirs is the kingdom of heaven."

- **Matthew 5:11–12:** "Blessed are you when others **revile you** and **persecute you** and **utter all kinds of evil against** you falsely on my account. Rejoice and be glad, for your reward is great in heaven, for so they **persecuted** the prophets who were before you."

As can be seen, God's blessings are much deeper and broader than the limited, selfish ones of the Prosperity Gospel.

Prosperity Gospel's Intrusion into Mainline Evangelicalism

Unfortunately, the Prosperity Gospel has made inroads into mainline Evangelical Christianity, and some of its seeds are sprouting up and growing among many Evangelical churches.

How can we know if some of the beliefs and philosophies of the Prosperity Gospel are influencing us? By carefully analyzing and asking ourselves what truths of the gospel we are omitting or neglecting.

Do we promote a version of salvation, like that of the Prosperity Gospel, which is salvation from problems, failure, and unhappiness, not salvation from sin and hell? Do we neglect the sinfulness of mankind, confession of sin, the consequences of sin, repentance, the judgments of God, the fear of the Lord, church discipline, the role of trials and suffering in the transformation process, discipleship, or hell? Moreover, are we so overly concerned about being positive and entertaining that we neglect the purity of the church and the truth of the gospel? If so, it's very likely the seeds of the Prosperity Gospel have crept into our midst and are influencing us.

Conclusion

In summary, there are two core concerns about Prosperity Gospel Theology: (1) the truths of the gospel it twists and excludes, and (2) the role of discipleship.

By omitting or twisting key truths of the gospel, many can be deceived and could very well wind up in hell.

By omitting or neglecting discipleship, it can severely diminish the avenue by which God transforms us into His image, presents us mature in Christ, and grants us His true blessings. If we neglect the role of discipleship, then we reject God's nature and image, choosing instead to retain the image of sin and remain spiritually immature.

Unlike Prosperity Gospel Theology, there are no shortcuts to acquiring God's blessings. They are not instantaneously acquired by miraculous methods, but conversely, come through a life-long perseverance of living out God's principles and commands through discipleship.

7. Misunderstanding Heavenly Rewards

"Do not lay up for yourselves treasures on earth, where moth and rust destroy and where thieves break in and steal, **but lay up for yourselves treasures in heaven**, where neither moth nor rust destroys and where thieves do not break in and steal. For where your treasure is, there your heart will be also" (Matt. 6:19–21).

When we fail to understand the big picture of life, it greatly affects discipleship. We wind up storing our riches on earth rather than in heaven.

God has given abundant revelation about heavenly rewards in Scripture. Running throughout its pages are rich illustrations and ample verses regarding this doctrine. In fact, it's a foundational theme of Scripture and one affiliated with the justice of God. It's only right that we are rewarded based on our actions and choices in this present life. Scripture teaches that according to how we live this life, we will be rewarded or punished in the next.

The Theme of Rewards in Scripture

The word "reward" or its variant is mentioned around 82 times in Scripture. In the Sermon on the Mount, which was Christ's longest and most famous sermon, He spoke about rewards nine times. In it, He emphasized the importance of storing up riches in heaven rather than on earth.

The Parable of the Talents also unfolds the truth of rewards (Matt. 25:14–30). In this parable, Christ gave certain individuals talents (abilities, gifts, time, resources, etc.) and then went away on a long journey. Upon returning, He settled accounts with those to whom He gave the talents. Some of these servants served well and doubled their talents. To them were given rewards based on their efforts and faithfulness. For the person who was lazy and chose not to serve God — even though he knew he would incur judgment—he was punished and sent to hell. This parable teaches that God will reward those who faithfully serve Him and punish those who don't.

At the end of the Book of Revelation, Christ talks about how He will bring rewards with Him upon His return: "Behold, I am coming quickly, and **My reward is with Me**, to render to every man according to what he has done" (Rev. 22:12, NASB).

The doctrine of rewards teaches that how we use the abilities, gifts, time, and resources that God gives us in this life will determine the rewards we will have in the next.

Christians and the Judgment Seat of Christ

Scripture teaches that all Christians will give an account for how they used their talents and served God at a place called the Judgment Seat of Christ. At this place, the believer is not judged as to whether or not they will be saved and going to heaven, but judged based on how they used their talents and served Christ in this present life. "For we must all appear before the judgment seat of Christ, so that each one may **receive what is due for what he has done** in the body, whether good or evil" (2 Cor. 5:10). This passage reveals the reality that each believer will stand before Christ and give an account for how they served Him in this life, and based upon how they served Him will determine the rewards they will receive in heaven.

There's another passage that sheds light on the Judgment Seat of Christ and what will take place there. It deserves a close look as it contains sobering words we should carefully ponder:

> According to the grace of God given to me, like a skilled master builder I laid a foundation, and someone else is building upon it. Let each one take care how he builds upon it. For no one can lay a foundation other than that which is laid, which is Jesus Christ. Now if anyone builds on the

foundation with gold, silver, precious stones, wood, hay, straw — each one's work will become manifest, for the Day will disclose it, because it will be revealed by fire, and the fire will test what sort of work each one has done. **If the work that anyone has built on the foundation survives, he will receive a reward. If anyone's work is burned up, he will suffer loss, though he himself will be saved, but only as through fire** (1 Cor. 3:10–15).

This passage teaches that some Christians will suffer loss when they appear before Christ to be judged for how they lived their lives and used the talents given them. They will still be saved and go to heaven, but they will suffer a loss of some kind. Some of these Christians might suffer loss because they served out of self-glory or wrong motives, and some might suffer loss because of laziness and unfruitfulness as seen in the parable of the talents.

Scripture teaches that heavenly rewards will be given to believers based upon their service to Christ. For those who have been diligent in serving and focused upon storing their riches in heaven, they will enjoy them forever. For those who lived carelessly, they will be saved, but will suffer loss of some kind.

The Difference Between a Gift and a Reward

What is the difference between a gift and a reward? A gift is something freely received and isn't based upon our effort or works but upon the kindness and love of another. However, a reward is given based on our efforts and works.

Scripture clearly teaches that salvation is a gift and is not based on works or effort in any way: "For by grace you have been saved through faith. And this is not your own doing; it is the gift of God, **not a result of works**, so that no one may boast" (Eph. 2:8–9). The only thing we must do to receive Christ's gift of salvation is to accept it.

Rewards, on the other hand, are given by God based upon

our efforts and service to Him. This is why the theme of rewards is found so abundantly throughout Scripture, and why Christ so emphatically encouraged us to lay up riches in heaven.

Misunderstanding Heavenly Rewards

I believe there are five main misunderstandings today negatively affecting the doctrine of heaven and rewards. These beliefs affect the role of discipleship and the eternal state of all believers. They are:

1. The belief that we can be saved by mere belief in God without producing fruit or showing any evidence of salvation.

2. The belief that heaven, and the rewards given there, will be the same for everyone despite how we live our lives on earth.

3. The belief that God's grace will wipe away all the consequences of choices made in this life so we can live negligently without suffering any eternal ramifications.

4. The belief that a Christian's freedom in Christ means they have the liberty to sin without any eternal consequences and accountability.

5. The misunderstanding or denial that all believers will give an account at the Judgment Seat of Christ for how they served God with their lives and used the talents He gave them.

These five misunderstandings are detrimental to discipleship. At stake are not trivial matters, but the loss of rewards that will affect our eternal state.

Consequences of Misunderstanding Heavenly Rewards

Because many believe in some or all five theological fallacies mentioned, they run the danger of doing just enough to get by in their Christian lives in the present. They conclude that they are going to heaven, and heaven will be the same for everyone, so why sacrifice this life's pleasures? In their view, the important thing is just making it to heaven. So, they'll tend to do just enough to get to heaven, but live their lives as they wish in the present.

I believe this mentality is seriously affecting the role of discipleship today, and for this reason, there are few strategic discipleship programs in our churches and little personal discipleship taking place. It might explain why 81% of Evangelical Christians don't read their Bibles regularly, why 61% of believers have not shared their faith in the last six months, and why the average time spent in prayer is 1–7 minutes a day.

After all, if how we serve God in this life doesn't really affect our life and rewards in heaven, then many will take the soft and pleasurable road instead. They'll just be content with going to heaven; believing it will be the same for everyone. As a result, the role of discipleship will be neglected because it's built on the premise that the sacrifice and effort invested in serving Christ in this life will be rewarded in heaven.

How Many Rewards Do You Want?

The sobering reality exists that each one of us has been granted the freedom to choose the amount of rewards we will have in heaven. It's not God's choice, but ours! He will simply be faithful in rewarding us based on how we used our talents in serving Him. Some will have many rewards and enjoy them for eternity, while others will have few or no rewards and live with that reality forever. Heaven will be wonderful and be the same place for every believer, but not all will enjoy the same amount of rewards there.

There are eternal consequences to the belief held by many that heaven and the eternal rewards given there will be the same for everyone. However, according to the Parable of the Talents (Matt. 25:14–30) and the Parable of the Minas (Luke 19:11–27), heaven will be the same place for all who enter, but it will not be the same experience. Some will have many rewards and be given oversight over much, while some will have few rewards and be given oversight over little or, possibly, nothing.

We Serve God Because We Love Him: Not Just to Get Rewards

I need to make it emphatically clear that we should not serve God just for His rewards, but because we genuinely love Him. God will only reward us if our motives are pure and we serve Him with grateful, overflowing love for all He has done for us.

Conclusion

We know that heaven will be wonderful for all who enter, and God will wipe away all tears there. However, I don't believe that when we are in heaven, He will blind our eyes to the clear reality that some will have few rewards while others will have many. That reality will be obvious and will last for all eternity. For those who suffer loss (1 Cor. 3:15), they will live with that consequence forever. They will miss out on the rewards they could have had if they had not been so distracted in this present life with laying up treasures on earth instead of in heaven. This is a sobering thought that should give us great pause.

When we enter heaven, what we did in this life and how we lived it will be locked in place for all eternity. We won't be able to go back and relive our lives and lay up riches in heaven like we should have just because we were foolish and didn't take time for God. After we realize our great error, it will be too late.

The misunderstanding of heavenly rewards has huge ramifications for our eternal state. As a result, many will be deeply regretful when they appear before the Judgment Seat of Christ and suffer loss, or receive few or no rewards.

8. Misunderstanding the Purpose of Discipleship

Many Christians misunderstand the purpose of discipleship, which in turn, leads to its neglect. They view it as applying primarily to "super Christians" and not to them. However, based on the texts of Scripture discussed so far, we can strongly contend that a person who is genuinely saved is also a disciple. The variant of the word "disciple" is mentioned 269 times in the Bible and the word "Christian," a scant three times. Therefore, the word "disciple" best fits the description of what a Christian is.

The purpose of discipleship is to become like Christ in our nature, knowledge, thoughts, desires, and purposes. It is God's plan for developing us into spiritually mature Christians and is not optional, but a command for all. Unfortunately, many Christians don't see it that way.

Discipleship is God's only plan for conforming us into His image. He has no plan "B"! He just doesn't wave a magical wand over us that produces instant maturity in our lives. On the contrary, God expects us to participate in the process of discipleship in order to become like Him. By neglecting discipleship, we are rejecting God's nature and image, choosing instead to retain the image of sin and remain spiritually immature.

The Neglect of Discipleship and the Great Falling Away

God warns that in the last days there will be a great falling away by many who claim to be believers. Christ said, "And then **many will fall away** and betray one another and hate one another. And many false prophets will arise and **lead many astray**" (Matt. 24:10–11). Moreover, Paul alerted, "Now the Spirit expressly says that in later times **some will depart from the faith** by devoting themselves to deceitful spirits and teachings of demons" (1 Tim. 4:1). The Great Falling Away will significantly affect Christians and churches who are neglecting discipleship because they won't have the discernment needed to recognize the false messages of our day.

Many Christians don't know what they believe because they don't read their Bibles. Also, many sermons today have a weak focus on the Bible because they are topical and primarily deal with felt needs. As a result, the foundational doctrines of Scripture are being neglected or viewed as impractical.

When asked to defend key doctrines like the truthfulness of Scripture, who God is, who Christ is, who the Holy Spirit is, what the essence of the gospel is, what the purpose of the church is, the events of the last days, the judgements of God, and moral issues, many Christians are hard pressed to provide answers. Moreover, many think that some cults are equal or similar to Christianity in their doctrinal positions.

Confusion and ignorance reign because discipleship is not encouraged, and most churches have no strategy for making disciples where these foundational doctrines could be taught. Many churches are more interested in gathering a crowd than in making disciples. They are more interested in meeting people's felt needs than their doctrinal and spiritual needs. As a result, doctrine and hard topics are ignored in an attempt to remove any negativity from the church atmosphere. Many churches want an atmosphere that is positive, uplifting, happy, and where people leave feeling upbeat and warm, so their preaching focuses more on the felt needs of their hearers than on doctrine.

Sound Doctrine and the Church Today

Although the focus God gives in the Pastoral Letters (1 and 2 Timothy and Titus) highlight the importance of sound doctrine (its theme is mentioned about 20 times), the focus today is more on topical messages that deal with felt needs. While preaching on felt needs is not bad in and of itself, it can produce weak believers who are ignorant of sound doctrine if it's their main diet. These believers can also become shallow and selfish, thinking that God and others primarily exist to meet their felt needs. In addition, they'll be more susceptible to the growing number of false prophets who are arising, and will continue to arise in the last days. It's not uncommon today for Christians to spend years in some churches and have no idea what they believe because they are rarely, if ever, exposed to doctrinal teaching.

I believe the neglect of discipleship and the disregard of doctrine will be the main causes for the Great Falling Away in the last days. People will simply have little biblical discernment to recognize the false doctrines that will creep in due to their ignorance of truth. Therefore, they will be easy prey for Satan and his lies. With the majority of Christians being biblically illiterate and knowing little about doctrine, they'll be easy targets for false teachers with fine sounding messages. Unfortunately, these false teachers will preach half-truths that will go unnoticed by many.

Conclusion

The purpose of discipleship is to become spiritually mature. How do we become spiritually mature? There's only one way, and it's called discipleship. It's not a game God wants us to play because He has nothing better for us to do; instead, it's His life vest that will rescue us from the raging waves of Satan's lies and protect us from the Great Apostasy of the last days. It will usher us into the abundant life, transform our nature, and give us wisdom and discernment to choose the best things in life instead of the good things. Moreover, it's the means whereby we will store up treasures in heaven and prepare for our eternal home.

By neglecting discipleship, we are rejecting God's nature and image, choosing instead to retain the image of sin and remain spiritually immature.

9. The Lack of Church Discipline

Most Christians would not associate church discipline with discipleship, but they are closely related. Discipleship entails both a forward and backward looking focus. It encourages believers who are right with God to move forward in their journey toward spiritual maturity, and it looks backward to seek out believers who are left behind in the process due to their involvement in sin. Church discipline is part of the "seeking out" aspect that rescues believers who are left behind and is an integral part of discipleship. When we overlook church discipline, we overlook a critical aspect of discipleship.

Sadly, the vast majority of Evangelical churches today do not practice church discipline. Albert Mohler comments on this trend by saying, "The decline of church discipline is perhaps the most visible failure of the contemporary church. No longer concerned with maintaining purity of confession or lifestyle, the contemporary church sees itself as a voluntary association of autonomous members, with minimal moral accountability to God, much less to each other."[77]

Today, we have a low view of the seriousness of sin! Immorality in the world is in a state of freefall, and Christians aren't that far behind. Why is this so? I believe one of the reasons is that there's no longer any consequences or accountability in the church for Christians who get involved in serious sin. As a result, sin runs rampant and is viewed as permissible. We have cancer in our church bodies, and most are content with allowing it to exist and even grow.

A permissive mentality that overlooks the seriousness of sin

---

[77]Albert Mohler, *The Disappearance of Church Discipline—How Can We Recover? Part One,* 2005, AlbertMohler.com, http://www.albertmohler.com/2005/05/13/the-disappearance-of-church-discipline-how-can-we-recover-part-one, Accessed 08/21/2015.

negatively affects discipleship because sin and disobedience are viewed as acceptable, with no negative consequences.

While the intent of this book is not a full treatment on church discipline, nonetheless, we'll look at a few principles about the role of church discipline in relation to discipleship.

What Is Church Discipline?

Church discipline can be described as a form of "intensive care" for **unrepentant church members who claim to be Christians**, but are involved in serious sin. Let me be clear; church discipline is **not** for unbelievers. It is also **not** for believers who repent and turn from their sins. Church discipline is only for **unrepentant church members who claim to be Christians**, but are involved in serious sin.

In order to rescue these unrepentant believers, serious measures should be undertaken to save them from destruction and devastation. It's an aspect of discipleship designed by God to be exercised when all other measures fail. It's an expression of genuine love and is to be administered in a loving, but firm manner. J. Hampton Keathley III, states, "Though church discipline appears unloving and harsh, it nevertheless rests upon the divine authority of Scripture and is vital to the purity, power, progress, and purpose of the church."[78]

Keathley adds, "The responsibility and necessity for discipline is not an option for the church if it obeys the Word of God, but a church must be equally concerned that Scripture is carefully followed in the practice of church discipline."[79]

John MacArthur affirms, "The purpose of church discipline is the spiritual restoration of fallen members and the consequent

---

[78] J. Hampton Keathley III, *Church Discipline,* Bible.org, https://bible.org/article/church-discipline, Accessed 10/08/2015.
[79] Ibid., Accessed 10/08/2015.

strengthening of the church and glorifying of the Lord. When a sinning believer is rebuked, and he turns from his sin and is forgiven, he is won back to fellowship with the body and with its head, Jesus Christ."[80]

Today, Many View Church Discipline as an Act of Hate

It's sad that the very means God has instituted for rescuing believers involved in serious sin from the grips of spiritual death is viewed as hate, rather than love. What a tragedy! As a result, the "Intensive Care Unit" of most churches is out of order, and numerous believers are dying spiritual deaths because its doors are closed.

Most would agree that God wants us to discipline our children so they grow up to be responsible and respectable. They understand this form of love when applied to children, yet for some reason, many Christians do just the opposite with fellow believers engaged in serious sin. They stand by and allow them to destroy their lives, damage the testimony of the church and of Christ, and do nothing. I don't believe that's true love. It might appear like love, but it allows destruction, not restoration, and how can allowing destruction be defined as love?

God disciplines those He loves and so should we: "My son, do not regard lightly the discipline of the Lord, nor be weary when reproved by him. For the Lord disciplines the one he loves, and chastises every son whom he receives" (Heb. 12:5).

Church Discipline in the Old Testament

We see the principle of church discipline in the Old Testament in the commands given to the nation of Israel to discipline and punish sin in its midst. In some cases, because of rebellion or lack of obedience to God's laws, individuals were

---

[80] John MacArthur, Grace to You, *Church Discipline*, www.gty.org/resources/distinctives/DD02/church-discipline, Accessed 10/08/2015.

excommunicated from being part of God's chosen people. This was a strong deterrent against sin: "But the person who does anything with a high hand, whether he is native or a sojourner, reviles the Lord, and that person shall be cut off from among his people. Because he has despised the word of the Lord and has broken his commandment, that person shall be utterly cut off; his iniquity shall be on him" (Num. 15:30–31).

Jesus and Church Discipline

Jesus said, "If your brother sins against you, go and tell him his fault, between you and him alone. If he listens to you, you have gained your brother. But if he does not listen, take one or two others along with you, that every charge may be established by the evidence of two or three witnesses. If he refuses to listen to them, tell it to the church. And if he refuses to listen even to the church, **let him be to you as a Gentile and a tax collector**" (Matt. 18:15–17).

Gentiles and tax collectors were people the Jews repudiated, avoided contact with, and viewed as sinful and unclean. When Christ told the Jews to treat an unrepentant brother involved in serious sin as a Gentile or tax collector, He was communicating the same concept as excommunication in the Old Testament.

The New Testament and Church Discipline

- **1 Corinthians 5:11–13:** "But now I am writing to you **not to associate** with anyone who **bears the name of brother** if he is guilty of sexual immorality or greed, or is an idolater, reviler, drunkard, or swindler — **not even to eat with such a one**. For what have I to do with judging outsiders? Is it not those inside the church whom you are to judge? God judges those outside. **Purge the evil person from among you.**"

  Here we see an example of church discipline wherein a Christian was having sexual relations with his father's wife, and the church in Corinth stood idly by, doing nothing (1 Cor. 5). Under the Holy Spirit's and the Apostle Paul's command, the Corinthian Church exercised church discipline on this sinful member. This discipline might seem harsh, but we see in 2 Corinthians that this man repented and was restored to fellowship with both God and the church (2 Cor. 2:5–8). Can you imagine the joy this brought to God and the Corinthian Church? Can you imagine the health it brought to countless lives by protecting them from sin's cancerous poison?

- **2 Thessalonians 3:14–15:** "Take special note of anyone who does not obey our instruction in this letter. **Do not associate with them, in order that they may feel ashamed.** Yet do not regard them as an enemy, but warn them as you would a fellow believer." This passage deals with believers who are unwilling to obey the clear commands of Scripture.

- **1 Timothy 5:19–21** (NASB): "Do not receive an accusation against an elder except on the basis of two or three witnesses. **Those who continue in sin, rebuke in the presence of all, so that the rest also will be fearful of sinning.** I solemnly charge you in the presence of God and of Christ Jesus and of His chosen angels, to maintain these principles without bias, doing nothing in a spirit of partiality." Here we see church discipline applied to leaders. Those who continue in sin are to be rebuked in the presence of all so that the rest will be fearful of sinning.

When we eliminate church discipline, we eliminate the fear of sinning. We remove a consequence God intended the church to exercise for deterring sin. As a result, sin can run rampant in our churches and grow like cancer, bringing destruction and death in its wake.

How to Treat Non-Christians Involved in Serious Sin

Many pastors and Christians seem confused regarding the difference between how God commands us to treat non-believers and believers involved in grievous sin. They lump both categories together and treat them the same. They fail to understand that God makes a clear distinction in Scripture between non-Christians and Christians, and has clear distinctions regarding His expectations of them.

For the non-Christian involved in serious sin (which is somewhat normal), God commands us to love and welcome them into our lives and churches. The doors of our lives and churches should be open to ministering to sinners just like Christ did. He was called "A friend of sinners" (Luke 7:34), and we should be too. However, we should not be friends with sinners to support them in their sin, but instead, we are to share Christ's Word with them and do everything possible to convince them to turn to Christ and repent of their sins.

God commands us to love all people, but He does not command us to love their sinful activities. In fact, He says just the opposite. The good news is that all sins can be forgiven through Christ's death on the Cross. However, these activities are still sinful. To tell people practicing sinful activities that their sin is okay is not love, but misleading. If we mislead them into believing a lie, then we'll give an account to God for doing so. Therefore, we are to love sinners and share Christ with them, but not endorse, celebrate, or support them in their sin.

How to Treat Christians Involved in Serious Sin

How should we deal with unrepentant Christians involved in serious sin? We treat them very differently than non-believers. It's different because, unlike a non-Christian, the Christian is born-again, knows God, has His Spirit and power within them — enabling them to do right — has God's Word that instructs them against sin, and has the church and believers guiding and helping them.

The non-Christian is dead in their trespasses and sins and unable to change without Christ's help. The Christian is alive in Christ and is blessed with all spiritual blessings in heavenly places (Eph. 1:3). Believers, therefore, have no excuse for falling into serious sin.

For those who call themselves believers, yet are involved in deep sin with no willingness to change, the church, and every Christian, should follow God's will in exercising loving church discipline in their lives (1 Cor. 5:11). This is God's remedy for rescuing hardened Christians who are involved in sin. It's a form of "intensive care" discipleship to be used for saving a sick believer who is in the grips of spiritual death.

Unfortunately, many Christians hold the view that we should treat non-believers and believers the same when they are involved in deep sin. They believe in a version of love that calls for just accepting, loving, encouraging, and praying for them.

Now while we are commanded to love, encourage and pray for our Christian brothers and sisters involved in serious sin, what do we do when they refuse to change? In their case, God commands us to exercise a different kind of love. It's a form of love that is disciplinary, a kind of love that seeks to save and redeem. It's called church discipline and is designed by God to rescue a hardened, unrepentant Christian from their sinful choices so that they don't destroy their lives, damage the testimony of the church, bring reproach to Christ, and fall into greater judgment from God.

John MacArthur states, "The goal of church discipline, then, is not to throw people out of the church or to feed the self-righteous pride of those who administer the discipline. It is not to embarrass people or to exercise authority and power in some unbiblical manner. The purpose is to restore a sinning believer to holiness and bring him back into a pure relationship within the assembly."[81] It's a form of discipleship for the purpose of restoration.

Misunderstanding Church Discipline

Probably the most misunderstood concept about church discipline is the belief that it's not love. But just the opposite is true! Church discipline, if carried out in a biblical manner, is a deep expression of love. It's love applied to a wayward sheep in order to bring them back to the fold. In the same way God disciplines those He loves, the church should also discipline those it loves. To not discipline is to not love.

Some Christians and churches feel that all an unrepentant believer needs is more knowledge, not church discipline. Their reasoning is based on the assumption that if we can just help them know more, then surely they'll come to their senses. They fear that if we exercise church discipline, then we'll surely lose them. This philosophy sounds loving and reasonable, but I don't believe it's the correct biblical response. What unrepentant Christians need is not more knowledge, but the willpower to obey what they already know. Church discipline helps provide the willpower they need.

For an unrepentant believer who knows the truth and is hardened in their sin, the only remedy left for them is church discipline. This discipline also involves the rest of the church's participation by stepping up the pressure on the unrepentant believer to repent and obey God. And as mentioned, it's a form of intensive-care discipleship for rescuing unrepentant believers from spiritual death.

In the same way we shouldn't stand by and watch a loved one in a boat go over a waterfall to their death, we shouldn't stand by and allow a brother or sister in Christ to fall to their spiritual

---

[81] John MacArthur, Grace to You, *Church Discipline,* www.gty.org/resources/distinctives/DD02/church-discipline, Accessed 10/08/2015.

death as well. To allow them to continue in their sin, damage the testimony and purity of the church, and bring reproach to the name of Christ is not biblical love. I believe it's biblical irresponsibility.

The Main Purpose of Church Discipline

Another critical misunderstanding about church discipline is the failure to realize that its main purpose is to protect the rest of the church from the cancer of sin and rebellion. It exists to rescue the unrepentant believer, but its primary function is to keep the rest of the church healthy: "Do you not know that a **little leaven leavens the whole lump**? Cleanse out the old leaven that you may be a new lump, as you really are unleavened" (1 Cor. 5:6–7). If sin in the church is allowed to spread, then the purity of Christ's church is affected.

Also, the destruction and pain the rest of the church can fall into by copying the behavior of an unrepentant sinner can be devastating. By exercising church discipline, we make a bold statement to the church that sin is serious and has no place in a believer's life. By not exercising church discipline, we allow just the opposite. Church discipline brings a cleansing effect on the church that is healthy; allowing serious sin to go undealt with and grow like cancer is not healthy. Many pastors are reluctant to exercise church discipline, thinking it will harm their churches, but just the opposite is true; it will bring health.

In Scripture, God reveals three main reasons why He is so concerned about purity, and therefore, commands us to exercise church discipline: (1) it rescues individual Christians from sin, (2) it protects the church from sin's destruction, and (3) it allows the church to have a greater witness to the world regarding who God is and how He desires mankind to live. When serious sin is allowed by those claiming to be His followers, God's message is damaged because the world sees no difference between how they and God's people live.

Conclusion

The lack of discipleship today in most Evangelical churches is affecting the level of spiritual depth among many believers. This in turn produces Christians who are more susceptible to being judgmental and hypocritical because their lives don't match their words. It then leads to the diminishing power of the church to speak out against society's sins because Christians are caught up in the very same sins that should be condemned.

We need to recognize that discipleship is what develops within us spiritual maturity. Without it, we'll be less effective in reaching the world as our message will be hindered by our lack of example.

Being a disciple of Christ is a call to obey His commands. If we fall into serious sin, then we should expect to be lovingly confronted by mature believers who love us enough to tell us so. When the church lovingly confronts sin in its ranks, it is not being hateful or judgmental, but loving.

Discipleship entails both a forward and backward looking focus. It encourages believers who are right with God to move forward in their journey toward spiritual maturity, and it looks backward to seek out believers who are left behind in the process due to their involvement in sin. Church discipline is part of the "seeking out" aspect that rescues believers who are left behind and is an integral part of discipleship. When we overlook church discipline, we overlook a critical aspect of discipleship.

10. The Belief in Salvation Without Discipleship

A proper understanding of discipleship begins with a proper understanding of salvation. If the true essence of salvation is misunderstood, then the importance and role of discipleship will be misunderstood as well. Many contributing factors are affecting the neglect of discipleship, but one of the most significant seems to be the misunderstanding of the relationship between salvation and discipleship.

Our actions and lifestyles are built upon our belief systems; therefore, if we have a faulty belief system, our actions will naturally follow.

Is Discipleship Optional?

Today, many Christians view discipleship as optional. Despite the fact that it was the central focus of Christ's and the Apostles' ministries, things have changed over the years. What does Christ teach about salvation and discipleship? Is the belief in salvation without discipleship biblical?

Dallas Willard claims that today Christianity as a whole tends to believe salvation is good enough to get us to heaven and discipleship is optional.[82] Willard elaborates on the state of Christianity today when he says, "For at least several decades the churches of the Western world have not made discipleship a condition of being a Christian. One is not required to be, or to intend to be, a disciple in order to become a Christian, and one may remain a Christian without any signs of progress toward or in discipleship."[83] In addition, John MacArthur believes that the contemporary teaching that separates discipleship from salvation

---

[82] Dallas Willard, *The Great Omission* (HarperCollins. Kindle Edition, 2009-10-13), p. 4.
[83] Ibid., p. 4.

springs from ideas foreign to Scripture.[84]

The Calls of Christ to "Follow Me" Combine Salvation and Discipleship into One Act

In the accounts where Christ uses the term "Follow Me," they include both a salvation and discipleship call. While some would like to separate Christ's call to salvation from His call to discipleship, they seem to be one in the same according to Jesus. In other words, salvation and being a disciple go hand in hand. Notice how Christ combines salvation and discipleship together:

> And calling the crowd to him with his disciples, he said to them, "If anyone would come after me, let him deny himself and take up his cross and follow me. For whoever would save his life will lose it, but whoever loses his life for my sake and the gospel's will save it. For what does it profit a man to gain the whole world and forfeit his soul? For what can a man give in return for his soul?" (Mark 8:34–37).

There are four other parallel passages where Christ makes the similar or same call to follow Him (Matt. 10:38–39, 16:24–26; Luke 9:23–25; John 12:25–26). In each call, Christ is addressing two groups: the crowd following Him and His disciples.

In Mark 8:34–37, Christ makes a sweeping statement to all, "If anyone would come after me, let him deny himself and take up his cross and follow me." These words would be argued by some to be a call to discipleship only. However, in the same call, Christ uses the terms "lose your life" and "lose your soul."

How would the terms "lose your life" and "lose your soul" relate to discipleship only? Losing your life and losing your soul would only make sense if the terms refer to salvation, for how could a disciple who is obediently following Christ through

---

[84] John MacArthur, *The Gospel According to Jesus* (Grand Rapids, Michigan, Zondervan Publishing House, 1988), p. 196.

denying themself and taking up their cross lose their soul? It seems clear that Christ combines both salvation and discipleship together into one call. He doesn't see two distinct aspects to the Christian life, but one. His call to salvation was a call to discipleship. Therefore, to be a follower of Christ is to be a disciple.

It would appear, then, that it's unlikely that one can be saved without being a disciple. Salvation, according to Jesus, seems to include much more than mental acquiescence to certain truths about God. It involves an active faith that expresses itself in following Christ. Therefore, salvation and discipleship are one and the same. To be saved is to be a disciple. To be a disciple is to be saved. Unlike some who would like to separate salvation from discipleship, in the calls of Christ to follow Him, they were not separated but combined.

A "Two-Tier" Form of Christianity

Bill Hull, who has written one of the most extensive books on discipleship called *The Complete Book of Discipleship: On Being and Making Followers of Christ,* is deeply concerned about the growing number of Christians who believe that discipleship is optional.

Hull asserts that we've established a "two-tier" state of Christianity. The first level is for those who believe in Christ and then "live primarily as they please," and the second level is for "serious followers" who choose the option of being devoted disciples.[85] He claims, "The church culture in the Global North — along with Australia, New Zealand, and South Africa — has largely accepted the idea of non-discipleship Christianity: people can be Christians without making any effort to submit to and

---

[85] Bill Hull, *The Complete Book of Discipleship: On Being and Making Followers of Christ* (The Navigators Reference Library 1, 2014, NavPress. Kindle Edition), Kindle Locations 700-703.

follow Christ."[86]

Hull continues, "The fact that we've developed this two-tier state of Christianity forces us to retrace our theological footsteps back to the actual message we proclaim. We need to ask ourselves, 'What kind of person does non-discipleship Christianity produce?'"[87]

Hull then elaborates on his claim by stating, "This common teaching is that a Christian is someone who by faith accepts Jesus as Savior, receives eternal life, and is safe and secure in the family of God; a disciple is a more serious Christian active in the practice of the spiritual disciplines and engaged in evangelizing and training others. But I must be blunt: I find no biblical evidence for a separation of Christian from disciple."[88]

As a result of the belief in a "two-tier" form of Christianity, many view discipleship as optional. Hull alleges, "They believe they can be saved without being a disciple because by and large, the modern gospel teaches that faith equals agreement with a set of religious facts. The problem is that believing in Jesus has no meaning if we don't follow Him in discipleship. Believing without discipleship is not believing; it is agreeing to a set of facts about a religious figure."[89]

Hull claims that preaching a gospel that excludes discipleship is a different gospel: "But because we've preached a different gospel, a vast throng of people think they are Christian/saved/born again when they really aren't! We've made the test for salvation doctrinal rather than behavioral, ritualizing it with walking the aisle, praying to receive Christ, or signing a doctrinal statement."[90]

David Platt shares this similar concern by stating, "Churches

---

[86] Ibid., Kindle Locations 700-703.
[87] Ibid., Kindle Locations 700-703.
[88] Ibid., Kindle Locations 572-575.
[89] Ibid., Kindle Locations 718.
[90] Ibid., Kindle Locations 740-742.

today are filled with supposed Christians who seem content to have a casual association with Christ while giving nominal adherence to Christianity. Scores of men, women, and children have been told that becoming a follower of Jesus simply involves acknowledging certain facts or saying certain words."[91]

From a biblical perspective, this view can run the risk of promoting a form of conversion that can easily produce false salvation and a lack of discipleship. It can give the appearance that we can be saved and then live our lives as we please. This mentality leads to the conclusion that we can have the desires of the flesh and heaven too — that we don't need to give up much to be saved. It violates the call of Christ to follow Him in discipleship because discipleship is viewed as optional. Consequently, the state of evangelicalism is suffering as a result, and today we have many spiritually immature Christians.

The Problem with Separating the Gospel into Parts

I admire those who separate the gospel into parts in order to better understand it. However, discipleship has been negatively affected as a result.

Instead of viewing the gospel as a complete process, there's a desire to separate the initial stage of salvation (belief and faith) from its other parts such as repentance, obedience, and fruit. In so doing, faith and belief are often elevated and clarified, while the expression of salvation as evidenced by repentance, obedience, and fruit, is overlooked or misunderstood as works. Instead of viewing the gospel in its entirety, it's divided up and dissected.

While careful analyzation of each part has its role, we can run the risk of losing sight of the big picture because we're so focused on the details. Therefore, it's important to look at the entirety of the salvation process to understand what it entails, not just one

---

[91] David Platt, *Follow Me* (Carol Stream, Tyndale House Publishers, 2013), p. 3.

part of it.

The gospel is only the gospel when it functions in its entirety. On the contrary, the gospel is not the gospel if only part of it is believed and practiced.

Conclusion

How does the belief that we can be saved without being a disciple affect discipleship? If we believe there are two aspects of salvation and that we can choose the salvation aspect but omit the discipleship aspect, then discipleship will be viewed as optional.

I believe being saved and being a disciple are one and the same. It's like a two-sided coin: on one side is faith in Christ and on the other side is following Christ. The act of following Christ is the biblical expression of genuine salvation.

I believe if we primarily focus on one side of the coin (belief only) and omit the other side of the coin (being a disciple), we can promote a false gospel. Both sides of the coin represent the coin in its entirety. Discipleship is the "following Christ" side of the coin. Naturally, if we omit the "following Christ" side of the coin we omit discipleship. This is the great danger of the belief in salvation without discipleship.

11. The Belief in Salvation Without Obedience

I believe the misunderstanding of salvation in relation to obedience is another central factor contributing to the neglect of discipleship today. As a result, many Christians are not engaged in discipleship because they believe they can be saved without obedience or submission to Christ. Is salvation without obedience biblical?

Dallas Willard quotes a statement by A. W. Tozer concerning the belief in salvation without obedience: "A notable heresy has come into being throughout Evangelical Christian circles — the widely accepted concept that we humans can choose to accept Christ only because we need him as Savior and that we have the right to postpone our obedience to him as Lord as long as we want to!"[92] Willard then goes on to state that "Salvation apart from obedience is unknown in the sacred scriptures. This 'heresy' has created the impression that it is quite reasonable to be a 'Vampire Christian.' One in effect says to Jesus, 'I'd like a little of your blood, please, but I don't care to be your student or have your character. In fact, won't you just excuse me while I get on with my life and I'll see you in heaven?'" [93]

John MacArthur has also spoken out about what he believes is a misunderstanding regarding the relationship between salvation and obedience. He claims that some theologians have proposed a gospel wherein one can receive eternal life yet continue to live in rebellion against God.[94] He notes, "They've

---

[92] A. W. Tozer, *I Call It Heresy* (Harrisburg, Penn.: Christian Publications, 1974, p. 5, quoted by Dallas Willard, 2009-10-13, *The Great Omission,* HarperCollins. Kindle Edition), p. 229.
[93] Dallas Willard, *The Great Omission* (HarperCollins. Kindle Edition, 2009-10-13), pp. 13-14.
[94] John MacArthur, *The Gospel According to Jesus* ((Grand Rapids, Michigan, Zondervan Publishing House, 1988), p. 15.

been told that the only criterion for salvation is knowing and believing some basic facts about Christ. They hear from the beginning that obedience is optional."[95] MacArthur refutes this belief by asserting, "The gospel Jesus proclaimed was a call to discipleship, a call to follow Him in submissive obedience, not just a plea to make a decision or pray a prayer."[96]

Not Everyone Who Says to Me, "Lord, Lord," Will Enter the Kingdom of Heaven

Christ has a sobering warning for those who assume they are saved but are not. He proclaims this reality with some startling words, "Not everyone who says to me, '**Lord, Lord,**' will enter the kingdom of heaven, but the one who **does the will of my Father** who is in heaven" (Matt. 7:21). Christ warns that it's not those who call Him "Lord" who will be saved, but those who do the will of His Father. He asserts that it's not what a person says, but what they do that matters, and that it's possible to acknowledge Him as "Lord," but not be genuinely saved. This verse counters the argument of some who believe we can be saved yet not obey. Christ stresses that true faith is active and should include obedience to be saving faith. He claims that mere mental assent does not save, but must be accompanied by obedience to be genuine faith.

Notice also that Christ says, "On that day many will say to me, 'Lord, Lord, did we not prophesy in your name, and cast out demons in your name, and **do many mighty works in your name?**' And then will I declare to them, 'I never knew you; depart from me, you workers of lawlessness'" (Matt. 7:22–23).

Christ states that many will not enter the Kingdom of Heaven because they are basing their salvation on works, not faith. They believe their "mighty works" will save them, not their faith in

---

[95] Ibid., p. 17.
[96] Ibid., p. 21.

Christ alone. Christ warns us that salvation is not by works but by grace.

We find, then, two factors that can result in false salvation: (1) belief in God without obedience and (2) basing our salvation on works and not grace. Christ warns of both dangers in this passage.

The Role of Obedience in Expressing True Faith

Christ taught that genuine salvation should result in obedience: "Whoever **believes** in the Son has eternal life; whoever **does not obey** the Son shall not see life, but the wrath of God remains on him" (John 3:36). Interestingly, Christ uses the word "believe" as synonymous with "obey." According to Christ, believing is obeying, and obeying is believing. They are one and the same.

In this text, obedience to the Son is critical to receiving eternal life, and without it, we are not genuinely saved. Salvation is a free gift given by grace through faith in Christ, but the fruit, or evidence of salvation according to Christ, is obedience.

The Sermon on the Mount and Obedience

Another powerful example regarding the importance of obedience in relation to salvation is found at the end of the Sermon on the Mount:

> Everyone then who hears these words of mine and **does them** will be like a wise man who built his house on the rock. And the rain fell, and the floods came, and the winds blew and beat on that house, but it did not fall, because it had been founded on the rock. And everyone who hears these words of mine and **does not do them** will be like a foolish man who built his house on the sand. And the rain fell, and the floods came, and the winds blew and beat against that house, and it fell, and great was the fall of it (Matt. 7:24–27).

The difference between the salvation or destruction of each house (our lives) in the parable rested upon whether or not they obeyed Christ's words or just heard them.

Now the significance of this passage is weighty. The Sermon on the Mount is the longest sermon recorded in the Gospels that Christ preached. Some theologians have equated the Mount of Beatitudes (the location where Christ preached the Sermon on the Mount) with the Old Covenant given on Mt. Sinai. It's believed by some scholars that in the same way God gave the summation of the Old Covenant on Mt. Sinai, Christ gave the summation of the New Covenant on the Mount of Beatitudes.

If the summation of the New Covenant entails the importance of doing and obeying what Christ taught, then it would seem logical that the gospel message of salvation would include the same. Therefore, a gospel message that permits mental belief only in God, and excludes the need for obedience, would fall far short of what Christ proclaimed.

The Parable of the Sower

Christ also spoke about the marks of a genuine believer in the Parable of the Sower (Matt. 13:1–23). Christ sowed seed (His Word) upon four different kinds of soils (people's lives). The first soil rejected the seed (God's Word), and the next two soils showed life for a bit, but then died out and didn't produce fruit. It was only the soil (people) that produced fruit who were truly saved. According to Christ, the mark of a genuine believer is fruit, not just belief and faith in God.

The Rich Young Man

Christ engaged a rich young man who knew much of the Bible, believed in God, had much of Scripture memorized, and even kept many of the Ten Commandments, but wasn't saved. Jesus used this encounter to teach that salvation and obedience go hand in hand. Matthew 19 recounts the meeting:

> And behold, a man came up to him, saying, "Teacher, what good deed must I do **to have eternal life**?" And he said to him, "Why do you ask me about what is good? There is only one who is good. If you would enter life, keep the commandments." He said to him, "Which ones?" And Jesus said, "You shall not murder, You shall not commit adultery, You shall not steal, You shall not bear false witness, Honor your father and mother, and, You shall love your neighbor as yourself." The young man said to him, "All these I have kept. What do I still lack?" Jesus said to him, "If you would be perfect, go, sell what you possess and give to the poor, and you will have treasure in heaven; and come, follow me." When the young man heard this, he went away sorrowful, for he had great possessions (Matt. 19:16–22).

Interestingly, the rich young man knew he wasn't saved, and Jesus knew it as well. There was no debate about that. However, despite the rich young man's knowledge of God, belief in Him, and obedience to some of the Ten Commandments, he wasn't saved. He lacked one thing: he was unwilling to submit to, and follow Christ. This passage indicates that belief in God, and even some Christian activity, isn't enough to save us. Faith must be accompanied by obedience in order to be genuine, saving faith.

Defining Who Is in the Family of God

After a long session of teaching about the Parables of the Kingdom, in which Christ had emphasized the importance of putting His words into practice instead of just hearing them, Christ was told that His mother and brothers were seeking Him. His response to them was quite fascinating: "But he answered them, 'My mother and my brothers are those who **hear the word of God and do it**'" (Luke 8:21).

Christ states that it's those who do His words that are part of His family, not those who merely hear His words without doing them. He stresses the fact that salvation and obedience go hand in hand.

Hearing Without Obeying Brings Greater Condemnation

Christ continually warned that hearing without obeying brings greater condemnation because we know what to do but refuse to do it. The following passage speaks of those who heard Christ's words but chose not to obey them:

> Then he began to denounce the cities where most of his mighty works had been done, because they did not repent. "Woe to you, Chorazin! Woe to you, Bethsaida! For if the mighty works done in you had been done in Tyre and Sidon, they would have repented long ago in sackcloth and ashes. But I tell you, it will be more bearable on the day of judgment for Tyre and Sidon than for you. And you, Capernaum, will you be exalted to heaven? You will be brought down to Hades. For if the mighty works done in you had been done in Sodom, it would have remained until this day. But I tell you that it will be more tolerable on the day of judgment for the land of Sodom than for you" (Matt. 11:20–24).

We also see countless examples of punishment and condemnation in the Old Testament for those who heard God's words but chose not to obey them.

Conclusion

Despite the verses that teach salvation and obedience go hand in hand, some today are teaching that obedience is optional and that one can be saved without obeying and following Christ. I believe this misunderstanding is a significant factor leading to the neglect of discipleship among many.

12. The Belief in Salvation Without Works

The belief that we can be saved without bearing fruit or showing any evidence of our faith is also contributing to the lack of discipleship. Many think that as long as they believe and have faith in God, they are saved. They cling to their belief as sufficient for salvation and believe bearing fruit and being a follower of Christ are optional. Is it possible to be saved, yet have no works or expression of that faith in our lives? Is belief in God enough to save us, or must our faith be accompanied by works to be genuine, saving faith? Is salvation without works biblical?

Is Belief in God Without Fruit Genuine Faith?

The Book of James strives to define faith and works, otherwise known as belief and fruit. It attempts to clarify what genuine faith is and how it's expressed. It's not teaching that works save us, but that true faith should include fruit that provides evidence of salvation. Notice how James clarifies that belief in God and faith without works do not save:

> But someone will say, "You have faith and I have works. Show me your faith apart from your works, and I will show you my faith by my works. You believe that God is one; you do well. Even the demons believe — and shudder" (James 2:18-19).

Notice how James says that our faith (salvation) is shown by our works. Notice also that despite believing in God and shuddering, the demons are not saved. This proves that it's not our belief only that saves us, but our belief expressed through obedience. Belief is the necessary beginning point in salvation, but if it's not expressed through works (fruit), it's not true faith and doesn't produce genuine conversion.

James also clarifies another critical aspect of faith:

What good is it, my brothers, if someone says he has faith but does not have works? Can that faith save him? If a brother or sister is poorly clothed and lacking in daily food, and one of you says to them, "Go in peace, be warmed and filled," without giving them the things needed for the body, what good is that? **So also faith by itself, if it does not have works, is dead** (James 2:14–17).

James clarifies that genuine faith must be accompanied by works (fruit) to be true faith, and if not, it is dead. For those who claim that belief is enough to save them, John MacArthur boldly responds: "The faith they are relying on is only intellectual acquiescence to a set of facts. It will not save."[97]

Defining Biblical Faith

What is true faith according to Scripture? Is it only mental belief about certain facts or does it entail more?

In Hebrews 11, we find the longest and fullest treatise on the definition and example of biblical faith:

- By faith, Noah **built** an ark.
- By faith, Abraham **obeyed** and left his country to follow God to the Promised Land.
- By faith, Sarah **received** power to conceive.
- By faith, Abraham, when he was tested, **offered up** Isaac.
- By faith, Isaac **invoked** future blessings on Jacob and Esau.
- By faith, Jacob, when dying, **blessed** each of the sons of Joseph.
- By faith, Joseph, at the end of his life **made mention** of the exodus of the Israelites and **gave directions** concerning his

---

[97]John MacArthur, *The Gospel According to Jesus* (Grand Rapids, Michigan, Zondervan Publishing House, 1988), p. 170.

bones.

- By faith, Moses, when he was born, was **hidden** for three months by his parents.
- By faith, Moses, when he was grown up, **refused** to be called the son of Pharaoh's daughter, **choosing** rather to be mistreated with the people of God than to enjoy the fleeting pleasures of sin.
- By faith, Moses **kept** the Passover and sprinkled the blood so that the Destroyer of the firstborn might not touch them.
- By faith, the people **crossed** the Red Sea as on dry land.
- By faith, the walls of Jericho fell after the Israelites had **encircled** them for seven days.
- By faith, Rahab the prostitute did not perish with those who were disobedient because she had **given** a friendly welcome to the spies.
- By faith, Gideon, Barak, Samson, Jephthah, David, Samuel, and the prophets **conquered** kingdoms, **enforced** justice, **obtained** promises, **stopped** the mouths of lions, **quenched** the power of fire, **escaped** the edge of the sword, were **made** strong out of weakness, became **mighty** in war, and put foreign armies to **flight.**
- By faith, women **received** back their dead by resurrection; some were tortured, **refusing** to accept release, so that they might rise again to a better life.
- By faith, others suffered mocking and flogging, and even chains and imprisonment, they were stoned, they were sawn in two, they were killed with the sword, they **went about** in skins of sheep and goats, destitute, afflicted, and mistreated.

The fascinating truth about all these examples of faith is that they are characterized by an action. Their faith was followed by doing something, not mere static belief. Each example is followed by a verb, a verb of action, a verb of obedience. Each person displayed works that bore witness to their faith.

Now it's critical that we clarify the difference between works done to earn salvation and works done as the result of salvation. Works done to earn salvation is what Scripture calls a "false gospel." Works done as the result of salvation is what Scripture calls "fruit." Works, therefore, are the result of our salvation, not what earns it. However, if our faith does not have fruit, it is dead.

John the Baptist and Biblical Faith

John the Baptist strongly rebuked those in his day who thought they could just believe in God and not bear fruit: "But when he saw many of the Pharisees and Sadducees coming to his baptism, he said to them, 'You brood of vipers! Who warned you to flee from the wrath to come? **Bear fruit in keeping with repentance**. And do not presume to say to yourselves, 'We have Abraham as our father,' for I tell you, God is able from these stones to raise up children for Abraham. Even now the axe is laid to the root of the trees. Every tree therefore that **does not bear good fruit is cut down and thrown into the fire**'" (Matt. 3:7–10). This verse teaches that faith without fruit is not saving faith.

Christ and Biblical Faith

Christ's most used phrase in calling people to salvation was, "Follow Me." "And **calling the crowd** to him with his disciples, he said to them, 'If anyone would come after me, let him deny himself and take up his cross and **follow me**'" (Mark 8:34). The term "Follow Me" is a call to action. It's a verb and entails more than belief. In a practical sense, following Christ cannot be done without some kind of action on our part, either spiritually or physically.

Fruit Is the Evidence of Genuine Salvation

Christ spoke about true and false prophets and how we'd know the difference between them. He said, "Beware of false prophets, who come to you in sheep's clothing but inwardly are ravenous wolves. You will recognize them by their fruits. Are grapes gathered from thornbushes, or figs from thistles? So, every healthy tree bears good fruit, but the diseased tree bears bad fruit. A healthy tree cannot bear bad fruit, nor can a diseased tree bear good fruit. Every tree that does not bear good fruit is cut down and thrown into the fire. Thus, **you will recognize them by their fruits**" (Matt. 7:15–20).

Christ says the way we recognize genuine believers from false believers is by their fruits. He also said that the false believers would be cut down and thrown into the fire. Therefore, those who don't produce the fruit of genuine salvation are not true believers. According to Christ, it's the fruit of a person's life, not their belief in Him that distinguishes a true believer from a false believer.

Genuine Faith Is Expressed by Action

Genuine, saving faith should result in bearing fruit. It does not entail just mental assent and mere knowledge, but some action on our part that results in doing the will of our Master. It results in good works!

Throughout the whole of Scripture, we see biblical faith that is obedient always brings blessings from God, but mere mental assent without obedience always brings His judgment.

For example, the reason the nation of Israel was deported to Assyria and Babylon was because of their lack of obedience. Most Israelites believed in God; they just didn't obey Him. Their mere belief in God did not save them from being deported and escaping His judgment.

Good Works Is an Expression of Faith

The most quoted verses on the foundational doctrine that salvation is by grace through faith in Jesus Christ and not by works is Ephesians 2:8–9: "For by grace you have been saved through faith. And this is not your own doing; it is the gift of God, not a result of works, so that no one may boast."

However, most disassociate Ephesians 2:10 from Ephesians 2:8–9. Ephesians 2:10 reveals what the result or outflow of Ephesians 2:8–9 should be: "For we are his workmanship, created in Christ Jesus for **good works**, which God prepared beforehand, that we should walk in them." By seeing these verses together, we learn that salvation begins with faith in God, but does not end there. True faith should be evidenced by works in a believer's life if it is genuine, saving faith.

Conclusion

I believe that, according to Christ and the rest of Scripture, genuine salvation should result in fruit bearing. We should desire to follow, be obedient, and please our Master. True faith should produce fruit in our lives that bears witness to the fact that genuine salvation has occurred. The fruit produced doesn't save us, but is a by-product of salvation.

How does the belief that we can be saved without bearing any fruit affect discipleship? If we believe we can be saved without being a disciple and bearing any fruit, then we run the risk of being false believers. We'll also neglect discipleship as our focus will not be on serving God, but on a version of the gospel wherein we believe we can be saved, but live as we wish with little or no accountability before God.

Therefore, can a person be saved and not produce any fruit? I believe the answer is no. Genuine faith produces fruit, not the absence of it.

13. The Belief in Grace Without Effort

Another factor contributing to the neglect of discipleship today is the common belief that grace is opposed to effort in our spiritual growth. We talk a lot about God's grace, forgiveness of sin, and our freedom in Christ, but don't talk much about responsibility, discipline, and perseverance. We focus on God's role in granting us grace but neglect our role in exerting effort.

Is the belief that God's grace is opposed to human effort true, or do they work hand in hand? Is it okay to be lazy and casual in our Christian lives because God will love us no matter what, or is this dangerous water to enter? Is it okay to presume upon God's grace and forgiveness, or is this a treacherous road to walk?

Grace and Effort

I believe God's grace, that enables us to grow in Christ, be victorious over sin, and arrive at spiritual maturity, is not opposed to effort. Grace is opposed to earning salvation and God's love, but it's not opposed to the human agent's cooperation with God by exercising effort in spiritual growth. We see throughout Scripture that God is not opposed to effort in doing His will.

Hebrews chapter 11 outlines all the great heroes of the faith and exhibits how their efforts pleased God. Each expression of their faith was accompanied by effort.

We also see in the Apostle Paul's life how he cooperated with the grace of God by exercising effort: "But by the grace of God I am what I am, and his grace toward me was not in vain. On the contrary, **I worked harder** than any of them, though it was not I, but the grace of God that is with me" (1 Cor. 15:10). Paul notes how he worked harder than the rest of the Apostles with the grace of God, yet he credits God for everything. In this verse, we see a wonderful relationship between the grace of God and human effort. They work hand in hand, God granting grace and the human agent working and applying His grace to their life.

The well-known verses of Philippians 2:12–13 also speak of the role of effort in relation to salvation: "Therefore, my beloved, as you have always obeyed, so now, not only as in my presence but much more in my absence, **work out your own salvation** with fear and trembling, for it is God who works in you, both to will and to work for his good pleasure." Working out our salvation means working to bring it to completion, not working to earn it. It means living out and applying God's Word in our lives, not just knowing something and remaining unchanged.

Working out your own salvation with fear and trembling speaks of the seriousness we should take in our pursuit of spiritual maturity.

In these verses, God expects us to exercise our effort for spiritual growth in Christ. As Bill Hull states, "Grace, then, is God's continued gift of enabling us to do good works and to give great effort. These are as much a part of his grace as the act of salvation or conversion."[98]

God's Grace and Human Effort

I believe the Bible teaches that living by faith encompasses two aspects: (1) what God does and (2) what we do in response to what God does. Scripture clearly teaches that we are saved by grace through faith and not of works (Eph. 2:8–9). In addition, it also teaches that we grow in our relationship with Christ by grace as well (2 Pet. 3:18).

Therefore, every aspect of salvation and every aspect of growth in Christ involves God's grace helping us in the process.

---

[98] Bill Hull, *The Complete Book of Discipleship: On Being and Making Followers of Christ* (The Navigators Reference Library 1, 2014, NavPress. Kindle Edition), Kindle Locations 718-720.

Without God's grace, we would have no desire to receive Christ or grow in Him. It's all accomplished by God working in us and granting us the desire to do His will.

God clearly fulfills His role in granting us grace to grow in Christ. However, He doesn't do everything for us, though He enables and grants us grace for everything. He expects us to have a role in applying His grace. As mentioned, we are commanded to "Work out our salvation." This means we are to exert effort and work with God's enabling grace. God expects us to do our part in working with Him; if we don't, we'll fail to reach spiritual maturity and remain stunted in our growth in Christ.

It's important to understand the difference between effort exerted to earn salvation and effort exerted as the result of salvation. Effort exerted to earn salvation is what Scripture calls a "false gospel." Effort exerted as the result of salvation is what Scripture calls "working out our salvation." Effort, therefore, doesn't earn our salvation, but is what God expects of us as we work out our salvation to become spiritually mature.

For those who misunderstand the true meaning of grace, they'll tend to neglect discipleship as they'll see it as opposed to grace. They'll hold the common belief that God's grace means He'll overlook our lack of obedience, remove the consequences of laziness, and hold us unaccountable for how we live our lives and use the talents He gives us.

Abusing God's Grace

Today, we have a tendency to abuse God's grace. There's a lot of talk among Christians about our freedom in Christ and God's grace. For some, this means they can acquire salvation and then live as they wish. They boast about the grace of God and their freedom in Christ. They assume that because of God's grace He now just winks at and overlooks sin. This simply is not true.

The biblical definition of freedom and grace are very different from what many think today.

The biblical meaning of freedom is the ability Christ grants us to overcome sin, not the freedom to be engaged in it. It's freedom over sin, not freedom to sin. It's the freedom and power to do what we should, not freedom to do as we wish.

The biblical meaning of grace can be defined as God's supernatural enablement that helps us live in such a way as to please God — not the grace to disobey and be unaccountable to the consequences of sin. God's grace empowers us to obey; it doesn't grant us the liberty to disobey and escape God's judgment.

Presuming upon God's Grace

For those who presume upon God's grace and elevate forgiveness over obedience, they overlook a fatal flaw in the life of King Saul. He consistently presumed upon the grace and forgiveness of God by disobeying and assuming God would just overlook his sin. As a result, God removed him as king over Israel and said these harsh words to him through the Prophet Samuel:

> And Samuel said, "Has the Lord as great delight in burnt-offerings and sacrifices, as in **obeying** the voice of the Lord? Behold, to **obey** is better than sacrifice, and to listen than the fat of rams. For rebellion is as the sin of divination, and **presumption** is as iniquity and idolatry. Because you have rejected the word of the Lord, he has also rejected you from being king" (1 Sam. 15:22–23).

In God's eyes, obedience pleases Him far more than asking forgiveness and presuming upon His grace. For the believer who chooses to live casually in their obedience to God, and disobeys because they are counting on His grace and forgiveness, they should take great pause. To presume upon and abuse God's grace and forgiveness is a serious sin in God's eyes.

God's Grace Does Not Remove Sin's Consequences

Many Christians confuse God's grace and forgiveness of sin with the removal of the consequences. They are very different functions. God certainly forgives and removes our sins as far as the east is from the west, but He doesn't remove the consequences of them.

King David is a stark reminder of how sin affects our lives. After he committed adultery with Bathsheba and murdered her husband Uriah, his life was never the same. He lost fellowship with God for a time, lost the son he had from his adulterous encounter, lost his moral authority, ceased to speak out against sin in the lives of his family and nation, remained virtually impotent as a spiritual leader, and lost the respect of others. God loved and forgave him, but there were monumental consequences for his sin.

Dietrich Bonhoeffer reveals a weakness he sees in Christianity today that abuses and presumes upon God's grace. It's the belief that Christians can be saved and then do as they please because they are under grace. He counters this understanding by stating, "The word of cheap grace has been the ruin of more Christians than any commandment of works."[99] Bonhoeffer claims that true salvation will encompass discipleship and works. He warns against the idea that salvation can be attained apart from obedience and summarizes such a view as "cheap grace."[100] John MacArthur echoes this same concern when he says, "Grace does not grant permission to live in the flesh; it supplies power to live in the Spirit."[101]

---

[99] Dietrich Bonhoeffer, *The Cost of Discipleship* (SCM Classics, Hymns Ancient and Modern Ltd., Kindle Edition, 2011-08-16), Kindle Locations 770-771.
[100] Ibid., Kindle Locations 770-771.
[101] John MacArthur, *The Gospel According to Jesus* (Grand Rapids, Michigan, Zondervan Publishing House, 1988), p. 31.

Conclusion

Many Christians today are neglecting discipleship because they believe that exerting human effort is not that important or is opposed to God's grace. They believe they can just coast along, living as they please, because God will forgive and remove the consequences of their lazy choices. In so doing, they are abusing and presuming upon God's grace, believing discipleship is optional. As a result, few are seriously pursuing a life that leads to spiritual maturity.

Conclusion to Chapter 2

In this chapter, we looked at 13 key factors contributing to the neglect of discipleship and spiritual maturity. In the next chapter, we'll define biblical discipleship by examining key phrases Christ used in calling people to follow Him. In the process, we'll understand what discipleship was like in the time of Christ and see how it vastly differs from discipleship today.

Chapter 3

Defining Biblical Discipleship

In This Chapter

In chapter 1, we analyzed the state of discipleship and spiritual maturity today, concluding that they're in critical condition and being grossly neglected. In chapter 2, we investigated the key factors contributing to the neglect of discipleship and spiritual maturity.

In this chapter, we'll define biblical discipleship by examining key phrases Christ used in calling people to follow Him.

---

1. The Meaning of Biblical Discipleship

"To another he said, 'Follow me.' But he said, 'Lord, let me first go and bury my father.' And Jesus said to him, 'Leave the dead to bury their own dead. But as for you, go and proclaim the kingdom of God.' Yet another said, 'I will follow you, Lord, but let me first say farewell to those at my home.' Jesus said to him, 'No one who puts his hand to the plow and looks back is fit for the kingdom of God'" (Luke 9:59–62). These words reveal the depth of commitment Christ demands in order to be His disciple.

What is biblical discipleship and how is modern day discipleship starkly different from that of Christ's day?

What Is Biblical Discipleship?

Joseph Crockett, in his article "Is There Discipline in Our Discipleship," states that the term "disciple" is derived from the Latin term, *discipulus*, and refers to a pupil, student, and follower. Related ideas include: to learn, to take, or to accept.[102]

James Samra, in his article "A Biblical View of Discipleship," proposes that the word "discipleship" is used in a number of

---

[102] Joseph V. Crockett, *Is There Discipline in Our Discipleship?* (Source: Living Pulpit, Online, March 1, 2014, ATLA Religion Database with ATLASerials, Hunter Resource Library), p. 9, Accessed 11/5/2014.

different ways in the Bible.[103] Sometimes it's used to denote educational training, and sometimes it signifies life transformation or that of becoming like one's master.[104] Samra summarizes this concept by stating that discipleship can generally be understood to mean "the process of becoming like Christ."[105]

Greg Herrick says, "The Greek term *mathētēs* generally refers to any student, pupil, apprentice, or adherent, as opposed to a teacher. In the ancient world, it is most often associated with people who were devoted followers of a great religious leader or teacher of philosophy."[106] The Hebrew word for disciple is *talmidim*.

As mentioned in chapter 1, Dallas Willard makes an astute observation by revealing that the word "disciple" occurs 269 times in the New Testament, and the word "Christian" a scant three times.[107] Willard defines discipleship as the foundational aspect of what it means to be saved and a true follower of Christ.

Klaus Issler defines biblical discipleship as the responsibility to teach all believers to obey everything Christ commanded. Issler states that the Gospel of Matthew records five major discourses by Jesus, from which six broad themes are taken. A summary of these discourses is found in the Great Commission where Christ says, "Teaching them to obey everything I have commanded you."[108]

The word "disciple" is related to the word "discipline." A disciple, therefore, should be a highly disciplined person who is

---

[103] James G. Samra, *A Biblical View of Discipleship* (Bibliotheca Sacra: 219-34, Publication Type: Article, Database: ATLA Religion Database with ATLASerials, Hunter Resource Library), p. 219, Accessed 11/5/2014.
[104] Ibid., p. 219.
[105] Ibid., p. 220.
[106] Greg Herrick, *Understanding the Meaning of the Term "Disciple"*, 2004, Bible.org, https://bible.org/seriespage/2-understanding-meaning-term-disciple, Accessed 08/13/2015.
[107] Dallas Willard, *The Great Omission* (HarperCollins, Kindle Edition, 2009-10-13), p. 3.
[108] Klaus Issler, *Six Themes to Guide Spiritual Formation Ministry Based on Jesus' Sermon on the Mount* (Source: Christian Education, Journal Date: September 1, 2010. CEJ: Series 3, Vol. 7, No. 2. ATLA Religion Database with ATLASerials. Hunter Resource Library), pp. 367, 368, Accessed 11/5/2014.

focused on following and obeying all the commands of God (Matt. 28:20).

Discipleship in the Time of Christ

In order to understand biblical discipleship in its fullness, we must see how it functioned in the time of Christ. Ray Vander Laan provides rich understanding in this area. He notes, "Discipleship was a very common practice in Christ's day and especially in the Galilee area. The people of Galilee were the most religious Jews in the world in the time of Jesus. This is quite contrary to the common view that the Galileans were simple, uneducated peasants from an isolated area. This perspective is probably due to the comments made in the Bible, which appear to belittle people from this area."[109] Vander Laan continues, "The Galilean people were actually more educated in the Bible and its application than most Jews were. More famous Jewish teachers come from Galilee than anywhere else in the world. They were known for their great reverence for Scripture and their passionate desire to be faithful to it."[110]

Discipleship Training Began Early in Life

Training for discipleship, as we would know it today, actually started very young in the life of a Jewish child. They would enter grade school (called Beth Sefer) at around 4–5 years of age, which was generally held at the local synagogue. The teacher at the synagogue was called a rabbi. At this level, they would mainly be instructed in the Torah (first five books of the Old Testament), learning to read, write, and memorize it. The rest of the Old Testament was referred to as well. Much of the Torah

---

[109] Ray Vander Laan, *Rabbi and Talmidim,* That the World May Know, www.thattheworldmayknow.com/Rabbi-and-talmidim, Accessed 08/13/2015.
[110] Ibid., Accessed 08/13/2015.

was committed to memory, and it's likely that by the time this level of education was finished (age 13), they had much of it memorized.[111]

After grade school, the best students would then continue on to middle school (called Beth Midrash). They would continue to learn and memorize the Torah, but would branch out and learn the rest of the Old Testament as well, committing much of it to memory.

After the Beth Midrash level, those who wanted to continue in discipleship would then seek out a rabbi who would accept them as disciples. They would often leave home to travel with him for a lengthy period of time. These students were called talmidim (talmids) in Hebrew, which is translated, disciple.[112]

Memorization Was a Key Factor in Discipleship

Memorization was important during Jesus' day because most people didn't have their own copy of the Scriptures, so they either had to know it by heart or go to the synagogue to consult the local village scroll. As mentioned, by the time a child finished the Beth Midrash level of education, they had most of the Torah, and much of the Old Testament memorized.

The common memorization technique involved rote, constant repetition, a practice still used to this day.[113]

A Disciple Imitated His Rabbi

Discipleship in Christ's day involved a heavy dose of imitation. A talmid (disciple) emulated his rabbi in all facets of life. His goal was to be like his rabbi. Vander Laan adds, "There is much more to a talmid than simply calling one a student. A

---

[111] Ibid., Accessed 08/13/2015.
[112] Ibid., Accessed 08/13/2015.
[113] Ibid., Accessed 08/13/2015.

student wants to know what the teacher knows for the grade, to complete the class or the degree, or even out of respect for the teacher. A talmid wants to be like the teacher, that is, to become what the teacher is."[114] That meant that students were passionately devoted to their rabbi and noted everything he did or said.

Vander Laan continues, "The rabbi-talmid relationship was a very intense and personal system of education. As the rabbi lived and taught his understanding of the Scripture to his students, they listened, watched, and imitated him to become like him. Eventually, they would become teachers themselves, passing on a lifestyle to their own talmidim."[115]

Discipleship Entailed Learning Much Scripture

The very few talmids that reached the status of a rabbi were extremely respected and sought after. Those who became rabbis were incredibly knowledgeable in Scripture, and many had memorized much, if not all, of the Old Testament. As mentioned, during Christ's day, they didn't have their own personal Bibles like we do today, so they had to commit it to memory to be able to reference and discuss it. As a result of memorizing so much Scripture, the rabbis were extremely knowledgeable in God's Word.

Those who wanted to learn from a rabbi also committed much, if not all, of the Old Testament to memory as well. This was a requirement to be a disciple as their discussions about Scripture didn't mainly deal with what the Scriptures said, but what they meant. Rabbis in the time of Christ would be equivalent to theologians today who hold at least one Ph.D. in theology.

To reach the status of a rabbi was a great accomplishment. They were the ones who decided biblical doctrines, practices, and

---

[114] Ibid., Accessed 08/13/2015.
[115] Ibid., Accessed 08/13/2015.

customs of the country. Their words were exceptionally authoritative and valued. Doug Greenwold says, "In the world of Pharisaism, rabbis were the teachers who had been given the authoritative role to interpret God's Word for the living of a righteous life—defining what behavior would or would not please God."[116]

Rabbis were affiliated as well with many different groups such as the Pharisees, the Sadducees, the Essenes, and others. For example, John the Baptist was a rabbi who had his own disciples (Luke 5:33), and the Apostle Paul was a disciple of Gamaliel before eventually becoming a disciple of Christ at his conversion to Christianity. Some rabbis reached notable status and had a strong influence in religious and government affairs.

Strict Devotion Was Expected

The rabbis expected strict, complete devotion and adherence to their teachings. They expected loyalty and obedience even beyond that given to their families. Greenwold states, "If a rabbi ultimately agreed to a would-be disciple's request and allowed him to become a disciple, the disciple-to-be agreed to submit totally to the rabbi's authority in all areas of interpreting the Scriptures for his life. This was a cultural given for all observant Jewish young men—something each truly wanted to do. As a result, each disciple came to a rabbinic relationship with a desire and a willingness to do just that—surrender to the authority of God's Word as interpreted by his rabbi's view of Scripture."[117]

Different rabbis varied in their views of Scripture, so students would choose their rabbis according to their recognition in the country and their theological positions. It would be similar today as to which seminary a student might choose for their graduate

---

[116] Doug Greenwold, *Being a First-Century Disciple*, 2007, Bible.org, https://bible.org/article/being-first-century-disciple, Accessed 08/15/2015.
[117] Ibid., Access 08/15/2014.

level of theological training. These rabbis, on occasion, would take their students on training trips that could last from several days to several weeks. These were intense times of training where all distractions from the busyness of life were set aside, and the students would focus entirely on the teachings of their rabbi.

The rabbis also had favorite teaching places, one of which  was on the Southern Steps that led up to the Temple Mount in Jerusalem. Tradition holds that even Christ taught His disciples on these steps. I've been blessed to visit this site, and while there, imagined how it must have been.

Theological Discussions Were a Part of Discipleship

It was common for the rabbi and his disciples (a group called Yeshivas) to wrestle significantly with the Word of God. These yeshivas would intensely dialogue and debate over an aspect of life and what Scripture said about it.[118] "It was a standard part of rabbinic teaching methodology."[119] Greenwold adds, "Studying their rabbi's view of Scripture and wrestling with the text to comprehend God's way for the conduct of their life was the main priority of a disciple and the yeshiva experience. Since all disciples had memorized most, if not all, of their Hebrew Scriptures in preparation for their Bar Mitzvahs at age 13, the issue was not what God's Word said, rather what it meant and how it was to be lived out."[120] During their times of intense

---

[118] Ibid., Access 08/14/2014.
[119] Ibid., Access 08/14/2014.
[120] Ibid., Access 08/14/2014.

dialogue and debate, these yeshivas would arrive at their theological convictions and doctrinal positions.

Transparency and Accountability Was the Norm

There was amazing transparency in these groups of yeshivas as they spent much time together in their teaching sessions and discipleship training trips. Doug Greenwold says it well: "Unlike many of our contemporary discipleship programs, there was no curriculum or agenda for this multi-year discipling experience. Rather it was a continual daily relational living experience where either the rabbi would ask questions of the disciple as he closely observed the disciple's life, or the disciple would initiate a discussion by raising an issue or asking a question based on some aspect of his daily life."[121] In this discipleship format, not only was theology passed on, but character, attitudes, and behavior.

The Meaning of "Believe"

As a disciple learned from their rabbi, they were placing their entire trust and belief in him. This process was called, "believing." Unlike today, the term "believe" had a very different meaning in the Hebrew culture. Once again, Greenwold states it well: "The Semitic understanding of 'believe' was not based on an intellectual assent to a creed, doctrinal statement, or series of faith propositions. Rather, to a first-century disciple 'believe' is a verb in which you willingly submitted to your rabbi's interpretive authority regarding God's Word in every area of your life. Thus, to say you were a disciple in the name of Gamaliel, meant that you totally surrendered your life to Gamaliel's way of interpreting Scripture. As a result, you conformed all of your life's behavior to his interpretations."[122]

The word "believe" in the Hebrew culture meant taking some

---

[121] Ibid., Access 08/14/2014.
[122] Ibid., Access 08/14/2014.

action, applying knowledge to daily life, and changing some attitude or perspective on life, not just mentally knowing something and remaining unchanged. Today, the word "believe" is used more as a noun and slants toward mere intellectual agreement or mental assent, which is a very different meaning than the usage in Christ's day.

Discipleship Meant Commitment

Taking into account the historical meaning of discipleship, we can now better understand the discipleship process Christ employed with His disciples. He called them to follow Him, be with Him, learn from Him, practice what they learned, surrender completely to Him, and to love Him more than their families, friends, and culture. It meant even being willing to die for Him if needed.

Therefore, a disciple can be summed up as a disciplined learner or student who chooses to follow Christ, their rabbi, to such a degree that they submit their entire life, will, time, plans, desires, dreams, character, and efforts fully to Him and His teachings. They are willing to deny themself, take up their cross, and obey all His commands with total abandonment. A biblical disciple is a person who gives complete devotion and loyalty to Christ above any human relationship or influence. It's a person who is willing to die for the cause of Christ on a daily basis, and once and for all if needed.

We see in the discipleship process during the time of Christ that there was a strong emphasis on knowing God's Word, relational mentoring, character, discipline, commitment, and devotion.

Discipleship in Christ's Day Versus Discipleship Today

How are Christians and the church doing today in regards to biblical discipleship? The contrast is quite staggering between discipleship in Christ's time and discipleship today.

Unlike Christ's disciples who knew Scripture exceedingly well and had much of it memorized, 81% of Christians today don't read their Bibles regularly and are largely biblically illiterate. Unlike Christ's disciples who were fishers of men and took the gospel to the ends of the earth, 61% of Christians today haven't even shared their faith in the last six months. Unlike Christ's disciples who prayed extensively, the average Christian today prays somewhere between 1–7 minutes a day. And unlike Christ and the Apostles who made discipleship a core part of their ministries, 81% of pastors have no regular discipleship program for mentoring their people.

It's clear to see that the value Christ and the Apostles gave to discipleship versus the value the average Evangelical church and Christian give it today is vastly different.

2. The Meaning of Follow Me

"And calling the crowd to him with his disciples, he said to them, 'If anyone would come after me, let him deny himself and take up his cross and **follow me**'" (Mark 8:34). What does it mean to "follow Christ"?

The most common phrase Christ used in calling people to salvation and discipleship was "Follow Me." It's mentioned 23 times in the Gospels. If this was the key phrase Christ used to call people to be His disciples, then it's crucial we understand it in order to understand discipleship.

According to the Gospels, Jesus spent approximately 70% of His ministry time around the Sea of Galilee, with the northern shore being His most traversed area. In fact, He even set up His home base during His early ministry in the small town of Capernaum, which is right beside the Sea of Galilee on the northern shore (Matt. 4:13). Scripture records that Christ called all of His 12 disciples from the Galilee area (Acts 1:11).

I've had the privilege of walking the northern shore of the Sea  of Galilee where Scripture records that Christ called four of the 12 disciples (Peter, Andrew, James, and John). I can see in my mind's eye this northern shore and can picture what it must have been like when Christ called His first disciples.

Picture a sunny day on the calm sea not far from the water's edge. Peter and his brother Andrew were fishing as they'd done for many years. Not far down the shore were James and his brother John mending their nets. These two pairs of brothers were all fishing partners. What happened next would change their lives forever:

> While walking by the Sea of Galilee, he saw two brothers, Simon (who is called Peter) and Andrew his brother, casting a net into the sea, for they were fishermen. And he said to them, "Follow me, and I will make you fishers of men." Immediately they left their nets and followed him. And going on from there he saw two other brothers, James the son of Zebedee and John, his brother, in the boat with Zebedee, their father, mending their nets, and he called them. Immediately they left the boat and their father and followed him (Matt. 4:18–24).

Now from accounts in the other Gospels, these four disciples had previously had other encounters with Jesus. Each encounter served them in knowing Him just a little better. So in their decision to follow Christ, they knew what they were doing and what they were committing to. However, unlike their previous encounters with Christ, this time, He asked them to make a commitment. He called them to a decision. They chose to take the boldest step they had ever taken and decided to obey and follow Christ. They left their nets, renounced all, and chose to be disciples of Christ. Their lives would never be the same again.

David Platt articulates what this calling entailed: "When Jesus called the first disciples, He was also calling them away from other things. By calling these men to leave their boats, Jesus was calling them to abandon their careers. When He called them to leave their nets, He was calling them to abandon their possessions. When He called them to leave their father in the boat by himself, He was calling them to abandon their family and friends. Ultimately, Jesus was calling them to abandon themselves."[123]

A Big Decision and a New Life

Following Christ would mean a totally new life for these disciples. They would learn to know Christ better, to deny themselves, to take up their cross, and to lose their lives for the sake of Christ. But in so doing, they would actually find their lives. They would be changed by Christ, and then through Christ's Spirit, they would change the world.

Like the original disciples, have we left behind what hinders us in order to follow Christ? Is Christ more important than our careers, more important than our possessions, more important than our families, and more important than our own lives? Do we know what He wants us to do and become?

To follow Christ assumes that He is our Leader and that we obey our Leader's orders. It assumes we do what we're told, that we set aside our plans, and that we die to ourselves and live for Christ. By doing so, Christ will change us, and then through His Spirit, we will change the world.

Following Christ Means We Follow His Example

The word "Christian" was a name given to the followers of Christ in Acts 11:26 and referred to those who were like Him.

In following Christ, we need to ask ourselves, "How did He live His life, what were His values, and what did He do?" In the same way the original disciples learned from Christ and modeled His life, we should do the same.

First Peter 2:21 says, "For to this you have been called, because Christ also suffered for you, **leaving you an example**, so that you might follow in his steps." We are to follow in Christ's

---

[123] David Platt, *What It Means to Follow Christ*, LifeWay, http://www.lifeway.com/Article/christian-living-what-it-means-to-follow-christ, Accessed 07-22-2015).

steps and be like Him in our actions, attitudes, values, and purposes.

Following Christ Means We Seek Him

In order to follow someone, we need to get to know them and understand what they want us to do. It implies we have a responsibility to take action in following that person's will and plans for us.

Instead of following our own plans, we are to follow those of Christ. We are to seek Christ's will above ours: "But **seek first** the kingdom of God and his righteousness, and all these things will be added to you" (Matt. 6:33).

When we put following Christ first, everything else in life will fall into place. If we don't, then everything will be out of sync and messed up. We'll live frustrated lives without purpose, fruitfulness, and joy.

Following Christ Means We Listen and Obey

In the same way the original disciples listened and obeyed Christ's voice, we should do the same as well. How do we do this today? We do it primarily by knowing God's Word and obeying it. Christ said, "Whoever has my commandments and keeps them, he it is who loves me. And he who loves me will be loved by my Father, and I will love him and manifest myself to him" (John 14:21).

Following Christ Means We Spend Time with Him

In the same way the original disciples spent time with Jesus, we should do the same as well. We should have a daily quiet time where we pray, read His Word, learn from Him, and spend time with Him.

Following Christ Means We Walk with Him

Unlike the original disciples, we cannot walk with Christ physically as they did. How do we walk with Him today? We walk with Him spiritually. The Bible calls this "walking in the Spirit." "But I say, **walk by the Spirit**, and you will not gratify the desires of the flesh" (Gal. 5:16), and "If we live by the Spirit, let us also **walk by the Spirit**" (Gal. 5:25). Walking in the Spirit means that we are in tune with Christ throughout our waking hours. We are conscious of His presence, of what He wants us to do, what He wants us to say, and the attitudes He wants us to have.

Following Christ Means We Set Our Minds on Him

"If then you have been raised with Christ, seek the things that are above, where Christ is, seated at the right hand of God. **Set your minds** on things that are above, not on things that are on earth. For you have died, and your life is hidden with Christ in God" (Col. 3:1–3). Following Christ means we set our minds on Him and seek heavenly things. It means we store our riches in heaven and are more concerned about God's Kingdom than this life.

Christians Today and Following Christ

Unfortunately, the statistics reveal that many Christians today are not seriously following Christ. One of the first truths we should realize in our Christian lives is the need to die to ourselves and live for Christ. But if this is the case, why are we so slothful when it comes to following Christ? Why do we try to get by with doing the least we can in our walk with God? Why are we not serious about discipleship or making disciples? Why don't we care much about knowing God through knowing His Word? Why are many Christians biblically illiterate? Why are many still babes in Christ after years of being a Christian? It appears it's because we are still following our own will and plans instead of God's.

Many Christians live as if they are practical atheists. They don't pray much, they don't read their Bibles much, and they don't think about God much. They don't want to be inconvenienced, but just want to live their lives as they please and then go to heaven after they've checked off all the items on their bucket list.

Could it be that the reason there are so many weak and baby Christians today is that instead of following Christ and giving up our lives for Him, we are saving our lives and keeping them for ourselves? God states that when we receive Christ, we die to ourselves and are now alive in Him. Our wills are now yielded to His, and we're no longer the bosses of our lives.

Following Christ means we go where He leads, we do what He says, and we submit to His leadership. Like the original disciples, we make a commitment to set aside our own wills and plans and choose those of our Master. We choose to take a bold step and become fully devoted disciples of Christ. We allow Him to change us so we can change those around us. We choose to "lose" our lives and, in so doing, "find" them.

3. The Meaning of Deny Self

"And calling the crowd to him with his disciples, he said to them, 'If anyone would come after me, let him **deny himself** and take up his cross and follow me'" (Mark 8:34). What does it mean to deny self?

The Greek word for "deny self" is *arnéomai*. It means to refuse, disown, or repudiate.[124] In general, it means to say no to yourself and to yield your rights and decisions to another. It means choosing what pleases Christ instead of what pleases yourself. One scholar has noted, "Used within the context of the imagery of taking up the cross and following Jesus, 'denying yourself' conveys the sense of a person disassociating himself from his self-interest to serve a higher purpose."[125] Similarly, it means to die to self.

"Denying yourself" and "dying to yourself" are synonymous terms in the Bible. When Christ used these terms, He was referring to anyone who wanted to come after Him and be His disciple. In the same way Christ was going to deny Himself and die on the Cross, He was telling those who wanted to come after Him to do the same.

S. Michael Houdmann states, "Jesus spoke repeatedly to His disciples about taking up their cross (an instrument of death) and following Him. He made it clear that, if any would follow Him, they must deny themselves, which means giving up their lives spiritually, symbolically, and even physically if necessary."[126]

---

[124] Helpmewithbiblestudy.org, *What Did Jesus Mean "Deny Yourself and Take Up Your Cross"?*
http://helpmewithbiblestudy.org/9Salvation/SanctifyWhatDoesItMeanToCarryCross,
Accessed 07/27/2015.
[125] Ibid., Accessed 07/27/2015.
[126] S. Michael Houdmann, *What Does the Bible Mean by "Dying to Self"?*
http://www.gotquestions.org/dying-to-self.html, Accessed 07/27/2015.

Denying self means that I am choosing Christ's will over mine. I am dying to my plans, desires, hopes, purposes, and pleasures, and choosing Christ's plans, desires, purposes, and will instead. It means I am no longer the boss of my life, but instead, Christ is.

The Example of Christ

Christ made the statement about denying self just after He had spoken to those present about how He was going to suffer, die, be buried, and rise from the dead (Luke 9:21–23). He was showing by example what it meant to deny self.

Denying Self Illustrated

Denying self or dying to self is a one-time event that should occur at the time we become saved, and then continue on a daily basis thereafter. Romans 6:3–4 speaks of how baptism symbolizes our death to self and adherence to Christ: "Do you not know that all of us who have been baptized into Christ Jesus were baptized into his death? We were buried therefore with him by baptism into death, in order that, just as Christ was raised from the dead by the glory of the Father, we too might walk in newness of life."

Dying to self is a one-time event, but it's also a daily event as well. Notice what Christ says, "If anyone would come after me, let him deny himself and take up his cross **daily** and follow me" (Luke 9:23).

The Apostle Paul illustrates this concept as well when he says, "I have been crucified with Christ. It is no longer I who live, but Christ who lives in me. And the life I now live in the flesh I live by faith in the Son of God, who loved me and gave himself for me" (Gal. 2:20). Here Paul reveals the lifestyle of a disciple. It is a person who has been crucified (dies to self-will) and now lives their life for Christ. It's now Christ who lives in them and runs the show; it's no longer they who are on the throne following their own will. They are denying themselves and allowing Christ to be in charge.

Denying Self Is Not Optional

S. Michael Houdmann states, "Dying to self is never portrayed in Scripture as something optional in the Christian life. It's the reality of the new birth. No one can come to Christ unless he is willing to see his old life crucified with Christ and begin to live anew in obedience to Him. Jesus describes lukewarm followers who try to live partly in the old life and partly in the new as those whom He will spit out (Rev. 3:15–16). That lukewarm condition characterized the church of Laodicea back then, but also many churches and Christians today."[127]

Some might think that denying self is purely symbolic. It's true it does involve a symbolic meaning, but it also has a completely literal meaning. History indicates that 11 of the 12 Apostles were martyred for their faith. Countless other believers have suffered death and severe persecution over the course of world history as well. It's even said that today there are more martyrs than at any other time in church history. When Christ spoke about dying to self, He was also talking about the possibility of physical death.

Jon Bloom conveys, "Not all who heard Christ's words to follow Him would necessarily die as martyrs, but all would have to die to themselves if they wanted to be His disciples. They would have to die to the desire for self-glory, die to the desire for worldly respect, die to the fear of man, die to the desire for an easy life, die to the desire for earthly wealth, and die a thousand other deaths as well to their earthly desires. Finally, they must die to their desire to save their earthly lives."[128]

---

[127] Ibid., Accessed 07/27/2015.
[128] Jon Bloom, *Let Him Deny Himself,* Desiring God.org., 2010, http://www.desiringgod.org/articles/let-him-deny-himself, Accessed 7/27/2015.

Denying Self Brings Life

The only things Jesus asks us to deny ourselves of are what will rob us of eternal joy. That's why the Holy Spirit said through Paul:

> For those who live according to the flesh set their minds on the things of the flesh, but those who live according to the Spirit set their minds on the things of the Spirit. For to set the mind on the flesh is death, **but to set the mind on the Spirit is life and peace.** For the mind that is set on the flesh is hostile to God, for it does not submit to God's law; indeed, it cannot. Those who are in the flesh cannot please God (Rom. 8:5–8).

Finding life and joy are found in saying no to our desires and yes to Christ's will for us. It's the opposite of what seems natural. It's the opposite of what most people do.

Christians Today and Denying Self

Today, many Christians are not denying self. When statistics show that 81% of Christians don't read their Bibles regularly, biblical illiteracy is at an all-time high, 61% of believers have not shared their faith in the last 6 months, and the average Christian prays around 1–7 minutes a day, it seems pretty obvious that many Christians are not denying themselves.

The reason numerous believers remain spiritual babies and are not growing in Christ as they should is because they are saving their lives instead of losing them. They are not denying themselves and saying yes to reading and studying their Bibles, praying, sharing Christ, serving, and storing up riches in heaven, but instead, are saying no to Christ and His will for them. For this reason, many Christians will fail to reach spiritual maturity and will have little or no rewards in heaven.

4. The Meaning of Take up Your Cross

"And he said to all, 'If anyone would come after me, let him deny himself and **take up his cross daily** and follow me'" (Luke 9:23). What does "take up your cross" mean?

Kurt Struckmeyer provides us insight: "Well, let's begin with what Jesus didn't mean. Many people interpret 'cross' as some burden they must carry in their lives: a strained relationship, a thankless job, or a physical illness. With self-pitying pride, they say, 'That's my cross I have to carry.' Such an interpretation is not what Jesus meant when He said, 'Take up your cross, and follow Me.'"[129]

Struckmeyer adds, "When Jesus carried His cross up Golgotha to be crucified, no one was thinking of the cross as symbolic of a burden to carry. To a person in the first-century, the cross meant one thing and one thing only: death by the most painful and humiliating means human beings could develop."[130] It was a one-way ticket to death.

Again, Struckmeyer states, "The cross was a particularly gruesome and humiliating device for brutally executing troublemakers. It was designed for people of the lower classes, for people who dared to challenge authority, and for people who threatened the status quo. It was intended to inflict prolonged pain and punishment. Bodies were left on the cross to rot and to be eaten by scavenger birds and dogs."[131] Moreover, they crucified those condemned to death in the most public places available so others would fear and submit to their authority.

Therefore, "take up your cross and follow me" means being

---

[129] Kurt Struckmeyer, *Take Up Your Cross,*
http://followingjesus.org/changing/take_up_cross.htm, 2007, Accessed 08/03/2015.
[130] Ibid., Accessed 08/03/2015.
[131] Ibid., Accessed 08/03/2015.

willing to die in order to follow Jesus. This is called "dying to self." It's a call to absolute surrender.

Christ's Example

Christ made the statement to His followers that they must take up their cross daily and follow Him just after Peter's great confession that He was the Son of the living God. Then following these words, He added, "The Son of Man must suffer many things and be rejected by the elders and chief priests and scribes, and be killed, and on the third day be raised" (Luke 9:21–22).

Christ told all those present that He was going to Jerusalem to be crucified and die on a cross. He was leading by example! He would then tell His followers that if they wanted to come after Him and be His disciples, they must be willing to do the same. They must be willing to die on a daily basis to their wills and plans, and be willing to die physically, if needed, as well.

The disciple's cross demanded death to self-will, self-interest, and self-seeking. The term, "take up your cross," speaks of the cost of discipleship and the cost of following Christ.

Contrary to what many Christians today might think, Christ doesn't call disciples to Himself to make their lives easy and pleasant, but instead, holy and productive. Willingness to take up your cross, in the same way Christ took up His, is the mark of a true disciple. Unlike many Christians today, first-century believers understood that taking up your cross had a clear and distinct meaning. It didn't mean you gave to Christ what was convenient; it meant you gave Him your all.

Taking up Your Cross and the Cost of Discipleship

How does "taking up your cross" apply to us today? It would involve asking ourselves the following questions to see if we're truly willing to take up our cross. Are we willing to follow Jesus if it means:

- Giving up some of our time?
- Giving our finances to Him?
- Serving Him and others?
- Losing some of our closest friends?
- Alienation from our family?
- Losing our reputation?
- Losing our job?
- Suffering for Him?
- Being persecuted for Him?
- Standing against the new morality of our culture?
- Losing our life?

These sobering questions reveal, in a practical sense, what many Christians are unwilling to give up for Christ. They might claim to be devoted believers, but in real life, they hold on to their lives and refuse to sacrifice much. They don't give up much time for Christ to read their Bibles, to pray, to share Christ, to speak the truth, to serve Christ, to develop their spiritual gifts and abilities, to be biblical fathers and mothers, to have family devotions, and to be faithful in church attendance. Instead, it appears they are more occupied with their jobs, getting ahead, school, sports, entertainment, and pleasure.

Taking up Your Cross Means Commitment

When Christ talked about taking up your cross, He was stressing the depth of commitment that following Him would entail. He was underscoring the price it would take to be His disciple. Naturally, we shy away from commitments like this and prefer a low cost, non-committal form of Christianity that is high in blessings and low in cost. We want all the riches of Christ, all the blessings He has to offer in this life and the next, but with the least amount of effort as possible.

All the riches Christ has to offer are available, but there's a price to attain them. Christ explained this truth when He used the term, "take up your cross." This term highlights the cost of following Christ, which in turn, leads to His blessings. Simply put, we cannot have the full blessings of God without the willingness to pay the price for them.

God's Blessings Have a Cost

There are two basic principles in the Christian life when it comes to the concept of blessings: (1) blessings come from God and (2) most blessings require a sacrifice to obtain them. Blessings are what God gives us based upon our love for Him and the sacrifices we make to follow Him. They are called sacrifices because they are not what our natural desires would choose.

Our flesh loves pleasure, fun, ease, and entertainment. It naturally doesn't like pain, suffering, difficulty, discipline, and hard work. Therefore, when we choose what Christ would have us do instead of what we would normally choose, then we're sacrificing our desires to do God's will. Without sacrifice, there are few blessings. When we attempt to attain God's blessings without sacrificing our will to do His, then we are trying to obtain His blessings by violating one of His unmovable, universal laws:

> Do not be deceived: God is not mocked, for whatever one sows, that will he also reap. For the one who sows to his own flesh will from the flesh reap corruption, but the one who sows to the Spirit will from the Spirit reap eternal life. And let us not grow weary of doing good, for in due season we will reap, if we do not give up (Gal. 6:7–9).

Discipleship is a sacrifice we make to follow Christ on a daily basis. To the degree we engage in discipleship will be the degree to which we reap God's blessings. To the degree we neglect discipleship will be the degree to which we forfeit His blessings.

The belief that we can attain God's blessings without any cost is appealing, but it's just not true. It's a belief completely opposite of what Christ preached. It's a belief that wants something for nothing.

Taking up Your Cross Involves Sacrifice

Sacrifice values eternity, but non-sacrifice values the temporal pleasures of this fleeting life. Moses clearly understood this principle: "By faith Moses, when he was grown up, refused to be called the son of Pharaoh's daughter, choosing rather to be mistreated with the people of God than to enjoy the fleeting pleasures of sin. He considered the reproach of Christ greater wealth than the treasures of Egypt, for he was looking to the reward" (Heb. 11:24–26).

The call on our part to sacrifice is a major theme of Scripture. In fact, it's the pinnacle and crescendo of the message of Romans: "I appeal to you therefore, brothers, by the mercies of God, to present your bodies as a **living sacrifice**, holy and acceptable to God, which is your spiritual worship. Do not be conformed to this world, but be transformed by the renewal of your mind, that by testing you may discern what is the will of God, what is good and acceptable and perfect" (Rom. 12:1–2).

In Scripture, we see God's continual eagerness to develop within us an eternal perspective to life rather than a temporal one. He desires to see us laying up our treasures in heaven instead of on earth. However, it seems today there's more focus on enjoying this present life instead of sacrificing this life for the one to come.

Taking up Your Cross Values Eternal Riches

Discipleship has at its core a focus on eternity, whereas non-discipleship has at its core a focus on this momentary life. Taking up your cross is the willingness to sacrifice the temporal riches of this life in order to obey God and gain the eternal ones. As Jim Elliot so wisely stated, "He is no fool who gives what he cannot keep to gain what he cannot lose."

For this reason, Christ rebuked those who sought Him primarily for the temporal riches of this life and not the eternal riches of heaven. He scolded them for seeking only the material blessings He offered and not the spiritual ones.

Shortly after Christ fed the 5,000, those whom He fed came looking for Him. Christ knew they were mainly interested in the earthly blessings He provided them, so He said, "Truly, truly, I say to you, you are seeking me, not because you saw signs, but because you ate your fill of the loaves. **Do not work for the food that perishes, but for the food that endures to eternal life**, which the Son of Man will give to you" (Matt. 6:26–27).

Taking up Your Cross Illustrated

Abraham understood the cost of following God and was willing to make enormous sacrifices to do so. He is called, "Our Father of Faith," and was willing to leave his homeland, his father, mother, relatives, and friends to follow God. He was willing to sojourn in a foreign land, leaving everything without knowing what awaited him. Moreover, he was even willing to give up his son, Isaac, his most cherished possession, that for which he had waited for most of his entire life to have. His example is amazing!

Genesis 22 recounts this incredible story: "After these things God tested Abraham and said to him, 'Abraham!' And he said, 'Here I am.' He said, 'Take your son, your only son Isaac, whom you love, and go to the land of Moriah, and offer him there as a burnt-offering on one of the mountains of which I shall tell you'" (Gen. 22:1–2).

Scripture records that early the next morning Abraham saddled his donkey, took his son, and headed out on a three-day journey to Mount Moriah to sacrifice his son there. How many times do you think Abraham glanced at Isaac during those long, dusty, three days, thinking about what he was going to do? Yet, despite his inner struggle, he plodded on.

Upon arriving at Mount Moriah, he climbed the hill (which is the same Mount Moriah upon which the temple would later be built by King Solomon), bound his son, and then prepared himself to sacrifice Isaac upon the altar he had made. As the knife was on its way down, "The Lord called to him from heaven and said, 'Abraham, Abraham!' And he said, 'Here I am.' He said, 'Do not lay your hand on the boy or do anything to him, for now I know that you fear God, seeing you have not withheld your son, your only son, from me'" (Gen. 22:11–12).

Abraham displayed his faith and obedience to God by his willingness to sacrifice his "all" on the altar. As a result, he was blessed beyond measure and became a foundational figure in Scripture—so much so that he's called our "Father of Faith."

But notice that these blessings were given to him as a result of the cost he paid to follow God, not as a result of doing his own will and then expecting blessings for nothing. The belief that we can obtain the blessings of God without paying the cost for them has no support in Scripture.

God calls us to be like Abraham, our Father of Faith. He tests us in order to know how much we love Him and to see to what degree we're willing to pay the cost to follow Him. We show our love to God by our willingness to follow Him, regardless of the cost.

Taking up Your Cross Involves Obedience

Taking up your cross means that we obey God regardless of the price. It means that no matter how difficult it is to read our Bibles daily we should do it. In spite of how hard it is to pray, we should press on. Regardless of how painful it is to tithe, we should obey. No matter what our loved ones and friends think of us, we should stand firm to biblical truth. In spite of how costly it is to be faithful in church attendance, we should be loyal. No matter how inconvenient it is to have family devotions, we should persevere. Regardless of how unhappy it makes us feel, we should stand strong in the face of ridicule. No matter how boring it might be to read theological books that help us grow in Christ, we should endure. In spite of the cost to be a disciple, we should pay it.

Christians Today and Taking up Your Cross

If we want to be like Christ, Abraham, the prophets, and the Apostles, then we must be willing to follow God regardless of the cost. Unfortunately, many Christians today are not willing to pay the price. They prefer a non-committal kind of Christianity. They favor a path of happiness, pleasure, and ease instead of paying the cost of discipleship. In so doing, they choose temporal riches over eternal ones.

In modern Christianity, we have a strong focus on the blessings of God, but a weak focus on the cost for attaining them. We highlight the riches of Christ but neglect the price to obtain them. In a nutshell, we want something for nothing. We talk about God's blessings but avoid the reality of what taking up our cross means.

It's a form of Christianity that only wants half the truth. It could be labeled, "Entitlement Christianity." It's the belief that we're entitled to happiness, ease, blessings, health, wealth, and prosperity — and if God doesn't deliver, we'll take our business elsewhere! We fail to understand that God blesses us on His terms, not ours. Yes, God loves to bless us, but only as we take up our cross and are willing to follow Him despite the cost. God is continually trying to get us to lift our eyes off the fleeting treasures of this life and cast them upon the eternal ones.

How about us today, are we willing to take up our cross and follow Christ? We'll answer that question by the choices we make and the cost we're willing to pay to be disciples.

Billy Graham has wisely concluded, "You see, Jesus doesn't simply call us to believe that He existed, or even to believe that He can save us. He calls on us to commit our whole lives to Him — to trust Him alone for our salvation, and then to follow Him as His disciples."[132]

---

[132] Billy Graham, *What Did Jesus Mean When He Said We Have to Carry a Cross?* Billy Graham Evangelistic Association, 2006, http://billygraham.org/answer/what-did-jesus-mean-when-he-said-we-have-to-carry-a-cross, Accessed 08/17/2015.

5. The Meaning of Save Your Life and Lose Your Life

"And calling the crowd to him with his disciples, he said to them, 'If anyone would come after me, let him deny himself and take up his cross and follow me. For whoever would **save his life will lose it, but whoever loses his life** for my sake and the gospel's will save it. For what does it profit a man to gain the whole world and forfeit his soul?'" (Mark 8:34–35). What does it mean to save your life and lose your life?

Christ spoke numerous times about the theme of saving your life and losing your life. In fact, He mentions it six times in the Gospels (Matt. 10:39, 16:25; Mark 8:35; Luke 9:24, 17:33; and John 12:25).

What Does "Save Your Life" and "Lose Your Life Mean"?

What does it mean to save your life and lose your life? The word "save" in Greek is sozo and means to save, keep safe and sound, or to rescue from danger or destruction.[133] The word "save" in this context is referring to keeping control of your life and remaining the boss of it. Saving your life has two basic applications:

1. For the non-Christian, it refers to the rejection of Christ and the truth of the gospel. They want to remain the lord of their life and do as they please, so they refuse to yield their life to Christ and make Him Lord. It's all about control, and they refuse to relinquish it.

2. For the Christian, it refers to those who choose, in some areas

---

[133] Biblestudytools.com, *The NAS New Testament Greek Lexicon*, http://www.biblestudytools.com/lexicons/greek/nas/sozo.html, Accessed 08/05/2015.

of their life, to do their own will over that of Christ's. They can do this for two reasons: (1) they are unwilling to do what they should do even though they know what God wants them to do or (2) they don't fully know what Christ would have them do because they are still in the growing process and are learning how to yield to Christ in different areas of their life.

The word "lose" in Greek is *apolesē* and means to destroy, to put out of the way entirely, abolish, put an end to, ruin, render useless, to kill, to declare that one must be put to death, to devote or give over to eternal misery in hell, to perish, to be lost, ruined, to destroy, or to lose.[134]

The phrase "lose your life" is what God wants us to do. It's the positive side of discipleship. It speaks of the **willingness** to give up control of our lives in order to follow Christ.

The phrase "save your life" is the negative side of discipleship and is the opposite of what God wants us to do. It's opposed to discipleship and refers to the **refusal** to give up control in order to follow Christ.

Saving Your Life and Losing Your Life Illustrated

The concept of saving your life versus losing your life is a central and foundational truth to the salvation/discipleship message Christ taught. To impart this essential concept, He used four illustrations to convey its important meaning and purpose in life:

1. Matthew 10:34–39: Family Division

2. Matthew 16:24–28: Gaining the World and Losing Your Soul

3. Luke 17:32–33: The Example of Lot's Wife

4. John 12:23–25: A Grain of Seed That Dies

---

[134] Lumina.bible.org, https://lumina.bible.org/bible/Matthew+10, Accessed 08/05/2015.

Now let's look at each of these illustrations Christ used in order to better understand the meaning of saving your life and losing your life.

1. Matthew 10:34–39: Family Division

"Do not think that I have come to bring peace to the earth. I have not come to bring peace, but a sword. For I have come to set a man against his father, and a daughter against her mother, and a daughter-in-law against her mother-in-law. And a person's enemies will be those of his own household. Whoever loves father or mother more than me is not worthy of me, and whoever loves son or daughter more than me is not worthy of me. And whoever does not take his cross and follow me is not worthy of me. Whoever **finds his life will lose it, and whoever loses his life** for my sake will find it."

Here Christ uses the illustration of family division to communicate His message of saving your life and losing your life. He says that choosing to follow Him will likely bring division and strife into our family relationships, and unless we're willing to follow Him instead of keeping our family relationships in peace, then we cannot be His disciple. He speaks of allegiance to Him rather than loyalty to our families.

Currently, in many countries choosing to follow Christ can mean total separation between family members and even death. I remember visiting Israel some years ago, and while there, my wife and I met a converted Christian from Islam. He told us that if his family knew of his recent conversion, they would most likely totally disown him and possibly have him turned over to be severely punished or killed. In his case, following Christ was costing him his relationship with his family. He had to choose between Christ or his family, and He wisely was choosing Christ.

In most Christian's lives, it won't cost them their life to follow Christ, but it might cost them family peace, their friendships, and their reputation. Choosing to follow Christ can be costly, but it's the price we must pay to be His disciple.

2. Matthew 16:24–28: Gaining the World and Losing Your Soul

"Then Jesus told his disciples, 'If anyone would come after me, let him deny himself and take up his cross and follow me. For whoever would **save his life will lose it, but whoever loses his life** for my sake will find it. For what will it profit a man if he gains the whole world and forfeits his soul? Or what shall a man give in return for his soul?'"

In this illustration, Christ talks about those who give their lives to acquiring wealth, power, popularity, prestige, pleasure, and all the luxuries this present world has to offer. They value the riches of this life rather than eternal ones. They store up their treasures on earth instead of heaven, and in the process, save their lives and lose their souls.

3. Luke 17:32–33: The Example of Lot's Wife

"Christ said, 'Remember Lot's wife. Whoever seeks to **preserve his life will lose it, but whoever loses his life** will keep it.'" What about Lot's wife? What did she do that would cause Christ to use her as an example of saving your life instead of losing your life?

Genesis 13:10 says, "Lot lifted up his eyes and saw that the Jordan Valley was well watered everywhere like the garden of the Lord, like the land of Egypt, in the direction of Zoar." While Sodom and Gomorrah were wicked cities during his time, Lot still chose to live close-by: "Now the men of Sodom were wicked, great sinners against the Lord" (Gen. 1:13).

Maybe Lot's wife influenced him to live close-by because she loved the bright lights and pleasures of Sodom, even though it was a wicked city. Later on, Lot chose to move into the city of Sodom, even though Scripture says his heart was vexed within him (2 Pet. 2:7). Later, God sent two angels to rescue Lot. They told him to get out of the city because God was going to destroy it. Even so, Lot lingered: "As morning dawned, the angels urged Lot, saying, 'Up! Take your wife and your two daughters who are here, lest you be swept away in the punishment of the city.'" But Lot continued to linger, so the men seized him, his wife, and his two daughters by the hand and brought them outside the city. "And as they brought them out, one said, 'Escape for your life. Do not look back or stop anywhere in the valley. Escape to the hills, lest you be swept away'" (Gen. 19:15–17).

The angels warned them not to look back at Sodom. The best meaning of this phrase is to "not look back to desire anything within it—none of its pleasures, values, activities, sins, and customs." Nonetheless, Lot's wife loved Sodom and all the pleasures it had to offer. So, as they were fleeing the burning city of Sodom, Lot's wife looked back: "But Lot's wife, behind him, looked back, and she became a pillar of salt" (Gen. 19:26).

By all appearances, Lot's wife had built her life upon earthly pleasures. She chose to save her life and ended up losing it. She had little desire to live for God and paid an immense price, of which, I assume, she still regrets to this day. For the person who is unwilling to submit to Christ and attempts to save their life, they'll pay the same price as Lot's wife.

4. John 12:23–25: A Grain of Seed That Dies

"And Jesus answered them, 'The hour has come for the Son of Man to be glorified. Truly, truly, I say to you, **unless a grain of wheat falls into the earth and dies**, it remains alone; but if it dies, it bears much fruit. Whoever **loves his life loses it, and whoever hates his life** in this world will keep it for eternal life'" (John 12:23–25).

In this passage, Christ uses a grain of wheat to illustrate the principle that the only way a Christian can bear fruit is by dying to themselves and living for Him. The words "truly, truly" mean: listen up, this is critically important, don't let this get by you! Christ implied that there will be no fruit in our lives unless we die to ourselves and live for Him. Therefore, those who wish to save their lives will lose them, but those who are willing to lose their lives will find their lives and bear much fruit.

They will be like the grain of wheat that dies and brings forth many more grains than just itself. If we live for ourselves, we'll just be one grain that will eventually be lost in the end, but if we'll die to ourselves and live for Christ, we'll produce much fruit and enjoy that fruit for all eternity.

These four illustrations show what Christ meant by saving your life and losing your life. Rarely does Christ illustrate a truth with so many examples, so this certainly was a key point He wanted to make clear.

Church Attendance and Saving Your Life

Regarding church attendance, Richard Krejcir quotes some disheartening stats done by the Institute of Church Leadership Development (FASICLD). Krejcir reports that:

- 20.5% of Americans frequently attended church in 1995
- 19% of Americans frequently attended church in 1999
- 18% of Americans frequently attended church in 2002[135]

Krejcir adds, "Now, by extrapolating the data and doing some statistical evaluation and adding some hope for revival, we can see the figures drop to 15% of Americans in church attendance in 2025, and a further drop to 11% or 12% by 2050. Soon, we will catch up with Europe, which currently is 'enjoying' two to four

---

[135] Richard J. Krejcir, *Statistics and Reasons for Church Decline*, 2007, www.churchleadership.org/apps/articles/default.asp?articleid=42346&columnid=4545, Accessed 08/07/2015.

percent of its population in regular church attendance. By the time these predictions come to pass, Europe may have no significant church presence at all."[136]

Church Leaders and Saving Your Life

Even many pastors are adopting a version of Christianity that embraces saving your life. Research done by Richard Krejcir reveals that almost 40% of pastors polled said they have had an extra-marital affair since beginning their ministry, and 70% said the only time they spend studying the Bible is when they are preparing their sermons.[137] Krejcir adds, "Focus on the Family reports that Christians in the United States lose a pastor a day because he seeks an immoral path instead of God's, seeking intimacy where it must not be found."[138] Moreover, LifeWay Research shows that 39% of Protestant pastors believe it's okay to get a divorce if a couple no longer loves one another.[139] And additional studies reveal that the average pastor only prays five minutes a day.[140]

The lifestyles and choices of some in leadership are undoubtedly contributing to the mentality that saving your life is more important than losing your life for Christ.

Christians Today and Saving Your Life

How are we doing today in this critical area of saving your life versus losing your life? Not so well according to the statistics!

---

[136] Ibid., Accessed 08/07/2015.

[137] Richard J. Krejcir, *Statistics on Pastors: What is Going on with the Pastors in America?* 2007, www.churchleadership.org/apps/articles/default.asp?articleid=42347&columnid=4545, Accessed 08/06/2015.

[138] Ibid., Accessed 08/07/2015.

[139] LifeWay Research, *Views on Divorce Divide Americans*, 2015, LifeWayResearch.com, http://www.lifewayresearch.com/2015/08/12/views-on-divorce-divide-americans, Accessed 08/19/2015.

[140] Deborah Beeksma, *The Average Christian Prays a Minute a Day; Prayer by the Faithful Helps Their Relationships*, GodDiscussion.com, 2013, Accessed 07/27/2015.

Could it be we've set aside Christ's foundational teaching on discipleship, and we're now living a form of Christianity that's very different from what Christ and the Apostles taught?

Today, many Christians are living a brand of Christianity where they are unwilling to give up much control of their lives. They value their time, money, friends, families, activities, lifestyles, dreams, entertainment, and sinful choices too much to let them go. They are choosing to save their lives instead of losing them. They are refusing to give up control of their lives to Christ.

6. The Meaning of Hate Your Father, Mother, Wife, and Family

"If anyone comes to me and **does not hate his own father and mother and wife and children and brothers and sisters**, yes, and even his own life, he cannot be my disciple" (Luke 14:26). What does it mean to hate father, mother, wife, and family?

The Role of Family During the Time of Christ

The importance of family in the Jewish culture played a much higher role than it does today in the Western world. Since the time of Abraham, the Jewish culture was family oriented. During their 400 years in Egypt, they lived as a very close-knit unit, bonded together by their unique circumstances in a foreign land.

Afterward, when they wandered in the Sinai Desert for 40 years, they lived within an even closer proximity, all learning the same lessons and sharing the same experiences.

Upon settling the Promised Land, they divided the land, and each tribe received a portion to inhabit. Then, each tribe divided their allotment of land among the family units within its tribe. The land given to each family unit would then normally have remained in their possession for hundreds upon hundreds of consecutive years.

Therefore, for example, a family living in Nazareth during the time of Christ would have had their ancestors living there for countless years before them. Each family would live in family units with parents, grandparents, great-grandparents, children, brothers, sisters, aunts, and uncles, all living in the same family complex or close-by. Unlike today, where people change locations regularly and move half way across the country, the Jews were not mobile, but instead, lived in the same town for generation after generation.

For this reason, it was virtually impossible to exist outside the family structure during the time of Christ. The family was everything. It was their support system, job provider, relationship center, and emotional stability structure. So when Christ said, "Unless you hate your father and mother, wife, children, and brothers and sisters you cannot be my disciple," His words would have sent shockwaves up and down the spines of His hearers.

What Does It Mean to Hate Family Members?

What was Christ saying by stating that we need to hate our father, mother, and so on, and how would His Jewish audience have interpreted it? Unlike us today, who don't quite understand these seemingly severe and harsh words, to the Jews, it was a common way of expressing a contrast between two concepts or loyalties. It was used in a comparative sense to describe such terms like "more than" or "less than," "first" and "second," and extremes such as "first" and "last." The terms love and hate, while appearing as opposites, is expressed in English by terms such as "love more" and "love less."[141]

Kyle Butt provides help on the meaning of the word "hate" by stating, "Numerous Greek scholars have added their combined years of study to the discussion to conclude that the word 'hate' (*miseo*) in Luke 14:26 does not mean 'an active abhorrence,' but means 'to love less.'"[142] Moreover, A. B. Bruce, in *The Expositor's Greek Testament*, states that the practical meaning of the word "hate" in this verse is "love less."[143]

The use of the Greek word *miseo* is also used many other times in Scripture to illustrate the concept of "loving more" or

---

[141] Biblicalhebrew.com, *Hate your Parents: Hate your Father, Matthew 10:37, Luke 14:26*, www.biblicalhebrew.com/nt/lovehate.htm, Accessed 08/08/2015.
[142] Kyle Butt, *Hate Your Parents—or Love Them?* Apologeticspress.org, 2004, apologeticspress.org/AllegedDiscrepancies.aspx?article=781, Accessed 08/08/2015.
[143] Ibid., Accessed 08/08/2015.

"loving less." In fact, Christ uses the terms "love more" and "love less" in a similar passage when speaking of discipleship in Matthew 10:37: "Whoever loves father or mother **more than** me is not worthy of me, and whoever loves son or daughter **more than** me is not worthy of me."

Therefore, a correct interpretation of "hating your father, mother, wife . . ." would be to love them less in contrast to our love for Christ. So, Christ wasn't telling his audience to literally hate their father, mother, wife, and so on. Instead, He was telling them that in comparison to their love and devotion to Him, the gap should be so wide and the distance so great between their love for Him and their most cherished family members that their love for family would appear as hate in comparison.

Choosing Christ over Family

Christ was using this contrasting terminology to drive home the truth that to be His disciple there cannot be any competing relationship that would come close to having the same place of loyalty and affection in our hearts as Him. Our love and devotion to Christ should be light-years away from that of the closest people in our lives on earth.

In order to be Christ's disciple, we must be willing to put Him above all earthly relationships. Therefore, if our family members or close friends will not follow Jesus, or even if they disown us for being Christians, we must still choose Christ over them.

Christ's Example

Christ not only spoke about the need to love Him more than anyone on earth, but He lived out and experienced what He taught. He was rejected by most of His paternal brothers, He was rejected by those in His hometown of Nazareth, He was rejected by Judas — one of His disciples — and He was rejected and crucified by His own people. He knew firsthand what it meant to love and obey God more than any person on earth.

When Christ faced the reality of the Cross, His commitment to the Father over His own will was lived out when He said, "Not My will be done, but Yours be done" (Matt. 26:39). That should be our life motto as well.

Christ's command that we love Him more than father, mother, wife, brother, or sister is not just limited to those in our close family circles, but also applies to any relationship in our lives that we might love and be influenced by more than Him.

Christians Today and Close Relationships

How are Christians today doing in the area of loving Christ more than any personal relationship on earth? For many, putting Christ and His commands above their family and friends is a deep struggle. Loving Christ more than anyone else is the ultimate test.

It's the same test God put before Abraham when He asked him to sacrifice his "all" (Isaac) on an altar to Him. It's the same test for us today. Therefore, if we have anyone in our lives who is hindering us from being fully devoted to Christ, we need to make a choice, once and for all, to choose Christ over them.

If we're going to follow Christ, we must not fear being ridiculed or marginalized for standing with Him and His Word. We must "hate" all others in comparison to our love for Christ.

7. The Meaning of Hate Your Life

"If anyone comes to me and does not hate his own father and mother and wife and children and brothers and sisters, yes, **and even his own life,** he cannot be my disciple"(Luke 14:26). What does it mean to hate your life?

Jesus taught this same truth with slight variations in Matthew 10:37–39, 16:24–27, Mark 8:34–38, and Luke 9:23–26, and 17:33.

What Does "Hate Your Life" Mean?

As noted in the previous section about what it means to hate father, mother, wife, and other family members, Christ was not telling His audience to literally hate their own lives, but was telling them that, in comparison to their love and devotion to Him, the gap would be so wide and the distance so great between their love for Him and their own lives that it would appear as hate.

Why is it important to "hate your life"? First of all, it's the only way to save it.

Jesus' words apply to everyone who wants to follow Him. He assumes that we all want to save our lives, but tells us that the only way to save them is to lose them for His sake and the gospel's. There's no other option! If we want true joy, meaning, purpose, fulfillment, and eternal rewards in heaven, then the only way to get them is through hating our lives.

What does it mean to hate your life, and how can we hate our life in order to find it? We find some excellent illustrations in the life of Christ and Scripture.

Christ's Example

Christ provides the perfect example of hating your life by laying down His life and being crucified for our sins. By giving

His life on the Cross, Jesus bore much fruit: "Truly, truly, I say to you, unless a grain of wheat falls into the earth and dies, it remains alone; but if it dies, it bears much fruit" (John 12:24). Christ used the example of a grain of wheat falling to the ground as an illustration of how a single grain of wheat, if it is planted and dies, will produce much fruit. In farming, it's quite normal for an average kernel of wheat to reproduce and multiply itself a hundred percent.

When Christ laid down His life and died, He produced countless fruit for all eternity. In the same way, when we lay down our lives, we bear much fruit as well.

How to Bear Fruit

If we save our lives and do what we want with them, then we'll be unfruitful, but if we lay them down, we'll bear much fruit. To the degree we die to ourselves, our plans, our wills, our desires, and yield them to Christ instead, is the degree to which we will be fruitful.

The way to measure whether or not we are dying to ourselves and hating our lives is by looking at how much fruit we're producing. If there's little fruit in our lives, it means we are saving our lives and not hating them. It means we are not doing what Christ wants, but what we want. God wants us to bear fruit, and the only way to do it is by dying to ourselves.

What Is Biblical Fruit?

What does the Bible refer to as fruit? It can be defined as the evidence in a person's life that reflects the result of actions and choices made. The following is referred to as biblical fruit:

- **Galatians 5:22–23 and 2 Peter 1:5–8:** The Bible refers to the development of Christian character as fruit.

- **Colossians 1:10:** Our knowledge of God's Word that results in good deeds is referred to as fruit.

- **Philippians 1:22:** Our labor and work for Christ are counted as fruit.

- **Romans 1:13 and 1 Corinthians 16:15:** Evangelism is considered fruit.

- **Hebrews 13:5:** We bear fruit with our lips when we praise God and glorify Him in our hearts, before non-believers, and with fellow Christians.

- **Romans 15:28 and Philippians 4:17:** Giving to the Lord's work is spoken of as fruit.

- **Matthew 3:8–10 and 7:15–20:** Repentance from sin and turning to the Lord is referred to as fruit as indicated in the ministries of John the Baptist and Christ.

Why We Love Our Lives

While Christians have been given a new nature at salvation, we do, however, retain our old nature. This old nature—called the sinful nature or the flesh—desires that which is contrary to Christ and our new nature.

When the Bible refers to our old nature as the "flesh," it doesn't mean that our physical bodies are sinful, but that our sinful nature, referred to as "flesh," is sinful.

Our flesh doesn't care about anything but feeling good and gorging itself on pleasure. If we allow it to dictate our choices in life, then we'll never align with God's will. We'll never submit to His authority, and we'll end up suffering enormous loss if we're Christians or wind up in hell if we're non-believers. But if we recognize that our fleshly desires are fatal to the soul and choose to live for God instead, then we'll end up with eternal rewards and joy.

When Christ says we must hate our lives, He is describing how we must hate our fleshly desires and refuse to let them control our priorities in life.

How to Lose Your Life in Order to Find It

We must realize that our fleshly nature is at war with the Holy Spirit and the new nature God has given us. This is why we continually have a battle going on inside of us. In order to win the battle, we need to walk in the Spirit: "But I say, walk by the Spirit, and you will **not gratify** the **desires of the flesh. For the desires of the flesh are against the Spirit**, and the **desires of the Spirit are against the flesh,** for these **are opposed to each other**, to keep you from doing the things you want to do" (Gal. 5:16–17).

We must put to death the desires of our flesh with God's enabling help: "For if you live according to the flesh you will die, but if **by the Spirit you put to death the deeds of the body**, you will live" (Rom. 8:13). If we walk in the Spirit and put to death the desires of our flesh, then we will find life and peace. We will, in essence, "find our lives." If not, we'll find pain and sorrow and "lose our lives."

In summary, hating your life means that instead of loving your life and living for the present, you give up your fleshly desires and live for Christ and your future life in heaven.

8. The Meaning of Gain the World and Lose Your Soul

"For whoever desires to save his life will lose it, but whoever loses his life for My sake and the gospel's will save it. For what will it profit a man if he **gains the whole world, and loses his own soul?** Or what will a man give in exchange for his soul?" (Mark 8:36–37, NKJV).

What does it profit to gain the whole world and lose your soul? This statement by Christ is really a "no-brainer" question and a simple one to answer. It was a question posed by Christ to show the stupidity of even asking such a ridiculous question.

But to make matters worse, Christ showed the absurdity of our rationale in that, while no sane person would be willing to lose their soul at the expense of gaining the whole world, they are willing to lose it for the hope of gaining just a fraction of it. How amazing! Who would be willing to lose their soul for just gaining a little bit of the "good life"? Of course, no one would, right? That's the point of the question. Who in their right mind would choose to lose their soul at the expense of a few fleeting years of pleasure? No one, right? Wrong! That's exactly what most do.

Is Gaining the World Smart?

Gaining the world for Christians means that they give a higher priority to their earthly affairs than seeking God and pursuing spiritual maturity. It means they choose to store up the majority of their riches on earth rather than in heaven.

Our souls are who we are, the part of us that's eternal. The term "world" represents materialism, pleasure, and prestige (1 John 2:15). No logical person would reason that a few years of wealth, pleasure, and prestige would be worth the cost of losing

181

their eternal soul. The math is simple: a few years of pleasure versus endless years of torment in hell? Even a 5-year-old can figure that one out.

Tragically, though, many surgeons, scientists, professionals, adults, and students can't do the simple math. With all their brilliance, they can't even do a simple math equation that a 5-year-old can do. They value a few fleeting years of pleasure above all the eternal glories of heaven and choose hell instead. Humbly said, that is the height of stupidity and foolishness. It's completely off the radar, incomprehensible, ridiculous, absurd, and ludicrous! Yet, it's what most people choose in this life. What a tragedy!

Gaining the World and Christians Today

How about us Christians? Can we do the math? Are we any smarter than the vast majority of people in this world who cannot? Can we figure out that a few fleeting years of pleasure in this life aren't worth the loss of eternal rewards in heaven? Unfortunately, according to recent statistics, many Christians can't do the simple math either. They are caught up in materialism, pleasure, and prestige, and are sacrificing their eternal rewards on the altar of a few vanishing years of gratification. They are deaf to the call of discipleship; and instead, are gaining the world but losing their eternal rewards in the process. How foolish! God warns us of this deadly trap in John 2:15–17:

> Do not love the world or the things in the world. If anyone loves the world, the love of the Father is not in him. For all that is in the world — **the desires of the flesh and the desires of the eyes and pride of life** — is not from the Father but is from the world. And the world is passing away along with its desires, but whoever does the will of God abides forever.

What hinders many Christians from putting discipleship as their highest priority in life? God says it's the desires of the flesh (materialism), the desires of the eyes (pleasure), and the pride of life (prestige) — all of which are enemies of discipleship. They are choosing the pleasures of the world that are passing away and ignoring the eternal riches and rewards of heaven.

Many Christians today choose to give priority to their nice homes, nice cars, retirement accounts, vacations, electronic devices, pleasure, and entertainment rather than being disciples of Christ and storing their riches in heaven. They are living for the here and now, not eternity! This is called saving, loving, and finding your life instead of losing and hating your life. For the person who chooses this life over the next one, all their pleasures will end when they die. They will have spent their years enjoying this life and will suffer the consequences in the one to come.

Gaining the World and Losing Your Soul for the Non-Believer

For the non-Christian, the clear meaning of gaining the world and losing your soul is simple to understand. Losing your soul speaks of the reality of hell, a topic that's very uncomfortable, yet spoken of repeatedly in Scripture. Christ spoke more about hell and the judgments of God than about heaven. He described hell as:

- A fiery lake of burning sulfur that is unquenchable and never goes out (Matt. 25:46; Mark 9:43–44; Rev. 21:8).
- Everlasting destruction away from the presence of the Lord (2 Thess. 1:9).
- Where people will gnash their teeth in pain (Matt. 13:50).
- Where the devil and his angels suffer (Matt. 25:41).
- A gloomy dungeon (2 Pet. 2:4).
- Where the worm never dies (Mark 9:48).
- A fiery furnace (Matt. 13:42).

- Where people will be salted with fire (Mark 9:49).
- A place of weeping (Matt. 13:50).
- A place of utter darkness (Jude 1:13).

Hell is a real place, and many will choose to go there as a result of rejecting Christ and attempting to gain the world's treasures. They'll choose materialism, pleasure, and the pride of life over the salvation of their souls and the eternal riches of Christ.

Although God defines success in life as being spiritually mature, most people define success in life as being wealthy, enjoying pleasure, and being well liked.

9. The Meaning of Being Ashamed of Christ and His Words

"For whoever is **ashamed of me and of my words** in this adulterous and sinful generation, of him will the Son of Man also be ashamed when he comes in the glory of his Father with the holy angels" (Mark 8:38). What does it mean to be ashamed of Christ and His words?

What Does "Ashamed" Mean?

The word "ashamed" comes from the Greek word *epaischunomai* and means apologetic, bashful, embarrassed, shy, timid, and hesitant. It's the sense in which we can be silent, fearful, reluctant, and ashamed by identifying and standing up for Christ and His words. It's the same word Paul uses in Romans 1:16 when he boldly proclaims, "For I am not **ashamed** of the gospel, for it is the power of God for salvation to everyone who believes, to the Jew first and also to the Greek."

The Apostle Paul and Not Being Ashamed of Christ

Paul paid a heavy price for not being ashamed of Christ and recounts it in 2 Corinthians 11:23–28:

With far greater labors, far more imprisonments, with countless beatings, and often near death. Five times I received at the hands of the Jews the forty lashes less one. Three times I was beaten with rods. Once I was stoned. Three times I was shipwrecked; a night and a day I was adrift at sea; on frequent journeys, in danger from rivers, danger from robbers, danger from my own people, danger from Gentiles, danger in the city, danger in the wilderness, danger at sea, danger from false brothers; in toil and hardship, through many a sleepless night, in hunger and thirst, often without food, in cold and exposure. And, apart from other things, there is the daily pressure on me of my anxiety for all the churches.

Paul also proudly stated when writing from prison in Rome for preaching Christ and the gospel:

> For I know that through your prayers and the help of the Spirit of Jesus Christ this will turn out for my deliverance, as it is my eager expectation and hope that I will not be at all **ashamed**, but that with full courage now as always Christ will be honored in my body, whether by life or by death. For to me to live is Christ, and to die is gain (Phil. 1:19–21).

Paul was certainly not ashamed of Christ and His words, and tradition holds that he was martyred as a result.

The Example of Others and Not Being Ashamed of Christ

The 12 Apostles also paid a high price for not being ashamed of Christ and His words. History records that 11 of them were martyred for not being ashamed of Christ, and John, while uncertain as to whether or not he died for Christ, was thrown into boiling oil and severely tortured.

Hebrews 11 recounts many of the Old Testament saints who suffered severely because they were not ashamed of God:

> Some were tortured, refusing to accept release, so that they might rise again to a better life. Others suffered mocking and flogging, and even chains and imprisonment. They were stoned, they were sawn in two, they were killed with the sword. They went about in skins of sheep and goats, destitute, afflicted, mistreated — of whom the world was not worthy — wandering about in deserts and mountains, and in

dens and caves of the earth (Heb. 11:35–38).

Today, in some parts of the world, many Christians are being martyred and persecuted at unprecedented rates. Why is this so? It's because they are not ashamed of Christ and His words. In fact, it's believed there are more martyrs for Christ today per year than at any other time in the history of the church. Estimates range from between 8,000–100,000 Christians who are now being martyred yearly for Christ.[144]

Moreover, it's estimated that from the birth of the early church to the present, 70 million Christians have been martyred for Christ.[145] All these chose to die for Christ rather than being ashamed of Him and His words.

Christians Today and Being Ashamed of Christ

The contrast between those who have chosen to be martyred for Christ instead of being ashamed of Him and His words, and many Christians today is staggering.

As mentioned, statistics show a whopping 61% of Christians have not shared their faith in the last six months, and nearly half (48%) of Christians have never even invited a friend to church. Many are also silent on key moral issues of our day and are choosing a path of peace and conformity rather than confrontation—a very different strategy than what Christ and the Apostles chose.

Many Christians today don't want to stir the waters, cause problems, or hurt people's feelings, so they idly stand by watching the moral decay and destruction from the sidelines. To them, it's not worth the friction. They are ashamed of Christ and

---

[144] Cath Martin, *70 Million Christians' Martyred for their Faith Since Jesus Walked the Earth,* 2014, ChristianityToday.com, http://www.christiantoday.com/article/70.million.christians.martyred.faith.since.jesus.walked.earth/38403.htm, Accessed 08/28/2015.
[145] Ibid., Accessed 08/28/2015.

His words and choose silence over engagement.

Many Christians today fear their friends, family, and culture more than God. Countless don't speak up for Christ because they are afraid of violating the new cardinal sins of political correctness, and fear being labeled judgmental, intolerant, dogmatic, or hateful.

Some Christians, however, don't speak up because they are simply ignorant of the truths of God's Word and don't know what to say. And sadly, some Christians are vocal about what they believe, but what they stand for is contrary to God's Word, so they wind up promoting what our culture says rather than what God says. They are babes in Christ tossed to and fro by the winds of false teachers and false philosophies circulating in our culture.

Conclusion to Chapter 3

In this chapter, we defined discipleship using key phrases Christ used in calling people to follow Him. In the next chapter, we'll discover the 14 essential components of discipleship that must be understood and practiced in order to be a disciple of Christ and attain spiritual maturity?

We're now coming to the heart of the book, so get ready to be challenged as we delve into the 14 essential components needed for growing in Christ!

Chapter 4

The Essential Components of Discipleship

In This Chapter

In chapter 1, we analyzed the state of discipleship and spiritual maturity today, concluding that they're in critical condition and being grossly neglected. In chapter 2, we investigated the key factors contributing to the neglect of discipleship and spiritual maturity. In chapter 3, we defined biblical discipleship by examining key phrases Christ used in calling people to follow Him.

In this chapter, we'll discover the essential components for the discipleship-making process that must be understood and obeyed in order to fulfill the Great Commission Mandate and attain spiritual maturity.

What Are the Essential Components of Discipleship?

I'm a long-term missionary in Mexico, and on one occasion, five churches asked me to provide leadership training for their pastors and leaders. The central theme was discipleship. However, as I began to ponder and pray about what I was going to include in this training, my own lack of understanding surfaced. I then began to research other notable theologians and pastors to discover what they would see as essential aspects of discipleship.

What I discovered was many different angles and approaches to the discipleship-making process. Some stressed knowledge as the key, some focused on evangelism, others on spiritual disciplines, and the list continued. Each one underscored their approach as the best and most biblical.

How about you as a reader? If a newer believer approached you out of respect for your maturity in Christ and asked you to disciple or mentor them, what would you include in the discipleship-making process? I think if we're honest, we'd say we're probably not certain. However, other than the essence of the gospel, is there a topic more important to understand?

First Things First

The essential components of discipleship function as vehicles which combine the grace of God and human effort for attaining spiritual maturity. They are not an end in and of themselves, but rather, provide a structure for attaining spiritual maturity. They are biblical, not mere inventions or ideas of people, and they exist to transform us into the image of Christ. These same essential components were used by Christ and the Apostles, and should be used by us as well.

If we practice these essential components with the intent of achieving spiritual maturity, then they will serve the purpose for which God intended. However, if we think that through mere ritualistic conformity to them that we will grow to maturity, then we are greatly mistaken. Christianity is a relationship with God, not mere conformity to a set of rules. Spiritual maturity, therefore, is impossible without the development of our relationship with God.

What Is Spiritual Maturity?

Spiritual maturity is not perfection, but the attainment of fullness, completeness, adulthood, or excellence in each of the essential components of the discipleship-making process.

Christ highlighted obedience as an overarching aspect of spiritual maturity in the Great Commission Mandate: "Teaching them to **observe all that I have commanded you.** And behold, I am with you always, to the end of the age" (Matt. 28:20). Spiritual maturity, according to Christ, is summed up by complete obedience to all of Scripture.

The Apostle Peter focused on knowledge, attitudes, and character as essential to spiritual maturity: "For this very reason, make every effort to supplement your faith with virtue, and virtue with knowledge, and knowledge with self-control, and self-control with steadfastness, and steadfastness with godliness, and godliness with brotherly affection, and brotherly affection with love" (2 Pet. 5–7).

In addition to Christ's and Peter's definition of spiritual maturity, the Apostle Paul defines spiritual maturity as:

1. A person who can understand and receive the wisdom of God from Scripture: "Yet among the **mature** we do impart wisdom, although it is not a wisdom of this age or of the rulers of this age, who are doomed to pass away" (1 Cor. 2:6).

2. A person who is mature in their thinking capabilities: "Brothers, do not be children in your thinking. Be infants in evil, but in **your thinking be mature**" (1 Cor. 14:20).

3. A person who has arrived at the measure of the full stature of Christ: "Until we all attain to the unity of the faith and of the knowledge of the Son of God, to **mature** manhood, to the measure of the stature of the **fullness** of Christ" (Eph. 4:13).

4. A person who can discern good from evil through the constant practice of using God's Word, and can understand and feed on the solid food (deep things) of Scripture: "But solid food is for the **mature**, for those who have their powers of discernment trained by constant practice to distinguish good from evil" (Heb. 5:14).

5. A person with a transformed mind: "Do not be conformed to this world, but be transformed by the renewal of your mind, that by testing you may discern what is the will of God, what is good and acceptable and **perfect**" (Rom. 12:2). This verse presents two options for each person: (1) be conformed to this world or (2) be transformed by Scripture to God's perfect will. Spiritual maturity is the process of moving from the conformity of this world to the conformity of God's will.

A spiritually mature person thinks as God thinks, acts like God acts, and values what God values. They have the same characteristics, attitudes, beliefs, and perspective of life that God does. They are led by the Spirit and submit to Him in all things. They love the Lord their God with all their heart, soul, mind, and strength, and they love their neighbor as themselves.

In summary, a spiritually mature person is someone who has arrived at fullness, excellence, and completeness in all of the 14 areas of the discipleship-making process outlined in this chapter.

Spiritual Maturity Is God's Purpose for Us

As mentioned, it's important to note that spiritual maturity is not the same as perfection. We will never reach that level in this life. However, it's a state of maturity that reflects, by and large, the image of Christ and His values. It's not like a popular bumper sticker that reads, "Not perfect, only forgiven." While this slogan contains truth, it overlooks the majority of our Christian growth to maturity after forgiveness and makes an excuse for bad behavior in the meantime.

Between being forgiven for our sins at salvation, and spiritual maturity, lies a wide gap. This gap is where we labor with the grace of God to attain spiritual maturity. We all begin as spiritual infants at salvation but should not stay there. We are called to much more than forgiveness; we are called to attain spiritual maturity. This is our goal and purpose in life: "Until we all attain to the unity of the faith and of the knowledge of the Son of God, to **mature manhood**, to the measure of the stature of **the fullness of Christ**" (Eph. 4:13).

God's deepest desire is that we would attain spiritual maturity. In fact, He sharply rebukes those who are slow or fail to attain it as seen in Hebrews 5:11–14:

About this we have much to say, and it is hard to explain, since you have become **dull of hearing**. For though **by this time** you ought to be teachers, you need someone to teach

you again the **basic principles** of the oracles of God. You
need milk, not solid food, for everyone who lives on milk is
unskilled in the word of righteousness, since he is a
child. But solid food is for the mature, for those who have
their powers of discernment trained by constant practice to
distinguish good from evil.

God was angry and rebuked these Hebrew believers because
they were slothful in attaining spiritual maturity. God feels the
same about us today! He expects us to become spiritually mature
within a reasonable length of time and is grieved when we fail to
do so.

God was also grieved with the nation of Israel for the same
reasons: "But they obeyed not, neither inclined their ear, but made
their neck stiff, that they might not hear, nor receive instruction"
(Jer. 17:23).

The Importance of Understanding and Practicing the Essential Components of Discipleship

If the Great Commission Mandate and summation of Christ's
ministry was discipleship (Matt. 28:19–20), and if the summation
of the Apostles' ministry was the same (Col. 1:28–29), then
understanding the essential components of the discipleship-
making process is paramount for fulfilling these commands.

God has designed discipleship as the vehicle to bring us to
spiritual maturity. That's why it was the summation of Christ's
and the Apostles' ministries. The essential components in this
chapter are servants of discipleship. They are the nuts and bolts,
the specifics, the structure, the application of discipleship for
attaining spiritual maturity. They are principles Christ and the
Apostles used and work for all people for all time.

1. Knowledge of God and Discipleship

Of all the essential components for discipleship, none is as important as the knowledge of God. While the others are critical, I believe this component rises above them all. Donald Whitney states, "No spiritual discipline is more important than the intake of God's Word. Nothing can substitute for it. There is simply no healthy Christian life apart from a diet of the milk and meat of Scripture."[146]

Why Is God's Word So Vital to Discipleship?

God's Word forms the foundation upon which all the other essential components rest. It's the main component God uses in the transformation of our mind, which in turn, leads to spiritual maturity. Alister McGrath, in his article "The Passionate Intellect: Christian Faith and the Discipleship of the Mind," centers his focus of discipleship on the importance of knowledge.[147] He claims that theology was once the "queen of the sciences" and held in the highest esteem, but is no longer the case. It has declined in recent decades, and this should give us pause.[148]

McGrath believes knowledge serves believers in both their own personal understanding of God and in providing greater effectiveness in sharing this understanding with others. McGrath adds, "Christians need to realize that there is an intellectual core to the Christian faith which requires a discipleship of the mind in

---

[146] Donald Whitney, *Spiritual Disciplines for the Christian Life* (Colorado Springs: NavPress, 1991), p. 24.
[147] Alister McGrath, "The Passionate Intellect; Christian Faith and the Discipleship of the Mind" (Source: Pro Ecclesia, 22 no 1 Winter 2013, pp. 118-121. Publication Type: Review ATLA Religion Database with ATLASerials. Hunter Resource Library), Accessed 11/5/2014.
[148] Ibid., p. 118.

order to understand."[149] He further states, "Christians should be guided by a rational faith which provides the foundation for all their understanding of God and life."[150]

We Are Commanded to Love the Lord with Our Minds

The greatest command is to "Love the Lord your God with all your heart and with all your soul and **with all your mind** and with all your strength" (Mark 12:30). God wants us to love Him, not only with our heart, soul, and strength, but with our mind as well. A strong case can be made that loving God begins with loving Him with our minds because it's through our knowledge of Him that we understand how to love Him with our hearts. However, many are ignorant of this truth and are biblically illiterate.

We've noted that the latest Bible reading statistics of Christians, according to LifeWay Publishing, are dismal at best. Only 19% of Christians read their Bibles regularly. That leaves 81% of Christians who are basically biblically illiterate. These believers are certainly not loving God with their minds.

Christians Today and Biblical Illiteracy

Albert Mohler shares his concern about the state of evangelicalism and biblical illiteracy by asserting: "While America's Evangelical Christians are rightly concerned about the secular worldview's rejection of biblical Christianity, we ought to give some urgent attention to a problem much closer to home — biblical illiteracy in the church. This scandalous problem is our own, and it's up to us to fix it."[151]

---

[149] Ibid., p. 119.
[150] Ibid., p. 119.
[151] Albert Mohler, *The Scandal of Biblical Illiteracy: It's Our Problem*, Christianity.com, http://www.christianity.com/1270946, Accessed 08/18/2015.

Researchers George Gallup and Jim Castelli state the problem bluntly, "Americans revere the Bible — but, by and large, they don't read it. And because they don't read it, they have become a nation of biblical illiterates. How bad is it? Researchers tell us that it's worse than most could imagine."[152]

The fact that the majority of so-called "Evangelical believers" rarely or never read their Bibles is staggering. It's no wonder many Christians today are "throwing in" with the new progressive morals of our culture and are spiritually immature.

Christians Today and Theological Illiteracy

Not only are many believers biblically illiterate, but they are theologically illiterate as well. They don't read theological books that would significantly deepen their knowledge of God and give them a correct worldview.

God has given gifted men and women to the church who have spent countless hours studying and writing books to aid us in becoming spiritually mature. However, only about 3% of believers read theological books and only about 10% read Christian, non-fiction books. Unfortunately, most Christians are indifferent and disregard these precious gifts of God, and as a result, choose to remain spiritually immature.

All the Components of Discipleship Rest upon God's Word

Every aspect of discipleship is linked to the knowledge of God's Word. Without it, we wouldn't know who God is, who we are, who others are, the purpose for our existence, the purpose for creation, where we have come from, where we are going, what God desires from us, and how we should behave. Some downplay the importance of the knowledge of Scripture, but in so doing, contradict the value Christ gives it.

---

[152] Ibid., Accessed 08/18/2015.

During Christ's day, discipleship had a heavy focus on the knowledge of the Bible. Most disciples had much, if not the majority, of the Old Testament, memorized. They would go on discipleship training trips to get away from the distractions of life and focus on learning Scripture from their rabbi.

Christ placed enormous weight upon knowing Scripture and emphasized it throughout His ministry. In fact, Scripture is so important to God that He calls Christ the "Word." "In the beginning was the Word, and the Word was with God, and the Word was God . . . And the Word was made flesh, and dwelt among us" (John 1:1, 14). Christ is the Living Word! To say that the knowledge of Scripture is not important is to say that Christ is not important.

Klaus Issler, in his article "Six Themes to Guide Spiritual Formation Ministry Based on Jesus' Sermon on the Mount," makes the knowledge of God's Word one of his six major themes of discipleship. He states that it was important for Jesus' disciples to know Scripture, and interpret it correctly, to be able to follow its genuine teaching.[153] He goes on to say, "Jesus' own life was bathed in Scripture since the phrase 'It is written' or some variation occurs 23 times on his lips."[154]

How Can We Know God?

There are two basic ways to know God: (1) by observing His creation and (2) by knowing His Word. Theologically, we call the field of knowing God through His creation "General Revelation." All rational humans can know general things about God through contemplating His creation: "For what can be **known about God** is plain to them, because God has shown it to them. For his

---

[153] Klaus Issler, "Six Themes to Guide Spiritual Formation Ministry Based on Jesus' Sermon on the Mount" (Source: Christian Education, Journal Date: September 1, 2010. CEJ: Series 3, Vol. 7, No. 2. ATLA Religion Database with ATLASerials. Hunter Resource Library), p. 372, Accessed 11/5/2014.
[154] Ibid., p. 372.

invisible attributes, namely, **his eternal power** and **divine nature**, have been **clearly perceived**, ever since the creation of the world, in the things that have been made. So they are without excuse" (Rom. 1:19–20).

Through creation, every person knows certain truths about God. They know He is all-powerful, eternal, and all-knowing. Scripture also records in Psalm 19 that "The heavens declare the glory of God, and the sky above proclaims his handiwork. Day to day pours out speech, and night to night reveals knowledge. There is no speech, nor are there words, whose voice is not heard. Their voice goes out through all the earth, and their words to the end of the world" (Ps. 19:1–4). We see, then, that through creation all mankind has been blessed to know certain things about God.

While what we can know about God through His creation is amazing, it is nonetheless, limited. We don't know the details about God, just the big picture. How can we know the details? Through learning and applying God's Word to our lives. Theologically, we call the field of knowing God through His Word, "Special Revelation."

It's special because it's unique and allows us to know God in His fullness. It also gives us understanding about who we are, the purpose for life, the plan of God for His creation, and our surroundings—all extremely important things to know.

In the remainder of this section, we'll look at why knowing and applying God's Word to our lives is so essential to the discipleship-making process.

The Bible Is Unique and Unlike Any Other Writing Known to Mankind

- **The Bible claims to be inspired and to contain the very words of God:** 2 Timothy 3:16–17 states, "All Scripture is breathed out by God and profitable for teaching, for reproof, for correction, and for training in righteousness, that the man of God may be competent, equipped for every good work." Also, 2 Peter 1:20–21 affirms, "Knowing this first of all, that no prophecy of Scripture comes from someone's own interpretation. For no prophecy was ever produced by the will of man, but men spoke from God as they were carried along by the Holy Spirit." Unlike any other writing known to mankind, Scripture claims to be the very words of God.

- **The Bible claims to be living**: Hebrews 4:12 asserts, "For the word of God is living and active, sharper than any two-edged sword, piercing to the division of soul and of spirit, of joints and of marrow, and discerning the thoughts and intentions of the heart." Scripture is living and active because God inhabits His Word and speaks through it. No other writing is like it.

- **Christ affirmed the Bible to be the very Word of God**: Christ continually made statements concerning Scripture, such as "It is written," "So that the Scripture might be fulfilled," and "Have you not read?" He also used it continuously in His ministry and teaching. "And he said to them, 'O foolish ones, and slow of heart to believe all that the prophets have spoken! Was it not necessary that the Christ should suffer these things and enter into his glory?' And beginning with Moses and all the Prophets, he interpreted to them in all the Scriptures the things concerning himself" (Luke 24:25–27).

- **Christ claimed to be the very Word of God**: John 1:1 boldly states, "In the beginning was the Word, and the Word was with God, and the Word was God." Then John clarifies Who the Word is: "The **Word became flesh and dwelt among us**, and we have seen his glory, glory as of the only Son from the Father, full of grace and truth" (John 1:14). Not only do we have the written Word of God that claims to be living, but this living Word also is a Person called Jesus Christ.

- **The Apostles affirmed the Bible as the very Word of God**: The Apostles asserted that Scripture was inspired and used it continually. For example, Peter quoted large passages of Scripture in his sermon on the day of Pentecost, as found in Acts 2:14–42; quoting Joel 2:28–32, Psalm 16:8–11, and Psalm 110:1. The other Apostles also used a heavy dose of Scripture in their ministries.

- **The New Testament writers affirmed the Bible as the very Word of God:** God fashioned the New Testament to rest upon the foundation of the Old Testament. Therefore, God inspired the human writers of the New Testament to quote the Old Testament an amazing 855 times.[155] Many of these quotes were by Christ Himself, which gives further validation that Scripture is inspired and is the very Word of God.

- **History supports the Bible as being the Word of God:** The Bible has been the most important writing in the history of mankind. From its inception until the present, it has been the most read, the most valued, the most copied, the most discussed, the most quoted, and the most sold piece of literature ever. It has ranked far above all other writings. Moreover, countless millions of people claim it has changed their lives and have been willing to die for it.

- **The Bible claims to be eternal:** The Prophet Isaiah wrote, "The grass withers, the flower fades, but the word of our God will stand forever" (Isa. 40:8). The Apostle Peter penned, "But the word of the Lord remains forever. And this word is the good news that was preached to you" (1 Pet. 1:25). Moreover, Christ proclaimed, "Heaven and earth will pass away, but my words will not pass away" (Matt. 24:35).

---

[155] Blue Letter Bible, BlueLetterBible.org, *Study Resources: Charts and Quotes,* www.blueletterbible.org/study/pnt/pnt08.cfm, Accessed 10/14/2015.

We Follow Christ by Following His Word

When Christ says, "Follow Me," He is telling us to follow Him and His commands. The original disciples entered into 3 ½ years of intense discipleship training with Christ, and then, after His death, His Spirit was with them as they continued as His disciples. Today, Christ primarily teaches us through His Word. However, the average believer spends little time learning from Christ through His Word. Therefore, they are unable to follow Christ.

Here's the latest Bible reading statistics of Christians according to LifeWay Publishing:[156]

- 19% read their Bibles daily or regularly
- 26% read their Bibles a few times a week
- 14% read their Bibles once a week
- 22% read their Bibles once a month
- 18% rarely or never read their Bibles

According to these stats, 81% of Christians don't read their Bibles regularly. That's unbelievable! And of the 19% who do read their Bibles regularly, many don't study or read it in-depth. Moreover, most don't read all of the Bible, but just parts of it as devotional reading.

In general, most Christians are eons away from being the kind of disciples who know and handle God's Word with precision and clarity as commanded in 2 Timothy 2:15. As a result, most Christians are babies or adolescents in their spiritual maturity, and are not serious about discipleship and becoming like Christ (Heb. 5:11–14). This is a severe indictment on the state of Christianity and discipleship today.

If the main avenue Christ used to teach His disciples was His

---

[156] Russ Rankin, *Study: Bible Engagement in Churchgoer's Hearts, Not Always Practiced,* Nashville, 2012, http://www.lifeway.com/Article/research-survey-bible-engagement-churchgoers, Accessed 07/23/2015.

words, and if the main avenue today is His words as found in Scripture, then most Christians today are extremely deficient in their ability to be disciples because their knowledge of Scripture is so desperately lacking. Unlike the original disciples who had much of Scripture committed to memory, many Christians today are biblically illiterate. Discipleship without a high dose of God's Word is impossible, as it's the main way Christ teaches us.

Following Christ means following His commands in Scripture. However, if we don't know His Word, we won't know His commands, so we'll be weak, ineffective disciples. We'll be disciples who grieve Christ instead of please Him.

God Expects Us to Know His Word

God instructs us in 2 Timothy 2:15 (NASB) to "Be **diligent** to present yourself **approved** to God as a workman who does not need to be ashamed, **accurately handling the word of truth**." God expects us to exert diligent effort in understanding and handling His Word, not to be indifferent and mediocre with it. 2 Peter 1:5 adds, "For this very reason, **make every effort** to supplement your faith with virtue, and virtue with **knowledge**." God commands us to know His Word, handle it correctly, and grow in it. In order to do this, we must be diligent and make every effort to know it.

The Importance of God's Word in Discipleship

As mentioned, Scripture is the most important component in the discipleship-making process because God supernaturally uses His inspired, living words to transform us into His image and bring us to full maturity in Christ.

The following are vital functions God's Word plays in discipleship and our growth in Christ:

- **It's food for our souls:** Matthew 4:2–4 asserts, "And after fasting forty days and forty nights, he was hungry. And the tempter came and said to him, 'If you are the Son of God, command these stones to become loaves of bread.' But he answered, 'It is written, Man shall not live by bread alone, but by every word that comes from the mouth of God.'" Scripture is the food that feeds our souls. In the same way our body hungers, the soul of a born-again believer hungers as well. Unfortunately, according to the Bible reading stats, 81% of believers are starving their souls, and by doing so, will never reach spiritual maturity.

- **It causes us to grow in Christ:** "But grow in the grace and knowledge of our Lord and Savior Jesus Christ" (2 Pet. 3:18). 1 Peter 2:2 adds, "Like newborn infants, long for the pure spiritual milk, that by it you may grow up into salvation — if indeed you have tasted that the Lord is good." Newborn infants have nothing on their mind except milk. We too, like newborn infants, should crave the Word of God so we can grow to spiritual maturity.

- **It renews our minds and changes our thinking:** Unlike any other writing known to mankind, Scripture transforms and renews our mind, which in turn, changes our behavior and brings us to spiritual maturity. Romans 12:2 declares, "Do not be conformed to this world, but be transformed by the renewal of your mind, that by testing you may discern what is the will of God, what is good and acceptable and perfect."

- **It strengthens our faith:** "So faith comes from hearing, and hearing through the word of Christ" (Rom. 10:17).

- **It gives us life:** "It is the Spirit who gives life; the flesh is no help at all. The words that I have spoken to you are spirit and life" (John 6:63). Also, Psalm 19:8 beautifully adds, "The precepts of the Lord are right, rejoicing the heart; the commandment of the Lord is pure, enlightening the eyes."

- **It instructs us in all matters:** "All Scripture is breathed out by God and profitable for teaching, for reproof, for correction, and for training in righteousness, that the man of God may be complete, equipped for every good work" (2 Tim. 3:16–17). Moreover, Psalm 119:105 states, "Your word is a lamp to my feet and a light to my path."

- **It protects us from sin and destruction:** King David attested, "I have stored up your word in my heart, that I might not sin against you" (Psalm 119:11).

- **It brings success in life:** God commanded Joshua to keep Scripture in the forefront of his life and meditate on it always so he would be successful: "This Book of the Law shall not depart from your mouth, but you shall meditate on it day and night, so that you may be careful to do according to all that is written in it. For then you will make **your way prosperous**, and then you will have **good success**" (Josh. 1:8).

Bible Intake

The role of Scripture in the life of a believer cannot be overemphasized. There are four key methods for acquiring it: (1) through reading, (2) through hearing, (3) through study, and (4) through memorization. The first three methods are the most common, and the last method, the least.

It's debatable as to whether or not Scripture memorization should be a separate and distinct essential component of the discipleship-making process as it has strong biblical and historical support. However, because it's part of the way we obtain the knowledge of God, I've included it in this category instead.

Personally, I've made Scripture memorization a part of my life and have experienced amazing benefits and blessings as a result. Not only has it sharpened my mental capabilities, but most of all, it has embedded the Word of God in my heart. I can say from experience that there's nothing like memorizing and meditating on God's Word. It's so rich, so powerful, so sweet, and so very life changing.

Conclusion

Bible intake is critical for attaining spiritual maturity and should not be neglected. To the degree we allow it to dwell in us richly and transform us will be the degree to which we will reach spiritual maturity. To the degree we neglect it will be the degree to which we will remain stunted and retarded in our spiritual growth.

2. Self-Discipline and Discipleship

Why is self-discipline so important that it's listed as an essential component of the discipleship-making process? Because it provides the structure, motivation, and perseverance necessary for attaining spiritual maturity, and the lack of it has been the downfall of countless Christians.

A strong case can be made that self-discipline is the most important factor needed for discipleship, and for that matter, life in general. Without it, none of the essential components of discipleship will be implemented and put into practice. Therefore, it can be argued that everything rests on discipline and without it, little else matters!

Donald Whitney boldly states, "I can say that I've never known a man or woman who came to spiritual maturity except through discipline. Godliness comes through discipline."[157] I believe Whitney is right. However, statistics today reveal that the average Christian has a definite lack of self-discipline. Due to this lack, many Christians are stuck in their journey toward spiritual maturity, and some will never arrive.

Discipleship Requires Self-Discipline

The word "disciple" is related to the word "discipline." A disciple, therefore, should be a highly disciplined person in following Christ. Without it, they will struggle.

As a pastor and missionary, I've seen firsthand the consequences the lack of self-discipline produces. I've seen people destroy their marriages, families, jobs, finances, health, bodies, and lives. I've seen countless people, who have wonderful hearts,

---

[157] Donald Whitney, *Spiritual Disciplines for the Christian Life,* (Colorado Springs: NavPress, 1991), p. 15.

live in pain and sorrow. Moreover, I've seen many Christians fail to reach spiritual maturity because they lack the self-discipline to attain it.

Self-Discipline Is a Key Purpose of the Book of Proverbs

Discipline is stated as a major theme of the Book of Proverbs: "For attaining wisdom and **discipline**; for understanding words of insight" (Prov. 1:2, NIV 1984).

A variant of the word "discipline" is mentioned 12 times throughout Proverbs, and the lack of discipline is mentioned numerous times: "And at the end of your life you groan, when your flesh and body are consumed, and you say, 'How I hated **discipline**, and my heart despised reproof!'" (Prov. 5:11–12).

Self-Discipline Is One of the Fruits of the Spirit

Galatians 5:23 states that self-control is a fruit that the Holy Spirit produces in the life of a believer. Self-control is synonymous with self-discipline. A self-controlled person is a disciplined person who makes themself do what they ought to do, not what they want to do.

Self-Discipline Is Related to Training

1 Timothy 4:6–8 uses the theme of training to convey the need for discipline in the Christian life: "If you put these things before the brothers, you will be a good servant of Christ Jesus, being **trained** in the words of the faith and of the good doctrine that you have followed. Have nothing to do with irreverent, silly myths. Rather **train yourself for godliness**; for while bodily training is of some value, godliness is of value in every way, as it holds promise for the present life and also for the life to come."

Here we see the value of discipline in training ourselves in godliness. However, most of us shy away from it. Bill Hull notes our tendency by stating, "Let's face it—discipline isn't something most of us like. We avoid discipline if we can, because it disrupts the normal and comfortable pattern of our life."[158]

Self-Discipline Is Related to Military Terminology

The Apostle Paul uses military vocabulary with Timothy in communicating the importance of self-discipline, enduring hardships, and being a tough soldier for Christ. He asserts, "Share in suffering as a good **soldier** of Christ Jesus" (2 Tim. 2:3). And again, "No **soldier** gets entangled in civilian pursuits, since his aim is to please the one who enlisted him" (2 Tim. 2:4).

According to the statistics of Christians today, self-discipline is lacking and needs to be built into our character if we're going to be deliberate disciples of Christ and reach spiritual maturity.

Self-Discipline Is Related to Sports Terminology

In 1 Corinthians 9:24–27, God uses sports language to convey the need for self-discipline:

> Do you not know that in a race all the runners run, but only one gets the prize? Run in such a way as to get the prize. Everyone who competes in the games goes into **strict training**. They do it to get a crown that will not last, but we do it to get a crown that will last forever. Therefore, I do not run like someone running aimlessly; I do not fight like a boxer beating the air. No, I strike a blow to my body and make it my slave so that after I have preached to others; I myself will not be disqualified for the prize.

The Apostle Paul uses the Olympic Games as a metaphor for the importance of discipline in our Christian lives. In the same

---

[158] Bill Hull, *The Complete Book of Discipleship: On Being and Making Followers of Christ* (The Navigators Reference Library 1, 2014, NavPress. Kindle Edition), Kindle Locations 445-447.

way athletes competing in these games would undergo strict training, we too must submit ourselves to spiritual training in godliness in order to be faithful disciples.

The Role of Self-Discipline in Discipleship

In Joseph V. Crockett's article "Is There Discipline in Our Discipleship," he stresses that discipline is the major theme of discipleship. Crockett attests that "Even if you are an athlete, the term 'discipline' may not invoke warm and fuzzy feelings of excitement, yet discipline is necessary, even though it may not be welcomed."[159] Crockett challenges, "Where is the discipline in discipleship?"[160] Crockett even goes one step further and states that "It is difficult, if not impossible, to follow Jesus, to be His disciple, without accepting, embracing, and embodying spiritual disciplines for Christian formation."[161]

Raymond Edman also has strong words for us today: "We need the rugged strength of Christian character that can come only from discipline: the discipline of spirit, of mind, of body, of society."[162] Today, we are a soft, indulgent society! All our modern conveniences and luxuries have eaten away at our strength and discipline, and we're paying a high price for it.

Edman goes on to boldly state, "Discipleship means 'discipline!' The disciple is that one who has been taught or trained by the Master, who has come with his ignorance, superstition, and sin, to find learning, truth, and forgiveness from the Savior. Without discipline, we are not disciples, even though we profess his name and pass for a follower of the lowly

---

[159] Joseph V. Crockett, "Is There Discipline in Our Discipleship?" (Source: Living Pulpit, Online, March 1, 2014, ATLA Religion Database with ATLASerials, Hunter Resource Library), p. 9, Accessed 11/5/2014.
[160] Ibid., p. 10.
[161] Ibid., p. 10.
[162] Raymond Edman, *The Disciplines of Life* (Minneapolis, Minnesota: World Wide Publications, 1948), preface.

Nazarene."[163] Edman is so bold as to state that an undisciplined person is unable to be a disciple. These are strong words, words worth pondering and absorbing, words worth putting into practice!

Bill Hull sums up the thinking of many when he says, "Most of us want to reap the harvest of discipline while living a life of relative sloth."[164] Without self-discipline, we won't attain spiritual maturity or accomplish much for the Kingdom of God, and we'll arrive in heaven with few or no rewards.

The Importance of Spiritual Discipline

Developing spiritual discipline should be a high priority in our lives because it's the gasoline that powers spiritual growth. Without it, we'll stagnate and run aground. Therefore, we should purposefully make spiritual commitments despite how tough they might be. For example, every believer should establish the spiritual discipline to at least pray and read Scripture daily. Additional commitments can be made such as Bible memorization, journaling, spiritual gift development, reading, and fasting.

Establishing spiritual disciplines are biblical and have been used for millenniums. They take the theoretical and make it practical. They put "feet" on discipleship, applying it to where the rubber meets the road. We can say, "We should," or "It would be great if," but that gets us nowhere. Discipline is what moves us.

Spiritual disciplines establish clear, measurable, biblical steps that lead us to spiritual maturity. Christ practiced them, and they are found throughout Scripture. Donald Whitney states, "The

---

[163] Ibid., p. 9.
[164] Bill Hull, *The Complete Book of Discipleship: On Being and Making Followers of Christ* (The Navigators Reference Library 1, 2014, NavPress. Kindle Edition), Kindle Locations 451-452.

Spiritual Disciplines are those personal and corporate disciplines that promote spiritual growth. They are the habits of devotion and experiential Christianity that have been practiced by the people of God since biblical times."[165] Whitney continues, "I will maintain that the only road to Christian maturity and godliness passes through the practice of the Spiritual Disciplines."[166]

Conclusion

Through self-discipline, we put into practice the principles that carry us to spiritual maturity. Without it, we remain spiritually immature. It provides the structure, motivation, and perseverance necessary for attaining spiritual maturity, and the lack of it has been the downfall of countless Christians.

A strong case can be made that self-discipline is the most important factor needed for discipleship, and for that matter, life in general. Without it, none of the essential components of discipleship will be implemented and put into practice. For this reason, it can be argued that everything rests on self-discipline and without it, little else matters!

---

[165] Donald Whitney, *Spiritual Disciplines for the Christian Life*, (Colorado Springs, NavPress, 1991), p. 15.
[166] Ibid., p. 14.

3. Obedience and Discipleship

The role of obedience is another vital component of discipleship. Without it, we go nowhere; with it, we go everywhere. The lack of obedience in the Christian life is one of the biggest roadblocks in our growth to spiritual maturity. Our choices are real and bring consequences in this life and the one to come. By obedience, we obtain God's richest blessings, and without it, we bring upon ourselves His discipline, displeasure, and judgment.

Christ's most used phrase, "Follow Me," calls for obedience, and it's impossible to follow Him without it. However, when 81% of Christians do not read their Bibles regularly, a whopping 61% of believers have not shared their faith in the last six months, 75% of church members do not attend a Bible study or small group, and the average Christian only prays somewhere between 1-7 minutes a day, it appears obvious that most Christians today are not obeying Christ as they should.

Discipleship and Obedience

Discipleship in the time of Christ called for strict adherence and obedience to a disciple's rabbi. No rabbi would even consider a candidate who was unwilling to pledge to him their total allegiance and obedience.

Christ employed this same concept in His call to discipleship: "And calling the crowd to him with his disciples, he said to them, 'If anyone would come after me, let him deny himself and take up his cross and follow me. For whoever would save his life will lose it, but whoever loses his life for my sake and the gospel's will save it'" (Mark 8:34–35). These verses call for obedience in the strictest manner. Christ knows that in order to follow Him, and be His disciple, we must have no other allegiance above Him. He calls for

213

completely devoted followers.

Obedience and Legalism

Obedience is often viewed by many Christians as cold and opposed to God's love and grace. Some react to a focus on obedience as a form of legalism (the belief that our efforts earn salvation and God's love). It's true that obedience to a set of rules does not earn salvation or God's love, but it does please Him and is vitally necessary for growth in Christ. Without obedience, we displease God and grieve His Spirit (Eph. 4:30).

If we truly believe that the wages of sin is death, then we must acknowledge that obedience saves us from sin's destruction.

Interestingly, when God gave the Ten Commandments and the Mosaic Covenant on Mt. Sinai, obedience was the cornerstone component God required: "Now, therefore, if you will indeed **obey my voice and keep my covenant**, you shall be my treasured possession among all peoples, for all the earth is mine" (Ex. 19:5).

As mentioned, some within Christianity are uncomfortable with a focus on obedience as they see it as a form of legalism. However, what does Scripture teach? Is obedience opposed to God's love and grace? Interestingly, God says they are not. Consider the following verses:

- **John 14:15:** "If you love me, you will keep my commandments."

- **John 14:21:** "Whoever has my commandments and keeps them, he it is who loves me. And he who loves me will be loved by my Father, and I will love him and manifest myself to him."

- **John 15:10:** "If you keep my commandments, you will abide in my love, just as I have kept my Father's commandments and abide in his love."

- **John 15:14:** "You are my friends if you do what I command you."

- **1 John 2:3–4:** "And by this we know that we have come to know him, if we keep his commandments. Whoever says 'I know him' but does not keep his commandments is a liar, and the truth is not in him."

- **1 John 3:24:** "Whoever keeps his commandments abides in God, and God in him. And by this we know that he abides in us, by the Spirit whom he has given us."

- **Matthew 5:19:** "Therefore, whoever **relaxes one of the least of these commandments** and teaches others to do the same will be called least in the kingdom of heaven, but whoever does them and teaches them will be called great in the kingdom of heaven."

God makes it overwhelmingly clear that our love for Him (which is the greatest commandment) is expressed by our obedience. To not obey God is not to love Him! He asks for our obedience because He loves us and it's the best for us. Keeping His commandments is the greatest way we can love ourselves as they bring us life and blessings. God does not see obedience as legalism that is opposed to His love and grace, but as the fulfillment and greatest expression of our love to Him.

Obedience and Knowing God

God says that the measuring stick for determining whether or not we actually "know" Him is through our obedience (1 John 2:3–4). Moreover, He says that obedience is the determining factor as to whether or not we are abiding in Him (1 John 3:24).

God expresses His love to us through His commands; we express our love to Him by obeying them.

Conclusion

The role of obedience is a critical component of discipleship. Without it, we go nowhere; with it, we go everywhere. The lack of obedience in the Christian life is one of the biggest roadblocks in our growth to spiritual maturity. God expects us to obey Him and is grieved when we don't. We show God how much we love Him through our obedience; we show Him our lack of love through our disobedience.

Obedience is a key factor in the discipleship process, and we'll get stuck in our spiritual growth if we don't take it seriously. If we presume upon God's love and grace, we greatly displease Him and damage ourselves in the process.

4. Abiding in Christ and Discipleship

What does abiding in Christ mean and how does it play such a key role as one of the essential components of discipleship?

Christ gave a vivid illustration of what "abide" means and its importance in John 15:1-6:

> I am the true vine, and my Father is the vinedresser. Every branch in me that does not bear fruit he takes away, and every branch that does bear fruit he prunes, that it may bear more fruit. Already you are clean because of the word that I have spoken to you. **Abide** in me, and I in you. As the branch cannot bear fruit by itself, unless it **abides** in the vine, neither can you, unless you **abide** in me. I am the vine; you are the branches. Whoever **abides** in me and I in him, he it is that bears much fruit, for apart from me you can do nothing. If anyone does not **abide** in me he is thrown away like a branch and withers; and the branches are gathered, thrown into the fire, and burned.

Christ uses the word "abide" five times in this passage. The word "abide" means to remain in, or stay connected to something. One author has noted, "To abide is to live, continue, or remain—so to abide in Christ is to live in Him or remain in Him."[167]

John MacArthur defines abiding in Christ as "Remaining inseparably linked to Christ in all areas of life. We depend on Him for grace and power to obey. We look obediently to His Word for instruction on how to live. We offer Him our deepest adoration and praise, and we submit ourselves to His authority over our lives. In short, Christians should gratefully know that Jesus Christ

---

[167] Gotquestions.org, *What Does It Mean to Abide in Christ?* http://www.gotquestions.org/abide-in-Christ.html, Accessed 10/20/2015.

is the source and sustainer of their lives."[168]

Grapevines and Abiding in Christ

The illustration of the vine and the branches in John 15 provides an incredible picture of what abiding means. A branch is completely dependent upon the vine for its nutrients and life. The moment it's detached, it quickly withers and dies.

Many years ago, I managed a vineyard and saw this firsthand. Often, due to the wind, a tractor, or other reasons, a branch would get disconnected from its vine. Within minutes, the branch would begin withering and dying. Grapevines are very different from other plants and are more susceptible to withering than most. That's why Christ used this illustration. He knew the Jewish culture was familiar with grapevines and would instantly understand His point.

Therefore, in the same way a grape branch withers and dies if it is not connected to its vine, we as well, will wither and die spiritually if we don't stay connected to Christ and abide in Him.

Walking in the Spirit and Abiding in Christ

Abiding in Christ can also be defined as walking in the Spirit or being led by the Spirit. "But I say, walk by the Spirit, and you will not gratify the desires of the flesh. For the desires of the flesh are against the Spirit, and the desires of the Spirit are against the flesh, for these are opposed to each other, to keep you from doing the things you want to do. But if you are led by the Spirit, you are not under the law" (Gal. 5:16–18).

Setting Our Minds on Christ and Abiding in Christ

Abiding in Christ means we are constantly setting our minds

---

[168] John MacArthur, *What Does It Mean to "Abide" in Christ?* Gty.org, www.gty.org/resources/Questions/QA161/What-does-it-mean-to-abide-in-Christ, Accessed 10/20/2015.

upon Him and His Word throughout our waking hours and seeking to obey Him. We take into consideration what He thinks, we pray for His help and guidance often, and we are in tune with His Spirit within us.

We don't wander far from Him throughout the day, are constantly checking in with Him, and are bringing every thought into obedience to Him and His Word (2 Cor. 10:4–5). We, in essence, live in the presence of God and pray without ceasing (1 Thess. 5:17). Praying without ceasing doesn't mean we do nothing else during the day but bow our heads in prayer; but rather, it carries the idea of living in the presence of God and attempting to please and obey Him in all things.

Seeking the Things Above and Abiding in Christ

Colossians 3:1–2 also helps us understand what the word "abide" means: "If then you have been raised with Christ, seek the things that are above, where Christ is, seated at the right hand of God. Set your minds on things that are above, not on things that are on earth." Abiding means we set our minds on God, on His Word, and on seeking His Kingdom. It values the things of God over the things of earth and continually makes adjustments that reflect this priority.

Conclusion

As alluded to earlier, John 15:5 says, "Whoever abides in me and I in him, he it is that bears much fruit, for **apart from me you can do nothing**." Without abiding in Christ, we can do nothing. We cannot be disciples, we cannot have right attitudes, we cannot grow in Christ, we cannot attain spiritual maturity, and we are absolutely helpless and dead. This is why abiding in Christ is so important to discipleship and should be one of its essential components.

5. Prayer and Discipleship

As we noted earlier, according to recent stats, the average Evangelical Christian prays between 1–7 minutes a day. In addition, Daniel Henderson did some recent research and discovered the following stats regarding Christians and prayer. He states the average person lives 77 years. That equates to 28,000 days, 670,000 hours, or 40 million minutes, and during their lifetime, they spend this time doing the following things:[169]

- The average person spends 24 minutes a day getting dressed. That equals 13 hours a month, 7 days a year, or 1 year in a lifetime.
- The average person spends 40 minutes a day on the phone. That factors out to 20 hours a month, 10 days a year, or 2 years in a lifetime.
- The average person spends 1 hour a day in the bathroom. That amounts to 30 hours a month, 15 days a year, and 3 years in a lifetime.
- The average person spends 3 hours a day watching television. That is 90 hours a month, 45 days a year, and 9 years in a lifetime.
- The average Christian spends less than 10 minutes a day in prayer. That equates to less than 6 hours a month, 3 days a year, and 7 months in a lifetime.[170]

What a tragedy that prayer, which should be our most important priority, receives the least amount of time and attention. Christians have time to talk on the phone 40 minutes a

---

[169] Daniel Henderson, *No Time to Pray,* Praying Pastor Blog, PrayingPastorBlog.blogspot, http://prayingpastorblog.blogspot.mx/2009/02/no-time-to-pray-no-time-to-pray.html, Accessed 10/16/2015.
[170] Ibid., Accessed 10/16/2015.

day and watch TV 3 hours a day, but can only pray less than 10 minutes a day. What's the problem? The only reasonable explanation is that it's not very important, and therefore, not a priority. Can you imagine how God feels about that? He's worth less than TV, phone time, the Internet, and almost every other activity!

Another recent survey shows even more disturbing news. It reveals that the average Christian prays just a minute a day: "It appears Christian prayers have apparently morphed into tweets to God."[171] Deborah Beeksma quotes the Rev. Nathan Shutes as saying, "My fear is that this generation has missed out on [being] prayer warriors. We have become an instant gratification generation. We tweet in 140 characters, and prayer can be just as short. Here are some numbers that ought to make you cringe; on the Baptist Board website, they say the average Christian prays a minute a day, and the average pastor prays five minutes a day. God have mercy on us for such little devotion to the Sovereign One of the universe. No wonder our nation is falling away from God."[172]

What Is Prayer?

Mary Fairchild suggests, "Prayer is not a mysterious practice reserved only for clergy and the religiously devout. Prayer is simply communicating with God — listening and talking to him. Believers can pray from the heart, freely, spontaneously, and in their own words."[173] Andrew Murray also enhances our understanding of prayer when he says, "Prayer is not monologue, but dialogue; God's voice is its most essential part. Listening to

---

[171] Deborah Beeksma, *The Average Christian Prays a Minute a Day; Prayer by the Faithful Helps Their Relationships,* GodDiscussion.com, 2013, Accessed 07/27/2015.

[172] Ibid., Accessed 07/27/2015.

[173] Mary Fairchild, *Basics to Prayer,* Christianity.About.com, http://christianity.about.com/od/prayersverses/a/basicstoprayer.htm, Accessed 10/16/2016.

God's voice is the secret of the assurance that He will listen to mine."[174]

Through prayer, we can be honest, open, express our frustrations, problems, joys, and sorrows. Prayer is simple, yet its effects are powerful. Prayer connects us to the ultimate power of the universe because it connects us with the Sovereign, Almighty God, Ruler, Owner, and King of it. No time spent in prayer is wasted; on the contrary, there is nothing more important we could do.

The Importance of Prayer in Discipleship

We see the importance of prayer all throughout the Bible. It's mentioned around 316 times and was a key characteristic of all godly men and women. Richard Foster, in his book *Celebration of Discipline,* claims that prayer is one of the most important aspects of discipleship: "Of all the Spiritual Disciplines, prayer is the most central because it ushers us into perpetual communion with the Father."[175] Moreover, Foster says, "All who have walked with God have viewed prayer as the main business of their lives."[176]

Jesus and Prayer

Unlike the average Christian, who prays around 1–7 minutes a day, prayer throughout the Bible is seen as a central focus of life. Christ set an impeccable example in His prayer life despite being, in very essence, God:

- He prayed regularly and on many occasions got away by Himself to spend time with the Father.

- After feeding the 5,000 and dismissing the crowd, Scripture

---

[174] Andrew Murray, Power to Change, Great Quotes on Prayer, http://powertochange.com/experience/spiritual-growth/prayerquotes, Accessed 11/16/2015.
[175] Richard Foster, *Celebration of Discipline* (HarperCollins, Kindle Edition, 2009), p. 33.
[176] Ibid., p. 34.

records, "He went up on the mountain by himself to pray. When evening came, he was there alone" (Matt. 14:23).

- Despite His busyness, He made time for prayer: "And rising very early in the morning, while it was still dark, he departed and went out to a desolate place, and there he prayed" (Mark 1:35).

- Before making the immeasurable decision to choose the twelve disciples, He spent a whole night in prayer to seek His Father's will: "In these days he went out to the mountain to pray, and all night he continued in prayer to God. And when day came, he called his disciples and chose from them twelve, whom he named apostles" (Luke 6:12–13).

- He stressed the importance of prayer to His disciples: "And he told them a parable to the effect that they ought always to pray and not lose heart" (Luke 18:1).

- Christ also overcame temptation and taught His disciples to do the same through prayer: "Watch and pray that you may not enter into temptation. The spirit indeed is willing, but the flesh is weak" (Matt. 26:41).

- We also find in John 17, the better part of an entire chapter, wherein Christ devoted Himself to prayer for His disciples and all who would follow Him afterward.

The Apostles and Prayer

Following Christ's example and teaching on the importance of prayer, the Apostles, and the early church also prayed constantly.

- Shortly after Christ's resurrection, the disciples continued in prayer: "All these with one accord were devoting themselves to prayer, together with the women and Mary the mother of

Jesus, and his brothers" (Acts 1:14).

- After the church was born on Pentecost, the early church devoted themselves to prayer: "And they devoted themselves to the apostles' teaching and the fellowship, to the breaking of bread and the prayers" (Acts 2:42).

- The lame man that Peter and John healed at the temple was a result of going to the temple to pray (Acts 3:1).

- After being persecuted for preaching the Word, the disciples, and the early church prayed for boldness to keep pressing on: "And when they had prayed, the place in which they were gathered together was shaken, and they were all filled with the Holy Spirit and continued to speak the word of God with boldness" (Acts 4:31).

- When faced with busyness and administrative challenges, prayer became a priority of the elders of the early church: "But we will devote ourselves to prayer and to the ministry of the word" (Acts 6:4).

- Prayer also accompanied each missionary journey by Paul and his companions: "Then after fasting and praying they laid their hands on them and sent them off" (Acts 13:3).

Christians Today and Prayer

The Bible is replete with examples of godly men and women praying. Yet today, the average Christian prays between 1–7 minutes a day. What a contrast! Samuel Chadwick states, "The one concern of the devil is to keep Christians from praying. He fears nothing from prayerless studies, prayerless work, and prayerless religion. He laughs at our toil, mocks at our wisdom, but he trembles when we pray."[177] It appears Satan is rejoicing

---

[177] Christian Prayer Quotes, *Prayer Quotations*, http://www.christian-prayer-quotes.christian-attorney.net, Accessed 10/20/2015.

over the lack of prayer in the lives of many Christians today.

Why should we pray, and why does it play such a large role in discipleship and our transformation towards spiritual maturity? Scripture provides, at least, six essential reasons:

1. By Prayer, We Have a Relationship with God

Having a relationship with the living God is the essence of the Christian life and our purpose for existing. It's what God sought to regain with mankind after their fall in the Garden of Eden and is a determining factor in whether a person is saved or not. The simple fact is that we cannot have a relationship with God without prayer. It's how we communicate and talk to Him.

Dan Hayes says it well, "I am first called to prayer because it is a key vehicle to building my love relationship with Jesus Christ. Hear me now — this is important. Christianity is not primarily rules. It is relationship."[178]

We are to love the Lord our God with all our heart, soul, mind, and strength. Christ exemplified this truth in His prayer life with the Father. He continually was in communion with the Father and walked every step while listening to His voice.

If we want to have a relationship with God, then we must pray. Samuel Chadwick states, "Prayer is the acid test of devotion."[179] It's in our obedience and commitment to commune with our Father that we show Him our true love.

2. By Prayer, God Gives Us the Power to Overcome Temptation

Christ provides compelling instruction, and an example, on how to overcome temptation. In Luke 22:39–46, Christ is facing His last hours on earth before being crucified. He is in the Garden

---

[178] Dan Hayes, *Motivating Reasons to Pray,* StartingWithGod.com, www.startingwithgod.com/knowing-god/motivating, Accessed 10/20/2015.
[179] Christian Prayer Quotes, *Prayer Quotations,* http://www.christian-prayer-quotes.christian-attorney.net, Accessed 10/20/2015.

of Gethsemane, embracing the reality of paying for the sins of mankind for all time and eternity. He begins this time by teaching His disciples how to overcome temptation: "And he came out and went, as was his custom, to the Mount of Olives, and the disciples followed him. When he came to the place, he said to them, '**Pray that you may not enter into temptation.**'" Then Christ practiced what He taught: "And he withdrew from them about a stone's throw, and knelt down and prayed, saying, 'Father, if you are willing, remove this cup from me. Nevertheless, not my will, but yours, be done.'"

Christ's temptation to avoid the pain of the Cross was so intense that His sweat became bloody: "And being in an agony he prayed more earnestly; and his sweat became like great drops of blood falling down to the ground." Despite His temptation, He remained in prayer, yielded to God's will, and was victorious over the Cross and death.

Afterward, He returned to His disciples to find them half-asleep. He then told them again about prayer and its role in temptation: "And when he rose from prayer, he came to the disciples and found them sleeping for sorrow, and he said to them, 'Why are you sleeping? Rise and pray that you may not enter into temptation.'"

Interestingly, Christ began His instruction on how to overcome temptation by telling the disciples about prayer, then showing by example how to do it, and then repeating His instruction again.

If we're going to be victorious over temptation, we need to follow Christ's example. Unfortunately, much of the time, prayer is not the first thing we do when confronting temptation, so we succumb and fall as a result. How much better we would be if it were our first line of defense. Dan Hays asserts, "What about seeing prayer as our first option so that God can give us courage and strength prior to our temptations? Certainly, if we would pray more, we would yield less to sin!"[180]

3. By Prayer, God Leads and Directs Our Paths

There are two general areas in life where we need God's direction: (1) in fully understanding truth and morals already revealed in the Bible and (2) in the practical areas of life that Scripture does not address.

God has already revealed much of His will to us through Scripture. For example, His will is that we become saved, are transformed into the image of Christ, attain spiritual maturity, and that we love God and others. However, in matters not directly revealed in Scripture, it gets trickier. Areas like whom we should marry, what job we should take, or what college we should attend, become harder to discern.

If we obey God in the areas already revealed in Scripture, then the areas not revealed will become much simpler to perceive. However, if we are disobedient to God's clear, revealed will in Scripture, then we'll struggle to find His will in other matters as well.

It's also important to note that Scripture provides wisdom and direction for finding His will by directing us to others. Proverbs 11:14 speaks of the role of counselors, Proverbs 1:8 shows the role of our parents, and James 1:5 speaks of directly receiving wisdom from God through prayer.

Through prayer, God will miraculously open and close doors in our lives. He loves us dearly, and when He sees His children seeking His Kingdom first and desiring above all else to please Him, He goes out of His way to supernaturally guide and direct their paths.

---

[180] Dan Hays, *Motivating Reasons to Pray*, StartingWithGod.com, www.startingwithgod.com/knowing-god/motivating, Accessed 10/20/2015.

4. By Prayer, We Accomplish God's Work

Charles Spurgeon declared, "I would rather teach one man to pray than ten men to preach."[181] Moreover, Andrew Murray claimed, "The man who mobilizes the Christian church to pray will make the greatest contribution to world evangelization in history."[182]

Prayer rallies the power of the Almighty and involves Him in our efforts. With Him, we are everything, but without Him, we are nothing. Christ said, "I am the vine; you are the branches. Whoever abides in me and I in him, he it is that bears much fruit, for **apart from me you can do nothing**" (John 15:5).

A careful look at Scripture reveals that everything accomplished for God happens through prayer. The births of Isaac, the Prophet Samuel, and John the Baptist all came through prayer. The wisdom of Solomon, the dedication of the temple, and the countless deliverances of Israel from her enemies came through prayer. The work of Christ, the works of the early church, and the spread of the gospel all came through prayer. Likewise, if we want God's blessing in our lives and ministries, it will only come through prayer as well.

5. By Prayer, We Are Victorious in Spiritual Warfare

The battle between good and evil and the reality of spiritual warfare is clear in Scripture. We see it in the life and ministry of Christ, the Apostles, and the early church. It is also specifically addressed in Ephesians 6:12: "For we do not wrestle against flesh and blood, but against the rulers, against the authorities, against the cosmic powers over this present darkness, against the spiritual forces of evil in the heavenly places."

It's through prayer that we tap into God's power and become

---

[181] Christian Prayer Quotes, *Prayer Quotations,* http://www.christian-prayer-quotes.christian-attorney.net, Accessed 10/20/2015.
[182] Ibid., Accessed 10/20/2015.

victorious over Satan and his evil forces. We are no match for them on our own, but we are more than conquerors over them through Christ.

Prayer is also the overarching armor in our spiritual warfare: "Praying at all times in the Spirit, with all prayer and supplication. To that end keep alert with all perseverance, making supplication for all the saints" (Eph. 6:17–18).

6. By Prayer, God Grants Us Peace

We find peace through prayer: "Casting all your anxieties on him, because he cares for you" (1 Pet. 5:7).

Additionally, "Do not be anxious about anything, but in everything by prayer and supplication with thanksgiving let your requests be made known to God. And the peace of God, which surpasses all understanding, will guard your hearts and your minds in Christ Jesus" (Phil. 4:6–7).

Prayer is what alleviates our worries and stress. It ushers God's peace into our hearts by taking our burdens, and concerns, and placing them on God.

Conclusion

By prayer, we have a relationship with God, overcome temptation, find God's will, accomplish much for God's Kingdom, are victorious in spiritual warfare, and receive God's peace. As the great prayer warrior E. M. Bounds says, "Prayer should not be regarded as a duty which must be performed, but rather as a privilege to be enjoyed, a rare delight that is always revealing some new beauty."[183]

Prayer is an essential component of discipleship, and without it, spiritual maturity is unattainable. We cannot grow in our relationship with God without communicating with Him.

---

[183] Ibid., Accessed 10/20/2015.

6. Mentoring and Discipleship

One of the central themes of discipleship during the time of Christ was that of relationships and mentoring. It was normal for a rabbi to take his disciples on trips that lasted from several days to several weeks in order to train them. They would dedicate this time for intense mentoring, teaching, practicing, and learning. All the distractions of life would be set aside for the purpose of interaction between the rabbi and his students. Teaching was highly relational and modeled, and the disciples would learn how to apply Scripture, in large part, by observing the conduct and practices of their rabbi.

What Is Mentoring?

Biblical mentoring is an informal relationship wherein a more spiritually mature person teaches and models godly, life-skills to others who are generally less spiritually mature. It can be formal, informal, take place in a group setting, take place in an individual setting, can be regular, or somewhat sporadic.

Examples of mentoring include small group Bible studies, Sunday School classes, youth group, one on one discipleship studies, accountability partners, and so forth.

The most effective mentoring takes place in a one on one setting, or in a small group where specific truths and life-skills are intentionally passed on.

Mentoring Provides an Example

Christ was a rabbi who modeled what He taught to His disciples. This was done as they spent time together, took trips together, lived together for periods of time, and served together. After learning from Christ, His disciples would then practice what they learned.

We see mentoring as a central focus for teaching and training in other examples from Scripture as well: Moses mentored Joshua, Naomi mentored Ruth, Elijah mentored Elisha, and Paul mentored Timothy. After Paul had mentored Timothy, he encouraged Timothy to mentor others: "You then, my child, be strengthened by the grace that is in Christ Jesus, and what you have heard from me in the presence of many witnesses entrust to faithful men who will be able to teach others also" (2 Tim. 2:1).

Modern-Day Discipleship

Discipleship in our day is very different from what it was in the time of Christ. Today, we primarily focus on teaching certain truths and think that after several classes on discipleship training we're finished. Normally, this is because we're focusing primarily on imparting knowledge and not on all the essential components of discipleship like character, attitudes, spiritual gift development, self-discipline, and so on.

Discipleship is much more than taking a class for several weeks and thinking we're done. Instead, it must be engaged in throughout our lifetime. We are never finished and must always be looking for new opportunities to grow in all the essential components of the discipleship-making process.

Mentoring in the Church

A number of recent scholars and theologians have highlighted the importance of mentoring in discipleship. Voddie Baucham Jr., in his article "Equipping the Generations: A Three-Pronged Approach to Discipleship," shows that Paul clearly instructs Titus to make disciples using a mentoring model.[184]

---

[184] Voddie Baucham Jr, "Equipping the Generations: A Three-Pronged Approach to Discipleship" (Source: Journal of Family Ministry, 2 no 1 Fall-Winter 2011, Publication. ATLA Religion Database with ATLASerials. Hunter Resource Library), pp. 74-79, Accessed 11/5/2014.

There are three key themes Baucham draws out from the Book of Titus that underscores what successful discipleship should entail:

1. Godly, mature men and women in the church
2. Godly, manly pastors and elders
3. Biblically functioning homes

Baucham stresses that each of these three themes represents one leg of a three-legged stool, and each leg is vital in the discipleship-making process.[185] His reasoning is as follows:

1. Godly, mature men and women in the church are those whom Scripture charges with teaching the younger men and women the truths of God.
2. Godly, manly elders provide the example to the flock and leadership within the church.
3. Godly homes are the best place for discipleship to take place as this is where most of life is lived.[186]

Each of these themes uses mentorship as the vehicle through which discipleship is carried out.

Relationships and Discipleship

James G. Samra, in his article "A Biblical View of Discipleship," stresses the importance of relationships in discipleship. He indicates that in the Gospels discipleship literally meant following Christ where He went and learning from Him in a personal setting. It involved learning to suffer with Christ, leaving all behind, seeing what Christ did, hearing what He said, being corrected by Him, and following His example.[187] Samara

---

[185] Ibid., p. 75.
[186] Ibid., pp. 76–77.
[187] James G. Samra, "A Biblical View of Discipleship" (Bibliotheca Sacra: 219-34. Publication Type: Article, Database: ATLA Religion Database with ATLASerials. Hunter Resource Library), p. 222, Accessed 11/5/2014.

affirms, "In the rest of the New Testament, because Christ is no longer physically present, discipleship involved imitation of other mature believers rather than literally following Christ (1 Thess. 1:6; 1 Cor. 11:1)."[188]

Samra also says that in the Old Testament there are some examples of what discipleship looked like as carried out in the likes of Moses and Joshua as well as Elijah and Elisha.[189] In all these examples, relationships and mentoring provide the environment wherein discipleship takes place.

Avery Willis, in his article "MasterLife: Discipleship Training for Leaders," stresses the role of relationships in the process of discipleship. Willis states, "Discipleship is accomplished through the practice of basic Christian disciplines under the guidance of mature, practicing disciplers . . . and is carried out in the context of a small group of approximately eight persons."[190] Willis' model uses mentoring as a key component of effective discipleship.

Conclusion

The example of Christ and other mentoring relationships in Scripture highlight the importance mentoring plays in discipleship. For this reason, it's one of the essential components needed in the discipleship-making process. Many affirm that we learn more by observing than by hearing. The mentoring relationship puts this truth into practice as it allows us to see the truth of Scripture lived out and applied to real life.

---

[188] Ibid., p. 224.

[189] Ibid., pp. 226–227.

[190] Avery T. Willis Jr, "MasterLife: Discipleship Training for Leaders" (Source: Theological Educator, no 28 Spr 1984, p 3-5. Publication Type: Article. Subjects: Baptists--Education; Christian life ATLA Religion Database with ATLASerials. Hunter Resource Library), p. 3, Accessed 11/5/2014.

7. Church Involvement and Discipleship

Why is church involvement one of the essential components of the discipleship-making process, and how does God use it to transform our lives and bring us to spiritual maturity?

The Church Is God's Invention

The church is not a new fad or invention of man. God birthed it on the Day of Pentecost, and it plays a unique role in His plan for believers. It consists of both the universal and the local church.

The universal church consists of all those who have a genuine, personal relationship with Jesus Christ: "For in one Spirit we were all baptized into one body — Jews or Greeks, slaves or free — and all were made to drink of one Spirit" (1 Cor. 12:13). The local church can be defined as found in Galatians 1:1–2: "Paul, an apostle . . . and all the brothers who are with me, to the churches in Galatia."

The church is God's caring community where believers find instruction, encouragement, correction, inspiration, and fellowship. Faithful involvement in church helps all believers attain spiritual maturity while a lack of it will stunt a believer's growth.

Church Involvement Develops Spiritual Maturity

"And he [Christ] gave the apostles, the prophets, the evangelists, the shepherds and teachers, to equip the saints for the work of ministry, for building up the body of Christ, until we all attain to the unity of the faith and of the knowledge of the Son of God, to mature manhood, to the measure of the stature of the fullness of Christ" (Eph. 4:11–13). Christ has given the church gifted men and women for the equipping of believers so that we might all attain spiritual maturity. Therefore, without their influence in our lives, spiritual maturity is unattainable.

Church Involvement Provides Sound Doctrine to Protect Us

In church, we find God's instruction for combatting the lies of Satan and our culture: "So that we may no longer be children, tossed to and fro by the waves and carried about by every wind of doctrine, by human cunning, by craftiness in deceitful schemes" (Eph. 4:14).

Church Involvement Provides Encouragement and Fellowship

Within the church, we find inspiration and encouragement in our Christian lives. As a famous illustration reveals, "A piece of coal removed from other burning coals will soon go out, but a coal left with other burning coals will keep on burning."

Dale Robbins asserts, "Receiving the preaching and teaching of the Word of God increases our faith and builds us up spiritually. Every believer knows what it is to face spiritual conflicts to their faith, and must realize the importance of being fed spiritually so that they can overcome the challenges."[191]

Church Involvement Provides a Unique Visitation of the Lord's Presence

Even though Christ resides in the heart of every believer, there's a special visitation of His presence when believers are gathered together. Consider the following verses:

1. The glory of the Lord filled the Tabernacle Moses built when the people of God were gathered together (Ex. 40:34).

2. The glory of the Lord filled the Temple Solomon built when the people of God were gathered together (1 Kings 8:11).

---

[191] Dale Robbins, *Why Christians Should Attend Church,* Victorious.org, www.victorious.org/pub/why-church-169, Accessed 10/21/2015.

3. The church was born on Pentecost as believers were gathered together (Acts 2).

4. When persecution faced the early church, they prayed, and the place shook with God's presence (Acts 4).

5. The missionary journeys of Paul and his companions were commissioned by the Lord when the church was gathered together (Acts 13).

6. Doctrinal decisions were made when the church was gathered together (Acts 15).

7. Many of the spiritual gifts are intended to be exercised when the church is gathered together (1 Cor. 12–14).

8. Prayer for healing is encouraged by calling together the elders of the church (James 5).

God moves in a unique way when believers gather, and we experience His special visitation when we're a part of it.

Church Involvement Is an Expression of Our Love for God

Dale Robbins says, "Going to church is a visible, tangible expression of our love and worship to God. It is where we can gather with other believers to publicly bear witness of our faith and trust in God, something that is required of all Christians (Matt. 10:32–33), and where we can bring Him offerings of praise, thanks, and honor, which are pleasing to Him."[192] King David wrote, "I will declare Your name to My brethren; In the midst of the assembly I will praise You" (Ps. 22:22).

Being involved in what God loves reveals our love for Him, and God certainly loves the church: "Husbands, love your wives, as **Christ loved the church** and gave himself up for her, that he might sanctify her, having cleansed her by the washing of water

---

[192] Ibid., Accessed 10/21/2015.

with the word, so that he might present the church to himself in splendor, without spot or wrinkle or any such thing, that she might be holy and without blemish" (Eph. 5:25–27).

God Commands Church Involvement

Because God loves us and knows what we need, He commands us to be involved in church for our own good: "And let us consider how to stir up one another to love and good works, not neglecting to meet together, as is the habit of some, but encouraging one another, and all the more as you see the Day drawing near" (Heb. 10:24–25).

Conclusion

In church, we receive from God and others critical components we need for discipleship, and we, in turn, give to others what they need for discipleship. We express our love to God and have the privilege and responsibility to minister to others with our gifts. Moreover, as we engage in this wonderful process, we move toward spiritual maturity.

8. Evangelism and Discipleship

Evangelism is one of the essential components of the discipleship-making process because it's part of the Great Commission Mandate. It's not just for missionaries in a distant land or those with the gift of evangelism, but for all. Everyone should participate in evangelism in some way or another.

Christ's Focus on Evangelism

The Great Commission Mandate includes evangelism: "Go therefore, and make disciples of all nations, baptizing them in the name of the Father and of the Son and of the Holy Spirit," (Matt. 28:19). Moreover, the corresponding text of Mark 16:15 tells us to "Proclaim the gospel to all creation."

We also see in the life and work of Christ His concentrated focus on evangelism. He was continually calling people to follow Him, revealing the passion of His heart: "For the Son of Man came to seek and to save the lost" (Luke 19:10). If we want to be like Christ, then we must have a passion for evangelism like He does.

We can measure, in part, our spiritual maturity by the level of passion we have for evangelism. If one of Christ's main purposes on earth was to seek and save the lost, it certainly should be one of ours as well.

Unfortunately, the majority of Christians don't share their faith or invite their friends to church. For this reason, Christ would sadly say to many Christians today the same thing He said to those during His day: "The harvest is plentiful, but the laborers are few; therefore, pray earnestly to the Lord of the harvest to send out laborers into his harvest" (Matt. 9:37–38).

Christ Called His Disciples to Be Fishers of Men

"And he said to them, 'Follow me, and I will make you

fishers of men'" (Matt. 4:19). The same message applies to us today. We are called to be fishers of men. A "fisher of men" symbolizes a person who evangelizes. They have a passion for reaching people with the good news of Christ, seeing them saved, reunited with their Maker, and rescued from sin's destructive domain.

For the person who neglects evangelism, it should give them great pause. How can they claim to love God and others, and care so little about God's passion for reaching the lost? How can they idly stand by as others destroy their lives, head for hell, and not warn them?

Most Christians Are Not Fishers of Men

In research done by Jon D. Wilke, the statistics regarding Evangelical Christians today who share their faith are troublesome. Wilke reveals, "When it comes to discipleship, churchgoers struggle most with sharing Christ with non-Christians according to a recent study of church-going American Protestants. The study conducted by LifeWay Research found 80% of those who attend church one or more times a month believe they have a personal responsibility to share their faith, yet 61% have not told another person about how to become a Christian in the previous six months."[193] Wilke continues, "The survey also asked how many times they have personally invited an unchurched person to attend a church service or some other program at their church. Nearly half (48%) of church attendees responded, 'zero.'"[194]

Many so-called Evangelical Christians are not only extremely negligent in sharing the gospel, but many don't even invite their unsaved friends to church. Christ said He would make His

---

[193] Jon D. Wilke, *Churchgoers Believe in Sharing Faith, Most Never Do,* LifeWay.com, http://www.lifeway.com/article/research-survey-sharing-christ-2012, Accessed 08/04/2015.
[194] Ibid., Accessed 08/04/2015.

disciples fishers of men. However, for many so-called modern day disciples, evangelism isn't even on their radar screen.

Christ Calls Every Believer to Be His Witness

Moments before Christ's ascension to heaven, as recorded in Acts 1:8, He repeated the Great Commission Mandate using slightly different words, "But you will receive power when the Holy Spirit has come upon you and you will be my witnesses in Jerusalem and in all Judea and Samaria, and to the end of the earth."

Notice carefully what Christ said, "You will be my witnesses in **Jerusalem** and in all **Judea** and **Samaria**, and to the **end of the earth**" (Acts 1:8). Another term for "witness" is "evangelize." Christ said some would be witnesses in Jerusalem (their hometown), some would be witnesses in Judea (a little larger circle), some would be witnesses in Samaria (their country), and some would be witnesses to the ends of the earth (foreign missions). Even though they were to be witnesses in different places, all had the privilege and responsibility to evangelize.

Paul instructed Timothy, who apparently was somewhat shy and timid, to fulfill his responsibility in evangelism: "As for you, always be sober-minded, endure suffering, **do the work of an evangelist**, fulfill your ministry" (2 Tim. 4:5). Even though it was uncomfortable for Timothy, he still needed to do the work of an evangelist.

God has given all of us the ministry of reconciliation: "All this is from God, who through Christ reconciled us to himself and gave us the **ministry of reconciliation**; that is, in Christ God was reconciling the world to himself, not counting their trespasses against them, and entrusting to us the **message of reconciliation**" (2 Cor. 5:18–19). In the same way Christ had the ministry of reconciliation (reuniting God with sinners), we have the same ministry as well.

Some feel evangelism is primarily for missionaries or others who have the gift of evangelism. While it's true some might have this gift, it does not alleviate others from participating in evangelism.

We Need to Speak, Not Just Show

A common belief today is that we should let our lives do the talking for us and evangelize primarily by "letting our light shine" before others. This belief does contain truth and is what gives us the right to share our faith, yet if we omit the balancing responsibility of evangelizing through speaking, we are misguided.

If letting our light shine was enough, then Christ, being perfect, would have just shown up, not said a word, and let His "light shine." However, Christ is referred to as the "Word" in Scripture who became flesh and dwelt among us (John 1:14). The spoken word is so important that Christ is called, the "Word." He spent His life speaking and did so much that John concluded his Gospel by stating, "Now there are also many other things that Jesus did. Were every one of them to be written, I suppose that the world itself could not contain the books that would be written" (John 21:25).

Virtually every example we see in Scripture where God wants to communicate something, He uses both a clean vessel (letting our light shine) and the spoken word. We need to be careful we don't allow the fear of evangelism scare us away from sharing the gospel through the spoken word and use the excuse of "letting our light shine" as a reason for not speaking and being bold for Christ.

Conclusion

Believers who are not involved in evangelism are believers who don't share Christ's passion for winning the lost. They are failing to obey Christ in fulfilling the Great Commission Mandate and display indifference to the fact that unbelievers are going to hell. If the purpose of Christ was to spread the gospel, then His disciples today should do the same. Nevertheless, the majority of Christians today are not fishers of men as Christ and His disciples were, and seem to loathe evangelism.

There's a huge disconnect today in the lives of many Christians between what they should do and what they do. The fact that the vast majority of Christians don't share their faith or invite their friends to church speaks volumes about their level of spiritual maturity and devotion to Christ.

9. The Inner Life and Discipleship

Why is attention to our inner life one of the essential components of the discipleship-making process? Because what takes place in our inner life is the truest expression of our life in Christ. It's where we apply and live out true spirituality.

According to Christ, an outward focus on keeping His commands with the intent to impress others has no value. He calls it hypocritical and vain: "You hypocrites! Well did Isaiah prophesy of you, when he said: 'This people honors me with their lips, but their heart is far from me; in vain do they worship me, teaching as doctrines the commandments of men'" (Matt. 15:5-9).

Our Inner Life Is the True Mark of Our Spirituality

In the Sermon on the Mount, Christ addresses the issue of the inner life as the mark of true spirituality. He speaks of anger, lust, divorce, oaths, bitterness, retaliation, loving our enemies, giving to the needy, prayer, and fasting, all from the perspective of the inner life before God versus mere external acts done before others to impress them. He warns that merely obeying His commands with the intention of impressing others does not please Him.

Lying deep within our hearts is the tendency to be more concerned about what others think of us than what God thinks. We often strive to impress others by appearing good on the outside, but are inwardly different. Many of the spiritual leaders of Christ's day were guilty of this snare as they did much of their service to God solely to impress others, with little concern for what God thought. They were full of pride and selfish ambition.

Unfortunately, we can be the same. Christ recognized this tendency within our hearts and addressed it with a strong rebuke: "Woe to you, scribes and Pharisees, hypocrites! For you are like whitewashed tombs, which outwardly appear beautiful, but within are full of dead people's bones and all uncleanness. So you also outwardly appear righteous to others, but within you are full of hypocrisy and lawlessness" (Matt. 23:27-28). We must take great care to serve with pure hearts that seek to impress God, not others!

The Importance of the Inner Life

Klaus Issler, in his article "Six Themes to Guide Spiritual Formation Ministry Based on Jesus' Sermon on the Mount," emphasizes that the key theme of the Sermon on the Mount is inner heart formation.[195] We can observe that virtually every theme Christ cites from the Old Testament is a clarification of the importance of the inner heart for the New Covenant. Issler sees the segment on the Beatitudes as a further verification of the importance of the inner life in the discipleship process.[196]

Dietrich Bonhoeffer devotes three chapters of his classic book, *The Cost of Discipleship,* to the topic of the inner life.[197] The inner life is where we live, where God knows our thoughts, motives, desires, and goals. When we bypass the inner life and attempt to "go through the motions" or "fake" our spirituality before others, we displease God and worship Him in vain.

Attention to Our Inner Life Protects Us from Legalism

When we neglect the inner life and pursue obeying God's commandments primarily to impress others, we risk the danger of falling into legalism and hypocrisy. For example, some Christians are boastful of their knowledge of Scripture and think they are

---

[195] Klaus Issler, "Six Themes to Guide Spiritual Formation Ministry Based on Jesus' Sermon on the Mount" (Source: Christian Education, Journal Date: September 1, 2010. CEJ: Series 3, Vol. 7, No. 2. ATLA Religion Database with ATLASerials. Hunter Resource Library), p. 370, Accessed 11/5/2014.

[196] Ibid., p. 371.

[197] Dietrich Bonhoeffer, *The Cost of Discipleship* (SCM Classics, Hymns Ancient and Modern Ltd. Kindle Edition, 2011-08-16), Kindle Locations 2163-2398.

more spiritual as a result. However, the problem is not that they are knowledgeable in Scripture, but that they have a desire to impress others with their knowledge.

It's the same with all God's commandments. If we do them to impress others, then we have completely missed the mark. This is why a focus on the inner life is so important. Without it, much of what we do can be vain and displease God.

Christ is certainly not telling us we shouldn't obey His commands, but stresses that if we obey them merely to impress others, then we have missed the point entirely. It all begins with pleasing God inwardly, and then we will live our external lives correctly.

The Inner Life and How We Live at Home

Interestingly, how a person lives in the privacy of their home, and how they treat others within it, is also viewed as an extension of the inner life by God. For this reason, God requires those aspiring to be elders or deacons to display their spirituality in their homes before being qualified to be leaders in the church: "He must manage his own household well, with all dignity keeping his children submissive, for if someone does not know how to manage his own household, how will he care for God's church?" (1 Tim. 3:4–5).

The Inner Life and the Lack of Spiritual Growth

God also indicates that if we neglect our inner life with Him, it will inhibit or block our ability to understand His Word and grow. This was a problem with the Israelites and applies to us today as well: "You hypocrites! Well did Isaiah prophesy of you, when he said: 'This people honors me with their lips, but their heart is far from me; in vain do they worship me, teaching as doctrines the commandments of men'" (Matt. 15:5–9).

Similarly, in the Book of Isaiah, God makes a connection

between the Israelite's inability to understand Scripture and their lack of attention to the inner life: "And the vision of all this has become to you like the words of a book that is sealed. When men give it to one who can read, saying, 'Read this,' he says, 'I cannot, for it is sealed.' And the Lord said: 'Because this people draw near with their mouth and honor me with their lips, while their hearts are far from me, and their fear of me is a commandment taught by men'" (Isa. 29:11, 13).

This same principle is confirmed again in Christ's ministry:

Then the disciples came and said to him, "Why do you speak to them in parables?" And he answered them, "To you it has been given to know the secrets of the kingdom of heaven, but to them it has not been given. For to the one who has, more will be given, and he will have an abundance, but from the one who has not, even what he has will be taken away. This is why I speak to them in parables, because seeing they do not see, and hearing they do not hear, nor do they understand. Indeed, in their case the prophecy of Isaiah is fulfilled that says: '**You will indeed hear but never understand, and you will indeed see but never perceive**.' For this people's heart has **grown dull**, and with their ears **they can barely hear**, and **their eyes they have closed**, lest they should see with their eyes and hear with their ears and understand with their heart and turn, and I would heal them.'" (Matt. 13:10–15).

Conclusion

If we honor God with our lips, but our hearts are far from Him, we too will struggle to understand Scripture and can even lose the knowledge and understanding of it we once had, thus, becoming spiritually blind. What a severe judgment from God! Moreover, we can displease God and worship Him in vain. This is why attention to our inner life is so important.

10. Spiritual Gifts and Discipleship

Understanding and practicing our spiritual gifts is another essential component of discipleship. Interestingly, they are not included as an essential component in other lists I researched. Why have I included them in this book? Because Scripture reveals their importance, not only in our own lives, but also in the life of others in the church.

What Are Spiritual Gifts?

Spiritual gifts are special abilities God gives to each believer for their own personal benefit and for the benefit of others. They are endowments that come in the form of grace and special help. They are supernatural enablements given by the Holy Spirit primarily for building up the body of Christ so that all may attain spiritual maturity.

Spiritual Gifts Have Been Given to All Believers

God has given every believer spiritual gifts. These gifts become part of who we are and how we serve God and others. Without understanding and practicing our spiritual gifts, we seriously hinder our own growth and the growth of others in the body of Christ. Ephesians 4:8–15 affirms this truth:

> When he [Christ] ascended on high, he led a host of captives, and he gave **gifts to men**. *These spiritual gifts have been given by God to* "Equip the saints for the work of ministry, for building up the body of Christ, until we all attain to the unity of the faith and of the knowledge of the Son of God, to **mature manhood**, to the measure of the stature of the **fullness of Christ**." *And* "Speaking the truth in love, we are to grow up in every way into him who is the head, into Christ, from

whom the whole body, joined and held together by every joint with which it is equipped, **when each part is working properly, makes the body grow** so that it **builds itself** up in love" (Eph. 4:8, 12–13, 15).

God has given each person spiritual gifts for attaining the measure of the fullness of Christ, which is synonymous with spiritual maturity.

A spiritually mature person is one who knows their spiritual gifts, and has honed and sharpened them for maximum usage in God's Kingdom. They use their gifts not only for their own personal discipleship development, but in making disciples as well. Spiritual gifts are God's special abilities for these purposes.

No spiritually mature person, therefore, would reject God's supernatural enablement for becoming and making disciples. After all, if the Great Commission Mandate to make disciples is taken seriously, then by default, we must take seriously God's gifts that help us fulfill His mandate. It is, therefore, impossible to be spiritually mature without understanding and practicing our spiritual gifts. For this reason, they are included as one of the essential components of the discipleship-making process.

What Are the Spiritual Gifts?

There are four main passages in Scripture that speak of the spiritual gifts: Romans 12:6–8, 1 Corinthians 12:7–10 and 12:28, and Ephesians 4:11–12. The following gifts are mentioned in these passages:

- **Romans 12:6–8:** "Having gifts that differ according to the grace given to us, let us use them: if **prophecy**, in proportion to our faith; if **service**, in our serving; the one who **teaches**, in his teaching; the one who **exhorts**, in his exhortation; the one who **contributes**, in generosity; the one who **leads**, with zeal; the one who does **acts of mercy**, with cheerfulness." Seven gifts are mentioned here.

- **1 Corinthians 12:7–10:** "To each is given the manifestation of the Spirit for the common good. For to one is given through the Spirit the utterance of **wisdom**, and to another the utterance of **knowledge** according to the same Spirit, to another **faith** by the same Spirit, to another gifts of **healing** by the one Spirit, to another the working of **miracles**, to another **prophecy**, to another the ability to **distinguish between spirits**, to another **various kinds of tongues**, to another the **interpretation of tongues**. All these are empowered by one and the same Spirit, who apportions to each one individually as he wills." Nine gifts are mentioned here.

- **1 Corinthians 12:28:** "And God has appointed in the church first **apostles**, second **prophets**, third **teachers**, then **miracles**, then gifts of **healing, helping, administrating**, and various kinds of **tongues**." Eight gifts are mentioned here.

- **Ephesians 4:11–12:** "And he gave the **apostles**, the **prophets**, the **evangelists**, the **shepherds** and **teachers**, to equip the saints for the work of ministry, for building up the body of Christ." Five gifts are mentioned here.

In total, there are 29 gifts mentioned. However, some are mentioned more than once. Considering this, there are 21 different spiritual gifts mentioned in these four passages.

- **Five Gifts Are Mentioned Indirectly in Scripture:** (1) celibacy (1 Cor. 7), (2) hospitality (Heb. 13:2), (3) missions (Paul's journeys), (4) intercession (Luke 18:1; James 5:17–18; 1 Thess. 5:17), and (5) casting out demons (Matt. 17:18; Mark 16:17; Acts 16:16–18, 19:11–16).

Adding the 21 gifts from the verses mentioned directly in Scripture to those mentioned indirectly, we arrive at 26 spiritual gifts mentioned in these passages.

Are All the Spiritual Gifts for Today?

My intention is not to deal with this question in this book, as time and space don't permit. Instead, my purpose is to simply mention the gifts found in Scripture in order to provide the most comprehensive, extensive information as possible. However, I will provide some clarification that might be helpful.

Those who believe all the gifts are for the whole period of the church are called "Continuationists" (from the word "continue"). Those who believe many of the gifts, but not all, are for today are called, "Cessationists" (from the word "cease").

What Are the Purposes of the Spiritual Gifts?

- **To bring us to spiritual maturity:** Ephesians 4:8–15 states that as each member of Christ ministers to one another using their spiritual gifts, believers are built up and move toward spiritual maturity.

- **To manifest God's presence:** Wayne Grudem articulates, "One of his [Holy Spirit's] primary purposes in the new covenant age is to manifest the presence of God — to give indications that make the presence of God known. And when the Holy Spirit works in various ways that can be perceived by believers and unbelievers, this encourages people's faith that God is near and that He is working to fulfill His purposes in the church and to bring blessing to His people."[198]

- **To build unity within the church:** In his letter to the Ephesians, the Apostle Paul encourages believers to be "Eager to maintain the unity of the Spirit in the bond of peace

---

[198] Wayne Grudem, *Systematic Theology: An Introduction to Biblical Doctrine* (Zondervan Publishing House, Grand Rapids, Michigan, 1994), p. 641.

until we all attain to the unity of the faith and of the knowledge of the Son of God, to mature manhood" (Eph. 4:12–13).

- **To reveal our interdependence upon one another:** The gifts are for the building up of the Body of Christ as each member understands and exercises their gifts. We are intertwined and dependent on one another. If one member suffers, we all suffer. If one member is weak, we all are affected (1 Cor. 12:21–26). This can also mean that if one member does not understand and practice their spiritual gifts, then the rest of the body suffers and can be hindered from attaining spiritual maturity.

- **To bring glory to God:** As each member understands and practices their spiritual gifts, the Body of Christ grows, and God is glorified. However, when believers are ignorant of their gifts or do not practice them, then God's glory is diminished in the church, and the Body of Christ suffers.

For these reasons, understanding and practicing our spiritual gifts is one of the essential components of the discipleship-making process.

The Need to Develop and Sharpen Our Spiritual Gifts

Not only should we know what our spiritual gifts are, but we should also develop and sharpen them so that we become masters at using them. The Apostle Paul said he was a master builder: "According to the grace of God given to me, like a **skilled master builder** I laid a foundation, and someone else is building upon it. Let each one take care how he builds upon it. For no one can lay a foundation other than that which is laid, which is Jesus Christ" (1 Cor. 3:10–11).

Paul was a skilled master builder. He had honed and sharpened his gifts and abilities in order to be the most effective tool as possible in the hands of God. He was extremely knowledgeable in God's Word, had impeccable character, was self-disciplined, hardworking, willing to suffer, persevered, and was completely devoted to the Kingdom of God and its advancement. We too should strive to be like Paul and become skilled master builders who know our gifts and use them with precision and excellence.

Conclusion

God has given each person spiritual gifts for attaining the measure of the fullness of Christ, which is synonymous with spiritual maturity.

A spiritually mature person is one who knows their spiritual gifts, and has honed and sharpened them for maximum usage in God's Kingdom. They use their gifts not only for their own personal discipleship development, but in making disciples as well. Spiritual gifts are God's special abilities for these purposes.

No spiritually mature person, therefore, would reject God's supernatural enablement for becoming and making disciples. After all, if the Great Commission Mandate to make disciples is taken seriously, then by default, we must take seriously God's gifts that help us fulfill His mandate. It is, therefore, impossible to be spiritually mature without understanding and practicing our spiritual gifts.

11. Serving and Discipleship

Why is serving one of the essential components of the discipleship-making process, and how does it help us attain spiritual maturity? Serving is essential as it fulfills several key purposes for our lives and existence.

God Created Us to Serve

"For we are his workmanship, created in Christ Jesus for **good works**, which God prepared beforehand, that we should walk in them" (Eph. 2:10). The very purpose for which God created us is to serve Him and others. For this reason, serving is one of the essential components of discipleship.

1 Peter 4:10–11 adds, "As each has received a gift, use it to **serve** one another, as good stewards of God's varied grace: whoever speaks, as one who speaks oracles of God; whoever **serves**, as one who **serves** by the strength that God supplies—in order that in everything God may be glorified through Jesus Christ. To him belong glory and dominion forever and ever. Amen."

When we fulfill the reason for which we were created, we find the greatest joy, meaning, and purpose in life. We also bring glory to God, bless others, and bless ourselves.

Christ Came to Serve

After a dispute among the disciples about who would be the greatest among them, Christ taught them a significant purpose for His earthly life and ours as well:

But Jesus called them to him and said, "You know that the rulers of the Gentiles lord it over them, and their great ones exercise authority over them. It shall not be so among you.

But whoever would be great among you must be your **servant**, and whoever would be first among you must be your **slave**, even as the Son of Man came not to be served but to **serve**, and to give his life as a ransom for many'" (Matt. 20:25–28).

Christ came to serve … and did so to such a degree that He died on a cross in His service to us.

Christ also illustrated the example of serving when He, being the Creator of the universe, humbled Himself and washed the feet of the disciples:

> When he had washed their feet and put on his outer garments and resumed his place, he said to them, "Do you understand what I have done to you? You call me Teacher and Lord, and you are right, for so I am. If I then, your Lord and Teacher, have washed your feet, you also ought to wash one another's feet. For I have given you an example, that you also should do just as I have done to you. Truly, truly, I say to you, a servant is not greater than his master, nor is a messenger greater than the one who sent him. If you know these things, blessed are you if you do them" (John 13:12–17).

If the purpose of God is that we would be transformed to become like Christ, then serving would rank as essential as it's who Christ is in His nature. If we want to be like Christ, then we must learn to serve as He does.

Laziness and Pride: the Enemies of Serving

God has nothing positive to say about laziness and pride as they kill a serving spirit. Key themes in the Book of Proverbs are warnings about the negative effects of laziness and pride. Both attitudes are self-seeking and end in ruin. Instead, God commands that we develop a servant's heart like Christ: "Do nothing from selfish ambition or conceit, but in humility count others more significant than yourselves. Let each of you look not only to his own interests, but also to the interests of others" (Phil. 2:3–4). He then gives us an example in Christ:

> Have this mind among yourselves, which is yours in Christ Jesus, who, though he was in the form of God, did not count equality with God a thing to be grasped, but emptied himself, by taking the form of a servant, being born in the likeness of men. And being found in human form, he humbled himself by becoming obedient to the point of death, even death on a cross (Phil. 2:5–8).

Christ was a servant, and He calls us to be one too. Laziness and pride must be resisted, and in their place, a servant's spirit developed.

Those who serve God and others will be honored: "If anyone **serves** me, he must follow me; and where I am, there will my servant be also. If anyone **serves** me, the Father will honor him" (John 12:26). What greater honor could one attain than that of the Father?

Conclusion

In the same way Christ is a servant, God created us to serve as well. When we fulfill the purpose for which we were created, we find the greatest joy, meaning, and purpose in life. We bring glory to God, bless others, and bless ourselves. However, the world says just the opposite. It says fulfillment is found in being served. It says power, prestige, and pride define greatness, not humility and servanthood.

Instead of following the world's self-serving attitude, we need to follow Christ's other-serving attitude. Spiritual maturity is other-serving; spiritual immaturity is self-serving.

We must take to heart God's will for us: "Do not be **slothful in zeal**, be **fervent** in spirit, **serve** the Lord" (Rom. 12:11).

12. Spiritual Attitudes and Discipleship

Spiritual attitudes have largely been overlooked in discipleship today. Why are they so important that they would be included as an essential component of discipleship?

Many years ago, I was involved in a children's ministry program in the church I attended and was continually puzzled by the leader's poor attitudes. She had been a believer for many years, was knowledgeable in Scripture, and appeared to be spiritually mature. Yet, she was grumpy, rude, harsh, and unpleasant. I wrestled with how this could be. As a young believer, it was all so conflictive to me. How could she overlook a major theme of Scripture, and why would her church put her in a leadership position having such great deficiencies in her attitudes?

Defining Attitudes

Attitudes can be defined as a mental state of mind, a way of thinking, a feeling, a way of behaving, a disposition, a demeanor, or an emotional state of being. Attitudes can be both positive and negative. They are the expression of our inner thoughts, feelings, emotions, beliefs, and values. Without exception, we always have some kind of an attitude.

Attitudes are the living outflow of our lives and always manifest themselves in a certain action or behavior. We will act a certain way depending on what kind of attitude we have at that time. Our attitudes are the reason we do what we do, obey or disobey, or feel what we feel. They are the servants of our will and affect how we interact and treat others.

Biblical Attitudes in Scripture

We see both positive and negative attitudes all throughout

Scripture. Galatians 5:22–23 lists several positive attitudes: "But the fruit of the Spirit is love, joy, peace, patience, kindness, goodness, faithfulness, gentleness, self-control."

Despite the likelihood of being in a cold prison cell in Rome, the Apostle Paul's main theme of the Book of Philippians is joy. Not only was Paul joyful, but he saw it as an essential part of our Christian life: "Convinced of this, I know that I will remain and continue with you all, for your progress and **joy** in the faith" (Phil. 1:25).

Philippians 2:5–8 (NASB) tells us to have the same attitude of humility as Christ: "Have this **attitude** in yourselves which was also in Christ Jesus, who, although He existed in the form of God, did not regard equality with God a thing to be grasped, but emptied Himself, taking the form of a bond-servant, and being made in the likeness of men. Being found in appearance as a man, He humbled Himself by becoming obedient to the point of death, even death on a cross."

Jesus also demonstrated the role of spiritual attitudes in His life. One author has noted, "He maintained a perfect attitude in every situation because He prayed about everything and worried about nothing. Jesus' attitude was never to become defensive, discouraged, or depressed, because His goal was to please the Father rather than to achieve His own agenda. In the midst of trials, Jesus was patient. In the midst of suffering, He was hopeful. In the midst of blessing, He was humble. Even in the midst of ridicule, abuse, and hostility, He 'made no threats ... and did not retaliate. Instead, He entrusted Himself to Him who judges justly.'"[199]

In the Sermon on the Mount, Christ speaks of key attitudes He wants us to possess such as being poor in spirit, mournful, meek, righteous, merciful, pure, peacemakers, and having a

---

[199] Gotquestions.org, *What Does the Bible Say About Attitude?* www.gotquestions.org/Bible-attitude.html, Accessed 10/23/2015.

willing attitude towards persecution.

Negative Attitudes

There are also many negative attitudes mentioned in Scripture that God commands us to avoid. 2 Timothy 2:3 states, "But understand this, that in the last days there will come times of difficulty. For people will be lovers of self, lovers of money, proud, arrogant, abusive, disobedient to their parents, ungrateful, unholy, heartless, unappeasable, slanderous, without self-control, brutal, not loving good."

Galatians 5:19–21 also mention several negative attitudes: "Now the works of the flesh are evident: sexual immorality, impurity, sensuality, idolatry, sorcery, enmity, strife, jealousy, fits of anger, rivalries, dissensions, divisions, envy, drunkenness, orgies, and things like these."

Attitudes Are a Choice

We have a choice in what kind of attitude we have at any given point in time, and the attitude we choose affects all factors of life.

Chuck Swindoll highlights the value of choosing the right attitudes: "This may shock you, but I believe the single most significant decision I can make on a day-to-day basis is my choice of attitude. It is more important than my past, my education, my bankroll, my successes or failures, fame or pain, what other people think of me or say about me, my circumstances, or my position. Attitude is that 'single string' that keeps me going or cripples my progress. It alone fuels my fire or assaults my hope. When my attitudes are right, there's no barrier too high, no valley too deep, no dream too extreme, no challenge too great for me."[200]

---

[200] Chuck Swindoll, *Strengthening Your Grip* (Word Books, Waco, TX, 1982), pp. 205-206.

Conclusion

Spiritual attitudes have largely been overlooked in discipleship today. Our attitudes are the visible expression of our inner thoughts, feelings, emotions, beliefs, and values. They directly affect how we interact and treat both God and others, either positively or negatively.

All the essential components of the discipleship-making process are linked to our attitudes. We can reach the highest level possible in each essential component of discipleship, but if we lack the right attitudes in each category, we will still be spiritually immature. This truth is strongly emphasized in 1 Corinthians 13:1-3: "If I speak in the tongues of men and of angels, but have not love, I am a noisy gong or a clanging cymbal. And if I have prophetic powers, and understand all mysteries and all knowledge, and if I have all faith, so as to remove mountains, but have not love, **I am nothing**. If I give away all I have, and if I deliver up my body to be burned, but have not love, **I gain nothing**."

All the essential components of discipleship must be carried along and bathed in godly attitudes, or they mean little, or nothing.

13. Character and Discipleship

Character is another essential component in the discipleship-making process that has been largely overlooked today, but is foundational to discipleship and extremely important.

Character Is Foundational

In biblical times, knowledge was built upon the foundation of Scripture and godly character. Critical character traits like honesty, respect, self-discipline, diligence, hard work, loyalty, responsibility, etc., formed the foundation upon which knowledge rested.

One of the ways character was taught was by using the Book of Proverbs. It was employed in Israel's educational system, and the study of it was a required subject.

The overall theme of Proverbs deals with character development. Its opening introduction states its purpose: "To know wisdom and instruction, to discern the sayings of understanding, to receive instruction in **wise behavior, righteousness, justice** and **equity**; to give **prudence** to the naive, to the youth knowledge and discretion" (Prov. 1:2–4, NASB). In these verses, wise behavior, righteousness, justice, equity, and prudence are foundational character traits.

I have come to the firm conclusion that character is more important than skills, giftedness, knowledge, social skills, and other important traits. Character is what determines how all our abilities are used, for either good or bad, and is the structure upon which abilities hang.

For example, a person could be extremely gifted musically, but if they don't have the character of self-discipline to practice, the conviction to produce wholesome music, integrity in their financial dealings, and a commitment to humility amidst success, they will be a total failure, causing severe damage to themself and others. With good character, abilities and knowledge can be acquired, but without it, all of life comes crumbling down.

The Importance of Character in Discipleship

Dallas Willard, in his book *The Great Omission,* speaks of the importance of character in discipleship when he claims, "God is greatly concerned with the quality of character we are building. The future He has planned for us will be built on the strength of character we forge by His grace."[201]

Beverly Vos, in her article "The Spiritual Disciplines and Christian Ministry," refers to the role of character in discipleship: "Through spiritual disciplines one builds great character, and therefore, the disciplines go hand in hand with the power of God demonstrated in one's life."[202]

What Is Character?

Character can be defined as inner traits we possess, aspects of our nature, our moral fiber, and our foundational makeup and essence. It's who we are and what we do in secret when no one is watching. Furthermore, our convictions and decisions are controlled by it.

In Scripture, several Greek words are used interchangeably in reference to character. The following are their usages:

1. *Dokimēn*: meaning approved, tried character.
2. *Ethē*: referring to morals.
3. *Aretēn*: meaning a virtuous course of thought, feeling and action, virtue, and moral goodness.[203]

---

[201] Dallas Willard, *The Great Omission* (2009-02-06, HarperCollins, Kindle Edition), p. 124.
[202] Beverly Vos, "The Spiritual Disciplines and Christian Ministry" (Source: Evangelical Review of Theology, 36 no 2 Ap 2012, pp. 100-114, Publication Type: Article ATLA Religion Database with ATLASerials. Hunter Resource Library), p. 113, Accessed 11/5/2014.
[203] Bible Hub, *703. Arête,* http://biblehub.com/greek/703.htm, Accessed 10/23/2015.

Interestingly, the word "virtue" is commonly used in the Bible when referring to character. It's an old English word translated by some newer Bible versions as "excellence." In Scripture, the word "godliness" is also used when referring to character.

Abraham Lincoln said, "Reputation is the shadow. Character is the tree."[204] Another author has stated, "Our character is much more than what we try to display for others to see; it is who we are even when no one is watching. Good character is doing the right thing because it is right to do what is right."[205] And Thomas Babington Macauley claims, "The measure of a man's character is what he would do if he knew he would never be found out."[206]

Character Is Part of God's Essence

God uses the essence of His character as a foundational reason for trusting Him when making covenants and promises with mankind: "The sovereign Lord confirms this oath by his own holy **character**: 'Certainly the time is approaching when you will be carried away in baskets, every last one of you in fishermen's pots'" (Amos 4:2, NET).

The Apostles Spread the Gospel Utilizing Godly Character

When the gospel was spread to the nations, the Apostle Paul said they brought it with deep conviction and character: "We know, brothers and sisters loved by God, that he has chosen you, in that our gospel did not come to you merely in words, but in power and in the Holy Spirit and with **deep conviction** (surely you recall the **character** we displayed when we came among you to help you)" (1 Thess. 1:4–5, NET).

---

[204] Character-training.com/blog, *What is Character?* http://www.character-training.com/blog, Accessed 10/23/2015.
[205] Ibid., Accessed 10/23/2015.
[206] Ibid., Accessed 10/23/2015.

Why Is Character Important in Discipleship?

God elevates character as an essential component of spiritual maturity. Notice that virtually every characteristic listed in 2 Peter 2 is a character trait or an attitude:

> But also for this very reason, giving all diligence, add to your faith virtue [character], to virtue knowledge, to knowledge self-control, to self-control perseverance, to perseverance godliness, to godliness brotherly kindness, and to brotherly kindness love. For if these things are yours and abound, you will be neither barren nor unfruitful in the knowledge of our Lord Jesus Christ (2 Pet. 1:5–8, NKJV).

This is a key passage we must take seriously for discipleship. It outlines a process that leads to spiritual maturity and fruitfulness. It mentions three essential components: (1) virtue (character), (2) knowledge, and (3) attitudes.

Developing Character Takes Time

Character is built over the long haul and is not an overnight process. God uses trials, suffering, persecution, and testing to develop His bedrock character within us. He wants us to be like Him, and He is a God of impeccable character.

Romans 5:3–4 says, "Not only that, but we rejoice in our sufferings, knowing that suffering produces endurance, and endurance produces **character**, and **character** produces hope."

James also speaks of its importance when he says, "Count it all joy, my brothers, when you meet trials of various kinds, for you know that the testing of your faith produces **steadfastness** [character]. And let steadfastness have its full effect, that you may be perfect and complete, lacking in nothing" (James 1:2–4).

Peter echoes the same theme as well: "Such trials show the proven **character** of your faith, which is much more valuable than gold — gold that is tested by fire, even though it is passing away —

and will bring praise and glory and honor when Jesus Christ is revealed" (1 Pet. 1:7, NET).

Character Is the Main Quality Required in Leaders

Character is so important that it's the primary quality required in elders and deacons: "Therefore, an overseer must be above reproach, the husband of one wife, sober-minded, self-controlled, respectable, hospitable, able to teach, not a drunkard, not violent but gentle, not quarrelsome, not a lover of money . . . He must not be a recent convert, or he may become puffed up with conceit and fall into the condemnation of the devil" (1 Tim. 3:2–3, 6).

How to Develop Character

Greg S. Baker claims, "Building good character is all about addition, not subtraction. What I mean is this: when it comes to change, our focus is usually on the aspects of our lives that are bad. We try to cut out or cut off these negative or bad qualities. We try to improve by subtraction. That is not how you build good character. It is the process of addition in your life that brings the character. In so doing, you automatically take care of the other negative aspects."[207] Baker adds, "The Bible teaches us this concept in 2 Peter 1:5–9. We are to add things like virtue, patience, love, kindness, faith, and so on. It is the process of adding these things to our lives that we gain the character to be fruitful in life."[208] Baker concludes, "So how do we develop godly character in our lives? You practice it until it becomes part and parcel with you. You diligently focus on what you want to add and then practice it until it becomes a habit."[209]

---

[207] Greg S. Baker, "How to Build Good Character," SelfGrowth.com, www.selfgrowth.com/articles/how_to_build_good_character, Accessed 12/14/2015.
[208] Ibid., Accessed 12/14/2015.
[209] Ibid., Accessed 12/14/2015.

On occasion, however, building character might include ceasing wrong activities in conjunction with building good character. Scripture says that we are to put off our old self and put on the nature of Christ:

> Put off your old self, which belongs to your former manner of life and is corrupt through deceitful desires, and to be renewed in the spirit of your minds, and to put on the new self, created after the likeness of God in true righteousness and holiness (Eph. 4:22–24).

In this passage, we see both putting off and putting on. Therefore, in some situations, we might need to cease certain negative activities in conjunction with building godly character.

Conclusion

Character is a foundational cornerstone upon which discipleship is built. It's part of God's essence and should be part of ours as well. Therefore, we should give utmost importance to developing character, as it's one of the principle components of discipleship. With good character, abilities and knowledge can be acquired, but without it, all of life comes crumbling down.

14. Stewardship and Discipleship

Stewardship is another essential component in the discipleship-making process. There exist three main areas in life in which we are given the responsibility to be stewards, and for which God will hold us accountable: (1) how we use our time, (2) how we use our money and possessions, and (3) how we care for and use our bodies.

What Is Stewardship?

Stewardship is the recognition that "The earth is the Lord's and the fullness thereof, the world and those who dwell therein" (Ps. 24:1). Everything that exists (time, material things, the spiritual world, principalities, and our own souls) are the Lord's. They all belong to Him and are given to us to manage and use for His glory and purposes. A steward is someone who manages what belongs to another. They are not the owners; they are managers who are responsible to the owner.

1. Stewardship of Our Time

Our time on earth is far shorter than most people think. Our lives are like a vapor that appear in the morning and evaporate by midday: "What is your life? For you are a mist that appears for a little time and then vanishes" (James 4:14).

King David aptly pointed out: "O Lord, make me know my end and what is the measure of my days; let me know how fleeting I am! Behold, you have made my days a few handbreadths, and my lifetime is as nothing before you. Surely all mankind stands as a mere breath! Surely a man goes about as a shadow!" (Ps. 39:4–6).

Our lives barely register on the timeline of eternity and how we use our time will determine our eternal state. Moses understood this reality and prayed, "So teach us to number our days that we may get a heart of wisdom" (Ps. 90:12). In addition, Moses, "When he was grown up, refused to be called the son of Pharaoh's daughter, choosing rather to be mistreated with the people of God than to enjoy the fleeting pleasures of sin" (Heb. 11:24–25).

A wise person will realize their days are numbered and will invest them in God's Kingdom rather than in the fleeting pleasures this life has to offer. God warned the Ephesian believers, "Look carefully then how you walk, not as unwise but as wise, **making the best use of the time**, because the days are evil" (Eph. 5:15–16).

Christians and Time Management

We live in unprecedented days where voices are screaming at us at every turn, vying for our attention and time. People's lives are extremely busy with countless activities and stimuli. One author has noted, "There's no doubt that the responsibilities and pressures of this world scream for our attention. The myriad of things pulling us in every direction makes it all too easy for our time to be swallowed up in mundane matters. Those endeavors that have eternal value, then, often are relegated to the back burner."[210] The busyness of our day affects how we spend our time and how much we invest in eternity.

To avoid getting lost in the distractions of life, we need to establish goals and make godly priorities. We must make biblical choices and establish firm convictions that become bedrock, non-negotiable commitments, and then do them regardless of the cost. We must make the essential components of the discipleship-making process priorities in our lives that we cling to daily.

In chapter 2, we talked about heavenly rewards and how the

---

[210] Gotquestions.org, *What Does the Bible Say About Time Management?* www.gotquestions.org/Bible-time-management.html, Accessed 10/24/2015.

use of our time in this life will affect the amount of rewards we will have in the next. If we are wise, we will carefully look at how we spend our time. By the statistics we have researched, the average Christian today needs to do some sober soul-searching and reassess how they are using their time.

2. Stewardship of Our Material Possessions

We will also be held accountable for how we spend our money and use our possessions. Stewardship reflects our commitment to God and our spiritual condition. We should never separate money and possessions from our spiritual life, for they are directly linked. How we manage what God has given us is one way of measuring our level of spiritual maturity.

If we use our money and possessions primarily for our own purposes, then that indicates we are still spiritually immature. It matters little how much Scripture we know or how faithful we are in attending church, if we disobey God in stewarding the resources He has given us, then we are still infants spiritually in this area. We see this affirmed in the Parable of the Talents (Matt. 25:14) and the Parable of the Rich Man (Luke 12:16).

Giving to the Lord Financially

A spiritually mature believer should be faithful in stewarding what God has entrusted to them. In the Old Testament, God required a minimum of 10% to be given to Him in tithes (tithe means 10%). In addition to the tithe, the Israelites gave free will offerings, temple offerings, and offerings for the poor. Some have estimated that the Israelites gave around 25% of their income to the Lord in some way or another. In addition to their giving to God, they also had taxes to pay, just like us today.

In the New Testament, we don't see a required amount of money that should be given to the Lord, but rather a principle encouraging generosity:

The point is this: whoever sows sparingly will also reap sparingly, and whoever sows bountifully will also reap bountifully. Each one must give as he has decided in his heart, not reluctantly or under compulsion, for **God loves a cheerful giver**. And God is able to make all grace abound to you, so that having all sufficiency in all things at all times, you may abound in every good work (2 Cor. 9:6–8).

A spiritually mature believer will be generous toward God, realizing they are His stewards and everything belongs to Him.

If in the Old Testament 10% was the minimum required to be given to God, then certainly in the New Testament He wouldn't expect less. I believe the principle of generosity encouraged in the New Testament would suggest we give beyond 10%.

For the person who fails to tithe and spends what they are stewarding primarily on themselves, God likens this to robbery. This was God's accusation to the Israelites in the Prophet Malachi's day. God said they were robbing Him, which is a serious crime. It's one thing to rob a person, but to rob God is entirely different! That's a crime of drastic proportions. God says:

Will man rob God? Yet you are robbing me. But you say, "How have we robbed you?" In your tithes and contributions. You are cursed with a curse, for you are robbing me, the whole nation of you (Mal. 3:8–9).

We are not the owners of what we possess, but God is. If we are not faithful in stewarding what belongs to Him, then we can actually be robbing God. If we are faithful in stewarding God's resources, then He will bless us beyond measure.

After accusing the Israelites of robbing Him, God gave them this promise if they would obey:

Bring the full tithe into the storehouse, that there may be food in my house. And thereby put me to the test, says the Lord of hosts, if I will not open the windows of heaven for you and pour down for you a blessing until there is no more need. I will rebuke the devourer for you, so that it will not destroy the fruits of your soil, and your vine in the field shall not fail to bear, says the Lord of hosts. Then all nations will call you blessed, for you will be a land of delight, says the Lord of hosts (Mal. 3:10–12).

3. Stewardship of Our Bodies

A topic neglected in stewardship, but spoken of repeatedly in Scripture, involves how we use and take care of our bodies. God takes this matter seriously: "Do you not know that you are God's temple and that God's Spirit dwells in you? If anyone **destroys** God's temple, God will **destroy him**. For God's temple is holy, and you are that temple" (1 Cor. 3:16–17). These are strong and sobering words—words to be taken thoughtfully! We can debate what "destroy" means in this context, but one thing is certain, it's not positive or something to be taken lightly.

Our Bodies Belong to God

God reiterates the importance of being good stewards of our bodies in 1 Corinthians 6:19–20: "Or do you not know that your body is a temple of the Holy Spirit within you, whom you have from God? You are **not your own**, for you were bought with a price. So glorify God in your body."

Our Bodies Are to Be Used for Good, Not Evil

One way we can be good stewards of our bodies is by using them for good and not evil: "Let not sin therefore reign in your mortal body, to make you obey its passions. Do not present your members to sin as instruments for unrighteousness, but present yourselves to God as those who have been brought from death to life, and your members to God as instruments for righteousness"

(Rom. 6:12–13).

Our bodies are to be used for God, not for sin or our own purposes: "I appeal to you therefore, brothers, by the mercies of God, to present your **bodies** as a living sacrifice, holy and acceptable to God, which is your spiritual worship" (Rom. 12:1).

Sexuality and Stewardship

A common way we can misuse our bodies is sexually: "The body is not meant for sexual immorality, but for the Lord, and the Lord for the body" (1 Cor. 6:13). Misusing our bodies sexually is a serious sin that is rampant in our day. Even many Christians are guilty of sex outside of marriage, adultery, and homosexuality.

Sexual sin is unlike other sins. When we sin sexually, we actually sin against and damage our own body: "Flee from sexual immorality. Every other sin a person commits is outside the body, but the sexually immoral person sins **against his own body**" (1 Cor. 6:18).

Dressing Our Bodies and Stewardship

How we use our bodies can also apply to how we dress or mark them. This is important as it can affect our testimony for Christ. In fact, God warns us that doing things that cause others to stumble is unloving (1 Cor. 8). When we dress or do things to our bodies that are extreme or uncommon, then we can damage our testimony and lose influence before others. For example, if we dress in a strange and extreme fashion, then Christians (and non-Christians) may dismiss our attempts to influence them for Christ due to our manner of dress. God wants us to have the widest audience and the largest platform as possible to minister to others. By dressing in extreme ways or doing questionable behavior, we can lose much of our testimony and influence for Christ.

A trend that is growing widely today is that of tattooing our bodies. There's a verse in the Old Testament I think we should carefully wrestle with before we casually mark our bodies: "You shall not make any cuts on your body for the dead or **tattoo** yourselves: I am the Lord" (Lev. 19:28). While Christians today are not under the Law given to the Israelites in the Old Testament, this verse nonetheless conveys, in some sense, God's feelings about marking our bodies.

I think we should also consider how marking our bodies might affect our testimony as well.

Taking Care of Our Bodies and Stewardship

We also should be good stewards of our bodies by taking care of them. Today, obesity is at an all-time high, over-the-counter drug consumption is unparalleled, junk food consumption is off the charts, and exercise is at an all-time low.

According to recent studies by the U.S. Department of Health and Human Services, many Americans are abusing their bodies. Consider the following statistics:

- More than 2 in 3 adults are considered to be overweight or obese.
- More than 1 in 3 adults are considered to be obese.
- More than 1 in 20 adults are considered to have extreme obesity.
- About one-third of children and adolescents ages 6 to 19 are considered to be overweight or obese.
- More than 1 in 6 children and adolescents ages 6 to 19 are considered to be obese.[211]

Today, we are abusing our bodies (God's temple) and little thought is given to how God feels about it. We look around, see the majority of people overweight, and think it's the new norm.

---

[211] U.S. Department of Health and Human Services, *Overweight and Obesity Statistics*, www.niddk.nih.gov/health-information/health-statistics/Pages/overweight-obesity-statistics.aspx, 2009, 2010, Accessed 10/24/1015.

Eating and Stewardship of Our Bodies

According to the previous stats, the majority of Americans are not good stewards of their bodies. What does God say about eating and stewardship of our bodies?

God is not silent on the issue and mentions it quite a bit in Scripture. The biblical term for overeating is "gluttony." Interestingly, God frequently uses gluttony and drunkenness together as sinful activities. Consider the following verses:

- **Proverbs 23:20–21:** "Be not among drunkards or among gluttonous eaters of meat. For the drunkard and the glutton will come to poverty, and slumber will clothe them with rags."

- **Proverbs 28:27:** "The one who keeps the law is a son with understanding, but a companion of gluttons shames his father."

- **Proverbs 23:2:** "Put a knife to your throat if you are given to gluttony."

- **Deuteronomy 21:20:** "And they shall say to the elders of his city, 'This our son is stubborn and rebellious; he will not obey our voice; he is a glutton and a drunkard.'"

- **Philippians 3:19:** "Their end is destruction, their god is their belly, and they glory in their shame, with minds set on earthly things." God says a gluttonous person makes food their god and has an earthly focus on life.

- **Titus 1:12-13:** "One of themselves, a prophet of their own, said, 'Cretans are always liars, evil beasts, lazy gluttons.' This testimony is true. For this reason, reprove them severely so that they may be sound in the faith."

As these verses reveal, God considers overeating a sin and calls it gluttony.

What Is Gluttony?

One author has commented, "Gluttony is generally defined as 'excessive eating.' In the Bible, the word 'glutton' and its variants are often mentioned alongside drunkenness. Therefore, it's clear that a glutton is someone who eats more than is healthy or eats excessively, and that such behavior is considered sinful. Gluttony is presented as an ongoing practice, not typically as a one-time activity."[212] In other words, gluttony is not overeating on occasion, but overeating regularly, and it's overeating regularly that leads to being overweight.

Why Is Gluttony Ignored Today?

S. Michael Houdmann contends, "Gluttony seems to be a sin that Christians like to ignore. We are often quick to label smoking and drinking as sins, but for some reason, gluttony is accepted or at least tolerated. Many of the arguments used against smoking and drinking, such as health and addiction, apply equally to overeating. Many believers would not even consider having a glass of wine or smoking a cigarette, but have no qualms about gorging themselves at the dinner table. This should not be!"[213]

As mentioned, gluttony and drunkenness are mentioned together in Scripture as sinful activities. We are quick to condemn drunkenness but tend to overlook gluttony. No pastor or church leader would be accepted in any church if they were a drunkard, yet they can be a glutton, and no one thinks a thing about it. The straight truth is that we have a double standard. We are biblical in one area and unbiblical in another.

---

[212] Compelling Truth, *What Is the Sin of Gluttony?* Compellingtruth.org, www.compellingtruth.org/gluttony-sin.html, Accessed 10/24/2015.
[213] S. Michael Houdmann, *Is Gluttony a Sin? What Does the Bible Say About Overeating?* http://www.gotquestions.org/gluttony-sin.html, Accessed 02/27/2016.

Overeating and Self-Discipline

S. Michael Houdmann weighs in again and states, "Physical appetites are an analogy of our ability to control ourselves. If we are unable to control our eating habits, we are probably also unable to control other habits, such as those of the mind (lust, covetousness, anger) and unable to keep our mouths from gossip or strife. We are not to let our appetites control us, but we are to have control over our appetites."[214]

Consequences of Overeating

- When we are overweight and do not take care of our bodies, we have less energy, strength, stamina, and ability to serve God. Productivity is lowered and money spent on poor health will result in poor stewardship of both our time and money. We also run the risk of dying prematurely, which shortens our time for serving God.
- Failing to be good stewards of our bodies can also sideline us from ministry, causing unnecessary pain in our lives and those around us.
- Being overweight is a symptom of a lack of self-discipline. It communicates to others a message of an undisciplined life. This is especially important for pastors and church leaders to understand because self-discipline is a foundation of the Christian life. When a pastor or church leader is a glutton, they are preaching by their lifestyle an undisciplined and unbiblical way of living to their congregants.

Houdmann asserts, "God has blessed us by filling the earth with foods that are delicious, nutritious, and pleasurable. We should honor God's creation by enjoying these foods and by eating them in appropriate quantities. However, God calls us to

---

[214] Ibid., Accessed 02/27/2016.

control our appetites, rather than allowing them to control us."[215]

Drug Use and Stewardship of Our Bodies

Over the counter drug use is at an all-time high. Estimates suggest 60% of Americans take at least one medication.[216] While much of the medication used today is useful and needed, we can still damage and abuse our bodies by using medication that's not entirely important. Just because a medication might be helpful, doesn't mean it's needed.

Also, it seems many Christians today believe drugs are the answer for all ailments, both physical and spiritual. Anti-depressant drug use is at an all-time high, and the concern is that many Christians are trying to treat their spiritual problems with drugs. I believe we need to be very careful about taking medication for emotional problems.

Our bodies are the temple of God, and He expects us to care for them. His words are quite harsh for those who don't: "Do you not know that **you are God's temple** and that God's Spirit dwells in you? If anyone destroys God's temple, God will destroy him. For God's temple is holy, and you are that temple" (1 Cor. 3:16–17).

Conclusion to Chapter 4

In this chapter, we looked at 14 essential components that must be understood and practiced in order to attain spiritual maturity. In chapter 5, we're going to get real practical! We'll take self-assessment tests to measure our level of spiritual maturity in each category, and provide practical ideas for how to grow in Christ and attain spiritual maturity.

---

[215] Ibid., Accessed 02/27/2016.
[216] Jessica Firger, *Prescription Drugs on the Rise: Estimates Suggest 60 Percent of Americans Take at Least One Medication*, Newsweek, 2015, http://www.newsweek.com/prescription-drugs-rise-new-estimates-suggest-60-americans-take-least-one-390354, Accessed 11/17/2015.

Chapter 5

How to Grow in Christ: Self-Assessment Tests and Practical Help

In This Chapter

In chapter 1, we analyzed the state of discipleship and spiritual maturity today, concluding that they're in critical condition and being grossly neglected. In chapter 2, we investigated the key factors contributing to the neglect of discipleship and spiritual maturity. In chapter 3, we defined biblical discipleship by examining key phrases Christ used in calling people to follow Him. In chapter 4, we discovered 14 essential components for the discipleship-making process that must be understood and obeyed in order to fulfill the Great Commission Mandate and attain spiritual maturity.

In this chapter, we'll talk about how to apply the essential components of discipleship to our lives in order to grow in Christ and attain spiritual maturity. This chapter is a "how-to" chapter. It will be very practical and provide help in the following ways:

1. It will have a spiritual growth assessment test for each of the essential components of discipleship in order to help you discover your spiritual maturity level in each category.

2. It will contain charts and graphs for visualizing and measuring your spiritual maturity in each category.

3. It will provide practical ideas for moving toward spiritual maturity.

4. It will provide action steps that can be chosen for applying the ideas for growth in each category.

5. It will build on the premise that a comprehensive approach to discipleship is the only way to attain spiritual maturity. This means we must grow in all the categories of the essential components of discipleship in order to be spiritually mature.

Now, let me briefly explain how each of the above suggestions function so you can get the most out of this book and begin accelerating your growth to spiritual maturity.

1. Spiritual Growth Self-Assessment Tests

God says in 2 Corinthians 13:5 to "**Examine yourselves**, to see whether you are in the faith. **Test yourselves**. Or do you not realize this about yourselves, that Jesus Christ is in you? – unless indeed, you **fail to meet the test!**" God expects us to analyze and examine ourselves to ascertain our level of spiritual maturity. For this reason, self-assessment tests are provided for each category, and an overall spiritual maturity test is provided at the end of this chapter.

At the beginning of each section dealing with an essential component of discipleship, a short self-assessment questionnaire is provided to help you see your level of spiritual maturity in that category. Please answer the questions honestly and then ask a close loved-one to answer it for you as well. Between all responses, you should get a good idea of your level of spiritual maturity for that category.

Please do this for all categories. At the end of this chapter, there will be a chart for adding up all your scores to see your overall spiritual maturity level. It is recommended to focus your efforts first on strengthening your weakest areas.

2. Charts and Graphs for Visualizing and Measuring Your Spiritual Maturity

The following chart provides an example overview of all the essential components necessary for attaining spiritual maturity. At the end of this chapter, a blank one is provided for you to mark on in order to see your spiritual maturity in each area and keep track of your progress.

Essential Components for Attaining Spiritual Maturity

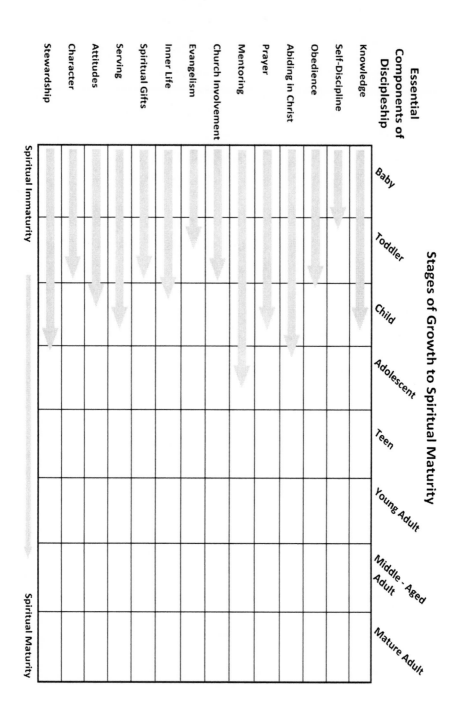

The next chart shows eight stages of spiritual growth: baby, toddler, child, adolescent, teen, young adult, middle-aged adult, and mature adult.

Please note that these labels have nothing to do with your own age. For example, you could be a "mature adult" in physical age, but a "baby" in your spiritual maturity. Similarly, you could be a "teen" physically, but be a "middle-aged adult" in your spiritual maturity. These labels are used solely for the purpose of identifying your spiritual maturity level, not your actual physical age.

Stages of Growth to Spiritual Maturity in (Example Chart)

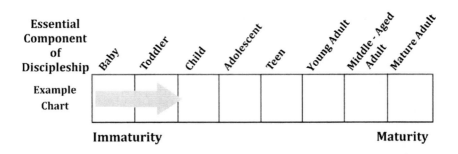

In addition, a similar chart (like the one above) is provided at the beginning of each essential component for discipleship to help you visualize your spiritual maturity in that category.

There will also be a blank chart provided after each self-assessment test for you to mark on so you can see your level of spiritual maturity for that category.

Nature of the Questions for the Self-Assessment Tests

In order to accurately discover your spiritual maturity level in each category, the self-assessment test questions must be asked from the highest level possible, or they won't provide accurate results. Therefore, the questions reflect what I believe should be the characteristics of a spiritually mature believer. There are only 10 questions per test, so there are many other great questions that could be asked but aren't.

3. Practical Ideas for Attaining Spiritual Maturity

After you've taken the self-assessment test for discovering your level of spiritual maturity in a particular category, then you'll find practical ideas for growth in that area.

4. Action Steps to Put into Practice

After taking the self-assessment test and looking at the practical ideas for growth in that category, then it's important to choose at least one of the ideas and begin doing it right away. Growth in Christ doesn't happen by merely knowing what to do, but by **doing** what we know we should do!

5. A Comprehensive Approach to Discipleship

The premise of this book is that in order to attain spiritual maturity we must approach discipleship from a comprehensive perspective. In other words, we need to grow in all the essential components of the discipleship-making process in order to become spiritually mature.

It was noted in chapter 1 that discipleship has been approached from a single-pronged or several-pronged perspective for much of modern day history, which has resulted in an unbalanced and weak outcome. Themes like knowledge, prayer, serving, and church attendance have been highlighted, while other themes like attitudes, character, spiritual gifts, and self-discipline have been overlooked.

A comprehensive approach to discipleship claims that we need to grow in all the essential areas in order to reach spiritual maturity. Spiritual maturity, therefore, is defined as being mature in all areas, not just a few.

For example, one can be strong in knowledge, but weak in their attitudes or character; this is not maturity. A comprehensive approach to discipleship advocates that we assess each category of discipleship to determine what level of spiritual maturity we have attained, and then give special attention to our weakest areas first. Then afterward, we can focus on all the other areas simultaneously.

God's Blessings Are Waiting!

What would change in the average Christian's life if they rightly understood the essential components of the discipleship-making process and practiced them? What if, instead of a single or a several-pronged approach to discipleship, we addressed it from a comprehensive angle? How might our lives be changed? How might our homes be transformed? How might the church be strengthened? How might the Kingdom of God be advanced? And moreover, how might God be honored and glorified?

Now, let's discover our spiritual level of maturity in each category of the essential components of discipleship and consider ideas we can begin to do in order to attain spiritual maturity.

It's time to grow! God's blessings are waiting! Are you ready to attain them and become spiritually mature?

1. How to Grow in the Knowledge of God

"For I desire steadfast love and not sacrifice, the **knowledge** of God rather than burnt offerings" (Hos. 6:6).

"But grow in the grace and **knowledge** of our Lord and Savior Jesus Christ" (2 Pet. 3:18).

Stages of Growth to Spiritual Maturity in Knowledge

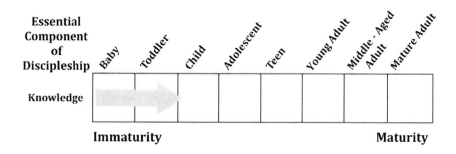

Self-Assessment Test for the Knowledge of God

Please take a moment to answer the following 10 questions to discover your spiritual maturity level regarding your knowledge of God. Answer each question using the following response options. Mark down your points earned for each question and then tally them up at the end to see your level of spiritual maturity in this category. As you take the test, avoid rushing. Answer the questions prayerfully and honestly. After you've taken the test, you might ask a loved one to take it for you as well. This will give you a broader perspective.

Points Possible per Answer

Never........................ 0 Points
Rarely .... 2 Points
Occasionally .... 4 Points
Frequently.............. 6 Points
Almost Always ...... 8 Points
Habitually .... 10 Points

1. I read the entire Bible at least once every year. _____

2. I memorize Scripture regularly. _____

3. I have a daily quiet time with God. _____

4. I study the Bible. _____

5. I read the Bible daily. _____

6. I can give a detailed overview of the Bible. _____

7. I know the overview of each book of the Bible. _____

8. I know and can defend the major doctrines of the Bible with clarity and precision. _____

9. I read Christian non-fiction books. _____

10. I read theological books. _____

Total Score _____

Now check your score against the following chart to determine your spiritual maturity level for the knowledge of God.

Spiritual Maturity Grade from the "Knowledge" Test

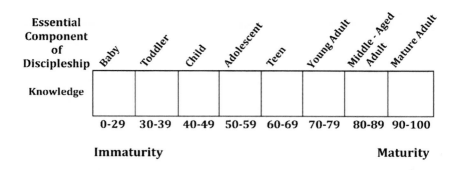

Essential Component of Discipleship	Baby	Toddler	Child	Adolescent	Teen	Young Adult	Middle - Aged Adult	Mature Adult
Knowledge								
	0-29	30-39	40-49	50-59	60-69	70-79	80-89	90-100

Immaturity   **Maturity**

My spiritual maturity grade for the knowledge of God:

I am a _____ spiritually.

Ideas for Growing in Your Knowledge of God

1. Establish a Bible reading plan for reading the entire Bible every year. You might consider the following options:

   - Reading the Bible chronologically.
   - Reading the Bible from beginning to end.
   - Dividing the Bible into three sections (Genesis–Psalms, Proverbs–Malachi, and Matthew–Revelation). Then read a chapter consecutively from each section daily.
   - Reading two chapters daily from the Old Testament and one chapter daily from the New Testament.
   - Reading the Old Testament once in a year and the New Testament twice in a year.

2. Start a Bible memorization plan. You can memorize selected verses, passages, chapters, and even entire books. It works great to get a 3x5 card, write your verse(s) down, and carry it with you. It's handy this way for memorization. You'll be surprised how much Scripture you can memorize in a year by

just memorizing a verse or two a week.

3. Read all the introductions to the books of the Bible in a Study Bible, on the Internet, or from other sources. This will rapidly give you an overview of the whole Bible.

4. Do a Bible study on the knowledge of God.

5. Read an Old Testament survey book. This will give you an overview of the entire Old Testament.

6. Read a New Testament survey book. This will give you an overview of the entire New Testament.

7. Read a solid, lengthy, systematic theology work. Systematic theology takes each major doctrine of the Bible and looks at all the verses that deal with that doctrine. It's indispensable for understanding the major doctrines of the faith. It's good to read several different systematic theology books to get a balanced view. Here are some suggestions:

   - Wayne Grudem's *Systematic Theology*
   - Charles Hodge's *Systematic Theology*
   - Louis Berkhof's *Systematic Theology*
   - Lewis Sperry Chafer's *Systematic Theology*
   - Gordon Lewis and Bruce Demarest's *Integrative Theology*
   - Millard Erickson's *Christian Theology*
   - Charles Ryrie's *Basic Theology*
   - Henry Thiessen's *Systematic Theology*

8. Read Old and New Testament theology works. These will aid you in understanding the big message and theme of both the Old and New Testaments (these are different from Old and New Testament survey books mentioned above).

9. Join an in-depth Bible study or start one of your own.

10. Read several books on how to correctly interpret the Bible (hermeneutics).

11. Take online Bible classes or even consider seeking an online Bible degree. There are many options available today, and

some are even free.

12. Purchase a good Study Bible, and read the introductions and commentaries it offers.

13. Listen to Bible college lectures. Many Bible colleges now have many of their Bible class lectures online and are free. Great options are Biola/Talbot Bible College and Seminary, and Dallas Theological Seminary. Their lectures can be accessed via YouTube or iTunes.

14. Read other theological books.

15. Read Christian, non-fiction books.

16. Look for someone in your church who is deeply knowledgeable in God's Word and theology and ask him or her to mentor you in this area.

Action Steps for Growing in Your Knowledge of God

Now prayerfully look back over this list, choose at least one idea, and make plans to begin doing it today. Then continually return in the future for implementing other ideas for your growth in the knowledge of God.

2. How to Grow in Self-Discipline

"Have nothing to do with irreverent, silly myths. Rather **train yourself for godliness**; for while bodily training is of some value, godliness is of value in every way, as it holds promise for the present life and also for the life to come" (1 Tim. 4:8).

"It is for **discipline** that you have to endure. God is treating you as sons. For what son is there whom his father does not discipline?" (Heb. 12:7).

Stages of Growth to Spiritual Maturity in Self-Discipline

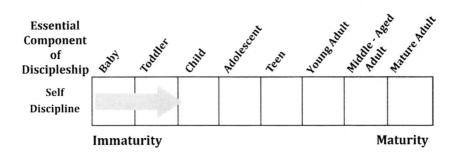

Self-Assessment Test for Self-Discipline

Please take a moment to answer the following 10 questions to discover your spiritual maturity level regarding self-discipline. Answer each question using the following response options. Mark down your points earned for each question and then tally them up at the end to see your level of spiritual maturity in this category. As you take the test, avoid rushing. Answer the questions prayerfully and honestly. After you've taken the test, you might ask a loved one to take it for you as well. This will give you a broader perspective.

Points Possible per Answer

Never .... 0 Points
Rarely .... 2 Points
Occasionally .... 4 Points
Frequently .... 6 Points
Almost Always ...... 8 Points
Habitually .... 10 Points

1. I am a highly disciplined person. _____

2. I manage my time effectively. _____

3. I finish tasks I've started. _____

4. I bring every thought into obedience to Christ and His Word. _____

5. I stick to commitments without giving up. _____

6. I make myself do what I know I should do. _____

7. I put my responsibilities first and pleasures last. _____

8. I am a hardworking person. _____

9. I display godly attitudes despite how I feel. _____

10. I keep my inner heart and exterior surroundings extremely neat, clean, and organized. _____

Total Score _____

Now check your score against the following chart to determine your spiritual maturity level for self-discipline.

Spiritual Maturity Grade from the "Self-Discipline" Test

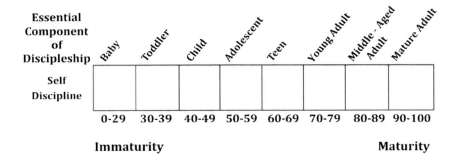

My spiritual maturity grade for self-discipline:

I am a _____ spiritually.

Ideas for Growing in Self-Discipline

1. Acknowledge your weaknesses.
2. Pray and ask God for His grace and help.
3. Tell others about your goal to be more self-disciplined.
4. Read books and articles about self-discipline.
5. Memorize Scripture that deals with self-discipline (self-control).
6. Establish spiritual disciplines in your life that you do regularly such as:

   • Reading Scripture
   • Praying
   • Fasting
   • Memorizing Scripture
   • Reading non-fiction, Christian books
   • Giving
   • Serving

7. Remove unnecessary activities and distractions in your life.
8. Make yourself the boss of your body and will, not vice-versa.

9. Practice tolerating physical and emotional discomfort.
10. Visualize the long-term benefits of being self-disciplined.
11. Share your desire to be more disciplined with a loved one and ask them to hold you accountable for developing specific self-disciplines.
12. Set clear, measurable goals and deadlines.
13. Complete unfinished tasks.
14. Start an exercising program.
15. Establish routines in your life.
16. Acquire, or make, a self-discipline logbook and record the start and end times of your tasks and projects.
17. Replace bad habits with good ones.
18. Get up and go to bed at regular times.
19. Plan out your days, weeks, months, and years in advance.
20. Start the habit of using "To-do" lists to get things done and be more efficient in your life.
21. Clean up and organize your surroundings.
22. Reward yourself for your victories and accomplishments.
23. Penalize yourself when you fail.
24. Make a "Checklist Chart" of your commitments and check them off daily in order to build good habits in your life.
25. Find an accountability partner to hold you accountable for your goals.
26. Do a Bible study on self-discipline.
27. Look for someone in your church who is spiritually self-disciplined and ask him or her to mentor you in this area.

Action Steps for Growing in Self-Discipline

Now prayerfully look back over this list, choose at least one idea, and make plans to begin doing it today. Then continually return in the future for implementing other ideas for your growth in self-discipline.

3. How to Grow in Obedience

"And by this we know that we have come to know him, if we **keep** his commandments. Whoever says, 'I know him' but does not **keep** his commandments is a liar, and the truth is not in him, but whoever **keeps** his word, in him truly the love of God is perfected" (1 John 2:3–5).

Stages of Growth to Spiritual Maturity in Obedience

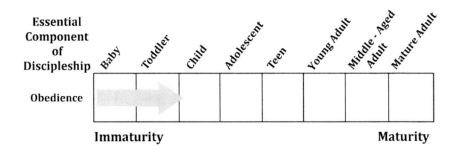

Self-Assessment Test for Obedience to God

Please take a moment to answer the following 10 questions to discover your spiritual maturity level regarding your obedience to God. Answer each question using the following response options. Mark down your points earned for each question and then tally them up at the end to see your level of spiritual maturity in this category. As you take the test, avoid rushing. Answer the questions prayerfully and honestly. After you've taken the test, you might ask a loved one to take it for you as well. This will give you a broader perspective.

Points Possible per Answer

Never....................... 0 Points
Rarely .... 2 Points
Occasionally .... 4 Points
Frequently............... 6 Points
Almost Always ...... 8 Points
Habitually............... 10 Points

1. I read my Bible daily. _____

2. I walk close to God throughout the day. _____

3. I pray daily for at least 20 minutes. _____

4. I am deeply involved in a church. _____

5. I regularly share the gospel with others. _____

6. I am highly self-disciplined. _____

7. I maintain a clear conscience. _____

8. I have a ministry where I serve God and others. _____

9. I display excellent, Christ-like attitudes. _____

10. I manage my time, finances, and body, excellently. _____

Total Score _____

Now check your score against the following chart to determine your spiritual maturity level for obedience to God.

Spiritual Maturity Grade from the "Obedience" Test

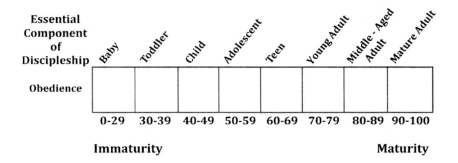

My spiritual maturity grade for obedience to God:

I am a _____ spiritually.

Ideas for Growing in Obedience to God

1. Prayerfully ask yourself how obedient you are to God and His Word.
2. Ask loved ones and close friends to rate you in how obedient you are to God and His Word.
3. If you are not faithfully reading your Bible, begin now. Choose a Bible reading plan and make a commitment to obey God in this area (see ideas from the "Knowledge of God" section).
4. If you struggle in staying close to God throughout the day, consider setting your watch or smart phone to notify and remind you of God.
5. Put physical reminders up that remind you of God.
6. If you are struggling in obeying God in the area of prayer, commit to a set time and a set amount of time for prayer each day.
7. If you don't share the gospel much, look at the section in this chapter called "How to Grow in Evangelism" and study what the gospel is and how to share it. Then pray and look for

opportunities to share your faith.

8. If you don't have a regular quiet time, make a commitment to do it faithfully each day.

9. If you don't give at least 10% of your income to the Lord's work, make a commitment to do so.

10. If you struggle in obedience in time management, finances, or taking care of your body, look at the section in this chapter called "How to Grow in Stewardship" and choose some ideas to help you be more obedient in these areas.

11. Prayerfully ask yourself if you allow Christ to control what you watch, read, hear, or think about, and commit to allowing Him more control over what you're putting into your mind.

12. Read books and articles about how to obey God.

13. If you have broken relationships and need to ask forgiveness, or need to forgive someone, make a commitment to be obedient in this area.

14. If you are not serving God, make a commitment to get involved in some ministry within your church or community.

15. Do a Bible study on obedience.

16. Look for someone in your church who faithfully obeys God in all areas of their life and ask him or her to mentor you.

Action Steps for Growing in Obedience to God

Now prayerfully look back over this list, choose at least one idea, and make plans to begin doing it today. Then continually return in the future for implementing other ideas for your growth in obedience to God.

4. How to Grow in Abiding in Christ

"**Abide** in me, and I in you. As the branch cannot bear fruit by itself, unless it **abides** in the vine, neither can you, unless you **abide** in me. Whoever **abides** in me and I in him, he it is that bears much fruit, **for apart from me you can do nothing**" (John 15: 4–5).

Stages of Growth to Spiritual Maturity in Abiding in Christ

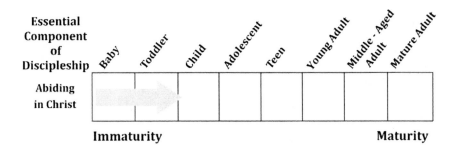

Self-Assessment Test for Abiding in Christ

Please take a moment to answer the following 10 questions to discover your spiritual maturity level for abiding in Christ. Answer each question using the following response options. Mark down your points earned for each question and then tally them up at the end to see your level of spiritual maturity in this category. As you take the test, avoid rushing. Answer the questions prayerfully and honestly. After you've taken the test, you might ask a loved one to take it for you as well. This will give you a broader perspective.

Points Possible per Answer

Never .... 0 Points
Rarely .... 2 Points
Occasionally .... 4 Points
Frequently .... 6 Points
Almost Always ...... 8 Points
Habitually .... 10 Points

1. I have a daily quiet time with God. _____

2. I seek earnestly to live in the presence of God. _____

3. I pray to God throughout the day. _____

4. I think of God throughout the day. _____

5. I make all my decisions based upon God's Word. _____

6. I bring every thought into obedience to Christ. _____

7. I display godly attitudes and character. _____

8. I live with eternity in mind. _____

9. I trust Christ and remain strong in trials and hardships. _____

10. I carefully listen for God's voice throughout the day. _____

Total Score _____

Now check your score against the following chart to determine your spiritual maturity level for abiding in Christ.

Spiritual Maturity Grade from the "Abiding in Christ" Test

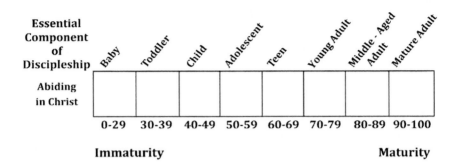

My spiritual maturity grade for abiding in Christ:

I am a _____ spiritually.

Ideas for Growing in Abiding in Christ

1. Start or be more faithful in a daily quiet time.
2. Consider some kind of reminder that causes you to check in with God throughout the day to be more in tune with Him. You might set a timer on your smartphone, put a picture somewhere, or establish a habit of praying and thinking about God more often. Daniel set aside a time to pray three times a day; maybe you might consider doing the same.
3. Seek an accountability partner to help you set your mind upon God more frequently.
4. Memorize Scripture that speaks of abiding in Christ (John 15:1–11; Col. 3:1–4; Ps. 1; Gal. 5:16–25).
5. Read books and articles on abiding in Christ.
6. Pray daily for God's help in learning how to abide in Him.
7. Saturate your mind more with Scripture, which will help greatly in causing you to think more about God.
8. Listen to Christian radio.
9. Listen to Christian music.
10. Listen to sermons on abiding in Christ.

11. Give up the activities in your life that are standing in the way of your full commitment to Christ.
12. Fast and pray to train yourself to abide in Christ better.
13. Reflect or journal on the activities of your day, thinking about how you used your time, how you walked with God, and what you could have done differently.
14. Do a Bible study on abiding in Christ.
15. Look for someone in your church who faithfully abides in Christ and ask him or her to mentor you in this area.

Action Steps for Growing in Abiding in Christ

Now prayerfully look back over this list, choose at least one idea, and make plans to begin doing it today. Then continually return in the future for implementing other ideas for your growth in abiding in Christ.

5. How to Grow in Prayer

"Rejoice always, **pray** without ceasing, give thanks in all circumstances; for this is the will of God in Christ Jesus for you" (1 Thess. 5:16–18).

"Continue steadfastly in **prayer**, being watchful in it with thanksgiving" (Col. 4:2).

Stages of Growth to Spiritual Maturity in Prayer

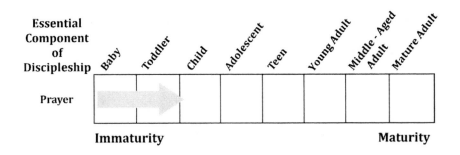

Self-Assessment Test for Prayer

Please take a moment to answer the following 10 questions to discover your spiritual maturity level regarding prayer. Answer each question using the following response options. Mark down your points earned for each question and then tally them up at the end to see your level of spiritual maturity in this category. As you take the test, avoid rushing. Answer the questions prayerfully and honestly. After you've taken the test, you might ask a loved one to take it for you as well. This will give you a broader perspective.

Points Possible per Answer

Never .... 0 Points
Rarely .... 2 Points
Occasionally .... 4 Points
Frequently.............. 6 Points
Almost Always ...... 8 Points
Habitually .... 10 Points

1. I have a designated prayer time daily. _____

2. I confess my sins and pray for forgiveness daily. _____

3. I maintain an attitude of prayer throughout the day. _____

4. I pray daily for at least 20 minutes. _____

5. I thank God for His blessings daily. _____

6. I pray for others daily. _____

7. I pray for God's help to walk closely with Him daily. _____

8. I listen for God's voice during my prayer times. _____

9. I pray with others for the needs of God's Kingdom. _____

10. I pray for my needs daily. _____

Total Score _____

Now check your score against the following chart to determine your spiritual maturity level for prayer.

Spiritual Maturity Grade from the "Prayer" Test

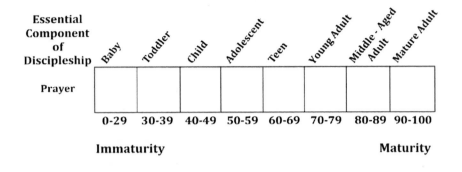

My spiritual maturity grade for prayer:

I am a _____ spiritually.

Ideas for Growing in Prayer

1. Set aside a fixed time for daily prayer.
2. Make prayer a daily habit.
3. Set aside a fixed place for prayer that is free from distractions.
4. Establish prayer topics to help you during your prayer time. Here are some ideas to include:
   - Confess your sins to God and ask Him to reveal unknown sin in your life, or things that are displeasing to Him. This may include broken relationships, wrong activities, mismanagement of time, neglect of God, laziness, allowing sinful things into your mind, and apathy.
   - Pray for the filling of God's Spirit in your life.
   - Pray for help in walking with God and setting your mind on Him.
   - Thank God for all His blessings in your life.
   - Praise God for who He is and what He's done for you.
   - Pray for family members.
   - Pray for unsaved loved ones and friends.

- Pray for missionaries, pastors, churches, Christian organizations, etc.
- Pray for your own needs.
- Pray for your ministry or ministries.
- Pray for government leaders.
- Pray for guidance and direction in your life.
- Pray for opportunities to evangelize.

5. Consider doing a "prayer walk" around some ministry, church, neighborhood, or place that needs Christ.
6. Join your church's prayer team and pray for needs that arise.
7. Start a prayer meeting.
8. Start a prayer journal and keep track of your own prayer requests and those of others. Your faith will be strengthened as you see God faithfully answer prayer.
9. Create a "prayer wall" and post your prayer requests on it.
10. Put prayer requests on your fridge.
11. Set aside meditative prayer times by going to the beach, going on a hike, going to a lake, or going for a walk.
12. Give up something this week to spend more time in prayer.
13. Make a commitment to fast and pray, setting aside a meal, or a full day.
14. Read books and articles on prayer.
15. Do a Bible study on prayer.
16. Look for someone in your church who faithfully prays and ask him or her to mentor you in this area.

Action Steps for Growing in Prayer

Now prayerfully look back over this list, choose at least one idea, and make plans to begin doing it today. Then continually return in the future for implementing other ideas for your growth in prayer.

6. How to Grow in Mentoring

"And what you have heard from me in the presence of many witnesses **entrust to faithful men** who will be able to **teach others also**" (2 Tim. 2:2).

"What you have **learned and received and heard and seen in me** — practice these things, and the God of peace will be with you" (Phil. 4:9).

Stages of Growth to Spiritual Maturity in Mentoring

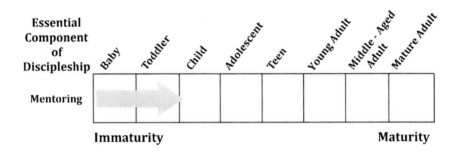

Self-Assessment Test for Mentoring

Please take a moment to answer the following 10 questions to discover your spiritual maturity level regarding mentoring. Answer each question using the following response options. Mark down your points earned for each question and then tally them up at the end to see your level of spiritual maturity in this category. As you take the test, avoid rushing. Answer the questions prayerfully and honestly. After you've taken the test, you might ask a loved one to take it for you as well. This will give you a broader perspective.

Points Possible per Answer

Never...................... 0 Points
Rarely .... 2 Points
Occasionally .... 4 Points
Frequently............... 6 Points
Almost Always ...... 8 Points
Habitually .... 10 Points

1. Currently, I am mentoring someone. _____

2. Currently, someone is mentoring me. _____

3. I have close friends who I allow to hold me accountable for spiritual growth. _____

4. I listen to feedback from others with open arms. _____

5. I am careful to admit my errors and ask forgiveness promptly when I've offended others. _____

6. I respond well to criticism. _____

7. I am skillful in teaching and mentoring others. _____

8. I know exactly what to teach others in mentorship. _____

9. I model what I teach. _____

10. I know God's Word thoroughly in order to give counsel and wisdom to those I teach. _____

Total Score _____

Now check your score against the following chart to determine your spiritual maturity level for mentoring.

Spiritual Maturity Grade from the "Mentoring" Test

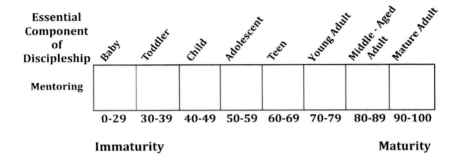

My spiritual maturity grade for mentoring:

I am a _____ spiritually.

Ideas for Growing in Mentoring

As mentioned in chapter 4, biblical mentoring is an informal relationship wherein a more spiritually mature person teaches and models godly, life-skills to others who are generally less spiritually mature. Mentoring can be formal, informal, take place in a group setting, take place in an individual setting, can be regular, or somewhat sporadic.

Examples of mentoring include small group Bible studies, Sunday School classes, youth group, one on one discipleship studies, accountability partners, and so on.

It should be noted, however, that the most effective mentoring takes place in a one on one setting, or in a small group where specific truths and life-skills are intentionally passed on. The following are ideas to consider for mentoring:

1. Pray that God would lead you to someone He desires for you to mentor.
2. Pray that God might lead you to someone who can be your mentor.

3. Develop a discipleship plan of the essential components you would use in mentoring someone (maybe this book would provide this for you).
4. Develop your own spiritual maturity so you can be a mentor who honors God and models what you plan on teaching.
5. Develop your understanding of what a good mentor or coach is and be a mentor who:

- Leads by example
- Has seasoned experience in order to share skills, knowledge, and expertise
- Has integrity
- Listens well
- Has a good reputation for developing others
- Has time and energy to devote to mentoring
- Has a learning attitude
- Demonstrates spiritual maturity
- Knows the strengths and abilities of their mentees
- Wants their mentees to succeed
- Communicates hope and optimism
- Provides guidance and constructive feedback
- Is respected
- Sets and meets ongoing goals
- Values the opinions of others
- Motivates by setting a good example
- Is skillful in teaching
- Provides insight
- Is accessible
- Criticizes constructively
- Is supportive
- Is specific
- Is caring
- Is admirable

6. Ask your pastor to encourage mentorship in your church.
7. Ask your pastor if you can start a mentorship program in your church.
8. Offer to teach a class in your church on mentorship.
9. Ask your pastor if you can put a sign-up sheet in your church lobby for those interested in being mentored, and another for those interested in mentoring.
10. Ask your pastor if he might preach about the role of mentorship in the context of discipleship.
11. Read books and articles on mentorship.
12. Develop a mentorship guide for training others in how to mentor.
13. Do a Bible study on mentoring.
14. Read again carefully the section "Discipleship in the Time of Christ" in chapter 3, which shows how mentorship functioned between Jesus and His disciples.

Action Steps for Growing in Mentoring

Now prayerfully look back over this list, choose at least one idea, and make plans to begin doing it today. Then continually return in the future for implementing other ideas for your growth in mentoring.

7. How to Grow in Church Involvement

"And let us consider how to stir up one another to love and good works, **not neglecting to meet together**, as is the habit of some, but encouraging one another, and all the more as you see the Day drawing near" (Heb. 10:24–25).

Stages of Growth to Spiritual Maturity in Church Involvement

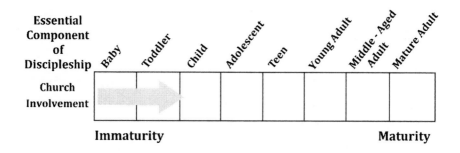

Self-Assessment Test for Church Involvement

Please take a moment to answer the following 10 questions to discover your spiritual maturity level regarding church involvement. Answer each question using the following response options. Mark down your points earned for each question and then tally them up at the end to see your level of spiritual maturity in this category. As you take the test, avoid rushing. Answer the questions prayerfully and honestly. After you've taken the test, you might ask a loved one to take it for you as well. This will give you a broader perspective.

Points Possible per Answer

Never........................ 0 Points
Rarely .... 2 Points
Occasionally .... 4 Points
Frequently............... 6 Points
Almost Always ...... 8 Points
Habitually............... 10 Points

1. I attend a Bible believing church. _____

2. I have a ministry in my church. _____

3. I have accountability partners in my church. _____

4. I am deeply involved in my church. _____

5. I attend a small group meeting. _____

6. I am open and honest with others about who I am. _____

7. I maintain a clear conscience with others. _____

8. I forgive others who have wronged me. _____

9. I am connected with others in my church. _____

10. I give financially to my church. _____

Total Score _____

Now check your score against the following chart to determine your spiritual maturity level for church involvement.

Spiritual Maturity Grade from the "Church Involvement" Test

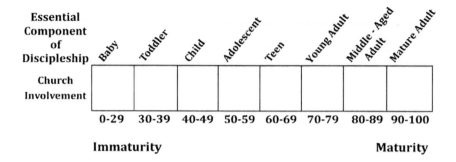

Essential Component of Discipleship	Baby	Toddler	Child	Adolescent	Teen	Young Adult	Middle-Aged Adult	Mature Adult
Church Involvement								
	0-29	30-39	40-49	50-59	60-69	70-79	80-89	90-100

Immaturity   **Maturity**

My spiritual maturity grade for church involvement:

I am a _____ spiritually.

Ideas for Growing in Church Involvement

1. If you can't fully support your church because it doesn't preach or follow God's Word, look for a Bible believing church you can be a part of and support with all your heart.
2. If you're not a member of your church, and they offer membership, join your church.
3. Look for a ministry where you can serve using your gifts and abilities.
4. Pray about starting a new ministry in your church.
5. Pray for your pastor and church leadership.
6. Get to know your church leadership team.
7. Give of your finances faithfully to support your church and obey God.
8. Be more faithful in church attendance.
9. Be careful about being critical and tearing the church down if you haven't been a part of building it up. Tearing down is easy, but building something up is hard work.
10. Commit yourself to loving and encouraging others in your church.

11. Pray about getting more involved in shouldering the load in your church.
12. Apply what you learn to your life. Don't just be a hearer of God's Word, but a doer of it.
13. Learn your spiritual gifts and use them.
14. Be a part of solving problems, not being one of them.
15. Be punctual.
16. Smile, be positive, and be warm to others.
17. Be friendly by greeting visitors and others in your church.
18. Be hospitable and invite people into your home for fellowship.
19. Read books and articles on church health and growth.
20. Do a Bible study on the purpose and role of the church.
21. Look for someone in your church who is faithfully involved in church and ask him or her to mentor you in this area.

Action Steps for Growing in Church Involvement

Now prayerfully look back over this list, choose at least one idea, and make plans to begin doing it today. Then continually return in the future for implementing other ideas for your growth in church involvement.

8. How to Grow in Evangelism

"For I am not ashamed of the gospel, for it is the power of God for salvation to everyone who believes, to the Jew first and also to the Greek" (Rom. 1:16).

"And he said to them, 'Go into all the world and proclaim the gospel to the whole creation'" (Mark 16:15).

Stages of Growth to Spiritual Maturity in Evangelism

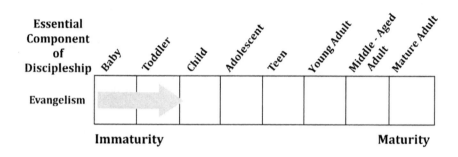

Self-Assessment Test for Evangelism

Please take a moment to answer the following 10 questions to discover your spiritual maturity level regarding evangelism. Answer each question using the following response options. Mark down your points earned for each question and then tally them up at the end to see your level of spiritual maturity in this category. As you take the test, avoid rushing. Answer the questions prayerfully and honestly. After you've taken the test, you might ask a loved one to take it for you as well. This will give you a broader perspective.

Points Possible per Answer

Never .... 0 Points
Rarely .... 2 Points
Occasionally .... 4 Points
Frequently .... 6 Points
Almost Always ...... 8 Points
Habitually .... 10 Points

1. I know each aspect of the gospel. _____

2. I have verses memorized for sharing the gospel. _____

3. I share the gospel regularly. _____

4. I look for opportunities to build relationships with those who don't know Christ. _____

5. I pray for unsaved loved ones and friends. _____

6. I am confident in my ability to share the gospel. _____

7. My heart is full of compassion for the lost. _____

8. I am willing to go anywhere to share the gospel. _____

9. I have a heart for missions. _____

10. I am involved in missions by either praying for missionaries, serving missionaries, or by giving to missions. _____

Total Score _____

Now check your score against the following chart to determine your spiritual maturity level for evangelism.

Spiritual Maturity Grade from the "Evangelism" Test

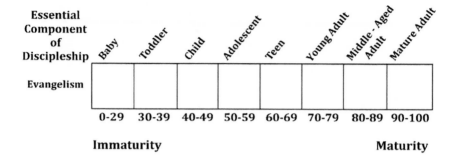

My spiritual maturity grade for evangelism:

I am a _____ spiritually.

Ideas for Growing in Evangelism

1. Write out your testimony about how you received Christ.
2. Practice sharing your testimony with loved ones or friends.
3. Share your testimony at church, in a small group, in a Bible study, etc.
4. Practice sharing the gospel.
5. Pray for opportunities to share your testimony and the gospel.
6. Read and study other Bible verses that focus on the gospel.
7. Read books on apologetics (how to defend your faith).
8. Get to know God's Word better so you are not embarrassed when sharing your faith and are more confident (2 Tim. 2:15).
9. Get to know the missionaries of your church.
10. Pray for missionaries you know.
11. Encourage the missionaries you know by sending them cards, giving them a phone call, etc.
12. Give financially to missionaries you know.
13. Consider serving as a missionary (either short-term or long-term).

14. Read books on great missionaries and the sacrifices they've made for God.
15. Read books and articles on evangelism.
16. Do a Bible study on evangelism.
17. Look for someone in your church who shares the gospel regularly and effectively, and ask him or her to mentor you in this area.
18. Study (memorize if possible) the following biblical presentation of the gospel so you can share it with precision and clarity:

Step 1: God loves us and desires that we would spend eternity in heaven with Him.

John 3:16: "For God so loved the world, that he gave his only Son, that whoever believes in him should not perish but have eternal life."

Step 2: Our sin and rejection of God separates us from Him.

Genesis 2:15-17: "The Lord God took the man and put him in the Garden of Eden to work it and keep it. And the Lord God commanded the man, saying, 'You may surely eat of every tree of the garden, but of the tree of the knowledge of good and evil you shall not eat, for in the day that you eat of it you shall surely die.'"
Isaiah 59:2: "But your iniquities have made a separation between you and your God, and your sins have hidden his face from you so that he does not hear."
Romans 3:23: "For all have sinned and fall short of the glory of God."

Summary of steps 1 and 2: We have lost our relationship with God our Creator, and as a result, have a sinful heart. We do not desire to please God and are selfish and sinful. Our greatest sin is that of not having a relationship with God and loving Him as our Father and Creator. If the greatest command in the Bible is to love the Lord our God with all our heart, soul, mind, and strength, then our greatest sin is not to love and have a relationship with Him. This is our primary sin (Matt. 7:21-23).

Step 3: The price for practicing sin and rejecting God is eternal torment in hell.

> Romans 6:23: "For the wages of sin is death, but the free gift of God is eternal life in Christ Jesus our Lord."
> Matthew 13:49-50: "So it will be at the end of the age. The angels will come out and separate the evil from the righteous and throw them into the fiery furnace. In that place there will be weeping and gnashing of teeth."
> Revelation 21:8: "But as for the cowardly, the faithless, the detestable, as for murderers, the sexually immoral, sorcerers, idolaters, and all liars, their portion will be in the lake that burns with fire and sulfur, which is the second death."

Step 4: God's remedy for our sin is abundant, eternal life through Christ's death on the Cross and resurrection from the dead.

> Isaiah 53:5: "But he was pierced for our transgressions; he was crushed for our iniquities; upon him was the chastisement that brought us peace, and with his wounds we are healed."
> Romans 5:8: "But God shows his love for us in that while we were still sinners, Christ died for us."
> Romans 6:23: "For the wages of sin is death, but the free gift of God is eternal life in Christ Jesus our Lord."
> Ephesians 2:8-9: "For by grace you have been saved through faith. And this is not your own doing; it is the gift of God, not

a result of works, so that no one may boast."

Step 5: Would you like to receive Christ and His gift of eternal life?

John 1:12: "But to all who did receive him, who believed in his name, he gave the right to become children of God."

John 3:36: "Whoever believes in the Son has eternal life; whoever does not obey the Son shall not see life, but the wrath of God remains on him."

Acts 4:12: "And there is salvation in no one else, for there is no other name under heaven given among men by which we must be saved."

Step 6: How to receive Christ as Lord and Savior.

1. Admit that you are a sinner in need of a Savior.
2. Believe that Christ died on the Cross to pay for your sins and rose from the dead to give you eternal life.
3. Believe that without Christ's payment for your sins you deserve hell.
4. Repent and confess your sins to God, asking for His forgiveness and grace.
5. Pray to receive Christ and His gift of salvation.
6. Give your heart and will to Christ.

Action Steps for Growing in Evangelism

Now prayerfully look back over this list, choose at least one idea, and make plans to begin doing it today. Then continually return in the future for implementing other ideas for your growth in evangelism.

9. How to Grow in Your Inner Life

"But the Lord said to Samuel, 'Do not look on his appearance or on the height of his stature, because I have rejected him. For the Lord sees not as man sees: man looks on the outward appearance, but the **Lord looks on the heart** '" (1 Sam. 16:16).

"So I always take pains to have a **clear conscience** toward both God and man" (Acts 24:7).

Stages of Growth to Spiritual Maturity in the Inner Life

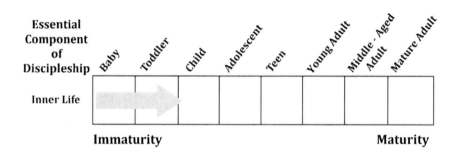

Self-Assessment Test for Your Inner Life

Please take a moment to answer the following 10 questions to discover your spiritual maturity level regarding your inner life with Christ. Answer each question using the following response options. Mark down your points earned for each question and then tally them up at the end to see your level of spiritual maturity in this category. As you take the test, avoid rushing. Answer the questions prayerfully and honestly. After you've taken the test, you might ask a loved one to take it for you as well. This will give you a broader perspective.

Points Possible per Answer

Never .... 0 Points
Rarely .... 2 Points
Occasionally .... 4 Points
Frequently.............. 6 Points
Almost Always ...... 8 Points
Habitually .... 10 Points

1. I am the same in public as I am in private. _____

2. Others can see that God is my highest priority. _____

3. There's nothing in my life I haven't fully surrendered to God. _____

4. I walk closely with God throughout the day. _____

5. I am highly concerned about obeying all of Scripture. _____

6. I replace sinful, impure thoughts with God's truth. _____

7. I maintain a clear conscience before God and others. _____

8. I confess all known sin promptly and ask God and others to forgive me right away. _____

9. I forgive others who hurt me and keep my heart clean of bitterness and resentment. _____

10. I read and meditate on God's Word to better understand His will and keep my life and heart pure. _____

Total Score _____

Now check your score against the following chart to determine your spiritual maturity level for your inner life.

Spiritual Maturity Grade from the "Inner Life" Test

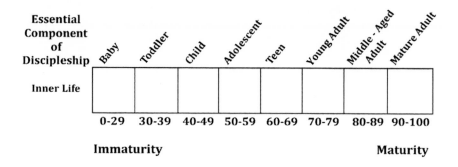

My spiritual maturity grade for my inner life:

I am a _____ spiritually.

Ideas for Growing in Your Inner Life with Christ

1. Prayerfully ask yourself how much of your Christian life and service to God tilts toward looking good before others instead of God.

2. Prayerfully ask yourself if you're more concerned with what others think of you instead of what God thinks of you.

3. Prayerfully ask yourself if you're guilty of the same tendencies as many of those during Christ's day who were hypocritical.

4. Give careful attention to starting or being more faithful in a daily quiet time where you:

   - Pray
   - Read your Bible with purpose
   - Memorize Scripture

5. Do a Bible search for the phrase "selfish ambition" and then meditate on Scripture that speaks of our tendency to be people pleasers rather than God pleasers.

6. Read the "Sermon on the Mount" (Matt. 5–7) that speaks of

doing our service to please God rather than others.

7. Ask loved ones or close friends to truthfully evaluate your life to see if you have selfish ambition.

8. Memorize Scripture that deals with pride and selfish ambition.

9. Prayerfully ask God to show you areas in your life where you are displeasing Him.

10. Read a book on the inner life that deals with how you can develop a heart that focuses on pleasing God and being a genuine follower of Christ.

11. Prayerfully ask yourself why you do what you do in your service to God and others. Is it to gain recognition or to please God?

12. Ponder over your life and prayerfully ask yourself if you have taken stands on biblical truths despite what others think of you.

13. Prayerfully ask yourself if some of your beliefs are held due to what others believe instead of what God's Word says.

14. Do a Bible study on the inner life.

15. Look for someone in your church who displays mature characteristics in their inner life and ask him or her to mentor you in this area.

Action Steps for Growing in Your Inner Life

Now prayerfully look back over this list, choose at least one idea, and make plans to begin doing it today. Then continually return in the future for implementing other ideas for your growth in your inner life.

10. How to Grow in Spiritual Gifts

"Now there are varieties of gifts, but the same Spirit; and there are varieties of service, but the same Lord; and there are varieties of activities, but it is the same God who empowers them all in everyone. To each is given the manifestation of the Spirit for the common good" (1 Cor. 12:4-7).

Stages of Growth to Spiritual Maturity in Spiritual Gifts

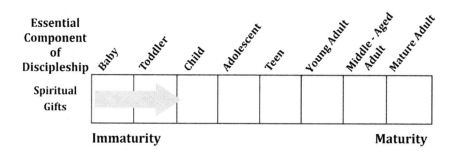

Self-Assessment Test for Spiritual Gifts

Please take a moment to answer the following 10 questions to discover your spiritual maturity level regarding spiritual gifts. Answer each question using the following response options. Mark down your points earned for each question and then tally them up at the end to see your level of spiritual maturity in this category. As you take the test, avoid rushing. Answer the questions prayerfully and honestly. After you've taken the test, you might ask a loved one to take it for you as well. This will give you a broader perspective.

Points Possible per Answer

Never .... 0 Points
Rarely .... 2 Points
Occasionally .... 4 Points
Frequently............... 6 Points
Almost Always ...... 8 Points
Habitually .... 10 Points

1. I know what all the spiritual gifts are in the Bible. _____

2. I know what each spiritual gift means and how God intends it to be used. _____

3. I know what my spiritual gifts are. _____

4. I am currently using my spiritual gifts. _____

5. I know the doctrinal positions on the spiritual gifts. _____

6. I am a master at using my spiritual gifts. _____

7. I am studying and learning more about how to better use my spiritual gifts. _____

8. I often think about new ways I could use my gifts. _____

9. I encourage others to use their spiritual gifts. _____

10. Using my spiritual gifts give me a deep sense of purpose in life. _____

Total Score _____

Now check your score against the following chart to determine your spiritual maturity level for spiritual gifts.

Spiritual Maturity Grade from the "Spiritual Gifts" Test

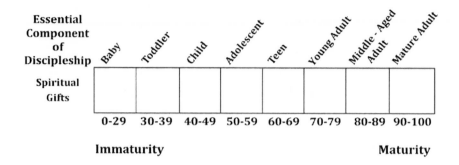

Essential Component of Discipleship	Baby	Toddler	Child	Adolescent	Teen	Young Adult	Middle-Aged Adult	Mature Adult
Spiritual Gifts								
	0-29	30-39	40-49	50-59	60-69	70-79	80-89	90-100

Immaturity   Maturity

My spiritual maturity grade for spiritual gifts:

I am a _____ spiritually.

Ideas for Growing in Your Spiritual Gifts

1. Do a Bible study on the spiritual gifts.
2. Take a self-assessment test to discover your spiritual gifts (there are many online from which to choose).
3. Take a Bible class on the spiritual gifts.
4. Ask your pastor to offer a class on the spiritual gifts.
5. Lead a Bible study on the spiritual gifts.
6. Write down your spiritual gifts and memorize them.
7. Ask others what they think your spiritual gifts are.
8. Pray and seek out how you can develop your spiritual gifts.
9. If you're not already doing so, offer to use your gifts within your church.
10. Do an in-depth Bible study on your particular gifts.
11. Seek out others who have your similar gifts and ask them to share with you about how they use their gifts.
12. Observe those who are mature in their use of the same gifts you have and watch how they use them.
13. Read books and articles on the spiritual gifts.
14. Read several theological books about the different doctrinal

positions on the spiritual gifts in order to understand all views (some believe all the gifts are for today while others believe not all of them are for today).

15. Pray about how you can develop your spiritual gifts in order to be highly skilled at using them.

16. Look for someone in your church who is faithfully using their spiritual gifts and ask him or her to mentor you in this area.

Action Steps for Growing in Your Spiritual Gifts

Now prayerfully look back over this list, choose at least one idea, and make plans to begin doing it today. Then continually return in the future for implementing other ideas for growth in your spiritual gifts.

11. How to Grow in Serving

"But Jesus called them to him and said, 'You know that the rulers of the Gentiles lord it over them, and their great ones exercise authority over them. It shall not be so among you. But whoever would be great among you must be your servant, and whoever would be first among you must be your slave, even as the Son of Man came not to be served but to serve, and to give his life as a ransom for many'" (Matt. 20:25–28).

Stages of Growth to Spiritual Maturity in Serving

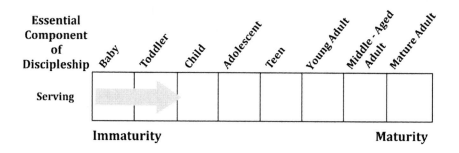

Self-Assessment Test for Serving

Please take a moment to answer the following 10 questions to discover your spiritual maturity level regarding serving. Answer each question using the following response options. Mark down your points earned for each question and then tally them up at the end to see your level of spiritual maturity in this category. As you take the test, avoid rushing. Answer the questions prayerfully and honestly. After you've taken the test, you might ask a loved one to take it for you as well. This will give you a broader perspective.

328

Points Possible per Answer

Never........................ 0 Points
Rarely .... 2 Points
Occasionally .... 4 Points
Frequently............... 6 Points
Almost Always ...... 8 Points
Habitually............... 10 Points

1. I have a ministry where I serve God and others. _____

2. I am a serving person. _____

3. I enjoy meeting the needs of others without expecting anything in return. _____

4. I see my painful experiences as gifts from God to better serve others. _____

5. I serve God and others through prayer. _____

6. Those close to me would say that my life is more about giving than receiving. _____

7. I am sensitive to the needs of others. _____

8. I volunteer my time on a regular basis. _____

9. Meeting the needs of others gives me great joy and purpose in life. _____

10. I feel deep compassion for those in need. _____

Total Score _____

Now check your score against the following chart to determine your spiritual maturity level for serving.

Spiritual Maturity Grade from the "Serving" Test

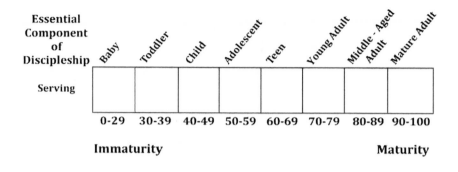

My spiritual maturity grade for serving:

I am a _____ spiritually.

Ideas for Growing in Serving

1. Memorize Matthew 20:25–28 and Philippians 2:5–8.
2. Ask God to reveal any area in your life where you lack a servant's heart.
3. Ask God to give you eyes to see the needs around you.
4. Prayerfully reflect on your desires to lead, and ask yourself if there might be selfish ambition on your part.
5. Instead of focusing on your needs, consider listening more and focusing on the needs of others.
6. If you're not already serving in your church, look for opportunities to get involved.
7. Learn what your spiritual gifts are so you know best how to serve God and others.
8. Pray about the needs of your church and consider talking with your pastor about how to meet those needs.
9. Read Christian books on serving.
10. Sacrifice one hour this week to serve in your church or neighborhood.
11. Look for ways you can serve those in your family.

12. Choose to do a random act of kindness for someone each day this week.
13. Ask for feedback on how you could be a better servant from your pastor, family, and close friends.
14. Ask your neighbors if they need help with something.
15. Look for widows or the elderly who might need a helping hand with projects around their home.
16. Consider serving at a food pantry or kitchen.
17. Serve on a short-term mission trip this year.
18. Serve someone by discipling and mentoring them.
19. Visit the sick in hospitals.
20. Visit shut-ins, the elderly, widows, etc.
21. Do a Bible study on serving.
22. Look for someone in your church who is serving faithfully and ask him or her to mentor you in this area.

Action Steps for Growing in Serving

Now prayerfully look back over this list, choose at least one idea, and make plans to begin doing it today. Then continually return in the future for implementing other ideas for your growth in serving.

12. How to Grow in Spiritual Attitudes

"But the fruit of the Spirit is love, joy, peace, patience, kindness, goodness, faithfulness, gentleness, self-control; against such things there is no law. And those who belong to Christ Jesus have crucified the flesh with its passions and desires" (Gal. 5:22–24).

"You should have the same **attitude** toward one another that Christ Jesus had, who though he existed in the form of God did not regard equality with God as something to be grasped, but emptied himself by taking on the form of a slave, by looking like other men, and by sharing in human nature. He humbled himself, by becoming obedient to the point of death—even death on a cross!" (Phil. 2:5–8).

Stages of Growth to Spiritual Maturity in Spiritual Attitudes

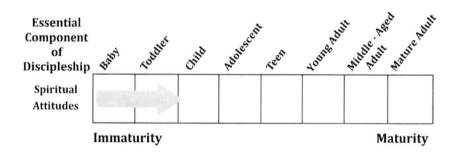

Self-Assessment Test for Spiritual Attitudes

Please take a moment to answer the following 10 questions to discover your spiritual maturity level regarding your attitudes. Answer each question using the following response options. Mark down your points earned for each question and then tally them up at the end to see your level of spiritual maturity in this category. As you take the test, avoid rushing. Answer the questions prayerfully and honestly. After you've taken the test, you might ask a loved one to take it for you as well. This will give you a broader perspective.

Points Possible per Answer

Never...................... 0 Points
Rarely .... 2 Points
Occasionally .... 4 Points
Frequently............... 6 Points
Almost Always ...... 8 Points
Habitually............... 10 Points

1. I display Christ-like attitudes.   _____

2. I am a loving, kind person.   _____

3. I am a joyful person.   _____

4. I am a peaceful person.   _____

5. I am a patient person.   _____

6. I am a friendly person.   _____

7. I am a serving person.   _____

8. I am a humble person.   _____

9. I am a forgiving person.   _____

10. I am a thankful person.   _____

Total Score   _____

Now check your score against the following chart to determine your spiritual maturity level for spiritual attitudes.

Spiritual Maturity Grade from the "Spiritual Attitudes" Test

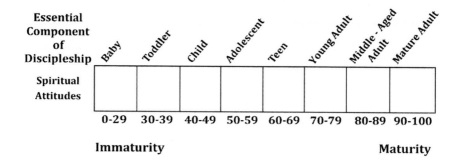

Essential Component of Discipleship	Baby	Toddler	Child	Adolescent	Teen	Young Adult	Middle-Aged Adult	Mature Adult
Spiritual Attitudes								
	0-29	30-39	40-49	50-59	60-69	70-79	80-89	90-100

Immaturity   Maturity

My spiritual maturity grade for spiritual attitudes:

I am a _____ spiritually.

Ideas for Growing in Spiritual Attitudes

1. Identify your default bad attitudes.
2. Identify the good attitudes that should replace your default bad attitudes.
3. Memorize Scripture that addresses your default bad attitudes.
4. Memorize Galatians 5:22–23, Philippians 2:5–8, Philippians 4:8–9, and Romans 12:9–21.
5. Do a Bible study on spiritual attitudes.
6. Identify godly attitudes mentioned in Scripture that we should develop. Here are some examples to consider: we should be loving, joyful, peaceful, kind, forgiving, humble, serving, encouraging, just, obedient, and respectful.
7. Make your quiet time with God a priority.
8. Ask God to help you identify and change your bad attitudes.
9. Share your desire to grow in godly attitudes with a loved one or close friend.
10. Carefully monitor your attitudes and replace them if necessary.
11. Prayerfully ask yourself why you have certain default bad

attitudes.

12. If you are bitter with someone, ask yourself why.
13. Forgive those who have wronged you.
14. Understand that forgiveness is normally both a one-time event and an ongoing process of continual forgiveness.
15. Pray for those who have wronged you.
16. Seek to do something good to bless those who have wronged you (Rom. 12:14–21).
17. Make a list of all the blessings God has done for you and thank Him.
18. Make a list of all the blessings others have done for you and thank them.
19. Thank God daily for His blessings in your life, even the trials (James 1:2–3).
20. Purpose to smile more, reminding yourself that smiling is a way to serve others, regardless of how you feel inside.
21. Get plenty of exercise.
22. Eat healthy food.
23. Get plenty of rest.
24. Find a prayer partner who you can share your needs with and will be faithful in praying for you.
25. Read Christian, non-fiction books on godly attitudes.
26. Look for someone in your church who displays mature, godly attitudes and ask him or her to mentor you in this area.

Action Steps for Growing in Spiritual Attitudes

Now prayerfully look back over this list, choose at least one idea, and make plans to begin doing it today. Then continually return in the future for implementing other ideas for your growth in spiritual attitudes.

13. How to Grow in Character

"But also for this very reason, giving all diligence, add to your faith virtue [character], to virtue knowledge, to knowledge self-control, to self-control perseverance, to perseverance godliness, to godliness brotherly kindness, and to brotherly kindness love. For if these things are yours and abound, you will be neither barren nor unfruitful in the knowledge of our Lord Jesus Christ" (2 Pet. 1:5–8, NKJV).

Stages of Growth to Spiritual Maturity in Character

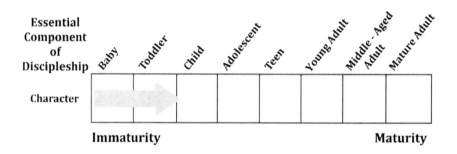

Self-Assessment Test for Character

Please take a moment to answer the following 10 questions to discover your spiritual maturity level regarding your character. Answer each question using the following response options. Mark down your points earned for each question and then tally them up at the end to see your level of spiritual maturity in this category. As you take the test, avoid rushing. Answer the questions prayerfully and honestly. After you've taken the test, you might ask a loved one to take it for you as well. This will give you a broader perspective.

Points Possible per Answer

Never .... 0 Points
Rarely .... 2 Points
Occasionally .... 4 Points
Frequently............... 6 Points
Almost Always ...... 8 Points
Habitually............... 10 Points

1. I am a person of impeccable integrity. _____

2. I do the right thing when no one notices. _____

3. I keep my word even if it cost me money, time, or inconvenience. _____

4. I obey God regardless of the cost. _____

5. I control my tongue. _____

6. I keep my composure when others attack me, irritate me, or say untrue things about me. _____

7. My motive in life is to serve God with all my being. _____

8. I am a truthful person. _____

9. I am a self-disciplined person. _____

10. I am a hardworking person. _____

Total Score _____

Now check your score against the following chart to determine your spiritual maturity level for your character.

Spiritual Maturity Grade from the "Character" Test

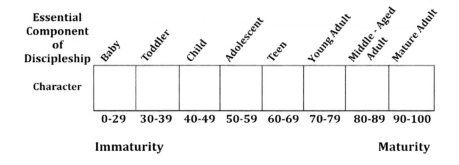

Essential Component of Discipleship	Baby	Toddler	Child	Adolescent	Teen	Young Adult	Middle - Aged Adult	Mature Adult
Character								
	0-29	30-39	40-49	50-59	60-69	70-79	80-89	90-100

Immaturity   Maturity

My spiritual maturity grade for character: _____

I am a _____ spiritually.

Ideas for Growing in Character

1. Do a Bible study on godly character.
2. Identify godly character traits mentioned in Scripture that we should develop. For example, we should be truthful, trustworthy, honest, loyal, self-disciplined, hardworking, generous, responsible, orderly, cleanly, organized, dependable, faithful, diligent, steadfast, and patient.
3. Identify your character weaknesses by prayerfully analyzing your life and asking trusted loved ones and close friends to help you see your blind spots.
4. Identify the godly character traits you need to develop.
5. Choose your worst character trait and commit to replacing it with the opposite godly character trait.
6. Ask God to supernaturally help you.
7. Practice new godly traits until they become habits.
8. Memorize 2 Peter 1:5–8.
9. Find the verses in Scripture that address your character weaknesses and memorize them.
10. Read a chapter of the Book of Proverbs daily and identify the

godly character traits found in it.

11. Read Christian books and articles on godly character, especially ones dealing with your particular weaknesses.

12. Lead a Bible study on character traits.

13. Make a checklist chart of the practical commitments you are making to develop godly character and check them off daily in order to build good habits in your life.

14. Look for someone in your church who displays mature, godly character and ask him or her to mentor you in this area.

15. Persevere, persevere, and persevere! Character takes time and isn't developed overnight. Be patient with yourself and stay committed to it for the long haul.

Action Steps for Growing in Godly Character

Now prayerfully look back over this list, choose at least one idea, and make plans to begin doing it today. Then continually return in the future for implementing other ideas for your growth in godly character.

14. How to Grow in Stewardship

"O Lord, make me know my end and what is the measure of my days; let me know how fleeting I am! Behold, you have made my days a few handbreadths, and my lifetime is as nothing before you. Surely all mankind stands as a mere breath! Surely a man goes about as a shadow!" (Ps. 39:4–6).

Stages of Growth to Spiritual Maturity in Stewardship

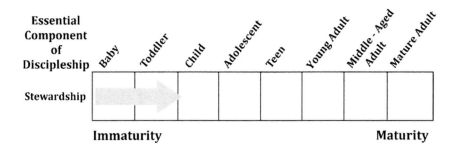

Self-Assessment Test for Stewardship

Please take a moment to answer the following 10 questions to discover your spiritual maturity level regarding stewardship. Answer each question using the following response options. Mark down your points earned for each question and then tally them up at the end to see your level of spiritual maturity in this category. As you take the test, avoid rushing. Answer the questions prayerfully and honestly. After you've taken the test, you might ask a loved one to take it for you as well. This will give you a broader perspective.

Points Possible per Answer

Never .... 0 Points
Rarely .... 2 Points
Occasionally .... 4 Points
Frequently............... 6 Points
Almost Always .... 8 Points
Habitually .... 10 Points

1. I manage my time well for God's purposes. _____

2. I am heavily invested in building God's Kingdom. _____

3. I am productive and accomplish much for God. _____

4. I let God control what I watch, read, hear, and think. _____

5. I take care of my possessions. _____

6. I am generous with my possessions. _____

7. I give at least 10% of my income to the Lord. _____

8. I am within my weight limit for my body size. _____

9. I exercise in order to take care of my body. _____

10. I eat healthily in order to take care of my body. _____

Total Score _____

Now check your score against the following chart to determine your spiritual maturity level for stewardship.

Spiritual Maturity Grade from the "Stewardship" Test

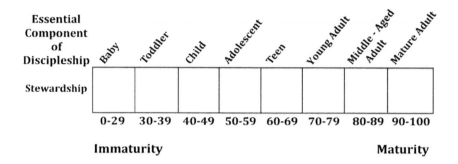

My spiritual maturity grade for stewardship:

I am a _____ spiritually.

Ideas for Growing in Stewardship of Your Time

1. Prayerfully reflect on how much time you spend on average on pleasurable activities each week.
2. Make a chart and keep track of how much time you spend watching TV, on social media, on the Internet, doing fun activities, doing nothing, and so on for a week or two.
3. Look at how you are spending your time and make a decision to be a better steward of it, realizing God will hold you accountable for how you've used this precious talent He's given you.
4. Make a choice to say no to the biggest item that is robbing most of your spare time, and choose to do something instead that is profitable and will serve God, others, or develop yourself.
5. Use a "To-do" list to be better organized.
6. Begin each month, week, and day with a planning time to set goals and log tasks that you should do.
7. Organize your life's activities by using a calendar-planning tool.

8. Cut out unnecessary distractions in your life.
9. Get plenty of rest by going to bed and getting up at regular times.
10. Set up a private zone in your home where you can get away to read, study, pray, meditate, think, and grow.
11. Practice not answering the phone, text messages, emails, etc., after a certain time of the day so you can better utilize your time for rest and personal spiritual growth.
12. Prioritize your goals and give more time to the most important ones.
13. If possible, delegate tasks and responsibilities so you have more free time for spiritual growth and serving.
14. Set a limit to the amount of time you will engage in pleasurable activities per week.
15. Read books and articles on time management.
16. Do a Bible study on time management.
17. Look for someone in your church who is good at time management and ask him or her to mentor you in this area.

Ideas for Growing in Stewardship of Your Possessions

1. Track what percentage of your finances you give to God's work.
2. Make a commitment to give at least 10% of your income to the Lord's work and make it a priority no matter what.
3. Do a Bible study on tithing and giving to God.
4. Read books on financial management.
5. Establish a budget and stick to it.
6. Repair items that are broken instead of buying new ones.
7. Do any needed home repairs that are being neglected.
8. Organize and clean up your surroundings.
9. Commit to getting out of debt.
10. Commit to not spending what you don't have.
11. Cut out needless spending in your life.

12. Eliminate unnecessary spending on pleasure.
13. Read books and articles where faithful Christians have given generously to God and how He has blessed them as a result (George Mueller, etc.).
14. Read Christian books on money management.
15. Look for someone in your church who is good at money management and is faithful in giving to the Lord's work, and ask him or her to mentor you in this area.

Ideas for Growing in Stewardship of Your Body

1. If you are overweight, prayerfully ask yourself why.
2. Commit to getting in shape physically.
3. Commit to a regular exercise program.
4. Commit to eating healthily.
5. Cut out your intake of junk food.
6. Drink water instead of soda, juices, sports drinks, etc.
7. Reduce your eating size portions.
8. Commit to going to bed and getting up at regular times.
9. Find an accountability partner to help you get in shape.
10. Instead of parking close to stores, park far away and walk.
11. Eliminate the poor habits that are causing you to be a poor steward of your body.
12. Read books and articles on how to take care of your body and get in shape.
13. Read the stories of others who have gotten in shape and how they did it.
14. Set clearly defined goals for getting in shape and on how to be a better steward of your body.
15. Do a Bible study on taking care of your body.
16. Make a weekly to-do list for getting in shape that might include the following:

- Workout five days a week
- Eat healthier foods
- Reduce food size portions
- Cut out processed foods
- Drink six large glasses of water daily
- Cut out soda and beverages
- Reduce or eliminate sweets
- Eat dinner before 7:00 p.m.

17. Look for someone in your church who does well at being a good steward of their body and ask him or her to mentor you in this area.

Action Steps for Growing in Stewardship of Your Time, Possessions, and Body

Now prayerfully look back over these three lists on stewardship, choose at least one idea from each category, and make plans to begin doing them today. Then continually return in the future for implementing other ideas for your growth in stewardship.

15. Overall Spiritual Maturity Chart

Now it's time to add up all the scores from each category to discover your overall spiritual maturity level.

Put your score in each corresponding line:

1. Score from Knowledge of God Test   _____

2. Score from Self- Discipline Test   _____

3. Score from Obedience Test   _____

4. Score from Abiding in Christ Test   _____

5. Score from Prayer Test   _____

6. Score from Mentoring Test   _____

7. Score from Church Involvement Test   _____

8. Score from Evangelism Test   _____

9. Score from Inner life Test   _____

10. Score from Spiritual Gifts Test   _____

11. Score from Serving Test   _____

12. Score from Spiritual Attitudes Test   _____

13. Score from Character Test   _____

14. Score from Stewardship Test   _____

Total score   _____

Total score divided by 14   _____

Now check your score against the next chart to determine your overall spiritual maturity level.

Spiritual Maturity Grade from the "Overall Maturity" Test

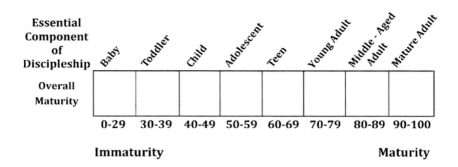

Take your overall adjusted score to find your overall level of maturity in the above diagram.

I am a _____ in my overall spiritual maturity level.

Now look back at the overall spiritual maturity chart and see where you scored the weakest. Next, look at the ideas for that area that you can begin to put into practice for growing toward spiritual maturity. Start with your weakest areas first and then address the next weakest area afterward. Keep doing this for all areas.

Remember, attaining spiritual maturity is a lifelong process so consider rereading this book. Keep focusing and putting into practice the ideas from this chapter in order to grow and attain spiritual maturity in all areas of the essential components of discipleship.

You might even consider using the last two chapters (or even the entire book) for a Bible study or small group resource for teaching others the essential components for attaining spiritual maturity.

On the following page, an overall chart for each category is provided. This will enable you to get an overall view of your spiritual maturity in each area.

Overall Spiritual Maturity Chart

Please put a mark (in pencil) to indicate your present level of spiritual maturity in each category. Consider working on your weakest areas first. Then return regularly to mark your progress and growth toward spiritual maturity in each category.

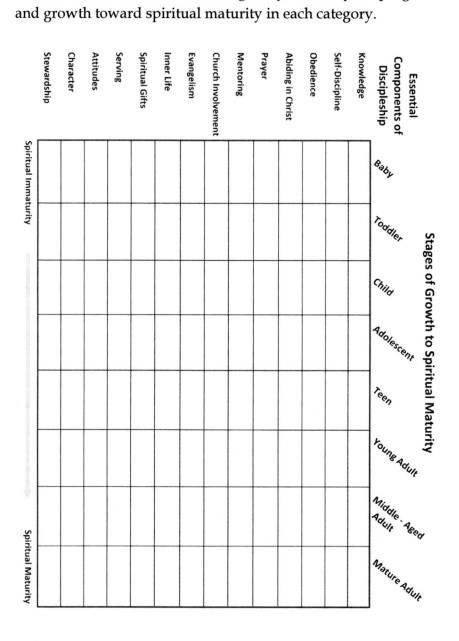

Conclusion

Today, we have many ways of defining success in life. Some define it as being a sports hero, others as being wealthy, others as being popular and well liked, and still others as being happy. How does God define success? He defines it as being spiritually mature!

Spiritual maturity is our purpose in life, not happiness, pleasure, possessions, prestige, or the fulfillment of our dreams. A lifelong commitment to discipleship is God's will for our lives and is what enables us to attain spiritual maturity. By neglecting discipleship, we reject God's nature and image, choosing instead to retain the image of sin and remain spiritually immature.

Now it's time to look in the mirror and sincerely ask yourself how much you want to fulfill God's purpose for your life in becoming spiritually mature. Today, there is more competition than ever, and most will get distracted with the cares of this life and remain spiritually immature. As a result, they will have few rewards in heaven. They will spend most of their time and energy focused on this life rather than preparing for their eternal home. How about you? Will you be one of them? I hope not! Are you willing to pay the cost to attain spiritual maturity? I hope so!

In closing, I want to encourage you to take some time to truly ponder and meditate on eternity and your life there. Reflect on how fast time is passing and how short life is. Reflect on eternity and its endless essence. Consider others who have passed away and think about how things are for them now in their eternal state, whether good or bad.

The only thing we're going to take out of this life is who we have become in Christ and our service to Him. We need to reflect prayerfully on the stanza from the poem by C. T. Studd that says:

Only one life, yes only one,

Soon will its fleeting hours be done;

Then, in "that day" my Lord to meet,

And stand before His Judgement Seat;

Only one life, twill soon be past,

Only what's done for Christ will last.[217]

May God truly grant you grace and strength as you strive to attain spiritual maturity and lay up for yourself treasures in heaven.

Thank you for reading this book and may God bless you for your desire to become spiritually mature!

"So teach us to number our days that we may get a heart of wisdom."
Ps. 90:12

"All flesh is like grass and all its glory like the flower of grass. The grass withers, and the flower falls, but the word of the Lord remains forever."
1 Pet. 24–25

"What is your life? For you are a mist that appears for a little time and then vanishes."
James 4:14

---

[217] C. T. Studd, *Only One Life Twill Soon Be Past,* http://hockleys.org/2009/05/quote-only-one-life-twill-soon-be-past-poem, Accessed 08/27/2015.

Bibliography

Acts 17:11 Bible Studies. *The Fear of God.* http://www.acts17-11.com/fear.html. Accessed 08/17/2015.

Baker, Greg S. *How to Build Good Character.* SelfGrowth.com. www.selfgrowth.com/articles/how_to_build_good_character. Accessed 12/14/2015.

Barna, George. *Growing True Disciples: New Strategies for Producing Genuine Followers of Christ.* Barna Reports. The Crown Publishing Group. Kindle Edition. 2013.

Barna Group. *The State of the Bible: 6 Trends for 2014.* 2014. https://www.barna.org/barna-update/culture/664-the-state-of-the-bible-6-trends-for-2014#.VdNGKTZRGUk. Accessed 08/18/2015.

Barrier, Roger. *What Does it Mean to "Fear the Lord?"* 2013. Crosswalk.com. http://www.crosswalk.com/church/pastors-or-leadership/ask-roger/what-does-it-mean-to-fear-the-lord.html. Accessed 08/15/2015.

Baucham, Voddie Jr. *Equipping the Generations: A Three-Pronged Approach to Discipleship.* Source: Journal of Family Ministry, 2 no 1 Fall-Winter 2011. Publication. ATLA. Religion Database with ATLASerials. Hunter Resource Library. Accessed 11/5/2014.

Beeksma, Deborah. *The Average Christian Prays a Minute a Day; Prayer by the Faithful Helps Their Relationships.* GodDiscussion.com. 2013. http://www.goddiscussion.com/110131/the-average-christian-prays-a-minute-a-day-prayer-by-the-faithful-helps-their-relationships. Accessed 07/27/2015.

Bible Hub. *703. Arête.* http://biblehub.com/greek/703.htm. Accessed 10/23/2015.

Biblicalhebrew.com. *Hate your Parents: Hate your Father, Matthew 10:37, Luke 14:26.* www.biblicalhebrew.com/nt/lovehate.htm. Accessed 08/08/2015.

Biblestudytools.com. The NAS New Testament Greek Lexicon.
http://www.biblestudytools.com/lexicons/greek/nas/sozo.htm
l. Accessed 08/05/2015.

Bloom, Jon. *Let Him Deny Himself.* Desiring God.org. 2010.
http://www.desiringgod.org/articles/let-him-deny-himself.
Accessed 7/27/2015.

Blue Letter Bible. BlueLetterBible.org. *Study Resources: Charts and
Quotes.* www.blueletterbible.org/study/pnt/pnt08.cfm. Accessed
10/14/105.

Bonhoeffer, Dietrich. *The Cost of Discipleship.* 2011-08-16. SCM
Classics Hymns Ancient and Modern Ltd. Kindle Edition.

Butt, Kyle. *Hate Your Parents – or Love Them?* Apologeticspress.org.
2004.
apologeticspress.org/AllegedDiscrepancies.aspx?article=781.
Accessed 08/08/2015.

Character-training.com/blog. *What Is Character?*
http://www.character-training.com/blog. Accessed
10/23/2015.

Christian Prayer Quotes. *Prayer Quotations.* http://www.christian-
prayer-quotes.christian-attorney.net. Accessed 10/20/2015.

Cole, Steven J. *Why You Should Hate Your Life.* Bible.org. 2014.
bible.org/seriespage/lesson-67-why-you-should-hate-your-life-
john-1224-26. Accessed 08/11/2015.

Compelling Truth. *What Is the Sin of Gluttony?* Compellingtruth.org.
www.compellingtruth.org/gluttony-sin.html. Accessed
10/24/2015.

Crockett, Joseph V. *Is There Discipline in Our Discipleship?*
Source: Living Pulpit. Online. March 1, 2014. ATLA Religion
Database with ATLASerials. Hunter Resource Library. Accessed
11/5/2014.

C. S. Lewis Institute. *Sparking a Discipleship Movement in America and
Beyond.* cslewisinstitute.org.
http://www.cslewisinstitute.org/webfm_send/210. Accessed
08/19/2015.

Dyck, Drew. *The Leavers: Young Doubters Exit the Church.* 2010.
    ChristianityToday.com.
    www.christianitytoday.com/ct/2010/november/27.40.html.
    Accessed 09/28/2015.

Edman, Raymond V. *The Disciplines of Life.* Minneapolis, Minnesota.
    World Wide Publications. 1948.

Eskridge, Larry. *The Prosperity Gospel Is Surprisingly Mainstream.* 2013.
    ChristianityToday.com.
    http://www.christianitytoday.com/ct/2013/august-web-
    only/prosperity-gospel-is-surprisingly-mainstream.html.
    Accessed 08/22/2015.

Fairchild, Mary. *Basics to Prayer.* Christianity.About.com.
    http://christianity.about.com/od/prayersverses/a/basicstopra
    yer.htm. Accessed 10/16/2016.

Firger, Jessica. *Prescription Drugs on the Rise: Estimates Suggest 60
    Percent of Americans Take at Least One Medication.* Newsweek.
    2015. www.newsweek.com/prescription-drugs-rise-new-
    estimates-suggest-60-americans-take-least-one-390354. Accessed
    11/17/2015.

Foster, Richard J. *Celebration of Discipline.* HarperCollins. Kindle
    Edition. 2009.

Gotquestions.org. *What Does the Bible Say About the Prosperity Gospel?*
    http://www.gotquestions.org/prosperity-gospel.html.
    Accessed 08/22/2015.

_____. *What Does It Mean to Abide in Christ?*
    www.gotquestions.org/abide-in-Christ.html. Accessed
    10/20/2015.

_____. *What Does the Bible Say About Attitude?*
    www.gotquestions.org/Bible-attitude.html. Accessed
    10/23/2015.

_____. *What Does the Bible Say About Time Management?*
    www.gotquestions.org/Bible-time-management.html. Accessed
    10/24/2015.

Graham, Billy. *What Did Jesus Mean When He Said We Have to Carry a Cross?* Billy Graham Evangelistic Association. 2006. http://billygraham.org/answer/what-did-jesus-mean-when-he-said-we-have-to-carry-a-cross. Accessed 08/17/2015.

Greenwold, Doug. *Being a First-Century Disciple.* 2007. Bible.org. https://bible.org/article/being-first-century-disciple. Accessed 08/14/2015.

Grudem, Wayne. *Systematic Theology: An Introduction to Biblical Doctrine.* Grand Rapids, Michigan. Zondervan. 1994.

Hayes, Dan. *Motivating Reasons to Pray.* StartingWithGod.com. www.startingwithgod.com/knowing-god/motivating. Accessed 10/20/2015.

Helpmewithbiblestudy.org. *What Did Jesus Mean "Deny Yourself and Take Up Your Cross"?* http://helpmewithbiblestudy.org/9Salvation/SanctifyWhatDoesItMeanToCarryCross.aspx. Accessed 07/27/2015.

Henderson, Daniel. *No Time to Pray.* Praying Pastor Blog. PrayingPastorBlog.blogspot. http://prayingpastorblog.blogspot.mx/2009/02/no-time-to-pray-no-time-to-pray.html. Accessed 10/16/2015.

Herrick, Greg. *Understanding the Meaning of the Term "Disciple."* 2004. Bible.org. https://bible.org/seriespage/2-understanding-meaning-term-disciple. Accessed 08/13/2015.

Houdmann, Michael S. *Is Gluttony a Sin? What Does the Bible Say About Overeating?* http://www.gotquestions.org/gluttony-sin.html. Accessed 02/27/2016.

_____. *What Does the Bible Mean by "Dying to Self"?* http://www.gotquestions.org/dying-to-self.html. Accessed 07/27/2015.

Hull, Bill. *The Complete Book of Discipleship: On Being and Making Followers of Christ.* The Navigators Reference Library 1. 2014. NavPress. Kindle Edition.

Institute in Basic Life Principles. *What Is the Fear of the Lord?* Iblp.org. http://iblp.org/questions/what-fear-lord. Accessed 08/15/2015.

Issler, Klaus. *Six Themes to Guide Spiritual Formation Ministry Based on Jesus' Sermon on the Mount.* Source: Christian Education. Journal Date: September 1, 2010. CEJ: Series 3, Vol. 7, No. 2. ATLA Religion Database with ATLASerials. Hunter Resource Library. Accessed 11/5/2014.

Keathley, Hampton J III. *Church Discipline.* Bible.org. bible.org/article/church-discipline. Accessed 10/08/2015.

Kinnaman, Dave and Lyons, Gabe. *Un Christian.* Grand Rapids, MI. BakerBooks. 2007.

Krejcir, Dr. Richard J. *Statistics on Pastors: What is Going on with the Pastors in America?* 2007. Churchleadership.org. http://www.churchleadership.org/apps/articles/default.asp?articleid=42347&columnid=4545. Accessed 08/06/2015.

_____. *Statistics and Reasons for Church Decline.* 2007. Churchleadership.org. http://www.churchleadership.org/apps/articles/default.asp?articleid=42346&columnid=4545. Accessed 08/07/2015.

LifeWay Research. *Views on Divorce Divide Americans.* 2015. LifeWayResearch.com. http://www.lifewayresearch.com/2015/08/12/views-on-divorce-divide-americans. Accessed 08/19/2015.

Lumina.bible.org. https://lumina.bible.org/bible/Matthew+10. Accessed 08/05/2015.

_____. https://lumina.bible.org/bible/Deuteronomy+10. Accessed 08/16/2015.

MacArthur, John F Jr. *Church Discipline.* Grace to You. www.gty.org/resources/distinctives/DD02/church-discipline. Accessed 10/08/2015.

_____. *The Gospel According to Jesus.* Grand Rapids, Michigan. Zondervan Publishing House. 1988.

_____. *What Does It Mean to "Abide" in Christ?* Gty.org. www.gty.org/resources/Questions/QA161/What-does-it-mean-to-abide-in-Christ. Accessed 10/20/2015.

Martin, Cath. *Evangelicals Admit Struggling to Find Time for Daily Bible Reading and Prayer.* 2014. Christianity Today. www.christiantoday.com/article/daily.bible.reading.and.prayer.is.a.struggle.for.many.evangelicals/36765.htm. Accessed 08/18/2015.

_____. *70 Million Christians' Martyred for their Faith Since Jesus Walked the Earth.* 2014. ChristianityToday.com. http://www.christiantoday.com/article/70.million.christians.martyred.faith.since.jesus.walked.earth/38403.htm. Accessed 08/28/2015.

McGrath, Alister. *The Passionate Intellect; Christian Faith and the Discipleship of the Mind.* Source: Pro Ecclesia. 22 no 1 Winter 2013. Publication Type: Review ATLA Religion Database with ATLASerials. Hunter Resource Library. Accessed 11/5/2014.

Mohler, Albert, R. Jr. *The Scandal of Biblical Illiteracy: It's Our Problem.* Christianity.com. http://www.christianity.com/1270946. Accessed 08/18/2015.

_____. *The Disappearance of Church Discipline–How Can We Recover? Part One.* 2005. AlbertMohler.com. http://www.albertmohler.com/2005/05/13/the-disappearance-of-church-discipline-how-can-we-recover-part-one. Accessed 08/20/2015.

Murray, Andrew. *Power to Change: Great Quotes on Prayer.* http://powertochange.com/experience/spiritual-growth/prayerquotes. Accessed 11/16/2015.

Neverthirsty.org. *Bible Questions & Answers.* http://www.neverthirsty.org/pp/corner/read2/r00664.html. Accessed 08/15/2015.

Ogden, Greg. *Transforming Discipleship: Making Disciples a Few at a Time.* InterVarsity Press. Kindle Edition. 2010.

Pew Research Center. *Evangelical Protestant.* Pewforum.org.
  http://www.pewforum.org/religious-landscape-
  study/religious-tradition/evangelical-protestant. Accessed
  08/19/2015.

Piper, John. *Prosperity Preaching: Deceitful and Deadly.* 2007. Desiring
  God. DesiringGod.org.
  http://www.desiringgod.org/articles/prosperity-preaching-
  deceitful-and-deadly. Accessed 08/23/2015.

Platt, David. *Follow Me.* Carol Stream, Illinois. Tyndale House
  Publishers. 2013.

_____. *What It Means to Follow Christ.* LifeWay.
  http://www.lifeway.com/Article/christian-living-what-it-
  means-to-follow-christ. Accessed 07-22-2015.

Pratte, David E. *Does God Promise Miracles to Give Us Healing and
  Prosperity?* 2011. Light to My Path Publications.
  www.gospelway.com. www.gospelway.com/god/health-
  wealth.php. Accessed 08/22/2015.

Rankin, Russ. *Study: Bible Engagement in Churchgoer's Hearts, Not
  Always Practiced.* Nashville. 2012.
  http://www.lifeway.com/Article/research-survey-bible-
  engagement-churchgoers. Accessed 07/23/2015.

Reardon, JoHannah. *What Does It Mean to Fear God?*
  ChristianityToday.com. Accessed 08/15/2015.

Robbins, Dale. *Why Christians Should Attend Church.* Victorious.org.
  www.victorious.org/pub/why-church-169. Accessed
  10/21/2015.

Robinson, Anthony B. The Renewed Focus on Discipleship: 'Follow
  Me'. 2007. Christian Century, 124 no 18 S 4 2007. Publication
  Type: Article. ATLA Religion Database with ATLASerials.
  Hunter Resource Library. Accessed 12/10/2014.

Samra, James G. *A Biblical View of Discipleship.* Bibliotheca Sacra
  April-June 2003. Publication Type: Article, Database: ATLA
  Religion Database with ATLASerials. Hunter Resource Library.
  Accessed 11/5/2014.

Statistic Brain Research Institute. *Television Watching Statistics.* 2015. www.statisticbrain.com/television-watching-statistics. Accessed 08/07/2015.

Struckmeyer, Kurt. *Take Up Your Cross.* http://followingjesus.org/changing/take_up_cross.htm. 2007. Accessed 08/03/2015.

Studd, C. T. *Only One Life Twill Soon Be Past.* http://hockleys.org/2009/05/quote-only-one-life-twill-soon-be-past-poem. Accessed 08/27/2015.

Swindoll, Chuck. *Strengthening Your Grip.* Waco, TX. Word Books. 1982.

U.S. Department of Health and Human Services. *Overweight and Obesity Statistics.* www.niddk.nih.gov/health-information/health-statistics/Pages/overweight-obesity-statistics.aspx. 2009, 2010. Accessed 10/24/1015.

Vander Laan, Ray. *Rabbi and Talmidim.* That the World May Know. www.thattheworldmayknow.com/Rabbi-and-talmidim. Accessed 08/13/2015.

Victory Life Church. VictoryLifeChurch.org. Intercessory Prayer — Praying Always. http://www.victorylifechurch.org/pdf/Intercessory_Praying_Always.pdf. Accessed 08/19/2015.

Vos, Beverly. *The Spiritual Disciplines and Christian Ministry.* Source: Evangelical Review of Theology, 36 no 2 Ap 2012. Publication Type: Article ATLA Religion Database with ATLASerials. Hunter Resource Library. Accessed 11/5/2014.

Whitney, Donald S. *Spiritual Disciplines for the Christian Life.* Colorado Springs, Colorado. NAVPRESS. 1991.

Willard, Dallas. *The Great Omission.* 2009-10-13. HarperCollins. Kindle Edition.

_____. *The Spirit of the Disciplines.* 2009-02-06. HarperCollins. Kindle Edition.

_____. *Transformed by the Renewing of the Mind*. Lecture given at Henry Center for Theological Understanding, 2012. https://youtu.be/jkzeUcnzYbM?list=PLApp3jRh1oAqt64uvfw4 J_Ps2lD8bYokR. Accessed 10/15/2015.

Wilke, Jon D. *Churchgoers Believe in Sharing Faith, Most Never Do*. LifeWay.com. LifeWay Research. http://www.lifeway.com/article/research-survey-sharing-christ-2012. Accessed 08/04/2015.

Willis, Avery T Jr. *MasterLife: Discipleship Training for Leaders*. Source: Theological Educator, no 28 Spr 1984. Publication Type: Article. Subjects: Baptists--Education; Christian life ATLA Religion Database with ATLASerials. Hunter Resource Library. Accessed 11/5/2014.

About the Author

Todd M. Fink is founder and director of Go Missions to Mexico Ministries. He received a Bachelor of Theology Degree from Freelandia Bible College (1986-1990), did studies at Western Seminary (1990-1993), received a Master of Theology Degree from Freedom Bible College and Seminary (2012-2013), and received a Ph.D. degree in Theology from Trinity Theological Seminary (2015).

He served as youth/associate pastor for 12 years at an Evangelical church in Oregon (1987-1998).

 Todd (Mike) is currently serving as pastor and missionary with Go Missions to Mexico Ministries in Mexico (1998-present) and is also an author, speaker, and teacher. He has a deep passion for God's Word and enjoys helping people understand its eternal truths. He is married to his lovely wife, Letsy Angela, and has four grown children.

Ministries of Go Missions to Mexico

HolyLandSite.com ~ Holy Land video teachings and resources

MinisteriosCasaDeLuz.com ~ Spanish resources for pastors

SelahBookPress.com ~ Book publishing

Connect with Todd (Mike)

Email: missionstomexico@yahoo.com

Facebook: Go Missions to Mexico

Websites:

- ToddMichaelFink.com
- SelahBookPress.com
- GoMissionsToMexico.com
- HolyLandSite.com
- MinsiteriosCasaDeLuz.com

Look for More Books Coming Soon by Todd (Mike)

- *Discovering the True Riches of Life*
- *Biblical Sites of the Holy Land: See Where the Bible Took Place*
- *Understanding the Fear of the Lord: How to Receive God's Richest Blessings in Your Life*
- *Understanding Heavenly Rewards: An Overlooked Truth*
- *Biblical Leadership: How to Lead God's Way*
- *Gender Roles in the Family and Church: What Does the Bible Say?*
- *Church Discipline: Intensive Care for Wayward Believers*
- *How to Share Your Faith: A Biblical Approach*

CPSIA information can be obtained
at www.ICGtesting.com
Printed in the USA
LVOW12*2309220416

484845LV00001B/1/P